I0788867

THE ULTIMATE ALEX DRAKE COLLECTION

BOOKS ONE THROUGH FOUR & BONUS PREQUEL

LEXXI JAMES

This is a work of fiction. Names, characters, places, and incidents are the product of the author's imagination. Specific named locations, public names, and other specified elements are used for impact, but this novel's story and characters are 100 percent fictitious. Certain long-standing institutions, agencies, and public offices are mentioned, but the characters involved are wholly imaginary. Resemblance to individuals, living or dead, or to events which have occurred is purely coincidental. And if your life happens to bear a strong resemblance to my imaginings, then well done and cheers to you! You're a freaking rock star!

To every little girl destined for adventure.

ALTER EGO

PREQUEL TO THE ALEX DRAKE SERIES

ALTER
EGO
AN ALEX DRAKE NOVEL
LEXXI JAMES

CHAPTER 1

PACO

Manhattan

AT NINE THIRTY on the dot, Paco Robles laid two choppy knocks on the door of his boss's office in the executive suite on the fifty-second floor before letting himself in.

Paco wasn't the garden-variety employee at Drake Global Industries. Technically, he wasn't on the books at all. His salary was completely under the table, and his access to offices, documents, and DGI's high-powered CEO, Alex Drake, was absolute.

No one but Alex had a clue who Paco really was or what he did, and that was just the way he liked it. Despite his role being undefined, absolutely everyone knew he was as close to the top as you could get in the multibillion-dollar global corporation without actually body-snatching the boss.

At his knock, a gruff heave came from behind the door. The sound gave Paco the mistaken assurance he could enter.

Once he'd swiped his access card on the wall panel and stepped inside, he instantly realized the error of his ways.

There was Alex in all his ball-busting glory. Suit on from the waist up, five-thousand-dollar slacks pooled around his ankles, he was currently focusing all his efforts into pounding the well-rounded ass of his latest conquest.

Paco could have silently backed out, but a discontented huff escaped him as he checked his watch. *You know the time, ass-wipe. You said nine thirty.*

Without breaking the rhythm of his bucking thrusts, Alex looked up and gave Paco a boyishly innocent shrug intended to deflect the daggers of his best friend's squint. And his ridiculous finger-shush was wholly unnecessary.

Paco rolled his eyes. *Like I'd embarrass the girl. It's bad enough she ended her day with you.*

After a short exchange of a dozen choice expressions between them, he left.

This was the side of Alex Drake he loathed. He used to hate all sides of the bastard, but that was a long time ago. When a man has gone through hell and back, it's easier to overlook his shortcomings.

All the world ever saw of Alex was the asshole side of him, but Paco knew the real him, the pieces that kept Alex from sleeping for days on end. And no matter how balls-deep he got inside a woman, no woman was getting close to him.

Or at least, not in a way that really mattered.

Twenty minutes later, a mildly sweaty and supremely apologetic Alex peeked his head into Paco's office. "Hey. You, uh, wanted to see me?" His chuckle was contagious.

"Not that fucking much of you," Paco blurted. But his jovial smile broke through as usual, despite his having to deal with the hellacious pain in the ass known as Alex Drake. Tonight was no different. "Let me guess. That would be Ms. Taylor."

Yet again. Another young woman who happened to have the last name that haunted Alex. Haunted them both.

Blinking away the past, Paco refocused on the here and now.

Alex was dealing with things the way he always did . . . deliberately. Methodically. Redefining OCD by practically fucking his way through the phone book, one Ms. Taylor at a time.

Thankfully, Alex never outright asked Paco to find the woman he really wanted. And Paco never offered. Their understanding was unspoken, and neither seemed interested in crossing that invisible barbed wire of a line.

Defeated, Alex gave him a pathetic shrug, not bothering to verbally confirm what they both already knew. Instead, he changed the subject.

"Hey, you're the one with unfettered access. What can I say? It's a double-edged sword. Speaking of swords—"

With both elbows on his desk, Paco plopped his head in his hands, working his fingers into each temple. Frustrated, he suggested the only solution that would alleviate his oncoming headache.

"Look, I just need to kick your ass. It won't take long, so I'll make it quick. It won't even muss up your hair any more than it already is, and I'll hold back enough to keep you out of the ER."

Laughing, Alex relaxed into the leather wingback chair opposite Paco's desk. "Maybe later. But my comment was actually business related." When Paco arched his brow with a stern glance of disbelief, Alex lifted a hand. "No, really. Charity called. We've got a bite."

If the hooker to the elite was calling Alex Drake with intel on someone trying to get a piece of the megamogul, Paco was all ears.

"Well, this I've got to hear."

CHAPTER 2

CHARITY

With barely a glance in the mirror, Charity settled on her outfit. An oversized sweatshirt hung just over one shoulder, and her favorite athleisure leggings were too comfy to pass up. Sweeping her long honey-blond hair into a scrunchie, she topped off the look with a smirk that softened to a smile.

Good enough. Not exactly the picture of a kept woman.

Maybe that was painting her position a little too rosy. A hooker by any other name . . . *would fuck as sweet.* That is, if she were ever given the chance.

For the past eighteen months, Charity had been living the life—and a lie—all because Alex Drake had decided to keep her. And what a life and a lie it had been.

Like clockwork, money showed up in her account on the first of each month . . . the first bank account she'd ever had. Some might call the money an allowance. To Charity, it was a small fortune she'd use to make a better life.

Her apartment in the heart of New York City's Upper East Side also came with the package. Its location on a quaint little street with classic brownstones sandwiched between chic high-rises placed her on an elite row.

Within walking distance of coffee shops and high-end shopping, the coveted location near Fifth Avenue was a hop, skip, and jump from priceless works of art on Museum Mile and the world-famous Met. A most unlikely home for a woman who'd spent years walking the streets and working the corners not too far from there.

With barely a penny to her name, Charity had been speechless a year and a half ago when she first stepped into the chic modern apartment. It boasted top-of-the-line stainless steel appliances and a kitchen island bigger than her bed. But nothing else. That is, until a designer showed up within minutes of her arrival. He asked about her preferences and showed her some photos and sketches. Within hours, truckloads of furnishings were unloaded and perfectly arranged to create an upscale apartment worthy of a home decor magazine layout.

It was all a dream come true. Like she had some crazy twenty-four-karat vajayjay that revirginized after each use.

Well, by now, that last part's probably the case.

Getting on all fours for her new benefactor wasn't just a natural assumption, but something Charity would want to do, over and over and over again, if for no other reason than to say *thanks*.

But strangely, nothing had happened between them. Nothing at all. In fact, she never really saw the man.

Besides, true revirginizing would take a year. *I think.*

And there had been someone in the last year. A brief, fleeting, incredible, mind-blowing someone who came and went so quickly, half of her wondered if it had really happened at all.

Only the upper half of her body wondered that. Charity's lower half still reeled from the aftershocks of a very real quake that rocked every part of her needy and lonely world. For as fiery hot as the night was, the morning after had left her wanting. And alone.

Still, loneliness beat the alternative.

Avoiding no more than fleeting glances at the scars on the back of her right hand, she knew all too well the consequences of her actions and her profession. And forever carried the reminder of how she'd come to know Drake Global Industries and the reclusive billionaire Alex Drake.

CHAPTER 3

CHARITY

Eighteen months ago

No problem.

Her blithely uttered words had haunted Charity weeks after she'd first uttered them to Stefano "Monty" Montgnaro. He was a regular client she saw a few times a month, whenever his traditional Italian wife and their three children went to visit her parents upstate.

Monty was rich and powerful, with looks that definitely screamed *pays for sex*. He had a proposition for her, and sure, it sounded cliché, but she couldn't refuse.

He hadn't threatened her to accept his "request" because he didn't have to. His reputation preceded him in more ways than one. Long ago, she'd found ways to avoid his inclinations for painfully rough sex.

Fix a drink. Wind him down. Avoid questions like *how was your day*, and sure as hell don't bring up the wife.

And if all else failed, a crushed-up Klonopin in a ready glass of cheap whiskey would at least make the two-hundred-pound gorilla manageable. But he paid well, and saying *no* came with consequences.

But fear wasn't Charity's motivator when she accepted his offer. Greed did all the talking. Double her rate wasn't good enough. Triple was more like it.

Triple! And cash up front—for a one-nighter. How could she say anything but *no problem?*

The photo he'd handed her didn't mean anything, and the name that went with it meant even less.

Monty didn't quite understand her indifference. "Don't you know who he is?"

Her head shake and shrug was enough to earn her his hard grip on her jaw. "Learn fast. You've got one week." Shoving her head free, he put a small case in her hand. "The guy has a different girl every night. You'll need to be really close to his phone—right on top of it is best—then press the button."

The only distinguishing thing about the clip-on device he gave her was a silver button at the top. Turning it to get a closer look, Charity thought the small gray box looked more like a garage door opener than anything else.

Half joking, she asked, "I'm not blowing something up, am I?"

He chuckled, his tone sarcastic. "Did I wipe my prints off it?"

"Then what is it?"

Monty's stern glare was enough of a warning. Talk time was over.

Tearing her clothes off meant their business discussions were finished. He'd be moving on to the less pleasant parts of their evening, dragging her with him.

Getting close to a guy was sort of Charity's thing. Soon enough, though, she learned that CEO Alex Drake was well protected and unapproachable.

With each passing day, her overinflated confidence shriveled to fear. The man was a fortress. Certainly, Monty would understand.

The week Monty had given her to accomplish her task came and went, and he returned despite her attempts to put him off.

"I need more time," she said, her voice cracking from her anxiety. "Just a little more time."

Monty's normally dark eyes grew even blacker with each passing minute of her excuses, and he repeated those two overconfident words back to her. "No problem."

The basic rule of business is no different from that on the street—underpromise and overdeliver. It should have been simple, but it wasn't. Instead, her overpromising was a dangerous mistake.

For a low-end hooker barely making ends meet with nothing in the world but her looks to lead the way, Charity was more than frustrated that a guy like Alex Drake was untouchable. And her time was up.

So, what happens to a girl who is all talk and no results?

Nothing. At least, not at first.

But letting Monty take her for a drive to get some air was her second mistake. And her nervousness quickly led her to mistake number three.

Charity welcomed the drink he offered her in the car. A few minutes after a swig from his flask, her body grew warm and she slumped back, feeling sluggish and heavy.

Confused, she watched Monty, then the road ahead. It was dark, which made sense with it being night and all. But it was darker than usual. *Are we leaving the city?*

With a deep inhale, she closed her eyes for a moment until she realized the car was pulling over in the middle of nowhere. Monty maneuvered the car through a maze of shipping crates, where he parked. His smile set her at ease.

She must have nodded off again but cracked open her eyes at the familiar sound of a lighter striking. Blinking, she refocused.

After lighting a cigar, Monty began babbling on and on about things that didn't make sense.

Is that Italian? And with every deep puff of that obnoxious stogie, annoying billows of smoke filled the luxury car. *Can't he at least crack open a window?*

Coughing, Charity tried pressing the button to lower her window, but his hand swooped to her neck. His rough fingers smoothed over her skin as he whispered more Italian in her ear.

The strong scent made her dizzier by the second, her headache increasing to massive, relentless throbbing. Her head dropped forward but didn't fall far. Something was wrapped around her neck, keeping her pinned to the headrest. It was tight, but loose enough she could wedge her fingers between it and her skin.

Getting free was a joke. Every move felt feeble and worthless.

Charity's panic gave her just enough to tug, then claw, until her desperation caused her to dig into her own flesh. Terrified, she cried out loudly, then louder.

"Let me go. Get me out of this." Her words were insistent and demanding before she softened her tone. If she said the right things, used the right tactic, Monty would be reasonable and sane. Wouldn't he?

But deep down, she knew. He wasn't releasing her. And the thought made her yank the binding harder.

The more she fought, the more amused Monty seemed as he watched her.

His cold laugh didn't last long, but a crooked smile stayed on his fat, hideous face the entire time.

He managed to pry one of her hands away from its desperate grasp, laying a long, unexpected kiss on the back of it before he pressed the glowing tip of his cigar to it.

The first burn seared through her skin as the pain ripped screams from her throat. Still fighting to get free, she was frantic to find she was helpless. Monty, however, was just warming up, taking his time and seeming to enjoy it much more than his disgusting rounds of sex.

Desperately, Charity pleaded with him to stop—begging and crying until her throat was raw and scratchy, and she was barely able to breathe. He only stopped long enough for a string of successive puffs to ratchet up the heat, making each new branding even more intense from the red-hot tip of his cigar.

Two more burns on her hand were just the beginning, and then he added a blade to the mix.

The torture lasted hours, with her night of hell finally ending as he dumped her mutilated body on the side of the road, miles from anywhere.

When she came to in the darkness, Charity dragged herself to her feet and headed numbly toward home, but the details were a little fuzzy. Exhausted and confused, she'd staggered in the direction of the city until a car pulled to a stop beside her.

Scared, she backed away, keeping her head low and letting her hair cover her eyes as she almost refused the ride. Charity wouldn't look at the driver's face, or her eyes, but kept her blurred vision fixed on the woman's clothes. Something about the unicorns on the lady's scrubs made her feel safe.

Nutjobs can't possibly like unicorns. Is she a nurse? Will she call the cops?

Hesitant, Charity considered her options, and the driver seemed in no hurry, letting her think it through. Eventually, she relented and got in.

The SUV was comfortably worn in, smelling fresh and sweet from the woman's perfume or body lotion. Its driver made idle chitchat, but when the first question came out about the hand she held protectively to her chest, Charity's street-smart instincts kicked into high gear.

Deny.

"I'm fine," she said softly, more than once, following it with a thank-you to avoid suspicion.

She noticed the soft twang in the woman's words, its familiar cadence soothing her for a moment before her guard went back up. *Kentucky.*

A sad smile warmed her face as she thought of her grandmother. Memories of Meemaw were filled with sunny days and laughter, fanciful stories, and butter cookies with sugar crystals sprinkled on top. Gone now, she was buried in a makeshift grave at the foot of a hill Charity would never find again in a million years.

Would her mother know where it was? And let's be honest, finding her mother would take a hell of a lot longer. She hadn't seen her mom since she was thirteen.

Overwhelmed by her own sorrow, she shuddered out a breath, missing her grandmother, but no tears fell. She was all cried out.

"Where can I take you?" the woman asked.

Stalling, Charity realized she didn't want to go home, but where could she go? "You can drop me off near Saint Joseph's. If that's not too far out of your way."

Only then did she notice how raw and quiet her voice was. But the woman didn't ask again, so she didn't repeat it, opting to reserve her strength—holding herself together long enough to last a car ride.

Asking to be dropped off almost a mile from her run-down week-to-week motel was crazy, but Charity felt like she had to. She held in the gasps that came with every painful step of the walk there. But if Monty was waiting, she didn't want anything to happen to her helpful unicorn.

Climbing the flight of stairs to her apartment nearly killed her, the pain causing her to wonder if a rib had cracked when he flung her from the car. But at last, she was home.

From the hole of a space she called the bathroom, the decrepit mirror reflected back her face. Monty left it completely untouched, yet had ensured his mark was everywhere else.

Struggling to see any glimpse of herself behind her swollen red eyes, Charity couldn't find a trace of the woman she'd been just a few hours ago. Maybe her face being spared was something to be grateful for, but the sight of herself just pissed her off.

It was typical Monty. Leaving her face for later gave her a warning of what would happen if she made trouble. That is, if he let her live at all.

But it was all she wanted to do. Make trouble. *And make that motherfucker pay.*

Her clenched fists released as fear forced her hand to the mirror. She opened it, relieved to find amongst the orange and white bottles the one she needed now before she made a hasty decision.

Swaying with pain and exhaustion, she stared at the bottle of Klonopin in her hand, thinking. Her overdose was three years ago. It had seemed accidental to the medical staff who had pumped her stomach. She wasn't suicidal. At least, that was what she'd told herself. And them.

But what happens the next time Monty comes by? Wants to touch me? Fuck me? He'll kill me if I refuse.

Charity's gaze traveled down her body. She couldn't bear to see how bad she was hurt beneath her clothes, and that was reminder enough.

He'll probably kill me anyway.

Emptying the container into her palm, she enjoyed a small swirl of satisfaction that lifted her rage as she scanned the pills in her hand.

What if I make trouble for that bastard, then beat him to the punch? Do I have enough to do it before he can get to me? How many did I take the last time?

Nodding silently to herself, she dumped the pills back in the bottle. All but two, that is. Tossing them in her mouth, she cupped a handful of water from the tap to chase them down, then headed to collapse, letting herself sink into the illusion of a safe bed and a good night's sleep.

CHAPTER 4

CHARITY

THE BLISS of oversleeping was soon overshadowed by fresh memories of the night before. Charity writhed through getting out of bed. Moving any part of her body hurt, and a hot shower made it worse, adding harsh stings to the ache of each cut and burn.

After a breakfast cocktail of painkillers and antidepressants, she headed straight to the heart of Manhattan and the towering obelisk that housed Drake Global Industries.

Of course, security wouldn't let a beat-up, crazy lady through, so this morning, Charity made sure she looked anything but. Her face was fine. Concealer and some makeup brightened her exhaustion and tamed her puffy eyes.

Her thick blond hair didn't need much to look elegant and neat. Twisting it into a bun at the nape of her neck was good enough. She could pass for a well-dressed woman with important private business with the head of security. *No problem.*

Again, those two words flickered through her mind, causing her to wince as she pushed through the clear glass doors.

Sure, women like her didn't exactly grace the halls of Manhattan skyscrapers —at least, not usually in the early light of day—but Charity could play the part. Black tights covered the welts on her legs. Her short skirt was plain black and more professional than the denim ones she owned. A flowy blouse at least made her look like she was fit to bring someone coffee, and a leopard-print scarf covered the scrapes and bruises on her neck.

Maybe a nobody like her would never have the power or influence to make a motherfucking asshole like Monty pay, but she could at least let someone know what he was up to.

That much I can do before . . .

The little bottle stayed nestled in her purse as she mentally counted the pills she'd seen in her hand yesterday. Subtracting two from this morning's count, she blew out a relieved exhale. *That should be plenty.*

But no sooner had she uttered the name Stefano Montgnaro than a security guard escorted her to an office on the fifty-second floor. On their way up, her runaway pulse convinced her that one more pill would help her keep it together.

At the nameplate outside the door, she struggled to focus her eyes. P. ROBLES.

His introduction was abrupt. "I'm Paco."

No title. Nothing else except to offer her a luxurious leather seat, a charming smile, and a small bottle of Voss water. Her security escort quietly shut the door, giving them their privacy.

"Charity," she said, accepting the drink. The cold glass bottle felt good in her grip. She flipped her hand, soothing her recent burns.

Skirting the horrific details of what she'd endured the past twenty hours, she shared what specifics she knew of Monty's plan. As she struggled through the sparse details and facts, her words were jumbled. Disjointed.

Frustrated, she muttered an exhaustive loop of, "Tell Alex Drake. Warn him about Monty."

Yes. Warn him about Monty.

Urgently, she shoved the gadget that looked like a little garage door opener in Paco's hand and grasped his forearms, shaking them. But he just calmly sat there, listening intently and not saying a word.

When she stopped talking, the silence between them suffocated her. Slumping back, she spat out, "I'm a whore."

Charity said it louder the second time, less concerned about the tears breaking free, and watched for a reaction. Nothing.

"Did you hear what I said? I'm a whore."

Why hide any of it? Shame. Guilt.

Fuck it. I'm so done.

The weight of Paco's pensive gaze solidified her decision. Standing, she stumbled as she tried to make it to the door.

His hand slipped in hers so gently, she froze. Slowly, he turned it so both of them could take a closer look. "Those are fresh."

His soft words knocked her back to her seat. Nodding, Charity looked away.

"Have you seen a doctor?"

With a shrug, she lied. "I'm fine."

"No. You're tough. You're numb. But you're definitely not fine."

A few quick knocks on the door made her bolt up, but Paco urged her back to her seat. "Come in."

Another man entered the office. Tense and on edge, he raked a hard look up and down her body , which hit a nerve.

Under her breath, Charity said, "I need to go." Clumsily, her awkward attempt at standing had all the grace of a giraffe on ice.

Paco slipped a strong arm around her, steadying her as he eased her back to the seat with the slightest shush. His reassurance quelled her panic. "It's all right. We're not going to hurt you. At all. Just rest. Okay?"

"Okay," she said numbly, breathing out a sigh as she obeyed. Nodding made her blinks heavier, and she sat back, less concerned about the man's continuing stare.

"Well?" he asked, studying her but directing his question to Paco.

By the way this man wore a suit, Charity wondered if he'd been sewn into it. The fit draped over his muscles, softening his rugged angles in a way that refined a tough guy without diminishing his strength.

This guy reeked money and power with a dark heat to his eyes that melted whatever walls she was fighting to keep up. Thankfully, his steely gaze returned to his not-so-private conversation with Paco.

Despite moving away and lowering his voice, Paco shared his observations, being specific and clear. "Her eyes are bloodshot and dilated. Speech slow, sometimes slurred. She's drugged. Could be self-induced to deal with whatever traumatic shit she's been through."

Is he a doctor? I don't need a doctor.

Self-conscious, Charity moved one hand under the other, but failed to cover the wounds before the man's alarmed stare fell to them.

"Jesus." He drew out the word, finishing as his fist opened to rake his hair. "All this because another ass-wipe is trying to get to me? Un-fucking-believable."

Get to him?

Blinking away her fog, Charity studied his face harder, matching it to one she'd seen in a photo. "You're Alex Drake?"

Although his jaw was clenched, his eyes softened as he nodded. "Yes. And we'd like to help you. If you'll let us."

"Sure you would." Her wry smile vanished and her wariness returned. "Why not? Everyone wants their own goddamn piece of Charity."

The puzzled crease in Alex's brow smoothed away as Paco explained. "That's her name. Charity."

"Oh."

When Alex stepped closer, she startled and pushed back into the chair, forcing it to tilt. But he didn't retreat and ended up squatting in front of her. His tender tone made her shoulders relax.

"I don't want a piece of you, Charity. But I do want a few things. I want our doctor to take a look at you. You'll like her. Her name is Valerie. She has her own practice but will break away to do this."

Charity shook her head, uneasy and eager to leave. But when Paco knelt beside her too, her anxiety melted away.

Paco's words were determined but tender. "She doesn't mind me sharing this when I need to. Valerie's had plenty of darkness in her past. She pulled through it and then some. You will too. And despite her scrubs, she's not a pediatrician. She just really likes unicorns."

"Unicorns?" Charity repeated the word to herself as the nearly forgotten encounter from the night before flashed through her mind.

"We all have to hold on to something, right?" Paco said. "She told me they stand for magic and wisdom. And miracles."

She was a miracle. Why can't I remember her face? But I remember those scrubs. And her voice.

Alex spoke, piecing through her memories. "Hey, don't worry. I promise you, she's seen it all and can help. And whatever you tell her will stay between you and her, though Paco might glance at the results of any tests she runs, just to make sure you're okay. I'd also like to get you somewhere safe tonight . . . and maybe longer. We'll see. Finally, Paco will check you out—"

Charity's eyes widened as she thought of the wasteland of damage he'd discover if she undressed.

"Check out your background," Paco said quickly to explain.

Relieved, she blew out a breath.

Alex stood up. "Afterward, we'll talk." Giving her a solemn look, he said, "It was nice to meet you, Charity."

With a meaningful nod to Paco, the powerful CEO left.

CHAPTER 5

CHARITY

A WEEK in a nice hotel could almost spoil a girl if she let it. But Charity was too savvy for that. Paco Robles would be visiting, and Alex Drake too. She gathered what little she had, preparing to head out after they left.

The meds from Dr. Valerie and any spare toiletries were shoved in her purse. The clothes they'd had delivered were nice—nothing too fancy but nothing too cheap. But her assumption was that nothing was hers, so she didn't bother taking any of those.

Why are they visiting me in the hotel? Time to pay the piper?

Frowning, she worried less about what they might want and more about what they'd see. Over the past several days, her body had dragged its way through a state of healing, and the bruises and burns weren't exactly invisible. But men were men. *Maybe they won't notice.*

Methodically, Charity closed every blackout curtain in each of the rooms, drawing them tight to avoid any light entering. Flipping on a single small table lamp, she decided she could pull it off.

Besides, who cares? An eviction was eminent. Nothing said thank-you like a fuck for the road.

But as they arrived in their tailored suits with their sweet hellos, she yearned to stay just a little longer.

What would it take for me to stay? For them to keep me?

As the men made themselves comfortable, the hotel chairs looked more like dollhouse furniture beneath their large frames. She stayed standing to hear the news, and neither of them seemed to mind.

"You won't need to worry about Monty any longer," Alex said, his words solid. Confident.

"That's a relief." Grateful, she grabbed two room-temperature no-name bottles of water, making a meager gesture at hospitality. "How—"

Paco narrowed his gaze, cutting her off. "No questions. And from this point forward, you've never heard of Stefano Montgnaro. Understand?"

Apparently, her weak nod wasn't good enough. Firmer, he repeated himself, emphasizing each word.

"Do. You. Understand?"

"Y-yes." She strengthened her tone with a definitive nod, acknowledging she'd just made an agreement she could never walk away from.

After a quick sip of his water, Paco resumed his charming smile. "Your background check came out clean," he said, surprise ringing in his words. "Cleaner than—"

"Most hookers?" she asked.

Nonchalant, he shrugged. "Probably. You're the first working girl I've investigated. But I was going to say your background check came out cleaner than most of the people who work for us. No arrests. No tickets or fines. And the good doctor Valerie screened your blood—no illegal substances. No criminal record of any kind except something sealed when you were a minor." He glanced at her, noticing her apprehension. "I didn't check that. That's your business. Unless, at some point you want to make it my business."

"What do you mean, make it your business?" Charity cocked her head, firming up some understanding of his status. "Are you an attorney?"

Shooting knowing glances at each other, both men laughed.

"Yeah. He's an attorney, and I'm the pope," Alex said with a grin, but Paco just shook his head.

"I'm a hell of a lot saintlier than you, asshole."

Wow. Her jaw dropped. She'd seen men banter and she understood male bonding . . . of an imaginative range. Without a doubt, these two were close. But a comment like that still took her by surprise.

Smiling for the first time in days, Charity relaxed, but still wondered how the coin flip would land. Which one would take her by the head, and who'd be banging her tail?

Alex finished a few big swallows of water, as if his thirst had been an afterthought. "Look, Paco and I wanted to talk with you about something."

Protective, Paco shot out, "But you can always say no."

I can say no?

"No." She blew out a breath, nodding.

"But you haven't heard the offer," Alex said, coaxing her to at least hear him out.

Realizing she'd been sending mixed signals, she clarified. "I mean, no—it's no problem. Really. I'd like to thank you both."

Quickly, Charity whipped off her clothes with gusto, as if there were a Guinness World Record at stake.

Shielding their eyes, both men avoided the lines and curves of her naked body. The room filled with a raucous roar of objections as *whoa* and *hold on there* were hurled at her as if she were a runaway horse.

Alex demanded she put her clothes back on, his booming voice having a boyish quality. "Please. We don't want to have sex with you."

With unfamiliar satisfaction, she savored the cheap thrill of making two wealthy and powerful men squirm in adorable discomfort, drawing out the task of dressing as they continued averting their eyes.

"You don't?"

Adamant, both shook their heads. She'd seen similar headshakes like theirs once or twice in her life. They reminded her of two schoolboys being confronted by an overflowing plate of steamed broccoli.

As she studied the men, figuring them out was easy.

Ah. Got it.

They're a couple. I'll bet they're into some kinky shit too.

Whatever. They're sweet. I'm totally down.

Waving his hand, Alex urged her to the small sofa. She sat, watching him regain his composure by checking the knot in his tie.

Clearing his throat, he released a long breath. "Charity, I think what we need is—"

"Bondage gear? A Saint Andrews cross?" Seductive, she popped a brow. "A sybian?"

With each suggestion, her enthusiasm expanded beyond the comfort of the men in the room. In apparent defeat, Alex dropped his face into his hands.

Paco chimed in. "We need a pinch hitter."

After thinking through his request, she reluctantly agreed. "Okay. I've never been much into pinching or hitting, but if that's what you want . . ."

Holding up a hand to stop her, Alex tried again. "We're looking for a mole. Someone to act the part of a high-end call girl. But we're not expecting you to . . ." Struggling for the right word, he finally settled on, "Do what you normally do."

Nodding, she asked, "So, you want something special?" She caressed his knee, but his massive hand quickly stopped her from blazing a trail up his thigh.

With Charity's wandering hand captured in his, he explained. "Special, yes. Sexual, no. You'll just be a front, and we'll cover all your expenses. Maybe we can come to some sort of an, um, arrangement?"

The lengths he was going to pussyfoot around evocative words got him a double scoop of sassy with a whopping side of smartass.

"Let me see if I'm catching your drift. You want me *on your staff.*" Her suggestive gaze locked on the fullness of his groin. His eye roll and Paco's chuckle only encouraged her. "And you could really use a girl like me in a choice *position?*"

Pinching the bridge of his nose, Alex stood. "I'm glad you're in better spirits. As much fun as this is, I'll let you two sort out the details." After giving her a stern look, he turned a sly grin on Paco. "Work it out. Let me know how it goes. And watch out for this one. We're dealing with a handful."

"That's what she said," Paco and Charity said in unison, laughing as their unintended chorus pushed Alex quicker toward the door.

Feeling feisty, she tossed out a few parting one-liners. "Is it because I love playing hardball? Or that I run things up the flagpole? Up and down, technically," she said under her breath with a wink at Paco. Bedding a few business douches had given her all the office lingo she needed for banter ammunition.

Grumbling, Alex stopped in his tracks. As the tycoon turned around, she caught the sexy half smile he sported.

Smirking, Paco whispered, "Here it comes."

The glint in Alex's eye lifted his previously serious demeanor to stratospheric levels of playful hotness. "All right, Charity. You want to know why we want you?"

Cracking his knuckles, he continued, grandstanding with the business chops of a tech tycoon and the charisma of a megastar lead singer. He pulled out every business saying on tap, spiking each of them with a suggestive leer.

"How about this? For starters, you'll put in the effort to peel back the layers. I'm sure you have the bandwidth to really give it your all. You seem ready to go the extra mile for a deep dive. We can count on you to be laser focused on raising the bar. Without a doubt, you'll do more than touch base, paying close attention to the low-hanging fruit. Finally, more than anything, I believe in your ability to . . ." His gaze fell to her crotch. "Think outside your box."

People say first impressions are the strongest. But watching the man of a million innuendos walk away after spanking her at her own game of dirty clichés?

It was a moment Charity would never forget.

CHAPTER 6

CHARITY

Present day

CHARITY'S COMPENSATION with DGI was more than she ever dreamed of, making her fake, no-sex, call-girl status the most respectable job she'd ever had.

When the first nosy neighbor hit her with *So, what do you do?,* Charity gave the only answer that came to mind, and it was in every way the truth.

Lottery winner.

She'd never take the risk of getting too chummy or drink too much around others. Her job was highly confidential, and she took it seriously. Her kept-woman status was a front. A decoy. She was there to lure out anyone trying to get a prostitute to breach the walls protecting Alex Drake.

Human nature seemed to intrigue the CEO. Monty was a bigger idiot than he was a coward. If a lowlife like him thought of hiring a hooker to go after Alex, chances were he wasn't the first to think of it, nor the last.

Charity's job was cemented. She was a lab rat, testing a theory to satisfy the CEO's curiosity. But that didn't mean she would slack on the job. This guinea pig was diving into the research full force.

Task one? *Spread the word.*

Pounding the pavement, she used a street team of people she knew to go viral with the news. If anyone asked for a job and Alex Drake was mentioned, she'd give her informant a thousand dollars to refer the client to her. Yeah, the false positives were staggering, and the few that panned out were unsophisticated enough that Paco managed to somehow remove them from her workload.

Task two wasn't hers. Mr. Robles took that one. *Get her a reputation, one that always preceded her.*

Charity's new online handle? @Pay2PlayGirl. She was the premier escort to the rich and famous . . . hooker to the elite. Thanks to some DGI publicist she'd never met, her social media presence was locked and loaded.

Occasionally, she'd sneak a peek at the feed. Discovering she may or may not have had a *date* with a royal made her envy the hype.

Day in and day out, she focused less on her job and more on her healing. Self-discovery. Growing. Learning.

For the girl who'd graduated from high school by the skin of her teeth—and the foreskin of a few choice blow jobs—she couldn't believe she'd be this interested in going back to school. But this wasn't about the War of 1812 or some protozoa shit. It was about her.

For the first time in her life, Charity let herself dive into the darker sides of her past, eager to push past whatever she found. The days flew by, one psych class at a time. Before long, it wasn't enough, and she doubled up on her course load.

Little by little, the small doubts and self-loathing that had always cluttered her mind transformed into compassion and understanding—both for herself and others like her. But she still had a job to do.

The phone calls with tips that used to fill her days were less frequent now, but she never strayed from the formula. When her phone's ringtone tore her from her latest textbook, she answered, "Pay to play. This is Charity."

A few words into today's conversation, she quickly agreed to meet the caller in person at a nearby coffee shop. Parsing the bits and pieces from the cryptic interchange, she realized this one didn't seem to fit the mold.

Color me curious.

Usually, the scumbag wanting a piece of Alex Drake would be a little scuzzier and a little less pretentious. So after she ended the call, Charity scrolled to the first contact in her cell phone favorites, labeled simply PLAYER NUMBER 1.

"Hi. It's Charity. I've got a live one, but not the usual. Let me know what you want me to do."

CHAPTER 7

CHARITY

CHARITY TOOK a calming breath as her snooty companion danced all over her last damn nerve, the woman alternating between pout and frown. Apparently, the triple-shot half-caff cappuccino with almond milk, three pumps of hazelnut, a half pump of vanilla, a drizzle of caramel, and a dusting of mocha still hadn't exactly met the mark.

"Take this back."

Accommodating, the friendly waiter whisked away her oversized cup, asking, "Sure. What's wrong with it?"

"I said a hundred fifty degrees. This is too hot. It destroys the flavor."

Charity offered the waiter a *for the love of God* grin. "Thanks, Josh." His nametag displayed his title of assistant manager.

Sweetly, she smiled back at her tablemate, imagining Josh letting the mug cool in the back for five minutes to fully absorb the flavor of his Mentos-fresh spit. "So, how can I be of service, Miss . . ."

"Just call me Natasha." Paranoid, the woman said this low, keeping on her oversized Jackie O sunglasses despite being indoors.

Don't worry. I've got your number. "Happy to, Natasha. Since that's your name."

Suspicious, Natasha pushed the glasses farther up the bridge of her perky nose as she looked around. "What makes you say that?"

Resisting an eye roll, Charity gestured to the woman's designer purse. "Your credit card. You already paid for your ten-dollar coffee. Planning a speedy escape? In case the waiter actually wants a tip?"

Wide-eyed, Josh set down the refreshed cappuccino.

Charity grabbed his hand, discreetly slipping him a twenty, then tugged a straw from his black apron. Patiently, she unwrapped it, taking a long sip of her chilled hibiscus tea while she waited for Natasha to speak.

A quiet millennium passed as Natasha scanned the room over and over, then finally lowered her nasally voice to a whisper. "I need you to find out about a man."

"I'm not a PI. What do you want? His dick size?"

Obviously, I wasn't hired for my tact. This mole is going in . . . balls to the DGI wall.

Gaping at her in utter shock, Natasha wasn't winning any points with her prolonged offense.

Charity let loose a huff of mild irritation. "Are you gonna tell me what you want, or do I keep going with twenty questions?"

"I want to know more about someone. About his . . . preferences."

Nodding her approval, Charity leaned in. "I'm not exactly on an hourly rate. I need specifics. You know, to quote you a price."

CHAPTER 8

CHARITY

As the security escort led Charity in, Paco's office seemed different. Or perhaps her memory of that day over a year ago had been tainted. The rich burgundy hues accented by neutral tones and crown molding were vibrant and pleasing, details she'd missed when she was here before.

It was big, but homey with photos, a sword collection, encased coins, and exotic souvenirs, all undoubtedly from extensive travels around the globe. The room wrapped her in a sense of warmth and safety.

The invitation to debrief Alex and Paco after hours was an opportunity she'd jumped on. So much had changed in the last year and a half, thanks to them. Paco had checked in on Charity every now and then and could see the subtle ways she'd transformed between each visit. But Alex never had.

Both men were seated at a conference table that overlooked parts of Manhattan she'd never seen. They stood as she stepped in, but her stomach knotted at how woefully underdressed she was next to them, choosing jeans and a plain black but fitted long-sleeve shirt for their meeting.

"I should have changed," she said shyly.

"Not on our account," Alex said, his insistence making her comfortable as he wrapped both hands around hers for a tender shake.

Paco pulled her into a sweet hug, releasing her to pull out her chair.

"So," Alex asked. "What have you got?"

Charity passed over her phone to Alex, unlocked to a photo of the sunglass-sporting, prim-and-proper Natasha, but he deferred to Paco.

"Let's let the man who never forgets a face take a look first."

Charity complied, wondering if the gorgeous and mysterious Mr. Robles could get any hotter. Paco's face filled with delight at the image, but he didn't interrupt her recap.

"Natasha. That's the only name she gave me. I tried to read her whole name off her credit card, but the light hit it as she slipped it back into her wallet."

Paco chuckled. "She could go by a few names."

"A con artist?" Alex asked.

Paco shook his head. "Nope. This one's even better. You wouldn't know her real name, though her uncle Cecil would be familiar to you."

Intrigued, Alex volleyed another question across the table. "I'm being set up by a perve?"

"I doubt he even knows. But this girl just applied for a job. Here." He handed Alex the phone.

"Let me guess. She wants to be vice president of anything at all. Rich kids—they think their wealth and a degree give them a free pass to a seat on the executive board."

"Wrong again." Paco sported a grin, releasing the information bit by bit. "First name, Natasha. Last name she gave DGI was . . ." He tapped out a light drumroll on the table. "*Taylor.* Some phony paperwork landed her application on my desk. We thought she was a corporate spy, so we've been watching her and waiting. But this makes more sense."

Alex looked at him, patient and clueless.

Paco beamed, replying with a song in his voice. "Somebody's husband hunting."

Alex gulped, undoubtedly from the weight of crosshairs on his wallet. "Me? I'm the most unworthy wedding catch of the century."

"You said it, brother. You never sniff around the same tail twice, and rarely even bother learning their names."

Alex scowled. "Hey, my mind is full of important crap like national security technology and how to maintain a competitive edge in the global space. If I remembered all the women's names I spend a little time with, some poor penguin is getting sacrificed, flicked off the brain iceberg, and gone forever."

Shrugging, Paco didn't seem to care. "Whatever. It's not like they mind.

Women are eager to overlook the occasional indiscretion when a man's net worth starts with a *B*."

"Occasional indiscretion? To be more indiscreet, I'd have to hire a publicist." Alex's momentary aggravation melted quickly and he looked over at Charity. "Okay. She wants some insights into Alex Drake. Use your imagination and give her something good."

NATASHA

Three weeks later

WATCHING ALEX DRAKE, the legendary CEO of Drake Global Industries, was intoxicating. Natasha couldn't seem to get enough of him. On the internet, that is.

Recently graduating from an Ivy League university came with consequences. The moment the diploma hit her hand, Natasha's dad and step-mommy number three cut her off. No black card. No new car. No upscale condo. Nothing.

Getting a J-O-B wasn't exactly rocket science, but it had never quite made her must-do list either. And then there was that whole bullshit of keeping one. With the bills piling up and an eviction notice in her hands, she recalled the advice of her great-aunt Vera that hit her like a ton of cash: *marry well.*

How well? A billion reasons told her to aim high.

Natasha's father was a measly millionaire. If she could pull this off, the mansions, private jets, Bentleys, and jewels she'd enjoy would be great. Showing up that bastard, however, would be the diamond crust on her blinged-out wedding cake.

But single billionaires weren't exactly a dime a dozen.

With a little market research and an eye on the bottom line, Natasha focused on Alex Drake. One womanizing asshole was another girl's treasure.

Who cares that he's got a never-ending line of eager beavers? The guy's rich. Hot and really, really rich. What more could a girl want?

With Charity's help, Natasha got all the answers she needed. Like cramming for a test with the answer key in hand, her snatch was ready to snag a billionaire.

But she didn't need Charity for everything. Hell, for as guarded as the man tended to be, he was a bit of a publicity whore. And unfortunately, *Big Al* had all the makings of a one-night stand.

Egomaniac.

Notorious womanizer.

Asshole of epic proportions when the mood suited him.

My kind of guy.

The megamogul attracted a revolving door of girls a few nights a week. Never the same girl. This guy wasn't exactly marriage material, with his status officially being SINGLE for over a decade.

But men were made to be molded. At least, their desires were. Because the way Natasha saw it, there wasn't one solitary thing on this man's body that needed refining. From the outside, Alex Drake could have been sculpted by Michelangelo.

The man was a god from every angle. In the rare shots of him in gym clothes, the rock-hard muscles of his body were pure eye candy. He had the legs of a marathoner, and that ass could only be earned by screwing women up against a wall six nights a week and twice on Sunday.

His bad-boy looks got him noticed, and his bank account made him a magnet for all the wet and wild women he could handle. But his heart remained a mystery. Maybe, like Natasha, he didn't have one.

Scanning the internet's sea of photos of Alex Drake's dates, she realized the man didn't seem to be looking for anything in particular in a woman. In fact, he wasn't particular at all.

Boobs: Full B through double D. *Check.*

Ass: The bigger, the better. *Check plus.*

Age: The alpha male liked them younger, but not too young, somewhere between the ages of twenty-four to twenty-six or -seven. At twenty-two, Natasha was two years below his threshold.

Will two years really make a difference?

Whatever. I was born to break down barriers.

Demeanor: Not too slutty. Or too senseless. And definitely not too sweet. Street-smart sassy was his type of sexy. *It's in the bag.*

Height and weight: Irrelevant.

Education: Inconsequential. *Maybe he just needs the right Ivy Leaguer.*

Obsession: Fetish rumors out the wazoo. Literally. And an obsession for the name Taylor.

Not for a first name, as in Swift. But a last name.

A woman with the last name Taylor seemed to get insta-access to the reclusive billionaire. At least for the night. He'd drop almost everything to get to know a woman better if an attractive body was attached to that name.

But Natasha wasn't into chasing rumors. Theories were meant to be tested. And what she needed was a hooker. Not for herself, obviously. She got plenty. And was straight.

I'm not defined by my freshman year.

Three weeks ago, hiring a prostitute to stumble upon him seemed prudent. With Charity, high-end happy endings could be arranged for a big fat pile of cash up front. But for surveillance and possibly satisfaction, she accepted a compromise. Half of the fee agreed to up front, and the other half would be due when she delivered the intel.

Like most men, Alex Drake had his habits. He regularly ordered a late dinner on Friday nights. Always to his office. The very same boring meal each and every time.

A Big Mac. No side. Apple pie. No drink.

What kind of psycho doesn't order fries?

Natasha took care of his regular delivery guy. She knew his minions wouldn't take a bribe. But the delivery man had to call out when his dog went missing, right? And the pup would only be gone for a few hours, so no harm done.

This gave Charity, aka Ms. Taylor, an in to deliver the food, show off her nametag, and report back everything that happened.

And what a report it was.

Direct access to the billionaire's Manhattan office had been a lot easier than Natasha expected. Charity did as she'd been told, delivering the grub to Alex's building with the nametag C. TAYLOR on prominent display. Security sent her right up.

And when she'd worn the nametag proudly, hoisted up by her full C cups, Alex noticed.

Natasha got an earful of all the delectably lewd details back at the coffee shop where they'd had their first meeting.

Fetishes were one thing. This guy turned out to be a straight-up freak. Wide-eyed and gawking, she'd eaten up Charity's account.

Apparently, Charity had easily been cleared to hand-deliver the meal straight to Alex's executive office. When she did, he tossed several hundred-dollar bills on his desk, paving the way to an offer she couldn't refuse. But first, he'd asked a few questions to break the ice.

Where was she from? Did she have any siblings? And a final question about fetishes removed any remaining icebergs in his path.

Frowning, Natasha asked, "He's looking for something. What?"

Charity shrugged. "Rich, powerful men don't like wasting their time. He was cutting to the chase, wanting to make sure he wasn't in the presence of a nun. And I'm a pro. I tailor my desires around those of my client. *No* rarely escapes these DSLs. I'll try anything once, and said so. He liked it, my willingness to explore. Then he tossed a ton of money on the desk, and we went at it."

Eager, Natasha lowered her voice and leaned in. "How much money?"

"Initially, a thousand. But trust me, it wasn't enough. That dude took me down a sexual rabbit hole so bizarre, I'm still not sure what the hell happened. I thought I'd seen it all." Blowing out a heavy breath, Charity pushed her hair from her eyes, opening them wide. "Apparently not."

Natasha drummed her fingers, revealing her impatience.

"Oh, right. You wanted details. Well, he started slow, probably because he knew I'd be a little . . . hesitant."

"Hesitant? You?"

Charity shelled out the torrid details, starting with what she called Drake's Dirty Sanchez.

Shocked, Natasha slapped her hand over her mouth, her imagination running wild. *Oh dear God, my complexion was not made for a poo mustache.* "You don't mean—"

"No," Charity said, assuring her with an insistent shake of her head.

Whether he was a billionaire or not, Natasha had standards. At least, that's what she told herself, realizing that a face full of crap set a new benchmark. But what she heard next barely qualified as any better.

Apparently, Alex Drake had a sexual appetite for, of all things, condiments. Natasha's mouth fell open as Charity continued.

"He opened his desk drawer. It was filled to the brim with those tiny little bottles you get with room service. Ketchup. Mayo. Even hot sauce. You can imagine my relief when relish wasn't his first pick, but champagne mustard wasn't much better. He likes his crunchy."

Perplexed, Natasha said, "Crunchy?"

"You know. It had those tiny little peppercorns in it."

"Mustard seeds," Natasha said, and her correction was met with a stern *who the fuck cares* glance.

"He explained what he wanted, and had me pull my panties off and shove them in his mouth. He wanted me to put my finger in the mustard, then wipe it under his nose, back and forth, while asking him if he liked that. Oh, and scolding him over and over for being a filthy boy. A dirty, filthy boy." Shifting uncomfortably, Charity clasped her hands. "And *that's* when things turned twisted."

Natasha sucked in a breath. *What the fuck? It gets weirder than this?*

"Without any warning, he dropped his pants—junk in the wind—and stared me down like a raging bull aiming at a matador, ready for the pounding. Giving me a stern look, he motioned for me to remove the wad of undies stuffed in his mouth, and then he stretched the lace to bind my hands."

Lifting her hands in front of her face, Charity demonstrated for effect. "Then he sucked my finger clean of all that nasty spicy mustard. I tried not to look too grossed out, but I don't have the best poker face."

Natasha heaved. *"Ew."*

"Right?" Charity rolled her eyes. "At least he didn't make *me* eat it."

As Charity's overly descriptive account kept coming, Natasha shivered in disgust, realizing that she might not have it as easy.

"With his custom-tailored, lightly starched shirt still on—tie and all—he demanded I reach underneath and up, pinching his nipples hard while telling him to take it. Oh, and call him Sally. So I kept doing it, even while he started jacking off."

Bewildered, Natasha finally pushed away the disturbing visual. "Why Sally?"

Charity shrugged with wide, rolling eyes. "Why any of it? But he seemed to like it. A lot."

Natasha huffed. "What a whack job."

"I still haven't told you the really weird shit."

"Holy fuck. There's more?"

"Oh yeah. So, he gets me into position. You know, typical bang-from-behind job. Then he pulls the panties off my hands and stuffs them back in his mouth.

With my hands on the desk, I waited. I knew he was serious when he slipped on a condom. His grunt was wild and animal-like as he pushed in, but then the sound changed."

"Changed how?"

"At first, I thought it was just a drawn-out moan. But when he got to pumping, I realized he was humming. There he was, picking up the pace, thrusting in and out as he hummed the tune of 'Row, Row, Row Your Boat.' Back and forth. With each beat of his thrusts."

Despite Natasha's blaring disbelief, Charity rushed to the finish line.

"I don't know. Somehow, it was catchy. At some point, I started humming along." Charity hummed the tune.

Unable to stop herself, Natasha joined in. *She's right. It is catchy.*

"Then we went into a full-on round, me starting with 'row' as he'd started 'gently' . . . down my stream."

The visual played out in Natasha's mind, and then she imagined herself in the mix. Humping. Humming. "I'm almost afraid to ask, but what happened next?"

"That was it. He came. And I went."

"Did he ask for your number?"

Charity's drawn-out head shake and blasé face said it all. "Frankly, I'm relieved. I'll stick with cracking the whip with my BDSM tribe and leave this gem to you."

Standing, Natasha threw out a quick, "Thanks."

Charity raised her voice. "Aren't you forgetting something?"

Looking around to be sure no one was watching, Natasha dropped her ass back into the seat and hissed, "I don't owe you anything. Sounds like you got more than you were due . . . from Alex."

"What he paid me isn't even half of what you owe me."

Natasha ignored her glare. "Please. You're a whore. You're used to getting fucked, and at least this time you had the privilege of being banged by one of the richest men in the world. If anything, you owe me. But let's call it even. Unless you want me to drop a dime on you with Vice."

Again, Natasha moved to head out, and this time, Charity didn't stop her.

CHAPTER 10

NATASHA

TAKING a low-level clerk job at DGI was easy enough when Natasha backed down her highest education level to a high school diploma. Although the work was well below the standards of her Ivy League education and family wealth, she wasn't there to make ends meet.

In the two weeks since the wild and bizarre revelations by Charity, Natasha doubled down on her goal—to meet Alex Drake.

Spinning in her chair in her cubicle and staring at the banking app on her phone, she blew out a disappointed breath. Willing the few hundred dollars in her checking account to magically multiply wasn't exactly a strategy. Time to catch his eye.

Her skintight skirts met the minimum length requirement of the DGI dress code in the company handbook. But they were totally wasted last week, as the busy CEO was out of town on business.

And even with him back in the office, the tycoon always surrounded himself with an entourage as he zipped to this meeting and that. Stalking a crazed workaholic killed her feet and her matrimonial buzz, but Natasha was getting closer . . . one epic fail at a time.

On more than one occasion, staging her way to *accidentally* bump into the boss reminded her of Thomas Edison's quote about not failing ten thousand times, but successfully finding ten thousand ways that didn't work.

So far, she'd found a couple. Literally two failures, and they were agonizing. *I'm in it to win it, but I'm not committing to inventing a light bulb.*

Natasha was so motivated, she could practically taste him. *I mean "it." Taste it. The money.* The idea of tasting him couldn't be separated in her mind from the various condiments he probably came with. Disgusted, she shuddered at the eventuality.

Attempt number one was so perfectly timed, it still perplexed her that it resulted in her first failure. With some approximation, she'd counted out twenty-three Drake-sized steps from the door leading from the executive parking deck to the lobby security desk. Stopping there every morning seemed to be his thing.

Chummy with the staff. Why bother?

Natasha's plan was foolproof. In a routine choreographed only in her head, at step eighteen, she'd trip right into him, but *save* his cup of coffee—his choice executive accessory. With her body pressed into his, her breasts spilling over, and a shy bat of her eyes, she fully expected his gratitude would lead to a dinner invitation.

But she hadn't anticipated that he'd stop, let alone back up, right at the perfect step. With nothing but his cup of coffee to catch her fall, she grabbed it on her way to toppling onto the security desk.

"Are you all right?" a low, gruff voice asked, filled with concern.

But it didn't belong to Chairman Moneybags. It was the monstrously huge chief of security, fumbling to wipe the coffee from his desk who asked after her welfare.

Checking his watch, Alex barely stopped. "Fife, I'll catch up with you later."

Disappointed, Natasha watched her quarry head to his private elevator. Who better to take out her frustrations on than a man a few echelons beneath her?

"Someone really needs to check these floors. I could've broken my leg. Sued the whole damn company." Reconsidering her statement, she took to limping halfway to the peon elevator. Just in case. *Always have a Plan B.*

Failed attempt number two was another issue in timing. Despite practicing the choreographed "trip" several times, she was intercepted by the hot Latin heartthrob who seemed to be fucking everywhere. The guy hung on Alex Drake like a much sexier second skin. *Why can't he be the billionaire?*

Planning on intercepting another of Alex Drake's afternoon routes, Natasha dressed that day in her flirtiest sheer white blouse classed up with a black lace bra beneath. Counting down with a *three, two, one*, she sprang full force from the snack room.

Rather than landing in the arms of Mr. Tall, Dark, and Wealthy, she smacked right into the hot, spicy, and ever so bite-worthy Mr. Robles.

Catching her stumbling body and dipping it like a dancer, he locked eyes with her in their impromptu tango as he asked, "Do you dance here often?"

For no reason at all, she giggled.

Inhaling as he held her, he took a deep whiff. "Chanel?"

Nodding, she stuttered, "Y-yes. It's Mademoiselle."

The moment was heaven. Paco's eyes were kind and gentlemanly. His strength wasn't obvious from the fit of his suit and lean physique. Yet he held her effortlessly in a prolonged dip, his arms wrapped around her.

In anticipation, she couldn't help but check out his lips. *God, he's going to kiss me.* Natasha's eyes fell shut, and her willing lips parted.

"Any day, Mr. Robles."

Alex's irritated bark seemed to motivate Paco. Whisking her up and into a spin before releasing her, he was off, hurrying after the boss.

Private dance lessons are a must for the future Mrs. Drake.

Finally, in a stroke of luck, Natasha's clerk duties gave her the break she needed—access to the executive floors, in particular, the office of the CEO. A small but heavy box needed to be delivered, and she snatched it from the hands of her coworker and took it to the fifty-second floor.

Having doublechecked her lipstick, hair, and bosom, she knocked. Then knocked again.

Nothing.

Not bumping into the elusive billionaire was fine. She'd make the most of her big break. Or break-in. The door was locked, but her access card would work. Clerks had access for deliveries.

One swipe, and the door unlocked. Peeking in, Natasha found the office was empty.

Confident that if anyone caught her—especially Alex Drake himself—the box in her hand was all the excuse she needed to justify her presence there.

The office was the biggest she'd ever seen, and she'd seen some doozies. Through several floor-to-ceiling windows, the views of Central Park were striking. But then again, they always were. From every angle.

Squinting, Natasha could almost make out her own family's corporate building clear across the expanse of lush trees, only interrupted by waterways and green spaces. From this vantage point, she barely saw the dots of tiny people moving this way and that down below, content that they were meant to stay far beneath her.

She turned and glanced around.

The office seemed elegant, yet understated. No photos or homey touches. The clean lines could have cost an arm and a leg or been a quick buy from IKEA. The oversized desk in a deep cherry wood was the only piece of furniture that looked to be worth an outrageous amount. The design wasn't familiar, but Natasha had grown up around enough opulent furnishings to know the really expensive stuff from the crap.

Moseying over to the desk, she set down the heavy box with a clank. Curious, she pried open the lid. Her hands flew up to cover her wide-open mouth.

Holy shit. Condiments!

The stacks of teeny-tiny jars made her eyes widen. *How many women does this guy go through?*

Easing herself into his chair, Natasha stared. The thought of sticking her finger into the icky goo of a condiment and smearing it anywhere made her shudder. *Gross.*

Casting her gaze around to absolutely anything else, she caught sight of the open planner on his desk. Before she could get a good long look-see, her cell buzzed with a text.

SUPERVISOR STEVE: Where are you?
NATASHA: Bathroom. Period. Gushing everywhere.

She added a toilet emoji and a dozen blood drops. *That should stop the texts.* After snapping a few quick shots of his calendar, she headed out.

CHAPTER 11

NATASHA

From across Gotham Hall, the grand banquet hall in Manhattan, Natasha fixed her gaze on the man who would be hers.

Tickets to the event started at five thousand dollars, and that was just for dinner and ambience. The fundraiser boasted a charity auction openly targeting a million-dollar goal for the event.

Obtaining a last-minute ticket was no easy feat. She could have gotten it legitimately, offering herself up as a date to any of half a dozen Wall Street yutzes who'd love to be photographed for the society pages with a blueblood like her on their arm.

But her eye was on the prize, and the last thing Natasha needed was the ball and chain of a date. So, using her wits, know-how, and a tank top, she found just the ticket she needed . . . bumming it off her uncle.

Uncle Cecil was good for three things—cash, cars, and charitable event tickets. Or at least he used to be. At her parents' insistence, he'd recently shut off the cash tap. And after one crash too many in his Maserati, the dude had suddenly gotten pissy about it.

But with enough cleavage and a lot of teasing, she got her ticket.

What? He's related by marriage, and everyone knows Auntie Lacie fucks around. Besides, it's not like I gave him a blow job.

As Natasha moseyed through the towering floral arrangements of creamy white and violet orchids to the tempo of the twelve-piece orchestra playing soft top-forty hits, she relished how everything about the gala screamed expensive. Lifting a flute of champagne from a harried waiter's tray, she pulled in a meditative breath that relaxed every muscle in her body.

It's good to be home.

Another tuxedoed waiter paused next to her, offering a tray. Carefully selecting a canapé that didn't reek of fish, she caught the eye of just the whale she'd snag.

As Alex Drake worked the room, his wandering gaze locked in on Natasha and raked up and down her body. There was no mistaking the hunger in his eyes. Batting her lash extensions, she smiled back.

I'll be engaged by the end of the week.

Surrounding him were a few social climbers she didn't recognize, and one guy she did. And that man started heading straight for her. Thinking about how Alex had barked at him, and how he was always on the CEO's heels, she reconsidered his position.

Must be his personal assistant. What's his name?

Then Natasha remembered. *Pablo.*

With a bright smile and a song in his voice, he said, "Mr. Drake would like the pleasure of your company."

"Of course he would." Handing the flunky her half-consumed glass of bubbly, she tucked her hair behind an ear and grabbed herself a fresh drink. The look on his face prompted her to explain. "Oh, that's really good stuff. Don't worry, I'll let Big Al know I said it was okay. No need to thank me, Pablo."

His smile stretched across his face. "How very generous of you, Ms. *Taylor.*"

Whatever he meant by stressing her supposed last name was something she'd deal with later. A billionaire was waiting for her.

Gliding elegantly toward him, Natasha hoped her upper-crust lineage was unmistakable. And by the looks of Alex's pearly-white smile, he was all in.

He's already eating out of my hands. And I haven't even graced him with a hello.

"Hello." The sexy timbre of his voice sent a shiver through her. Whatever the hell she was about to say was gone.

"Uh, uh . . . hello."

He didn't wait for more words, taking her hand in his. "It's such a pleasure to meet you. Ms. Taylor, is it?"

"Hmm? Oh, uh, yes. That's me." Collecting herself, she said, "But you may call me Natasha."

Alex smiled. "May I? And of course, you know Paco from your waltz in the hall." He reached out to tilt Paco's hand, turning the champagne flute just so, as the sugar-berry lip gloss on its rim shimmered.

He has to know it's expensive.

With a half-cocked smile and a popped brow, Alex asked, "May he call you Natasha too?"

"Huh?" Confused, she looked at the two men, not quite grasping the peculiar intent behind their smiles.

Oh God. Is he proposing a three-way? Not that I'm a prude, or would mind a delectable sample of all this hot and spicy beef, but seriously? Chatting about this . . . out in the open and in front of everyone? How about a little discretion?

"Paco!"

An attractive man with quite the looker on his arm strolled up to clap a hearty pat on Paco's back. The man was immediately recognizable, and she prayed her gasp was silent.

Trevor Stuart had made her top-ten list of most eligible rich bachelors, but just barely. His gaming company's banner year jumped him ahead three spaces to a solid number ten—until that very morning, when his engagement was announced.

Natasha's initial gawking turned to a sneer.

I can't believe he's with this fake-boobed bimbo. Ogling the woman's baseball-sized diamond ring, she redoubled her resolve to have one much bigger on her finger. Soon.

"Trev," Paco or Pablo said, "this can't possibly be the woman we've heard so much about. Anna Lindsey, your work in robotics precedes you. Alex and I would love to steal you away to the dark side if you'd ever consider leaving the gaming world."

This dude seriously needs to stop kissing their ass and work on mine. And what's with Alex and me?

Skeptical, Natasha bounced her gaze between Alex and Paco. *They're definitely weirdly close.*

When the conversation suddenly quieted, Natasha froze when she realized all eyes were on her, and she vaguely thought she'd heard them ask something.

What was it they said? Think!

Alex's dimple popped as he smiled again. "Oh, this is Ms., um, I'm so sorry, what was your name again?"

A quick rush of fury burned her cheeks but abated quickly with the short mantra that always got her through anything.

Ten flawless carats. Ten flawless carats.

"Natasha," she said before waking her smile.

"That's beautiful," Anna said. "What do you do, Natasha?"

Unprepared, she pulled in a quick breath as her eyes widened. Sure, she could lie without a second thought. But she couldn't get caught in one just yet.

On the DGI books, she was an entry-level clerk, but there was no way those words were coming out of her mouth with this crowd. And her degree was left off the application. The social security number was a bit tricky, but fake paperwork about an upcoming annulment seemed to explain away the name discrepancy.

"This young lady just graduated from Wharton," Alex said, lifting his glass in a toast to her.

Impressed, the small crowd murmured appreciatively, but Natasha's normal pride for her alma mater was snuffed out by nervousness. *How does he know that?*

Suspicious, she stared at Alex's right-hand man. Squinting, she asked herself, *Does Pablo know?*

Or was it Paco? Pablo . . . Paco. He's sexy, but a nobody. Whatever.

"I'm dying over that Lamborghini outside. I was really trying to hold off on buying one, but it's so sweet," Trevor said, gushing about her favorite car. A Lamborghini was one of the first things on her to-buy list as soon as she tied the knot. "Though I'm not sure I can pull off yellow."

"It's a Lambo," Paco said with a smile. "Anyone can pull it off. And driving around in that bright beast definitely brightens my day."

His revelation made him unbelievably magnetic.

Natasha took a step toward him, barely noticing that Alex was stepping away. The heat of Paco's Latin accent and the obvious chiseled physique barely hiding beneath his fitted suit made her move closer.

Painting on her most seductive smile, she asked, "You have a Lambo?"

"A Lamborghini? Me? No." Paco laughed off her comment. Leaning in, he said, "This will be lucky number three."

His wink was all she needed to hook her arm around his. He didn't seem to mind. *Why would he? I'm a prize.*

Seeming to enjoy her touch, he ran his gaze over her lovingly. "Don't we make quite the attractive couple?"

His boast to Trevor and Anna gave Natasha a boost. Her posture straightened with the assurance of a woman bred for the finer things.

Clinking her champagne glass to his, she beamed. "We certainly do." Her extra mouthful of bubbly was just the cherry to top this delicious cake.

Locking his dark gaze to hers, Paco added, "If only I weren't gay."

Champagne nearly shot out her nose as she choked down her swallow. "You're gay?" burst from her lips, the timbre of her tone distinctly asking if the matter could be negotiated.

"And my date has finally arrived."

Spotting the hunky beefcake heading for them, Natasha reeled as the hits kept coming. Now she had to cross lick-worthy number five off her list.

Six-foot-four-inch ebony god with the dreamy chocolate eyes Grant Evans? He's gay too? Goddammit!

Removing himself from Natasha's clutch, Paco greeted his guest with two cheek-to-cheek kisses, and returned her untouched, still half-full flute of champagne to her limp hand. Her lipstick stain remained intact.

"Do you mind taking care of that? I'll make sure to put in a good word with *Big Al.*"

Big Al. Snapped back to her original goal, Natasha scanned the room in haste. *Fuck.* Alex Drake was nowhere to be seen.

No, no, no. Tell me he didn't leave.

Her feet quickly carried her past the small clusters of chitchatting hobnobbers to see if she could catch a glimpse of the elusive Mr. Drake. She raced around the grand banquet hall, cursing her three-thousand-dollar stilettos with every step.

In a secluded corridor, a floor-to-ceiling inscription bathed in the glow of old-fashioned lights caught Natasha before she passed it. She mumbled a few words, as if reading the chiseled stone letters aloud would give her some clarity.

. . . know that your own money, rewarded for its service, returns to you as strength and surety for the years to come.

Under her breath, she huffed. "What the fuck does that mean?"

"It's like a riddle, isn't it?"

Startled, she whirled around, catching the tall, dark figure staring at her with a half smile.

"Gotham Hall used to be a bank."

Curious, Natasha said, "Really?"

"Yup." Alex strolled casually to the massive plaque, stopping beside her and looking up. "These lofty words met everyone who entered the bank since it was built in the eighteen thirties. Gave them confidence that their money would grow in these walls. Their pennies would bloom and make them richer and richer."

"So, it outgrew its money? Where'd it move to?"

He scoffed. "It didn't. These words are nothing but a big, steaming pile of bullshit. Greenwich Savings Bank dissolved in 1981. At the time, it was the sixteenth largest deposit holder in the country with one point five billion dollars."

"How could a bank fail with that much money?"

Matter-of-factly, he said, "Oh, you know. Recessions. Deregulation. A leak that they were about to be sold. Greenwich Savings lost a third of its deposits when the news came out. A run on the bank is the fastest way to lose half a billion dollars in three days."

Noticing he'd again pronounced the word to rhyme with *sandwich*, Natasha couldn't help but correct him. "Don't you mean *gren-ich*?"

Obviously amused, he smirked. "Everyone walks away from a story with a different lesson. But you're used to homework . . . after four years of college."

Defensive, she asked, "How do you know that?"

Alex towered over her, the heat of his body kicking up her pulse, forcing her lips to part to take a needed breath.

"I know everything because I do my homework. Like I know the correct pronunciation of your last name. You've pronounced it *TAY-lor*. But everyone knows if you sound it out correctly, it sounds like *JAY-me-son*. Of the Long Island Jamesons."

Caught, Natasha didn't meet his eyes. Instead, she turned on her heel, simply saying, "Excuse me."

Lightly, Alex wrapped his large hand around her arm. "Leaving so soon? But I haven't even given you my proposal yet."

CHAPTER 12

NATASHA

FROM GOTHAM HALL, the ride was an unnerving silent eternity. Natasha couldn't help staring at Alex, wondering what would happen. She'd prepared herself for the worst. Well, at least the worst she could imagine.

A far cry from a Lamborghini, his Rolls-Royce seemed to age him. Like, he could be her father. Mulling it over, she wondered how many women he'd been with. Had any of them called him Daddy? Trying it on for size, she mouthed the word to herself.

"Did you just say *Daddy?*"

His chuckle brought a ripe heat to her cheeks.

"No." Natasha lied, denying it outright. *The fucker has hearing as sharp as a dog's.*

As he pulled the car into a private garage at DGI, she froze.

Shit. Nobody proposes at an office. Without a doubt, he wanted his quickie at the bone zone to have a view. Disappointed, she tried not to pout too hard to avoid future wrinkles around her lips.

Parking practically in the center of the massive garage, he got out. Gentlemanly enough, he opened her door, but she didn't budge.

"I'm not a one-night stand."

"Whoa," he said, smugly scoffing. "Who said anything about an entire night? Don't get too comfortable there, missy."

Indifferent, he headed to an elevator, whistling the catchy tune to "Row, Row, Row Your Boat."

Without many options, Natasha followed, picking up the pace as he didn't seem like the patient type.

His executive office was becoming familiar. Though she'd seen the jaw-dropping views and would have loved to see them at night, the blinds were all closed. The lights were on before they entered, nearly at gas-station levels of blinding.

"You said something about a proposal." Her insistence was born of both irritation and jitters. Something about the way he gazed at her felt dark. Dirty. Thinking of Charity's description of Drake's Dirty Sanchez, she shivered a silent *bleh*.

Alex rounded his desk to sit in his executive chair, his comfort apparent as he leaned back, propped his elbows on the armrests, and steepled his fingers.

There she stood, doing her best to control her breathing. His gaze moved up and down her body, but the look he gave her wasn't lust.

What is it? Measuring me up?

Insecure, Natasha stood taller, then second-guessed her outfit. But if he was the kind of guy she thought he was, a loose skirt was just up his alley. Or technically, the fastest way up *her* alley.

As she stood there, she took the opportunity to study him back.

Alex was attractive. Like, really, *really* attractive. He filled out a suit so well, it was as if she could see every chiseled muscle in his chest. If she ran her tongue up the side of his neck to the hard angles of his jaw, would the stubble bother her?

The stark contrast between the dark man before her and the men she'd dated —boys by comparison—set her mind to wondering what it would be like. To be taken by him.

As Natasha waited in front of his desk like any other employee, her gaze wandered to his lap. Maybe today, this employee would be getting a billion-dollar bonus.

"Come here."

His demand was menacing, making her shiver in a way she couldn't understand. Or resist. Not comprehending why, she obeyed.

Standing up and moving behind her, out of view, he deepened his voice. "Put your hands on the desk."

Again, she didn't question it, or object. Or even play hard to get. *What's wrong with me?*

The heat of his hands warmed the cheeks of her butt before pulling her skirt above her waist. The coolness of his office breezed against her flesh, a stark contrast to the heat of his touch that rubbed softly, then vanished.

For the first time in years, Natasha felt herself getting wet. She braced for impact. *It's the bang-'em-from-behind move Charity mentioned.*

Before anything happened, she started humming with a subtle sway to her ass. *Row, row, row your boat . . .*

To her dismay—and disgust—a tiny room-service-size jar of mayonnaise was set in front of her.

Wide-eyed, she panicked. *Nooo. Not the Drake Dirty Sanchez. And with mayo. Ew.*

Next to it, he slid a small stack of hundreds. A very small stack. By the looks of it, three hundred dollars was the extent of her enticement.

Furious, Natasha balked. "Don't you think I'm worth more?"

His tone firm, he said, "I'm not even sure you're worth that."

"But you gave—"

A firm smack of his hand hit her ass. The sting sent a shock wave throughout her body, instantly shutting her up. As soon as she eked out a second sound, his hand hit the other cheek.

God, I want this man to fuck me. This is the closest I've been to an orgasm in ages. Well, by someone else's hand.

"Hmm? You were saying?" Suddenly disinterested, he moved to the sofa, leaving her. "I gave someone something? Probably. I tend to do that with the ones I like. The ones who seem a little extra special. I don't pay spoiled little brats to snoop through my stuff and behave badly. If anything, you should be paying me for your lesson."

Uncertain, Natasha watched him as he swiped the latest *Forbes* from the decorative table before him, thumbing through it without looking back at her.

Wading through a thick pool of confusion and bullshit, and wishing she didn't want another spank, she grabbed the jar of mayonnaise.

Hesitating for only a few seconds, she hurled the condiment hard across the room. Though it was perfectly aimed at his pompous head, that weak arm of hers that her tennis coach warned her about failed her again. The little jar thudded along the carpet several feet short of him.

Throwing a *tsk-tsk-tsk* her way, he raised a brow over the magazine before chastising her. "O for two. Oh, wait. There was also Paco. That's O for three."

Furious, Natasha stomped over, shimmying her skirt back down as she fumed. "You're an asshole."

"That's what they tell me." Tossing the magazine aside, he eased onto the tufted leather sofa, casually slinging an arm over the back. "And you, my dear, are an Ivy Leaguer who'd rather bang her way to the top instead of earning it. You have the smarts and connections to blow a hole through corporate America, and you want to piss it down the drain? Fine. You want to take to whoring and trade your dignity away? Here's the deal. The street value of your prim little puss isn't worth the price of a venti latte. But the photos and videos I took of you bent over my desk are worth a hell of a lot more."

Photos? Videos?

Swallowing the ball of regret lodged in her throat, Natasha couldn't speak, her thoughts strangling whatever words she tried uttering. His smug smile made her wish her aim had been better with that damn jar.

Regaining her composure, she shot back, "What do you want, fuckhead?"

"Fuckhead?" Alex asked, feigning shock. "Wow, you kiss your uncle Cecil's ass with that mouth?"

Rage flamed across her neck and cheeks. "How do you know about that?"

"Sorry, I thought I was clear. I do my homework. But then again, that wasn't exactly a secret."

Drawing on a sweetness usually reserved for just that uncle in question, Natasha batted her eyes. "Look, I don't have money. My family cut me—"

"I'm not exactly hard up for cash, and I know your issues with your family."

"Wow, you weren't kidding when you said you do your homework."

Alex shook his head. "I barely needed to. You keep airing your family's dirty laundry and can't stop bashing them on Twitter."

Slamming her eyes shut before rolling them, Natasha hated where this was going. "Then what? What is it you want?"

The delight in his eyes sent her mind reeling. His smile hid some devious secret she wasn't sure she'd like.

Finally, he spoke. "To offer you a little deal."

CHAPTER 13

NATASHA

Natasha watched Alex's comfortable stroll back to his desk. As he removed his blazer to hang it on the back of his leather chair, she surmised that God's gift to women was preparing to bestow her with the legendary package in his pants.

"I assume you have protection." Natasha's tone vacillated between hope and trepidation. She sure as hell didn't have anything on her.

"Oh, we won't need a condom between us."

Her mouth agape, she wondered if this was just the lotto win she needed. Stretch marks would suck. And breastfeeding was O-U-T. But a baby would mean a lifetime guarantee of the good life.

Suspicious, she sensed something was off. "Why don't we need a condom?"

Alex's boyish smile widened to a full face of mischief. "If I tell you, I'll spoil the surprise."

Her unsettled pout seemed to have an impact on him.

"Here's the deal. I'm not going to tell you what we're doing until you unconditionally agree that you'll do it."

Natasha's eyes flew open wide. "You want me to agree to something I don't know? Why would anyone in their right mind do that?"

Grinning, he said, "Because there's ten thousand dollars in it for you if you do. It would've been twenty, but you stiffed someone I like."

Goddamn Charity.

Natasha took a firm stance, crossing her arms and bowing up to a man twice her size who seemed to be mocking her with a mirrored pose. "I'm not agreeing to anything unless I know the terms."

Nonchalant, he lifted a brow. "At least you're sounding a little like someone with a business degree. I'll tell you what. You can ask me three questions, the kind that require a yes or no answer. I'll give you those to decide if you're in or out. But at the end of it, either you're walking out of here with nothing, never to darken the door of my global empire again. Or you're mine for two hours, at the end of which you walk away with the cash."

From the inside pocket of his high-end suit, he tugged out a bundle. "Ten thousand dollars," he said again, reminding her of the stakes of her decision.

As it landed on his desk, Natasha could practically smell the condiment ambrosia.

Loosening his tie, he bent over to pick up the tiny jar of mayonnaise. "What should we do with this?"

Before she could utter the disgusting term out loud, he tossed the jar in the trash.

Her shoulders relaxed with relief. *Oh thank God.*

"Now, your questions."

"Three questions, huh?" Pursing her lips, she eyed the chess master up and down, thinking about why he wouldn't want a condom. "Are you planning to fuck me in the ass?"

"Decent guess. But it's a little too, I don't know, unimaginative for a girl like you. So, no."

He's getting creative. Whatever. This guy's a freak.

Nervous, Natasha asked, "Are any food products involved at all?"

"Food *products*? That's vague. Makes me think of gas station roller food. Hmm . . ." His sadistic smile curled up. "Let's go with no. Last question."

She took her time thinking it over, rummaging through every detail of Charity's account.

No Drake Dirty Sanchez. Nursery rhyme timed to his thrusts . . . I've had worse. And shoving my panties in his mouth would be a bonus to shut his smug trap up. But what would be imaginative? What else does he want?

Natasha's palms started sweating before she asked the last question. Studying his eyes, she mused aloud. "Are you going to hurt me?"

Those bright eyes she'd been watching turned darker. "No," he said, insistent in letting the word land firmly between them.

A second later, the glint in them returned.

"Now, little girl, you're out of questions and out of time." Fanning the bills in front of his face, he asked, "Are you sticking around . . . or walking out?"

CHAPTER 14

NATASHA

"You could just tell me what I'm in for." Natasha kicked up the charm with a few flutters of her lashes.

"Where's the fun in that? You've been scheming for weeks to bust into my world. In case you didn't get the memo, my empire—my rules. And in another minute, the choice won't be yours. This little deal turns into a pumpkin in sixty seconds. Fifty-nine. Fifty-eight."

"What if I leave before the two hours is up," she asked quickly, popping her hands on her thighs in a last-ditch effort to stall.

"Then I send the photos straight to *Page Six* with every tawdry detail of your plan to bed me. And you've only got a few seconds left."

He had to be playing her. "Oh, but you won't just send them anyway?"

"I won't."

"What? I'm just supposed to take your word for that?"

Shrugging, Alex smiled with the confidence of a man used to playing hardball, and just enough of a smartass smirk to sink her gut. He had her.

Unlocking her hands, Natasha made a break for the door. *Fuck him.* Determined, she grabbed the handle.

But the warm thought of ten thousand dollars in her grasp stopped her from turning the cold metal doorknob. *It's ten thousand dollars. Fine. I'll fuck him. Or let him fuck me and pray the son of a bitch doesn't fuck me over.*

"Staying?" he asked, waving the stack at her hypnotically.

Frowning, she nodded.

"Then let's get started. There's something I've been meaning to try." His mind seemed to turn as he said the words, as if he'd only just considered it. "And, well, it's a little different from what women usually do for me." With a chuckle, he huffed. "I mean, it's a *lot* different from what women usually do for me."

Great. Rolling her eyes, Natasha asked, "No NDA?"

A knowing half smile curled his mouth. She was getting used to the way it sprouted a dimple, but the bump in her heart rate still caught her off guard.

"There's my little business major talking again. In my world, nondisclosure agreements aren't worth the paper they're written on. People always want to blab. It's like you just can't trust anyone anymore."

His devious grin widened across his face as he caught her gaze. "But I trust you, Natasha. Besides, even if you told everyone about all the little deeds you and I would be sharing, there isn't a person on the planet who'd believe you. I'm not even sure I'd believe you." His uncertain shrug was joined by a wink.

Rolling up his sleeves, he tugged off the tie he'd loosened moments ago. His eyes wandered her body but didn't hold the remotest look of lust. He might as well have been a physician as he said, "Remove your clothes, but keep your bra and panties on." Until he reconsidered, dropping his gaze to her feet. "Louboutins?"

"Yes." The tone of her response wasn't the usual pride that rang out when she acknowledged the genius master of a shoe designer. Instead, it was an uncomfortable syllable, questioning and afraid.

"I like them. Leave those on too."

Oddly, Natasha might have been bashful about blatantly stripping in front of the man, but there was no need. Alex wasn't looking at her. Instead, he casually strolled to the sofa and rearranged a pillow before pulling a gray faux fur throw from a large drawer in the coffee table.

Standing there, she watched as he removed his shoes, setting them aside. But his clothes stayed on, making her wonder if she'd be peeling them from his skin.

Maybe he wants me to start with a lap dance. Mulling it over, she knew her moves weren't horrible, but dancing wasn't exactly her forte.

But he said this would be different. *If he's never had a lap dance before, he'd be the only guy on the planet who hasn't.*

Still in his shirt and slacks, he lay down on the couch. She cocked her head as he turned on his side, facing the cushioned back.

"You ready?" he asked.

With a drawn-out breath, Natasha said, "Maybe," and made her way over.

There she stood, in front of a guy turned away from her as if about to take a nap. Perplexed, she hadn't a clue where this was going.

"What . . . do you want me to do?"

"Dim," he said, confusing the hell out of her until the lights began darkening. "Lie down."

The deep grumble sent a shiver down her spine, right to her tingling lady parts. Like a festive holiday, it had been a while since her shrubby snatch lit up like a Christmas tree, but tonight it sent throb after heated throb to her eager core. And just like the once-a-year holiday, the anticipation was equally as thrilling.

The sofa was nicely spacious, but not oversized. With the way he filled it, even resting on his side, she could only squeeze on by spooning him. Pressing herself against his back gave her a good feel of every muscle that could have been carved of pure marble.

"Like this," Natasha whispered, barely able to get the words out at all.

"That's fine. Comfy?" he asked.

"*Um . . .*" Stealing a cheap thrill, she squeezed her body in a little closer, wrapping herself in his warmth and a whiff of the lightest cologne on his neck. Inhaling a deep, lingering breath, her lips released a raspy *yes*.

"Can you see the clock from here?"

Her eyes searched the room in the dim light, finding the small vintage clock resting on the mantel. Only then did she noticed the dazzling flames of the fire warming the room.

"It's ten fifteen."

"With the time since you agreed, I'll give you fifteen minutes. You can leave at midnight, Natasha. And I'd prefer that you don't dawdle. Understood?"

"Got it. Don't let the door hit my ass on the way out. But I still don't get what we're doing."

"As mind-blowing as this might be for you, *this* is what we're doing. See, I have trouble sleeping—"

Eagerly, she offered her sage advice. "You should try a Percocet with Ambien. And if you're already resistant to that combo, chase it with a little vodka. You'll sleep." She patted the mass of bicep and tricep muscles before resting her hand on them.

He gave her a disturbed glance over his shoulder. "Great idea. If I want to slowly turn into a med- and booze-dependent zombie." Nestling his head back to a spot that seemed to settle the throbbing vein in his neck, he started again. "As I was saying, I have trouble sleeping. The past few weeks have been especially bad."

"Diabolical scheming will do that to an evil dictator."

Natasha's smart-aleck words made his hand whip back. The smack on her ass nudged her closer. Unfortunately, his hand didn't linger.

"So," he said, "for the remainder of our time, all you're going to do is lie there. But if you're cold, there's a blanket."

What? "You're going to pay me ten thousand dollars just to snuggle?"

The last thing she needed was a cover. His body was hot, and her needs rolled over her own body like a wildfire.

"Hmm . . ." He mulled it over. "You may also lightly stroke my hair. Just to soothe me."

"May I?" Her sarcastic words fell flat. Thinking it over, she offered a suggestive alternative. "You could . . . do more. If it'll help you sleep."

Natasha wrapped her leg around him as she peered at the rugged lines of his profile. Her non-begging had to elicit some sort of reaction, right? But if he had one, it was well masked in the closed eyes of a man trying to nod off.

Alex said nothing. Not then. And not during the remainder of their time together.

For some of that time, she was bored out of her mind. But for the most part, she liked it. Watching this magnificent specimen as his breaths softened, raising and lowering his chest in a seductive pattern that kept her fascinated gaze fixed.

Another glance at the clock only confirmed that time was slipping away too fast.

Alex Drake was the single most frustrating and fascinating man she'd ever met. Was he interested in her? For more than a stand-in binkie?

Somehow, deep down, Natasha got how unusual this was compared to what he usually expected of women. Did that make her different? Special? Or just uninteresting?

Midnight came and went, but instead of leaving, she quietly tugged up the blanket. Snuggling into him, she was ready to nod off when his sudden shift to his back knocked her off the couch and onto her ass on the soft carpet. The sharp *hey* that popped from her lips didn't seem to disturb the sleeping king.

Mission accomplished.

He's asleep.

Discouraged, Natasha found the sofa no longer had space for both of them with his body splayed across it. Tucking the luxe blanket softly around his body, she marveled at the broad-shouldered stud one last time, burning the memory in her mind of each line of his face. A sudden shiver sent her scurrying for her clothes.

The cash in her hand was nice. Natasha measured its weight, casually bouncing it as an unexpected sense of longing moved her gaze back to Alex.

What if she stayed? Or came back tomorrow?

What if he's pissed that I'm still here past midnight? Or wants to renege on our deal and keep the cash?

Stuffing the money deep in her cleavage, she headed out. As soon as she tiptoed out of the office and quietly shut the door, a whisper shot across the hall.

"Over here."

Natasha followed his voice through the dim hallway. "You?" It was, once again, the hot and unfortunately gay Paco.

"Me." He huffed out the word, his scowl giving him a distinctly parental air. "Come on. I'll take you home."

Not having a ready alternative and wanting to see the bright yellow Lamborghini for herself, she let him. Like the drive with Alex, this one was quiet until she remembered she hadn't given him her address.

"Oh, I live at—"

"I know where you live. It's in your employee file. Here."

It was too dark to make out the contents of the large folder he handed her, and she had no idea where the light switch in the space-age car was. "What's this?"

"A letter of reference."

Furious, Natasha screamed. "That asshole's firing me?"

Calmly, Paco said, "Easy on the eardrums. And no, he's not firing you. But with your qualifications, he's pretty certain you're not interested in continuing as a clerk. This letter also serves to show that you were in a short intern position. It's common, coming right out of school, and prevents you from having to explain what you were doing at the company."

Squinting at a man who barely acknowledged her glare, Natasha asked, "So, I could stay at DGI if I want?"

"Yes . . . if you want," he said, bright with enthusiasm. "As a clerk. But between you and me, we've seen better clerks."

No argument there.

Taking a moment of silence to think it through, she wondered more about Rip Van Winkle and his mysterious sidekick. "So, you two are close?"

"Not as close as the two of you were tonight." Paco glanced at her. "So I assume." Rolling the car to a stop, he said, "This is you. I'll get your door."

As he helped her out, she again cursed him for being a smoking-hot gentleman wrapped in a rainbow.

"You're on the fifth floor," he said, as if she didn't know. "When you get up there, wave down so I know you got home safe." His attention fixed to his cell, he essentially dismissed her.

A few steps toward her building, Natasha started the slow temptation of overthinking things. "Why did he do this?"

Does he like me?

Keeping his eyes glued to a text his thumbs feverishly tapped out, Paco answered. "It doesn't matter. You're never going to see him again. Besides, he's Alex Drake. Why the hell does he do anything?" With a stern glance at her, he left her with a warning. "Figuring him out is a waste of time. I stopped trying to get inside the head of that bastard a long time ago."

He resumed his texting. Begrudgingly, she went inside.

Waving down to Paco, Natasha was disappointed that he didn't wave back before getting in his big yellow beast and driving away. Seeing him again probably wasn't happening either.

Emptiness making her lethargic, she shuffled toward her favorite puffy pink chaise and plopped down. Her *Bitch, You Wish You Were Me* notepad had a fuchsia pen holding it open to her list.

Grasping the pen between her fingers, she finished off the *x* in Alex's name by scrolling two half circles over the top, transforming the letter into a two-tailed heart.

A second later, she took her time thinking through the evening. Sure, he was handsome and charming in a *God's gift to women, assholish* sort of way. Her nose scrunched as she marked through his name, and after another thought, Grant Evans as well.

That's better.

Meditating through a long inhale, Natasha circled number two on her list. "Davis R. Black," she said under her breath. Reading the word *Chicago* next to *Black Technologies* made her frown.

It wasn't her favorite city. And the guy had to be the biggest geek alive, making his money in some sort of lame military technology. Positive at least one room in his house had to be filled with Star Trek crap and dorky magician stuff, she blew out a longwinded sigh.

It was late. And she had a long day ahead of her.

She chucked the DGI folder in the trash before making her way to a bed crowded with pink faux fur pillows and a sheer white canopy net. "Mrs. Natasha Black. Beats the hell out of Mrs. Pompous Womanizing Asshole."

CHAPTER 15

CHARITY

CHARITY HAD BEEN in only one executive office before—Paco's—and it was magnificent. By comparison, Alex's was twice the size but sparse, with clean lines and a contemporary look that said little about his personality or personal life.

Paco gave her the warm feeling of family, but she knew he carried that air with him wherever he went. Alex Drake was another story, a mystery wrapped in a ten-thousand-dollar suit and a well-crafted smile that probably lingered long after the sentiment behind it had gone. A self-appointed guardian of the woman he barely noticed.

It was the strangest feeling—wanting to make them proud. Make *him* proud.

In a cream-colored vintage chiffon dress that cost next to nothing, Charity felt a definite step up from her usual embarrassingly casual look. This one nailed old Hollywood to a tee. The couture lines fit her like a glove, clinging to all her curves without making her look cheap.

On her way to his office, she floated through the building like she belonged there, hoping her walk was coming off as elegant and classy. But no matter what she wore or how she cleaned up, the CEO scarcely noticed the difference, never changing his demeanor.

One way or another, I'm getting your attention. At least for half a second.

"This view is mesmerizing," she said, staring off into the distant lights twinkling in Central Park.

Busy clicking away at a keyboard at his desk, Alex mindlessly acknowledged her statement with, "Mm-hmm."

While they waited on Paco's arrival, Charity found that aimlessly gazing off at the city couldn't hold her interest. She'd much rather watch Alex.

He was so engrossed in his work, staring at him didn't seem nearly as intrusive as it might have. Watching him, she wondered if he ever looked at a woman with as much passion and fondness as he did for his computer screen. Like a ten-year-old with a video game, it probably took a lot to tear him away.

Curious, Charity moved closer, wanting to check out whatever captured his attention. Holding back a giggle, she learned he really was playing a video game. Of some sort.

"What is that?"

"Huh? Oh, this? It's a cryptographic simulator with a built-in algorithm to increase difficulty and shift statistical probability with each successive achievement level." When she hit him with a blank stare, he translated. "It helps me learn codebreaking by increasing the difficulty each time I get it right."

"Oh. Cool." *In a geeky spy sort of way.*

Without another glance, he shut down the mishmash of patterns displayed across his screen. Turning his attention to his cell resting on the massive desk, he said, "Sorry, I didn't mean to be rude. It looks like Paco should be up here in a minute."

In a single, swift move, Charity hiked her skirt high and straddled the unsuspecting billionaire.

Protectively folding his arms over his chest as a barrier, Alex arched a stern brow. "Didn't we already have a talk about this?"

Gleeful, Charity nestled herself into his crotch. "We did. But I just want to fuck with Paco a little."

At the telltale sound of two abrupt knocks, Alex conformed to Paco's new terms for entering the office at night, shouting, "Come in."

On cue, she began riding him like a mechanical bull set to high, while he casually wove his fingers behind his head.

Grinning from ear to ear, Alex said nonchalantly, "Hey, Paco."

In an exaggerated defensive move, apparently terrified the vision would instantly turn him to stone, Paco slammed his eyes shut and covered them with his hand. "Dammit! Why the hell would you tell me to come in?"

Alex shrugged. "It wasn't my idea."

Hesitantly, Paco spread his fingers just wide enough to see Charity dislodge herself from Alex's lap.

Straightening her elegant dress, she giggled. "I couldn't resist. And Alex was a good sport, though it felt a little like I was assaulting an unsuspecting priest. You know, Paco, for as tanned as you are, you blush easily."

He heaved out a sigh. "Hey, I'm just glad to see you weren't really scraping the bottom of the barrel."

Alex brushed off the insult. "Nope. She's not that desperate."

Charity's smile lit up. "For you, Alex Drake, anytime, any place." Not wanting to be rude, she said, "You too, Paco."

As Alex roared with laughter, Paco gave her a droll look.

"I know you've got all sorts of magic brewing under that skirt, but unless you've grown a cock, it's a polite pass for me."

Wrapping Paco in a big hug, Charity said, "No matter how hard I try, I just can't seem to satisfy all the people all the time."

He waved her off with both hands. "You know me, Charity. I never mix business with pleasure."

"For the love of God . . ." Her huff was exaggerated. "Can't we for once forgo business?"

"Not today, Ms. *Taylor*." Alex led both of them to the comfort of the seating area.

Paco frowned. "Taylor. The name of a thousand women. You know, this means the collective minds of greedy women everywhere have figured out you're in the market for a certain Ms. Taylor?"

Ignoring the comment, Alex made his way to the bar, waving a bottle of Woodford Reserve their way. With their nods of approval, he poured three glasses.

"I don't think they've put it all together. They just know women with that last name tend to . . . I don't know, pique my interest." He flashed a boyish grin and handed out the crystal lowballs. "I can't help it. It's a weakness. Hey, I'm entitled to one."

Paco prolonged his eye roll. "Sure. Just one. And your little fixation didn't start as a weakness. It's your insane obsession that's made it the weakest link. The last thing you need is a vulnerability—for yourself or DGI."

Studying Charity, probably because she dropped her guard enough to reveal the curiosity in her eyes, Paco said, "I'm here to protect Alex. Even from himself."

Charity nodded, understanding.

Paco shifted his gaze back to Alex. As it sometimes did, his tone turned somber. "Want me to take care of it?"

Trying to keep her eyes from widening too much, Charity looked down. *Like how he took care of Monty? I thought Natasha was a see-you-next-Tuesday too, but that seems an extreme response to a pretentious kid.*

Alex smiled, shaking his head. "Right. Like you could stop the gears of the giant Big Apple rumor mill. It's out there, and it is what it is. And it brought me right into the greedy little mitts of Natasha. You know me. I can spot an opportunity a mile away, and this was too much fun to pass up. It distracted me from …"

He trailed off, and the men exchanged a look of understanding. Charity didn't know what Alex was referring to, but she still gathered its importance.

Alex chuckled. "Besides, this one had fun written all over it."

Charity's outward curiosity couldn't be helped, so Paco explained.

"This guy walks the shortest damn tightrope between two extremes. At one end, he's overworked and irritated as shit. At the other, he's bored senseless and desperate for a distraction. He hates vacations and hardly ever sleeps. I don't care if you bang college kids, but I'm over all this next-level babysitting crap."

Choking on his bourbon, Alex spoke through his coughs. "For the love of God, I did not have sex with that girl."

Both Charity and Paco hit him with sarcasm, raising the *bullshit* flag with a series of squints, *right*, sarcastically drawn-out nods, and *if you say so*.

"I'm truly wounded that you two don't trust me." After donning a sad look and clasping his hands dramatically to his heart, Alex turned to Charity. "Well, at least you got the last laugh. Okay, I've kept you in suspense long enough. How about I have a little dinner delivered, and I'll tell you both exactly what happened."

Alex's sly grin let them know his reputation just got ramped up a notch, in the most disturbing and diabolical way.

Seated with Paco and Alex in his office at an executive table worth more than an average car, Charity couldn't believe they let her pick such a casual meal for delivery in the midst of the elegant setting. The three of them chowed down on the finest, most authentic Italian pizza, calamari, and handmade spumoni in the city as Alex laid out the play-by-play.

His words were a detailed, descriptive, and surprisingly PG-rated account of the fun he'd had with Natasha. Pointing his spoon at Charity before digging at the last of his ice cream, he asked, "Did she stiff you like I said she would?"

Her *yup* was matter-of-fact. Unimpressed, she said, "Threatened me too."

Paco nodded. "That girl's classy all the way." Checking his watch, he added, "I've got to head out."

Charity adored how Paco kissed her cheek. He had to do this with absolutely everyone. Make them feel important. But she let herself feel special in the moment, believing there was more heart behind his habitual gesture. "Is this where you change into skintight latex and search the city for damsels in distress?"

"Yes," he said, kissing her other cheek to complete their farewell. "And it takes a whole lot of lube and baby powder to get in that sucker, but the look is totally worth it." To Alex, he simply said, "Later," before heading out.

Charity bit her lip, looking down at the leftovers.

"What?" Alex asked, a worried scowl creasing his forehead.

Embarrassed, she shook her head, hoping he'd let it go, but no such luck.

With an insistent glare, he said, "Go on, spit it out."

Under his demanding gaze across a conference table of leftovers, it didn't take much to pry the confession from her. "I hate wasting food. I know it's tacky to ask—"

Alex raised a palm at her without a word, then stood up to step over to the bar. Returning with several reusable paper totes from a local upscale grocer and some Ziploc bags, he tossed Charity half his handful and kept the rest for himself.

As they each filled their bags, Alex started talking, almost to himself, sharing a few little-known facts that were unexpected and surprising.

"I hate waste—in any form. It's the reason I'm good at what I do. I started this company with scraps. Other companies wanted to throw out so much stuff. Some even paid me to take their surplus. Long line cable. Electrical casings. Specialty nylon and engineering-grade plastics. Even office supplies. If I took stuff off their hands, they paid less in dumping fees." His smile was half proud, half humble in a way that only Alex could pull off. "Nine out of ten new companies fail. I was always the last man standing. I got half a million dollars of startup inventory my first year."

She quelled her wide eyes, shifting them to the task at hand. "At least we finished the spumoni. No soupy Ziplocs here." Her banter was a weak disguise to hide just how awestruck she was at the man. She'd thought her hero worship couldn't tick up any higher, and yet it had.

With his shirtsleeves still buttoned tight, Alex grabbed the unused napkins to wipe down the table himself. Charity at least tried to swipe the towels from him. At his playful snarl, she held her hands up in defeat, letting him assume the role of cleaning lady. Apparently, the man had no patience for a pecking order between them.

"I can't believe you don't have a cleaning crew."

Apologetically, he blew out an *eh* under his breath, continuing to wipe away. "I abuse them on a regular basis. Lots of late-night meetings. I insisted they take off early today."

"I'm guessing with full pay. Plus tip."

Alex said nothing in return, as if any attention paid to a good deed would be his downfall. Charity smiled, content to simply watch him.

A stunner to look at, Alex was a deadly combination of down-to-earth and dangerously attractive, and his never-ending muscles really sealed the deal. But the dark circles under his eyes overshadowed his finer points, leaving a hot mess that looked like he'd been dragged through the mud a few times before slipping on his suit and tie.

This was Charity's first long look at him, and she took her time. Behind his polished exterior was a man who needed something. Maybe it was something she could give.

Checking his watch, he caught her off guard. "How much does Natasha owe you?"

He can't seriously want to give me more money.

When he swiped a keycard across a panel behind his desk, the wall opened to a room that lit as soon as he entered. "Well," he called out, "how much?"

"I'm not sure."

"Bullshit."

Hearing him sing that word from his not-so-secret room made her laugh. Covering her smile was unnecessary, as he was preoccupied with stuffing a wrapped stack of hundreds in a small bank pouch.

"Do you need a ride?" he asked. "I can have a driver here in ten minutes."

I think we both do.

Without overthinking it, Charity asked, "Would you mind driving me home?

I mean, you definitely need an excuse to get out of here before midnight. Otherwise, you'll wake up over there. Again," she said, casually motioning to the sleek leather sofa, whose smooth lines and stiff cushions made for stylish accents but a piss-poor bed.

When her knowing gaze met his, he frowned at the couch.

Nodding, he agreed. "Let's go."

The quiet drive through the city made her mental gears crank faster.

The pouch in her lap was heavy. With an inconspicuous lift in both hands, she decided the weight indicated some outlandish amount of cash. Remembering the bank wrapper on it she'd seen before he dropped it in the bag, she wondered.

How much is a brick of hundreds? It has to be a lot. At least, a hell of a lot more than that butt-munch Natasha owes me.

Subtle in twisting her head, Charity sneaked a peek at the off-duty billionaire. She followed the rugged lines of his jaw down to his chest and arms, blown away by the magnificence of every inch.

She'd be damned if his suit wasn't reinforced with spandex to hold in all that glory, as every muscle seemed desperate to bust free. Then her gaze fell to his hands, gripped at ten and two on the steering wheel.

How did I not see those before?

Staring harder, she was thankful for the intermittent flashes from streetlights and storefronts that gave her a glimpse at the darker side of the man she'd spent a little time with. His hands were strong and rugged, but more surprisingly, completely covered in random faded scars.

His subtle shift of attention from the road ahead to her stare shooed her nosy eyes away. *Shit.*

"What's on your mind?" The soft drop in his tone was encouraging, but men like this only shared what they wanted. Snooping was never a good look.

With her hands clasped tightly around the thick pouch, Charity mentally searched for the best way to break the increasingly awkward silence.

"You gave me too much money," she calmly blurted after an exhaustive minute.

Braving a glance back at his face again, she was relieved to see his half-cocked smile didn't seem cross. But a wall had gone up between them that was palpable.

Does he know that wasn't what I was thinking? Whatever gears turned in his head, she wasn't sure what they were churning out.

Alex didn't bother with a response, letting that lickable dimple do his smirking for him. The luxury ride was slowing to a stop, managing to roll up right in front of her building's entrance. Premium spaces like that were never vacant. It was obvious the man had the power to part pussies and parking spaces alike.

"This one, right?"

It was only then that it occurred to her that he hadn't asked for her address. Sure, the man paid for the place, but it wasn't like he ever visited her there.

"Yes," Charity said, undoing her seat belt. She had no reason to stay glued to the luxurious leather seat. But desperate to rekindle a closeness with her benefactor, like a schmuck, she remained in place.

A second later, Alex killed the engine and was out of the car, strolling around to let her out. Like a goddamn chauffeur.

Oh God, or like a date. Double shit.

Panicking, she shoved the door open wide, nearly slamming it into the man in the process. "Fuck. I'm sorry. I spaced. I didn't mean to—"

"Not a problem." He waved away her concerns. "My catlike reflexes have saved these jewels more than once. Though my assailant is usually a whole hell of a lot bitchier. Everything all right?"

Not meaning to, Charity shook her head.

Frowning, he pocketed his hands. "How can I help?"

CHAPTER 16

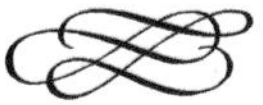

CHARITY

As CHARITY APPROACHED the door to her apartment with Alex, it suddenly dawned on her the sort of impression she was about to make. She was a lot of things, but neat freak sure as hell wasn't one of them.

With that in mind, she couldn't help blocking the doorway with her body, pretending to fidget with the lock. He wasn't exactly pressed up against her, but the proximity of all that manliness was close enough that the distance did little to shield her from his overbearing heat. It radiated like the goddamn sun. With little choice, she pushed the door open wide, allowing him to enter at his own risk.

The upscale accommodations were much nicer than she could afford without the Drake scholarship fund. Still, pouring any surplus funds into her undergraduate classes meant the high ceilings and city view could only be seen by traversing a sea of textbooks, notepads, and crumpled pieces of paper littered across the room.

"Psychology?" Alex asked, flipping through random pages of a book he picked up off the floor.

"Yeah." Quick to straighten up, Charity pressed the bank pouch into his chest, exchanging it for the textbook in his hand. Stuffing it, along with sweats, shoes, an errant bra, three other textbooks, and everything else she could fit in her arms, she rushed through tidying up.

Luring him there wasn't about showing off how well she was doing in school, especially when she was older than her peers by seven or eight years. Though she liked the approval in Alex's eyes. His smile wasn't one of longing, but she clung to the tiniest hope that he might be pleased.

The prolonged racket of dumping this and that into the hall closet meant clearly she was a poor candidate for adulting. With a nervous smile, she couldn't help but caress and hide her scars, a tic she'd developed whenever she wondered how poorly she stacked up against the rest of New York.

But Charity's scars paled in comparison to her companion's. His hands were covered with them, and perhaps that was why they'd been less noticeable at first. The webbing on his skin was much older than hers, worn to blend better, but still wrapped his rugged hands. The effect toughened him despite his tailored suit.

What would cause that? How far up do they go? And . . . are the rumors true?

To avoid getting caught staring again, she filed her wonderings away for later.

"Can I offer you a drink?" she asked. Her casual tone was meant to be relaxing. Compelling. She might have overdone it a little, coming off a smidge calculating.

Alex cocked his head, mulling over her simple question much longer than he should have. "I need to drive, but don't stop on my account."

The ice-cold vodka from the freezer was in her hand a second later. As much as Charity would love to shove a jumbo straw into the bottle and have a go at it, pouring two fingers into a lowball seemed classier. Out of politeness, or just to avoid drinking alone, she filled a similar glass with ice and water, handing it to him and offering him a seat.

With a sip and a patient smile, he kept himself several feet away from her, using the space of the sectional to maintain a *professional* distance.

Charity decided with a man used to navigating the grabby waters of Manhattan socialites, the direct approach might work best. "Can I be offensively blunt?" The mouthful of vodka she swallowed warmed her chest, soothing the niggle of apprehension.

"Please. The more offensive, the better." His smile charmed the words right out of her.

"You look exhausted. I'm guessing you haven't slept in days. Maybe weeks." When his long blink conceded her point, she leaned in. "And I think I know exactly what you need."

"I think I know where you're going with this." He pushed aside her unspoken suggestion with a polite shake of his head. "I rarely even take aspirin. Drugs aren't my thing, but thanks."

She scooted closer, cautious in taking his hand. The strength of his hand melted her. It had to show in her eyes. "That's not what I'm talking about."

With a huff, he asked, "Charity, please tell me you didn't get me up here to psychoanalyze me.

"God, no. Freud was a freak."

"Palm reading?"

"No."

"Acupressure?"

Sighing at his adorable stalling tactics, she said firmly, "No."

"Because by the way you're holding my hand, I couldn't possibly understand what you want. Especially since I think I made myself clear a long time ago."

Gently squeezing his hand, she gave him the best puppy-dog eyes of her life. "Please. Hear me out."

Calmly, he sat back, generously leaving his hand in hers. The beast might be at bay, but he was likely biding his time to tear something apart. Would it be her idea?

Or me?

Centering her thoughts, she carefully chose her words to come off as objective as possible. Imagining herself in a lab coat and thick-rimmed glasses, she tried to keep the discussion clinical. "I think you're overworked and under . . . stimulated. What you really need is a no-holds-barred release."

Patting her hand with a sweetness that came off paternal and patronizing, he said, "Thanks for the offer, Dr. Charity. In case you somehow missed the memo, I get plenty."

"No, you pound plenty. Minimal stimulation, minimal spew." Wincing, she realized that might have pushed her analysis past medical and straight to vulgar. "Or how about minimal investment."

He leaned in to mock her. "Is that your professional assessment? Are we back to our old game? I can already hear it coming. I only get out of it what I put into it."

"Look at yourself. Your eyes are carrying more bags than a baggage handler at La Guardia. So, why not let me do what I do best?"

"Spread crazy-ass rumors and be my mole? I'm for it one hundred percent. Have sex with you? Absolutely not."

"Why not me?"

"Why not you?" The rhetorical question was delivered with a laugh. "Paco wasn't bullshitting. I don't mind a trip to pound town, but I'm not about to get close. It's hardly a secret. I barely know their names, but your name, I know. Consider yourself disqualified, and my fruit absolutely forbidden." He stood, dropping the pouch to the sofa.

All Alex's overwhelming protectiveness did was reinforce her defiance.

"You can't keep paying me for *not* having sex with you. This place and your personal tuition assistance program are more than enough." Pointing at the pouch with a clear disinterest in touching it, Charity continued. "I don't even know what outrageous amount is in there, but I know it's crazy. And for what? Pulling a gag on some rich bitch? Seriously, call it my gift to society."

For whatever reason, he listened, and her lofty look at the bag in question gave her the courage to ask, "How much is in there?"

Easing himself back to the sofa, he drew a breath that finally led to an answer. With a coy shrug, he said, "A hundred thousand dollars."

Shocked, she felt her jaw drop open. Any notion of a response other than stunned silence was long gone.

Alex explained. "Look, all I want to do with my money is make sure the underdog gets a good, sporting shot at a win every once in a while. Believe it or not, I can account for every cent I've given you. And by the way you live, so can you."

"What do you mean?" she asked, genuinely wondering if there were cameras planted throughout her place.

No biggie, if so. I just want to know.

Alex slid the pouch closer to her. "You've had the resources to do a lot of things. Extravagant shopping. Lavish trips. But you haven't used any of the money to spoil yourself."

"Why would I? You and Paco spoil me enough."

"Charity, you haven't even bought a car. And unless we need you for a meeting, you never use the DGI drivers that you're more than welcome to. Whenever you go to class, you walk or take the bus." His clear distaste for public transportation came out in his tone. Taking a moment, he sucked in a breath, cooling his jets. "The last big check I handed you was signed right over to a women and children's shelter."

Lifting a brow, she bypassed his last comment, cutting right to the question echoing in her head. "How do you know I walk and take the bus?"

Charity's pointed question caused him to clasp his hands, explaining away his insights with an executive demeanor. His answer was matter-of-fact, clarifying the reality of the world she'd been kept in.

"Because you work for me, and on some of my most discreet jobs. It makes you vulnerable. You've met one Monty, but I've met thousands. I know what's going on with you because it's my business to know, especially when you're taking twice the course load and coming home exhausted through the dark streets of New York City at night. Do I have to remind you what can happen?"

His fingers steepled, pointing to her hand. Forgetting who she was with, Charity covered it. A year and a half later, and the side effect of shame still lingered.

Stern, his eyes met hers. "That shit's not happening on my watch. Look, let me set your mind at ease. I don't know exactly what you're going to do with this cash, and I don't care. But I know what you've been doing is important, to you and to others. Without a doubt, you won't snort it up your nose or shoot it up your veins. And buying a Birkin or Louboutins seems to be the last thing on your mind. You're at the beginning of really doing something, changing lives for the better. I'm not interested in managing you or checking how you spend it. This is your money . . . to do with as you please. No strings attached. Okay?"

After a long minute of thinking it through, Charity came to terms with her decision. "Okay." A sly grin spread across her face, as if she could legitimately make a demand. "On one condition."

CHAPTER 17

CHARITY

Charity knew her ultimatum was silly. Laughable. It couldn't be more comical unless she sported a big, fat pair of clown testicles over her skirt. But between her slow sips of vodka and the nice guy masquerading as an a-hole, could she be entitled to a piece of Alex Drake? A small, vulnerable corner of his soul she'd always protect?

"Fine," he said, playing along with a good-natured chuckle. "Give me your demands."

My demands. Hmm.

Sweetly, Charity fluttered her eyelashes, debating a few distractions. "Could you find a safe hiding place for that? If I put six figures in a bank account at once, red flags go up left and right." When he didn't snap to it, she said, "I know this place is safe. But with that much cash around, *I* won't be able to sleep. I was going to stash it under the mattress, but it seemed too obvious."

The contemplation in his rigid jaw melted to a smile. "Sure. I'll slip the pouch behind an air vent. It'll only take a minute."

"Oh, no rush." *We're going to need more than a minute.*

"Let me find a low wall vent. It'll rest just inside." Crossing the room, he scanned the walls and floors, inspecting each vent one after the other. "They're all floor ones in here, but I might have luck in another room. Let me check around. Do you have some tools? I'll need it for the screw."

Oh, I know the tool you'll need for the screw.

To avoid suspicion, Charity simply nodded. "I think there's a vent that'll work in the master bathroom. And there's a small tool bag under the sink."

Pouch in hand, he followed the nudge of her chin down the hall to her bedroom. She stayed on his heels, but not too close. The slightest inkling of her little scheme, and he'd be gone faster than a case of cock rings at a BDSM convention.

As he got to work, she busied herself with her own agenda, softly shutting the door between them.

"I like your pink tools," he hollered. "I didn't know I could screw and get so in touch with my emotions." His muffled voice carried through the door she'd softly shut.

In a low voice, Charity said, "Oh, you're about to have a breakthrough."

"What breakthrough?" he hollered, not letting a closed bathroom door interfere with their conversation.

"I said I hope you don't break through . . . the wall . . . or anything." *Fucker really does have the hearing of a dog.*

Relying on the element of surprise, she kept up the small bits of conversation, asking if he might check the wobbly towel rack and possibly kill any lurking spiders.

Rushing her task, Charity worked feverishly. With a few seconds to spare, her butt hit the mattress just as he stepped through the door.

"All set," he said. Wide-eyed, he froze, a buck in her headlights.

Thanks to a new pair of strappy white heels, she wasn't completely naked. But her best sexting attire caught him more off guard than she'd imagined, and his stare was disturbing. He wasn't looking at her body. Instead, his intensity was focused straight on her eyes.

With one leg crossed over the other, she leaned back on the bed, hoping the sultry pose disguised her need to avert her eyes. Imagining herself on a beach in Saint Tropez, she wore a comfortable smile, grateful to the vodka gods for taking the edge off.

Whimsically, he broke the silence. "Should I get more cash?"

"Depends. How freaky are you getting?"

Curious, she had to see his reaction. The second she looked back, his eyes locked on hers. Though her breath hitched and her lips parted, his gaze told her nothing. It was the best poker face she'd ever seen.

Alex stepped closer, seeming to peer past her facade and half-truths, crumbling the walls she'd spent years building.

Softly, he asked, "What do you want, Charity? What could you possibly want from a man you haven't seen in eighteen months, who you'll probably never see again after tonight?"

And that was that. In just a few words, he stripped away any closeness between them. The exposure of offering herself held little value to a man who had everything. The charade was over. She'd never be more than a hooker.

Charity sat up, letting out a long breath to keep a determined little tear from running free. *At least he's being honest.* "I'm sorry. A man like you has his pick of better women—"

"Stop," he whispered.

His warm hands took hers, squeezing gently before releasing them. Cupping her cheeks, he offered her tenderness that was a far cry from the man shooting her down a moment ago.

"Diamonds aren't born of other diamonds. It takes unbelievable pressure and resistance to form something so brilliant and beautiful. You've got more character than most of New York, and your stunning beauty comes from your strength. I'm my usual asshole self for not wanting to get completely lost in your body. This isn't about you, Charity. It's about me. You're entitled to more than I can give. I'm not cut out for a relationship. The truth is, I don't deserve one."

"Because of the woman you keep looking for?" she asked, and his quiet stare was enough of an answer. "Look, let me set your mind at ease—reassure you using your own words. I'm not here to hurt you. I'd like to help you, if you'll let me. To do with as you please, no strings attached. Okay?"

She was ready to welcome all of him, if only he'd let her. Despite his closeness, that wall of his was still high, keeping an emotional divide between them.

Finally, he spoke. "You didn't give me an answer. What do you want?"

"To give you this. Whatever it is that *you* want, that I think you need. No expectations. No judgment. And if you're worried about feeling indebted, don't. Think of it as a one-time business transaction. The money in the bathroom might be just enough to cover the rate of a high-end pay-to-play girl catering to the elite."

"Plus tip," he said with a smirk. "You're certainly persuasive at pleading your case."

Alex's half smile was knowing. Naughty. But proving her worth would take more than a sales pitch. Her act had to be one that no one had shown him.

Slow enough not to scare away her big game, Charity smoothed her hands up the stiff muscles of his chest, doing just enough to loosen his tie. His expression was more questioning than comfortable, but it was enough leeway for her to carry out her insistent task.

Carefully, she slipped the tie over his neck and head. Dangling from her finger, the deep blue silk was richly woven, holding the knot just where she needed it.

"Hang on." It was the first time any concern showed on his usually unflinching brow.

"Don't worry. Just this. Nothing else. What you need is a change of pace. Word on the street is you like taking a woman from behind. A straight blow job occasionally, but a grade-A ass shot is your preference."

"Well, the latest word is that I like my girls tasting like Dijon and am into nursery rhymes. You can't believe everything you hear."

Tugging the tie over her head, Charity arranged it at the right spot.

"Voila!" Once she'd cinched the knot, her blindfold was sexy and warm, carrying the lightest cologne and the strongest musk of pure man. "You can do anything. Be comfortable. Be yourself. I can't see a thing."

The heat of his body rolled over her so softly, she could wrap herself in it and let everything else go. *Just . . . forget.*

His voice deepened. "And what makes you think I want your eyes covered?"

Charity's crossed leg rocked, caressing the side of his. *The rumors. About why you hide your body.* "Lucky guess." Lucky indeed, with a hunch that seemed to be paying off. He was still there.

In true Alex Drake form, the man of a million and one one-night stands tested the waters. "What if I want something a little different? A little . . . unconventional?"

His fingers lightly stroking the base of her neck made her gasp. Not the pretend gasp or sighs she'd done too many times to count, but a very real reaction to his sizzling-hot finger against her needy skin.

"Unconventional is my middle name."

Alex moved closer, his breath making her skin pebble as she held in a shudder. At the low vibration of his words against her neck, she dropped her head back, half expecting a kiss.

"I want to know your desires, Charity. And girls who lie don't interest me. You know what you want. Are you willing to tell me and see where it goes?"

CHAPTER 18

CHARITY

Am I willing to tell him?

It was clear that however Charity responded, Alex would see right through some fabricated story just to get him off. No doubt about it, the truth was unconventional. It happened all the time, but no one ever chatted it over first.

Here goes nothing.

"I'll make you a deal," she said. "I won't say a word. Not one peep. You can imagine I'm anyone else. Treat me like her. Call out her name if you want. Even Ms. Taylor."

Alex's response was soft and honest, bringing on a dozen more questions better suited for another time. *If there is another time.*

"I don't know her name. Not her first name, anyway." The mattress shifted as he sat beside her. "All I've known sexually are one-way streets. I need something more. I have to know . . . what do you get out of this?"

Licking the fullness of her lower lip, Charity handed over a quick answer to a deeper desire. Whether or not she could make a memory real—replace it with the here and now—was a gamble she was willing to take.

"I'll return the favor. To me, you'll be someone else."

If it were up to her, Alex would consume every needy corner of her wanting mind tonight. Their time together would fill the void left by an unforgettable encounter that happened months ago with someone else, but never left her thoughts. With Alex, she could lose herself, reliving the sizzling memory of another lover.

For a drawn-out moment, he seemed to be deciding. As his searing breath swept across her neck to her ear, she turned toward him, again ready for a kiss. But he still wasn't going there. Not yet, anyway.

He let his whisper warm her lips. "Lie back."

Speechless, Charity succumbed to every raw emotion pent up inside her for months. Willing her tense muscles to relax, she was swallowed by the softness of the comforter as a hot finger skimmed the length of her torso.

Her squirm was unintentional, but she knew where his big, thick finger was heading. And it was almost there. This wasn't what she wanted. It was bad enough he'd been her chauffeur earlier. Pleasing *her* wasn't the point.

This isn't about me. "I—"

"Quiet," he said, gruff and stern. "Remember, not a word."

And in that second, she understood. The knit in her brow deepened as her game played out. Again, she was both the town bike and village idiot. She'd laid down rules for a mastermind who loved games.

God, I hope I don't regret this.

"You and I have something in common, Charity. We've both fucked and been fucked, and it's a lifestyle that doesn't lend itself to letting people in. I haven't sat back and enjoyed the feel of a woman in a really long time. The minute I make the slightest attempt at really pleasing anyone, in her mind, the relationship has started. She's practically setting a wedding date and looking up Harry Winston rings. But this . . ." His finger made a long, hot serpentine trail across her skin. "This is exactly what I want."

Teasing her thighs, his sensual finger had an effect unlike other men. Her wetness was escaping too fast.

Objecting, she panted. "This is supposed to be about you. You don't have to—"

In a strong, swooping grasp, his firm hand held her mouth shut. It was his gentleness that spiked her pulse and made her breath shudder.

"Shh," he said, resting his weight on her body.

The silkiness of his suit rubbed against her. Only moments ago, the fit was so molded and polished, it could pass for pure steel. But now it was as deceptively soft as he was.

"Now, Charity, I thought you'd be a woman of your word, so I'll give you a choice. I'm going to remove my hand from your mouth, and either you're telling me to leave, or we're both getting exactly what we need."

His body rolled beside hers, and she nearly lost her mind from the loss of his heat. His fingers feathered her skin just below her belly, ready to claim her, yet keep her distant.

Abruptly, his skating fingers stopped. Cold.

Charity knew exactly what he was waiting for because he was Alex Drake. He wanted his java spiked, his women hot, and his good deeds unmentioned. And in this moment, his demand was unconditional.

He needed her surrender, or he was gone.

CHAPTER 19

CHARITY

BITING HER TONGUE, Charity gave him the only assurance he'd understand. To proceed, Alex wasn't looking for a nod or a sound, or even a word. He was a man of action, and her body had to do the talking.

Spreading her legs had never been an issue. But tonight, the movements of her body were those of a woman opening herself up to a whole new experience. She cared for him. And she'd do almost anything for the titan who could use a night of just being a man.

Like the parking space and perhaps hundreds of women before her, she erased all barriers to entry. Draping one knee over his body, she opened herself, ready to get up close and personal with the hand that legends were made of. Between her welcoming parted thighs and ready wetness, her green light had to be blaring.

At first, Alex skimmed her with a slow, teasing touch at her entrance. Spreading her building wetness across her plump folds, his fingers were everywhere she needed them to be, skyrocketing her to the brink. With a desperate thrust of her hips, she chased his elusive finger. But it was gone, an apparent punishment for her impatience.

Disappointed, Charity retreated with a whimper. Her fevered breaths filled the air as she smiled, enjoying every second of this penalty way too much.

Again, those captivating fingers slipped through her core, erasing every thought from her mind. He smeared her sensual dew in the most delicious back and forth strokes up to her clit, where a tender round of circles forced her back to arch.

Fisting the comforter, she stopped any more movements than that, staving off the release she so desperately chased. It was all so good. Too good. Slowing her breathing, she managed to hold off her building climax.

But through the boundless waves of ecstasy, there was something about his touch. She knew it. She'd had it before. Just like the notes of a fine wine, or jazz, his movements were so unusual and distinctive, the brilliant complexity became identifiable. Familiar.

Or is it in my head?

Who the fuck cares? His touch is perfect.

God, how much does he charge by the hour?

His fingers pressed in. Not one or two like he was respecting her delicacy. Instead, his three thick fingers shoved in deep, filling her with a rush that pushed right past politeness and straight on to the roughness of a good, deep fuck. Each thrust was its own hot, firm invasion where pain and pleasure collided.

Charity struggled for air, rocking against the hand that gave her a ride that consumed every part of her tingling existence. And it was everything. Just like . . . *the last time.*

The ball of his thumb was pure ecstasy on her clit, circling until there was nothing but sensation pulsing through every nerve of her body.

As she rode his hand into oblivion, nothing mattered. Nothing existed. Nothing but the heat building within her like a wildfire in the midst of a dry desert. Tumbling in one crashing wave upon another, she reveled in the delirium that could almost set her free.

His touch woke every remnant of her raw and honest desire. Ripping through her unapologetic lips was the one word she didn't mean to say. Her breathy whisper released it without her permission, and the body that caved from the euphoric explosion instantly filled with regret.

"Jordan."

Alex waited until Charity's shudders ended before shifting her limp body below the plush comforter. When he tugged his tie from her head, her sleepy gaze met his for a second before he headed to her bathroom.

After barely enough time to do a quick cleanup, he reappeared with a gentle grin. His loose tie was back over his shirt with just the right amount of *give a damn* for the early hours of the morning.

Suspecting he must have noticed the fleeting frown she didn't hide fast enough, she finally mustered two words. "I'm sorry."

Taking a seat on the bed, he gave her hand a tender squeeze. "You have nothing to be sorry about. Jordan is very, very lucky," he said warmly.

Suffocating the full weight of her sadness in a controlled breath, Charity threw her arm over her eyes, desperate to cover a tear. "If only she knew I existed." Pining for the return of her mysterious one-night stand seemed hopeless.

It took a second of silence for her arms to lower. Apparently, the *she* reference that Charity had just tossed him filled his ruggedly handsome face with intrigue before taking a hairpin turn to revisit their encounter.

His words were softer than she'd ever heard. "I didn't mean to push you into this."

Giggling, she corrected him. "I believe you read the pressure valve backward. You didn't push me into anything. At all."

"I mean, if your natural tendency is . . ." He paused, choosing his words carefully. "Women."

The polite lift of his brow caused Charity to laugh louder than before, and something about his boyish attempt to correct his perceived misstep had her hands caressing his cheeks in an instant.

"Hey," she said, reassuring him. "My natural tendency is people. In every form imaginable."

His eyes widened as he mouthed the words back to her. Micro-expressions flitted across his face as he mentally explored the continuum of *every form imaginable*.

Finally breaking away from the intellectual mix-and-match options, he turned to her with a curious grin. "So, we're good?"

"No," Charity said with a scoff. "We're sure as hell not good. I was supposed to help you get over your shit. Enjoy yourself. Relax." Her yawn followed a long stretch beneath the blanket, emphasizing her point. Stacking her hands behind her head, she waited for his response.

"Trust me, you gave me exactly what I needed. And then some." He kissed her head and moved for the door, ready to head out.

"And then some? Does that mean you owe me?" Charity's words were playful, but she wanted one last second of their closeness as it ended. Their time was nearly up.

He needs at least one wisecrack for the road.

Alex leaned against the door frame, seeming to contemplate her question a minute too long. Finally, he gave her a lasting glance and a cryptic smile with a riddle in one word.

"Maybe."

Killing the remainder of the lights, he let himself out.

CHAPTER 20

PACO

Six months later

PACO DELIVERED his trademark pair of choppy knocks to Alex's office door, but he was sure the man could identify him by little more than his shadow, footsteps, and breathing. He heard the soft *come in* and sighed, worried about how each day Alex's usual happy demeanor seemed to fade a little more.

Alex didn't acknowledge him. Instead, he stood silently before the panoramic skyscraper view, losing himself in the downpour against the lights of a metropolitan backdrop. The plummets of heavy raindrops and occasional flashes of lightning were always beautiful from behind the double-paned windows that silenced even the loudest weather.

Paco headed to the bar to pour a bourbon for Alex. After a quick debate, he opted to shake things up with a Chopin vodka for himself instead of his usual Grey Goose. And then there was the third glass.

The pour was usually dealer's choice, but knowing who'd be finishing that one off, he poured another bourbon, well past two fingers.

This might start as a business meeting, but it wouldn't end as one. Looking up, Paco decided to tackle business first.

"We're starting a new trust test next week."

"What's that?" Alex didn't move but readily engaged.

"We have a few positions that require higher than normal sensitivity and trustworthiness. We need to know where people stand. Dozens applied. We're setting a series of Alex Drake wallets in their path. We want to know who will return it. Who will snoop through it. Who will outright steal some or all of it. And who might just try to parlay the info on the dark web for a tidy profit."

Alex barely nodded, but Paco caught the grin of approval in his reflection. "Any concern from legal?"

"Nope. When they applied for the positions, they signed an agreement to a series of random tests of trust, with the consequences of a discovered breach leading to actions that may—and possibly will—result in termination."

"They signed that?"

"Every last one of them, with Gina walking through the document and reading it aloud before they signed. She's pretty burned out on reciting it."

"What are you putting in the wallet?"

Laughing, Paco answered. "For starters, a fake ID of yours with the most hideous photo of you we could find. Then the usual—trackable credit cards, a note with passwords and usernames to fake accounts, and two thousand dollars in marked hundred-dollar bills."

For the first time since Paco entered, Alex turned around. His five o'clock shadow was nearing the stage of a scruffy beard, and his normally meticulously styled hair was tousled. "Okay. Let the games begin."

Paco remembered the last time Alex was this disheveled. And the time before that. And the time before that. Every year, this date hit him hard, but at least he'd be shielded from his own torturous thoughts with the distraction of back-to-back meetings all week.

"Let's make a toast," Paco said.

With a solemn nod, Alex joined him at the end of the conference table. The two sat next to each other, and the crystal glass with the extra bourbon sat between them.

"Ten years," Alex said, forcing out the words.

"Ten years." Paco sighed, swallowing his emotions as they both clinked their drinks against the lone lowball on the table.

Despite their suits and status, in a grand office looking out over the world, both men tossed their drinks back, eager to hit the ground numbing. No one could move past the memories, but a shot or two of hard liquor at least calmed them enough to get through another series of days where life went by.

"You need another," Alex said with an eye on Paco's glass.

Reluctantly, Paco agreed. "Just one more. And about half as much as I gave you. Your tolerance is crazy high for a guy with your build."

"Did you just call me feeble?"

"No. I called you a lush. You've been slipping it in your coffee in the mornings lately."

Alex handed the glass back to Paco, then helped himself to the glass with no owner. "What are you, my mother?"

"No, I'm your warden. You've got a full week of meetings. I said take some time off. Like the spoiled dictator you are, instead you double-booked your fucking week. Your online calendar looks like a goddamn bingo sheet."

Sipping more slowly and savoring the taste, Alex gave him a smartass smile.

Paco shot back his own sneer and raised him with a hairy eyeball. "You know I'll be taking half those meetings."

"Hey, misery loves company."

"Apparently."

Alex looked away, his glassy eyes lost in a faraway stare.

Don't you fucking go there.

Setting down his vodka, Paco grabbed Alex's attention with a reference to a certain tall blonde. "Charity says 'hi.'"

Alex's distant gaze vanished. He returned to the present, his eyes brighter as he engaged in the conversation. His lips turned up in the smallest smile. "Did she? I forgot to ask. How was her graduation?"

"It was terrific. We had dinner afterward. I gave her our gift."

"You make us sound like a couple."

"Speaking of which, *that* was one of her first impressions of us. An old couple into kinky shit."

"Hey, we're not old." Alex defiantly waved his glass at Paco.

His outsized gestures were undoubtedly the result of hitting the aged Woodford before Paco had joined him for a drink. It wouldn't surprise him if the workaholic hadn't had a bite of food all day. Or any sleep the night before.

With a hearty laugh, Alex said, "But Charity got the last bit right. How'd she react?"

"How do you think she reacted? She kicked me in the nuts and told me to fuck off."

Their chuckles filled the space, lifting the heavy mood between them.

"No, really."

"Really? Well, her scream was so loud, and her hugs and kisses went on and on . . . and on. So much so, the people at the table next to us thought I'd just proposed and congratulated us. And in true Charity form, she thanked them and gave me a huge kiss right on the smacker."

"Tongue?"

"No, thank God."

"I'm glad she liked it."

"Who wouldn't like the deed to an upscale apartment on the Upper East side? I like a hand on my ass as much as the next guy, but I said if she didn't behave, I wasn't giving her my gift."

"Your gift?"

Nodding, Paco gave him a humble shrug and sipped a little more. "She's got the bug for school. You covered her undergrad, so I figure I can cover her grad work. You know, Valerie says the outreach program they're collaborating on is growing faster than they can handle. Practically overnight."

That got Alex's attention, bringing him completely back to the here and now with a vibrant energy Paco hoped would last. It was good to see him like this, talking like it were any other day.

"Are we in?" Alex enthusiastically asked.

"Oh yeah. We're in. But off the books. If DGI's name is on it, they'll get all the wrong publicity. They're doing good things. If they need anything, Charity promised she'd ask. But if she doesn't, Valerie's no wallflower."

Studying Alex more, Paco threw out a question, half hoping it was nothing. "You and Charity. Did something happen?"

The blank expression staring back at him said volumes and yet nothing at all. Typical Alex.

It surprised Paco to hear him say, "Charity's too fine a woman for the likes of me."

Thank God for small favors. I hate when Alex bangs them and things get awkward. Then what?

With just enough vodka to double-dare him, Paco dove headfirst into the obvious, but slid in with the truth. "I'm here for you. Whatever you're battling. Whatever you need. But something's off. Or am *I* off?"

Alex thoughtfully rubbing his scruff was unusual. As if it had only just occurred to him that Paco might be on to something, not quite realizing himself that anything was noticeably wrong.

Predictably, the deep breath that followed was Alex's typical stalling tactic, giving him the time to decide what he'd share. What he'd keep to himself. What, perhaps, he was just now coming to terms with.

After a contemplative minute, Alex said, "I don't know."

Something about the way he blew out those three little words gave Paco pause on grilling him further. Patiently, he waited, ready to listen.

Repeating himself with an uneasy shake of his head, Alex further emphasized his thoughts. "I don't know what it is."

After a minute, Paco's worry got the better of him. "I, uh . . . notice you've stopped dating. Or should I say, stopped marathon dating. Either you got serious and you're hiding her from me because I know too much, or her last name is Taylor. You've had me check into a dozen of them. Did one fit the slipper?" Though he secretly knew the answer to that question, he needed Alex's take.

"It's not that." His disappointment rolled off each word.

"Has something else happened? Are you okay?" Worried, Paco expressed a bigger concern. "Are you sick?"

Scoffing at Paco's fears, Alex patted his shoulder, giving him some well-needed reassurance. "No sicker than usual. And only in my head."

His weary laugh was met with an equally deflated one. Then he hit Paco with what had to be the truth.

After another swallow, Alex said softly, "I feel edgy."

What's that look in his eyes. I've seen that look before, but not in years. Not since . . .

Banishing the memory from his mind, Paco kicked that Pandora's box just out of reach. "Edgy is understandable."

"No." Alex waved off Paco's excuse. "It's . . . different. Tangible. In the air. Don't you feel it?"

With anyone else, a question like that might sound insane. But sitting across from each other and bonding over drinks was evidence enough that the man had a strong hold on his sanity.

Alex Drake was the reason they sat together now. And, as one of them was a billionaire and the other had a piggy bank eagerly catching up, say what you want, but no one could argue with results.

But facts were facts. It was the one time Paco couldn't connect with whatever his friend was going through, readily chalking it up to Alex being Alex. Sleep deprivation and working to exhaustion? It had to take its toll.

Paco shook his head.

"No?" Alex blew out the word, his angst riddled with disbelief.

He took another mouthful, and Paco added it to his mental tabulation. Alex was clearly outpacing him.

He's mellow. Not even close to last year, or the year before. But we're early on this slippery slope. You can't fool me, AJ. Not now. Not ever.

"You know what I'm in the mood for?" Paco asked.

"Wow." Alex struggled with the question, taking another slow sip before answering. "Seriously, that question could have literally any answer." Thinking for another second, he asked, "Can I at least buy a vowel?"

"Tapas."

"Huh?"

"Tapas. You know, the appetizers."

Alex's eyes slowly shifted from side to side, as if he were mentally running through the menus of every restaurant in a ten-block radius. "You want to hit a restaurant? I don't even know where we'd find one open at this hour with tapas."

"I do. Best damn restaurant in the city for them. My place. Tapas will be the perfect complement to your booze-on-booze dinner. I'll whip some up while you drink yourself slaphappy, until you eventually pass out and I bust out the Sharpie. We'll hit the ground running hard tomorrow, after I tag you on Instagram and your phone wakes you by blowing up. I'm thinking *money heist* mask meets *kitty cat*."

Alex shot him a solid smirk, the kind that used to irritate the shit out of him. "You don't trust me to be alone."

Tossing back the last of his vodka, Paco told the truth. "Damn straight."

EPILOGUE

ALEX

STARING himself down in the mammoth mirror of his luxury bathroom, nothing but an exhausted shadow of a man looked back. Another week down, and Alex wasn't any better. He'd kept every minute of the work week jampacked with a myriad of things that would help him breathe through one more day.

But it wasn't enough.

It was two in the morning. He'd spent three hours in his penthouse gym, pushing himself to exhaustion. But after all that and a hot shower, a disappointed glance at himself said it all.

Nothing was helping.

If anything, the bottled-up energy fueled an attack. At least he finished a shave before the trembling in his hands overtook his control. With his fists balled on the coolness of the marble bathroom counter, he rode the waves of intense anxiety until they passed.

Eventually, they always passed.

Unsettled, he pulled himself from his reflection's hazy glare, hating how his eyes always gave him away. At least to Paco.

Alex didn't give a damn what the rest of the world thought, but Paco was a different matter.

The last thing Alex Drake needed was bad publicity. If DGI's stock value dropped an eighth of a point because he couldn't get his shit together, he'd look forward to a good long ass-kicking by the only guy who'd take a fucking bullet for him.

Tilting his head a little to the left, then the right, he gave himself a final pass. With enough coffee and the right Tom Ford suit, in a few hours, he would look presentable enough.

Saying a silent prayer to the mercy of the universe, he clung to his last shred of hope that he wasn't going crazy. Even if he lost his mind, he still had faith in his ability to pull a miracle out of his ass and play the part of Alex Drake, CEO.

Surrendering to the inevitable, he killed the lights before he padded out of the bathroom. His king-size bed nailed opulence, but never quite made the grade when it came to carrying him off to sleep. Like all the other nights, he eventually got in anyway.

Hands clasped behind his head, Alex stared aimlessly at the dark ceiling and shadowy walls that always closed in on him.

The pounding in his ears reminded him that it would be another Woodford-spiked-coffee morning. If he was lucky, he'd get ninety minutes of sleep—the least he'd managed since tapas night. Overthinking things was his mind's jungle gym, looping through the scenarios and questions that hadn't stopped haunting him on and off for a decade.

But tonight, Alex took a mental detour. *Have I lost my mind?*

The erratic echoes of his own instincts continued pummeling him with one word.

No.

If I've lost my marbles, then I've lost all of them because this feels goddamn real.

It wasn't the first time he'd been carried away with a feeling.

The last time I was too fucking late. Better late than never is bullshit, and I've been paying for it every day of my life since.

But I wasn't wrong.

And I'm not wrong now.

It could be any one of a million things. But it all traced back to that name. *Taylor.* He gave himself a short leash to think about her for a moment, indulging once again in his obsessive fascination.

Is she even single? Married? With a hopeful notion, he considered another option. *Divorced?*

Is she happy?

On the spectrum of his last two encounters, would she be more like Natasha? Or like Charity?

What would she look like now?

Her hair. Her skin. Her smile. His mind always tried filling in the blanks.

Was that why he'd had so many different women over the years? A crazy rich man's game of trying her on for size. Sketching a model of her from every new possibility.

Alex had indulged in a heavy diet of voluptuous women for the past decade, aiming to satisfy his libido over his heart. A quick romp and a consolation prize from Cartier helped keep every relationship under twenty-four hours and at arm's length. *Okay, cock's length is more apropos.*

Maybe she's out there right now. Sleeping peacefully here in New York. *But even if she is, she doesn't need her life disrupted by a bastard like me.*

Believing this woman could somehow change everything had all the signs of a madman grasping at straws. The sick desires of a lunatic desperate for redemption and forgiveness from some woman he'd never met.

If she could possibly be the key to unlocking his only path to freedom from the darkness of his existence, why not just find her? He had every resource imaginable at his fingertips. Operatives. Investigators. Google.

Instead, Alex made an almost daily decision that any movement in that direction would be a step too far.

No. I can't force this. The coin flip is in the hands of fate.

As he finally dozed off, picturing her hair a touch more chestnut this time, he couldn't help one last fleeting thought, proposing a deal to heaven or hell, or whoever would listen. Because, who knows? Maybe for once, destiny would lend a hand. Wasn't he owed at least that?

Put her in my path. I'll take it from there.

BOOK 1: ACCESS

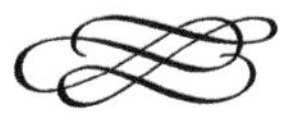

AN ALEX DRAKE NOVEL

ACCESS
AN ALEX DRAKE NOVEL
LEXXI JAMES

CHAPTER 1

MADISON

Madison Taylor was always on time, yet today of all days, she was edging dangerously close to being late for an interview she'd wheedled her way into getting. The job opening hadn't even been announced. Instead, she'd come upon it in the happenstance, chain-of-events way so many great opportunities tend to occur.

And it was all thanks to a very pissed-off but well-dressed lady ranting nonstop on her Bluetooth in the bathroom last week.

The woman, oblivious to the presence of anyone else during her conversation, had chattered on and on. Unbothered by the occasional hand-washer or intermittent flushing, she kept talking, and her conversation had captured Madison's undivided attention. From inside her own stall, of course.

"Fuck that bastard. So I took a few bucks from his wallet? Like he'd miss it between buying companies and islands and shit. I type a hundred forty words per minute and do the work of three people while looking smoking hot in my fifteen-hundred-dollar blazer . . . and they fire me? Drake Global Industries can kiss my perfectly Brazilian-waxed ass."

Her blazer costs fifteen hundred bucks? That's almost a month's rent!

Honestly, Madison had long since stopped peeing, but she couldn't tear herself from the seat. From the slit between the door and the wall, she watched the woman in her unmistakable red-bottomed Louboutins pace in and out of view.

Ms. Dressed-to-Impress barely breathed between expletives as she continued her tirade.

Avoiding confrontation had become Madison's happy place. Normally, any amount of shouting was the surest way to an armful of hives. And being raised by a gunnery sergeant dad hadn't exactly helped matters.

Her nonconfrontational nature was part of the reason her butt stayed planted in place, but not the only one. Deep down, she was way too chicken to ask this woman what she was dying to know, preferring instead to park it in a restaurant bathroom stall, letting her vagina air-dry. Maybe if she lingered a little longer, the universe would satisfy her curiosity.

Who should I contact about the new job vacancy at Drake Global Industries?

In a moment of calm, the woman listened intently, softly twirling the end of a cigarette clockwise, then counter-clockwise between her lips, over and over again.

The NO SMOKING sign was enough of a deterrent to keep her from lighting up, and the activity seemed to satisfy some deep-seated need enough to prevent her from puffing to her heart's content outside, thankfully keeping the conversation within earshot.

"Well, Gina Sawyer can kiss my ass too, because she said under the circumstances, she couldn't give me a reference. What a crock of steaming-hot bullshit!"

Bingo!

That little tidbit was Madison's ticket straight to the big leagues. Or at least a shot at them.

A week later, she'd scored an interview with the very same Gina Sawyer mentioned. Thrilled to learn Ms. Sawyer was the director of human capital at DGI, Madison was doubly ecstatic that the job hadn't actually been advertised.

Her request for an interview was, well, incredibly easy. The guy on the other end of the call, Andi with an *i*, explained that Ms. Sawyer wouldn't be back for a week, but he'd go ahead and pencil Madison in.

"Ms. Sawyer's always saying I need to be more proactive, so I'm taking the bull by the fucking horns. She's out this week, but how will Monday at eight a.m. work?"

"Yes, that'll be great!"

"Monday it is." Clicks followed as Andi tapped furiously on his keyboard before he added a few words of advice. "And don't be late. Ms. Sawyer hates tardiness. She also hates puppies, smiles, and happiness in general. You picking up what I'm putting down? Just email your résumé to our HR account today, and you should be good to go. Good luck."

The butterflies in her stomach fluttered madly as Madison got the picture loud and clear. Sucking in a breath, she reminded herself of his words.

Don't smile. Don't bring up puppies. Be ready for a ball-busting interview. And don't be late.

Early Monday morning and definitely not late, Madison hit the ground running. Literally. She'd been raised in Small Town, USA, where city blocks were just a hop, skip, and a jump long. So she'd never get quite used to the Big Apple, or the concept of New York City blocks. The streets alive with bustling cars and hurried people were formidable, stretching endlessly into the distance.

Confused, she emerged from the subway flustered, realizing she'd gotten off too soon, with three insufferable blocks uptown to go. Shoving her doubts to the very back of her mind, Madison sucked in a can-do breath, determined to push onward and upward.

Three blocks. That's not too bad.

Yeah, if she weren't wearing stilettos.

It wasn't like she had a ton of options. Scrounging around her sparse closet and modest wardrobe for something suitable for an interview, she quickly realized corporate-ready shoes were her shortcoming. After passing over a few casual and workout shoes in her closet, she'd decided the ones on her feet were her nicest, most business-appropriate pair. Even if she showed up a little out of breath, she'd look sharp, professional, and like she belonged in the welcome embrace of corporate America.

Sunny and bright, the morning was electric. Energy pulsed through Madison's veins, pushing her pace to a confident stride. A quick check of her phone confirmed her suspicion. At this rate, she wouldn't just be on time, she'd be early.

For some, a thought like that might have downshifted them to settle into an easygoing stroll. But not Madison, and definitely not today. Each breath filled her with optimism and excitement, and the anticipation of a whole new life.

In no time, the towering Manhattan obelisk that housed Drake Global Industries was straight ahead.

"DGI." She sighed, eyeing the gorgeous building of steel, stone, and glass that stretched clear up to the sky.

Charged with pure adrenaline, she rushed around the corner, ready to push through the entrance and hit the interview head-on. Instead, she smacked into something midstep. Like crashing into a wall, she was stopped cold.

Stunned, she bounced back, realizing she hadn't run into a wall—merely a rock-solid man.

"Watch where you're going," the deep voice grumbled before its owner vanished into the building.

Nearly knocked down, she heard herself meekly shout after him, "Sorry."

On second thought, that jerk should have watched where he was going. Butthead.

There Madison stood, again wallowing in her inability to push back when pushed. Or shoved.

Okay, technically, I ran into him, but still.

It was too late to make a scene anyway. And the tragedy of going another day without standing up for herself was quickly overshadowed by the stain of injustice.

And coffee. The tall, dark-suited man with his brick-wall body had left her a parting souvenir before disappearing behind the double glass doors.

Wincing at the injustice of it all, Madison slammed her eyes shut with a huff. A long, dark stain now streaked down the front of her pristinely pressed white silk blouse beneath the black jacket. Her serious attempt at a power suit was two shakes from being shitcanned.

Lightly brushing off a few drops, she assessed the damage. He hadn't spilled much coffee on her, but what there was had hit all the wrong places, striping every ruffle on its way down. And that wasn't the best part. No, the definite *pièce de résistance* was the slightly familiar and overwhelming scent of bourbon.

Panicked, Madison glanced at her watch. With thirty seconds to spare, she had roughly five minutes to figure something out. In her haste, she nearly slammed into another passerby as she rushed into the building.

Keep it together, girl.

Quickly, she found sanctuary in the nearest restroom. Surrounded by the opulence of the marble floors and gold-trimmed faucets, she grumbled mentally that the only way she'd be more out of place would be if she were wearing athleisure wear and flip-flops.

Appalled, she stared at her reflection.

Her hair, which had been so beautifully swept up less than ten minutes ago, was now in shambles. Although part of its condition might be attributable to her brisk three-block jog, the rest was the definite result of the wrestling-feder-ation-caliber body slam.

Half the clips she'd carefully placed now dangled pathetically from loose wisps of hair. The remainder were gone, leaving no hope of recreating the polished and professional updo Madame YouTube had helped her through.

Her black suit itself seemed fine. Twisting to the left and right, Madison nodded, pleased with the condition of the bargain find. But the blouse wasn't so lucky.

With a skunk stripe down the front and all the aromatics of an Irish pub, the only plausible explanation would be that her day drinking had begun well before the crack of dawn.

In a frantic whirl of sheer determination, she stripped her blazer away, ridding herself of the blouse just as someone walked in. Breezing by Madison, the sophisticated woman made her way to a far end stall, shaking her head in disapproval. Another *sorry* escaped Madison's lips before she could help herself.

Determined to keep the tiniest tear restrained, she closed her eyes and took a deep, calming breath.

Do not panic.

Momentarily centered, she looked around. Her last streak of luck from a semipublic bathroom led to today's interview. Staring her reflection down with the right blend of tenacity and naivety, she forced herself onward.

Let's do this.

Biting her pouting lower lip, she shoved her only silk blouse deep in her purse, crossing her fingers in the hope she could rescue it with a soak in the kitchen sink later. Sighing, she hoped her Michael Kors bag wouldn't permanently reek of *eau de booze*. Breathing in a cautious whiff, she desperately wished the zipper still worked.

Making a hasty check of her lacy nude camisole, she found it was thankfully unscathed. The upside of all those semi-outdated but adorable ruffles on the blouse? They managed to soak up every last drop of java, sparing her undergarment. Without overthinking it, she slipped the black blazer back on, securing it with the single silver button.

Turning this way and that, she sized up her new look. Her impressive cleavage totally nailed it. For naughty librarian, she had the job. But for a Fortune 50 company, it wasn't exactly the ideal interview ensemble.

Pulling back her shoulders, she stood proud and tall. Slowly, her composure crumbled. Then more intentionally, leaving her to hunch forward completely.

I give up.

As usual, Madison's boobs were front and center, always drawing more attention than she preferred. Convincingly optimistic, she nodded.

It's totally fine. This will work.

But as her insecure fingers kept fidgeting with the blazer, trying without success to hide her cleavage, a flush reminded her that her time was up.

Ms. Sawyer hates tardiness replayed over and over in Madison's head, looping steadily to the beat of her thumping heart.

Quickly, she yanked the remaining hair clips from her hair, tousling her wavy locks and letting them gently cascade in a *just got out of bed* look that went beautifully with her peekaboo breasts.

Determined not to care, Madison sucked in a breath and raced out the door, rushing to the front desk with barely a minute to spare.

CHAPTER 2

MADISON

A BIT OUT OF BREATH, Madison arrived at the security desk. "Hi, I'm here for an interview with Ms. Sawyer."

The guard nodded with barely a glance at her and picked up the phone. His badge displayed his name and title—FIFE, CHIEF OF SECURITY. The man was intimidating from every angle, but his smile softened him enough just enough to be approachable.

He wrapped up the quick call, clearing Madison for access. As he stood to give her directions, he finally took her in and his mouth dropped open, practically hitting his desk with a clang.

Flustered, Madison breathed through her embarrassment as his eyes steadily focused on her breasts. Suddenly aware of each of her heaving breaths in and out from her brisk jaunt over, she refrained from crossing her arms over her chest. A move like that would just draw even more attention.

Clearing her throat, she straightened her blazer, trying to calm both her breathing and her nerves. Ignoring Fife's annoying grin that thankfully was drool-free, she took the keycard he handed her.

"What's this?" she asked, waving the rigid plastic back and forth to break his hypnotic glare at her boobs.

"Oh." He shook off his watchful fascination. "Um, when you get in the elevator, hold it in front of the magnetic pad on the wall. It's your access to the executive suites. Press *E* after the pad turns blue."

With a soft *thanks*, she hurried over to the glass-walled elevator and got in. There, a bright silver pad glowed blue as soon she waved the keycard in front of it. Only one of the elevator buttons lit up.

A second after Madison pressed *E*, the elevator whisked upward with a soft whirring sound. From the growing height, the lobby looked beautiful as beams of morning sunlight bounced off the marble floors and metal-accented furnishings. She'd been much too distracted to take notice when she entered, but the glass skyscraper and its dancing sunbeams left her breathless.

As the ground level retreated and the people bustling along it shrank into tiny little specks, she started wondering what exact floor she was going to.

With a quick glance at the panel, she realized there were fifty-one marked buttons that hadn't lit up. The bright blue *E* made fifty-two.

As the humming faded and the elevator slowed, Madison sucked in a deep breath, swallowing hard as it stopped. A melodic ping hit the air, and the doors slid open to reveal a large foyer. Soft music played faintly in the background, and a clean but subtle fragrance reminded her of a hotel where she'd briefly worked.

The receptionist sat at a large desk straight ahead. Far ahead. Nearly a New York City block ahead.

Slumping her shoulders, Madison didn't have to check her watch. By this point, she was definitely late.

With a few rushed steps forward, she winced as the clickety-clack of her heels on the polished marble echoed. In this expanse of an outrageously grand entryway, every tap was painfully obnoxious.

Madison tried masking the noise with a rapid succession of tiptoed steps, which only worsened the effect and ended with her tripping over her own feet as she practically swan-dived into the desk.

With catlike reflexes and a big mental thank-you to whoever was watching over her, she caught herself. Smiling, she stood up straight and held out her hand to shake that of the preoccupied woman behind the desk.

The receptionist kept her hands to herself and greeted her with barely a look. "Good morning, Ms. Taylor. Ms. Sawyer is ready for you." With the slightest nod backward, she directed Madison toward the glass-enclosed office behind her.

Timidly, Madison looked up, just then noticing the eyes of the no-nonsense woman locking on hers. Even from across the room, through walls of thick glass and a receptionist desk between them, the woman's cold glare was abso-freak-ing-lutely intimidating.

Madison imagined being part of a *National Geographic* documentary, where the cheetah, ready to tear the poor defenseless gazelle to smithereens, pauses. Patiently, the cheetah waits, bearing witness as the gazelle fumbles wildly, desperately trying to re-posture itself in some lame attempt to be slaughter-worthy.

Even through the transparent wall, the woman's popped brows showed every bit how very much undecided she remained on the matter.

Rebalanced, Madison moved toward the office and let out the smallest gasp as she wobbled. Clear as day, she felt it. One of her heels was loose, torn a little from the sole.

Dammit, I love these heels.

As carefully and as quickly as possible, she walked over, limping a little to inconspicuously keep her shoe on.

With soft brunette curls and a hard-as-nails grimace, Ms. Sawyer remained on a phone call. She looked up briefly but didn't otherwise acknowledge Madison. "All I know is if you can't have drivers on time for your biggest client, I have ten other companies ready for the work."

Oh, perfect. Ms. Sawyer's already upset. Nervous, Madison hid her jitters behind a shy smile.

With the phone call ended, Ms. Sawyer pursed her lips, seeming to consider her alternatives before finally gesturing an impatient wave toward the chair, impolitely indicating Madison might sit.

Holding in a breath, Madison sat as properly and straightly as possible. The scene began to take on some twisted version of Alice in Wonderland. *Take this breath, and my breasts get bigger. Take the next, and my blazer shrinks smaller, smaller, smaller.*

Between struggling through every stifled breath and her feet absolutely killing her, she just wanted this day to be over already.

GINA SAWYER was engraved on an intricate crystal nameplate, centrally displayed on the front of her cherrywood desk. The oversized desk could have easily doubled as a dining table, but the top remained unsettlingly bare.

Only a Louis Vuitton planner and a space-age screen sat front and center. She fiddled with a thin golden pen as she made faces at her computer screen.

Pronounced in her eye roll, Ms. Sawyer commenced the interview in a bored singsong voice, repeating a line she'd obviously said a time too many. "So, why do you want to work at Drake Global Industries?"

Quick as a whip and fully prepared, Madison gushed about all things DGI, rattling off market-share statistics and historic accolades like a pro. Her advanced degree in googling set her on a sure path to success. Hopefully, Ms. Sawyer would be wowed and impressed, and practically fall all over herself with "When can you start?"

But even if Ms. Sawyer wasn't, Madison couldn't help but be a little impressed with herself. Raving about how DGI had paved the path for technological innovations in global telecommunications, she desperately wanted to be a part of it. A part of something interesting and important, and so much bigger than this small-town girl in the heart of New York.

Thanks to the publicity churn of an overexposed company, Madison was on her game. Her recitation was half shareholder's presentation, half sermon, as she ambled down the path of how DGI was postured for enterprising leaps in the next era. Despite her enthusiasm, her well-rehearsed speech was abruptly cut off.

"Look, cut the crap. What do you really want?"

Ms. Sawyer's tone was cutting and confrontational, causing Madison to freeze. Blubbering incoherently, she stammered as her voice finally betrayed her, completely giving out.

Her sudden case of speechlessness somehow provoked her unexpected nemesis, who gave her an irate glare. Turning back to her monitor with a few annoyed blinks, Ms. Sawyer tapped at the keyboard tucked beneath the surface of her desk.

"Obviously, I didn't clear you for this interview, and my *former* assistant seems to have gotten the last laugh after all."

Squinting, she scrutinized the screen.

"Basic background investigation. Madison Taylor. Temping for the last year here and there. Barely any college. And, oh yes, all the while moonlighting as a waitress in the evenings, which I'm assuming is to make whatever ends you have meet."

Madison could feel the flush rise up her face. Hearing her less than impressive credentials read aloud was bad enough, but it wasn't like she'd tried hiding anything. So, why did she suddenly feel exposed and embarrassed? And ashamed?

Of course, her break into the big leagues was a bit too good to be true.

Hearing her lackluster credentials aloud, she realized her hopes were obviously idiotic.

Why would anyone give me a chance?

Ms. Sawyer's eyes locked on Madison's helpless gaze. Swallowing her uneasiness, Madison slowed her breathing to suppress the tears welling up. Any second now, the flood was coming.

Don't cry. Don't cry.

Clasping her hands, Ms. Sawyer leaned in. "Look, it's not the lack of experience, though, that doesn't help. As impressive as the long list of minimum-wage jobs are, that's not what's really keeping us from making a love connection today. Oh, and it's not even, well, all this."

She gestured with a frown at Madison's blazer and camisole, taking in a deep whiff.

"It's the glorious combination of all of it wrapped up in an obvious overindulgence of night-to-day boozing it up. As much as I hate good-byes, I'm afraid this is the end of the road."

Dismissing Madison without a word, Ms. Sawyer returned to her computer, typing away and decidedly going on to more important matters.

Madison couldn't help but wipe a few determined tears from her eyes as she stood. "Sorry to have wasted your time," she said, her voice wavering. Pressing her weight on that wobbly heel, she needed a moment.

Sorry? Again? Really? What the hell do I have to be sorry for?

Fueled by a fury that wouldn't be ignored, she huffed out a long, pissed-off breath.

She'd already said sorry to the rock-solid waste of a suit whose splash of coffee helped her blow this interview. Then to Little Miss Judgey in the bathroom. Now her chronic apologizing was to the high-and-mighty Gina Sawyer. And for what? A high work ethic and getting body-slammed by a Neanderthal?

Despite Madison's puffed-up posture, ready to give this woman a piece of her mind, Old Stonewall Sawyer hadn't moved. Instead, she seemed perfectly content to continue ignoring Madison. It was just the tipping point to make her blood boil over.

Loudly, she cleared her throat, then bit the inside of her cheek to keep the stubborn little tears from flooding out.

"Hey!" she said loudly, but there was no response. "You know what?"

When Ms. Sawyer continued to ignore her, Madison decided she had to keep going. In a miserable attempt to steady her voice, she squeaked out, "I'm not sorry. You people think you can look down on all us hard workers who make your day better, no matter how crappy our day is going."

Getting a head of steam, Madison kept going, her voice firming more by the second. "And by the way, you missed a few jobs on that background investigation. I worked at Starbucks to pay for those college classes, making hot venti lattes for coldblooded people like you. And I cleaned bathrooms and scrubbed toilets at a few restaurants you've probably frequented, so say what you want because I'm used to your shit."

Whipping the silk blouse from her purse, she waved it high and proud like the goddamned American flag, and Ms. Sawyer finally deigned to look up.

"Oh, and the reason I look and smell like *this*," Madison said, wildly gesturing at her own spilled-out breasts, "is because another jack-hole who works in this building crashed into me on my way in, dousing my beautiful clearance-sale white Chanel blouse with a full-on hit of his Kentucky coffee. So, I'm not sorry for any of it. I'm just sorry I wasted my time coming up fifty-two floors only to break my heel, when I should've shoved it up your executive butt."

Proudly thrusting out her lingerie-clad chest, she whirled around, standing tall with her dignity as she made her grand exit. Within a few steps, Madison heard Ms. Sawyer's phone buzz, and her bravado faded.

Only then did it occur to her that while she was giving her version of the preamble to the Constitution, high-and-mighty Ms. Sawyer was probably instant-messaging security. Nervously, Madison quickened her unsteady pace to the elevator.

"Ms. Taylor!" Ms. Sawyer called out.

Oh God, she's going to tell me there are cops waiting for me in the lobby. Maybe threaten me with jail on some trumped-up charge to satisfy her sadistic pleasure. And without a doubt, she'll top it off with the elite cherry of that smug-ass smirk.

Ignoring her name being called, Madison made a beeline to the elevator, desperately stabbing at the call button over and over until the door opened. Inside, she hit the *G*, but the elevator refused to move.

Ms. Sawyer raced out of her office. "Hey! Wait a minute!"

Why won't the door close? Oh, the access card.

Madison feverishly waved it and *G* lit up. With a single tap of the now blue button, the car dropped, swiftly arriving at the lobby. Relief poured out of Madison with an audible breath as the doors opened.

Composed, she pulled herself together, stepping out slowly and carefully in her haphazard attempt at a sophisticated gait in a wobbly shoe.

Halfway to the exit, she heard her name again.

"Ms. Taylor!" Miraculously, Ms. Sawyer was now in the lobby, barely an arm's length from Fife.

How the hell did she get here so fast?

Laser-focused on the exit, Madison picked up the pace. As coolly as her weak stiletto heel would let her, she set her sights on the door.

Steps from freedom, that loose little heel bit it, betraying her and landing her squarely on her greatest asset, right in the middle of the lobby floor.

Ms. Sawyer and Fife raced over, looking down at her. *Of course.* Her epic fail of an escape had to be the icing on their cake.

Defeated, Madison softly said, "Look, I'm leaving. You don't need security."

All six feet four inches of Fife bent over, swooped her up like a rag doll, and gently placed her dead center in front of Ms. Sawyer. Face-to-face, Madison gave her a blank stare.

Ms. Sawyer grabbed her hand, shaking it vigorously. "Welcome to DGI, Ms. Taylor."

Confused about what was happening, Madison could feel her brow furl to a tight knot.

Sporting what seemed like a genuine smile, Ms. Sawyer pulled her closer. "You have the job. And call me Gina."

Fife affirmed her new corporate status with a nod and a wink.

CHAPTER 3

ALEX

Thirty minutes earlier

"Where the fuck is my car?"

Alex Drake, the self-made billionaire and world-renowned telecommunications genius, hated being late. Almost as much as he hated being outsmarted or poor, but not nearly as much. Lateness was his downfall. A tragic vulnerability.

At least being late was a supremely rare occurrence, thanks to a zero-tolerance policy and a treasure trove of expensive watches.

The on-again, off-again reminder of his tortured past was making an encore appearance today. His unforgiving heartbeat pounded through his body, making his hands tremble and deafening his ears. It was an inescapable reminder.

It was the one vulnerability that never let up. Never gave him a break.

Lately, it had taunted him more and more, always lurking just below the surface, ready to emerge when he least suspected it. Still, he should know by now it would happen at the most inconvenient times and places.

Checking his vintage Omega Speedmaster, Alex breathed out a quiet *fuck*. Crumpling in the middle of the crowded sidewalk outside his own goddamn building would be fucking inconvenient, for sure. He could practically see the headline.

CEO COLLAPSES UNDER THE WEIGHT OF BEING A COLOSSAL DICKHEAD

Technically, he wasn't late. He was early. But with his irritation and edginess ratcheting up beyond control, the fists hidden deep in his pockets balled tighter.

The signs were all too familiar. A panic attack was coming, and faster than usual. *Too fast.*

With a desperate sip from his disposable cup, he found his recent tactic to self-medicate was failing. A few shots of bourbon in his fresh Sumatra just wasn't cutting it this morning, and every staggered breath meant he was running out of time.

He couldn't wait for a car.

Furious beyond reason—because the last thing this circumstance called for was being rational—he hit the third favorite on his phone.

"If I have a driver on call 24/7, then why the hell am I standing on the street corner like an asshole? New driver! Now!"

A tremor ran through his body, forcing him to make a hasty return to his building. His last-second about-face resulted in his solid build flicking off whoever just bounced into him.

Goddammit. "Watch where you're going."

Barely hearing the faint *sorry* above the roar in his ears and what was becoming an intolerable blaring of the busy street, he hightailed it inside. Blinded by every glimmer of light, he had to get away. *Now.*

Sucking in a deep breath, he bolted back into the building. *My building.* Manhattan's testament to his empire. And today, his sanctuary.

With few in his inner circle, no one knew the real Alex Drake. The ones who called him AJ were few and far between.

The man he'd been when DGI was just a pipe dream called Drake Cable & Comm seemed like a lifetime ago. The little garage start-up-that-could took jobs in high-risk areas of the globe, amassing market share and quick cash.

It was a path built from unprecedented financial gains, but at what cost? Risks were easy when you didn't care if you lived or died. The more dangerous the venture, the better. His track record was flawless, save for the single greatest, most devastating personal loss of his life.

Others might have forgiven him. *That's their call. Not mine.*

Hyperfocused to the max, Alex had built his life around profits and deals, filling every void with cash—and the voids were deep and vast. He'd long ago buried any hope for healing or redemption. For happiness. Or love.

To his credit, climbing to the top without outright annihilating others was preferred, but some things were unavoidable. Such is life. And if Alex Drake was anything, that son of a bitch was a fast learner.

A decade ago, life converged at the intersection of crush or be crushed.

Even if the crushing was just the weight of the world around him, hardening his armor was nothing more than a natural measure of self-defense. He could preserve the bits and pieces of the old Alex, pushing onward while saving whatever slivers could be spared in the aftermath.

The problem was, he'd become the only inmate of his custom-tailored luxury prison. No matter how gilded, all prisons are ultimately lonely.

"Good morning, Mr. Drake," rang across the lobby from the usual choir.

Detached and determined to keep his stride brisk, he held it together just long enough to refrain from a full-blown run.

His feet picked up the pace as he closed in on his private elevator tucked behind the security desk. Intentionally, it was designed to blend invisibly behind the wall.

As he swiped the access panel, his hand squeezed the embossed platinum-plated access card until his knuckles turned white. Without looking, he knew his embossed initials on the corner would be imprinted on his palm. This wasn't his first rodeo through the past.

At the fifty-second floor, he stepped through the door to his lavish penthouse office overlooking Central Park. The sweeping views of lush trees and tranquil water were always enough to capture and calm him. At least, for the moment.

He could always lose himself in the view. The magnificence of it soothed his heartbeat, luring him from the heavy toll and endless anxiety that empire-building and burying a past tended to bring.

After a few meditative breaths, he was relieved when his mind cleared. Stronger, he could come to grips with dealing with the day. A sudden jolt in his pulse kicked his instincts into high gear.

It's not over. Proceed with caution.

What if I was out when it happened? Not somewhere . . . safe?

Quickly, he scrolled through his phone, frowning as he clicked the contact of a higher-ranking favorite.

"Paco. You need to take a meeting for me. Check my calendar. Twenty minutes. The usual place."

He didn't bother thanking his stand-in. The man knew the deal and understood. *He always understands.*

Suddenly free for an hour or so, Alex eased into the seat at his oversized desk, running a hand across the smooth wood surface. He sucked in a deep breath with an entirely new wave of thoughts awakening.

Again, his pulse quickened. Different from the blood-pressure spike on the street, this wasn't unwelcome. His lips curled up as he reminisced about all the tantalizing women he'd had bent over the custom-carved cherrywood desk.

Seeking the company of a beautiful woman was unnecessary. The endless string of luscious distractions always sought him out, appearing from out of nowhere, and in spades. He could take them or leave them, allowing himself the indulgence when the mood struck him. And showing them the door when the mood was over.

Exchanging numbers never happened. He'd make do with the not-so-cheap thrills an abundance of nameless, faceless ladies could provide. And the desk in front of him? It was the only part of his life he'd let them close to. His demand for privacy was unyielding, and his home was strictly off-limits. No one got close to him there, because no one got close to him. Period.

Call it unprofessional, but the lap of his empire's luxury seemed to satiate everyone's needs. And satisfaction was guaranteed, at least for the much younger ladies.

Come. Don't come. He didn't care. In the end, they walked away with a sweet kiss, his boyish grin, and a nice little something-something from Cartier as a quick consolation prize and very final farewell.

After checking his watch, he sent a direct message.

ALEX: Gina, I need that new driver ready for lunch at Le Bernardin.

GINA: On it. And he'll be early.

ALEX: I'm sure he will. You have a definite je ne sais quoi with our service contractors. Must be your remarkable charm. Speaking of which, how's your new assistant?

GINA: Oh, you need to see for yourself.

Curious, Alex flipped on his monitor. Years ago, some lunatic demanded his contract be paid in full, and when Gina refused, he pulled a knife on her. Earning herself the nickname Tough as Nails, she talked him off the ledge. But the whole incident pissed everyone off, no one more than Tough as Nails herself.

At the end of the day, DGI didn't have enough to prosecute or sue. Sadly, it was her word against his. A week later and at Gina's rather loud insistence, cameras were installed in key locations throughout the skyscraper, with several in and around her office.

Spying on employees wasn't exactly Alex Drake's speed. When necessary, he had people for that. But every now and again, Gina would rope him into something sure to lift his spirits.

Alex moved closer to the monitor and with a two-fingered swipe, expanded the view.

ALEX: Is she holding what I think she's holding?

GINA: Yup.

Fascinated, Alex watched the young assistant with her hands below the desk, hastily scrambling and unscrambling a Rubik's cube, over and over again, and checking her watch after each go.

ALEX: She's fast. Competition level. So, are you thinking what I'm thinking?

GINA: Well, I'm thinking she's not the sharpest pin in the cushion. I mean, she's trying to hide what she's doing, holding her hands under the desk. And yet she's oblivious to the fact that the wall behind her is made entirely of glass. Obviously, I can see everything.

After a second, the dancing bubbles began again.

GINA: I'm predicting I'm about to lose an assistant, and not because I get the benefit of firing her cubing ass. Nope, you're going to poach yet another one of my assistants for other areas of the firm.

ALEX: It's like you're in my head. Any military background?

Smiling, Alex watched Gina's shoulders slump, letting her head fall back in exaggerated defeat. She dragged her keyboard to her lap, and her fingers flew across the keys.

GINA: Yes. Secret clearance. Music to your ears. Geeks unite. So, where's this one going?

Watching the assistant's next spin whirl faster than the last, Alex rubbed his chin with his thumb.

ALEX: Not sure yet. Get with the assessment team and see if there's any aptitude for coding or crypto.

GINA: Of course. Since I've had her for a week, why not?

He practically heard every note of her irate tone.

ALEX: Hey, I'm saving you from serious jail time. Another few days of watching this, and you'd strangle the kid with your bare hands. And it's not just geeks. Justin Bieber can spin a cube in under two minutes.

GINA: Fine. If you're done sharing how you and the Biebs have so much in common, I need to call the car service before my next appointment. My boss will do his own murdering if they're late.

Amused, he couldn't help a slight chuckle that Gina was this peeved. Leaving it at that was completely out of the question. He teed up an easy shot that would ease her mood.

ALEX: Aw, c'mon. Tell me how you really feel?

With no more prompting, Gina moved her hand inconspicuously behind her head, as if to fix her hair. Discreetly, she used the opportunity to show Alex how he was "number one."

Somehow, the international sign for *go fuck yourself* always made a grin spread across his face. Not too long ago, Gina let it slip that she never imagined her request for monitors would lead to giving her boss the finger more often than not. She confessed it was a total perk.

Getting flipped off usually meant the webcast was over, but the elevator opening caught his eye. Stunned, Alex couldn't take his eyes off the screen.

Even across the distance and through the glass walls, Gina's cameras picked up the shapely legs and voluptuous body of a whole new mesmerizing, delicious distraction.

What do we have here?

Like Fife before him, Alex fixated on the hypnotic lull of her beautiful porcelain breasts, firm yet softly jiggling with her every suggestive step.

Something about her gait seemed nervous. Unsure? Unusual with the overly confident lot of candidates that came and went.

Closing in on the reception desk, the shy little temptress tripped, eliciting a subtle laugh from a nearly giddy Alex.

Oh, there goes her heel.

His hand hovered over the monitor's power button, not quite ready to shut it off. He cursed the fuzzy video feed, making him wish he'd invested in a slightly higher resolution system.

The scene unraveled, bit by tantalizing bit. By Gina's thoroughly unamused demeanor, she was about to do what she did best.

Gina wasn't exactly hired for her people-pleasing skills. She was essentially a behemoth of a gatekeeper, defending his corporate fortress like a 300-pound bouncer. Whoever the scantily clad Ms. Blazer was, Alex knew one thing for certain. She was on her way to being bounced out.

But, God, what a beautiful bounce it would be.

Front and center for a showdown, he ignored the erratic spikes in his heart rate. Consequences be damned, his eyes were staying glued to the screen.

Fuck, look at her. How can I not?

Every alluring sway of her body tantalized him, and the relentless throbbing in his pants pressed with need. This pretty young thing was well on her way to getting her perfectly round ass handed to her on a platter, and he ached to be the tray.

But something else held his unblinking gaze. Something about this girl was different. Interesting. Undeniably magnetic. With a strange familiarity that made his mind race.

Her sweet pouty smile sent his head into overdrive. He could imagine it in about a billion different scenarios. And the longer he stared, the dirtier each naughty little thought became.

Transfixed, he propped an elbow on the desk, resting his chin on his fist.

Sooner than expected, she stood, obviously unhappy. Unsatisfied, he frowned at the completely anticipated conclusion.

He huffed under his breath, disappointed at the premature end to their brief and very one-sided time together.

I give it twenty-four hours. If I can't get her out of my head, Gina always has her contact information.

After taking a single step to the door, the woman whipped her body around. The beautiful dancer-like turn stole his breath and caused him to raise a brow.

A second later, her demeanor transformed from a polite little interviewee into one hell of a half-naked fireball, exaggerating every movement and capturing his wide-eyed amusement.

Fuck me. Naughty librarian. Nailed it.

He turned the volume louder. Catching the tail end of his little spitfire going on and on about how Gina was an asshole made his smile widen.

Yup! Gina hasn't lost her touch.

His thumping pulse reminded him again how his unpredictable state could spiral out of control at any moment. With a deep understanding that there were worse ways to go, he sucked in a calming breath but stayed glued to the screen.

Lifting the warm cup to his lips, he filled his mouth with a healthy swig, savoring the flavor. Transfixed by her feisty moves and delicious jiggles, Alex ignored the subtle pounding in his ears.

"Oh," she said loud and clear, punctuating her words around a semi-erotic dance of wild gestures. "The reason I look and smell like *this . . .*"

God, don't stop moving like that!

". . . is because another jack-hole who works in this building crashed into me on my way in, dousing my beautiful clearance-sale white Chanel blouse with a full-on hit of his Kentucky coffee."

Shit. Instantly, Alex's grin vanished. Forcing down the mouthful of the Woodford-spiked Indonesian Sumatra, he swallowed his guilt with an audible gulp.

I'm the jack-hole.

A second later, he panicked as she scurried away. His fingers couldn't hit Gina's number fast enough.

"Gina, hire her. Now!"

"Yes, Mr. D." Gina's shout was loud, making its way to his ear just as she killed the call. "Ms. Taylor!"

Holy fuck. What did she say?

Snatching the screen, he spat out a few more expletives, aggravated that *Ms. Taylor* was hightailing it farther and farther away. Before Gina could reach her, the main elevator was carrying her swiftly to the ground floor.

Intently, he watched the scene unfold. Gina was doubling back, scurrying toward his office. A step ahead of her, he flung his office door wide.

Before Gina could ask, he nodded a hurried approval. With that, she flew past his office, stealing his private elevator for the hot pursuit.

Relieved and a little rattled, he blew a huge sigh through his lips as he rubbed at the tension in the back of his neck.

Resting against his door until it closed, the name that launched a thousand one-night stands echoed through his mind.

Ms. Taylor.

In a last-ditch attempt to stomp out his growing hopes, he reminded himself that *Taylor* was a common enough name. Hell, with his trail of conquests, he should know.

Maybe it was of no consequence. At all. Just another dead end. It's not like his diligence in working through the on-again-off-again Taylor-of-the-Month club ever panned out.

But he couldn't shake it . . . *that* feeling.

I have to know.

Unconvinced he hadn't toppled over into certifiable insanity, he teed up a text to Paco, then paused. *What the hell is her first name?*

With a quick check of Gina's calendar, he had it. And decidedly, he liked it. A smile settled on his lips as he whispered, "Madison."

ALEX: Need you to check out a woman.

PACO: Women are your area. Not mine.

ALEX: Last name Taylor.

PACO: Taylor? Sure. It's been a hot second since the last dozen Taylors I've checked out. But at the moment, I'm a little busy covering someone's ass at a meeting.

Smug and confident, Alex didn't respond. He didn't have to. He just needed to take a breath, sit back, and let Paco come to the decision he always came around to.

PACO: First name?

ALEX: Madison.

The bubbles on his phone screen bounced, then stopped, then bounced again. Impatient, Alex huffed, knowing that Paco was in a vicious cycle of typing, erasing, retyping, re-erasing. Finally, his text arrived.

PACO: How about you take the day off?

ALEX: How about you fuck off?

Insistently, his phone buzzed. *Of course.*

Who knows what excuse Paco came up with to tear himself away from the meeting. Likely, his discreet under-the-table texting wouldn't convey the exact message Paco needed transmitted. No doubt, he wanted to talk Alex off the ledge.

What he didn't know was that Alex was in the throes of freefalling into the familiar hold of a full-on manic state.

Heated, he answered the call. "Need to hear me say it? Fuck off!"

"Seriously, I'm worried about you. No bullshit. You've got to let this go."

Alex paused just long enough to avoid lashing out and going completely apeshit on the man. "I hear what you're saying. Now try hearing me. Mad-i-son Tay-lor. Just . . . find out."

Even he was annoyed at the unexpected whine in his tone. Cutting the conversation short, Alex hung up.

Uncertain he was doing the right thing, he dragged his hands across his mouth and cheeks, settling there in disbelief. Paco's great advice was quickly shoved to the sidelines. His mind was made up.

I'm right this time. I can feel it.

The talk with Paco reignited his edginess. With a watchful eye, he monitored the mild tremble in his hands. Glaring, he willed it to stop, and a second later, it did. The surprise made him content, but not cocky. But the pounding was still there, deep in his head.

Out of habit, he rubbed his brow before lowering his hands to his temples. Applying light circles of pressure to the throbbing, he knew he couldn't spend the rest of the day ping-ponging out of control and between emotional extremes.

With a ton of meetings that would take him well into the evening, he needed to get it together. Paco couldn't take all of them. *Focus.*

Oh, he was focused, all right.

Madison Taylor. His eyes closed as doubt crept in. *Could it be her? What are the odds?*

Even if she's not *the* Taylor, the draw to *this* Taylor was indescribable. Compelling.

Or is it just that she's attractive? Very attractive.

Sexy? With her lush locks lying across those breasts ready to bust loose, Alex took a breath. *Definitely sexy.*

But he'd seen sexy a hundred times over. What was it that made her different? Perhaps the way her raw emotions played out in every passionate move was enough to captivate him.

The vision of her behind his eyes was still so fresh. So ready. He could use it. Calm the erratic energy surging through every part of his body. A willing hostage, his mind surrendered completely to thoughts of her. And once again, his pulse spiked.

If he didn't get a grip before lunch, the meeting that took months to arrange would be sunk.

So, why not? Get a grip, that is.

Too much was on the line, and a quick run was out of the question. Low on options and time, Alex took hold of the perfect pressure valve, ready for a release.

Fuck it. She's perfect. She's mine.

Eager to lose himself in thoughts of her, he rested back in his chair. Instantly, his shoulders relaxed as his emotions drifted from wonder to desire. Visions of her beautiful breasts and full lips filled his mind.

The throbbing readily shifted from his head, rushing down to his other head. His cock bulged hard against his pants, eager for an escape.

"Dim." The bright lights of his office softened and the shades lowered, covering the panoramic views. Covering the bases, he called out, "Lock," and the bolt on his office door engaged, giving him the privacy he needed.

Unzipping his trousers, Alex caressed the heaviness in his hand, easing back into the reclining seat.

His eyes closed, he stroked, succumbing to the tantalizing vision of those pouty, luscious lips. Soft skin. Gorgeous ass that begged for his touch. He imagined how her seductive moans would fill the air as he peeled the blazer from her skin.

Tugging that suggestive camisole down, he'd quell a fiery, hard nipple with his mouth, suckling gently, then harder in the moment. His rod would press slowly through her willing, full lips.

God, that feels good.

Thoughts of her beautiful mouth made him stroke faster. Alex could practically touch her—taste her—the warmth of her mouth was all around his cock. Pumping tight and fast, his own friction built the sensation. Heat spread throughout his body, and his balls tightened.

Rapturous, erotic thoughts flickered through his mind like a film. He had to have her. Take her. Take care of her?

"Yes," pushed through his lips without hesitation. Take care of her as no man had. Or could.

God, what is it about her?

What if everything could change? Be turned right?

It all feels so right.

Intoxicating thoughts of having her—keeping her—closed in on him. He could feel the softness of her delicate hands around him with every stroke. Deep in her mouth, he pumped himself harder.

Make me come, Madison.

His fantasies swallowed him. His balls pulled up as his thighs stiffened, quaking by the orgasm crashing through him, his essence coating her lips and throat. He ignited, slamming his other hand down on the desk. Every tense muscle in his electric body was set free.

The edginess and stress were gone. But so was she.

Breaking from the spell, Alex opened his groggy eyes. Clear as day, he saw the reality of the situation. The only thing he'd coated was a good part of his perfectly tailored Armani pants.

Heaving, he looked around, then barked out, "Time?"

"The time is eleven o'clock," said the seductive automated voice of his virtual assistant.

Barely able to catch his breath, he grabbed a few tissues from the drawer.

Swiping at his pants with them, he cursed as he managed to make the streaks noticeably worse.

With an irritated huff, he kicked off his shoes and stood, letting his unsalvageable pants fall to the floor. He slipped off the matching blazer but was content to keep his shirt on.

Taking a staggered step to the wall behind him, he swiped his access card across the panel, habitually slipping it back into the breast pocket of his shirt.

The wall opened, revealing the hidden room. Soft lights flooded the interior, illuminating a massive closet filled with suits, shirts, shoes, and coats, most still new with tags. Ties from Armani and Gucci hung from an array of hooks, matching the general blues and dark grays of the suits of each meticulously designed and color-coded section.

In the corner was another panel, which also required Alex's access card. With a quick swipe, it opened, revealing three shelves. The top shelf held eight high-end vintage watches. Just the ones he favored.

The second shelf held a cluster of Cartier and Tiffany & Co. boxes. Nothing ends a one-night stand better than a bauble worth more than a car.

Finally, at the very bottom of the secure case was the root of all evil—a staggering pile of cold, hard cash. Crisp new hundred-dollar bills were wrapped in hundred-thousand-dollar stacks of ten-thousand-dollar bundles, neatly assembled in rows.

His jaw was tense with indecision. Abandoning further deliberation, he erred on the side of generous, tearing open a bundle and snatching ten grand free.

Unlike the black suit he'd worn earlier, a deep blue one caught his eye. He nodded approvingly, satisfied with the style and color for the remainder of the day.

It meant his Omega Speedmaster no longer matched. Perusing his options, he half considered a Vacheron Constantin before settling on a Patek Philippe, better matching a sleek belt and new untouched shoes.

Satisfied, he dressed and returned everything to its previously secured state. Then he stepped to an adjacent and rather lavish bathroom where he washed and dried his hands, checking them again for even the subtlest signs of a shake.

Certain the worst of his tremors was over, he straightened the tie that had loosened and made a last once-over of his appearance. Returning to his desk, he leaned over his computer to send one last message.

alex: Gina, have them clean my office before I return.

The time caught his eye. Quickly, he slid the ten-thousand-dollar stack into the pocket of the discarded blazer, ensuring the end of the hundreds were in clear view.

Not giving the cash a second thought, he strolled to his elevator, which had returned, awaiting his arrival. Everything in Alex's life was programmed for his gratification. Well, everything that could be programmed.

He knew that within half an hour, two people would enter his office. Besides the usual wipe down and vacuuming, they'd remove the clothing and shoes from beneath the desk. These two cleaners were the oldest employees of DGI. They'd seen many suits and shoes, though never for this reason.

Gloved, they'd feverishly work. Their jobs were confined to cleaning the executive floor, while the rest of the building was handled by a major contractor.

Whenever they found clothing on the floor, their long-standing and explicit instructions were well understood, but known only to them.

CHAPTER 4

MADISON

A month later

FAST-PACED AND EXCITING, Madison's job challenged her in ways she'd never imagined work could. She was originally hired as a management intern, but her intuitive skills in analysis and trending surprised even her. Within two weeks, she'd been reassigned as an executive analyst.

The move was sudden and unexpected. She'd even been presented with a signing bonus. In her mind, signing bonuses were reserved for athletes, recording artists, and people who cleaned up toxic waste.

Thankful for the bonus, she'd caught up on some bills and bought a few new outfits, hedging her bet by holding on to most of her windfall. Doubt always gnawed at the back of her mind. More than anyone, she knew the drill. Life happens, and this dream job might vanish as quickly as it had appeared.

Making the most of every thrilling little bit of DGI life was priority number one. Time flew by as Madison poured herself into work, learning absolutely everything she could about the fascinating company.

Forgoing lunch became a natural consequence of ingesting every ounce of corporate history. Who needs food? Work filled her more completely than anything had in a while.

Passion? Obsession? To-may-to, to-mah-to.

Often the first one in the office, she enjoyed jockeying for position with Fife for who'd be the last one out. Most days, it was Madison for the win.

And to add a ribbon of chocolate to life's three-scoop sundae of a future, the news she'd been on pins and needles waiting on had finally come. Her lease application for a nicer one-bedroom apartment in the heart of the city was approved.

Translation? She could ditch her two party-girl roommates for a centrally located pad overlooking a much quieter street. The one-bedroom apartment was within walking distance of coffee shops, quaint bookstores, and the DGI skyscraper that still filled her with excited little butterflies every time she stepped into it.

Her vision of life in the big city was coming true. It was everything she'd dreamed of when she abandoned a comfy small-town existence for the crazy allure of New York City.

Blame Broadway and every romcom ever featured there.

And coming and going worry-free of traffic gave her a few extra zzz's each day. Not hours, but just enough to let her escape into a steamy romance novel late each night.

With all big cities, there were risks. Despite her hop, skip, and jump to and from work, easy going couldn't always be in the cards.

Three yawns in, Madison stretched in the ergonomic comfort of her office chair and checked her phone. It was late. With a dreamy glance out the window, she noticed the sun was still shining, but barely.

Like most evenings, she crossed the empty lobby, a little *hoorah* leaping into her mind as she spied the empty security desk. *Yes! Four-for-0 this week.* Her title of Last Woman Standing was undisputed.

The silence of the vast lobby was barely broken by the sneakers she'd changed into for the walk home. Not super fashionable, but she really needed to preserve her work heels. Sighing, she still missed her pretty little stilettos. Her personal sacrifice to the great DGI gods.

With a quick flip, she swiped her access card to leave. The building would be locked down after Fife left, and anyone remaining would need to badge out for the door to release.

Rounding the corner of the building, she made a hasty dig in her purse to be sure she had a five-dollar bill, ready to give it to Joe. The homeless man often lingered at the corner at the end of the building. He'd apparently been a staple of the block for years.

Nicknamed G.I. Joe due to the vintage BDU jacket he sported from a war long gone, he was purported to be harmless. But the harmless, homeless veterans were always on her mind, haunting her since the loss of her brother, Jack.

Whenever she could, she'd either give Joe a few bucks or a meal, or both if she could swing it. Today, though, she left the money in her purse when she saw Joe wasn't alone. Tucked into a ball on the sidewalk, Joe could barely defend himself against the three guys huddled around him in some jacked-up rugby scrimmage.

Laughing, two of them shoved him with their feet, warning him about returning. A third guy puffed his cigarette through a scowl only a mother could love. His tossing his cigarette at Joe was the last straw for Madison.

Without thinking, she ran up to them, shouting, "Hey, leave him alone!"

The three men turned toward her. Slowly, their sadistic smiles widened as they met her eyes.

Shit, now what?

The big one with the cigarette and disturbingly thick forehead jeered. "Well, well, well . . . looks like Supergirl has arrived."

Her heart pounding, she gulped hard at his approach.

Before she could step back, another one grabbed her forearm. "How 'bout you let a real man show you a good time?"

Alarmed, she tugged, desperate to be free of his hold, but his firm grip remained wrapped around her wrist. Undeterred, Madison yanked back with the full force of every bit of strength in her body.

She toppled back as if freed, slapping her arm into yet another man. This one caught it.

"What seems to be the problem?"

The low voice boomed with a take-no-shit tone, sending an untimely jolt straight to the very worst parts of her under the circumstances.

Looking up over her shoulder, Madison lost her breath, taking in the ruggedly handsome stranger standing behind her.

Holy crap. It's Alex Drake.

Panicked to find her arm still stuck to his chest like a fridge magnet, she shyly drew it back but he grasped it. Apparently, releasing her wasn't part of his plans. And the longer he held it, the harder it was for her to breathe.

Calmly but firmly, he nudged her behind him, barricading her from the three men with his own body. Only then did she slip from his hold. Stepping forward, he put more space between her and the cluster of bullies.

Starstruck and in disbelief, Madison watched, frozen. She should be running. Getting help. Something. Anything.

But her little tennis-shoed feet weren't budging an inch without his say. Beyond a shadow of a doubt, this man had control. She had no idea what was coming, but every instinct told her whatever he was about to do, she'd never forget it. He was there for one reason.

To protect me.

CHAPTER 5

ALEX

It had been nearly a month since Alex's last episode, but with pure adrenaline pumping through his veins and the Madison of his dreams behind his back, he stood confident. Perhaps arrogantly so.

The risk was worth it. She was more than worth it. And exercise never provoked his condition, so unleashing a righteous ass-kicking should calm him right down.

"Hey, we were just showing the lady a good time," the biggest asshole said, staring up at Alex.

With a few inches on the guy, Alex smiled as the son of a bitch gave him one hell of a snarl. Reflexes ready and hackles raised, Alex was primed to give him a pounding.

Whether in the back alley or the boardroom, the Hulk in Alex was always ready to pounce. Too ready, which occasionally posed an occupational hazard. But today, all signs pointed to *fuck yeah*. All that adrenaline reinforced him.

The deadly heat of Alex's glare belied his half-cocked smile. Stepping forward, he didn't blink, not stopping until their noses were barely inches apart.

"Well, party's over," he said, a growl lacing his words. "I suggest you and your minions head on out." Alex's tone was as fair a warning as they were getting, the coil before the strike.

"Hey, no problem." The bastard backed off just enough to pull back a punch.

The lame move was totally expected. And for Alex, it might as well have been in slow motion.

The guy attempted a pathetically wide jab at Alex's head. Sure, Alex was a black belt in three separate martial arts, but none of that was necessary. Swiftly leaning to the right, he eased out of the way just enough to deflect the blow, using his attacker's momentum to shove the guy hard into the granite wall of the side of his building. Full force. Headfirst.

Stunned, his attacker collapsed to his knees, eliciting a stifled chuckle from Alex. Casually straightening his blazer, he then rubbed the wall, coyly checking it for scratches. When he gave the other two a quick stare-down, they backed away, raising their hands in worried surrender.

Behind them, Alex caught two of New York's finest racing over, plus Fife was now rushing to the scene, his usually pleasant demeanor gone. Alex recognized the no-nonsense glare of the former SEAL's combat days.

The two hooligans bolted from the scene, abandoning their friend. The cops grabbed him, forcing him to his feet.

"Not an issue, gentlemen," Alex said, figuring the ass-wipe had probably learned his lesson. That, and the last thing he needed was a crime report at his own goddamn doorstep. "My friend just fell. He's pretty clumsy, so I'm sure he'll tread lightly the next time he walks by this part of town."

Reluctantly, the cops released the douchebag. Grumbling in defeat, the man staggered away.

Determined to make the most of their brisk run over, the cops turned their attention on G.I. Joe. "Hey, buddy, you can't be here. Get going."

Again, Alex intervened, smoothing his words with a cool layer of diplomacy.

"Gentlemen. This guy's not hurting anyone, and by the tiles he's lying across, I believe he's technically on private property. So, unless the owner has an issue, which *I* don't, then under the laws of the State of New York, he's free to lounge, eat, unaggressively panhandle, and discreetly urinate on the building as long as he doesn't expose himself." Alex unleashed his most charming smile. "Gotta love New York City laws, right?"

Dismayed and shaking their heads, the boys in blue looked at each other, then smirked back at Alex and yielded with nods. "Hey," one of them said, "if you want him here, trust us, he's yours. He's a hell of an accessory for your monumental skyscraper."

Their sarcastic laughs thinly veiled their mild irritation.

Annoying the cops hadn't been Alex's intention. Busting their butts each and every day was the life they lived. The last thing they needed was another pompous prick showing them up. He'd never mock their determination to "protect and serve."

Sincere apology sweetened his tone. "Look, I appreciate it. And you. How about when your shift ends, you can be my guests at the 21 Club?" He handed them each his card. "Tonight, or whenever. Just show them this card, and they'll take care of you."

Alex wasn't sure they'd take him up on it, but they thanked him nonetheless. And he'd take care of them one way or another. He always did.

With a glance at their badges, he filed their names away, adding them to a growing list of people to look after. *Someday.*

He shook their hands, then watched them tip their hats to Madison, Fife, and even Joe, before they each pocketed his card and returned the way they came.

"Fife, take Ms. Taylor inside. I'd like a private chat with this guy."

With a step toward Joe, Alex was surprised to be blocked. Madison moved between them, locking her bright doe eyes straight on him.

"Mr. Drake, I'm so sorry you had to get involved, but I can help him."

Her concern for Joe was obvious from her wide-eyed pleading and the subtle lines in her brow. She was worried, and Alex couldn't believe what it was doing to him.

So many feelings were swirling around inside him, but one raw emotion surged up through him more than anything else. Something he rarely experienced when dealing with people, and even less with women.

For the first time in ages, he was genuinely intrigued.

Madison's concern apparently didn't escape Joe, who'd been sitting silently until that moment.

"Hey, don't worry, doll. AJ will take good care of me."

Madison and Fife looked at Joe, then Alex, obviously confused by Joe's reference.

Their hesitation gave Alex an excuse to lean close to Madison's ear, keeping his voice just above a whisper. "Apparently, I look like someone he knows."

Damn, she smells good.

Still, Madison wasn't budging an inch, and if she kept it up, the bulge in his pants was ready to show her more than an inch.

Firmly, she stood her ground. Based on her crossed arms and stubborn stance, she had no intention of going anywhere.

"Look, Ms. Taylor, I'm not sure why you're so concerned, but you needn't be. He'll be fine."

Alex had a pretty good idea what she was thinking. Between his MMA moves and his hard-charging, no-bullshit reputation, she was apparently afraid to leave him alone with Joe.

A second later, she started pleading. "Mr. Drake, he's a veteran. Please don't hurt him."

Alex couldn't hold back a smile. "I'm not going to hurt him."

A knot formed in her brow, telling him that the object of his little fixation must have thought he was being patronizing. Admittedly, it might have been the tiniest bit patronizing.

The doubt clear on her face was endearing.

Beauty and *balls. Fuck, she's adorable.*

Unable to shed his smug grin, Alex solemnly raised a palm in the air. "I swear to God I won't hurt him."

Madison backed up, as if half expecting a lightning bolt to strike him down from the sky.

With a small step forward, he was in her space. One glance in her big, beautiful eyes stole his breath, and he gripped her upper arms.

The shiver that ran through her body made him want to take her. *Right here, right now, for all the world to fucking see.* But glancing at Fife, and then Joe, he scratched the idea.

Instinctively, he softened his touch, smoothing his thumbs back and forth. It seemed to set her at ease. Her lips parted, audibly catching a shallow breath. And, God, it took every ounce of willpower to keep himself from plunging a deep kiss past a polite pretense and straight down her throat.

Instead, he handed her off to Fife, shooting the man a stern look. "Get her inside."

Fife's arm swooped around her, replacing Alex's grip. As his chief of security pulled Madison safely into the building, Alex watched her twist around to look back. Something in him deflated as he realized she was looking at Joe.

As if on cue, Joe shouted, "Don't worry. AJ and I are gonna catch up."

Once Fife rounded the corner with Madison in tow, Alex again straightened his suit and adjusted his tie, still watching to ensure Madison hadn't doubled back.

Sterner than usual, Alex said, "Joe?"

"Yeah, AJ?"

In a short, casual stroll, Alex stood before Joe, then tugged at his slacks to squat down. The vantage point allowed an eye-to-eye discussion.

Alex let out a slow huff. "You know you can't piss on my building, right?"

Grinning, Joe reassured him. "Right, AJ."

They both enjoyed an extended chuckle as Alex reached into the breast pocket of his suit. He always kept Marlboros in a silver case, although he never indulged. Ready and waiting, they were there to appease various clients and random women who were so inclined.

But today, he pulled one out and offered it to a grateful Joe, lighting it for him and wrapping his hand around it to ensure the light breeze didn't steal the flame before Joe could savor a puff.

Joe relaxed, giving Alex enough leeway to ask a question.

"So, how do you know Supergirl?"

CHAPTER 6

MADISON

"F IFE?" Madison said, still reeling from being escorted back into the building like a child.

"Yes, Ms. Taylor?"

"I *was* actually on my way out."

She eyed his hand on her shoulder, and with an uncertain shrug, he promptly removed it.

"Well, I guessed that since you carded out, but Mr. Drake told me to bring you in," Fife said as he headed toward his desk, and she followed.

"I carded out because I thought you were gone."

"I just had to do some paperwork," he said, pointing his large index finger toward the bathroom.

"So, how did you know to come outside?"

"Oh, I saw it all as soon as I returned." Turning the screen, he showed her his monitor, which displayed the live footage from eight separate angles, including the current feed from the exterior.

Scooting next to Fife, she took a better look. The cameras were trained on Alex and Joe. Studying the screen hard, she saw that Alex seemed to be handing Joe a cigarette, then lighting it for him. Their conversation seemed friendly and casual.

Are they laughing? They look like two old friends.

Feeling an inch tall and even worse for wishing there was audio, Madison bit her lip.

How could I have pegged him so wrong?

She knew his history practically by heart. Alex Drake was the founder and CEO of a global multibillion-dollar empire. Yet, she'd considered his intentions to be no better than those of her assailants.

Deeply immersed in the silent conversation, she watched as things seemed to be wrapping up. Madison couldn't help the feelings coming over her. Most of all, she was intrigued.

Alex concluded their chat by pulling out his wallet, then handed Joe what seemed to be its entire contents. The bills were definitely hundreds. A lot of them.

With that, he turned to return to the lobby, sending Fife into a slight panic. With a gentle shove, he moved Madison to the other side of the desk, hiding the fact they'd been watching Alex's "private" conversation.

With the boss approaching, both acted abnormally nonchalant. As Alex stepped closer, Madison couldn't help notice him averting his eyes.

"Ms. Taylor needs a ride home, Fife." Ignoring her and seeming collected but pissed, he said nothing else. And she hated it.

Trying to make amends for having irked the man who had just rescued her, she forced herself into the conversation.

"Mr. Drake, I can't thank you enough for what you did back there, but a company car isn't necessary."

His deep breath was audible, and the air of annoyance surrounding it was almost more than she could bear.

He looked back, hardening his eyes with a glare. "You might not feel it's necessary, but when I see people on my staff getting manhandled right on my property, let's just say I'm not letting you traipse home alone."

"I meant I can get a Lyft. I don't want you or the company further inconvenienced."

"This isn't a debate, Ms. Taylor."

The pesky little hives growing beneath her sleeve were an instant response to his loudness.

"You want to lose your fucking mind and stand between a homeless guy and three thugs intent on beating the crap out of someone, next time do it off my property. It's a liability to this company . . . and to me. So, unless you've got some badass kung-fu skills you can whip out from beneath that skirt, I strongly suggest you take the car."

Abruptly, he ended the conversation, heading toward the executive garage. Before the door shut behind him, he repeated himself. "Get her the car, Fife."

Watching him walk away, which did she hate more? Him for being a total bastard, or herself for having a hand in making him one?

Fife stepped up, interrupting her internal debate. "You'd actually be doing me a big favor if you let me drive you home. My car's a little sketchy right now, and that means I get a company car for the evening. Okay?"

Nodding, she let out a sigh. "Yes, of course. Thanks."

Once in the car, Fife yammered on and on, giving it his all to reassure her. "Hey, don't let it get to you. Mr. Drake might be a rich blowhard, but he's a blowhard that cares, and that should count for something, right?"

Forcing a weak smile, Madison couldn't reply. Between being exhausted, irate, sullen, and embarrassed, she took several deep breaths, determined to keep from overreacting.

Her gaze drifted down to her skirt. She imagined cupping her hands around her mouth, shouting into it like a megaphone. "Yoo-hoo? Badass kung-fu skills? Are you up in there somewhere? No? Okay. Just checking."

Dammit. I hate when attractive, condescending men are right.

Barely traveling two blocks to her building, Fife was already slowing down to drop her off. "Have a good night, Ms. Taylor."

It was only then, as Fife wished her a good night, that she began to wonder.

How, in a company with tens of thousands of employees, did Alex Drake know my name?

Frustrated, Alex sat in his private garage, the unrelenting pulse pounding through his body not letting him leave. He sat in his car, considering his second unbelievably terrible encounter with the beautiful Ms. Taylor.

"Madison," he said, correcting himself under his breath.

Inadvertently, he'd won a battle he hadn't meant to enter. But did he lose the war? Hurting her was never his intention.

Still primed from the scuffle on the street, his fight-or-fight-harder instincts kicked into high gear, refusing to be contained.

Lyft, my ass. Is she out of her goddamn mind?

The mere mention of a Lyft shot him to a new, uncontrollable level of totally losing his shit.

What the fuck was she thinking? If she'd hopped into a Lyft, how the hell would he know if she got home safely? And sending a dozen off-the-clock operatives in pursuit would be crazy. *Right?*

Clear as day, he saw himself, pacing all goddamn night like a keyed-up prom dad.

Let her think I'm an asshole. Join the club. It's for her own good.

The fresh thought of that man's hands on her had his mind spinning. *She needs protection.*

With the unrelenting pounding in his ears, he prepared for the worst, slumping into the soft leather seat of his Rolls-Royce Phantom. He didn't bother trying to start it. His trembling hand stopped him cold. For the moment, driving was a lost cause.

Motionless, he sat in the empty, silent garage. There was nothing to do but brace for impact. Ride it out.

As usual, the numbness washed over him. Then the cold. At some point, the trembling would ebb. He wiped his eyes and rubbed his face, dragging his fingers anxiously through his hair.

Painfully, a sentence echoed in a growing loop through his head, but he couldn't—*wouldn't*—bring himself to finish it.

If anything happened to her . . .

CHAPTER 7

MADISON

THE NEXT DAY, wearing office-ready slacks and carrying pepper spray in a pink lipstick-style canister, Madison headed to DGI—on foot—determined not to be afraid of her own shadow.

On the way in, she grabbed two egg-swiss-and-turkey-bacon croissants from the local deli, ready to share one with Joe. If the other didn't get eaten for breakfast, it would be fine for lunch. Nerves always wreaked havoc on her appetite.

But as she neared the towering headquarters, panic swept her to a run. Security guards were now prominently posted at each end of the building. Armed guards.

Where's Joe?

Within a few steps, she relaxed. Hidden at first behind the massive stature of a *don't fuck with me* security guard, Joe was propped up against the side of the building where he usually was. Filled with relief, she caught her breath.

Smiling, Joe looked up. "There's my Supergirl."

If only. "And there's my G.I. Joe. Here."

He took the warm sandwich she handed him, tucking it carefully into the pocket of his raggedy BDU jacket.

Worried, Madison squatted next to him. "Not hungry?"

Is he injured?

141

"AJ got me one earlier, but I'll save this one for lunch." He gave his pocket a few light pats, happy with his prize.

Madison exchanged a smile with Joe, then headed into the building. Thoughts of Alex Drake filled her head, like they'd done for most of her sleepless night.

Well, Mr. Drake, you might flaunt that asshole armor, but there's a knight in there. Somewhere.

Cheerful, she stepped up to the security desk. "Good morning, Fife."

"Good morning, Ms. Taylor. Hey . . ." He motioned for her to lean in, and Madison did, ready to receive a discreet message. "The boss wants to see you. He's in conference room 214."

Unsettled, Madison winced. *I'm so fired.* With a helpless look, she thanked Fife.

Well, it was nice while it lasted.

Apprehensive, she made her way to the second floor. Most of the meeting rooms in the building were glass walled, where anyone could see the goings-on. But room 214 was private, with a multitude of entrances.

Because DGI often hosted meetings where the confidentiality of the participants was highly prized, keeping their comings and goings under wraps was of the utmost importance. With an abundance of rumors and conspiracy theories, employees often speculated who visited, as well as how they came and went.

Rumors of hidden exits that led to other buildings popped up in whispered water-cooler conversations, and speculation about an extensive tunnel system sometimes crept in, perhaps leading to the White House. Or Area 51.

Finding the door slightly open, Madison peeked inside before mustering the courage to knock. Half seated on the edge of the massive cherry conference table was a man too gorgeous for words. She gawked in pure appreciation. It wasn't until he checked his watch that she snapped out of it.

With a hard swallow against the dryness in her throat, she laid a few light knocks on the oversized door.

"Come in."

The boom of his voice shot across the room, sending her pulse into a tizzy as she struggled for air. The frenzy of nerves in her stomach meant that breakfast croissant might not be eaten until dinner.

Entering, she found the room flooded with a comfortable brightness. The blinds were closed, but light glowed through the sheer shades.

Alex's face was rugged. Chiseled. And his bright eyes shined in this light. The lines of his face showcased a life of raw reality, amplifying a sexy-as-hell bad-boy presence mildly tamed by the soft lines of his custom-tailored suit.

Anxious, Madison stopped just inside the doorway, too shy to move, remaining at the perfect distance to admire every inch of the hot package known as Alex Drake.

Well, if this is the end, I guess there are worse ways to go.

Alex stood, but instead of buttoning his blazer in the customary fashion, he removed it.

Why is he taking off his jacket?

"Ms. Taylor, come in and close the door."

His jacket is off, and now I'm coming in and closing the door? To be clear, I don't have enough money on me for a lap dance.

Slowly, she complied, but kept her gaze locked on Alex as she did. He rolled up his sleeves, revealing just the tease of his muscles.

"Y-you wanted to see me?" Her voice cracked slightly, part fear of being fired, and part stammering like a front-row fan at a rock concert.

He gave her a quick once-over, and her breath hitched. Expressionless, he crossed his arms. "Well, I can see by your sensible sneakers that you opted to walk to work. Tough as nails, huh?"

She took the taunt, but after a night to think it through, she had a few choice things to say. And in her mind, it was now or never.

"Mr. Drake, I just need to say something." Uneasy, she let out a slow breath. "I apologize for not being more gracious about your offer yesterday. You were right. I was impulsive, and though what happened certainly wasn't my intention, I did end up putting myself, this company, and you in a precarious position. And for that, I am truly sorry."

He took a minute, eyeing her as he seemed to ponder her apology. Finally, he replied with a, "Hmm."

Did he say *hmm?* Or *mmm?*

Wait, why would he say mmm?

Allowing his lips to relax into a soft grin, he said, "But it's not going to change your behavior, is it?"

The question seemed innocent enough, but trick questions always do.

Its seriousness weighed on her. If she said it wouldn't change her behavior, she could be fired for something buried deep within the DGI personnel manual, some mention that under no circumstances could an employee ever put DGI in any form of risk.

On the other hand, if she conceded, assuring him that her behavior would change, well, it would be an outright lie. And Madison Taylor was no liar. Mostly because she was atrocious at it.

Cautiously, she said, "I'm not going to be a captive of my own fear, if that's the question."

Something in the glint in his eye and the widening of his smile calmed her. Like, he got it. *Could he possibly relate?*

"Let me tell you what I think, Ms. Taylor."

Madison braced for impact, gripping the back of a conference chair for support. Her eyes widened as he headed toward her.

"I've been replaying what I saw yesterday, and something about it is really bugging me."

Another step closer, and he was barely an arm's length away. "May I?" he asked, eyeing her arm. His intention remained unclear.

Unsure what she should do, she extended her arm, holding his attention, prepared for a handshake.

In a sweep, his hand wrapped firmly around her forearm, and she gasped in surprise. His playful eyes met hers, but he didn't release her. And she wasn't trying to get away. Patiently, she let him hold her, and his touch sent a tingle straight to the very center of her core.

"When you pulled away yesterday, you were wearing a very flimsy blouse."

Indignant, Madison rebuffed whatever the hell it was he was suggesting. "I didn't invite him to grab me, if that's what you're getting at."

Struggling, she tried pulling her arm back, but it was hopelessly locked in the strength of his immovable grip.

"No, what I mean is the fabric wasn't very, um, substantial. If you really had broken away from him, his hand would have closed, and he'd be left clutching your blouse. It would have torn by the time your arm swung into my chest. See?"

He demonstrated with her blouse sleeve.

She caught on, nodding as the epiphany hit her. "He let me go."

Alex nodded back, seemingly satisfied that she understood. "He let you go. He used the momentum of your pull to push your arm into my chest."

With that, he pulled her arm into his chest, replaying the events of the day before. She couldn't help but notice the mass of solid muscles concealed beneath his pressed white shirt.

Yesterday, she hadn't noticed, too engulfed in the dangers of the moment.

But today was a whole new story, and her all-consuming awareness kept her arm absolutely glued to him. *Big-time.*

Indifferent to her schoolgirl gawking, Alex proceeded with his impromptu lecture. "Whenever you're in a situation like that, and hopefully you'll never be again, you need to take a moment and look at his hand."

Exaggerating his demonstration, he displayed his hand. It drew attention to more than his lesson. Despite his pristine manicure, his hands were marked by rough, faded scars that trailed up his arms.

What would have caused that? She peered shyly at his face. Were they the superficial evidence of much deeper damage?

Her gaze focused on his lips. While she'd been dreamy-eyed and curious, he'd apparently been talking the entire time.

"Focus," she heard him say, "on the thumb. That's your escape strategy. You're going to reverse karate-chop out through there in one quick motion . . ." He prodded her to try it.

Without overthinking it, she did, quickly freeing her arm. Pleased, she stood taller.

Again, he wrapped his hand around her arm, methodically bringing in one finger at a time, then firming his grip. Checking in with her, he asked, "Is that too tight?"

"N-no, it's fine." *God, it's more than fine.*

Madison breathed through the warmth rushing up her neck and face. Something about this very hands-on lesson was taking a turn for the naughty, but she wasn't about to admit it.

Jesus, this isn't a date, Madison. He's taking time out from his insanely busy schedule to not fire you and possibly save your life. Focus.

Reining in her mental bad behavior, she followed his words.

"Now, try." His tone was encouraging, and his eyes softened as he spoke.

Confident, she tugged a little toward the thumb-exit he'd pointed out, but nothing.

She sucked in a breath and tried harder. Then much less politely. No dice.

With a ridiculous amount of bravado, she really struggled to set herself free, playfully popping her foot up to nearly touch his thigh for a second—pantomiming her Oscar-worthy act of making a significant effort.

She caught his chuckle. Who wouldn't be amused? She was a teensy little sprite, trying to wrestle out of the hold of a smoking-hot giant.

Alex feigned a yawn while effortlessly maintaining his grip.

She gave up with an admission of defeat. "Okay, okay . . . I can't get away."

"Right. And with a behemoth like that guy yesterday, if he wanted to keep you held, he'd still have you in his grubby talons. So, you're going to do something unexpected that won't take much strength. Not that you're not strong, but your aggressor will probably be stronger. A lot stronger. So, you're going to block your natural tendencies to pull away, and surprise him with a swift little move that should put him on the ground. Ready?"

"Ready," she lied, her response coming out more like a question. Unconvinced, she really couldn't imagine escaping from such a strong grasp.

Not that I'm complaining. She softly sucked in a breath and bit the corner of her lower lip.

Alex paused, glancing at her mouth and then her heated cheeks before he continued. "Okay, I've got you. You're going to put your free hand on top of mine, forcing my hand to stay there."

She watched closely, then did as he directed. As Alex monitored her technique, she stole a few glimpses of his face, studying his tough and uncommonly striking features.

The urban legends about his allure over women are 150 percent true.

He nodded with approval, forcing Madison to squelch a giggle. He was approving her technique, not her musings. But she half supposed that if she dared to say it aloud, he'd probably nod just the same.

"Now, swing your arm around, and back-grab my wrist with your captured hand. Think of it as a variation of *wax on*, but where you end up having both hands grabbing him, and his arm and body will pivot involuntarily. It's a reflex. You then use the leverage of your position to force him to the ground."

Methodically, he walked her through the moves in slow motion, drawing Madison in. She noticed more than the complexity and effectiveness of each move.

Alex Drake's not just a guy with cool fighting skills. He's had some serious tactical training. He might have even taught it.

Captivated, she welcomed the tenderness of his tone and patience of his teaching. It all played out like a lesson Jack might have given her. If he were still here. In the oddest way, Alex reminded her of Jack, and she suddenly really missed her brother.

Pulling herself together, she concentrated, following the leader through a series of complicated steps. With very mild adjustments, Alex guided her as she moved through the technique.

Then out of nowhere, it clicked. *I've got it.*

Working through the move slowly at first, she thrilled as her confidence built. She whipped through it a little faster and more forcefully, instantly swinging his body and contorting it to the floor.

"Okay, okay, I give!" he shouted playfully.

Delighted at her success, she couldn't help the giddy squeal that escaped her throat.

Alex returned to his feet, giving her a disapproving glance that clearly said, *God, you're such a girl.*

Eager to please, she wiped her face of everything but pure stoic professionalism. "Yes, I think I understand now. Thank you, Mr. Drake."

Her sudden shift to a serious demeanor drew a belly laugh from Alex. His dancing gaze darted met hers, and he closed the distance between them.

Her heart skipped a beat as she melted under his stare, sure that if she played poker with the man, every move she made would quickly give her away.

CHAPTER 8

ALEX

ALEX DRAKE always had the amazing wherewithal to be good at practically anything. Whether engaging in major corporate wheeling and dealing or simply playing a hand of Texas Hold 'em, he was a natural, due in part to his uncanny ability to read people.

For years, he'd honed his nonverbal communication skills, knowing it would pay off, and it gave him the upper hand in almost any situation. But today, his usual advantage was crumbling under the sweet suggestive bits of his very own kryptonite.

With a laundry list of silent tells, Madison was his, and his will to resist was evaporating. He was all too ready to let go. Open his world. Unlock his heart.

But why?

He'd been approached by countless women over the years. Overtly, sometimes demanding, in the way one-night stands tended to be. But this . . . well, this was something entirely different. Irresistible. New.

Between the rapid pulse in Madison's wrist and the dilation of her pupils, her attraction to him was transparent. Compounded by the increased fullness of her lips as she slowly sucked in the lower one before biting it, he found himself fighting an internal tug-of-war he was willing to lose.

Between defending her and desiring her, he was dangerously close to falling for a woman he barely knew—and falling hard. So Alex concentrated, desperate to stay focused.

"Good. You're free. What do you do now?" he asked. Realizing he was a little too close, he summoned all his strength, keeping himself a safe few inches from her magnetic pull.

God, her lips are so fucking kissable.

Interrupting his stare, Madison stammered. "I . . . I . . ."

"Yes, Ms. Taylor?" His tone softened, and his eyes captured hers.

"I . . ." Her focus fell to his lips, and she licked hers ever so slightly.

What I wouldn't give for just one taste.

Ready to take her into his arms and never let go, he kept his voice low. "Go on."

Tenderly, he looked down at her, willing to lose all control. *What is it about her? Something different? Familiar?*

The electricity between them sparked with a connection that was undeniably real. Tangible.

Fighting the insane need to take her in his arms, he tamped down his desires and listened with the patience of a saint.

If I push her, I might lose her.

Despite the unrelenting attraction to her magnetic curves, her next words definitely got his attention.

"I, um, guess I'd kick him in the balls?"

At those words, his body instinctively tensed. Despite his captivation with her, just the thought of being on the receiving end of that move was the wake-up call he needed to free him from her allure.

Why are the prettiest ones always so evil?

Deliberately, he took a step back and rolled his sleeves down. Clearing his throat, he put his blazer back on.

"Not a bad suggestion, but not your best option." Still turned away from her, he buttoned his suit jacket, taking a few seconds to regain his composure. "No, Ms. Taylor, your best option is to use those stylish Brooks for their intended purpose." Turning back, he gave her a stern warning. "Get as far away from your assailant as possible."

Nodding, she boldly stepped toward him, and he welcomed her with a grin. "That's probably a good idea. I'd only kick him in the balls if I had my badass kung-fu skills with me."

Her teasing smile reminded him that he owed her an apology.

"Look, about that. I'm sorry for what I said. You didn't do anything wrong. I was just upset, but I was wrong to take it out on you."

"No need to apologize. I mean, you were right, after all." Madison's smile transformed as her eyes widened. "You were *right*."

Her lips say I was right, but her eyes say she wants to kick me in the balls. It's a trap.

Ready to hand over a bigger apology, he sucked in a breath, prepared for full-on grovel mode. And maybe dinner. He'd do anything to get that beautiful smile back on her face.

Before he could speak, she cut in.

"You know, I'm probably not the only woman—or person, for that matter—in this multibillion-dollar company who doesn't know how to defend themselves."

"Yes. So?"

"So, sixty percent of our revenue comes from national defense, and not just our nation's, while twenty-five-percent of our work is in active contingency areas. All of our buildings have full gyms with training rooms that are barely used, on top of which we have an aggressive military recruiting program."

"All true." Not quite connecting the dots, Alex stood, riveted by her knowledge of his company. Madison hadn't been there that long, barely a month, but seemed to be a walking DGI encyclopedia, rattling off information like she'd majored in the subject.

And just when I didn't think she could get any sexier.

"Well, what if employees with these unique skills volunteered their time to teach varying levels of self-defense or martial arts, or both? It reinforces the image of a strong company that's also focused on employee protection and support. This would give us a recruiting advantage, and a public image that says strong companies start with a strong workforce."

Alex looked at her one last time, staring deeply as if he could see straight to her soul. Her shudder was nearly invisible, but it kept a satisfied smile on his face. There she was, giving him full witness to all the vulnerabilities she masked.

She's not just beauty and balls after all. She's got brains too. I'm going to marry this girl.

Strolling past her but keeping his eyes forward, Alex opted to hide his insistent desire to whisk her into his arms. Instead, he opened the door.

~

Madison couldn't take much more of Alex's darkening gaze but she stayed put, desperate to show her strength . . . and hide her shiver.

Decidedly, he looked away.

Again, he looks away? What would it be like to let go and lose myself in his strong arms and dark eyes?

Bitterly cold, he walked past her, avoiding her eyes at all costs, but damn near scorching her with his hot body so close.

Did I upset him? Maybe threatening to kick him in the balls was crossing the line.

Watching him walk away was disappointing and disheartening, but glorious all the same.

Alex opened the door but didn't turn back. His voice commanding, he left her with a few parting words. "Make it happen, Ms. Taylor."

As the sound of his footsteps retreated down the hall, Madison broke out in a little happy dance. Rocking her moves with a hushed *yes, yes, yes*, she froze when her quirky twirl in place made her worst nightmares come true.

In the doorway, a small crowd was gathered, eagerly awaiting their use of the conference room. They seemed to enjoy her impromptu audition, filling the room with a chorus of *awws* as she cut her performance short.

Scrunching her face, Madison forced a grin, masking the heat of her cheeks as she pushed her way through the applauding group.

CHAPTER 9

ALEX

CALMING the elated pep in his step, Alex entered his executive floor conference room.

Attentively, Paco and a small team sat up straighter in their seats upon his arrival. Leather-bound folders were perfectly positioned in front of every chair, providing detailed plans and a full itinerary for Alex's twenty-eight-day corporate trot across the globe, starting way before sunrise the next Monday.

Alex made himself comfortable at the head of the table, unable to erase the giddy smile pasted on his face, or evade the observation of Paco's amused eye.

Focusing on the work ahead, Alex opened the binder, a cue to his chief operating officer that he might proceed.

"Fourteen countries in twenty-eight days?" Dana said. "Just verifying you're good with that."

"Actually . . ." Alex flipped through the first few pages, scanning the itinerary for a small opportunity.

I need a day. No, two.

Unable to find an opening, Alex did what he does best. He made the opportunity he needed. "I'm not. Add Paris and Milan, in that order."

"Yes, sir," a senior analyst responded, quickly scribbling on his notepad. "Tack on two days to the end?"

Alex sped through the overview, rechecking himself. The last thing he needed was to make a long trip longer. "Yes," he said, more adamantly this time.

152

Nodding, he clasped his hands. "Thirty days even. Sixteen countries with France and Italy added. That'll work. Now, let's walk through the strategies for each location."

As three enormous monitors lowered from the ceiling, dark but transparent blinds descended across the panoramic windows, still allowing views of the city's skyline. The monitors came to life, simulcasting the meeting to DGI offices around the world, with nearly two hundred executives hanging on the plans ahead.

Rick, the VP for global strategy, activated the presentation, ready to go through the massive report in exhaustive detail. "We'll start in South America, make our way across the Middle East to Asia, then ricochet back via Europe to meet key stakeholders. Locations and detailed agendas start on slide five."

With the presentation in full swing, Alex caught a text lighting up his phone. Not missing a word of Rick's report, he read and began a reply to the text as he asked, "Rick, I thought the Japanese were good with the initial plan. Why the extra day?"

"No change in the original deal," Rick said. "They requested a brief discussion on Project Venator on behalf of a major client. The meeting will tack four hours onto the next day but should prove quite lucrative. That, and they insistently requested a dinner the first night, as well as a presentation in your honor."

A shy grin showcased all the enthusiasm Alex would ever express, balancing his approval with humility. "Lucrative always works, and I appreciate their hospitality. I look forward to it. Please continue."

Rick did so, and Alex resumed a quick text tennis match with Paco.

PACO: Paris AND Milan? You're hardly the shopaholic. Business or pleasure?

ALEX: Business is always a pleasure.

PACO: You might be fluent in five languages, but votre français est merde. Très atroce. Perhaps you'll need a translator.

Alex pulled back his laugh to a stifled huff, conceding that his French, indeed, was not only atrocious, but complete, undeniable shit. Whatever. No matter how many languages Paco was fluent in, he still wasn't going on this trip.

ALEX: Hardly. Mandarin is the new language of money but won't be needed as both parties I'm meeting speak Italian. And with me out of the country for nearly a month, you'll be covering roughly 120 meetings.

PACO: Exactly 128, asshole.

ALEX: Hey, I'm not hitting Dubai, so it's not like you're missing the real shopping.

Avoiding more probes into his European detour, Alex set the phone face-down, determined to ignore any further texts or annoying glances from the Paco peanut gallery.

Alex looked up. In the lower right corner of the center screen, he found the page number of the slide presentation. *Eighteen. Of two hundred twelve.* Without a doubt, his ass would be planted in that chair for several more hours.

Giving in, Alex motioned the attendant for coffee.

CHAPTER 10

MADISON

One month later

WORKING at DGI was a dream come true, and Madison couldn't be happier. Well, not unless the sexy CEO who monopolized her dreams finally came around to sweeping her off her feet.

Grounding herself in reality, she blended seamlessly into the fabric of the tight-knit DGI team. Corporately, she excelled, which was as much of a shock to her as to anyone.

Trending analysis came easily to Madison, opening a surprising career path in a field that some might call monotonous. Or outright boring. But she was good at it and loved unlocking new opportunities for DGI's global expansion.

Her insights were strong, coming from a mixed bag of experience, natural intuitiveness, and an instinctive knack for understanding people.

And in a blink, that tiny spark of an idea for a small starter class on basic self-defense took off, exploding into full offerings twice a day, four days a week, with options in different techniques and skill levels.

In a company built by military veterans, it was easy to find a cadre of instructors willing to volunteer their time and eager to share their knowledge. The students were thankful, showering Madison with praise for such an amazing idea. But she took the success in stride.

No one's more grateful for a sense of purpose than this girl.

Keeping busy every second of every day filled a painful void in her life, and taking a beginner class or two helped. The instructors took her under their wing, flocking protectively to her side.

Their comradery gave her a few strong shoulders to lean on, but still, she wasn't eager to share. Grateful for the option, she opted to keep a small corner of her private life safely concealed. Yet without saying a word, they all approached her with caution and compassion. Deeply, they understood her loss.

Keeping busy had become Madison's coping technique, and she'd soon earned the solid reputation as a diligent workaholic. It afforded her a way to stay in the here and now, and away from the past.

And it was *almost* enough to keep Alex Drake out of her mind.

But every now and again, she couldn't resist rubbing her wrist, losing herself in the reverie of his hand wrapped around it. Of him. His strength. His smile. His scent.

So I sniffed the man. Who can blame me? It's not like I set out to catch a whiff of his tall, dark, CEO-ness. In my defense, he entered my airspace. And he smelled amazing.

He is amazing. And I'm just another dime-a-dozen analyst on his payroll.

Wake up, Madison—and smell the workweek.

Casually bumping into him in the hall might have been nice. Or perhaps in the lobby at the end of the day. With a slight pout, she once again decided cyber stalking was tempting, but out. If fate was on hiatus, so be it.

So, like most mornings, she started the day with piss and vinegar, and a hearty plop into her soft leather chair. With a swift spin, she prepared to tackle another non-Alex-filled day.

As the dizzying spin of the chair slowed, she found an entirely new challenge to this particular workday. A little box from Tiffany & Co., placed neatly in the center of her desk, stared up at her with that seductive *come hither* look of that telltale robin's-egg blue.

She picked up the box with a giddy smile and then a suspicious glare. Studying it closely, she easily convinced herself the too-good-to-be-true offering couldn't possibly be what it seemed.

If Jack had taught her anything, it was to balance every new challenge with a strong amount of optimism and a healthy dose of skepticism. Squinting, she tipped the scales to full-blown doubt.

Unsure of what exactly to do with the little tease, she set it aside, leaving the pretty package on the corner of her desk. For the rest of the week, she worked around it, every so often allowing herself to curiously admire it.

A week later, the swirl of her chair slowed to reveal another box had appeared. A big sister to the first.

Did someone add water?

As with the first precious box, Madison shied from temptation—no matter how much it tempted her with its glossy color and sexy black print.

With two outrageous desk ornaments neatly stacked, she now had a small pile going. Like some ultra-high-end Harry & David tower. Or an important piece of Andy Warhol pop art.

And if, by some miraculous stretch of the imagination, these really were from Tiffany & Co., leaving them untouched was of the utmost importance. After all, her patience seemed to be paying off. A few more weeks, and her worst-case-scenario treasure trove would be sky high.

After a few days of smiling at the boxes only to have them ridiculously tease her back, today Madison found a whole new adventure waiting. Tented on her desk was a small note. No envelope. With no markings on the outside.

It stood attentively next to the two boxes. With a curious glance around, she unfolded it.

Aren't you going to open the boxes?

The boxes, like the note, had shown up first thing in the morning, before she'd arrived. Which was really, really early. Madison had been raised by a kind but crusty gunnery sergeant. Bright and early was part of the package in the Taylor household.

Hardwired to work hard and learn harder, Madison was usually the first in the building. More often than not, she beat Fife in. Which meant that whoever the culprit was, they either worked way too late or were insanely early.

Or sleeps here. Kudos to being one-upped by a fellow workaholic.

Madison also considered access to her office. With nothing of value there, she never locked it. But every floor was highly restricted, with each employee's access coded into their card. If you didn't belong on a floor, you weren't getting there. Madison worked on the fifty-first floor, just below the CEO and VP suites.

Despite its vast size, there were fewer than a dozen offices on her floor, and only five had occupants. Three belonged to women, one to a gay man who often carried on about his wonderful husband, and hers. Two of the women had boyfriends and the other was married. Systematically, Madison had eliminated all the most obvious suspects.

Again, she read the note, studying the clean strokes of the uppercase handwriting as if it hid some clue. Gently, she bit her lower lip, thoroughly contemplating its suggestion.

If these boxes are really from Tiffany's, that means they probably contain incredibly expensive jewelry. That's sort of ridiculous. Sure, Tiffany jewelry just shows up. Because that's the kind of stuff that happens. All the time.

Taking the smallest box in her hand, she inspected it closely, then gave it a gentle shake near her ear.

It could be some sort of test? Or prank? A bizarre new form of corporate hazing. A camera likely waited to expose her. No matter what, this was most definitely not a small tower of diamonds. But maybe . . .

Snatching up her phone, Madison checked the internet. She tapped in the keywords *corporate, espionage, recruiting,* and *tactics.* Perplexed, she stared.

Seven hundred thousand results? Corporate espionage is going freaking viral.

Hurriedly, she scanned the results, one by one, leading her disapproving squint to end in a long nod. *This is exactly the type of tactic a corporate spy would employ.*

Deep in her search, she jumped at the startling ping of an alert on her desktop screen. The announcement of a new message nearly made her drop her phone. Catlike, she saved her phone from yet another screen crack, though nothing would save it from being distressed and outdated.

Carefully, she placed her phone on her desk, breathing out in relief. Crisis averted, she glanced at her monitor.

ANONYMOUS: Hi.

MADISON: Hi.

ANONYMOUS: I left you the boxes.

Flushed, Madison froze. *Oh my God, the corporate espionage recruiter is here in the building right now.*

ANONYMOUS: *I'm actually contacting you about some serious company business.*

Yup, here we go.

ANONYMOUS: *I'm taking an employee morale survey. What Starbucks beverage would make you happiest right now?*

Amused and smiling, she considered it. *Okay, not exactly the tactic I imagined. Actually, it's a hundred times dirtier. Luring me with Starbucks. Have you no shame?*

MADISON: *Right now? Well, in an effort to support employee morale, I'd have to say an iced matcha latte with almond milk.*

ANONYMOUS: *The green drink? Really?*

MADISON: *Hey, don't knock it. It's incredibly refreshing. My messenger app isn't quite identifying you. Who is this?*

ANONYMOUS: *Rather than just outright tell you, how about we meet? And if for any reason you're not interested, you go about your work and I'll go about mine. No questions asked.*

Madison's fingers lifted off the keyboard. *Should we meet?* When she took a bit too long to respond, Anonymous resumed typing.

ANONYMOUS: *Look, if I tell you who I am right off the bat, you might be less interested.*

MADISON: *Really? Why?*

ANONYMOUS: *Because I look like Igor and need to bribe women with lavish gifts to spend time with me.*

Quietly, Madison laughed. His comment conjured memories of a Halloween long ago. That year, her father had dressed as the mad scientist; her brother, Jack, was Frankenstein's monster; and Madison was relegated to be the lowly Igor.

Really? Igor? She'd be an amazing monster. She was born to play the monster. Ask anyone. But Jack was eight years older. And taller. His selection was obvious.

But Jack could never bear her crying. Or her wrath. So when she absolutely refused to do Halloween that year, her brother found a solution like he always did, and this one was perfect.

He'd be the monster for the first part of trick-or-treating, and they'd switch during the second half.

Willingly, he'd assumed the role of Igor, delighting her as he propped her high on his shoulders. To everyone, he introduced her as Frankie. In turn, she introduced him as her loyal servant, Igz.

For years, the nicknames stuck. Whenever someone had the upper hand, that person would be declared Frankie, and the other would be Igz.

Truth be known, Jack should have been the Frankie more often than not, but he often carried the title of Igz. That was her brother. Always giving her the upper hand. He did it so often that Frankie became one of her steady family nicknames. In fact, her dad still called her Frankie.

A sad smile lifted Madison's lips. Jack always took care of her, and she really missed that about him. She missed him.

Realizing it had been a hot minute since she'd typed, Madison postured her fingers to respond when another message beat her to it.

ANONYMOUS: But my close friends call me Igz.

Stunned, she lost her breath. Dizzy and in disbelief, she reread the line.
Does he know?
How could he know?
There's no way this is a coincidence.
Espionage recruiter or not, she had to know exactly who this was.

MADISON: You don't have to bribe me with gifts. We can meet. Have coffee or something.

*ANONYMOUS: I vote for "or something," but I guess a funny green drink
will do.*

Strangely, her smile returned, widened by his forwardness. Even with her anxiety in full swing, Madison was amused. Oddly charmed. But this round of anonymous speed-dating would have to wait.

Approaching footsteps pulled her back to reality. Work was beckoning.

Through the glass wall, she saw a uniformed deliveryman headed toward her office, a vendor keycard hanging from his lanyard.

MADISON: Hey, I've gotta run. Coffee sometime sounds great.

ANONYMOUS: Yes. Sometime soon.

The deliveryman peered in. "Madison Taylor?"

"Yes," she said, stylus in hand, ready for whatever required her signature.

Instead, he handed her a venti-sized clear plastic Starbucks cup with a creamy green iced liquid inside. Taken aback, she had nothing but a blank stare for the deliveryman.

Quickly, he reassured her. "Don't worry. The tip was already covered. Enjoy, and have a great day!"

She whipped back to her computer screen to find Mr. Anonymous was offline. She didn't have a chance to thank the charming spy.

A little deflated, she did what any girl in her position would do. Smiling, she wrapped her lips around the straw, sucking in a slow sip of the scrumptious drink. The flavor instantly set her at ease, and let out a little hum of delight.

Corporate spy or not, until I know for sure, next time I'm telling him I also like paninis.

CHAPTER 11

MADISON

DAYS LATER, Madison was still distracted, fixated on the last messages from her virtual pen pal. Likewise, the little blue boxes continued to taunt her. There they sat, constantly reminding her of her anonymous admirer, and their anonymous small talk, followed by a deliciously anonymous drink.

But even as Friday came and went, Mr. Anonymous hadn't returned. Poof. Gone.

What exactly would that missing person poster look like?

All weekend long, Madison spent the time between chores and romance novels wondering about her mysterious friend. But as the days became a week, then two weeks, she'd had enough. Back at work, those sexy blue boxes double-dog-dared her to get to the bottom of it.

Game on.

Thinking he might have given her an accidental clue during their dialogue, Madison dusted off her best detective skills. She started by striking up conversations with random employees entering the break room, beginning with what she considered to be her most likely lead.

First, she asked about the morale committee. Was there one? And if so, who ran it? The responses ranged.

Some said, "Morale committee? What a great idea." Others came back with, "We're paid too much to need morale." And then there was the "Like I need one more bullshit thing wasting my time. Additional duties as assigned, my ass."

The only real conversation she got was from some guy buried behind an international copy of the *Wall Street Journal*. As soon as she asked about the morale committee, he carried on and on, brimming with enthusiasm . . . entirely in Chinese.

Flustered, she needed a new tactic. Thank God the man never popped his head up from behind the paper. He would have gotten a good look at Madison's frustrated eye roll at yet another dead end.

When his ramblings subsided, she meekly but politely excused herself, thanking him shyly with *sheh-sheh*—the only Chinese she knew.

Redirecting her investigation meant a new strategy. Next stop? The IT department. The super-geeky and ultra-friendly techie twins were always up for a challenge, and a possible favor.

The tech guys were apparently called twins because they look eerily similar, with the same 1960s NASA engineer glasses and button-up, short-sleeve shirts. Although, by age, they could easily be father and son.

Their side-by-side rolling chairs only added to their singular persona. Playing to the hype, they shared one nameplate with "TRex" prominently displayed on it. The term was a hybrid of Ted and Rex, their actual names.

When Madison explained what she needed, Ted volunteered their services on behalf of himself and Rex. "We can help!"

With a not-so-subtle glance shared between them, they seemed to be hatching an idea. By their expressions, it had to be diabolical.

Rubbing his hands together with sinister glee, Rex said, "For the right price."

As if on cue, Ted rolled his chair to a wall cabinet and pulled open a middle drawer. Rex just smiled.

If he pulls out a metallic bikini and Princess Leia hair buns, I'm out of here.

Instead, he grabbed a glossy sheet of paper and unfolded it before handing it to her. Glancing at it, Madison was surprised and relieved to see it was a Girl Scout cookie order sheet.

"We're not supposed to have this out, but my daughter can really use some sales, if you don't mind."

Eagerly, Madison perused the list. It hadn't changed much since she used to sell these little gems. Committing to a box of Thin Mints, she handed over a ten and the cookies were hers.

The box didn't stand a chance. Before Ted could give her change, Madison had the box popped, a sleeve torn open, and two cookies shoved in her mouth.

The men just stared.

"Sorry, I haven't had lunch," she mumbled through a mouth full of cookie.

By their wide-eyed gaze, she could see herself through their eyes. The *nom-nom-nom* sounds escaping her overflowing mouth, with cookie crumbs flying everywhere. Cookie Monster Madison in all her glory.

When she offered the open end of the sleeve to the fellas, they pounced with appreciation for a mid-afternoon snack.

Pointing a cookie at her, Rex piped up. "We're just glad to see a girl eat. We've heard rumors that your kind stopped doing that."

"Not this girl," Madison said, flipping another cookie into her mouth like a chip.

Snacked up and raring to go, TRex let Madison know that an anonymous message account was totally possible.

Yes, that's the sort of smoking-gun tidbit that brought me here.

And there were only a handful of ways one could do it from within the DGI firewalls.

Ted offered more. "They'd have to be either a guest user or a privileged user. Guest users are rare for us. We don't like outsiders on our networks. Privileged users . . . well, there might be a few dozen."

Now we're getting somewhere.

"We're happy to look into it, but . . ."

"But?"

Rex shrugged. "Well, as soon as we figure out who they are, we have to report it. It's technically grounds for immediate termination."

Immediate termination? Well, hell, I don't want to get anyone fired. I mean, what if it's not espionage? What if he's just really, I don't know, shy?

Covering her tracks, Madison played it off as research. For a course she was thinking about taking. Apparently, that was nerd code for a barrage of questions and free tutoring offers.

Without actually naming a school, professor, major, or course, Madison skated through their friendly interrogation and avoided more questions by flipping the script.

"Hey, is there a volume discount on the cookies?"

She must have hit the right note, because Ted's eyes lit up enthusiastically as he followed the smell of money. With her order placed, he explained that he only kept a minimum inventory onsite to satiate the usually predictable level of demand. He handed her the only remaining box and promised to deliver the rest in a few days.

Cookie booty in hand, Madison hightailed it back to her office. Realizing she'd wasted her entire lunch break chasing a phantom, she fended off any hangry tendencies by allowing herself just one more cookie.

Decidedly, she kicked off her heels, halting the investigation for the time being, and forced her focus back to work.

A few shakes of her mouse refreshed her screen. Staring once again at the unchanged messenger window, she couldn't help but wonder if there was a genuine reason he hadn't chatted back.

What if something happened? Maybe . . . he was caught? Possibly fired? Jailed?

After a sigh and blank stare at her screen, her wondering was rewarded.

ANONYMOUS: How was your drink?

Unintentionally, Madison beamed. *He's back. Totally not incarcerated.* If Mr. Anonymous was a privileged user, there's no way he'd be recruiting a new analyst for some extreme corporate spy game.

Smiling, she revved up for round two.

MADISON: Amazingly refreshing. Thanks. You certainly know how to make an impact.

ANONYMOUS: You wouldn't open those two little blue boxes brimming with potential, so I figured I'd better step up my game. Buy a girl a drink. With that out of the way, are you ready for "something else"?

MADISON: Something else? Wow, you must be the president of the morale committee.

ANONYMOUS: I do what I can.

MADISON: So, you're back?

ANONYMOUS: Yes. I didn't mean to disappear on you. A few things came up out of town. If it's any consolation, I had no fun at all.

MADISON: Two weeks and no fun? Sounds like you're the one who needs the gifts.

ANONYMOUS: Who needs gifts when I'm looking forward to "something else"?

His casual banter drew her in. Despite her aversion to office romances, she couldn't help it. He was funny and sweet, with enough of an edge that she was dying to find out who he was.

But one bad date, and work could become a perpetual land mine of awkward situations.

Been there. Done that. Got the T-shirt.

She held back a response, relieved to see Mr. Anonymous taking off the pressure by typing. A second later, she realized the pressure was just beginning.

ANONYMOUS: Hey, you know Gina?

MADISON: Tough-as-Nails Sawyer? Mr. Drake's VP of human capital?

ANONYMOUS: So, you know her. Great!

Maybe this was her in. *Come on. Throw me a bone.*

MADISON: Yes, I know Ms. Sawyer. How do you know her?

ANONYMOUS: Gina and I go waaay back. We've worked together for years.

Well, that wasn't much of a clue.

ANONYMOUS: Anyway, she'll have something for you late Friday afternoon.

MADISON: What is it? Should I call her?

Maybe this guy's in HR. Madison thought she'd signed all her onboarding paperwork, but it was possible in the hundred or so pages that she might have missed one signature.

ANONYMOUS: Nothing urgent, and it won't be there until Friday. She leaves at six that day, but she won't have it until after 5:30. Small window. Don't forget.

Smiling, Madison turned up the heat.

MADISON: I don't know.

ANONYMOUS: You don't know?

MADISON: I'm terribly forgetful. Remembering might be tough without a calendar invite. Mind shooting me one?

There are no anonymous calendar invites.

ANONYMOUS: I have a feeling you'll remember. Besides, if you know who I am, you'll never get out of your office and make friends.

Giggling and astonished, she pressed for more.

MADISON: You heard I was asking around?

ANONYMOUS: Maybe I did. Maybe I didn't. Maybe I caught you asking about me. Or maybe, just maybe, you asked me about me.

Thumbing through a mental picture book of everyone she'd spoken with, she kept her cool.

MADISON: That's a lot of maybes.

ANONYMOUS: You covered a lot of ground.

Stumped in this stalemate, she played one last card.

MADISON: So . . . no hints?

ANONYMOUS: No hints. Need another green drink before I go?

MADISON: No thanks. Is "something else" off the table?

ANONYMOUS: Definitely not. Gotta run.

He punctuated his statement with a little emoji running man. And again, Mr. Anonymous was gone.

Pouting, Madison scanned the calendar, noting with no surprise that today was Monday. She huffed in frustration. Without a doubt, the delicious anticipation meant sleep for the next few days was a lost cause.

CHAPTER 12

MADISON

BY LATE FRIDAY AFTERNOON, Madison had completely lost track of the time, immersing herself in the quarterly market analysis report.

Simultaneously, both her computer and phone reminders pinged her. In the midst of an incomplete calculation, she decided that any more work on it would definitely wait.

Five thirty. Friday. Finally.

With a few keystrokes, she messaged Gina's assistant, requesting access to the executive floor. A few moments later, she received a confirmation her card was good to go.

The elevator doors opened as Madison arrived at the fifty-second floor. Seeing Madison through the glass wall, Gina stood, ready to greet her, a marked difference from their last encounter. Her assistant must have just left, but Gina waved her in.

"Good evening, Ms. Taylor."

Madison was usually the one on the service side of industry, so being addressed so formally by a superior threw her off.

"Please, call me Madison," she said as she handed Gina a box of cookies.

"Thanks, Madison. How much do I owe you?" Gina asked, pulling out her purse.

"Not a thing. Seriously, you're saving me from myself. I'm already a sleeve deep in these scrumptious goodies. And let's just say there's plenty more where those came from."

"Thanks, I'm starving. And there's something waiting for you through those doors." Gina didn't skip a beat, tearing into the box of cookies as her phone buzzed. She glanced at the text. "Shit, my wife's threatening to head to the restaurant without me. You can use the room to your heart's content. Pretty much everyone's gone."

Pretty much? "So, who's left?"

"Oh, I almost forgot." Gina grabbed a card from her desk, handing it to Madison with one hand while dialing her wife with the other. "Baby, I swear I'm on my way. No, I didn't eat," she fibbed after choking down a cookie.

And with that, Gina raced away.

Madison's chance to ask about the identity of her mystery admirer vanished. *Well, maybe this is the big reveal.* She pulled the note out of the envelope, her intrigue building.

I'm batting 2-0 on you opening boxes,

so I guess I'll go big or go home.

Try these on for size.

She headed through the door leading to some sort of washroom. But washroom definitely meant different things to different people.

Apparently, places that sold slushies and roller food had an entirely different type of restroom—the polar opposite of the fifty-second-floor executive lavatory. The space was an absolute palace, with an Italian leather chaise positioned in its center. With twenty-foot ceilings and skylights, the room was impressive and bright.

Mahogany walls were intermittently graced by floor-to-ceiling mirrors, giving Madison a head-to-toe eyeful of herself. A little intimidated, she smoothed her hair, trying to look less frazzled in the elegant space.

Looking around, she realized the toilets and sinks were down a small corridor, with private stalls enclosed by stately arched wooden doors. Tasteful gilded fixtures were abundant, giving an Old World touch to the room.

On a lavish chaise were two boxes. One was the size of a shoebox, and the other more suited for a garment.

Like a child on Christmas morning, Madison pounced on the largest, giving it a quick shake. Giddy, she tore the lid away, rummaging through the delicate layers of silver tissue. Inside was a stunning black lace dress that could have graced the cover of *Vogue*.

Whipping up the exquisite gown, she accidentally knocked the smaller box onto the floor. Panicked, she scooped it up, praying she hadn't broken something fragile or pricey.

Or worse, fragile AND pricey.

Carefully, she set it on the chaise. The box was intricately rigged with a hinged lid. When she opened it, a pair of shoes lifted out, spotlighted by an LED hidden in the lid. The stiletto heels were secured with a small tension groove.

"Oh," she said with a sigh. *They're beautiful.*

As Madison studied them like a curator inspecting fine art, her hand flew to her lips, covering her gasp. The resemblance was astonishing.

These were the shoes—*her* shoes—that had broken the day she was hired. She looked closer, realizing they weren't *her* shoes after all. These were much nicer—but were an identical replica of her old shoes.

Clearly, hers hadn't returned from the landfill, miraculously repaired. Those were goners. No matter how she'd hoped and prayed after pouring a hell of a lot of superglue on that heel, the break was final.

Ceremoniously, with thankful words and an ache of regret, she'd thrown them away. Her beloved seven-year-old heels were so precious, they'd only seen the light of day a few times. And no matter how they cut into her heels and pinched her toes, they always looked new.

But now, in their place was a perfect brand-new pair, practically dancing the cha-cha in the spotlight. Oddly, the box and shoes were devoid of a brand name or logo.

Judging by the soles, this pair had never touched the ground. Enchanted with excitement and whimsy, she had to slip them on.

The fit was pure magic, more so because unlike her old pair, this one had the comfort of an Ugg slipper, caressing her foot like a cloud.

I guess that makes me Cinderella.

And as much as they worked with the suit she was wearing, her fairy godfather had a gown ready to go, one that beckoned her to try it on.

Here goes nothing.

Madison shed her corporate ensemble and pulled on the slinky gown with an overlayer of fine lace. The dainty fabric practically melted onto her skin and hugged every curve, making a bra impossible to pull off.

Promptly, she slipped off her bright pink bra and put the dress back on, watching the design fall into place. Though not usually one to linger over her reflection, she couldn't help it. The look was flawless.

Admiring the view, she smiled wide as her gaze worked its way up from the precious shoes to the sweeping cut of the beautiful gown.

Abruptly, the good vibes stopped at her face.

Oh my God, what's that?

She squinted, taking a closer look at her mouth. "Oh, you've got to be kidding."

Nothing says enchanté *like Thin Mint in the teeth.*

A knock at the door meant there'd be no digging it out at the moment.

Battling a mild panic attack, Madison held a hand to her racing heart as her anxiety ratcheted up to the stratosphere. Touching the door handle ever so slightly with the other hand, her fingers stalled. But the slight rattle of her hand on the lever was enough to give her position away. She heard a soft voice call out, the naturally deep tone soft and coaxing.

"Madison?"

It wasn't until that moment that she realized she'd been holding her breath. When his low voice called her name again, she exhaled, relaxing her tension even more. His deep voice was more than warm and relaxing—it was recognizable.

I know the man behind the curtain.

She slowly pulled open the heavy door, shyly peering through the space as it widened. His dark, majestic presence gazed down at her.

"Mr. Alex Drake, the great and powerful wizard of Igz?"

"Yours truly," he said, leaning his head against the door.

The moment stilled.

Taking her time, Madison reveled in his tender expression. The lines of his face were softer than she remembered, and his lips smiled with a charm that could melt panties from a mile away.

Calmly, she waited as his gaze swept over her before returning to her face. His eyes were dark and suggestive, piercing deep into her soul as he invited her to his.

She stood there, gawking at a man too delicious for words. Comfortable. Smiling. He had to feel it. The electricity between them.

God, I could lose myself in this man.

Madison couldn't help prolonging her stare, even as Alex broke the spell to check the time.

"Is everything okay?" he asked. "Are you still getting dressed? I was—" He glanced down, oddly staring a little too long at his watch as his facial expression twisted.

Her gaze swept down, then away as she smothered a giggle.

Yup. He definitely feels it.

She pretended not to notice as the tent in his slacks did its damnedest to make her acquaintance.

Rushed, Alex continued, and she met his eyes with her full attention. "Uh, I was going to show you something, but if you don't come out soon, we're going to miss it."

She ignored him as he casually pocketed his hands in a poor attempt at a magician's flip of the wrist. Apparently, dragging his Louisville slugger to an inconspicuous position would take a little more than sleight of hand.

Grateful that her gown concealed her own weeping core, she turned away. She'd imagined him a million times . . . from the isolation of her cold bed and her hot hand, but nothing prepared her for the reality of him.

The man standing here was handsome and funny, and bigger than life in more ways than just his package. With the warmth of his smile and the heat of his body, she was without a doubt going to be putty in those big, strong hands of his.

At least, a girl can hope.

Madison struggled for control of her face, not wanting to risk widening her smile. If she did, this gorgeous man would get a full view of her pearly whites rimmed in chocolate.

Straining, she kept her teeth hidden behind a wall of pursed lips. Any smile, no matter how small, would reveal all the signs of a well-crafted hobo disguise. Stubbornly, she pressed her lips together a little tighter.

He backed away with a frown. "You seem concerned. Is it because of our first encounter?"

Losing the war with her smile, she rushed to the corridor, eagerly finding the furthest sink. She called back, "No, of course not. You were incredible. You really saved me, and Joe."

"I mean the time before that."

Curious but preoccupied, Madison asked, "What time before that?" She peeked her head back from the hall. "Sorry, I just . . . I need a moment to freshen up. I'll be right back."

She knew her departure was abrupt, even rude, but leaving the tall, dark, and handsome CEO with the seductive scent couldn't be helped.

"I'll just be a second," she called out, hoping to reassure him enough to keep him from leaving.

As she ran the tap water and scooped some into her mouth for a swish, she barely made out his side of the conversation.

"Look, I know I kind of just sprang this on you, and if you're uncomfortable at all—"

His gallant ramblings to put her at ease were cut short by her quiet gargle, followed by the loudness of spitting in the sink.

Hmm, if he heard that, he's probably thinking that sound usually comes after a bit more intimacy.

Satisfied after a final check of her teeth, Madison returned to the waiting hunk. She blew out a breath, feeling much more relaxed.

With his blazer unbuttoned and his tie noticeably loosened, every bit of him seemed defeated. Maybe giving up on whatever he had planned.

"Sorry." She smiled wide and explained. "I had a small smudge of Thin Mint I needed to get off my teeth." She stepped closer. "I didn't quite hear you." Hopeful, she lifted her gaze to meet his.

Alex stood taller, towering over her with the solid body of the most attractive man she'd ever seen. His gaze might have been disarming, but the dimple that appeared with his boyish grin made her absolutely weak in the knees.

"Thin Mint, huh? Well, I think you may have missed a spot." The ball of his thumb gently rubbed the outer edge of her bottom lip, wiping what could only be an indiscernible smudge of chocolate from her mouth.

Madison held herself steady, giggling between smooth swipes, letting him finish. He followed the gesture with a ridiculously exaggerated display of diligently examining his thumb before sucking it ever-so-slightly clean.

God, that's hot.

He popped his brow, businesslike as he asked, "Who's your supplier?"

I can't rat out Ted.

"Oh, I've got friends in high places." Wide-eyed, she shocked even herself with the preposterousness of the comment, considering the man she was speaking to.

"Do you now?" Playful and knowing, his eyes lit up. "Then it *must* be Ted."

Frozen, Madison couldn't think of a word to say. Obviously, nothing happened at DGI that Alex Drake didn't know about. Timidly, she asked, "If you know, then why is he so secretive?"

"Because he sells a crap ton of cookies that way. Forbidden fruit and all. Seriously, he and his daughter outsell everyone else in the troop by three to one. Let's take you, for example. How many boxes did you buy?"

"Um, six . . ."

Both his eyebrows lifted high. "Six?"

". . . teen. Sixteen, actually, but he cut me a deal."

Alex gave her a spirited smirk. "Soon you'll be outbuying me."

"Well, I'm a sucker for a great deal and a good cause encased in mint-choco-latey goodness."

Exaggerating a sly shift of his eyes to the left, then the right, he leaned in. Confiding in a deep, authoritative tone, he shared a bit of wisdom. "Be leery of a Ted in sheep's clothing . . . and watch out for his poker game."

"Noted." Madison nodded, filing away for later the possibility of a future poker game.

Alex returned to the task at hand. Her heart raced at his insistence.

"Seriously, I need to know how to lure you out of here." He leaned closer, his lips nearly touching her ear as he whispered, "I could carry you on my shoulders, if you like."

Madison tempered her astonishment with intrigue. "That! That right there. What made you say that?"

Folding her arms, she kept them light and loose. *Is he guessing? Or does he know?*

He rebuttoned his blazer and displayed all the signs of a man ready to leave. Giving her a tender smile, he said, "Let's just say I've got friends in high places too."

Alex's tone was gentle and easy, and in a strange way, sentimental. It made her want to get to know so much more about him. Then his elbow leisurely winged out, inviting her to take it.

Instantly, her arms unlocked, and her hands couldn't help but wrap around the warmth of his arm. She enjoyed nestling her fingers in the inner crease of his elbow, clinging to the strength of his bulging bicep.

Leaning against him comfortably, she let him lead her out of the room, arm in arm. "The way I figure it," she said, "either you're a mind reader, or . . ."

"Or?" He slipped his warm hand over hers, melting her completely into submission.

Breathless, she took a second before continuing. "Or you've paid way too much to get information on me that's absolutely worthless. Possibly bribing all the moms in my hometown. Although they wouldn't need much enticing. Your smile and a bit of *pass the prosecco*, and those ladies would sing like the cast of *Mamma Mia*."

"Well, now I feel like I've missed an opportunity. And information always has value," he said as they stopped at his office door. "I've built an empire recognizing that things others think are worthless might, in fact, be absolutely priceless . . . like this."

A warm rush spread across her neck and face as he seemed to be leaning in for a kiss. Instead, he moved in to open the door, making way to his very dark office.

"Open blinds," he commanded.

As the blinds obeyed, the glow of a radiant setting sun filled the room, with glints of gold flashing here and there on every bit of glass and metal in the expansive room. The panoramic wall of windows showcased breathtaking views of the Manhattan skyline and Central Park below.

The honey-drenched sky captivated Madison until a curious glance around led her gaze straight to a familiar tower. The two Tiffany boxes patiently waiting on the oversize executive desk stared back, taunting her yet again.

Too easily, he peeled away from her grasp.

Spoilsport.

Alex grabbed the larger of the two boxes, bouncing its weight in his hand. It wasn't until that moment she considered it might actually be heavy with no-kidding diamonds ready to adorn her wrist.

With the box displayed in his open palm, he presented it to her.

Studying his eyes, she found the irresistible glint that sparkled all this time had lost its shimmer, and the grand gesture began to feel expectant and empty. For the first time since the pretty box appeared in her life, her interest in it waned.

I just want to get to know him.

After a moment of pondering, she reluctantly took it. Erring on the side of hope, she didn't open it. Instead, her fingernails tapped gently across the top of it as her gaze wandered to the wall of windows.

"You said something about the first time we met. How *do* we know each other?" she asked, half wondering if he was toying with her, like a cat might with a mouse before swallowing it whole.

"How about I make you a deal?"

Alex stepped closer behind her as he spoke, and his warm breath feathered over her cold shoulders, sparking a shiver. Her breathing hitched as his hot palms ran over her bare upper arms, warming them as he softly caressed.

He has to know what the heat of his body is doing to me.

"If it doesn't come to you after we've gotten to know each other better, I promise I'll tell you how we met. And tell you everything else."

The last word hung in the air after he finished. *What else is there?*

Madison whirled around and stepped back to more fully face him. The cold window against her back startled her, propelling her body right into his. Helplessly caught in his embrace, she silently cursed the lovely blue box still in her hands, now sandwiched protectively between their chests.

"Well," she said, "you've gone to an awful lot of trouble. I mean, the dress. The shoes. Seems like a lot just to get to know a girl."

CHAPTER 13

ALEX

ALEX RELISHED the memory of doing all this. For her.

Madison's dress size was a breeze. In fact, estimating it from the video footage of her in Gina's office wasn't even necessary. The views of her curves from every angle were burned in his memory like a fresh branding.

Still, he watched the video more than once to reassure himself of her size. But the replay of her passionate moves relieved his stress a hundred times better than booze.

Some guys focused on sports stats, but Alex Drake was all about perfection and precision. And without a doubt, this girl was perfect. Madison Taylor was precisely a 36-C. By the jiggle, every bit of her voluptuous bosom was a full C, and borderline D.

The dress was his own design—a doodle he sketched out during the staff meeting from hell before his trip. The dainty little number was a sublime blend of Victoria's Secret meets Audrey Hepburn. Like Madison, the gown was elegant with a fiery, sexy edge. During his layover in Paris, an eager designer was just as captivated by the footage, and created a gown that molded to her like a second goddamn skin.

God, I want to tear it off her.

The shoes were a bit tougher, yet something in her expression when they broke told him they were important. After pulling the feed from the lobby, he shot the video to his on-call clothier. They analyzed it from every angle, then advised him that his chances were best with a referral to an Italian shoe designer.

With a frenzy of emails, around-the-clock phone calls, a can-do attitude and an obscene amount of cash, their existence was solidified. By his final stop in Milan, her ensemble was complete, culminating in the vision he now adored before him.

Alex gazed down at her and grinned. "It was no trouble at all. You're easy to please."

The sweet smile that unfurled on Madison's skeptical face conveyed every ounce of her disbelief as she tugged up the box still trapped between them. "And this? Unless this is some sort of memory jogger on how we met, let's get to know each other before you shower me with lavish gifts. Though the occasional matcha latte is definitely appreciated."

Accepting the gift's return, he took it to his desk. After replacing the box with its mini-me, he admired them for a moment before turning back to her.

Alex stayed put, perplexed but pleased. He needed a moment—and not just for the nagging bulge trying to burst free from his slacks. For the first time in, oh, ever, a woman wasn't after his money or status. And though clearly interested, she wasn't chasing him. Everything about Madison Taylor filled him with a caring protectiveness he'd never imagined.

A feeling he suspected would just continue to grow.

She faced him, her body limned with the amber paint of a setting sun that backlit her in an angelic glow. But somehow, even though haloed in the moment, he knew a fiery, seductive devil lay in wait below that innocent facade.

Nothing about this woman was naive or contrived. He knew it, and his cock knew it too.

This temptress will be the death of me.

Those soft curves and inviting smile of hers made him lose his damn mind. But this had to be different. *She* was different. With a determined vow he wasn't sure he could keep, he decided that nothing would be rushed with her. Everything had to be beautiful. Lasting. Immensely pleasurable.

All for her.

Intensely, Alex watched Madison, and she remained still, letting him run his gaze over her body. He hungered to satisfy her deepest desires.

Everything about her, here and now, was breathtaking, backdropped perfectly as the last rays of sunlight slowly disappeared beneath the horizon.

CHAPTER 14

MADISON

UNDER THE HEAT of his dark gaze, Madison turned away to stare unseeing out the wall of glass. "So, Mr. Drake, is this what normally happens when you bring a woman to your executive suite?"

Swallowing her nerves, she realized that definitely sounded less suggestive in her head. But she let the question linger in the erotic pull between them.

Hey, it's not my fault. That smoldering hunk of man knew exactly what he was doing. Breathing on my neck. Rubbing my arms. Smelling crazy good.

Chilled, she shivered, hoping to hell Alex would come closer already.

She sensed more than heard him stalk toward her. His body was close, but he didn't touch her. He didn't have to. The heat of him burned through her from behind, soaking her core.

His words were low, rumbling gently over her. "Listen, Madison."

Alex combed his fingers through her hair, sliding her tresses forward, over her shoulder. His breath singed the now exposed sensitive nape of her neck, and she gasped. Massaging her skin, he spoke softly.

"You're right. I've had lots of women here, and I've given many of them gifts. But I've never chased them. They've all chased me. And when I wanted it over—and I *always* wanted it over—a small token softened the blow. They left happy, and I moved on. Until now." His hands slid down her arms to her wrists, where he wrapped them with a squeeze. "Until you."

Until me?

Alex dropped a tender kiss on her shoulder, and she found his restraint unsettling.

He's holding back.

Desperately, she wanted him. Needed him. Her body pressed back against his, and the boldness of her movement changed the gentleness of his kisses and his hold.

His lips were everywhere, nibbling her shoulders, strong against her neck, pillowy against her cheek. Saying so much, and yet nothing at all.

Madison ignored the battle playing out in her head. In case her mind didn't get the memo, the match was fixed.

I get it. This isn't just my boss. This is the CEO of the company. If this goes south, life could be hell. But, God, does this man feel good.

Seriously, it should be illegal to feel this good. He touches me, and it's like he knows me. Knows everything. What I'm thinking . . . feeling . . . needing. And, boy, am I needing.

The spark in her hoohah was about to blaze out of control, with Firefighter Alex's name written all over it.

She bit her lip, arched her back, and reached down to claw at his thick thigh like a leopard in heat. Her other hand reached back, fisting his hair and tugging his head closer. Not wanting to muddle her message with a mixed signal, her moves demanded whatever he held back.

Mind, lay low. Body is breaking all the rules and bracing for Alex Drake impact.

When she spun around, his lips descended on hers, invading her mouth as his tongue broke through in long licks and forced strokes. She breathed him in, stroking his tongue with hers before he stopped and pulled back slightly.

"Madison," he said low. "Are you sure? I don't know what it is about you, but I know that once I start—with you—I don't think I can stop. And I don't just mean tonight." His forehead rested on hers as he stole a soft kiss. "If you have any doubts at all, it's fine. I can back off. Take it slow. Anything you need. Just tell me."

Smiling her reassurance, Madison licked her lips, his taste still fresh on them. She looked up, seeing the doubt behind his dark eyes and tense brow.

Her lips brushed ever so softly over his as she whispered into his mouth, "I'm all in."

His kiss burned back, awakened with a rush that crushed against her lips. His strong hands teased her with a touch that trailed from her neck down the sensitive skin of her back.

Alex hesitated only for a moment before swiftly releasing her zipper, letting gravity drag the gown to pool at her feet.

She moaned with need, feeling his hands warm every curve as he controlled her. A maestro to her impulses, he was masterful in every touch, as if he'd handled her for years.

This man had never before held her, but in every touch, he knew her. Her body was rapturous, moving in tempo to his will. Every sensation was filled with something she'd never known. She trusted how he handled her. She trusted him.

A soft kiss pressed to her lips. "If anything displeases you, I have to know. Understand?"

There it was again. A darkness to Alex's eyes that seemed worried and protective.

"Yes." She heaved out a breath, coaxing his lips back to her mouth.

He cupped a breast, caressing its weight before his mouth made its way to it. His lips nibbled across it, licking her nipple to a firm peak before grazing it with his teeth. She gasped hard as he suckled it, burning it with the heat of his mouth.

Heavy, her head leaned back against the window as his tongue sliced a line down her, pebbling her skin as he reached her core.

Her body burned in his hands, falling against the coolness of the window behind her. A harsh gasp escaped her throat as his breath melted her.

Dropping to his knees, Alex nuzzled his face into her plump wetness, kissing and licking her through her panties. The slightest whimper escaped her lips as his mouth brushed the top of her thong. Taking the slight band in his teeth, he tugged it down.

His powerful hand scooped up her thigh, balancing it over his shoulder. She stroked his hair as he knelt before her, and savored how he seemed to revere her.

With a long lick, he buried his face in her wetness.

"Oh my God." Madison pulled in a breath, gripping his hair and willing herself to hold off the rush of an orgasm.

Smearing her juices up to her clit, his fingers circled it. Massaged it. Then he pulled back just long enough to meet her eyes with a smile.

"Not yet," he said softly.

"Not yet," she whispered, submitting to his sweet demand.

After a tender kiss to her swollen pussy, Alex stroked his fingers against her, hot as they worked back and forth. Again, that dangerous tongue made a long lick before forcing its way deep inside. Her gasp rose to a cry.

Deliberately, he pulled out, teasing her entrance with his fingers before shoving one in. He gave her a few glorious pumps, hitting her spot over and over before pulling away.

After a swipe to her clit, he wrapped his lips around it before plunging two fingers so far in, she struggled for air.

Grinding her hips and following his seductive direction, her body swayed. Dizzy, she could feel herself coming completely undone by him.

It was all too much. His touch. His lips. *And, my God, that tongue.* She climbed higher, straddling Alex's mouth as she rode the waves of ecstasy across his lips.

Her panted screams tore through the room while her body collapsed from the eruption. Her inner walls shuddered, crushing his fingers to a stop deep inside her.

Tenderly, he lapped her gently, laying tender kisses here and there as she floated down. Finally, his fingers slid free.

Careful and slow, he eased her leg down until her foot met the floor. Caving beneath the weight of pure ecstasy, her body made a heavy slide down the cool glass until he caught her, sweeping her into a cradle tight in his arms.

Her head fell into the crook of his neck, and she nuzzled him, savoring his closeness. Her lips left kiss after kiss against his skin.

Alex carried her to a soft leather sofa, laying her down before resting his blazer over her. Her body stretched into the warmth it provided.

"I have a blanket if you'd like one."

Dazed and happy, she bit the fullness of her lower lip as she smiled and shook her head.

He sat next to her, and she couldn't help reaching up to stroke the hard lines of his jaw. He pressed his lips to her palm. His fingers slid a few strands of hair away from her face, tucking them behind her ear.

"What about you?" Madison asked, barely able to lift her heavy lids.

"There'll be time," Alex said softly, assuring her as he stroked her cheek.

Closing her eyes for just a moment, every muscle in her body relaxed. She held tight to her smile as she drifted to sleep.

CHAPTER 15

PACO

PACO ROBLES always strolled into DGI with the swagger of a man without a care in the world, regardless of the weight he carried on his shoulders each and every day. At nearly midnight, with no one around, his swagger was for his own benefit. He'd earned that swagger the hard way and proudly flaunted it, even with nobody watching.

His confidence was derived from knowing where all the bodies were buried, a consequence of owning the shovel and doing the digging. He'd been Alex Drake's heavy for the better part of a decade. With Alex, Paco managed to elevate himself, devoting much of his free time to smoothing away any of his remaining rough edges. A whore to nice things, but not status, he could easily distinguish a fine champagne from a Napa knockoff, yet usually preferred a frosty mug of whatever was on tap.

Some days Paco felt like the right-hand man of a mob boss, and other times he just felt like the fucking cleanup crew for whatever shit landed in Alex Drake's lap.

Paco was well paid for his talents, with his greatest gift being his ability to become a chameleon. He could dress down and blend into a crowd, or easily charm a boardroom full of the most powerful CEOs in the world. He commanded center stage when required, but more often than not, remained cloaked in his power of invisibility.

Swift with his camera phone, and discreet with a wide array of covert surveillance equipment, he captured whatever he couldn't commit to memory, which didn't leave much.

With a background in street fighting and mixed martial arts, what Paco lacked in bulk he made up for in speed and precision force. And still, few knew anything at all about him.

Aside from Fife, Paco was the only other person whose keycard gained him entrance to the boss's personal elevator, office, and the great Alex Drake himself. As one of only three people with unfettered access to the entire building, Paco came and went as he pleased, wherever and whenever he wanted.

Gina knew his salary was off the books, with prompt cash-only payments every Monday. No records were kept, electronic or written. No one ever questioned any requests he made, and any asks were to be considered those of Alex Drake himself.

Tonight, Paco's task was easy enough, but it weighed heavy on his mind. Making his way to his office on the executive floor that he might as well consider home, he slipped past Alex's office with a contemplative glance at the door.

Entering the comfort of his own luxurious space, Paco relaxed. He'd made every square inch of the room a reflection of his life. Souvenirs from all over the world were strategically placed to amplify their significance and importance.

Dropping into the plush executive chair, he pressed a button, relaxing back as it fully reclined. He gave himself the leeway to close his eyes, but he wouldn't sleep.

Patiently, he waited.

CHAPTER 16

MADISON

C OOL AIR DRIFTED over Madison's skin, waking her in the darkness. Disoriented, she lifted her head to glance around.

Instantly, her hands slid up and down her body. She was naked, in an empty office with just the peek of a flame rolling in a fireplace she hadn't noticed earlier.

With a soft yawn and a stretch, she reached around the sofa, then down to the floor, finding the blazer that had slipped off. She pulled the coat to her face with a soft moan.

As she inhaled his scent, the sweet seduction of the night came back, over-taking her in a swirl of unbelievable sensations. Relaxing into a cozy replay, she was startled when a few sharp raps at the door pulled her from her dreamlike retreat.

Still groggy, she smiled, her heart beating faster as she whispered, "Alex."

Slowly, the door opened.

"Miss Madison?" a male Latino voice said softly.

That's not Alex.

Panicked, she watched the door open with wide eyes. *Crap.*

"Just a minute," she called out, trying desperately to remain calm.

In haste, she threw the blazer around her shoulders, slipping her arms into it and wrapping it around herself like a kimono. As the man entered, she hopped to her feet, suddenly realizing she was still in the stilettos. Somehow, they seemed a touch dressy paired with the oversized jacket.

"Sunrise lighting," he said, his voice smooth and commanding.

Worried, she wrapped the blazer a little tighter as the room began to glow.

The man stepped in. His face filled with a warm smile, giving way to friendly eyes that remained trained on hers. "I'm Paco Robles. I'm here to help you with anything you may need."

Deflating, Madison couldn't help a twinge of disappointment. The man was kind, professional, and completely unfazed to find a half-naked woman in Alex's office this early in the morning.

Methodically, he scanned the room, then headed straight toward the scene of the hot and heavy crime. Scooping up her gown, he took care to lay the delicate lace carefully over his arm. She breathed a quiet sigh. Thankfully, her panties had mysteriously vanished.

She couldn't read the change in his expression, but something on the desk caught his eye.

"Unopened?" he asked, motioning to the blue boxes still on the desk. "I don't blame you on the earrings, but you really need to look at this one before you decline."

Gently, he hung the gown over the back of the chair, freeing himself to take the larger box in both hands. Eager and smiling, he carried it to her, taking a seat on the sofa and patting the space next to him, inviting her to sit. Slowly, she did.

Mesmerized as he handled the box, she watched as his fingers moved like a magician showing off a spellbinding trick. Swiftly, he opened it, pouring the contents into one hand. Another box slipped out, in the same gorgeous blue, but velvety.

With just the right amount of ceremony, he held it before them, lifting the hinged lid slowly. Her mouth fell open, releasing an embarrassingly loud gasp.

"My sentiments exactly," he said, nodding with reassurance. "Tiffany and Company, ten and a half carats of brilliant square-cut diamonds set in eighteen-karat white gold."

A second later, the tennis bracelet was out of the box and he clasped it around her wrist. Admiring the bling, he reached for her hands, squeezing them as he met her eyes. "Hey, if you don't want the earrings, can I have them?"

Madison couldn't help but giggle as she played along. "Absolutely. Why not? Diamonds for everyone."

Paco joined in, laughing as he popped to his feet and headed back to the desk. Instead of retrieving the other box, he walked past it and faced the wall.

"Are you in a time-out?" Madison asked.

"Working here? Every day of my life," he said, a jovial ring to his tone.

She watched as he swiped an access card across a panel she'd only just noticed. The wall opened to another room. "Sunrise lighting," he said again.

Fascinated, she watched the enormous room light up. She stepped closer, a crazy curious moth to this super-secret flame.

"Miss Madison, here is where you can get ready to start your day. Panoramic views of the city, and the lighting will adjust as the sun rises."

It was a bathroom, but some crazy luxe version with state-of-the-art fixtures and more space than her living room and kitchen combined. *Alex Drake must live here.*

"This is the shower," he said, "with room for you and seven of your closest friends. Three rainfall showerheads, eighteen settings with programming and music options. And if you want to take a ride on the wild side, you have your own personal waterfall."

As he said the word *waterfall,* a surge of water poured out from the wall above to the smooth stone floor below.

"Infinity bathtub, in case you prefer a soak. Over here is the toilet. If the lid is closed, it'll open as you approach. The controller is in the wall. Heated and cool seat options, and temperature and steam options for the bidet."

A vajayjay steam? That might be where I draw the line. Maybe.

"This is what I like to call the magic mirror."

Paco headed to a wall of mirrors and picked up a remote. He pointed to the center mirror and pressed a button. The center third of the mirror transformed into a television, set to the local news. He clicked it off.

"And whatever you need—dryer, lotion, perfume, makeup—just press this button on the remote, and it works like your phone. Speak into it, and whatever drawer it's in will pop open. An outfit will be waiting for you when you're done."

With that, he departed.

Madison couldn't quite process the amazing room and all its glory. A sliver of sunshine peeking over the horizon meant Saturday was definitely here. She wished Alex were too.

As she realized she *really, really* had to go, it suddenly occurred to her that

her first priority was to quickly master the space-age console controlling the
toilet.

CHAPTER 17

MADISON

AFTER THE SINGLE most amazing shower of her life, Madison was overcome with a sinking feeling deep in the pit of her stomach. The reality of the morning after.

Perhaps the party was over. Mr. Robles had to be Alex's charming cleanup crew.

Pushing past her disappointment, she made a determined effort to enjoy all this luxury while it lasted. Whisking the remote from the sleek stone counter, she shyly said, "Hairbrush . . . oh, and a dryer, please."

Instantly, the dryer came out from a panel behind the wall, while a drawer filled with ten different brushes opened from below.

Trusting the magic mirror to fulfill her every demand, she asked for lotion. Another panel opened, filled with creams and lotions plucked straight from Ulta. The same with the makeup and perfumes.

After going through her morning routine, now armored with the finest luxuries the mirror bestowed, she moved to the cute little number hanging behind the door.

As magically as he promised, Mr. Robles had an outfit waiting. They were the special sorts of goodies that only a jaunt through Barney's or Bergdorf's could provide.

The little summer dress was both classy and sexy, with built-in padding to avoid the need for a bra, and just the type of flowy skirt she loved. A delicate thong and a sweet little clutch were also part of the package.

Rounding out the look were a very unpractical pair of strappy heels that managed to make every pair of shoes she'd ever owned look like flip-flops. She read the labels of the shoes and purse, shocked.

Louboutin? And Hermès?

Even if she wanted to protest wearing all these unbelievably stunning clothes, she had no alternatives at the moment. And if this were the end of her Alex Drake story, these were a pretty remarkable stash of consolation prizes.

That being said, they were of little consolation. Sadly, the prize she coveted most slipped away in the night.

Madison glanced at the mirror one last time, ignoring her pout. Out of habit, she swept her hair behind one ear. Her naked earlobe made her wonder.

What was in the other box?

As soon as she stepped to the door, it opened. The rich aromas of bacon and coffee that met her nose gave her a whole new sense of purpose. A lavish breakfast was set up at the conference table, just waiting for her to dig in.

A loud grumble from her tummy reminded her that her dinner last night had consisted of a sleeve and a half of cookies for her main course, and Alex Drake for dessert. Real food was an absolute necessity.

But first, priorities. The little blue box on Alex's desk was calling her name. She reached over to pick it up, but found it slightly open. Peeking inside, she couldn't believe her eyes.

It was empty.

Madison glanced around, assuming the contents had somehow spilled from the desk onto the floor, but her round of millionaire egg hunt turned up empty.

A familiar chime sent her on a new hunt, following the sound to find her phone. It sat next to an elegantly covered plate of food, with her purse from the night before lying behind it. The phone was compelling, but a second growl from her stomach assured her the message could wait.

She sat and removed the heavy lid. Hidden beneath was a beautiful buffet with yummy written all over it. The plate held two hard-boiled eggs, bacon, sausage, and a mini-croissant next to a small blueberry scone. A steaming pot of coffee sat next to a porcelain cup, flanked by crystal salt and pepper shakers, and a bottle each of chilled Voss still and sparkling water.

Moaning with bliss as she chomped on a crispy piece of bacon, she sighed as her phone resumed its incessant buzz-and-chime combo. She checked it to find the time was 9:30 a.m., and that she had a dozen missed calls and twenty-two text messages.

"Oh my God. Sheila's bridal shower!"

No time to finish, she stuffed her cheeks full of the mini-croissant and snatched a piece of bacon for the road. Before she raced out, she retrieved a shiny new penny from her purse. With a kiss to heads, she placed it next to the monitor on Alex's desk, heads side up.

As she rushed out the door, Madison couldn't help but notice the contents of his trash. The headline of the *Wall Street Journal* were the only words in English. *Is the rest in Chinese?*

Curiosity aside, she had things to do and places to be. Hurrying past Gina's office toward the elevator, she heard the suave voice call after her.

"This way's faster."

Trusting that her new friend, Mr. Robles, knew his way around much better than she did, she backtracked and followed him to a hidden second elevator.

"Your chariot awaits," he said, the car ready and waiting.

She stepped in, surprised as he joined her, pressing the button labeled *L*.

"Thank you. I'm terribly late," Madison said, prepared to explain how her best friend's bridal shower was happening and she was supposed to be picking up the cake, but she absentmindedly trailed off as her gaze landed on his ears.

His tanned earlobes were now sparkling, each adorned with two carats of shimmery elegance.

He raised an eyebrow, pulling his lips into an adorable smirk. "You said I could have them."

I did say that, didn't I?

They reached the lobby in seconds, and the elevator doors opened behind the security desk.

"I'll drive," Paco said, leading her to the executive garage.

Madison followed, in too much of a hurry to notice the luxuriousness of the car they'd gotten into. Her first clue was the telltale image of a charging bull on the steering wheel.

The strong growl of the Lamborghini seemed loud enough to wake the city, leaving Madison awestruck at the power reverberating clear through her seat. The second she clicked her seat belt in place, they raced onto the bustling streets of a Manhattan morning. Nervously, she clutched the door handle, and her observant driver slowed in response.

"Hey, you've got nothing to worry about. If you're in a car with me, consider yourself safe. Cars are my passion. I like my cars like I like my men—fast, powerful, and sexy when wet."

"Mr. Robles?" she asked.

"Please, call me Paco," he said, charming her with his smile.

"Paco, I'm sorry to ask, but do you mind if we drop by—"

"A bakery for Sheila's cake, and then to the restaurant for the bridal shower? I got you, girl. Cake's already been delivered, with flowers and a gift basket of Moët, gourmet chocolates, two Broadway tickets, and a card from you. We'll be at the restaurant in about fifteen minutes. You'll be right on time."

Blinking, Madison just stared at him.

He glanced at her. "Too much? I can keep the tickets if it would make you more comfortable," he said with a chuckle.

Nervously, she followed suit at his absurd display of selflessness. "I'm seriously afraid to ask how you know all that."

With a finger to his lips and a coy *shush*, he said, "I never reveal my sources." His smile grew wide. "Let me ask you something. Have you ever wondered what it would be like to have your every wish granted, and every desire anticipated? Well, Miss Madison, you're about to find out."

"I am?"

Dozens of questions whirled through her mind. But timing was everything, and Paco was pulling the car to the curb in front of the restaurant, where a gaggle of Madison's friends casually waited outside. Between her hot Latin driver and the sexy beast of a car, she instantly realized what this must look like.

Her friends' mouths dropped open as they stared. She smiled nervously, struggling to figure out how the hell to open the door. Suddenly, it opened for her.

Feeling sheepish, Madison stepped out, taking Paco's extended hand. He discreetly slipped an access card into it.

In a low voice, he said, "There's a message on your phone with my number. Text me when you're ready to leave."

Before any of her girlfriends could swarm him, he peeled away, the high-performance engine roaring down the city street.

Surrounding her instead, they tossed her question after question, giddy with enthusiasm at the man now labeled as her date.

"It's not like that. He's just a friend from work. Trust me, I'm *not* his type. And before you even ask, neither are any of you. Let's get set up."

As they headed into one of the private rooms, Madison found it filled with gorgeous rose-and-peony flower arrangements, a table ready for gifts, a champagne station, and dozens of appetizers. "Oh my gosh, I'm sorry I wasn't here to help. It looks amazing."

"Hellooo," one of her friends said. "We just walked in with you. We didn't do this."

Madison and the girls looked at each other blankly.

"Maybe we have the wrong room," Madison said slowly, wondering aloud.

But the CONGRATULATIONS, SHEILA sign on the table was flanked by the basket of goodies Paco promised.

Hiding her glee, she knew exactly who the culprit was behind this over-the-top display. Protectively, she went into stealth mode. And nothing helped a covert operation like a full-on booze distraction.

Armed with a glass of bubbly from the champagne station and a knife, she clinked the glass. "Well, someone put a whole lot of effort into what will be an amazing shower. And I for one am grateful."

The space filled with joyous laughter and the pops of champagne corks as the girls helped themselves to the glorious array of bubbly. When Sheila walked in a moment later, Madison handed her a glass.

"To the most gorgeous and amazing bride-to-be. To Sheila!" She held her glass high in the air, and the tinkle of glasses clinking sounded around the room.

With the food served, Madison enjoyed the never-ending feast, a few more glasses of champagne, and several rounds of avoiding questions about Paco or the party.

Bullet dodged.

Faint chimes and a string of buzzes pulsed from her phone. Downing the last of her glass of champagne, she checked her phone, seeing two text messages from different numbers.

UNKNOWN NUMBER, RECEIVED AN HOUR AGO: Text me back when you're ready to be picked up. PR

UNKNOWN NUMBER, RECEIVED 1 MINUTE AGO: Need you. Go to the room next door.

Forking a strawberry, Madison dredged it through the remaining buttercream frosting on her plate, savoring the very last bite of her second slice of cake.

"Be right back," she whispered to Sheila, then slipped away. But before she could knock on the door down the hall, the door swung open. "Alex!"

It was all she could say before he whisked her into the room and pulled her to the heat of his body. His eager kiss lingered as his tongue swept through her lips in long, languid strokes. He finally released her mouth and they both blew out satisfied breaths.

Leaning his forehead to hers, Alex said, "I missed you." He kissed her again, smoothing his hand over her cheek. "How's the party? Is everything acceptable?"

Scolding him playfully, she said, "I think you know *acceptable* isn't exactly the right term."

The muscles holding her against him tensed before he pulled back, and a furrow appeared across his brow.

Melting into a smile, Madison caressed his face, dropping her thumb to soothe the dimple in his chin. "No, it's not acceptable because it's remarkable. Beyond belief. But how did you know?"

She hoped her words came off as more curious than concerned and suspicious. But they were likely heavy with the weight of everything she wondered.

"When I moved your purse to the table, your phone slipped out. A text was on the screen confirming this morning's party of twenty at Le Reve's. I didn't want to wake you, but I didn't want something missed on account of me. So I called the restaurant and made sure you were taken care of." Boyish and sweet, Alex asked, "Is that, um, suitable?"

Madison kissed him, tightening her embrace and enjoying the feel of the man in her arms. With his hot hands caressing her back, there was no room to keep up her guard.

Between them, it didn't feel like he was playing games. Even if he'd done nothing for her event, her reaction would have been the same. She didn't need any of it. Having Alex here was more than enough.

With a charming half smile, he asked, "So, I take it that's a yes?"

In response, she kissed him again, much slower this time. The warmth of his lips and the heat of his body melded with his scent, the scent that was distinctly Alex Drake. An intoxicating swirl that made her weak in the knees and wetter than a river in a rain forest.

It was all too much—his rugged good looks, tempting body, generosity, and kindness, all wrapped up in a scorching kiss and stone-hard bulge pressing into her like a battering ram. Madison wanted him more with every second that passed.

Again, they pulled away for a desperate breath. He was staring at her lips, and she licked them.

"What do you want?" she whispered.

"I'm dying for your mouth," he said, brushing his knuckles against her full bottom lip. His eyes met hers, patient as he waited.

"Yes," Madison said breathlessly, enjoying the feel of his fingers on her kiss-swollen lips.

Releasing her, he locked the door and led her to a wingback chair tucked in the corner of the room. Before he could undo his belt, she gripped his hands, placing them at his sides.

"It's your turn," she said, watching as his eyes darkened in approval.

Taking her time, she slipped off his slacks and boxers, letting them fall to his ankles. Then she sat him down, kneeling before him, reverent in worshipping his thick cock heavy in her hands. He pulled her into a kiss, plunging his tongue through her lips, and priming her mouth for more.

She swiped her tongue wide across the fullness of his head, savoring the delicious drop at his tip that tasted a hundred times better than that bite of frosting had.

Alex's hands were on her, forcing her dress down to expose her breasts, aching for his touch with hard, puckered peaks. Gently, he cupped and caressed the soft, weighty mounds, increasing the pressure enough to make her body hum, and she moaned.

He plucked one before pressing it in his fingers. A soft squeal escaped her, and he repeated the teasing pinch with her other breast. Before losing much more control, she dropped her head, hungry for the rigid firmness of his shaft.

The second her mouth engulfed him, he sank back with a groan. His fingers wove into her hair, guiding her, and pushing her further with a deep growl.

"Yes," he insisted.

Having him like this, Madison moved with passion and longing, her body squirming with need. Her wetness seeped past her panties, her pussy ripe and ready, weeping for more.

She hollowed her cheeks, sucking hard and stroking his massive rod in tandem. He murmured her name, and she bobbed faster. But she had to see his face.

For a moment, she pulled away from his thick, silky shaft, letting her hands wrap him, balancing the clockwise and counter-clockwise strokes together. She worked them faster.

"God, Madison, you're going to make me come." His face was beautiful and relaxed.

Determined, she returned her mouth to him, sucking the living sin right out of that gorgeous cock. Without breaking her rhythm, she could feel him—dragging her skirt up, inching it across her back. His fingers swiped in circles across her ass and thighs. She squirmed, desperate to keep her steady pace.

His tender touch pushed her hips to a wanting rhythm, moving in unison with her head sliding up and down his length. Her back arched and her body moved, craving his penetrating touch.

His daring finger slid beneath her thong, grazing her between her cheeks before discovering her slick folds. He pressed a finger in, causing her to quiver and release a muffled squeal.

After a few pumps, he pulled her panties down, letting them fall to her knees. He smeared her wetness up and down her swollen pussy before plunging two fingers deep inside. Moaning around his shaft, she sped up as he fingered her— fucked her. His touch was so tender and yet so hard, she'd give anything to find her bliss in the sweet torture of his touch.

Faster, he pushed his pace, and her mouth raced to match his stride. They both groaned in pleasure. He would be hers. And unconditionally, she was his.

Her core quivered, tightening in a wave of pulses around his fingers. Slowing her breaths but maintaining her rhythm, she found holding out was becoming impossible.

When he pressed a third finger to her clit, the spasms rocked her, followed by a muffled succession of screams, and she forced him deep in her throat.

Out of control, her entire body shuddered, crashing her turbulent climax around his fingers and grinding them to a halt. But as he nudged her head just the slightest bit deeper, he exploded. She savored every last hot drop of him down her throat.

Drawing his fingers from the tightness of her core, he swept her onto his lap, cuddling her with soft kisses before sweeping his tongue in and tasting himself from her mouth.

Lazily, she watched as he sucked his fingers clean, lapping up every last drop of her sweetness. Madison was breathless as his gaze danced back at her.

His hand caressed her, moving down her body to the long line of her thigh. He snagged her panties, pulling them off her legs, and slipped them into his pocket.

After a few wonderful minutes resting in each other's arms, he stood, still cradling her tightly. Setting her in the chair, he replaced the dress back over her bodice, then whispered in her ear.

"I want you in my life, Madison. And not just for today."

Their kiss was slow. She clung to the ebbing seduction.

Breaking away, he rubbed his nose against hers, and his eyes twinkled as he smiled. "At whatever pace you're comfortable with."

Spent, she could only agree with a subtle nod.

Alex stood, straightening his shirt and blazer, then smoothed his hair from the steaming hot-sex god of a moment ago. Casually, he strolled behind her, warming her shoulders with his hands, and melting her with a quick massage. Her heavy eyes closed as she moaned.

"I have to go, beautiful. Rest, but not for too long. Your friends will wonder where you are."

He kissed her lightly on the head, then left.

~

Madison did her best to compose herself as she checked her hair and face in the reflection of her phone. Slipping out of the room and back into the bridal shower, she wondered if her escapade was obvious from her beaming smile or shaky walk.

As soon as she stepped in, Sheila shouted, "Maddi, I almost left. Where have you been?"

Breathing through the flush rising in her cheeks, she apologized. "Sorry, something came up." *Big-time.* "I was longer than I thought I'd be."

But only because he was longer than I thought he'd be.

CHAPTER 18

MADISON

MADISON SHOT A TEXT TO PACO, and in an instant the rumble of the Lamborghini announced its presence from down the street. Somehow, the magnificent beast looked distinctly different.

As the scissor door lifted, she leaned down to ask, "Did your car change color, or was it red when you dropped me off?"

Laughing, Paco said, "I can't be seen wearing the same outfit twice." Gesturing to his suit, he emphasized that he'd also changed his outfit, though the flashes of brilliance remained on his dazzling ears.

Madison got in. "Okay, Mr. Mind Reader, where do I want to go now?" she asked, curious as to the extent of his precognition.

"Obviously, you *think* you want to go home. You've had a long day and you need to put your feet up, maybe lounge in a hot bath and get to bed early. Am I right?"

He is so right, it's scary. Like he's known me forever. Or maybe he just knows that any woman would want that after a long night followed by a long day.

She hid her giggle, wondering how many more times she could think of something *long*.

"But we're not doing any of that just yet," he said, handing her a small box.

"Oh, you shouldn't have."

Her excited statement ended on a down note when she opened the box.

Madison lifted out the pair of used leather gloves, unsure what to think of them. They were fingerless, with a pattern of tiny holes punched across the top.

"I'll give you three chances," he said, inviting her to guess with a ridiculously adorable popped brow and thoroughly evil smile.

"Golfing?" Madison said, giving him a confused look.

"Nope."

"With this car and these gloves, we could be making a music video?"

"Good guess, with definite future potential, but not today."

Noticing their size, Madison slipped them on, which fit like, well, you know. Scrunching her brow, she thought aloud.

"Well, I can't be helping you bury a body." She wiggled her fingers. "Nothing's covering my fingerprints."

"So, you won't be my patsy? Noted. But I'm not giving you a hint."

"Oh, I don't need a hint. Obviously, you're letting me drive your car, and don't want my grubby hands mucking up your steering wheel." She smirked, knowing if she was going to bomb the last guess, she'd wrap it in a hopeful suggestion.

"Now who's the mind reader?" Paco said before taking a sudden turn onto an isolated road.

Madison held her breath. "Really? You're going to let me drive your car?"

"Look around," Paco said as he pointed out the lush density of vegetation surrounding them. "No, I'm going to have you help me bury a body."

The seriousness of his tone made her wonder for half a second, before she caught the tiniest hint of a smile.

The road opened to what seemed to be a secure area. NO TRESPASSING signs were posted along a border of twelve-foot-high double-chain-link fence topped with ropes of razor wire. The place had *we're not fucking around* written all over it.

The car rolled to a stop at an unmanned gate. A lone post held a small call box, a camera, and a swipe pad with DGI embossed on it.

Paco swiped his badge and the gate slid open. He revved the car forward, accelerating around several curves with a broad smile on his face. Once they drove through a mini forest, the tree cover ended to reveal a private runway with several hangars far ahead. At one end, he parked, opening both doors with the press of a button.

"Ready?" he asked.

No. Maybe.

"Yes," Madison said with a slight nod as she stepped out. Nervous, she headed to the driver's side as Paco stood waiting to help her in. "Wait. I don't think I can do this."

"Sure you can."

"I mean . . ." She blew out a long breath, hating to admit to a feminine short-coming. "I don't know how to drive a standard."

"Yes, you and ninety-two percent of America. Lambos are all automatic. The highest performance automatic on the planet, in my opinion."

Automagically, Paco closed her winged door. Trying to hide her uncertainty, she bit her lip and hoped her arm didn't erupt in her usual wave of itchy patches.

As Paco slid beside her in the passenger seat, that door closed as well. Step by step, he ran through a crash course on the mechanics of the display and functions.

"This is a massive piece of machinery. Are you sure you want me driving it?"

Seriously, he leaned in, and she gave him her undivided attention.

"Miss Madison, before you start driving, there are three things I need you to understand. One, you can't hurt anyone or anything. Look around," he said, and she did. "We're on a private runway in the middle of fucking nowhere. And you couldn't flip this baby if you tried. Okay?"

"Yes, okay." Madison deliberately relaxed her shoulders with a sigh of relief.

"Good. Two, I'm not just going to let you drive so you get a quick high like we're a couple of kids at an amusement park. I want to teach you a few tricks with this car, share with you some really cool shit, but I can only do that if you listen to me very carefully and trust me without question. Got it?"

"Got it." Feeling more confident, Madison nodded. "And three?"

"Three, the gloves you're wearing aren't just to keep your grubby little hands from mucking up my steering wheel. That's only half the reason."

Madison exaggerated her eye roll.

Gently, Paco lifted her hand and continued. "Those gloves were previously owned by the remarkable Cha Cha Muldowney, also known as the First Lady of Drag Racing. She'd go from a dead stop to two hundred twenty-six feet in five and a half seconds. She'd break two hundred sixty miles per hour in a hot pink car, kicking ass and looking damn good doing it. She was brave in the face of adversity, and fierce to those who dared to challenge her. Channel her spirit and glamour at all times when you drive this car. I certainly do. Clear?"

"Yes," Madison said with sass, trying on Paco's badass vibe for size.

As he nudged her with a sexy smile and waggling brow, Madison started the engine. Her body jolted, startled at the strong growl emanating from the car and vibrating her ass. Loudly, she giggled.

Taking command and easing her breaths, she looked over at Paco, inspired by his insistent nod communicating, *Get it, girl!* Slamming her foot on the gas, she peeled off, squealing with delight as the car hit ninety miles per hour in seconds.

Although she couldn't hear him, Paco windmilled his arm in the air, shouting over and over what looked like, "More! More!"

Madison hit 120 miles per hour before slowing, flipping a U-turn, and gunning it even harder. Her smile stretched from ear to ear. At the end of the runway, breathless with exhilaration, she slowed as Paco motioned for her to come to a stop.

He gave her a huge grin. "Having fun?"

Too winded for words, she nodded.

"Ever heard of a J-turn?"

"No, but I'm familiar with a three-point turn. Is it like that?"

"Yes," Paco said excitedly. "Think of it as a three-point turn without the middle point. We're going to start in reverse. When you get to about thirty-five miles per hour, you're going to whip the steering wheel like this without letting up on the gas. This will lock the front wheels. Then yank the steering wheel hard in the exact opposite direction. As soon as the front of the car has slid a hundred eighty degrees from the direction you were in, pop it into drive and gun it. Got it?"

Blankly, she blinked. Catching on to the sheer depths of his lunacy, she blurted, "No! I got none of that. At all. I have no idea what you just said."

"Cool, then this will be way more fun than I thought. Oh, and if we really want some fun . . ." He opened the glove compartment and pulled out a satin blindfold. "One of us can wear this. Hmm, who should it be?"

Pointing back and forth between them and silently mouthing *eenie meenie miney mo*, he began sliding it over his head. With a nervous yelp, Madison yanked his arm down.

"Oh, you want it. Okay!" Paco leaned over with a playful growl as she resisted. Sternly, he reminded her of his words. "You said you'd trust me implicitly. Crazy trust test time. Put it on."

Reluctantly, Madison took the blindfold and put it on. After a few seconds, she opened her eyes from behind it.

"Hey," she said, shocked by the discovery. "I can see through this. Or have you somehow bestowed me with the power of X-ray vision?"

"Yes, you can see through it. So begins your afternoon of lessons. Lesson one. Things aren't always what they seem, or nearly as scary as they appear. Okay, lesson's over. Give that baby back. I'm going to need it for a little fun time later."

As he tossed the blindfold back into the glove box, Madison caught sight of more of his little props. *Did I just see fuzzy handcuffs? Not judging, and definitely not asking.*

Paco drew her attention. "So, let's go over this one more time, and then give it a try. In reverse, start driving, and when you get to thirty-five miles per hour, grab the steering wheel like so. Yank hard, then yank in the opposite direction. Once you complete the turn, lock the wheels, shift into drive, then accelerate to the end of the runway. Ready?"

"As ready as I'm gonna be."

Madison put the monstrous beast in reverse and pressed timidly on the gas. At the pivotal speed, she started yanking the steering wheel, but Paco pulled it much more forcefully.

The car began to spin. She yanked the wheel in the opposite direction just as forcefully, locking the wheels without needing Paco's assistance.

"Good," he said, and returned his hand to his lap.

With the car now facing the opposite direction, she popped it into drive, slammed her foot to the gas, and floored it, propelling the precision machine to 135 miles per hour before easing it to a stop.

Proud as a badass peacock, she beamed. Her heart pounded out of her chest, and her head spun, making her dizzy with excitement. "Oh my God, that was incredible!"

"You did pretty good. Ready to try again on your own?"

"Yes!" she exclaimed, then caught the *on your own* part. Feigning confidence, she sucked in a breath.

Paco pointed ahead. "Good. Pull up there, let me out, and let's see what you've got."

She nodded, grinning with the giddiness of a girl who was bypassing the line and getting to ride the awesome roller coaster again. When she pulled up to the vacant area he instructed, he got out.

Paco leaned in, giving her a few more instructions. "Do it twice. Once going down there to the end, then once again on your way back. Go really freaking fast and hurry up. If I break a sweat out here, I'll be super cranky." He stepped away, and the door shut.

Madison got the car into position, and slowly rolled in reverse.

Bond. Madison Bond.

After testing the waters with a bit more gas, she pressed her foot hard, going for broke. With Paco watching, the Lamborghini moved with surprising ease as she executed the maneuver twice, once down, and a second later, once back.

With all the thrill and speed of a Formula Rossa roller coaster, the buildup climbed to the point of full throttle, and in seconds was sadly over. Still giddy in the aftermath, she returned to pick up Paco.

Although she pulled up right next to him, his utter annoyance was apparent. Arms crossed and head shaking, he stalked to the driver's side. As the door winged up, he tapped his foot in irritation.

Dramatically, he slid his sunglasses down his nose to glare at her. "You may have kicked ass with that last J-turn, but this ain't your car, Miss M."

Dropping his vexed facade and exchanging it for a wide grin, he offered his hand to help her out, which she quickly accepted. Keeping her composure was impossible. Once her feet touched the ground, she bounced gleefully, shouting a *hell yeah* as she bopped over to the passenger side.

As he drove off the runway and out of the foreboding entry point, Paco resumed his lesson. "And that leads us to lesson two. You're capable of more than you think. There are great things in store for you, Miss Madison. Trust your instincts. Always."

Awestruck, she stared. "So, do you prefer Yoda or Sensei? Um, I don't mean to sound ungrateful, because this was utterly amazing, but why did you teach me all this?"

For the first time since she'd met him, Paco looked somber, the shine draining from his eyes.

"What's wrong?" Madison asked. "Was it something I said?"

"Oh, it's just my RBF," he said, forcing a smile.

"You have a resting bitch face like I have a third boob. What is it?"

CHAPTER 19

PACO

Paco looked over, melting at the familiar warmth in Madison's eyes.

He got it—why Alex had been drawn in so quickly. It was as clear as the perfect button nose on her face. Her eyes and her smile, whipped together in a perfect recipe of sincerity and understanding, made keeping his guard up around her impossible.

But he needed to pull it together. For all their sakes.

"Let's just say I really wanted to teach this to someone once. Someone very special. But I lost the chance." He took a needed breath. Looking at her, he shared a harmless bit of honesty, even if its full meaning would be lost on her. "I guess I just didn't want to miss the chance again."

Still in her seat belt, Madison leaned over and rested her head on his shoulder in a silent display of empathy.

Paco's heart sank. Sometimes, there are no words for loss. Just understanding. In that, he and Madison would be forever connected.

His glassy eyes remained focused on the road, but he rested his head on hers as they quietly made their way back into the city.

Paco drove around the corner, heading toward Madison's apartment. The street was a hellacious labyrinth of double-parked cars and crowds of overzealous pedestrians. He looked up, quickly finding her humble abode crammed amongst the squeeze of windows climbing six stories high.

Teasing her, he slowed, then sped past without a glance. When she gave him a worried frown and a soft touch on his forearm, he broke out in a practiced maniacal laugh.

"Don't bother asking. We're doing exactly what I said you would do. Promise."

"Really? Because I believe you distinctly said something about lounging in a bath and an early bedtime." After a second of Paco continuing to keep her in suspense, she asked, "Can you at least give me a hint?"

"There's something you need to learn about this inner circle. We're vaults. Bat those big pretty eyes all you want, but there will be absolutely, positively no hints."

The irritation pouring from her scrunched-up face and pouty lip was too adorable for words. And he didn't need to snap a shot with his phone to remember. Every face he'd ever seen would be permanently filed away for safekeeping.

And today, the many looks of Madison Taylor would forever be locked away in a very special corner of the vast vault of his mind.

CHAPTER 20

MADISON

MADISON ADMIRED her new friend's handsome face long after he'd turned his attention to the road. His instructions were clear and wrapped around her like a warm blanket. Trust your instincts.

I trust you, Paco Robles.

With a few quick turns, they were nearing the DGI skyscraper as he asked, "Do you have that card I gave you?"

Carefully opening her elegant Hermès clutch, Madison pulled out the little card he'd handed her earlier, waving it with a smile.

"Good, you'll need it."

"I will?" she asked, realizing they were now passing DGI's headquarters.

"Yes," he said before she could ask the question. "We're going the wrong way for that too." Her amused glare made him chuckle. "And that's all you're getting out of me for now."

Between the warm sunshine beaming through the windshield, the purr of the engine lulling her in the leather seat, and the closeness she felt with her new friend, Madison couldn't stifle the yawn that crept up on her. She wrestled with a few heavy blinks before sinking back and swearing to close her eyes for just a moment.

Madison woke to Paco killing the engine. Shaking off her disorientation, she took a curious glance around. They were in a very private, very upscale garage with custom lighting and a glossy finish to the designer floors.

Her door opened with Paco standing outside. "We're here." Again, he offered a hand to help her out, which she accepted with a gracious smile.

"Where?" Madison asked, not recognizing it.

"Where you'll be staying . . . unless you object. I confess, my driving lesson was to keep you occupied until Alex finished this up for you. Use your card over there."

Madison headed to an elevator, ready to give the panel a swipe with the card she held. In an instant, Paco's hand covered hers, stopping her before she could complete the move.

A solemn expression overtook his face, though his smile remained intact. "You have my number. If you need to leave for any reason, text me. No questions asked."

Curious, she gripped his hand in both of hers. "You're concerned?"

Insistently, he shook his head. "No. Not about leaving you here. But I know how fast this is all happening for you. Each step is a decision. Maybe a hard one. Maybe one you shouldn't have to make right away. I don't want you worrying about having second thoughts. You're entitled to them. If an hour from now or a week from now, you want your space, I'll be your chariot and will happily lead-foot you anywhere you want to go."

Madison took a breath, thinking through his sweet offer. There was a kinship between them. This polished man in his pristine suit and Italian shoes cared for her with a warmth that she couldn't put her finger on, like a best friend she'd known for years. Almost like family.

"Look," she said, leading with complete candor. "You and I don't know each other. But I feel like we do."

He nodded with a grin. "I feel the same way," he said with a humble tone that seemed uncommon and special.

"Which means I know I can level with you on this. And that somehow, you'll understand. This connection I feel with Alex, it's like the one I feel with you."

Playfully, Paco lifted a brow. "Not exactly."

Madison giggled. "No, not exactly. But it's there. It's tangible. I sense it with everything I am, and I can't explain it, but I feel like I don't need to." She took a solemn breath. "Have I mentioned my brother, Jack?"

Serious and reserved, Paco shook his head.

"We lost Jack, and I think of him a lot. Did he do everything he wanted his last day? What if it's my last day?"

"It's not." Paco's voice was defiant and stern, his hard expression revealing his panic.

Calmly, she shushed him with a grin. "All I mean is if it were, maybe I'd forgo the run and have a second slice of bridal shower cake. Maybe I'd get behind the wheel of a car worth more than my apartment building and floor the gas pedal. And maybe, just maybe, I'd take a chance on the sweet man at the office who goes out of his way to get me my favorite drink when he should be more concerned with running his global empire. See? Easy decision."

Paco pulled her in for a warm hug. "Yes, Miss Madison. Easy decision."

They both pulled in a deep breath as they leaned into each other. Even though she was sure Paco sniffled, Madison said nothing, focused on controlling her pesky tears.

Finally, he released her. "Well, what are you waiting for? That key card isn't going to swipe itself."

Giddy with the growing butterflies tickling her insides, she swiped. The doors slid open, revealing a similar panel inside the elevator. Nodding as he stepped in beside her, Paco encouraged her to swipe again, so she did. With no buttons to push, the doors closed and the car lifted them quickly.

When the doors reopened, Madison stood there, overwhelmed at the sight of the luxury penthouse apartment overlooking the city. Pale blush roses were set in vases throughout a room of expensive furnishings, exquisite paintings, and bronze figurines that looked antique. The wall of windows showcased a view of Manhattan's skyline that was breathtaking.

Stunned, Madison froze to stare, so Paco gently led her in. His hand lightly pressed the small of her back as she stammered out, "W-wha—"

"Welcome home, Miss Madison. Enjoy discovering. Dinner will be served at seven o'clock. Your bath is already drawn and will hold its temperature for about an hour. And it bears repeating—call or text me if you need anything. At all."

With a quick kiss on each of her cheeks, he stepped back into the elevator.

Still at a loss for words, Madison could only question him with her wide eyes.

Brushing aside her unasked question with nothing more than a grin, he said, "And don't lose those gloves. You'll need them again." He winked at her just before the elevator doors shut.

Did he say home?

∽

The vastness of the penthouse apartment was remarkable, but that paled in comparison to its contents. The furnishings and art were exquisite, yet warm and cozy. Books were abundant in each room, some new and some old, and many with bookmarks, as if they'd been re-shelved mid-read.

Meandering through the halls, she stepped shyly into the master bedroom. The breathtaking space was flooded with light from the floor-to-ceiling windows as well as four oversized skylights. Wonder and a tingling blush filled her as she stared for a minute at the oversized bed.

Wait. What kind of billionaire lets a strange woman loose in his place? I could be a crazy woman. Rifling through his stuff. Stealing his shit. Jumping on his bed. With. My. Shoes. On.

And if Madison was in for a penny, she was hell-to-the-yeah in for a pound. Tiptoeing, she stepped into what she presumed was Alex's closet. But she was very, very wrong.

Oh my God. The semi-palace held a wide range of elegant women's clothing, tags intact. Frantically, she flipped through a dozen or so in disbelief. They were all in her size.

It was as if Rodeo Drive had backed up a truck and unloaded its load of high-end clothes and accessories right into the elegant room. A wall of shelves held an unbelievable variety of shoes for every season, arranged by color and heel height, and again, all in her size. But it didn't hold every pair.

Inside a special alcove, a pedestal sat below a spotlight, showcasing the pair Alex had given her. Smiling and sentimental, she brushed them softly with her fingertips. Glancing around, she still couldn't believe her eyes.

I can practically do a J-turn right here in this space. This closet is nearly the size of my apartment.

The center of the closet was taken up by an island with a much smaller version of the DGI access panel. When she hovered her card across it, it opened, a reverse Venus flytrap exposing boxes from Tiffany's and Cartier.

Looking down at her wrist, she decided the diamonds wrapping it were plenty. She swiped the panel again and the island closed, keeping all its wonders safe and sound.

Curious, Madison followed the sound of a slight rumbling from the other end of the closet. She emerged into a bathroom with a huge white bathtub front and center, surrounded by water flowing from its infinity edging.

The rumbling was from a series of Jacuzzi jets, pulsing lavender-scented water in an intoxicating swirl that she had to touch. It felt like heaven.

A side panel displayed the temperature, with the ability to adjust it up and down. *I am not messing with perfection.* Next to the temperature panel was a plush robe with *MT* embossed on the pocket.

She looked around. Half the towels were embossed with her initials, and the other half labeled *AD* in identical stitching.

Next to the bathtub, a bottle of champagne was chilling in a bucket of ice beside a single flute. A small table next to it held a tray of chocolate-covered strawberries, cheeses, and artisan crackers. A little note with MADISON handwritten on it was tucked on the tray, and she opened it.

Enjoy your bath. See you tonight.
Alex

Seeing his name made her smile.

The note? The bath? And the outrageously gorgeous apartment?

What's a girl to do?

Perhaps this wasn't *home* in all that the word entailed. But for the moment, it was wondrous and warm, and made her feel more comfortable than she'd ever felt before. And it wasn't about the things. It was all Alex. He was sweet and thoughtful, and went so far out of his way to make her welcome, she couldn't help but feel close to him.

Madison knew, more than most, that life was short. It all begged to be savored. And savor it, she sure as hell would.

CHAPTER 21

MADISON

AFTER INDULGING IN A BATH, sipping champagne, tasting some delectable straw-berries, and slipping on a little black dress that flawlessly walked the fine line between elegant and casual, Madison was ready to see Alex.

There was still time before dinner, and she wasn't exactly sure when he'd be there. *Home,* she reminded herself.

To fill the time, she lost herself in the penthouse the way one loses their day in a fine museum. The furnishings and art were stunning yet subdued, and in a strange way, exactly to her liking. Each item was something she would have chosen. You know, if she had unlimited resources and a penchant for really expensive stuff.

She admired how every piece seemed to be placed in the exact spot she would have put them. Even the book on the side table, lying perfectly off-center beneath the lamp.

The Count of Monte Cristo. Her favorite.

She picked it up, thumbing through it nostalgically. Heaving a sigh, she finally flipped back to the very first page, and her smile vanished. The beautiful inscription there was handwritten in cursive.

Love you always.
Grandpa Mike

Reeling in shock, she closed the book and carefully inspected the cover and spine before reopening it. Stunned, she stared in disbelief.

This is my book. From Grandpa Mike. A book that up until that day had been in her apartment, tucked away in a drawer next to her bed.

Alarmed and clutching the thick vintage book, she scanned the room, wondering exactly what she'd walked into. In one corner of the room was a sleek black baby grand piano, its top adorned with about a dozen framed photos.

A fairly small one caught her eye. In it, she and her father seemed to be posing, and holding up another photo. Squinting and frustrated, she couldn't make out the photo-within-the-photo, but three people were in the smaller image.

It's too fuzzy. I can't tell who they are. But that's my dad, and that's definitely me at fourteen or maybe fifteen.

Undeniably, the two of them were smiling, posing for the shot. She had only the faintest recollection of the photo being taken, and none of whatever it was they were holding. The more she tried recalling it, the more of a blank slate her mind became.

Her head was swimming with emotions and questions. Mostly questions.

Despite her initial thoughts, *how* might not be the biggest question. She got it. Alex was a billionaire whose company specialized in reconnaissance and surveillance, data mining, and, of course, investigating. He certainly had the resources.

No, the biggest question was *why*.

Retracing her steps back to her purse, she pulled out her phone and snapped a shot of the interior of the book, then the photo.

She sent the images to the number Alex had texted from earlier, making her point with only three capital letters.

MADISON: WTF?!

CHAPTER 22

PACO

At 6:30 P.M. SHARP, Paco picked up Alex from his last meeting of the day in the Lamborghini, a common practice they both found helpful. The drive allowed them to catch up on any recent developments at work, and on whatever else was on their minds, with a casual familiarity they both preferred not to reveal at the office.

To the outside world, Paco and Alex were merely employer and employee. Only they knew the depth of their friendship.

Even with the long hours, nothing beat carrying on with work in a half-million-dollar car. Paco could get places quickly, and pretty much park wherever the hell he wanted.

He alone was trusted with highly confidential transactions, covert reconnaissance, and anything that required just the right touch when hundreds of millions of dollars were on the line.

Today, a few documents required Alex's signature. The slightest premature leak of the information contained within them could impact DGI in a very long-term and detrimental way.

And what these documents contained, if taken out of context, could incite semi-mass hysteria. Crash global markets. Kill their stock value overnight. Place DGI in the international hot seat for years to come.

But this was Alex, and how he rolled. *Just another day.*

Conversely, if tidbits of information needed to hit the streets, Alex had the connections and Paco had the network. They scattered leaks strategically, planting each in an optimal climate with pinpoint precision. DGI's stock value, corporate growth, and global presence were solidified.

And with each notch on the DGI bedpost of lucrative transactions, an equally impressive bonus always followed, flowing straight to Paco's offshore bank account.

A speed reader, Alex breezed through the documents, signing here and initialing there, easily multitasking when a text alert diverted his attention. With a quick glance, he read his phone while signing, and his signature stuttered, scrawling clear off the page.

"Fuck," he muttered under his breath.

Paco, witnessing Alex's faux pas, dismissed his concern. "Don't worry. I have a second set for just these times when you stroke out during an important signature." Helpfully, he reached over to point out the binder's second tab.

"No, *this!*"

Scouting about for a place to park, Paco pulled into the nearest valet drop-off point, in front of a restaurant. As the valet scurried to let him out and take the keys, Paco lowered the power window.

"Hey, I just need to sit here for a minute," he said, handing the man a hundred-dollar bill. Raising the window, he ignored the gush of gratitude and focused on the text Alex just received. He pulled it closer, getting a better look at the images.

Letting out a long breath, Paco handed back the phone. "Are you going to tell her?"

Pensively, Alex stared off in the distance. "Not yet."

Paco unleashed a controlled amount of irritation. "Why not? You said yourself you didn't want to hide everything at your place, or start a relationship on the wrong foot. So, here you are. At this point, I'm not sure you can avoid it."

Alex just maintained his faraway stare, seeming to contemplate the damn good advice. After a minute or two of silence, he made his decision.

"What I can't avoid . . . I might be able to delay." Alex's statement came off as a question, with a distinct tone of requesting Paco's advice.

Paco looked away, making up his own mind without being pressured by the weight of their past. He knew the importance of the unasked question. With an unsure shrug, he finally conceded with a nod.

"Let's go," Alex said as he sent a text, most likely to Madison.

With that, Paco peeled away from the restaurant.

CHAPTER 23

MADISON

DEEP IN THOUGHT, Madison sat gazing out the window, staring unseeing at the Manhattan skyline. *I need answers.* But deep down, she wavered, hating confrontation.

The waiting was making her nervous and edgy. There was no stopping the hive rash from breaking out on her arm. She stifled an itch and rested her head back against the chair as she waited.

For the eighth or ninth time in a row, she read Alex's text.

ALEX: Please don't go. I'll be there in fifteen minutes. Maybe faster. Paco's driving.

Rattled and still unsure how to even handle this bizarre situation, she sucked in a breath as the bell rang.

He's ringing the bell?

Getting her bearings, she headed toward the elevator as another set of soft pings hit the air. *How do I answer it?*

Without her intervention, the elevator opened. The soft murmur of unfamiliar voices broke the silence. Several people entered pushing stainless-steel rolling carts, halting as soon as they saw her.

A tall man wearing a catering apron addressed her. "Good evening, ma'am.

We have instructions to set up in the small library, unless you prefer a different location?"

Not sure of what to say or do, she just nodded. "Sure. Thank you."

She followed them as they seemed to know their way around, setting up at a table with two chairs in a day room off to the side.

Feverishly, they worked to get a four-course meal set up at the table overlooking the city. As their arranging was coming to a close, Madison panicked, ready to scramble for her purse and give them a tip. But the moment they'd finished, they departed like food ninjas in the night.

Delectable wafts of food emanated from the elegant dinner setting. Several assorted plates were covered with silver domes, hiding the food beneath. Moët chilled in a polished stand, and a low arrangement of pale pink roses decorated the center of the table.

Before she could step forward and peek at the dishes emanating savory scents, the elevator pinged again.

She stepped out, frozen in place as Alex entered the apartment. He looked every bit the total package. A sweep-you-off-your-feet kind of guy with rugged good looks and a touch that absolutely undid her.

But was this all just the pretty wrapping to something much darker?

Everyone has a past. Could his be worse? Is he a stalker? How did he get the book and the photo? And what about the nickname he knew? Or my name, for that matter?

Alex's eyes, tortured and desperate, locked with hers, but he didn't move. Madison's heart raced out of her chest as their lovers' standoff played out.

CHAPTER 24

ALEX

ALEX KEPT Paco waiting in the car for a few reasons. He might need a wingman. Or a witness . . . in case he needed something signed. Or, God forbid, if Madison needed a ride.

But as he stood, not budging from the entrance to his penthouse suite, his gaze remained fixed on hers. Alex focused to keep his breathing steady. Controlled.

God, not now.

Desperate to suppress the growing pounding in his ears, he pushed aside his panic as he stared deep into her gorgeous, worried eyes. He needed to quiet his thoughts, push away the darkness and pain, and focus on nothing but her.

An episode, even a small one, would take center stage at the worst possible time. Madison couldn't find out about his weakness like this.

I have to be here for her. Protect her.

Alex could see as plain as day she was suppressing her own reactions. *Justified reactions.*

Sure, he'd seen her lash out once, but none of that was her nature. She'd snapped at Gina because she'd been pushed and provoked, and mostly because of him. And even then, Madison's first instinct was to leave.

She had to be considering it. Bolting as fast as possible away from this asylum and its inmate.

Please don't go.

Mindful, his gaze fell from her doleful expression to her hand on her arm. Instantly, her scratching stopped. *Her hives are back.* Despite the obvious itch driving up her skin, she was staying.

Relieved, he stepped closer.

"Alex, I'm not sure what's going on, and I'm not sure how long I can downplay the full extent of my total freak-out, but I'd really like to hear whatever it is you want to tell me. To understand it. All of it. How did you know my name? And about Igz? And how did you get my book? And the photo? Did you . . . did you break into my apartment?"

"No, on my life, I didn't." He had to embrace her, reassure her, but the doubt in her eyes stopped his advance cold. "I can only imagine what you're thinking. The answer is no, I didn't take your things."

"Then *how?*" Madison's expression demanded answers, her eyes searching his desperately.

Uneasy, Alex began to pace. *How do I tell her? And still keep my word?*

The terms were unwritten—barely a contract, if you asked Paco. But to Alex, it was a contract, a verbal agreement he would keep . . . no matter what anyone else thought.

Again, he took a step toward Madison, covering her shoulders with his hands and gently coaxing her to sit in a chair. He took a knee before her, grasping her hand with a tender caress.

Thinking fast, he had an idea. "Look, will you stay here for five minutes? Just don't leave. I'll be right back."

Madison studied his eyes, and patiently, he awaited her decision. He pled with his eyes, and when she finally nodded, he jumped to his feet.

Leaving the room, he made a quick call. "Meet me in my study."

In the room he used as his home office, Alex typed a quick letter and hit PRINT, ready to give Madison Taylor an offer she couldn't refuse.

"You rang?" Paco asked, sarcastic as he entered, obviously leery of the scheme before Alex even uttered a word.

Flatly, Alex had to say it. "I could really use your support."

"How about we start with my skepticism and see where it goes?"

Determined, Alex whipped the fresh printout to his desk, penned his name, then handed it to Paco. "Sign this."

Paco took half a second to scan the single-page document. Looking back at Alex with a heated glare and pursed lips, he tossed it back onto the desk. "Nope."

"Sign it!"

"Have you lost your fucking mind?" Paco shouted.

Concerned, Alex shushed him, motioning toward the open door with a reminder of Madison not too far down the hall.

"Come on. Just sign it."

"Not happening. Go ahead—cancel my black card. Get someone else. I'm not signing it."

Cautiously, Alex proceeded. Paco's flight mode could flip to fight mode at a moment's notice.

Defenseless and showing it, Alex stood open armed and pleading with all he had. He didn't want a fight. But he stayed behind his desk, not wanting to get his ass kicked either, in case Paco was ready to pound some sense into him.

With a heavy breath, Alex considered his words and actions carefully. Then he said the one word he rarely said to the man, hoping with all his might it had some meaning between friends.

Softly, he said, "Please."

Paco began rambling, something he only did when he was that perfect storm of freaked-the-fuck-out and completely comfortable letting it all go.

"Everything about this screams *bad idea.* You barely know her. *We* barely know her. Do I have to go down the full spectrum of possible ramifications? One wrong move and DGI could be cut off at the knees, practically dissolving everything we've all worked so hard for over the last decade. If I sign this, DGI might die a very quick death. You can't take this back, Alex."

Quietly, Alex calmed his emotions. "I've never asked you for anything."

"I know that!" Paco revealed his anger in a wild flailing of his arms, but refrained from shouting. "Goddammit, you think I don't know that?"

"I have to do this. Show her what's in my heart."

"Yeah? Didn't anyone ever tell you that the heart is the fucking Achilles heel of business? I'm here to protect you. You might be the majority shareholder of DGI, but I'm fucking second in line. If I do this, I might be failing you more than I ever have."

The somber meaning of his words hung heavy between them.

Direct and confident, Alex softly said, "It's her."

Paco's squint and pursed lips meant only one thing, and Alex smiled.

"Give me a goddamn pen before I change my mind." Signing, Paco said, "I always knew we'd go down in a ball of flames. I just never imagined I'd hand you the kerosene."

"Look, if we're going down like the Titanic, your ass is on a lifeboat. I'll take the hit alone."

"Let's get one thing straight. We go down together . . ." Paco's somber tone belied his knowing brow and cocky grin. "Or not at all."

Smiling with gratitude and patting Paco's shoulder, Alex said, "Do me another favor. Don't start blinging out your life preserver just yet."

CHAPTER 25

MADISON

Five minutes earlier

MADISON WATCHED as Paco stepped off the elevator. Before heading to meet Alex in his study, he paused to give her an assured smile and lifted a single finger, requesting her patience for a minute.

She didn't know exactly why, but seeing Paco was a relief. Not enough of one to stop the incessant itching on her arm, but it made her feel better anyway.

Waiting was torture, giving her mind time to come up with a million questions. At the top of the list were, *What's Alex doing? And why does he need Paco?*

Still, Madison wasn't exactly making a break for the door. Alex had her book and her photo. A photo of her teenage self might have been creepy, but her dad was in the shot.

She thought for a moment. When was the first time she and Alex met? Could it have been a long time ago, with her dad?

Madison needed answers, and so she'd wait it out, come hell or high water. At least, she thought that until Paco began shouting. His words came through loud and clear.

"Have you lost your fucking mind?"

Did Paco just discover something? About Alex?

The remainder of his words were muffled, but his tone was insistent, the sound of someone thoroughly pissed off.

It should have been her tipping point—enough for her to scurry away and never look back. But she had to stay. To get to the bottom of it.

As both men returned, Alex handed her the printed document with fresh signatures.

Madison read it, forcing herself to breathe. Done, she shot a look of disbelief to Alex, then Paco. Perplexed, she looked back to Alex.

Finally, she had the presence of mind to speak. "I'm not sure what to say, but I guess I'm with Paco. Because I'm pretty sure you've lost your fucking mind."

CHAPTER 26

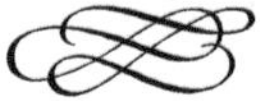

MADISON

The letter bearing today's date read as follows:

To Whom It May Concern,

I, Alex Drake, being of sound mind, do hereby agree that if I ever lie to Madison Taylor, everything I have and everything I own, including my personal and corporate holdings, will immediately and unequivocally be transferred to her for whatever purpose she deems fit.

Signed,

Alex Drake
President and CEO
Drake Global Industries

Witnessed:
Paco Robles

Madison bounced a concerned glance between the two men, then landed her glare on Paco, pouring every bit of *you've got to be kidding* straight at him. He shrugged, raising a *talk to the hand* palm to her face, his expression clearly expressing *don't even start.*

Alex returned to his bended-knee position before her, taking her free hand in both of his. "Madison, I promise you that the book and photo, as strange as it may sound, were given to me. I didn't take them . . . *or* have someone take them for me."

They both glanced at Paco.

"Why are you both looking at me?" Paco puffed up, seeming indignant at the implication. "Hey, these pristinely manicured nails are waaaay above petty theft."

Madison studied Alex's eyes, more confused than ever.

"The bottom line, Madison, is that I can't tell you, at this moment, why I know the things I know or have the things I have, but I promise you it's not what you're thinking . . . whatever you're thinking." Alex caressed her face in his hands, pulling her forehead to his. "I swear, every single thing is on the up-and-up. I just need a little time before I explain . . . and I *will* tell you everything. Please, will you stay?"

Between the warmth of his hands and the desperation in his eyes, Madison contemplated Alex's request for all of thirty seconds. *Yes.* Surprising even herself, her acceptance came out as another question.

"How much time?" she asked cautiously.

"Thirty days. And I'll tell you absolutely everything. All of it."

"Thirty days?" she said, considering his request.

If there was one thing Madison knew, it was people. After years in the service industry, she practically had a sixth sense for knowing who to trust and who to back away from. Her track record was solid.

Beyond a shadow of a doubt and for no reason at all, she trusted Alex Drake. A man she barely knew. But one who apparently trusted her with his home, and possibly the future of his company.

This is crazy.

With a deep breath and a silent prayer, she decidedly threw caution—and maybe common sense—to the wind.

"Okay. Thirty days," she said, acquiescing with a wave of raw emotions as his lips landed on hers in an impassioned kiss.

Interrupting, Paco cleared his throat. "Look, you both seem to have this sorted, so I'm just going to head out." He made a casual stroll to the elevator as Alex called after him.

"Hey," Alex said.

Paco turned back as the doors opened.

"Thank you. And if I didn't mention it earlier, nice earrings."

Grinning, Paco entered the elevator, letting the doors slide shut as he tossed back his defense. "She said I could have them."

CHAPTER 27

MADISON

Grateful at seeing Madison satisfied, at least for the moment, Alex couldn't avoid the direction of his relief. He was charged and more than ready to take her in his arms and never look back. Not like the others.

With any other woman, sex was just a trade-off. He got the no-strings-attached hookups his overactive libido needed, and they got what they wanted. Usually jewelry. Sometimes cash. The occasional gift of a flashy car ended a few of his booty calls.

But there was never intimacy, because Alex could never be intimate without trust. At least never again, a decision he'd made a very long time ago.

No one's getting close.

But Madison was different. He felt it in every fiber of his being and clear to the depths of his soul.

Look at her.

Even with a closet filled to the rafters with high-end jewels, the only piece on her was the extravagant tennis bracelet, and only because Paco had wrapped it around her wrist.

Madison was everything. Brave and honest, regardless of the consequences. Kind. Generous. She endeared herself to him even more, seeming practically oblivious to the fact she had all the makings of the girl next door wrapped up in the appearance of a fucking *Sports Illustrated* model.

She was perfect. In every single way.

Laying one passionate kiss on her lips after another, Alex was so damn grateful that she returned them willingly. Freely. Even passionately and enthusiastically.

His arms embraced her, pulling her tightly against him. Every soft curve of her body begged to be discovered. But a hot meal waited in the next room.

"You hungry?" he asked, stroking her cheek softly with his knuckles.

Madison remained quiet, not saying a word as she shook her head. Her slight smile widened, and the fullness of her lips invited his return. With each of her deep breaths, the rise and fall of her chest was subtle. Seductive. Whatever questions or doubts that remained between them seemed to fade away, leaving room for his lust and her surrender.

She was his.

And he wanted nothing more than to be hers.

Lifting her from the chair, he stood, cradling her in his arms. Making his way to the master bedroom, he was glad she'd be the very first to ever share his bed.

He set her on her knees on the large mattress, skimming a finger down her spine. His tongue pressed through her lips, parting them to explore, tasting her with deep, sweeping strokes.

He stripped off his pants as she tugged free his tie. But as she plucked each button and opened his shirt, his instincts overwhelmed him, forcing his hands around her slight wrists.

She has to stop.

It suddenly occurred to him just how different this would be, taking a woman face-to-face. The last time was over ten years ago. A quick bang from behind always avoided the inevitable questions, or comments, or expressions. No chance of puzzled glances. Or worse, pity.

But Madison was staying. He wanted her—all of her. Could he give all of himself in exchange?

Unable to move, he kept his hands around her wrists, helplessly locked in her gaze.

Smiling, she contemplated him with eyes filled with reassurance. He loosened his grip, and her still restrained hands moved through the unbuttoned portions of his shirt, slowly prying them apart.

She has to see it. See me.

Lightly, her fingers grazed the extensive scars that crossed from one side of his chest to the other. Her smile waned, but her eyes filled with tenderness as she freed another button.

"You want me to trust you?" she asked softly while sliding her hands through his grasp, beating him at his own game. Doing something unexpected.

Cautiously, she traced his wrists with her fingers, using the lesson he'd taught her to circle them and pivot the grasp to her control, sweetly forcing his surrender.

His muscles relaxed. His resistance disappeared. And slowly, he let her lower his arms, taking his hands in hers.

"Then trust me," she said, bringing the palm of his hand to her cheek before nuzzling it and pressing a kiss to his palm. Lovingly, she undid his cufflink. Again, she repeated her soft seduction.

Could he do anything but completely give in?

CHAPTER 28

MADISON

INSTINCTIVELY, Madison understood. Whatever they were about to share would be new and unrivaled. And more beautiful than anything she'd experienced in her life.

In no hurry, she cherished their closeness, taking in his raw emotions and returning a feeling that filled her, spilling out into tender kisses and devouring him with every touch.

With the last button undone, she ran her hands over the firm angles of his abs, delicately moving them across the tight muscles of his chest. Unconcerned, she glided her fingers across his scars, and he let her. Shoving the shirt past his chiseled shoulders, she pushed it away, brushing a soft kiss to his lips as it fell to the floor.

Hooking her finger between his slacks and the heat of his skin, she tugged him closer, undoing his pants and releasing him from the rest of his clothes.

Naked, he stood before her, his chest heaving as he otherwise remained absolutely still. Madison ran her gaze from the angst of his eyes all the way down, taking him in with wonder and awe.

His body was magnificent. Perfect.

She licked her lips, again meeting his eyes in the hopes she could allay whatever negativity might be torturing him inside his head. Fear. Doubt. Hurt. The sliver of self-loathing breaking through. None of it mattered.

Eagerly, she explored him. Her hands drifted here and there over the faded tracks that marked him, before she laid light kisses along his chest, brushing her lips across all of him.

Swiftly, his hand wove through her hair, stopping her. The torment in his eyes melted. His mouth crashed against hers, invading her, his kiss rough and deep, taking her to the very brink with nothing more than his forceful tongue sweeping long strokes through her mouth.

As he tore her dress from her body, she heard the rips as his rushed hands moved carelessly, urgent with need. Still tightening his fist on her hair, he smoothed a strong hand over her sex, cupping it over the soaked wetness of her panties.

Standing before him in only her panties and heels, Madison lost herself in the heat of his touch. She was pulsing with need, ready to come right in his hand if this gorgeous god of a man wasn't careful.

With the lightest lick, he swirled her breast, then sucked in her nipple. As he forced a finger deep inside her, she moaned.

"Oh God."

The tender grip of his teeth on her nipple was too much. Her hips bucked, and she rode the burn of his hand uncontrollably.

Hurriedly, he grabbed a condom from the drawer and tore it free. Even with his finger sweetly fucking her, she needed to taste him first. She kicked off her heels and knelt before him. Sucking him in, she milked him gently with her mouth as she savored the scent and taste that were uniquely his. Satisfied, she took the condom and sheathed him with both hands, rolling it down his thick shaft.

Laying her back, Alex parted her legs, prying them open as he watched her arch, bracing for the pleasure to come. He inched out his finger, sucked it clean, and groaned low. The tip of him, firm and stiff, teased her opening, but he didn't press in.

Instead, he tore free the lace between her legs, tossing it aside as he pinned her down with his weight. The tip of him teased her, gliding back and forth before prying her swollen lips apart.

His thumb circled her sensitive clit, the pressure sending her higher. Panting, she fisted his hair. When he filled his mouth with the fullness of her breast, the sensation nearly sent her over the edge as his finger pushed past her tightness, again plunging deep inside.

"Alex!" She cried out, pleading with her tone as her body writhed beneath him. Desperate, she arched her back and wrapped her legs around him, ready to take absolutely everything this man had to give.

He teased her by withdrawing his finger, tracing her slick folds up and down with his shaft, forcing her to buck, begging shamelessly as she chased his cock with need and determination.

Finally, he pushed inside. As he shoved in every bit of his length, the air was forced from her lungs in a staggered cry. His width stretched her as he fucked her over and over, sweetly driving himself deeper.

Her wet folds engulfed him, the euphoria closing in on her as he shoved in to the hilt. With his thumb rubbing circles into her clit, her body rocked with him, clinging to every sensation as his lips seared her neck and shoulders. She sucked her own wetness from his lips as his mouth met hers. Then he pulled out.

"Please, Alex . . ."

The second she opened her eyes enough to meet his dark gaze, he sank deep inside her, splitting her wide in one swift move.

"Yes!" she cried as his cock tore through her.

Driving in and out, he hit her spot over and over until her nipples tightened painfully and her body shuddered. He wrecked her with each cruel pass, speeding up in a way that brought her to the brink before he slowed, settling her in a quiet ache only long enough to catch her breath.

Again, he pulled out, leaving just enough to cover his crown in her folds and slickness. Ready to finish the job herself, Madison had barely grazed the swollen lips of her pussy with her fingers when he yanked her arm high over her head, stretching her quivering body drenched in a sheen of sweat.

Her eyes met his dark, hungry gaze before his body crashed around her, tearing her into a thousand blissful pieces as he raced to a relentless rhythm.

"Now," he commanded, his voice low and stern as he rode her senseless and back again. "Come for me, Madison."

Her body erupted, obeying his gruff demand.

Alex jolted, his own climax catapulting her to the stratosphere as a second wave rushed through her, instantly tingling every nerve and filling her vision with clusters of stars. Her body shuddered as her walls tightened around him.

His mouth engulfed hers, muffling her raspy cries as he suckled her tongue and shattered her to oblivion.

Deep inside, she could feel him, pulsing desperately to empty all of himself inside her. Her muscles spasmed around him, milking him of everything he could give. With a final thrust, he pushed her beyond any fears or doubts, making her body light and her mind free until nothing else mattered.

I am his.

~

Side by side, Madison and Alex lay panting in the dark, holding hands. She was spent in every way. Physically. Emotionally. Her body was heavy and exhausted.

Alex took a deep breath and pulled her hand to his lips, brushing his mouth against her fingers before laying a kiss on her lips. "You sure you're not hungry? I could bring the food in here."

She shook her head, weaving her fingers tighter through his. "Alex, whatever it is you have to tell me, you can. I won't judge you."

Releasing a deep breath, he rolled to his back. She watched as he gazed at the ceiling, lost for a moment in thought. She followed, rolling herself on him, tangling her leg between his and laying soft kisses along his chest before nuzzling her head into his neck.

Softly, he stroked her hair, running his hands through it and down to the small of her back. Contented, he rested it there. With a kiss to her head, he began to speak.

"I'm guessing Paco spent the afternoon giving you a few lessons. Well, here's a lesson he taught me a long time ago." Pulling her hand to his lips, he kissed it, then clasped it to his chest. "Never make a promise you're not sure you can keep."

Madison's brow tightened as she took this in.

He's worried I'll judge him. Did he do something wrong? How wrong? Was it illegal? Immoral?

And what if he's right? What if I can't keep from judging him?

But she remained silent in the dark, thinking through what he'd said, certain that if Alex listened hard enough, he'd hear every wheel turn in her mind. And a lot of wheels were turning, spinning out of control with question after question.

A second later, Alex surprised her with a subdued chuckle that grew to a loud laugh.

Dumbfounded, she shot him a confused glare. "What?"

"So, do you remember our first encounter?"

Perplexed, Madison gave him a blank stare, her curiosity piqued. "No."

"Well, it's part of the reason we're together, but not all of it."

His quiet smirk was adorable. Intriguing.

Patiently, she waited for him to continue. Instead, he pulled his hands back neatly behind his head, seemingly satisfied to plant a seed with just enough water to grow.

"And?" Madison said hopefully.

"*And*, I have thirty days. You agreed. We sealed it with a kiss. And then some." He planted a small peck on her growing pout. Whispering to her lips, he said, "That's it for now."

"That's it?" Equally amused and annoyed, Madison asked, "Has anyone ever told you you're a tease?"

Grinning, he peered at her from the corner of his eye. "I've always wondered how to keep a drop-dead gorgeous woman in suspense. Now I know."

Flipping her willing body onto her back, he managed to draw a giggle from her as he gently rested his body on hers. For the moment, he quelled her light irritation with a kiss, melting every one of her emotions into pure submission.

This man will be the death of me.

Staring seriously into her eyes, he said, "Thirty days gives us time to get to know each other. But during that time, I want you to feel at home. Really at home. Have anything you desire at your beautiful little fingertips." He took each of her fingers to his lips, kissing them one by one.

Crinkling her nose, she shot him a look of pure determination. "Well, it might seem like a long time to be in suspense, but I'm not going to be distracted by all this glitz and glamour," she said, exuding a hard-core, take-no-prisoners demeanor. Insistent, she handed him the terms. "You have exactly thirty days, Mr. Drake."

Warmly, he kissed her again. "Thirty days." He saluted smartly, then continued. "I won't let you down, Ms. Taylor."

You'd better not, Alex Drake.

And with that, they began another round of consummating their month-long deal.

BOOK 2: EXPOSED

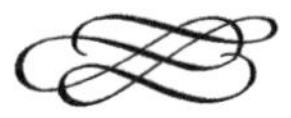

AN ALEX DRAKE NOVEL

EXPOSED
AN ALEX DRAKE NOVEL
LEXXI JAMES

CHAPTER 1

MADISON

Madison caught the sly tone in her best friend's knowing voice. Sheila might be a reporter for the *New York Times*, but today her investigative skills were focused on getting the goods on Madison—her best friend and soon-to-be maid of honor.

Patiently, Sheila skated her finger along the rim of her half-consumed latte, her eyes dancing with anticipation as she waited.

Making a casual turn away, Madison focused on scanning the city streets from their perch at the corner café. Avoiding Sheila's see-right-through-you eye contact at all costs was pretty much impossible with the superhuman weight of her stare.

Madison shrugged, her lips breaking the leaf-decorated foam of her cappuccino as she savored an extra-long sip from the oversize mug. "I'm not sure what you mean."

"Right," Sheila drawled. As if ready to expose a cover-up, the diligent reporter leaned in. "Sure. The ridiculous smiling. The pep in your step. The glowing skin. I get it. You want to keep it on the down low. But you know that sooner or later, I'll figure out who he is."

Undoubtedly, Sheila was right. Always accurate in reading Madison's deepest thoughts, it didn't help that Sheila was a legitimate bloodhound when it came to sniffing out the truth. And keeping secrets was the last thing Madison wanted.

But sharing her secret with anyone, let alone an up-and-coming reporter like Sheila, was completely out of the question.

With a meditative breath, Madison let Sheila attempt her Jedi mind tricks, maintaining a stoic poker face. Madison rarely kept things from her best friend, and she knew Sheila was probably putting two and two together as they sat. With where Madison worked and how long she'd been floating on air, perhaps she was naive to think her new relationship with her boss would stay under wraps. But if Sheila figured it out on her own, it was fair game.

"Wait!" Sheila bounced in her chair, the riddle solved. "Holy shit, I get it. I know your big secret. You're dating . . ."

Madison sucked in a deep breath, ready for Alex Drake's name to fall from Sheila's lips. If Sheila connected the dots, Madison couldn't possibly deny it. Not convincingly, anyway. Instead, she braced for impact, her head already in an anticipatory nod of agreement before Sheila finished her sentence.

"A woman."

"Yes . . . *what?*" Madison's shy smile and modest blush vanished as she mentally repeated the last few lines of their conversation. *Did I just acknowledge being in a relationship with a woman?*

As Madison's head quickly shifted from nodding to shaking, Sheila's tone was reassuring.

"Look, if you're not ready to come out, I'm a vault. But really, we'd all be good with it." As Madison clasped her hands and placed her elbows on the table, leaning forward to correct the misunderstanding, Sheila piled her hands on top. "We're happiest when you're happy, and you're obviously happy."

Madison weighed the cards she held. On one hand, if she protested, Sheila and their other friends would just keep pestering her for her new significant other's identity. And it wasn't as if Alex had urged her to keep it under wraps. He hadn't.

If anything, he'd always made suggestions for them to go out. In public. Where absolutely anyone and everyone could see them. Together.

Just the thought made Madison's arms itch, but she resisted the urge to scratch. The truth was, she just wasn't ready to share this secret. Instead, she held it close, preserving the precious revelation like cherishing a wish in the seconds before blowing out the candles of a birthday cake.

On the other hand, perhaps playing along was the path of least resistance.

Satiated for the moment, her friends would at least give her some breathing space. The ploy would buy a little time to get to know Alex better. In private.

And it wouldn't be an outright lie, would it? Madison didn't exactly say she was dating a woman. Sheila did. Madison could just, well, conveniently not deny it.

Tugging her hands delicately away like a Jenga piece, she gave her friend a smile.

"Well, um . . . I'm not saying I'm with a woman," she said, and Sheila blinked at her in confusion. "And I'm not saying I'm with a man . . . um . . . in particular." Madison's answer was becoming so tangled, she started confusing herself.

"So, you're not with anyone?" With a suspicious squint and lifted brow, Sheila took a slow sip of her drink.

Madison swallowed the lump in her throat, desperate to mask her every tell. Was it working?

As if sensing her uncertainty, Sheila stared back, studying Madison and searching her eyes for a clue to the truth.

I hate lying. Not just because it's deceptive and wrong, but because I suck at it.

Could she backpedal without tripping up? "Perhaps it's best I leave it at that."

"Leave it at what?" Sheila strummed her fingers on the table until she froze and her eyes lit up with enthusiasm. "Oh, you're *curious.*"

Sheila's slow, assured nod nearly convinced Madison to go ahead and confess. But she resisted. Wanting to avoid another ride on this merry-go-round of a guessing game, Madison decided to settle into her new label. At least for the time being.

I mean, it's true. By nature, I am a curious person. Sheila obviously inferred Madison's bi-curious status. *But that's not what I said.*

Newly attuned to the fine print, Madison spoke carefully. "I'm curious in general, sure." Her reply sounded much more like a question than a statement, but she went with it.

Squealing with delight, Sheila caught herself. Knocking her enthusiasm down half a peg, she leaned in closer. "Hey, I get it. I've dabbled in, you know, curiosity."

Choking on her froth, Madison widened her eyes, panicked that Sheila was undoubtedly ready to unburden herself with a rich assortment of endless and highly detailed visual descriptions.

Luckily, the waiter broke in. *Thank God.*

"Ladies, can I get you anything else?" Swooping between the two of them, he cleared the emptied plates.

Relieved, Madison breathed her sigh through a smile, never imagining how thankful she'd be for an interruption to girl talk. "Sheila, I've really got to get back to work." Reaching for her latest Hermès clutch, she pulled out the matching wallet, prepared to pay the bill.

"No, no, no, girl. This one's on me," Sheila said, handing the waiter cash. "No change, thanks."

"Thank *you*, ma'am," he said, delighted with the fat tip as he carried the neat stack of plates and cups away.

Both ladies stood. Madison stepped over, not fully prepared for Sheila's sweeping hug, which lingered as she happily rocked Madison to and fro before leaning back.

"And if you ever need to talk with someone who's, you know, been *there*," Sheila glanced at their crotches, "I'm here for you."

Madison followed Sheila's eye movements before snapping hers shut, desperate to kill whatever image might intrude into her thoughts. *That which has been thought can't be un-thought.*

"Okay, then," Madison said hesitantly. "I do so appreciate that, girl. Well, gotta run."

Madison checked her ten-carat diamond bracelet as if it were a watch, intent on scampering away. Extricating herself from the warm hug, she turned to head off, propelled faster with the light smack of Sheila's hand on her ass.

"You do you, girl!" Sheila called out a little too loudly for Madison's comfort. "And bring whoever you want to the wedding."

Madison waved back awkwardly, lowering her head while letting her thick tresses drape over her burning cheeks as she headed down the street.

As she approached the towering skyscraper that housed Drake Global Industries' New York City headquarters, she marveled at how her life had become an unbelievable whirlwind over the past few weeks. The dinners. The shopping. The traveling. It was overwhelming, but she'd done her best to take every bit of the opulence in stride.

Alex Drake had money. That much was clear. But as strange as it sounded, the lavish lifestyle this billionaire could afford her wasn't nearly as appealing as the man himself.

It was hard not to be a fangirl in his presence, but Madison cherished every here-and-there opportunity to get to know the reclusive man better. Those moments weren't showy or lavish, and they meant everything. How he managed to make mundane, everyday life feel new and magical was beyond her.

He adored her as no one had, as if she were the first woman to really be in his life. *And maybe I am.* But was there a reason for that? She tamped down her anxiety as much as she could, but it stubbornly remained in the back of her mind, threatening to come front and center at the slightest bump in the road of their relationship.

And as much as their blossoming relationship was wonderful, it was all so private. Extremely private. It wasn't as if they'd signed a nondisclosure agreement or anything, but neither of them pressed the other too hard to shout their relationship from the rooftops.

Madison wasn't eager to go public. She knew her credibility might fly out the window at DGI if water-cooler gossip hit the halls about her personal relationship with the boss. And Alex just seemed contented to keep her all to himself. Who could blame him?

And if things between them detoured from happily-ever-after, not only his image, but DGI's as well, might suffer an unintended consequence or two. Or a million. On top of which, their relationship was all so new. Only a few weeks.

Now, by the calendar of public opinion, some might argue this alone was more than impressive. It represented an Alex Drake Olympic-level world record. A notorious bachelor and womanizer, a Drake month of dating might as well be a dog year.

But worst of all, there was the secrecy. Maybe *secrecy* was too strong a term, but why was he waiting to tell her "everything else," as he put it?

What else is there? And what's with the book? And the photo? Or how we met? Or the whole making myself "at home" in his lap of luxury?

She'd noticed the novel *The Count of Monte Cristo* in his penthouse home, an inscribed gift many years ago from her grandpa Mike. Why would Alex have it? And the mysterious photo of her as a bright-eyed teen in one of the last moments with her dad before her parents' divorce. Why couldn't she remember it?

Shocking revelations had been piling up, kept just out of reach. When Madison demanded answers, Alex gave none. None in that moment, and none for the next month. But in thirty days, she'd have all her answers. All she had to do was stick around. And in a show of good faith, he handed her a contract. One she couldn't refuse.

I, Alex Drake, being of sound mind, do hereby agree that if I ever lie to Madison

Taylor, everything I have and everything I own, including my personal and corporate holdings, will immediately and unequivocally be transferred to her for whatever purpose she deems fit.

Obviously, the man was insane. And just like that, Madison had moved in with him. How could she not? Because they were a perfect match—her crazy to his insanity. Could he possibly know he was the first man she'd ever lived with?

Normally, she'd have towering emotional walls built high around herself, preventing anyone from getting too close. Always protecting herself from a life where loss was inevitable. But with Alex, there were no walls. She'd eased into his life with cozy familiarity and had never been so comfortable. So at home. It should really bother her, but it didn't. At least, not enough for her to leave.

I'm falling. Hard. For a man I barely know. Which makes me certifiable. Possibly idiotic. But the thirty days I promised him are nearly up, so ready or not, answers are coming.

Despite all the other questions that pelted her mind daily, none of these was the most significant. The biggest remained the undisputed heavyweight question of all time.

Why me?

As quickly as these questions arose day in and day out, Madison just as persistently whack-a-moled them down. Per their agreement, all her answers were only a few days away. With that, she opted to focus instead on the monster of a question at hand.

Sheila's wedding was right around the corner. Madison was the maid of honor, and a plus-one would be required. The question of the hour danced through her mind.

Should I bring a man, or a woman?

CHAPTER 2

MADISON

Fidgeting, Madison stood as solemnly as possible in front of her boss's desk, desperate to keep a straight face.

"Let me get this straight." Alex sat at his desk, resting his elbows comfortably on the arms of his custom-made leather chair as his fingers steepled to his chin. A cocky-ass smirk spread across his face, drawing out a smile of her own that Madison couldn't hide. "You want to date a woman?"

"No!" she exclaimed, rolling her eyes at his misunderstanding.

"Oh, you just want to dip your *toe* in to test the waters. Or is this more of a *plunge* into the deep end?" Exaggerating a swan dive with one hand, he slid the fingers into the grip of the other, then suggestively pushed his fingers in and out of the clasped hole.

Madison shook her head, ignoring the heat his provocative miming stirred beneath her skirt. Sure, she was annoyed—more at herself than at Alex. Mostly because she couldn't hold back a laugh, no matter how she tried.

When Alex stood up, straightening and buttoning his blazer in that completely normal and sexier than hell way he always did, she bit her lip. He strolled around his desk to her, and her breath hitched as his warm and somewhat patriarchal hand landed her shoulder.

His expression somber, he cleared his throat. "Seriously, I support you. And if you need an innocent bystander to walk you through the delicate intricacies of pleasuring a woman, well . . . count me in." His selfless offer and cheesy grin were incorrigible.

God, he's such a man.

But he wasn't done. Lifting her hands, he held them against his chest. "Whatever you need, just name it." His deep tone coupled with those mesmerizing eyes somehow always made him less annoying and more adorable.

And don't even get me started on that boyish naughty grin.

Pulling her close, he lightly rubbed her nose with his. A delicate peck on her lips came next, which led to the most irresistible kisses down her neck.

"Well, there is *something* I need," Madison said, trying not to submit completely to Alex's intoxicating advances. *Though my panties are melted to oblivion.*

"Mm-hmm. Name it, you kinky little vixen." Alex made his way lower, rumbling out a delighted moan as he left a trail of searing kisses between her breasts. Cupping her fullness from the outside, he pressed her cleavage to his softly whiskered face.

Madison's breathing stuttered, partially from the touch of his lips rubbing across her décolletage, but mostly from the butterflies filling her stomach. "I need . . ."

"Yes? What do you need?" His tone was low and deep as he stood tall again, his hands making their way to the round curve of her ass, pulling her into him. His firm erection pressed against her skirt, coaxing her core and making her wetter by the second.

"I need a date for the wedding, but . . ." Exasperated, Madison let out a breath, averting her eyes. Her gaze dropped to his desk, seeing the penny she'd left weeks ago still in place. The heads-up coin stared back at her, reminding her to stay true to her feelings while guilting the hell out of her. She struggled to finish her sentence.

Alex pulled back, ducking his head down just enough to catch her gaze. Again, she tried looking away. His fingers lifted her chin, encouraging her eyes to meet his.

"But?"

A slow sigh escaped her lips, releasing a buildup of low, continuous pressure she'd been holding in.

"But I'm not sure we're ready for a public appearance." Searching his eyes, she forced out the last of her words. "Are you?"

With a fresh set of those damn nervous hives prickling up her arm, Madison waited, apprehension filling her as she waited for his reply.

CHAPTER 3

MADISON

Nervous anticipation hung in the air between them as Alex took his time giving her an answer. Too much time.

But, what if he actually wanted to go to the wedding with me? *Could I bring him? Would I bring him?*

The fame of Alex Drake's impressive corporate climb and financial status only slightly paled in comparison to his notorious womanizing. Those juicy topics would undoubtedly cause continuous gossip during the wedding reception, most likely overshadowing the wedding itself.

Topping it all was their relationship. A magical combination of attraction, seduction, romance, and even that elusive concept—trust. A show of trust handed to her on a silver platter by an irresistible man offering an insane contract.

It was a huge leap of faith—moving in with him, falling for him, a man she barely knew. What she did know about him was that Alex Drake was convincing. She could have anything and everything at her fingertips, and he asked nothing in return except to take a month to get to know him better.

Nothing to lose. Except maybe my heart.

Despite trying to get to know Alex better, she only saw the things he let her see. Aspects of the man still eluded her, a side of himself or his past that he seemed reluctant to share. It kept him isolated. Shielded.

What's thirty days anyway?

Agreeing to wait a month for an explanation almost seemed trivial. But now she couldn't fight her curiosity. She needed to know what he meant when he referred to "the first time they met," some incident that despite her best efforts, she couldn't recall. She was also dying to know about the parts of him that stayed hidden. And everything else.

Those were his exact words. *Everything else.*

They echoed through Madison's mind, worming their way through her thoughts until nearly consuming her. Then that minute would pass and she could think of something else. Like Sheila's wedding.

With a deep breath, Alex swept a few wispy strands from Madison's face, studying her as she waited for his take on whether to take their relationship public. She looked up at him, unable to smooth the creases in her brow. If his walls were up, hers would be up too.

"I understand," he said so convincingly, she almost caved. "So, I get to keep you all to myself?" Scooping both her hands in his, he kissed each before pulling them to his chest. "I'm the luckiest man alive."

Ah, the dreaded diversionary tactic. I know it well.

Without much more leverage on whether they were taking their relationship public or not, Madison had two choices. She could either confront him outright about his thoughts on the matter, or she had to let it go. The awkward silence that followed made her reluctantly opt for the latter.

Giving her a peck, Alex offered a suggestion. "Hey, if you want to go down the path of bi-curiosity, I'll bet Gina knows someone who would love to be your *date,*" he said, lifting his eyebrows and grinning devilishly. "Fancy night out, free food, maybe some heavy petting after a few drinks."

Playfully, Madison smacked his arm, pretending not to be annoyed at him. "Not exactly what I had in mind."

"Just offering suggestions. Can't a boy dream?" Alex gave her a mischievous look.

Madison gave him a pout that always had the opposite effect than intended. "Alex, I'm not taking a woman as my date, no matter how convenient it might be. I'm straight and I'm proud," she said, staunchly drawing a line in the sand.

Leaning in for a nuzzle of her neck, he murmured, "And don't I know it."

She made a feeble attempt to push him away before welcoming his advances. But before she could get swept away in the undertow of his passion, she stopped him, pressing her palm to his chest. "Wait, do you have time?"

He gave her a perplexed frown. "I thought that's why you dropped by during my one free spot today. Don't you have access to my calendar?"

"No," she said, nearly adding *crazy head* to the end of that sentence. Of course she didn't have access to his calendar. The man was a multibillionaire. A mogul. Obviously, his calendar was private.

Alex pulled away for an instant, tapping out a few effortless keystrokes at his computer before devoting his attention back to her. "You do now. Complete access." His lips were on hers before she could object. "And I've cleared my calendar."

The heat of his lips left a trail of seductive prints across her skin that cooled much too quickly for her liking, and the steady pooling between her legs promised a full surrender.

Softly, his lips brushed hers as his fingers made their way down her back to her skirt, then traced the tantalizing line separating her butt from her thigh, causing a shiver. That seductive finger worked slowly across her leg to the front. There, it lingered at her center, drawing lazy circles beneath her short, flowing skirt.

There was no keeping that man away from her newly moistened panties. He lightly stroked his patient fingers back and forth across her mound, until her wetness saturated the expensive silk undies she'd worried were too pretty to wear.

I can't confront him now. He's using his secret weapons to distract me. His touch. His warm breath on my skin. The Empire State Building hiding in his pants. This man knows my weaknesses. The biggest one being him.

Her head fell back but her gaze stayed on him. The heat of his hand was on her chest, and by the smile on his lips, the way her breathing raised and lowered her cleavage seemed to be to his satisfaction.

The steady ringing of his desk phone barely interrupted the pulsing of his fingers with its distinctive chime. Though the phone stopped briefly, it rang again. Simultaneously, his cell phone cut in with the ping of an incoming text.

"It might be important," Madison whispered.

"The hell it is." Alex softly growled, sliding his finger from the outside of her panties to beneath, taking his time enjoying the hot dew coating his fingertip.

Undeterred, he worked up and down her slickness, massaging her soaked folds before pushing a thick finger deep within her core. Her loud gasp couldn't be contained.

As her body rested against his other large hand across her back, he steadied her, letting her body relax and respond. His rigid finger pulled back and pushed in, over and over, as his thumb made its way to her clit, desperate for his touch. Her body rocked in his hold, chasing every touch against her needy, wanting core.

He pressed his tongue through her lips, both muffling her whimpers and enticing her to suck. The ringing started again, as did the text pings from the cell deep in his pants pocket. She had no complaints about the delicious vibration accompanying his solid cock against her sex, but the distracting tone was annoying.

Slowly, his fingers pulled out and his lips were off hers, but instead of letting her go, he pulled her in, scooping her up in an instant straddle around him. Effortlessly, he whisked her to his high-back leather executive chair, seating her gently in the worn comfort of it.

Finally, his cell phone rang. Alex snatched it from his pocket, his gaze fixed on Madison, his expression fervent and hungry but his tone businesslike and controlled. "I'm busy."

His calm words caused her to bite the smile from her lower lip.

He held the phone pressed to his ear, listening while he stroked Madison's thigh. One after the other, he lifted each of her legs over the armrests, and she let him as the silky fabric of her skirt fell away. His front-row view of her plump, ready pussy didn't make her shy. Eagerly, she watched his gaze darken. As his lips took a turn for the naughty, nothing mattered but pleasing him— right here, right now.

Her eyes widened as he knelt before her spread-open legs. Phone in hand, he silently lapped up her sweetness, not bothering to mute the line.

Madison let out a gasp as quietly as possible, hearing a muffled voice coming through the phone. Her master of multitasking emerged with her wetness glistening on his lips and chin.

Alex spoke into the phone with a deep, raspy voice, fixing his eyes on Madison's. "I'll come when I'm good and ready," he said before hanging up.

Finally.

Pocketing the phone, he returned to bury his face between her legs, his stubble rough against the tender skin of her inner thighs. In a long sweep, his tongue sliced into her, jolting her to cry out as quietly as she could. Desperate, she reached over her head, grabbing the headrest and using her strength to pull up just enough to spread her legs wider. Madison needed more, longing for him to fill her eager, aching core.

He took his time running his tongue back and forth before twisting it through her tightening walls. After a few lashes along her smooth crevice, he lifted his gaze, admiring her face as her heavy lids batted back.

"*Now* I'm good and ready," he growled, manipulating the chair to a recline.

He pulled a condom from his pocket, setting it on the desk next to that heads-up penny. She watched, hungering as he unfastened his belt, loosened his pants, and slipped them and his silk boxers to the floor. He wasn't exaggerating on that call. Every hard inch of him was ready.

Madison licked her lips, slid herself higher on the chair, and braced for his thick, heavy cock to press inside, stretch her walls, and make her his.

Alex leaned over her, first working two fingers through her wet tightness while circling her throbbing clit with his insanely talented thumb. She sucked in her lower lip and gently bit, breathing through the silent scream and panting as he unleashed his sweet torture.

"But they're waiting for you, and it's probably a huge deal," Madison said with a husky moan.

Alex lowered his head, groaning low in her ear. "Why, Ms. Taylor, are you referring to what I've got in store for you? Because I can't wait to present my huge deal to you."

With her breathing ragged and erratic, Madison struggled to speak. When his fingers slipped to just the right spot, her back arched and her body quaked under the attention of his controlled, intense movements.

"The, uh, business deal," she stammered out as reasonably and logically as possible, with what was sure to be a mind-blowing orgasm taking hold. "I—I know it's important."

But, oh my God, I'm close.

Close, but knowing Alex the way a girlfriend of about a month did, Madison was certain he wouldn't send her over like this. Not without him.

His hungry gaze was everywhere. The flush of her cheeks. The rise and fall of her chest. The lust in her eyes. But his rhythm didn't change. And it wouldn't. Not until he was ready.

"They're early. When they want ten million of my dollars, they can fucking wait. I've got a bigger priority," he said, slowly withdrawing his fingers to make way for his seeping rod.

He took barely a second to roll on the condom before burying himself inside her. She struggled for air as he pulled back out, then shoved every inch into her. She'd been desperate for that pleasure.

Laying his body over hers, Alex quickened his thrusts. His lips brushed hers, then across her neck until his breath was in her ear.

"I need you to come for me, Madison," he said in a low, gruff tone. A tone that carried her through each hard new thrust. "You can take all the sweet time you need."

His words set her on fire as an electrifying shiver raced across her body. She might have been able to hold out a short while longer, but his growled desire for her orgasm ignited something deep within her. Her body yielded to please him.

He pumped faster, timing his rhythm to the erotic circles his thumb made around her clit. Even when her pussy shuddered and her walls tightened around his thick cock, he kept going, bringing her to an even higher peak as he nibbled the sensitive skin on her neck.

Low, Alex demanded, "Now."

Her pussy shuddered, spasming tightly around his cock as her orgasm swept over her.

"Yes, Madison, yes."

She whimpered seductively, urging him on, and when he covered her mouth with his, she sucked on his tongue. Her wetness was still fresh, making her moan as she sucked. The fullness of his cock hit her everywhere as his body exploded in a series of husky sounds and forceful jolts.

He pulled back from her lips, both of them gasping. Catching his breath, he whispered, "You're the only woman I want, Madison. The only woman I will ever want."

Maybe it's the tender kisses he always gives me afterward. Or the way he says my name. Or maybe it's me, being shattered into a million blissful pieces and unable to fully pull myself together again. Whatever the reason, I believe him.

After a few minutes' rest, she looked into his eyes, gently stroking the dampness of his hair. "Should I slip out the back?"

Alex breathed out a light chuckle. "With me still inside you? I think that might draw a bit of attention." Resting his forehead on hers, he kissed her sweetly, then the sadist agonizingly pulled away.

Filling her lungs with a deep breath, Madison smiled as she undid herself from her spread-eagle yoga pose. Alex ducked into his office washroom as Madison sat up. Dizzy, she stayed seated for a moment, straightening her clothes as she scanned the floor. When Alex returned, he tapped her shoulder.

"Looking for these?" he said, teasing her while dangling a pair of panties from his sinfully talented finger. Before she could snatch them back, his hand closed around them as he whipped them away. "I need a distraction during the exhaustive meeting I'm about to start. These will at least make the day bearable. And I can use them to wipe my tears when I transfer ten million dollars to this startup," he said, dabbing his eyes with her panties before pulling them to his nose for a naughty inhale. A hum of pleasure vibrated from his chest as he savored her scent.

Before she could reach for them again, he pushed them in his breast pocket, an impromptu, crotch-up pocket square. Madison tucked them in a little deeper, smiling in flattered amusement. His strong hands cupped her face as he kissed her, melting her one last time.

As Madison made her way to Alex's private elevator, she was a little surprised when he waltzed in behind her. "Are you following me?" she asked coyly as she swiped her access card, selecting one floor down.

"To the ends of the earth."

This man will be the death of me.

He cupped her cheek, then caressed her neck as he held a kiss to her lips while the doors closed, then reopened a few seconds later.

"About the wedding," he said, holding her hand as she stepped off the car and turned. "Whatever you want, I'll make it happen. Just wish it."

The elevator doors shut on her handsome admirer, and Madison's smile vanished. Desperately, she wished for the one thing—the only thing—she wanted from him.

I wish I knew what you're keeping from me.

CHAPTER 4

MADISON

HAVING LOST part of her morning to the man with the boyish charm and sinful hands, Madison bellied up to her computer, ready to roll up her sleeves and jump into work. But an email from Alex was all it took to distract her again.

As her heart thumped and butterflies fluttered, she opened it. The automatic text had her biting her lip.

ALEX DRAKE, CEO, INVITES YOU TO SHARE HIS CALENDAR

Madison couldn't possibly accept, but she couldn't *not* accept. He'd know, because important people like him always knew.

Despite her reluctance and apprehension, she tapped the RETURN key, not realizing the system would launch today's schedule as soon as she did that. Ready to click the little *x* in the upper right corner to close the view, she found herself staring at one entry in particular.

SAMANTHA. EXECUTIVE SUITE 5010

Madison blinked at the screen, trying not to make too much of it. But the meeting was private, marked with a little lock. Did he mean to give her full access?

It's fine. He meets with lots of people.

But all the other entries included the nature of the meeting. This one had nothing but a woman's name and a vacant executive suite that was only used for out-of-town VIPs who needed a desk.

Instantly, Madison called the only person who could give her perspective.

"Hey, girl," Madison heard along with a million clicks of typing through the phone.

"Hi, Sheila. I need to ask you a question. One of my colleagues is seeing someone—"

The typing stopped. "Oh, this is gonna be good. Cheating, right?"

"What makes you say that?"

"Because it's my freaking specialty."

Ignoring the comment, Madison pressed on. "Anyway, she found a suspicious meeting with another woman on his calendar."

"Uh-huh," Sheila said, taking that all-too-familiar tone of *I know where this is going.* "How did your colleague *accidentally* access his calendar?"

Confident, Madison said, "It wasn't an accident. He gave her access. Which he obviously wouldn't do if he was hitting it with someone else, right?"

"And this is why I always say men do this to themselves. Dumbass."

It took all Madison's willpower not to defend her man in that moment.

"Let's give the man the benefit of the doubt," Sheila said. *Yes. Perfect. Exactly what we should do.* "How long have they been dating?"

Sheepishly, Madison muttered, "Not long," as her head fell to her hand.

"Well, how long have they known each other?"

"Um . . ." This wasn't looking good. "They kind of . . . sort of . . ."

"Just met. Got it. What's the name of the other woman?"

"Just to be clear, we don't know that she is *the other* woman." Madison reread the entry. "The appointment is with Samantha. Why?"

"No reason. But *Samantha* sounds sexy. And where's the meeting?"

"In an office."

"Mm-hmm."

"Don't salivate. This isn't a story. Just a colleague looking for advice."

"I only salivate when I know I'm on the right track. It's sort of why I love my job."

Madison sucked in a breath, regretting the question before it left her lips. "What would you do . . . if it were you?"

"Maddi, let me get this straight. You're asking an investigative reporter what she would do when confronted with a situation ripe with the overwhelming stank of suspicion?" Letting the silence sink in, Sheila huffed. "Need I say more?"

"No," Madison said, deflated.

"Besides, she could drop by. If she works in the building, there's no harm in stretching her legs, right?"

"I guess not." Madison could easily rationalize the harmless break to get away from her screen.

"Any chance of a front-row seat? I could even grab my camera, snap some shots. Maybe this guy will think twice when his face is plastered all over social media as a cheater cheater, pumpkin eater."

Still protective for reasons she couldn't explain, Madison said, "Sorry, girl. She sort of wants to tackle it alone."

"Just let her know. Keying a car is an actual crime. And my way is so much more satisfying."

"Sage advice." *And a hard pass. On both accounts.*

"Anytime. Oh, my editor's coming. Gotta run. Later."

"'Bye." Madison sank back into her chair to think about it. She clicked the *x* in the upper right corner, closing Alex's calendar, but still saw the words in her mind's eye as clear as day.

The discouraging fact was that she barely knew Alex. She had to be smart. Do this, or always wonder about it.

I'll just walk by.

Saying a silent prayer that she was blowing this whole meeting with Sexy Samantha out of proportion, she waited until the indicated time and began her own investigation. Sticking with a leisurely, casual stride, she headed down the halls of DGI, straight for a room with the door closed and the glass walls frosted. Or mostly frosted.

After a minute of surveillance, she discovered a discreet place to peer through a small strip of the glass wall that was transparent. The problem? It was big enough that anyone inside the room looking that way would see her. And yet it wasn't enough of a deterrent to stop her.

Wide-eyed, Madison wasn't sure what to make of it. There was Alex. And apparently, there was Samantha.

Madison had to admit that Samantha *was* sexy. Seated with her luxurious locks spilling from a ponytail, the woman had both her hands in Alex's, and all Madison could do was watch.

CHAPTER 5

MADISON

WITH WIDE EYES and her palms pressed to the cool glass, Madison studied the two, having no idea what to make of it.

Alex sat at the small round conference table. Not wearing his blazer and with his sleeves rolled up, he seemed to be in a serious conversation. One that apparently involved tremendous amounts of support from Sexy Samantha. And hand holding.

After another minute of watching their discussion and having zero luck with reading lips, Madison's eyes widened as Alex jumped up from his seat. Charged with excitement, he raked both hands through his hair as he spoke with a booming voice.

Unconcerned but attentive, Samantha didn't react or seem overly concerned with his outburst or his sudden sporadic pacing. Having spent whatever emotions he had on the moment, he returned to his seat and back to Samantha.

With a keen eye, Madison studied the two.

Were they working? Were they friends? Perhaps they were friends. Which would explain how Samantha maintained a charmed smile during his outburst. And how her words could soothe him, convincing him to relax back in his seat. The whole hand-rubbing thing she was doing could be considered sweet.

Or seductive.

Or maybe I've got to stop asking Sheila for advice.

Determined, Madison shook her head, pressing her ear hard against the glass. She was barely able to make out two words.

"Not enough."

What wasn't enough?

Was it about work? Or them? Is there a "them"?

Alex and Samantha's ongoing conversation was fairly uneventful. Even boring. No *gotcha* or *aha* moments. For that matter, it looked like a friendly conversation that could have happened any number of places in the building, such as the lobby. A conference room. Alex's office.

Why here?

Madison looked up and down the halls. Only then did it occur to her that no one else had passed by. This wing was quiet. In fact, it seemed mostly vacant, safe from prying eyes.

Well, except Madison's.

This is ridiculous.

Before she could step away and return to her real work of the day, Alex stood. He rolled down his sleeves and checked his watch, the meeting suddenly over. That's when Samantha stood too, then wrapped her arms around him for a hug.

Despite the flush overtaking her cheeks, the erratic pounding in her chest, or her feet being half a step from bolting, Madison took half a breath. Then a full one. This hug was happening, but nothing else. No hand on the butt. No boob grab. Not the remotest sign of a kiss.

Sexy Samantha had gone out of her way to give what could be perfectly described as a bro-hug. Barely leaning in. Ass out. Pat to the upper back. No contact whatsoever with anything south of the equator. Samantha kept the hug brisk and deliberate, backing away with a polite smile and a fair amount of distance. A far cry from first base.

Madison was ready with a *friend zone* ruling until they opened the door. His voice low, Alex said, "I'd walk you out, but you know how it is."

"Oh yes," Samantha said with an elegant laugh, her voice soft and raspy. "Being seen with me? I know a few dozen reporters who'd love that scoop." She winked, as vixens often do, and hurried away.

After he spent a few moments straightening his tie and slipping on his blazer, Alex left the room. Madison counted thirty seconds before heading the same way herself, confident she'd avoid anyone at all as she took slow steps to the elevator, her head down as she contemplated everything she'd seen.

"Madison?"

Caught, she froze and looked up, but managed to speak. "Alex. Hi."

His hands in his pockets, he took a quick glance around and stepped closer, so much so that she was forced to crane her neck to take in the intensity of his dark eyes. Heat poured from him, blanketing her body.

"What are you doing here?" he asked.

Spying. "Stretching my legs."

He bent quickly, his lips meeting hers in a quick peck before she could object or speak, or move, or breathe. "It's perfect I'm seeing you."

"It is?" she whispered, uncertain.

"I have a surprise for you. There's an overnight bag in your office with a fresh change of clothes. We'll take off whenever you want today for a long weekend, and will come back Tuesday night."

"But I've got a few meetings . . ."

"I've got a few meetings myself . . ." Alex's lips nibbled hers, silencing her, his hands still in the pockets of his slacks. Tenderly, his mouth moved over hers, brushing her full bottom lip before teasing her with barely a lick. Just a taste, a delectable hint of everything her body wanted more of.

Madison could feel the growing wetness between her legs. Then he backed away, creating distance between them with the opening of the elevator doors.

A man with a wheeled utility cart exited, nodding politely as he passed the two.

"After you." Politely, Alex extended an arm, then patted his jacket with a huff. "Dammit, my phone. Madison—"

"Go," she said, realizing he must have forgotten it in the room.

Disagreeing with a firm shake of his head, he tried stepping into the elevator with her, but she pressed her palm to his chest.

"You've spent way too much time seducing me today."

Alex kept an arm on the elevator door, preventing it from closing, but setting off a faint chime. "Oh, I've just begun. As soon as you're done today, head to my elevator, hit *R*, and the seduction will continue."

With that, he released the doors, waiting until they fully closed before stepping away.

CHAPTER 6

MADISON

WELL PAST FIVE O'CLOCK, Madison worried less about Samantha and more about how long Alex must have been waiting. Her last meeting of the day ran late, and couldn't exactly be interrupted with *Gotta go—secret rendezvous with the CEO. Later, gators.*

And the bag Alex had packed for her and left in her office was missing one particular item. Madison wasn't exactly used to frolicking around commando, but she was already in a rush. For this man, she suspected she'd probably do a whole lot more.

She bounced impatiently on the balls of her feet as the elevator lifted in agonizing slow motion. After about ten years, the doors opened to a rush of crisp, fresh air on the rooftop, high above the streets of Manhattan.

Ahead of her, Alex leaned back against the glossy surface of a luxurious fifty-two-foot black helicopter, unhurriedly scrolling through his phone.

He looked up. "Ready, beautiful?"

Elated, she ran full force into him. His arms wrapped tightly around her, willing her into a long, soothing kiss.

"For absolutely anything," she said, pressing another eager kiss to his lips.

She savored it, sinking into this and every kiss as if they both felt the same— like each might be their last. Under the late-day sun, they took their time, letting the kiss linger before slowly melting away.

"Well," he said with a recovering breath, "if that's the kind of greeting I get with this, I'd better let you sit up front with the pilot."

Madison couldn't help planting her eager lips back on his, filling this kiss with all the energy and excitement of the new adventure to come.

Gently, Alex pulled back from her smiling lips, letting his finger brush her full lower one, plump and sensitive at his touch. "Hey, if we don't stop now, we'll never leave." He lifted her chin for another soft peck, then moved to unlatch the door and help her in.

Madison settled into the leather bucket seat, taking in all the unusual gadgets and brightly lit buttons. She admired how they crammed the console, knowing each had a mysterious purpose that must take years to master.

In a few long strides, Alex was on the other side of the aircraft, entering to take the seat next to her. "I'll just sit here for a minute while you buckle in."

Madison took the cue while he handed her a headset. With a short examination of it, she slipped it on. Casually, he pulled on an identical one.

"Can you hear okay?" he asked into the attached mic.

"Yes, perfectly."

Her eyes growing in wonderment at the sight of so many switches and doodads, she eagerly awaited the pilot who could explain it all.

Why might some light up while others didn't? What were the dials for? And what was with the joystick? Staring, she considered how the long arm that extended from the floor was both massive and suggestive, but she managed to tame her naughty smile.

The displays and controls captured her interest until her gaze drifted to Alex. Puzzled, he let out a small huff of impatience as he considered the console.

"I wonder what this does." Carelessly, he flipped a switch, and the display turned on. "Hmm, what about this?"

Another flip, and a few more buttons lit up. Madison caught the grin that instantly gave him away.

Clicking his own seat belt firmly in place, he asked, "Are you *sure* you're up for anything?" Alex seemed to enjoy surprising her, sharing secrets little by little to reveal more of himself.

Captivated, she asked, "You're the pilot?"

He flipped a few more switches and checked some levers overhead, then his delighted eyes met hers while he spoke into his headset. "November-One-Seven-Delta-Golf departing the Manhattan downtown district. Request permission to transition your airspace to the north."

Another voice broke through. "November-One-Seven-Delta-Golf, stand by."

Alex took her hand and brushed his lips softly against her knuckles, sending a tingle up her arm.

"November-One-Seven-Delta-Golf, you're cleared into the class bravo airspace. Cleared to transition to the north. Maintain twenty-five hundred feet. Safe flight, Mr. Drake."

Still holding her knuckles to his lips, he kissed them and replied, "Thanks, Neal. Give Carolyn and the kids my best." He set Madison's hand back on her lap, and they were off.

Holding her breath, Madison watched as the DGI symbol on Alex's midtown helipad shrank into the sea of high-rise buildings. As they rose high above Manhattan, everything about the biggest city she'd ever been in looked strangely small.

"If there's anything you want a second look at, just let me know."

She nodded, too enthralled to speak. Though she'd flown on planes a few times, this vantage point was entirely different. So much more was visible—like being on the wings of an eagle midflight over the city.

His voice rumbled low over the headset. "Take the cyclic."

Madison whipped her head around, seeing him motion to the joystick.

"Go ahead. Just hold it steady." When she slipped her hands nervously around it, Alex clasped both hands behind his head. "I'm just gonna take a little nap."

"What?" she cried, her pitched voice filled with terrified elation.

"You're doing great. You've got about twenty minutes, then I'll take it back as we get closer."

Her grin widened, and Alex gently swept her hair back behind her ear. She beamed even more, realizing he was getting a better look at her. She loved the way he looked at her, but it was these penetrating gazes that somehow always turned up the heat in her cheeks, painting them in a warm blush.

After a while, the buildings became fewer and farther between, overtaken by the lush green of grass and trees, broken here and there by the blues and whites of rivers. Alex's stroke on Madison's hand nudged her enough to relinquish control.

Based on the direction of the setting sun, Madison knew they hadn't veered from their original northbound heading. Though she'd never been here, the stunning beauty of the land was instantly recognizable. The Adirondacks welcomed her, instantly giving her a sense of peace and relaxation.

She pulled in a breath as she took it all in from her bird's-eye view. "It's gorgeous. Are we going camping?"

"We are. We'll be camping in a six-bedroom luxury cabin on a lake owned by a friend of mine. But if you prefer something more rugged, I'll do my best at moose calls."

Madison pretended to sigh with disappointment. "I guess a luxury cabin might do. But only if there are s'mores," she said, unveiling a giddy excitement that always seemed to encourage him.

Alex reached back, retrieving a small paper bag from the seat behind them. He handed it to Madison, who opened it to stare in disbelief. Inside were chocolate bars, graham crackers, and some of the biggest marshmallows she'd ever seen.

"Oh, you got me s'mores?"

Aghast, Alex stared at her. "No, I got *me* s'mores." He slowly pried the bag from Madison's hands and returned it to the back seat. "But I could be enticed to trade."

"Trade?"

He straightened and did his best at being aristocratic. "Well, I happen to be a collector. A collector of rare undergarments."

"Rare?" she asked, genuinely perplexed. *Like, vintage?*

"Rare, indeed. You see, I only collect undergarments that have touched the erogenous zones of your body."

"Oh, I guess I do see."

Madison's expression dropped, her downturned mood enough to prompt him to grab the bag and eagerly return it to her hand. Still in character, she declined, realizing Alex hadn't intentionally forgotten to pack her panties. It was an oversight. One she intended to use.

Through the playful veil of her thick, batting eyelashes, she gave him a remorseful glance with an exaggerated sigh.

"Well, I was really looking forward to some of that chocolatey chewiness. But at the moment, a trade's just not possible." Licking her lips and adding a full pout, she pulled in a deep breath. "Sadly, I'm not wearing any, um, collectibles."

His creased brow and tight lips transformed to a wide-eyed grin. And amongst the incoming evergreens and fresh air, Alex suddenly had two cyclics to contend with.

CHAPTER 7

MADISON

THROUGH A BREAK IN THE FOREST, a plush green glade came into view. Two people—a man and a woman—waved. The woman's wave eclipsed the man's, excited bursts with both arms as she jumped several times to get their attention. With a shy smile, Madison waved back.

Behind the friendly duo was a stunning property. The magnificent structure and likely architectural feat was what Madison assumed Alex meant by the "cabin."

The front of the lodge-style mansion featured abundant tall windows separated by log walls and large stone accents, while the back of the fortress overlooked the still blue of a crystalline lake. Circling for only a moment, the helicopter hovered in for a landing.

Waiting out the unforgiving gusts kicked up by the rotor blades, the couple hurried from their distant spots to greet them. The man and woman, dressed down in flannel and jeans, both contrasted with the elegant home and complemented it. Their smiles beamed as they greeted Madison and Alex.

Alex hopped out first, kidlike in leaping off the platform. He jogged around to Madison's door and lifted her by the waist, spinning her onto the ground.

With a swarm of butterflies flitting in her belly, she smoothed her hair and tugged at her outfit, eager to make a good impression. Aside from Paco, her new friend and Alex's right-hand man, these were the first of Alex's friends that he'd introduced her to.

As the couple approached, the burly man wearing glasses, a scruffy beard, and a warm smile blurted, "So, this is your sexy new baby!"

Madison felt every bit of the heat rising in her cheeks, certain everyone could see the redness warming her face. Instantly, the auburn-haired woman tugged her into a warm embrace.

"He means the chopper," the woman whispered in her ear, and relief poured from Madison in an audible exhale. The men were too engrossed to notice, making their way to the helicopter.

Madison overheard Alex explain it was the Sikorsky 76-D, and that custodial rights could always be arranged for a favor.

Just how many people owe this man a favor?

"Hi, I'm Jessica Bishop, but everyone calls me Jess. And you must be Madison." Jess gestured for them to head to the house, looping a sisterly arm through Madison's as if they were long-lost relatives catching up. "We've heard so much about you."

You have? Madison concealed her surprise and focused on the incredible home they were strolling toward. "Wow, your place is magnificent."

"I know, it's a bit much, but the land has been in my family for years. I come from a long line of mountain people. Simple-life lovers. Then Mark swept me off my feet, and after years of persistence, convinced me that a *log cabin* would suit the space well. Four years and three architects later, here's Mark's tribute to the simple life. Our home away from home for years now."

Jess presented the palace as only a knockout of a spokesmodel would. Her beauty was natural and effortless, unpretentious yet stunning.

Seeing Jess in this light, Madison guessed she was in her forties, a gorgeous beauty loosely concealed beneath her casual clothes. Without a bit of makeup, she somehow reminded Madison of what Marilyn Monroe or Ann-Margret might have been like on a lazy weekend between sex-bomb shoots.

As the men headed back, raucous with the laughter of an obvious tight bond, Madison turned to greet them. Extending her hand in a do-over, she relished a restart to their conversation, unconcerned of any possibility that the handsome lumberjack might lead with a comment on her degree of sexiness.

"Jess was just telling me about all the work you put into this beautiful property. It's amazing, Mr. Bishop."

The mister might seem formal, but after years of working in the service industry, old habits died hard—always address people formally first, until asked to do otherwise. Sometimes it felt stiff and uncaring, but she always warmed it up with a genuine grin.

As he gripped her hand firmly, his reaction became pained. With sudden exaggerated force, both of Mark's hands flew dramatically over his heart, as if struck by a crossbow at a hundred yards.

"Et tu, Brute? Et tu?"

Madison blinked rapidly, concerned about her apparent faux pas and wondering what the hell she'd done wrong, but Jess and Alex just laughed.

Unsympathetic, Jess laid a few firm claps on her husband's back, chiming in with a big, cheesy grin. "Don't mind him. It's hard for the male ego when we marry them but won't take their name."

Alex slipped his arms around Madison's waist, pulling her back against the heat of the front of him. Instantly, she relaxed into his embrace, receiving a few quick kisses to her temple. "You can just call him Mark. Though I hardly recognized you, man. You look like a grizzly bear with glasses."

"Hey, the mountain life changes you, brother." Mark gave that shaggy beard of his a few strokes, making Madison wonder what Alex would look like if he let his scruff really go. "No shave in almost two weeks. The longest I've ever gone. But I'll clean up in a few days before heading back to the office."

With a knowing glance at Madison still wrapped in Alex's arms, Mark continued. "Well, Madison, welcome. It's great to finally meet you, and to see Alex so happy." He shifted to give Alex an accusatory squint. "And I'm sure you're glad to be up here without feeling like a third wheel."

Alex grinned, shaking his head. "Hey, I was *very* happy to be a third wheel. Dragging me up here wasn't exactly roughing it. And I wasn't bringing someone here until it was the right someone."

The wild thumping in Madison's chest left her speechless.

They're all friends. Good friends. And the place has been here for years. What does it mean? Something? Anything?

Trapped between confusion and elation, she turned in Alex's arms, searching his eyes for an answer. Without saying a word, he pressed his warm lips tenderly to hers.

Perhaps he said more than he intended. Is he ready for this? Am I? Am I making too much of it?

Maybe this was more, more than either of them were ready for, if they really sat down and mapped out all the plusses and minuses of diving headfirst into the chemistry that sparked like the Fourth of July between them.

But everything was perfect. Comfortable. Right.

In the surrender of their growing kiss, the world melted away. Madison barely noticed as Jess and Mark turned and walked toward the house, giving her and Alex as much time and space and sweeping kisses as they needed.

CHAPTER 8

MADISON

DINNER PREP that evening was nothing like Madison might have imagined. Alex and Mark spent an hour slaving away in the kitchen while Jess and Madison got to know each other better.

Despite her repeated attempts to chop vegetables or clean up, the men continued shooing Madison away, insisting she relax and be pampered. On her last attempt, Alex promptly marched her butt out of the kitchen, sending her off with a kiss, a generous pour of aged cabernet, and the sweetest swat on her backside.

Amused and apparently accustomed to being waited on hand and foot by the two otherwise high-testosterone alphas, Jess encouraged her to give in. Reluctantly, Madison succumbed to the deep berry swirl of the red in her hand, headed to Jess for a clink, and finally curled up alongside her on the overstuffed sofa.

"Madison, can I ask you, do you come from a service background? Food services or hospitality?"

Madison gave Jess a bashful shrug. *Is it that apparent?* "Yes. That's pretty much my entire background. How'd you know?"

"Me too. It's written all over your need to help in the kitchen. Trust me, while you're here, the boys won't let you lift a finger."

"Wow, we'll have to drop by more often."

"Anytime. I love the girl time, and I rarely get it up here."

Jess was easy to talk to, unpretentious and open, and she shared freely about her life. She wasn't the kept woman some might think, and the nonprofit she'd started years ago helped vets to that day. It also happened to be how Jess and Mark met.

"It was a fundraiser. Love at first sight, which might have been clear to anyone watching, but denial was my game," Jess said, her giggle equal parts sentimental and naughty as she reminisced. "We were strangely inseparable. I called myself his 'heart hostage' and kept trying to push him off. If I vanished off the face of the earth, a stampede of lady contenders would've been vying to be by his side. But Mark was just so damn tenacious."

Madison sighed with pleasure. *Is there anything better than a love story?*

"Nobody thought it would last," Jess said. "I'm pretty laid back, and couldn't care less about how many bazillions he had. And when we married—the mountain woman and the megabucks tycoon—it was hard to keep up with all the hushed chatter. How long would we last? How much would I get if we divorced? Five different divorce attorneys handed me their business cards when I was out shopping. They followed me and found me, like stalking was cool so long as it was in my best interest."

"That's insane."

"Mark wanted me to have a bodyguard, but there was no need. I grew up with five brothers who taught this girl how to aim for the groin and make it hurt."

Taking a long sip of her wine, Madison reminisced for a moment about her own brother and the lesson Jack gave her on how to successfully deliver a knee to the jewels. It made her smile.

"But at the end of the day," Jess said, "it's Mark's passion that drives him, not his profit. He knows that I'm in love with him, not his billfold. If he lost everything tomorrow, he'd still have me. And somehow, I feel like it's the same with you and Alex."

"Oh." Madison buried her elation at Jess's words behind a restrained smile and another sip of wine. Could she and Alex really be on par with Jess and Mark? "Why do you say that?"

"Well, for starters, you work."

Madison shrugged. "At Alex's company."

Finishing off the glass, she set it down and grabbed the nearest throw pillow, hugging it to her chest. Curling her feet up under her, she let the effects of the bold red set in as she relaxed back into the plushness of the sofa.

Jess gave her a knowing look. "Yes, but if I know Alex, and I'd like to think I'm one of the few who know him pretty well, I'm sure he's made it abundantly clear that you don't have to. Am I right?"

Madison nodded, trying to hide her surprise. Nobody knew that Alex had offered her the lap of luxury. *His* lap of luxury. And as alluring as his offer was, she'd declined it over and over again, afraid of letting herself fall for a man with the reputation of keeping his women temporary and at arm's length.

Selfishly, she had to have more than the fleeting spoils and disposable consequences of being a kept woman. Keeping her job was a small step to having all of Alex Drake, while holding on for dear life to herself.

"And yet you continue to work. My guess is you do it to learn and grow as your own person, driven by your passion. Same as all of us." Crossing one leg over the other, Jess took a sip of her wine and leaned in. "Let me ask you something, Madison. If Alex lost everything tomorrow, would you stay with him?"

Madison's nod was immediate and unequivocal, though the question lingered in her mind. Could Alex lose everything? It was difficult to imagine, but in this day and age, anything was possible.

"I think, no matter what, I'll always be here for him. It's hard to explain, but with Alex, I feel a connection. It's something I can't deny and I can't explain. It's just there." Madison smothered a light laugh, but freely smiled. "I feel silly saying it because our relationship is so new. And there are still so many things I don't know about him."

Averting her gaze, Jess took an extra-long sip of wine.

Madison had a feeling Jess knew more than she'd ever say. She seemed loyal that way.

Finally, Jess said, "Alex has had his shields up a long time. It's hard living a life where you're not always sure who you can trust. But he trusts you, Madison, which is maybe the biggest step I've ever seen the man take. He might be a kickass CEO to the rest of the world, but I think in your hands, he's pretty much putty."

Jess's words made Madison smile. Her gaze dropped, and she noticed a small framed photo next to the wine bottle. Looking closer, she realized it was their men posing in front of the Statue of Liberty, younger versions of themselves.

"So, how about Alex and Mark," she asked. "How did they meet?"

Jess set down her wineglass and stood, her light expression taking on a more somber look. She turned away, taking a few deliberate steps to the mammoth stone fireplace. With the long arm of the poker, she pushed at the logs, losing herself in the spark and roar of the flames. Whatever secrets she was harboring seemed to be well guarded, as if they weren't hers to share.

Eventually, she returned the poker to its wrought-iron caddy and turned back, keeping her response vague. "Oh, they've known each other for years. Like brothers. They can tell you more over dinner, but they've leaned on each other time and time again. In their circle, trust is a priceless commodity, and the trust they have in each other is limitless. There's nothing they wouldn't do for each other. Speaking of trust, are you ready for tomorrow?"

Madison recalled the conversation she and Alex had in the helicopter before they arrived. He'd arranged an activity for them tomorrow, something she'd never tried before. The lump that rose in her throat at the thought of it could only be forced down with a large swallow of cab.

"As ready as I'm going to be, I guess."

Can anyone really be ready for this?

Anxiety had been Madison's steady companion for many years, as constant and normal as eating, sleeping, and breathing, sticking to her like her shadow.

But the nervous energy she had for what was to come was different—a raw mix of fear and thrill, reinforced with a strong dose of faith that knew no bounds but had no beginning. Faith that this unconventional idea would be worth a try. Faith that thirty days with Alex would be worth a try.

Even a decade later, the wave of hurt that shattered her over and over again at the memory of her brother, Jack—the loss never failed to leave her numb, but she always managed to paste on a smile and tackle another endless day. Numbness was good. Isolation was better. But being with Alex was like pure oxygen, giving her one easy breath after another.

Like so many things in Madison's life, Alex somehow seemed to sense and understood her grief and anxiety. Was that why it was easy? Because he could see past her well-practiced facade?

They never discussed it. She never let him in. So, how did he know? How could he possibly know to ask her how she was coping? *Coping*, he'd said. Not coped. Not the past-tense presumption everyone else used.

And Alex Drake saw everything. The indiscernible shrug she would give in response that should have moved his questions along. The avoiding glance to hide the burning tears in her eyes. The soft shudder of her breath that did all it could to stave off the inevitable breakdown.

It was enough for Alex to see her agony. See it and offer her a different way out, an alternative to fighting her feelings—to take on the domination of each raw emotion head-on. To push past everything she'd fooled herself into thinking she controlled, and finally let go.

That was what tomorrow's activity could give her, Alex had promised, and she was both terrified and eager to give it a whirl.

Jess reached over to pat Madison's arm. "Don't worry about it. You're in terrific hands. Alex actually taught me and Mark. He'll earn your trust."

I believe you.

When the boys barged in wearing the widest grins and outlandish chef's hats as they announced dinner was served, each woman headed to her man.

As they made their way past the kitchen, with each square inch of gourmet countertop pristine despite the frenzy of cooking going on not long ago, Madison couldn't help but beam at two titans of industry being so handy in the kitchen.

Alex led her past an eat-in seating area that offered no food at all, and out to an oversize deck overflowing with candles and flowers. There, they'd arranged a spread with so much food, the two couples would have to nibble on it for the entire long weekend just to make a dent.

The flickering candles reached high, snapping up the last beams of sunlight that were quickly simmering behind the lake. Taking a seat, Madison accepted the peck Alex placed on her cheek, and continued reconciling Alex Drake, masterful CEO, with Alex Drake, the man.

Jess discreetly pointed out the men's matching KISS THE CHEF aprons, as if they could be missed, and leaned over to whisper, "You thinking what I'm thinking?"

Madison lifted her wineglass and tapped it gently to Jess's. "That we're staring at dessert?"

"*Bon appétit,*" she said with hints of an Adirondack accent and a resonating clink.

"So, are you ready for tomorrow?" Mark asked Madison, and when she nodded meekly, he gave her a reassuring wink. "You know, Alex Drake might look the part of a titan of industry and world-renounced CEO, but he's also managed to convince me that this, how shall we put it, *unconventional method* can help."

"Hey, I only said it helped me," he said, modest in his admission.

"There we were," Mark continued, "a ragtag group of vets desperate to dig ourselves out from being explosive, or reactive, or desolate, or numb. We didn't want much. Just a single freaking day without anguish would be nice."

Alex shrugged. "Back then, the concept was new. A way to deal with PTSD that didn't have to do with sharing your feelings."

"We're guys," Mark added. "No one ever accused us of being in touch with our feelings. But the beauty of this was that a bunch of macho guys could get behind it. Everyone who heard about it was all in."

"Family members were all in too. And this wasn't a 'treatment.' No one was there to analyze reactions or keep count. This was a lifeline of hope for people at their wits' end." Alex beamed. It was the first time since she'd known him that she detected unapologetic pride.

Mark patted him on the back. "For some of us, it was something . . . sometimes the only thing . . . we could look forward to in order to feel normal. For others, it brought calm, peace of mind, and solace."

"Does it do that for you?" Madison asked gently.

Thoughtfully, he replied. "For the first time in a long time, it gave me purpose. A purpose I needed. Help others. Give back. Make a difference. Save people where I ... I missed the chance before." He took a large sip of wine before Madison pressed a kiss to his lips.

"I'll get us some cappuccino," Mark said.

"I'll help." Jess and Mark rushed to the kitchen as Alex fed her a fresh strawberry.

The deck was softly lit by torches, but it was what was beyond it that captured Madison's attention between easy chatter about each of their lives and the sinful bites of delicious food. As darkness closed in, Madison could still see the woods just beyond the lake, and wondered if this was the reason they all loved it here. It was more than a tranquil paradise where nature harmonized with the people in it.

It was private. Secluded. No one made pretenses, and everyone settled comfortably into the contentment of just being themselves. In a world of power players and corporate climbers, Madison was a nobody. But here, she breathed easier, knowing that even a nobody would be welcomed, just being herself.

Alex's warm hand wrapped around hers, pulling her back from the distance her mind drifted off to. His smile was contagious, and she gave him a wider one in return.

Madison relished the intimate glances they shared. The hidden moments where the world vanished and nothing existed but them. Those intimate seconds that wove them together with each passing day were everything, where she could learn more about the reclusive man, and settle into the comfort of the two of them growing even closer.

CHAPTER 9

ALEX

THAT EVENING, Alex stood on the balcony off the guest room wearing only his warm flannel pajama bottoms, splitting the set and leaving the top for Madison. It had become a comfortable routine back at his place.

Back home.

Here at Mark and Jess's, which had become his home away from home over the years, the decor was rustic and woodsy, with modern wood beams and stone accents throughout. Expansive glass paneling wrapped around the balcony, providing a seamless view of the evergreen forest in the distance.

With the sliding doors set invisibly past the edges of the wall, there was no divide between the heated room and the chilly outdoors. The fresh air would float through the room and then swirl back out, wafts of warm and cool air softly skimming the bare skin of his chest and back.

The setting was serene, but Alex could feel the strain of his knuckles, growing whiter with each passing minute of clutching the rail for dear life.

Sporadic tiny bursts from fireflies blinked against the darkness of the pines, giving him too little to focus on. So he stared off, concentrating on pulling in each breath. The tug-of-war with his body was a fight—one he battled nightly to win.

Not now, he insisted to himself again and again. *Not now*. Deep breath in. *Not now*. Slow breath out. Each breath was ragged but he pressed on, barely controlling the erratic spikes of his runaway pulse.

Even when the sweat streaming down his forehead, neck, and back burned like ice, Alex remained still. Calm. The episodes passed faster that way, when he focused and didn't move.

The relentless thumping of his own heart in his ears always deafened him, which he turned into a game. Counting the beats kept him sane. As if ticking off the days in his body's prison, he waited out the wave without losing his remaining sanity.

It will pass. It has to.

Shattering his focus, a sudden high-pitched mechanical squeal broke through the silence, which always happened when the guest shower hadn't been used for months. The sound was annoying as shit. But tonight, it was his saving grace, alerting him that he had a little more time to get himself under control.

Madison can't see me like this.

Desperate, he picked up his cell phone and punched at the same number over and over again, barely waiting for it to be sent to voice mail before swearing under his breath and trying again. "Goddammit. Pick up, Mark. Fuck."

Frustrated, he hurled his phone as far out into the darkness as he could. Gripping the handrail again, Alex closed his eyes as he focused, focused, focused.

On Madison.

The softness of her long wavy hair when she'd first wake up. The fullness of her lips when they pressed against his. The sparkle that lit her eyes every time she saw him, and the smile that always followed. She was the first woman he'd brought up here. She'd caught on to that. Did she know she was the first woman to move in with him? The only woman? With Madison, everything felt right.

Yes. Madison.

He sucked in an even deeper breath, filling his lungs and holding it. Slowly, the tremors that racked his body finally subsided.

Her footsteps were light, but he could gauge her distance behind him. When her hands slid around the tension in his torso and her cheek rested against his bare back, he released his breath in a long, slow exhale.

Opening his eyes, he noticed the darkness of the tree line twinkling with distant fireflies again. Her warm lips pressed against his back, and his heart rate slowed from its unbearable high of just seconds ago.

A last labored breath was all he needed—giving him an extra moment before facing her.

CHAPTER 10

MADISON

Madison emerged from the bathroom, greeted by the sweet scent of fresh air blending with the hickory logs ablaze in the fireplace. The flannel top was right where she expected it, waiting for her on the corner of the bed, just like at Alex's place.

Back home.

She pressed the snuggly soft fabric to her nose and inhaled the familiar smell of cedar, wondering how many times Alex had worn these pajamas here at the cabin over the years.

Her breath hitched, as it always did whenever she saw him. He stood tall against the backdrop of twilight, every muscle in his solid back ripped and carved, drawing her in and lighting a desire so strong, she could never hold back.

Needing him was more than anything physical, though an outsider looking in might not know it. In this moment, he was distant, carried far away in his own thoughts. She'd give anything for a peek into whatever was pulling him far from here. From her.

Something was bothering him. Feverishly, he seemed to be attacking his phone with his thumb, impatient and muttering. Shocked, Madison watched him heave the phone out into the darkness.

Frowning with confusion, she said nothing, because what was there to say? *Are you all right?*

It was the same question that made her cringe when people asked, making her want to bare her teeth at them. *Sure. I'm fine. Barely able to eat, sleep, or breathe, but everything's hunky-dory. Move along . . . nothing to see here, folks. Nope, nothing to see.*

Maybe she and Alex were alike in that way. Maybe not. It didn't matter. In that moment, Madison had two choices. Run . . . or stay.

In a few quiet steps, Madison closed in, skimming her fingers across the small of his back, then smoothing her hands around to the flat of his sculpted abs. Securing her hold around his waist, she pressed her cheek to his back before placing a tender kiss to his skin.

With her arms wrapped around him, his thundering heartbeat slowed and his quick breaths leveled off. As did hers.

Though his hand covered hers, he barely turned his head, taking an unusual pause before speaking. "Hey, if you have any reservations about tomorrow, it's okay. No pressure."

No pressure. And we aren't going to talk about what's upsetting him, because "no pressure."

"No," she said slowly, "I want to do it. From what you've said, it might help me sort a few things out. Issues I've had problems dealing with."

Madison hesitated to talk more about her quest through self-exploration. Burdening others seemed like a chore more than a relief. The last thing people needed to know about was her personal hell of anxiety and panic attacks fueled by loss and pain.

"Let's do something," he said.

Alex turned and moved inside for a moment to pick up a small ottoman. His smile was comforting, but she wondered why he'd bring it out to the balcony's edge.

"Here." He grabbed her hand, urging her to stand on it. Then, with some unspoken plan, his hands firmed around her hips, turning her to face the woods.

The railing was tall, but only met her at the kneecap. She took a nervous look down, balancing on one foot and then another before easing into the confidence she was safe. Alex's hands lingered on her hips, reinforcing her position.

"Did you ever see *Titanic*?"

"With Leo and Kate?" she asked with a casual familiarity as if I knew the megastars personally.

"Remember the scene where they were on the bow of the ship? She stretched her arms way out, embracing the air and the sensation of being one with everything around her. The sunset. The ocean. Having faith in everything in the moment."

"She had faith in him," Madison said. If there was one thing she loved, it was a great love story.

Pulling in a breath, she played out the scene, taking all her lessons from high school drama to the next level. She stretched her arms wide, looking out into the darkness with vivid recollections of the orange-and-blue sky in the scene. The ship as it sailed across an endless sea. The breathless moment of that amazing onscreen kiss.

With strength and intention, Alex leaned her body forward, giving her the smallest taste of how it might feel. "This is what you'll do tomorrow. Just think of that scene, and you'll be fine."

His hold on her hips tugged her back until she stood tall again on the ottoman. Both of his hands moved ever so slightly higher, slowly inching up the hem of the soft shirt and baring her ass.

Madison's giggle was instant. "My view is spectacular. How's yours?" She shot him a playful glance over her shoulder.

"Getting better and better." His murmurs of approval deepened as a breeze swept across the bare skin of her butt.

"Is there anything I can do to help?"

Without warning, he yanked her back, letting her willing body fall into the cradle of his arms. "I can think of a few things."

His mouth met hers with a tenderness that pried her lips open, urging her to take the smallest tip of his tongue as he stole a taste. The next sweep was rushed and hungrier than the first. The feel of his searing lips as they molded with hers sent electricity everywhere, lighting a wildfire throughout her body.

With a few steps into the room, he spread her across a plush rug close to the logs roaring in the stone fireplace. Soft pillows and blankets had been scattered near the hearth, making the rustic space feel romantic and sensual.

As Alex joined Madison, she skimmed her fingers over his skin. Fascinated, she explored every line and curve of his shoulders and chest, while his hand slid across the sensitive plane of her inner thigh.

His hand moved in a slow path to the fullness of her ass before pulling her in, taunting her aching pussy with the heat of his flannel-encased erection pressing hard to her core.

With each button of her shirt he tugged away, he explored another new area of exposed skin with his lips, nibbling across her breasts, then up her neck. Her shirt was open and undone when he asked, "How's this for camping?" His warm whisper didn't linger at her ear, and his hot kisses quickly trailed down.

"Oh, it'll be perfect in a while."

Mid-kiss, he stopped. Amused, he pinned her with a playful glare.

"And just what, Ms. Taylor, would make it more perfect?" he grumbled, tracing a long line across her collarbone, between her breasts, then nearly to her wetness before pulling his sinful finger back. Opening her shirt, Alex exposed one breast at a time, then stroked her peaked nipples lightly with his tongue. "Hmm?"

The bite to her own lip didn't help getting her words out. With heavier breaths, Madison tried again. "Well, uh, usually when people camp, it's beneath a big, open sky."

"Interesting," he murmured across her neck. "Did you want to go outside?" This time, he let the tip of his teeth graze her nipple before he lapped it with a heated lick.

"N-no. But, uh, this will all be perfect as soon as you have me seeing stars." She moaned, arching her back as he popped her full breast into his mouth, suckling her as she began a slow ride against the strength of his thigh.

"I'll do my best," Alex said, working his fingers along the wetness weeping from her folds.

When he swiped his wet fingers across her clit, she moved in harmony with his hand, taking in every circle—every blissful sensation—across her desperate bundle of nerves.

"I need you," she whispered, running her fingernails tenderly across the skin of his neck as she begged.

He removed his pants, letting her see the thick fullness of his dick, its tip glistening. "I'm yours, Madison," he murmured against her lips.

She watched as he moved to retrieve a condom, not bothering to tear it open or put it on. Not yet. His was a body to be admired, and admire it she did, losing herself in every sculpted muscle. Eventually, she pulled her gaze away from his abs and chest to finally meet his eyes.

Kneeling, he took her in, his dark, hungry gaze holding more than heat and desire. Beyond, she could see the longing. Like he'd never had her before. As if she'd never been his.

She gave him a tender smile, hoping every worry and doubt between them could disappear. *I will always be yours, Alex Drake.*

He remained still, patiently allowing her to drink him in with her eyes. And her journey along the dips and valleys of his body was unrushed. Alex Drake was a work of art. Etched to perfection. Strong, yet vulnerable. Willing to let her in, but not weak.

She understood how precious a gift was his trust. He was the epitome of power, yet he'd relinquished all of it to her mercy. Giving himself over. Being truly exposed.

In return, her desire for him was unyielding. She wanted to be anything and everything he needed. Be completely his.

But of all the emotions swirling within her now, the one taking over was lust.

With a suggestive lick across the fullness of her lip, she slipped her hand through his inner thighs, tugging his body forward to her eager, waiting lips. The drop on his tip needed a long lick before he forced himself through to the back of her throat.

"Yes, Madison." He dropped his head back, a low rumble leaving his throat. His fingers wove through the thickness of her hair until her position and pace mirrored his wants. Just the rhythm made her wet.

Alex's movements were masterful, controlled, as he turned her on her back, keeping his throbbing cock in her mouth. She gasped with anticipation as his head made its way to the throbbing between her legs.

The first lick made her shiver. The second made her hips rock and sway, as every touch between her legs had her climbing. Chasing. Keeping the rhythm of her mouth closely matched to his, and fighting every impulse that pounded her swollen pussy.

Because coming was not an option. Not yet.

When his mouth devoured her clit, her submission was imminent. Their bodies intertwined, locking in the depths of their erotic feeding. The lashes of his tongue were amplified as his fingers smeared across her—rubbed her—invaded her.

And with increased pace, Madison stroked and sucked, taking him deeper while tenderly teasing the sensitive skin of his sac.

The taste of Alex was stronger as he forced himself further in. And the fingers he slid through her swollen folds were too much, hitting the one spot that could always make her shatter at his whim.

She tried to match his pace, but it was elusive. His tongue focused on her pulsing clit, and his relentless fingers strummed her spot, coaxing her orgasm ahead of his own.

Uncontrolled, her climax ripped a cry from her mouth, pulling her from his bulging cock with a gasp. Her throaty screams filled the air, while she rode his face and fingers through her ecstasy.

"Are you seeing stars yet?" he growled naughtily, still enjoying licking the swollen lips of her soaked pussy, while keeping his fingers firmly in place.

"Yes," she cried at the top of her lungs. "Yes. Yes."

Her eyelids fluttered, opening enough for her to realize the balcony door was open and had been . . . *the entire time.*

"Oh my God, I didn't mean to be so loud." Madison panted, breathless and embarrassed, wondering what Jess and Mark must be thinking.

With a final swipe along her walls, Alex had her back arching and legs trembling as he pulled his fingers from her. Her body writhed from the loss. As he kissed his way back to her face, she couldn't help but draw him in, aroused as her lips tasted the fresh dew of her own essence.

"Well, they're about to hear a whole lot more," he said low.

Condom in hand, he slid the sheath on. With more control than any man should have, Alex glided the head of his rigid cock in and out, teasing her folds before plunging it to the hilt.

Again, her whimpers kicked up to screams. "Yes. God, yes."

With a steady pace, his lips plucked at a nipple, letting it snap back from a light tug of his teeth.

"I'm close," Madison murmured. "So close . . ." Her body moved with his, needy for every sensation. Every touch.

Alex's pace quickened and his thrusts became rougher. Harder. Deeper. And she couldn't hold back.

Her eyes fluttered and her back arched. "Please. I—I have to come again."

"God, yes," he said, filling her, pounding her, taking her to the brink with circle after circle along her clit.

Both tumbled deep into the erotic abyss, riding each other's waves and crying out as loud as their bodies would let them. Each sensual movement was ecstasy. Then his hot release erupted in a series of heavy thrusts that threatened to tear them both apart.

After their heaving breaths slowed and their bodies cooled, Alex slipped away for a moment, returning with a thicker blanket for Madison, though he seemed to prefer the gentle breeze, comforted in the swaddle of the fresh night air. He slipped a pillow gently beneath Madison's head before taking one for himself, keeping a loving watch on her as she peered at him through eyes heavy with satisfaction.

Wincing, she whispered, "I'm positive they heard us." Giggling, she pulled the blanket up over her face, hiding the heat blazing across her cheeks.

Undeterred, Alex tugged the bedding, pulling it down. "Beautiful, I'm sure the penguins in Antarctica heard us."

His playful laugh ended in another kiss on her lips. Nuzzling into the warmth of his chest, Madison gazed at the fireplace with its bright sparks and dancing flames as her mind drifted.

A few words floated up from her subconscious, often silent but always there. She shoved them down, avoiding the wonder of Alex—or at least, avoiding it for now. Carried off to an exhausted sleep, she only faintly heard the thought now.

Who is Alex Drake?

CHAPTER 11

MADISON

Madison couldn't recall exactly when or how she moved from the floor, but there she was, snug in the plush, oversize bed, enjoying the sunlight that warmed her skin as she yawned. With a glance around and no sounds from the bathroom, she realized Alex had to be gone.

And not just gone. All traces of their campground escapade had been magically erased. Even the fireplace seemed undisturbed, cool and untouched.

Did I dream it?

She lifted the covers and took a good look at herself. Though Alex's flannel pajama shirt still wrapped her arms, it didn't cover much else, remaining unbuttoned and open.

Nope. Not a dream.

A huge smile stretched her cheeks as thoughts of his stubble wreaking havoc on the insides of her legs played back. With a stretch, she revisited her afterglow until a few knocks interrupted her luscious jaunt down memory lane and her own hand massaging her thigh.

"Madison, you up?"

Surprised, Madison froze for a second before her fingers worked feverishly, refastening one button after the other. Realizing her frazzled work ended in a total misalignment of the two sides, she abandoned working on her clothes and pulled the comforter high.

"Come on in, Jess."

Bright as a spring daisy, Jess strolled in with two mugs of coffee in hand. How her bed head and flannel robe managed to make her look like a pinup, Madison would never know.

"Morning," Jess said with only the slightest yawn. "Alex said you might like a little coffee."

"Mmm, yes, please." Madison leaned over for a long stretch, receiving the steaming mug with eager hands.

Like long-time friends, Jess plopped on the bed next to her, taking a refreshing sip from her own cup. "So, Julia Child and Betty Crocker are rustling us up some breakfast, but be warned. Those boys can really cook. Everything you see will look amazing, but don't eat more than a bite."

"Why not?"

"For what you're doing today, you'll be walking a fine line between eating enough to have something in your tummy and overfilling the tank—risking a mid-event upchuck."

"Toast and bacon it is." Madison nodded, already battling bouts of queasiness whenever she thought about the day ahead. The last thing she needed was that sort of lasting impression.

"Breakfast should be ready in about fifteen minutes," Jess said with a few light pats on Madison's knee through the overfilled comforter. With her coffee in hand, she headed for the door.

"Um, Jess, before you go." *I have to know.* "Did you and Mark hear anything last night?" Nervous about the response, Madison winced as she held her breath.

"Hear anything?" Jess's pursed lips and uncertain glance revealed nothing. "I'm not sure. What would it have sounded like?"

The cries of *oh God* and *yes, please, yes* looped through Madison's mind as her answer stalled. "Oh, I don't know, just, you know . . . anything. Anything out of the ordinary."

"Well, we usually sleep like logs, so we don't hear much. But last night? What were we doing? Oh, we were too wrapped up in a ton of hot, sweaty sex to hear a thing."

Madison relaxed, giggling.

"What can I say?" Jess said with a wink before she headed out. "I'm a screamer."

~

This was it, the moment of truth.

Madison couldn't quite believe what they were doing. What she was doing. The toast and bacon had plenty of time to settle, but instead, they did flips in her belly, sending sweat to her hands and wild pulses to her heart.

I don't know if I can do this.

The emotions racing through her were fickle, shifting from *daredevil thrill* one minute, to *freaked out and ready to call it quits* the next. Then to *hell yeah.* Then to being worried she'd pee her pants.

Between her thundering heartbeat and near hyperventilation, Madison focused on what was needed most. Controlling her bladder.

If I ever do this again, the second cup of coffee is a hard pass!

Alex took his position behind her, though he felt a million miles away as he shouted, "You okay?"

Convincingly, Madison nodded and then held up her thumb.

His voice loud, Alex kept her motivated. "Just do what I told you. If you don't get there, it's no big deal. But I'm ready when you are."

Keep calm. Big breath in. *I can do this.* Slow breath out.

Madison's mind quieted, and the wind in her face gave her the strangest sense of peace. For the moment, that was a good thing.

Alex's lessons had been gentle, reminding her that reactions are personal. One person might laugh. Another might cry. Some had even ended their session in gut-wrenching screams. Or jubilant shouts. Maybe all of the above. Maybe none of these at all. Anything was possible. And everyone was right.

"We feel what we feel," were his words, and Madison knew he was bracing her. Preparing her for some lack of control that wouldn't be shamed and shouldn't be held in. "Just . . . let it all out. It'll help you let go."

This was the Alex she had to know. The man who helped others without any kind of spotlight. Founding a group dedicated to helping as many as he could, most of them vets.

Embracing the moment, Madison closed her eyes and did as they'd rehearsed, the scene on the bow of the ship in *Titanic.* Throwing her arms wide, she summoned the courage to open her eyes and let it all go. Control. Fear. Doubt.

The goggles she wore gave her a bird's eye view of everything, including her life. A life that was meant for more than wading through the weighty sludge of pain. One that needed to be lived.

Pushing past the tightness in her chest, she leaned forward. Took a step. And fell.

It was faster than she could have imagined, and she panicked at first, then plummeted with terrifying elation and abandon. Freefalling ten thousand feet was one hell of a way to let everything go. And away they went, falling to the earth at a dizzying speed without a care.

She'd nearly forgotten Alex until his body shifted and tightened against her. As it was in all areas of their relationship, Alex Drake had her back, one tandem leap at a time.

Skydiving was a rush she couldn't understand. Madison didn't shout or laugh. The only clue she gave Alex that she was conscious and hadn't fainted was that her arms remained rigid, flying free from her sides.

Awestruck, she took in every sensation, imagining herself, not so much in gravity's hold, but more in a spirited freedom of flight. *A hundred twenty-two miles per second*, she recounted in wild disbelief.

"Ready?" Alex said, shouting.

Nodding, she pulled her arms in, wrapping her hands tight to the straps of her harness. The surge of adrenaline that followed pervaded every cell of her body.

I've got this. I'm ready.

Alex took the lead and deployed the drogue parachute. It was the beginning of the end, reducing their speed while prolonging the sensation of the freefall.

A pop sounded as the final larger chute deployed, jerking them up gently before slowing them with its drag. Alex grabbed the toggles, easily steering them with strength and skill. The dizzying freefall descent was slower now as they glided to the open field—the drop zone. Jess's little body waved up at them, and the picturesque field grew closer by the second.

As the ground closed in, Madison prepared. In front tandem form, she lifted her legs, stretching them in front of her, so Alex could take the lead in landing them.

Gliding into the lush, green grass, the landing reminded Madison of a slip-and-slide, zooming freely to the end. She knew Alex would have both knees bent, taking the brunt of the force as he dragged them to a gentle stop.

Falling back, Madison could feel her cheeks draw into a wide smile, but her exhilaration faded quickly, disrupted by a few tears that gathered in the rim of her goggles.

Jess was ready, running over to them to help collect the parachute as Alex unclipped it and removed his harness. His goggles off, he gave Madison a concerned glance.

She couldn't move. Or speak. Or understand anything that was happening.

Instead, she just rested against him, letting him remove her goggles and untether her from the harness. His thumbs gently whisked away her runaway tears, letting her come to terms with her confusing emotions in her own time.

Checking in, he asked, "How do you feel?"

Madison couldn't control the creases in her brow, but she could feel them. Her emotions tumbled over each other, moment by moment, shifting their weight from one feeling to the next.

It's too much.

Her body felt lifeless. Heavy and weak. Alex stroked her arm, but she could see he was studying her.

I don't want him to worry.

She tried a small movement, but he held her in place.

"It's all right," he said low. "Stay still. I'll be right back." Gently, he rolled her body off his and laid her down on the grass.

Madison watched as he moved over to Jess and asked softly for a blanket. Saying how they'd enjoy some time alone for a bit, but that two bottles of water would be appreciated.

Alex was again by her side, and the bottles of water appeared, though she didn't recall seeing Jess. Lifting Madison's head, he offered her a sip.

Swallowing, she looked away, ashamed that more tears were escaping. "I'm sor—"

"Hey," he said, sitting beside her and taking care to wipe the tears from her face. "You're fine. We don't have to talk, remember? We feel what we feel. And we can stay here as long as you like."

Madison again hadn't noticed Jess until she felt the warmth of the cashmere throw on her shoulders. Before Madison could thank her, Jess was gone.

Tucking the lightweight blanket around her and up to her chin, Alex seemed content to stay lovingly away. With an insistent pull, she drew his body closer to hers. To lie beside her.

"I'm not going anywhere," he said, laying tender kisses along her cheek. "We have all the time in the world, Madison Taylor. I'll always be by your side."

A comment like that might have garnered a reaction an hour ago. But not now.

With the sun shining and birds chirping, she knew she needed to snap out of it, hop up, and enjoy the day. But she was paralyzed, lost in a journey that wouldn't be done until every last emotion was acknowledged and assessed until it faded away.

So, she lay there, weeping with this remarkable man, losing herself in the changing shapes and colors of the clouds high up in the sky.

CHAPTER 12

MADISON

MIDWAY through her first morning back at work, Madison's messenger window popped up with a welcome message. Not from Alex, but welcome, nonetheless. Alex's right-hand man, Paco Robles, had quickly become her bestie. It was only then that she realized she hadn't seen him in over a week.

Paco: Hey, a good girl like you wouldn't happen to know anyone who plays poker and doesn't mind healthy stakes?

The twenty seconds she waited before replying was the best she could do at a virtual poker face.

Madison: My poker's not terrible, though it's been a while. Got a game?

Paco: Yes! Lost our fourth to love and marriage. If you're good for Wednesday evenings, I'll add you to our group.

She checked the calendar.

Madison: Tonight's Wednesday.

Paco: Exactly. Game day. We'll have your induction ceremony tonight.

Madison: What's the buy-in?

Paco: Normally $1000. Alex has a tab.

Madison: I'm good. My piggy bank is all kinds of plump at the moment. And it'll be fatter after tonight.

Paco: Game on, girlie!

Madison: See you there.

Fired up, she rubbed her hands together, prepared to count her winnings. *It's totally in the bag.*

As the valet rushed to open Madison's door, she sprang from her Lyft with a shy *thanks*. Taking in the magnificence of the Carlyle Hotel, she found the iconic building brimming with elegance and history, and right in the heart of Manhattan's Upper East Side. One glance up, and the fancy skyscraper seemed to be barely a tiptoe from touching the sky.

Though another man held open a side door, Madison politely declined, opting for a fun spin through the revolving door. She landed just inside, surrounded by the Old World grace of stately potted palms, black marble floors, and crystal chandeliers.

After another glance at the cryptic text from Paco, she headed to the concierge.

Paco: Ten paces to the concierge desk.

I think he forgot a step.
With the concierge at the desk already giving her a helpful smile, Madison strolled over. "Hi. I'm not sure—"

"Good evening, Ms. Taylor. I believe this is for you."

As he handed over a deep red envelope, Madison smiled. Her name was scrolled across it with a smiley face in the *o*.

"Thank you," she said.

"My pleasure. Is there anything more I can do for you?"

Madison shook her head, satisfied for the moment with the mystery of a note. Inside the envelope was a card, but no key. On the fancy Carlyle stationery, the handwritten note held seven smart-ass words.

Don't lose your money too fast, Taylor.

She flipped the card over, noticing the bold strokes that gave the brief instructions a sense of suspense and intrigue.

Private Elevator.
Penthouse.

Penthouse? Of course.

Madison headed toward the elevator, taking her time to study the paintings lining several walls. As she reached it, she realized she wouldn't be alone in the car. This elevator had an operator, just as it had fifty years before. Like the concierge before him, he knew exactly where she was going.

When the elevator stopped, it opened to a lavish suite of magnificent scale, with high ceilings that showed off every inch of rich wallpapered and wain-scoted areas, brocade drapes, and exotic rugs. Each piece of furniture perfectly offset the opulent architecture, and still preserved a coziness. A warmth.

"Hello?" Madison called out as she took a few careful steps in.

"Well, here's a hustler if I've ever seen one . . . and not in the prostitution way."

Silver-tongued and as suave as ever, Paco entered, looking as elegant as his surroundings. Daringly, he wore his satin smoking jacket *sans* shirt, its pattern a rich peacock-colored paisley that only he could pull off. Taking in his black satin pants and gold smoking slippers, Madison imagined this was as dressed down as the man got shy of being buck-ass naked.

Noting the two pink cocktails he carried, Madison reconsidered his outfit. *If this turns into a strip poker game, I'm out of here.*

"Thanks for inviting me," she said, and they exchanged a light kiss on the cheek.

"Hey, Madison, glad you could join us," Ted said as he and Rex walked in, enjoying their own bottles of beer.

The dynamic duo of DGI's IT division were often referred to collectively as

TRex due to their strangely similar appearances, even though they had to be ten years apart in age.

"Paco's been great about letting us use his place for our weekly game," Ted said with another sip.

"It's stunning," Madison said, admiring it again.

"Thanks. Grey Goose cosmo?" Paco asked.

Graciously, she accepted, determined to pace herself. But after her first sip and an exaggerated *mmm*, she sipped again. *Okay, pacing myself is crazy talk.*

"What's in the bottom," she asked.

"Two Griottines cherries, because I had a feeling you'd like it extra sweet," Paco said with a smile.

"Okay, but you're not allowed to use your infamous mind-reading during the game." Madison held up her champagne coupe for a toast, solidifying their new card-sharp camaraderie.

Paco clinked with his twin cosmo, and TRex brought their beers in. She took another sip of the recently poured drink, fresh with itsy-bitsy ice chips still floating at the top. The refreshing and energizing imbibement was just what she needed to relax.

"Before we go to the card room . . ." *Because, of course, a place like this has a card room.* "You have a little something to remove, Miss Madison," Paco said rather insistently.

Since she'd first taken in his chiseled abs showcased in the elegant smoking jacket open clear to his navel, Madison had loosely considered a convenient exit strategy in the event this did turn out to be a strip-poker game. Just in case. Mentally flipping through several alternatives, she settled for the old standby, *a sudden case of diarrhea*, to quickly excuse herself.

Looking anxiously around for the nearest bathroom, and on the brink of asking, she noticed Paco's not so subtle glances down. Her gaze quizzically followed his to her own feet. Then to his. Then to the delightful feet of the dynamic duo.

Smoking slippers. They were all wearing gold smoking slippers, each with their initials embroidered on top.

A burst of relieved laughter left her lips. Well, relief coupled with amusement at seeing Ted and Rex's matching ensembles paired with such elegant slippers. They'd managed to carry off hiker-meets-NASA engineer, topped off by the royal family.

The fun of kicking off her heels and sliding each foot into these pillows of heaven was only made better by admiring her own monograms in the top. *Best princess poker tournament ever.*

Paco led them to a room filled with golden art deco accents, red wallpaper, and black drapes, obviously decorated by the Queen of Hearts himself. The octagonal felt-lined card table was ready, with small side tables for each player brimming with charcuterie, berries, finger pastries, and an area for each of their drinks.

Paco took his seat opposite from Madison, and Ted and Rex naturally fell into place on each side of her. Paco's hands were a whirl as he manipulated the cards, flipping them between shuffles, and showing off in a way that seemed purely for Madison's delight. She watched, fascinated by the magician who could pull her smile from thin air.

Finally, he dealt. "Five-card draw. Nothing wild. Ante up."

As everyone tossed a few chips into the center of the table, Rex leaned over to Madison. "And if you lose all your money, you still get to play."

"I love it. How long do you play for?" she asked.

"Until Ted starts his usual string of incessant yawns. A few hours at most," Paco teased.

CHAPTER 13

PACO

AFTER A FEW ROUNDS OF DRAWING, calling, and folding, an uneasy and slightly irritated feeling crept over Paco. His poker Spidey sense, that uneasy feeling of being played, was in full swing.

"Madison, did I hear you're the maid of honor at a wedding?" Ted asked. "That sounds fun."

"Well, yes. I just need a date."

Paco coughed up his sip of cosmo, practically choking it out his nose. Rex leaned over to lay several hard pats on his back. Determined, Paco grunted his breathing into submission, trying not to fly off the handle.

"Why don't you have a date?" he said sharply, his indignation coming off a little stronger than intended. "I thought you *were* seeing someone."

"Well, yes, I am." Madison's feeble attempt at calm and collected didn't exactly soothe his alarm. "I am definitely seeing *someone*. But, well, I'm just not sure we're ready to take things to the next level."

"The next level?" he asked, giving her a blank look.

"Mm-hmm. You know. We haven't exactly decided to go . . . public."

"We? So, it's a joint decision? As in both of you." Paco held his cards high, intentionally covering most of his subdued, pissed-off expression, though there was no masking his paternal tone of disapproval.

Madison's already covering for Alex and his pervasive asshole streak. What the fuck is wrong with him? I am so going to kick his ass.

Studying her, Paco didn't miss much as she sank lower in her seat and started fidgeting with her arm. *Shit. I'm triggering her hives.* Paco figured he had about ten seconds to make it right before Madison bolted with some lame excuse.

I'd bet a c-note she'll go for the old daring diarrhea escape.

He'd deal with his own feelings later, likely with a size twelve shoe up Alex's ass. For now, he'd seduce her with, of all things, an obvious mistake. He'd paid attention, round after round. Madison Taylor was a cunning little card counter. Just like him. Except, she used her superpowers to lose.

With renewed energy, Paco shuffled and dealt a fresh hand. It took about half a second for Ted and Rex to fold.

"Raise," Paco said, smiling confidently at Madison. He raised a brow, show-casing his most charming dimples, double-daring her to play.

"Raise, huh?" Madison let out a laugh.

He knew it, and it was written all over her face that she knew it too. His hand was pure shit.

"Just to be crystal clear," she said smugly, "you said raise?"

"Yeah, girl. I said raise." He defiantly polished off his drink, then flipped his glass, forcing the cherry to fly through the air and land squarely in his mouth. He chomped it, channeling a smart-ass schoolgirl popping gum.

"Oh, challenge accepted." Madison pushed her chips forward, mimicking Paco's suave demeanor, and finished off her own drink.

But as she attempted the final move, flipping the glass to toss the cherry into the air, she overshot, forgetting there were two. Flying high, one cherry landed squarely in her wide-open mouth, but the other took an Olympic dive straight down her blouse, lodging securely in its new nesting spot deep between her breasts.

Wide-eyed, she scanned the room as if hoping no one had noticed. As usual, the TRex twins played it as cool as Paco imagined they could. Ted kept his stare on the felted table, studying it intently. Meanwhile, Rex appeared to be counting the tiles of the coffered ceiling. Paco laughed under his breath.

"Where's the " Madison stood as Paco pointed down the hall to the nearest bathroom, then rose with Ted and Rex while she rushed away from the table.

As she exited the room, Ted and Rex breathed out loud sighs of relief, and Paco placed reassuring hands firmly on their shoulders. "Well, gentlemen, I'm pretty sure the evening will only go downhill from here."

Ted and Rex nodded in vehement agreement before tidying up and scurrying out the door. They shouted their good-byes to Madison and left.

Paco took a moment to refresh his drink, then headed to the balcony to reel in a few emotions that were begging to break to the surface.

Madison's meek little steps approached. "Hello?"

"Out here," Paco called out, luring her to the balcony.

Her gasp of delighted approval gave him a strange sense of pride in his place. Approval wasn't in his vocabulary. He never sought it out. But somehow, it felt good, and he took in the sweeping city views differently, noticing every bright colorful twinkle across the skyline.

"God," she whispered, "and I thought this place couldn't get more amazing."

As a gust of crisp evening air hit them, Madison shivered a little. Paco took the opportunity to drape an oversize pashmina across her shoulders. She pulled it tight as she stood next to him on the balcony, looking out into the dazzling sparkles twinkling in the darkness.

"So, did everything come out all right?" Paco said, teasing her.

"Yes, and became a casualty of the three-second rule. So, I take it I scared the fellas off?"

"Hey, best poker game ever," he said, assuring her with a shoulder nudge. "If you want a cappuccino or nightcap, I could call Enrique to come up."

"Enrique?"

"Yes, my pool boy."

Madison beamed. "You have a pool?"

Pure mischief laced his words as he sang, "*Nooo*," and they both chuckled. "But he makes a great cappuccino, among other things."

Paco hung his head, turning somber. "Listen, sorry about grilling you earlier. I didn't mean to. I was just . . . disappointed in a certain someone." He looked over, catching her wince.

"I'm sorry, Paco."

"Sorry? *You* have nothing to be sorry about," he said, wrapping his arm around her shoulders, rubbing her tension away.

"I'm just, I don't know . . . not ready for what it means to bring the worldly Alex Drake to a wedding as my date."

Paco stood quietly. The best way to get information was always through silent, attentive listening. That, and he couldn't tip his hand that he'd assumed the opposite.

"Bringing Alex to a wedding when I'm the maid of honor is like bringing him home for Christmas dinner during a family reunion. There'll be a lot of attention. And questions. And what do I say? We're still getting to know each other, and there's so much still . . . unanswered."

Clasping his hands tightly together, Paco leaned on the railing, looking out and away. He could tell her. Answer all those unanswered questions. Give Madison the peace of mind she deserved.

But Alex asked her for a month, and she'd accepted. It was their agreement, not his. Like it or not, this was Alex's call. And whether he'd ever admit it to Alex's face, Paco respected the hell out of the man. So much so that he wouldn't interfere.

Despite being shoulder to shoulder, he could feel Madison's distance. She'd give in, but at the cost of pulling away.

"I'm making such a big deal out of this," she said, wringing her hands. "It's ridiculous. I'll just invite him."

Paco gave her a paternal look. "Not on my account. You're perfectly entitled to your feelings. Validated, even. You want the whole story first, to know what you're getting into, and that's fair. Besides, having a date for a wedding isn't a big deal. And if you're very nice, I might have another option for you."

That put the shine back in her eyes. "Really?"

"Yes. But I need to check a few things first. No matter what, you'll have a date for the wedding, and Alex will be fine with it."

Madison looped her arm through his, leaning her head on his shoulder. Comfortable with him. The way it should be.

"You're like an incredibly stylish guardian angel. Thank you." Madison smothered a yawn as she spoke. "I should get going."

"Why? I have a ridiculously fabulous guest suite. Stay. You know Alex will be working at least three more hours. I need to chat with him anyway about business, and I'll let him know. Check it out. It's the last room down the hall."

"You sure?"

"Have you ever known me to be unsure?" He eyed her with the confidence of a man who had never been wrong. Even to his detriment.

Her warm smile kept him in the moment, and her soft peck good night on his cheek tugged his heart hard enough that she'd own that piece of it forever.

❧

As Madison made her way to the guest suite, Paco caught the faint buzz of his cell. *Perfect timing.* He answered quickly, eager to chat.

"How's the game?" Alex asked, faking his way through wanting to hear about Madison.

Paco knew way too much about the situation with the two of them. Their month-long agreement was almost done, and this was the longest they'd been apart since entering said agreement. Without a doubt, it was eating Alex alive, torturing him from the inside out, though he'd never let on.

"Game's over. I offered Madison my guest suite tonight. Said you'd be preoccupied with work for several hours more, but I thought her staying here would be best, with this whole wedding thing. Madison didn't want to get into it, but I know it's killing you."

Alex let out a long sigh. "She's not ready to go public, and I don't blame her. She has no idea who she's in bed with. Literally. How can I expect her to trust me when I'm obviously hiding the past?"

Exhausted, Paco tossed out a loaded question and his best advice. "Why not just tell her?" Saying he had nothing to lose would be pointless. Paco would do it differently, but this was Alex's call. "Thirty days is almost up anyway, and this full-on delay of the inevitable is doing nothing more than adding a daily row of cinder blocks to the growing brick wall between you."

Alex took his time considering Paco's words, like he always did before coming to the exact same conclusion, no matter what the topic.

"You're right," he said, acquiescing as if he had a choice. But Paco's smug grin lasted for half a second, with his words barely making a dent in Alex's emotional shield. "It's better she stays there tonight."

Yup. He's getting a shoe up the ass.

"Fine," Paco said. "Well, in other news, I've got a plan B lined up for this whole wedding fiasco, but I'm giving you the courtesy of disapproving. Doesn't mean I'll listen, but you're free to share your feelings. If you have any."

"What can I say? You're my plan B kind of guy. I trust you implicitly."

"Good. I've got a great little number for Madison's pic."

"Pic?"

"Yup. For her dating profile. I'm thinking of leading with *Have a boyfriend but need a guy for the night.* I'll let you know how it goes."

"What kind of plan B is that?"

"Oh, now you care. What happened to 'I trust you. Implicitly.'"

"Fine," Alex said, letting Paco imagine the vein bulging from the middle of his forehead.

Evil scheming—check.

"Fine, what?" Paco asked, faking genuine surprise.

"Fine. I'll take your fucking afternoon-talk-show shrink advice. I'll figure out something tonight."

"*And?*" Paco said insistently.

"And I'll tell Madison everything. *Tomorrow*. I'll tell her tomorrow."

CHAPTER 14

ALEX

ALEX HUNG up the phone and lay back in bed. Shirtless, he glided his hand mindlessly over the scars across his chest as he let his thoughts drift. Each flaw and welt in his skin had, over time, become him. The point at which his past and present always converged. A testament. A reminder.

There are no second chances.

Are there?

Memories flipped though his mind like photographs, each image making his heart pound harder, pulsing loudly in his ears. He shuddered and his eyes slammed shut.

Fuck. I can do this. I have to do this.

The soft chimes of his phone tugged Alex back to the here and now, announcing a FaceTime request from *her*. Wiping away the beads of sweat from his brow, he sucked in a breath and answered.

Madison's image filled the screen, with soft eyes and a warm smile that always managed to chase away the demons inside. She was here. He could relax.

"Hey, beautiful," he said, his normal, nothing-to-worry-about facade in place. "Did you win big?"

"Hardly. And the game ended abruptly when I made a cherry disappear deep into my cleavage."

"What kind of poker is that?"

"Texas Hold'em."

"Well, I'd love an encore performance of seeing how you hold 'em."

"I bet you would."

"Might the big winner be free for lunch tomorrow? I'm taking some time away from the office, and I'd love to take you to your favorite place, wherever that might be."

"Well, since I'm about as picky as a goat, how about you surprise me with something you love. Something that makes you feel like home."

You make me feel like home, Madison.

"Deal." He watched her take two subtle yawns, which always meant she was seconds from falling into a deep sleep. "See you tomorrow. Sleep well."

"You too." With that, Madison kissed two fingers and pressed them to the screen.

He let her hang up, lying there with nothing but an emptiness so strong, he had to stop himself from racing over there, busting through the door, and curling his body up against hers.

Alex had the night to figure things out. Not that he would sleep, with his most common bedfellow being insomnia. He continued pushing past the flashbacks from a decade gone, turning away from the play-by-play loop that normally plagued his mind. Fighting for control against his quickening pulse and the perspiration gathering on his face and neck, he got out of bed.

Rather than succumb to the undertow of dark recollections, Alex did what he always did. Pushed himself to exhaustion. In his penthouse gym, he flipped a switch. Hit with bright lights, he paused for a second to allow his eyes to adjust.

Moving past the other equipment, he opted for his fail-safe. The Zero Runner. It was the one machine that would give him the benefit of a ten-mile run while preserving what was left of his knees. Kicking up from zero to a heart-pounding pace, he felt his tension ebb.

How the fuck will Madison not blame me when I blame myself? Or not hate me when I . . . I hate myself? Or . . .

Alex upped his pace, trying to run as far away from the past as possible, despite it being planted so firmly deep inside him.

Or leave? Is there a hope in hell she won't leave?

CHAPTER 15

MADISON

IN THE EARLY hours of the midmorning workday, Madison escaped to catch a quick break. Stealing just enough time to sit alone in an isolated corner of the local artisan coffee house gave her a respite between analyzing charts and trend analyses. She had exactly twenty minutes to lose herself in a tall, dark roast cappuccino, catch up on a little reading, and relax a little before the next two hours of studying eye-crossing graphs.

"May I join you?" The annoying voice was recognizable, but completely unwelcome.

Madison glanced up from her seat at the intimate café table to see Frank Seaver looking down on her with a disgusting grin. Seaver was a senior vice president of Excelsior/Centurion, or E/C, the largest competitor of DGI.

He was known for being sharp as a whip, a mediocre dresser, and one of the biggest assholes of all time, often flaunting his expertise by mansplaining his way through every conversation with a woman.

Seaver constantly bandied his title about, using his status in the reckless and manipulative way common to bullies, the acts of a desperate man eager to secure his position as president of the company one day. One day very soon, if all his bragging were to come true.

Without knowing him well, or really at all, Madison *knew* his kind. Years in the service industry might not count for much on a résumé, but they gave her a solid foundation for instantly gauging *people*. The good, the bad, and the buttheads.

Over the years, Madison had fine-tuned her own sixth sense about people, and this guy was bad news. She'd only seen him once or twice at DGI, but between his slovenly appearance, the bits of food that always seemed to be stuck in his teeth, and the way he looked every woman up and down—present company included—absolutely made her skin crawl.

"I'm actually waiting for someone," Madison said firmly, hoping her assertive tone would cover the lie.

True to form, he ignored her, promptly plopping his pompous ass in the seat next to hers and scooted his chair uncomfortably close.

Oh my God. His breath.

"Oh, you're waiting for me," he said before snapping his fingers for the waitress. Shocked, Madison stared. *How rude.*

The annoyed server ambled over to take his order. "You snapped?"

"Large black coffee in a to-go cup," he said without looking at her, instead leering so hard at Madison's body, she set a menu between them.

If he tries to move it, he's getting a fork in his hand.

"As I was saying, you're waiting for me."

The young woman returned with his coffee, and Seaver promptly retrieved an obnoxiously large old flask from his inside blazer pocket.

Taking one whiff as he poured the amber liquid into his cup, Madison felt her blood boil, driving a wave of heat straight to her cheeks.

This is the jack-hole who almost cost me the job at DGI. Nearly knocked me over, dumped most of his liquor-laced coffee on my blouse, and didn't bother looking me in the eye before bolting away. Well, maybe he's irritated the barista enough to ensure booze isn't his only add-on.

"And *why* would I be waiting for you?"

As much as Madison wanted to toss her own coffee right into his smug face, she knew Seaver's reputation. His pastimes included obsessing over the bottom line and initiating corporate wars against his enemies. If he was targeting her, it had to do with DGI. Like it or not, it would be worth her time to listen.

Holding back her repulsion at the food stains clinging to a shirt that hadn't been washed, oh, ever, Madison sat attentively.

"Let's just say I'm about to make you a very wealthy woman," he said, sliding his palm onto her knee.

Rather than jabbing a fork into his chubby, hairy hand, she gently lifted it to the table, keeping hold of it in the pretense of paying the man some attention. Choking back the bile rising in her throat, she asked, "And how exactly are you going to do that?"

Madison forced a smile that Seaver returned—chunks of food and all.

"Well, I understand you just might have the upper hand at DGI. Am I correct?"

Frank Seaver was many things . . . arrogant, opinionated, and smelly. But *wrong?* A jackass like him didn't climb the corporate ladder by accident. *He's up to something.*

She probed him for more. "I'm just an analyst, so I'm really not sure where you're going with this, but I'd"—*gulp*—"love to know more." She wasn't sure how long she could keep this up, but painted on a smile that she hoped gave him an assurance he could tell her anything.

"My dear, do you know what a proxy vote is?"

Madison's eyes widened as her mind began spinning. *The son of a bitch is angling for a hostile takeover. But why approach me?*

Contemplative, she covered her emotions. Her concerns. "Maybe," she said, looking up as if struggling to think. "It has something to do with a person giving their voting power to someone else. I think."

What's he up to?

His smile emerged, brimming with the charm of a crocodile. "Very good. And for the kind of proxy voting I'm after, I'd like to make you an offer. For your vote."

Wary, Madison took a moment to think. Her DGI retirement shares would be pretty much worthless with her junior status at the company, and couldn't come close to what a hostile takeover would require. And there was no way this guy was stalking his way through the corporate directory, one employee at a time, trying to get their votes.

Frustrated, she blew out a breath. *Can he just get to the point already? Maybe there's a way to speed this along.*

"I'm afraid you're wasting your time. I'm not nearly the stakeholder you think I am." Madison didn't have to fake her baffled expression. Genuinely dumbfounded, she studied him for a moment. The man didn't come close to living up to his reputation.

Their discussion now over, Madison waved for the barista, but ever the charmer, Seaver swatted her away. After digging through a very worn leather attaché that had probably once belonged to a Roosevelt, he pulled a piece of paper from it.

From where she sat, Madison could see it was a copy of a piece of paper that had been crumpled in spots, with large tears from one side to the other. Tape seemed to be holding it together like pieces of an aged treasure map. Overly dramatic for the circumstances, he slid it to Madison.

What the hell? In her hands was a copy of the contract Alex had given her—the one relinquishing all he owned if he ever lied to her. *But I threw it away.*

After her first night at Alex's penthouse, she'd torn it up and tossed it without a second thought. It should have been gone forever.

An unexpected breeze from the shop's door opening nearly snatched the paper from Madison's hand, and she gripped it harder. "Um, where did you get this?"

"Aw, naive little girl, a savvy businessman never reveals his secrets." He sneered, triumph lighting his beady eyes. "And from your reaction, I'm guessing you didn't realize you are the new majority shareholder of DGI."

The nudge was all she needed to pretend to be in the dark, diligently examining the document as if for the very first time.

"For argument's sake," she said, "let's imagine this is a legitimate contract. Which is crazy. As I read this, in order for this, well, insane transaction to occur, Alex Drake would need to somehow lie to me. He hasn't."

"Oh, but I assure you, he *has*."

The only thing keeping Madison from vomiting at Seaver's disgusting tone was that good organic free-trade java shouldn't be wasted.

Again, he reached into the battered attaché and pulled out another piece of paper. This time, it was an image of a photograph, printed on standard letter-size paper from what looked to be a home printer. Despite the fact the guy was low on magenta, the image was unmistakable.

Front and center of an obvious wedding photograph stood an exotic and strikingly beautiful woman, maybe the most beautiful Madison had ever seen. Dressed in white and with a tulle veil pulled back behind her head, she carried a lavish bouquet of pale roses. On both sides of her stood the men who had become staples in Madison's everyday life—Alex and Paco.

Seeing the image managed to rip Madison's heart from her chest for this asshole to dissect. What made it worse was that the picture was beautiful, filled with joy and happiness. So perfect, it could be a layout for a national bridal magazine.

By the looks of Alex and Paco, this snapshot had to be recent. The salt and pepper strands at Alex's temples—the ones she'd run her fingers through so many times—were as much in view as his wide smile and sparkling eyes.

Maybe it's older than it looks. Maybe not.

Forcing a sip of her coffee down her throat, Madison choked back her tears and took a deep breath before responding.

Without looking up, she kept her voice steady, despite her pounding pulse and her breaking heart. "He never said he wasn't married."

Disgusted, she said it. No matter what was happening between her and Alex, she was merely a pawn to Seaver. But this pawn was determined to protect DGI from a scumbag like him.

"Loyal to the end? A noble quality, though somewhat misplaced. Oh, I promise you, we're going to take all that pain and anger of yours and transform it into cold, hard cash. He'll pay. He'll hurt. I swear."

The man practically hissed the last words, oblivious to the fact that Madison wasn't conceding. *God, read the room.*

Confident, he pulled out another photo, placing it on top of the first one. Unlike the laser-printed wedding picture, this was a real no-kidding photo, yellowing and slightly torn at one corner.

Growing number by the second, she picked up the small picture and took a good, long look. The bastard had the nerve to be pleased with himself, propping his elbows on the table as he grinned smugly at her. Like a sadistic ringmaster, Seaver obviously reveled in wounding a creature before breaking its spirit. And this blow cut her to the core.

Madison let out the slightest gasp but remained as silent as possible, taking in the image through the blur of tears. *This has to be fake. Doctored. It can't be real.*

Impatient for the first time since sitting down, Seaver pointed at the image and began what had to be a well-rehearsed monologue. "That there's your brave brother, Jack. Valiant soldier. Dedicated son. Remarkable brother. Taken too soon. And next to him, well, you probably recognize that man. Don't you, Madison?"

She said nothing, barely registering her recognition of Alex.

"Alex Drake didn't just hire you, my dear. He hired you to play you the same way he played Jack. Well, not exactly the same," Seaver said with a smirk.

Desperately, Madison scrutinized the photo, partially to pull back the tears that threatened, and partially to figure out how this could be possible.

Her brother was in uniform, his freshly minted lieutenant bars indicating this had to be months before his death. And the man next to him was a much younger but still unmistakable Alex Drake, who had one arm around Jack's shoulders. The arm of another person was also around Jack's shoulders, but from the other side. But the picture was cropped, and that person might never be known.

The furious look she shot at Seaver had no effect. In fact, he seemed pleased, smiling as he sipped his coffee. But her glare wasn't moving from him, and after a minute, he leaned in. In a full breath of coffee, cheap booze, and halitosis, he snarled his words.

"Your anger is misdirected. But you can take it out on Alex Drake—the man responsible for your brother's death."

In an instant, she dropped her gaze. There was no stopping the tears, so why bother trying?

Biting her lip, Madison struggled to make sense of it. Any of it. She and her father had both investigated Jack's death for years, but the government had closed ranks. Her family had learned nothing about the cause of Jack's death or the circumstances surrounding it. Not one thing.

Maybe a mogul like Alex Drake could shut down an investigation. But could he be a murderer? He obviously knew Jack—why not tell her so?

Every second she thought it through pushed more of a single emotion to the surface. The one she'd been fighting. The one nagging at her for weeks—doubt.

I don't know Alex at all.

With her last shreds of composure, she held it together enough to ask, "Can I keep these? Verify their authenticity?" Madison's voice was so low, she wasn't entirely sure Seaver heard her.

"Of course, my dear." With that, he stood. "Nothing is possible without you. Our relationship will thrive on openness and trust for many, many years to come."

She felt his hand stroke her hair, but was too engrossed in a tidal wave of feelings to slap it away.

Seaver huffed out a laugh. "I'll help you get the closure you need while making you rich beyond your dreams. Let it soak in. Call me when you're ready. I'll take it from there."

He left his pristine, high-gloss business card on the table before tossing out a crumpled ten-dollar bill, letting it land in a wad in her coffee cup. Finally, he swaggered out of the coffee house, his footsteps taking forever to disappear down the block.

Madison collected the photos and pieced-together contract and tucked them into her bag, then pulled out her wallet. Her hands shaking, she slipped out a twenty as the barista hurried over to stop her.

"He paid, hon. You're good."

I'm good? The last thing I am is good.

On the verge of uncontrollable bawling, Madison laid the twenty-dollar bill on the table. Wide-rimmed dark sunglasses would be her only defense against the tears now flowing freely.

"He's not buying my coffee. Or me."

CHAPTER 16

MADISON

IN A DAZE, Madison wandered the city, eventually ending up where she'd started. A place she felt safe. The only place she could sink into the quicksand of emotions on the verge of engulfing her. And the only place that had nothing to do with Alex Drake. At all.

Exhausted, she found herself back home.

As soon as she walked through the door of her apartment, she collapsed under the weight of devastation. Her crying seesawed between light and controlled sobs to hysterically bawling. The worst came when she thought of Jack.

All her sorrow and pain poured out in the back-and-forth loop that replayed every detail of the days after her brother's death. The military notification. The return of his effects. The delivery of his remains. The funeral.

But the tragedy that didn't end with him. Jack was everything, and the shock waves of loss hit everyone, ripping her family apart.

After Jack's death, her father could barely function, and her mother couldn't bear living with a ghost of a man while dealing with her own loss of their son. The divorce happened so fast, tearing Madison from her father. Visitations were occasional, at best. Rebuilding that relationship took time. Madison hadn't just lost her brother—she'd also lost her father, and in many ways, she'd lost herself.

Barely fifteen at the time, she'd dealt with everything the way any teen would. Day by day, as best she could, not having much of a say or a choice. Her days were spent building a life around the hole in her heart, but never really filling it.

And today, that hole had been ripped open with cruelty and raw pain, shattering a very vulnerable side of her soul.

A long time passed before she had the strength to move from the spot she'd collapsed in. Little by little, she found enough strength to pick herself back up. Aimlessly, Madison scanned the untouched room.

Her apartment was exactly as she'd left it nearly a month ago. She'd moved into Alex's luxury penthouse before completely unpacking. Boxes were everywhere, stacked here and there, their contents waiting for her attention. She'd been too wrapped up in launching her career. And a new life. And her relationship with him. *Too goddamned wrapped up in Alex Drake.*

Well, not today. Today, right now, this moment was about Jack. And her family. About honoring the life of her brother and bringing all she had out into the light. Every photo. Every memento. Reclaiming the world she'd been robbed of. But . . .

What about the book?

Her book. From her grandfather. Another loss.

I have to get it back.

Across the small space, the microwave clock in the kitchenette gave her the time. A few hours lost, but the day could still be salvaged. Alex would still be at work. The penthouse would be empty.

I can run in and out, but then what? What happens after that?

Pushing back her uncertainty, she didn't know and didn't care. Seeing the finish line wasn't important. This was a fresh start.

In haste, Madison grabbed her bag and flung open the door. About to bolt, she was stopped by the liar himself. Alex Drake stood there, staring down at her, holding his fist in mid-knock.

Seeing him now was too much.

It wasn't the anger and rage that consumed her. It was regret. Regret at gazing into those mesmerizing eyes and remembering the first time he'd knocked on a door that she'd opened. The first tender moments of something meaningful. Magical. Unlocking his world so completely, he'd captured her heart.

But now? Seeing the gorgeous man—the manipulator—was the last thing she needed.

CHAPTER 17

ALEX

"Madison, my God. We've been worried." Concerned, Alex studied her eyes. They were red and swollen and . . . unfamiliar. Wild. Dark. Maybe enraged. "What's wrong? What's happened?"

Opening his arms wide, Alex took a step toward her, ready to embrace her. But wide-eyed, she backed away. When his panic surged into overdrive, his instincts took over, shifting his approach from concerned boyfriend to trained operative.

Instantly, he dropped his arms and softened his demeanor. Focusing, he relied on the skills that always took over in a crisis, defusing the fragile situation he now found himself a part of. He took a step back to give her space as his mind spun with one too many worst-case scenarios.

What the hell is going on?

Alex took small, deliberate steps, crossing the threshold and entering, but left the door ajar, showing Madison she was free to leave or stay. That she was safe.

The lines in her brow deepened as she shifted her gaze from Alex to the door. Maybe her anxiety was stronger than he thought. It could be a panic attack. But it felt like fear.

She doesn't seem to know me. And she's afraid.

She had to open up. Forcing her out of this wasn't the answer. Whatever the hell this was, it would take patience. And time.

Alex steadied his voice, lowering it to a calm, commanding level. "Madison, please talk to me. You can tell me anything. What happened?"

Her expression was contorted. Conflicted.

With very slow movements, he motioned toward the sofa, silently asking if they could have a seat. When she gave him a begrudging nod, he made his way around a few boxes to the couch. Though there was plenty of room on the seat next to him, his gestured invitation was met with no response. No movement. No sound. Subtly, he offered the chair across from him, giving her any possibility to relax and sit.

Madison held out for a moment, pulling in a shuddering breath before lowering herself onto a chair across from him. Her glare was desperate. Exasperated. And by the look of those swollen, red-rimmed eyes, she'd been drained of every emotion and tear. Still, she clutched at her purse for dear life, creating a barrier between them.

Alex recognized the signs. *Shock. She's in shock. Coaxing her too quickly might backfire.*

"Take all the time you need," he said calmly, almost hypnotically, before lowering his elbows to his knees, leaning forward and trying like hell to gain any shred of insight.

Madison's clothes were intact. No sign of struggle. No contusions. No marks. Nothing from an impact. Nothing physically traumatic to give him a clue at what could have happened to her. Nothing other than her big, beautiful eyes, ravaged by tears.

Contemplative, Madison studied Alex without a word until finally, her gaze lowered. After what seemed like an eternity, she cleared her throat, beginning with a question.

"How did you know where I was?"

Pointing to the purse she clutched like a teddy bear, he gave her a soft, matter-of-fact response. "Your corporate phone has a tracker. We had a lunch date. I thought you might have been tied up, but when I heard you'd missed several meetings and hadn't used your keycard to reenter the building, I panicked. Madison, please, can you tell me what's going on?"

After another small eternity of silence where Alex could do nothing but be patient and sit still, Madison finally spoke. "Tell me something, Mr. Drake. Are you married?" she asked, and the sight of her trembling lower lip killed him. She was heartbroken, and he had no idea why.

Surprised, he sat up straighter. "No, I'm not. Why would you think that?"

Glaring at him, Madison dug into her purse and whipped out what seemed to be Exhibit A. "Looks like the happy couple and his best friend."

Alex took the photo. Tamping down his alarm, he raked his fingers through his hair, controlling the tremble as his hand worked the tense area of his neck.

"That's exactly what it is," he muttered under his breath, staring hard at the image.

The matter-of-fact tone of his admission was probably the worst thing he could do with Madison, but he couldn't do more. *It can't be. Not again.*

Abruptly, Alex stood. Raising his voice startled her, but this was as controlled as he could be at the moment. "Madison, where did you get this?" He thrust it at her, snapping the sheet abruptly.

Pissed off and defiant, she snatched it back. "Is that all you can say? You're married, shacking up with me like I'm a kept woman, and all you can ask is where I got this? Who the hell do you think you are?"

Blankly, Alex stared. "Madison, there's a lot going on here, but please believe she's not my wife. I can expl—"

"Then whose wife is she? God, with all the secrets and bullshit, you'd think I'd be okay with this. News flash. I'm not."

Madison's voice was cool and cutting, but its venom made something completely clear. She might have been his at one point, but she wasn't his now.

The click of the door shutting gave Madison a jolt, and she spun toward it as the printout she held slipped from her fingers and landed at Paco's feet. Worry dulled his usually cheerful demeanor as he glanced at Alex, who had nothing for him but an apologetic look.

After locking the door, Paco scooped up the picture, his expression hardening as he stepped closer to Madison. "Yasmin isn't Alex's wife. She's mine."

CHAPTER 18

ALEX

ALEX WATCHED as Madison reeled from her raw emotions. *"Yours?"*

Before Paco could respond, Alex cut in.

"Madison, it's a long story, too long to explain now, but this is very, very important. Where did you get this?" When he tried stroking her arm, she whipped it away, so he did the only thing he could think of. He begged. "Please."

Not wasting time, Paco pulled out a small old-school flip phone. With an authority that seemed natural to him, he said three words. "Omega is compromised." Then he hung up.

The gravity of the situation was suffocating. There was no way for Madison to know. To comprehend.

Timidly, she said, "The man who gave me that also gave me this." Pulling the small photo from her purse, Madison reluctantly held it up to Alex.

Paco moved closer, eyeing it too. The glance he and Alex exchanged was solemn.

And then she said it, words Alex could never unhear. A question that came from the only woman he'd let in, see him unshielded, know how damaged he was. It shattered any hope of a future for them. There was no turning back.

"Alex, did you—" She choked back her tears. "Did you have something to do with my brother's death?"

Stunned, Alex stood there in disbelief. Paco stepped in, ever protective of his best friend, even with Madison. But the trembling hand Alex lifted stopped Paco cold.

It was Alex's turn to step back, to look at this woman like a stranger, and defend himself to the only person who had the power to be both his judge and jury. With a deep breath, he barely uttered the word, "No."

It was then that Alex realized the truth. Despite opening his world to Madison—his life—she didn't know him at all. Maybe, somehow, that was unfair. If he took a step back and looked at this objectively, maybe her perspective was understandable. But still, the accusation hit him like the blast wave of a nuclear bomb.

Since they first met a couple of months ago, he'd wrestled with how to tell her the whole story. The tragedy he and Madison shared. The senseless chain of events that bound them, bringing them all through a world of anguish to arrive at this very point. Yes, unpacking years of pain was inevitable. But he'd never imagined she'd assume he was remotely involved in Jack's death. Or worse, responsible.

Devastated and settling into his own fresh hell of shock, Alex switched back to autopilot—his last bastion of self-defense. Slipping back into a way of life he'd thought was over, dealing with the crisis of the moment, while suffocating everything else until it was lifeless and numb.

For people like Alex, life was a string of old habits that keep one day rolling into the next. He knew what he needed to do. What the situation demanded of him. And right now, he needed to leave.

Emotionless, he moved to the door. "Paco, stay with Madison. I'll take care of Yasmin."

But just as he stepped outside the apartment, Paco caught up and his strong grip wrapped around Alex's arm, holding him in place.

"What do you mean? Madison needs you." Paco leaned closer, lowering his voice. "And you need her."

The slight tremble that started quickly grew until it rocked through Alex, steadily overtaking his body in a full quake. In one sharp move, he broke free, his open palm landing on Paco's chest. "We don't have time for this. Omega requires cleanup. Epsilon is being activated."

Controlled, Paco held his wrist, huffing out his annoyance. Even though Alex had forty pounds on his friend, he was no match for a pissed-off Paco, and they both knew it.

"Goddammit, Paco!"

Instantly, Paco's expression morphed from faithful friend to *go fuck yourself*. Releasing Alex, he scowled as he crossed his arms across his chest.

"I'm sorry," Alex said, knowing he'd gone too far. If anyone had suffered, it was Paco. He had every right to demand to take point for protecting Yasmin.

Looking away, Alex shoved his hands in his pockets, a feeble attempt to mask how bad the tremors were getting. His voice calmed. "Look at Madison. She can't even make eye contact, let alone have me anywhere near her. I'm no good here. I'm—" Alex cleared his throat and clenched his teeth, trying hard to conceal the flush he could feel rising up his cheeks, and the heat saturating his ears.

Relenting, Paco unfolded his arms. After all their years together, he obviously knew what Alex needed now. Space. The quiet and isolation of a drive would let him breathe. Snap him out of it quicker.

"Okay," Paco said, clapping his back.

"I'll take care of Yasmin, I swear." Alex's words were factual but pleading, and he laid a reassuring hand on Paco's shoulder. "Nothing will happen to her. This isn't a full compromise. We don't know how much has been exposed. It's just . . . a precaution."

"I know," Paco said, perhaps trying to convince both of them.

Businesslike and focused, Alex retrieved his phone. "And you—you take care of Madison. Find out what happened. And . . ."

He glanced through the doorway. Despondent, Madison paced in her living room, wiping fresh tears from each cheek.

"Tell her—tell her everything." With a glance that exchanged their understanding, Alex rushed out, hurriedly pressing his phone to his ear.

CHAPTER 19

MADISON

MADISON LOOKED up to find Paco entering. Alone. Her shoulders drooping with a combination of relief and disappointment, she tried to control her shaking body and hold back her tears as she spoke.

"Paco, I don't know what's going on, but if I've done something that put someone in danger—"

In a few long strides, he wrapped his arms around her, rocking her with a tight hug. Her trembling subsided in his hold.

"Hey, you haven't," he said softly, which only made her sob harder. "Shhh. Yasmin will be fine. Alex will take care of it. He always does."

"He will?" It felt traitorous to say it again. To doubt Alex. Openly. But she had to hear Paco's response. To know.

He pulled away enough to look her in the eye, his expression unyielding. "Yes, he will. Look, Madison, it's really important that we know who's been pushing all this to you. It's a dirty little trick we call playback. They're feeding you misinformation in a way that looks real, but it's all smoke and mirrors to manipulate you. Gain intel." He cupped her cheek and forced her sad eyes to meet his. "We don't have a lot of time. We need to know who's after Yasmin."

Madison broke their embrace to grab her handbag and retrieve the battered contract, which she passed to Paco.

"As far as I know, they're not after your, um, wife," she said, and when he smiled at her hesitation, she told him the rest. "I think they're after Alex."

319

"Who are?" Paco asked as his phone buzzed. He took a moment to check. "It's Alex," he said, answering and turning on the speakerphone. "I have you on speaker. Madison shed some light on the situation. I'm not sure we're blown. Maybe just inadvertently exposed."

"Then what's this about?" Alex asked, his voice sounding steady and calm.

"Apparently, it's personal." Paco urged Madison with his eyes.

"Alex," she said, struggling to speak. "I th—think they're after you."

"Is that all?" he asked in that casual tone she'd gotten to know. It was easygoing. Reassuring. His way of protecting her. "This isn't my first rodeo. But I usually tend to keep my enemies closer. Who's targeting me?"

Disappointed to admit it, Madison said, "Frank Seaver."

"There's more," Paco said. "He had the contract you gave Madison."

Blubbering, Madison wanted to clarify. To explain. But she had no explanation. "I swear, I have no idea how he got it."

"Shhh." Paco rubbed her back gently, soothing her. "Alex, you still there?"

"Yes. Still here. I might be pushing a hundred miles an hour away from you two, but I'm not going anywhere."

His words lifted her heart in a way she couldn't understand. But this was Alex. The guy who'd said those same words when she fell apart after the parachute jump. As if he'd say it over and over again for the rest of their lives if he had to.

"Look," Alex said. "Epsilon is in motion. It's a good idea to maintain course. I'll wrap that up, which will probably take another two hours. If you don't hear from me, we'll circle back at the penthouse. But can you give me a moment with Madison?"

As requested, Paco toggled off the speakerphone, then handed the phone to her and stepped away. Her gaze followed him for a minute in the small space as he seemed to be deciding if he should step outside. Instead, he seemed to find the perfect excuse to slip inside her bedroom.

"Madison?"

"Yes, I'm here. Alex, I'm—"

"Don't say a word. Just listen. I know you're confused and unsure, and that's my fault. All of this could have been avoided if I'd just told you everything up front. But, as you're probably figuring out, it's complicated. I'm complicated."

"No, you're—" She paused, afraid to finish. *The only thing I need right now.*

"I'm ready to uncomplicate things. Seaver's gunning for a hostile takeover bid. They'll end up offering me a golden parachute, a huge lump-sum buyout to ensure I walk away quietly. Considering my options, maybe walking away isn't the end. Maybe, beautiful, it's a beginning. For us."

"What?" Madison asked softly. "Alex, what are you saying?"

A golden parachute? That's insane. A pile of money that would push him out of Drake Global Industries forever?

"You can't step down from DGI. You *are* DGI."

From memory, Madison could recite every major corporate milestone. List every office throughout the world. Every award. Alex Drake had built a garage startup into a billion-dollar empire. His fingerprints were on every achievement and honor. Without Alex Drake, there was no Drake Global Industries.

I can't let this happen.

"Truth is," he said, "I've been fighting for a lot of years now. I don't want to fight anymore. I want to wake up and know that I haven't wasted another day on meaningless work. To know that at the end of the day, I've got something wonderful to look forward to." He paused a moment. "And I know it's unfair to say it, but I don't care about any of it. I just want you, Madison."

She couldn't think of what to say or do, but this was one grand gesture she couldn't accept. "Alex—"

"Paco can tell you anything you want to know. Everything. And tomorrow, I've cleared my calendar. If you want to talk, or meet, or anything at all . . ."

She could hear the interruption of an incoming call. Someone else was demanding his attention, and she knew it was important.

"Madison, I'm sorry, but I need to take this. Just know that I'm here for you. I'll always be here for you."

With that, the call ended, and the phone clicked back to the home screen. Alex was gone.

Staring hard and wishing him back was no use. A whimpering sigh escaped her. So much had been left unsaid.

When Paco emerged from her bedroom, wearing one of her oversize T-shirts, pajama pants, and fuzzy pink slippers, Madison's instant smile was unavoidable. It was obvious the man could never be trusted with her stuff. The pale pink T-shirt had a queen logo across the front, making it doubly apropos.

He hopped on her couch, crisscross-applesauce style, and encouraged her to do the same. When she did, he took both her hands in a firm grip. He held them to his chest, meeting her eyes with a tender expression.

"There's a lot for us to talk about. I'd rather be comfortable if I'm going to bare my soul tonight. How about you put on some pajamas while I rustle up snacks and drinks?"

With a relieved inhale, Madison nodded in agreement, but snacks might be a problem since she hadn't lived there in weeks. Plus, a stocked refrigerator? Uh, serious backburner stuff there.

"I don't think I have any groceries. And any I do have are probably a science experiment just begging for a YouTube channel."

The doorbell rang, and Paco jumped to his feet to answer as Madison followed. The delivery man outside was loaded down with an assortment of deliciously fragrant Chinese food, and a large brown paper bag filled with a bottle of Grey Goose vodka and all the fixings for Paco's sexed-up cosmos, including the ice and glasses. *Because the man is an absolute genie.*

"We're all set." After a quick inventory, Paco motioned the delivery man to the small table, where he carefully set the bags.

As Madison rummaged through them, he yanked her by the hips, shooing her away.

"Change first. Comfy jammies and comfort food to get us through this night." Under his breath, his voice was strained. "We're gonna need it."

It was clear Paco was trying to dress up a pile of crap with her favorite foods and some warm comfort. As he worked to set everything up in the cramped space, she gave him a hug from behind before dutifully obeying and reacquainting herself with her comfiest loungewear.

With the bedroom door cracked open, she could hear Paco clanking about and fixing their drinks. In his best Bette Davis impression, he drawled, "Fasten your seat belts. It's going to be a bumpy night."

The man was freaking adorable. She could hear him give the cocktail shaker a fierce rattle before pouring. Peeking out, she caught him downing one, pursing his lips with disapproval at the empty glass before drinking the other. Apparently, their impending discussion had a two-drink minimum.

"Hey, save some for me," she called out.

"Don't worry. There's plenty where that came from." Soon, there was another rattle of the shaker as he promptly fixed another round.

Paco looked up as Madison returned. She wasn't exactly the girl next door. More like the girl next door's comfy cousin. Her wavy locks were wound into a bun on top of her head, and her pink fleece robe was tightly cinched, revealing only the bottoms of her flannel pajama pants and fuzzy panda slippers.

Hands on her hips, she admired the slight wobble to his stance. "And exactly how many am I trailing by?"

"Three," Paco said with a strong roll of his *r*. Curiosity washed over his expression. "What's under the robe?"

"Oh, just a shirt."

"Come on . . . let's see your go-to undisputed number one comfy shirt of all time."

With a roll of her eyes, Madison loosened her robe, tugging it open to reveal a very worn and extra-snug E.T. THE EXTRA-TERRESTRIAL T-shirt. When Paco's eyebrows rose with amused judgment, Madison sternly cautioned him. "Not a word."

On cue, one eyebrow dropped. The judgy one. The amused one held its ground, prompting her to explain.

"Jack gave it to me for my eighth birthday. It's my favorite movie of all time, and wearing it somehow always makes me, I don't know, feel better. Like everything's going to be all right. And before you go thinking *E.T.* is juvenile, Neil Diamond wrote the song 'Heartlight' because it's such a beautiful movie."

Paco seemed to be feeling every ounce of the effects of that third cocktail. Genuinely fascinated, he asked, "Really?"

CHAPTER 20

MADISON

With cocktails poured, Chinese food in hand, and "Heartlight" softly playing from Paco's phone, Madison and Paco both tended to their boxes of chow mein, each equally adept at using chopsticks. Paco ate quietly, quelling any conversation for most of the meal. Even his chewing was unnervingly soft.

Done picking at her food, Madison set the takeout box on a side table. Staring at Paco, she wondered how long he intended to stall with this girls-night-in setup. Or how bad the blow was to come.

Paco finished off a last mouthful of noodles and stood. Gathering the remnants of their meals, he tossed them in the garbage can in the kitchen, then grabbed the tall bottle of liquid courage on his way back.

He took a breath, stopped the music on his phone, and returned to his place on the couch.

Beseeching him with hopeful eyes and a wry smile, she wasn't sure what to ask or how to start, but thankfully didn't need to decide. After a swig straight from the vodka bottle, Paco wedged it between his lotus-crossed legs, then started with a question of his own.

"Madison, what do you know about Jack's death?"

After a few seconds, she forced out an honest response. "Nothing at all, I guess. The military wouldn't say a word about what happened or even where he was or what he'd been doing."

Thoughtfully, Paco sipped from the bottle again. "Where's that picture you had?"

Madison took it from the end table and carefully handed it to him. Taking a moment to look it over, he smiled slightly before he turned it toward her. Holding it up to give her another look, he let it dangle from his fingertips with his knuckles facing her.

"What do you see?" he asked.

Her gaze followed the figures in the photo, first examining Jack and then Alex. Uncertain, she looked back at Paco, shaking her head slightly.

Shrugging, she said, "I see Jack and Alex. It had to be right after Jack's commission as an officer. And Alex is much younger than now, maybe about the same age as Jack. It had to be just . . . before."

She didn't elaborate on *before what*. It was clear Paco understood.

Insistent, he held the photo higher. "Look again, Madison."

He wasn't angry. If anything, his tone was softer. Sincere.

Madison did as he asked, determined to find whatever she had to be missing.

Following the line of the mystery man's hand, her eyes caught the smallest clue, and she leaned closer. Gasping, she made the discovery. The one Paco nodded to as she searched his eyes for confirmation.

As Paco held the photo for her, his expression melted, and she reached out to traced the ring on his finger. His pinky ring. It was the same one on the hand of the man just out of the photo. The man was Paco.

"You were there?" Madison asked, watching the exaggerated nods of a man pickled and boozed.

"I was there," he said somberly. "I was there when it happened. All of it. Every—" He choked up, pinching the bridge of his nose hard, not quite stopping his own tears from forming.

"Why are you cut out of the photo?" Madison wondered aloud, her finger tracing that side of the photo and noticing for the first time that the edge was frayed. It was subtle, but up close looked as though the paper had been creased repeatedly, then torn.

With a huff, he took another swig. "I'll get to that. But I need to start with the night it happened. The night Jack . . ."

Snapping his eyes shut, Paco took a moment, and Madison laid a hand on his knee. Regaining his composure, he started again, now running his thumb over Jack's smiling image.

"Jack and I were recruited separately. They were seeking military members who possessed . . . special skills, you could say. Well, except Alex."

"Alex?" Madison traced a finger over his image. "Why isn't he wearing a uniform?"

"Because Alex wasn't military. He wasn't one of us." Paco pulled the photo closer and blinked to regain his focus. "God, I hated that son of a bitch back then."

His rough words were oddly endearing. Paco took more than a swig before continuing. It was enough of a gulp to push him past his discomfort and continue.

"So, there we were, the three of us in a Jeep, in the pitch black of night, right in the heart of BFE, when Alex's Spidey sense kicks in. The man could feel things. Anxious, he insisted on taking a look around. That didn't go over well with Jack, who told him to keep his ass in the Jeep."

"That sounds like Jack," Madison said, remembering him fondly.

"At which point Alex hopped out."

"Which sounds like Alex."

"Yup. Alex didn't care. None of us answered to each other. And Jack and I . . ." Paco trailed off, looking at Madison as he chose his words. "Jack and I always had each other's back, and loyalty was a big deal with him. Just like with you."

With the tip of his finger, he lifted her chin as he motioned to the windowsill. A handful of pennies were neatly stacked in rows. It was a family pact she thought nobody knew about.

"I knew the consequences of not backing Jack. But I couldn't shake it. I grew up in the streets. Fighting is in my blood. Like Alex, I could feel something headed our way." Paco's expression was soft and apologetic before he dropped his gaze. "I wanted Jack to be right."

After a heavy breath, he pushed out the rest. "Alex and I both left the Jeep, tracking in opposite directions away from Jack's position. That's when it happened. Alex noticed something. Something neither Jack nor I did."

"What?"

Paco looked away, as if seeing the tragedy projected on a screen before him. "Signaling. Small white lights in the distance. They knew where we were. Alex raced toward the Jeep, screaming for Jack to get out. I ran back too, but we were both too late. The RPG hit. I could see him. Jack tried getting out, but couldn't clear the blast. The force of the explosion threw him, pelleting him with shrapnel as it threw his body far from me. Alex was closer, catching the white hot bumper right in the chest. It burned clear through his clothes, branding his skin. I was the luckiest, or the most damned of them all."

It took another swig for him to keep going.

"I got hit in the head with something." Pulling his hair back, he revealed a scar along his hairline. "But never knew what. It knocked me out cold. It was Yasmin who discovered me, a local girl. She and I both thought Jack and Alex were dead, so she led me to a cave in a small hill, hiding me there with no other plan beyond that. She brought me a little food and water, probably her own meal for that day. And within twenty hours, a cleanup crew arrived. They picked up my tracker. That's when I learned Jack and Alex had been medevac'd to Germany. They were both alive. At least, for the moment."

Madison scooted closer to Paco, weaving her fingers through his and resting her cheek on his shoulder. His head, heavy from the booze, fell willingly on hers. He squeezed her hand, rubbing light circles along her thumb.

"By the time I got to Germany, Jack was barely holding on. Alex, though stable, was unconscious most of the time, thanks to morphine. He only woke for moments here and there, but just enough to see me give Jack one last good-bye." He took another gulp from the bottle.

Madison pulled away enough to look at Paco, watching fresh trails of tears stream down his cheeks before dropping into his lap.

"I kissed Jack. One last time before he passed."

It took a second to take that one in. Madison had never considered that her brother might be gay, but hadn't really thought about his sexuality at all.

It did explain why despite invitation after invitation to homecomings and proms, Jack never went. And it gave her even more insight into the pieces of a puzzle that had never quite clicked together. Her mind flipped through dates and places. Overheard conversations. Letters.

Yes, the letter. Perhaps she had a revelation of her own to share.

Cupping Paco's face, Madison gently swept her thumbs across his tears. For a passing second, she left a tender kiss on his cheek, then hugged him tightly. "It was you."

Paco pulled back. "What was me?"

"Jack mentioned you." She took both of his hands and squeezed. "He told us about you. Wanted to introduce you to us when he got back. But we didn't know who you were. Not even your name." She squeezed a little tighter. "All he said was that you were, and I quote, the love of his life."

Paco lowered his forehead to hers, and they sat there a moment, soaking it all in.

"I have to tell you the rest," he said with a shiver, and Madison grabbed the nearby throw and wrapped it around his shoulders.

"Alex had a much longer recovery, and they were about to send me back to the States. But I visited Alex, wanting to see him before I left, and gave him the book. That way, he'd have something to pass the time. And to remember Jack by."

Madison was puzzled. "A book?"

Paco just looked back, giving her a *keep up* expression. "No, not a book. *The* book. You know."

"Oh my God." Hopping to her feet, she headed to her bedroom. There, on the dresser, was the book in question. *The Count of Monte Cristo,* exactly where she'd left it.

She grabbed it and returned to Paco, who was now sprawled across the length of the couch with the blanket pulled up to his chin. Squinting open one eye, he lifted his feet, letting her sit down before resting his legs across her lap.

Pausing to pull in a deep breath and release it, Madison opened the cover, and there it was. The identical inscription that their grandfather had penned in both her copy of the book . . . and Jack's.

Love you always. Grandpa Mike.

This was it. The answer. The first time she'd doubted Alex was about the copy of this book with the same inscription that she'd found in his penthouse. Believing it was hers, she'd demanded to know where he'd gotten it from and didn't believe his story, but everything he'd said was true. It was given to him. And it wasn't her book after all.

Repeatedly, she shook her head in amazement. "Of course. Jack had a copy too. I guess I should have known. Grandpa Mike always made sure we had the same gifts. Mostly to keep me from having a freak-out, because I always had to have exactly what Jack had." Her fingers walked across the inscription. "But why didn't Alex just tell me?"

Paco chuckled. "Oh, that." He stacked his hands behind his head, laughing at the memory. "That would be because your older brother insisted."

Wide-eyed, Madison considered his statement, convinced that the thought of Jack having any say in her future dating had to be the ramblings of a thoroughly intoxicated man. She was a teen when Jack died, so for him to make any demands of Alex regarding her was ridiculous. Her skeptical expression pressed Paco to explain.

"One night, we were all playing five-card stud, and just, you know, shooting the breeze. As usual, Jack starts going on with his Frankie stories. Frankie this. Frankie that. Which, by the way, were so freaking adorable."

Madison couldn't help but smile at the memory of the nickname her brother had given her when they were kids.

"Alex, being the cocky bastard he was, popped off that when you grew up, he was going to marry you. He said it just to piss Jack off, and it worked. The thought of Alex being Jack's brother-in-law was enough to make him double-down."

"Sounds about right."

"But Jack gave you a lot of credit. Said a slick-talking womanizing bastard like him didn't stand a chance with his Frankie."

Awkward.

"And that's when Alex had to go into some story about the Italian twins, and —" Paco quickly cut himself off, obviously feeling the weight of Madison's glare. "But that's not the point," he said, recovering quickly. "The point is that Jack threw Alex a challenge. If by some twist of fate Alex ever met you—once you were of legal age, of course—"

"Of course."

"Jack was sure Alex wouldn't last thirty days with you, and that you'd never want to be with such a money-hungry, skirt-chasing son of a bitch. Oh—" Despite the Botox, Paco's brow furled.

With his hand smacked hard to his lips, he apologized. "Sorry. That's sort of a direct quote. And for whatever ass-backward reason, Alex took it literally. Maybe because those were some of the last words Jack ever said to him. Like he'd made a commitment."

"Because that's Alex Drake. A man who keeps his commitments," Madison said before giving Paco a curious look. "But that doesn't explain the photo."

"Oh, why I'm torn out of it? I was visiting Alex, giving him the book. Even in his condition, in pain and being pumped full of every legal opiate known to man, he was sharp. He overheard a conversation. A cover-up was about to go down, and Jack was chosen to be the fall guy for an operation gone very, very wrong. Seriously, those idiots thought dead men wouldn't talk. Well, I sure as hell wasn't dead."

"Who?" Madison asked, not sure she wanted that answer.

Paco only shrugged. "I don't know, and back then, I didn't care. But if I was going to take on this battle, I had to protect everyone else from the backlash. If those bureaucratic assholes would pin this on a dead veteran, nothing was sacred, and a smear campaign would be way too easy for them. And I didn't know you—or your family. I had no idea what you'd think of me and Jack. So I figured I'd take on the fight alone. No collateral damage. I tore myself out of the photo but left the Jack-and-Alex half in the book. I knew Alex would like some memory of Jack. And I burned my side of it."

He thought for a minute, then wiped his eyes again. "You know, the saddest part is, it was the only photo of us together. Anyway, I made it to the Pentagon, and managed to get in front of all the key players. Threatened them with everything I had, which between us girls, wasn't fucking much. But I swore I'd talk. Welp, the sons of bitches kept their word, all right. They doctored Jack's official record to say that he separated from the service months before the operation. That meant no life insurance payout to his family. No combat casualty payment. Any benefits he would have left you and your family evaporated into thin air. Nothing but his name. Jackson Daniel Taylor."

It was insane. But Paco had to be so alone in all of this.

Patting his feet resting in her lap, Madison said, "I can't believe everything you did. I wish I could have been there for you . . . *we* could have been there for you."

Paco shook his head. "All Jack talked about was his family. About you." He sat up a little and reached out to caress her face. "I knew you'd need closure. You'd need to know Jack died with honor, even if you didn't know all the details. So, the veteran's funeral was arranged. I scraped together whatever money I could to make sure he had a beautiful service."

Perplexed, Madison stared at him. "Wait, I thought the military paid for his service."

"If the record said he died on active duty, they would have. Close to one hundred percent. But they screwed him, so he got a veteran's service instead. Still beautiful, but the benefits only covered transportation from Germany to Dover, and I still needed to get him home. Plus, the casket needed to be paid for, and several other things. I knew Jack had been sending money home, so it wasn't like you were swimming in dough."

Paco slumped back. "I didn't want to intrude on your family's privacy, so I did what I do best." He clumsily sipped again, spilling a little on his cheek, which

Madison wiped up with her sleeve. "I became invisible. I worked behind the scenes with the funeral director, making sure that whatever your family needed was covered. Money was never discussed. I pawned the few gold chains I had, and some other things I could live without. At one point, I almost thought I'd have to give this up." He wiggled his pinky, highlighting the ring. "But it's just some cheap pot metal. Jack found it somewhere in Italy. Worthless to pawnshops, but priceless to me."

He planted a big kiss on the ring, then slipped it off just enough to give Madison a glimpse of the skin beneath. "See?"

Giggling, she gently caressed the green-tinged skin with her fingertips.

Beaming at her, his eyes glistened with tears. "You were so young. When I saw you, it reminded me of what Jack would have looked like at your age. Well, probably with shorter hair," he teased, wrapping a loose tendril of her hair around his finger, and sinking deeper into his comfy spot.

"After you and your family left, all I could think about was Yasmin. She was barely older than you. So young, yet so brave. She risked her life saving me. It was too late for Jack, but maybe not for Yasmin. I needed to do something. And that's when Alex Drake blew back into my life, and together . . ." Dramatically, he counted off with his fingers. "We found the girl. Rescued the girl. *I* married the girl. We thwarted one—no, two kidnapping attempts on Yasmin, and built a multibillion-dollar empire, *and* . . ." Paco looked around. "Uh, where's your bathroom?"

Quickly, Madison pointed to the bedroom, where the only bathroom was. "Through there. Do you need help?"

Fumbling his way toward the bedroom, Paco doubled over in laughter. "No, girlie. As helpful as you are, I've got this."

As soberly as possible, he disappeared into the bedroom, then instantly popped his head back out, leaning hard against the frame of the door.

"You know, about a year ago, Alex became obsessed with finding you. Really obsessed. Well, not obsessed with *finding* you, so much as wondering if you might miraculously pop into his life. Somehow. I guess finding you would've been too fucking easy for a guy with a global reconnaissance business."

"Seems to be a man who likes a challenge."

"But every time a woman crossed his path with the last name Taylor, he had me check into her. See if it was you. Jack never mentioned your name, just your nickname, Frankie. And I . . . I never told him I knew you. I mean, knew where you were."

Curious, Madison asked, "Why not?"

Fighting gravity, Paco slid down the door frame a little, then managed to pull himself back up again. "Because after Jack died, Alex nearly died too. Not just physically. It took a lot to get him out of the dark. For a time, nobody could even mention Jack without Alex lashing out or breaking down."

That makes two of us.

"Somehow, he felt responsible. Like if he'd just done things differently. Or reacted faster. I guess I wasn't quite sure he'd be good for anyone, least of all you."

With an accusatory finger pointed at her, Paco stood taller. "And *someone* helped him get him out of that dark, dark place, missy." A smile lifted his lips. "And it's someone *you* know," he taunted before disappearing into the bedroom again.

Madison heard several thuds, with items being knocked about. Obviously, Paco was finally making his way to the bathroom, one knocked-over item at a time.

The suspense was too much. "Wait," she called out. "Who do I know that helped Alex?"

Paco shouted back. "Dan."

Dan? "Dan who?"

"You know. Dan." A second later, he called out, "Taylor."

With that, Madison heard the bathroom door snap closed.

Dad?

CHAPTER 21

MADISON

COUNTING DOWN THE MINUTES, Madison impatiently awaited Paco's return.

Seriously, how long does it take to pee?

Flush? *Check.* Wash hands while faintly humming "Happy Birthday"? *Check and check.*

Finally, she could hear the bathroom door opening, but Paco didn't emerge. Another sixty seconds ticked by before she went to check on him.

There, having discovered a bed that was just right, Paco had pushed the covers to the side and passed out, one clear-coat-pedicured foot dangling over the other.

Tiptoeing to him, Madison laughed at the slightest little vodka-induced snore. About to bring the covers over him, she paused, again noticing his ring.

I guess that makes you my brother-in-law.

With a faux-down comforter, she tucked him in and kissed him gingerly on the temple. His suit jacket and pants were laid out on the other side of her full-size bed, delivering a rare once-in-a-blue-moon opportunity.

Making her way to the nightstand, she silently slid open the drawer, pulling out an aged envelope as quietly as possible. With a few items of cheap jewelry, pens, an old pack of gum, and some cosmetic samples piled on top of it, she wasn't quiet at all. But Sleeping Beauty snored on, blissfully undisturbed.

The stamp on the envelope was beautiful, designed with flowers and a single word. *Italia.* It was the last note from Jack, mailed to her over a decade ago.

After pressing her lips to it, Madison slipped the envelope into the pocket of Paco's custom blazer, ensuring it peeked out, but knocked over his slacks in the process.

Delighted, she recognized the key fob that fell onto the floor. Embracing the temptation of the heavy little device, she pushed aside the technical term for what she had in mind. *Grand theft auto.*

"I swear I'm just borrowing it," she whispered. Returning to the living room, she grabbed her bag and headed out, admiring the bright yellow Lamborghini parked at the curb.

He's seriously a little too trusting of this neighborhood.

After the driving lesson Paco had recently given her, she had the mechanics down, taking off with the rumble of the car drilling straight into her crotch. It was then that she bothered glancing down. There she was, in what could possibly be a half-million-dollar car, classing it up in her comfiest PJs, fuzzy robe, and smiling panda slippers.

For a hot second, turning around crossed her mind, but she rejected the thought.

It's New York. Like anyone would bat an eye.

At the next red light, Madison grabbed her earbud and tapped the third favorite on her phone. After two and a half rings, her father picked up.

"Hello? Frankie?"

His voice made her smile, and the nickname pulled her right back to the simpler time of being his little girl. "Hi, Dad."

"Is everything okay?"

A twinge of guilt hit her when she realized it had been some time since they'd last spoken. The day she arrived in New York, in fact. "Yeah, Dad. Everything's fine. I was just thinking that it might be nice to drop by and catch up sometime."

"Jellybean, that would be great. When are you thinking?"

"Well, I need to check something, but is tomorrow too soon? Would that be all right?"

"Of course. I'd love it, but don't you have to work?"

Typical Dad. Worrying about the big city swallowing his little girl whole. And probably wondering if she might be on her way to moving back home.

"Well, in a way, this might end up being for work. It's hard to explain. I'll call you tomorrow morning with the details."

"Sure," he said cheerfully. "Anytime. I'll always be here for you."

You, and another guy I know.

After extending the silence with a smile, she heard, "Frankie? Did I lose you?"

"Still here, Dad. Can I ask you something? Years ago, was there a guy you helped out through a tough time?"

"Well, that might be a long list," her father said with a sigh. "Our vets are a tough lot, but under the right pressure, even the toughest steel will fracture and break."

Carefully, Madison considered her words, not wanting to tip her hand. If she were too eager, he'd see right through her. And this wasn't the time to bring up her relationship status.

"Maybe this will help. The guy I'm asking about wasn't a vet, but might have been wounded. In combat." She paused, thoughtful in considering the scab she might be scratching at. "It was someone who . . . knew Jack. Was with Jack . . . on his last assignment."

Now it was her dad's turn to stretch out the silence. She could feel him holding back. But whether it led to something would be his call, not hers.

Finally, he spoke. "I think you might mean AJ."

"No, it's—"

Wait. Another puzzle piece fell into place from back when Madison first started working at DGI. What was that the name G.I. Joe had mentioned when Alex rescued him from some thugs on the sidewalk outside their headquarters? *AJ and I are gonna catch up,* the homeless man had said.

"Yes. AJ. That's him. Can you tell me about AJ?"

"Frankie," her father said once he'd finished his story, "I can't wait to see you. Love you, honey."

"Love you too, Dad."

With the call disconnected and her destination approaching, Madison checked overhead, scanning the Homclink panels and pressing a button. Nothing happened. When she pressed a second button, the large door directly ahead of her rolled upward, welcoming her. Her smile beamed as she rolled into the familiar penthouse garage.

Just counting the cars parked there wasn't a foolproof way to know for sure if Alex was home. Six cars, spaciously parked throughout, didn't always mean he was there. He'd call for a car service more often than not so he could work during his commute, making the most of every hour of the day.

She pulled the access card from her purse. Though she'd used it that very morning, the rigid edges felt different in her hand. A few hours ago, she was on her way back here to return this card to Alex—ready for one last visit with the sole purpose of leaving it all behind, including their relationship.

And now? Now everything had changed.

When the elevator rose and then opened to the penthouse, the luxury apartment felt warmer, strangely calming and yet energizing her all at once. The feeling surrounded her, wrapping her in a sweet comfort and familiarity. She was home.

"Paco, I'm in the office."

Madison's pulse kicked up at the sound of Alex's voice, and she hurried down the hall, her plush panda slippers muffling her steps. Stepping inside his office, she found him deep in thought, studying two of his three desk screens. He hadn't heard her enter.

Clearing her throat, she said, "It's not Paco."

In an instant, Alex jumped from his chair and rushed over, stopping short of a sweeping embrace as he noticed her head-to-toe ensemble.

"Madison. I'm . . ." He hesitated, taking all of her in.

"Not a word," she said, pointing a solemn finger straight at his nose.

Crossing his arms, Alex released a hand to smother his lips, keeping his remarks—and chuckle—to himself.

Smart man.

"Good. Now it's your turn to not say anything and just listen." She took in a needed breath, settling the butterflies fluttering in her stomach, holding them still before setting them free. "I know you think all of this could have been avoided if you'd just told me everything to begin with. And I get it. It's complicated . . . maybe more complicated than even you realize." Her remark barely scratched the surface of so many things, including Paco's confession.

Daring to take a step closer, Alex smiled, his eyes bright with hope.

"But *I'm* not ready to make it uncomplicated. At least, not if that means DGI continues without you. A dirtbag like Frank Seaver can't buy me, and I would hope to God he couldn't buy you either." Madison pulled down the large hand covering Alex's mouth and tightened both her hands around it. "Please tell me I'm right."

His other hand caressed her cheek, stroking her face as his eyes drank her in.

"You're right," he whispered to her lips before pressing a kiss there, lightly at first. Then he deepened the kiss, running his hands through her hair and across her back, pausing to pull away just enough to press his forehead to hers.

"I thought I'd lost you," he said softly, and their lips met again.

Her body relaxed into his. "I thought I'd lost myself. I didn't trust you because I didn't trust myself, or my own instincts. Instead, I believed a slimeball like Frank Seaver, even though I knew he was manipulating me." Cringing, Madison became furious all over again at the thought of letting a contemptable puppet-master rope her in. "I hate that a schemer like Frank Seaver swayed me so easily. Especially after that scumbag nearly cost me my interview with DGI."

Alex's brows drew together. "What do you mean?"

"The morning I arrived for my interview, we had a full-body slam into each other. The bastard spilled his coffee all over me—*spiked* coffee. Left me smelling like an Irish pub."

With a deep sigh, Alex dropped his head. "You, uh, don't say."

"I had to go into the executive suites of DGI with no blouse on under my blazer, just my camisole . . . *and* interview with Gina. I'm sure you can imagine how that went."

"Oh, I can picture it. I mean, I can imagine your frustration."

With his head down, he led her to sit on the contemporary settee. Surprised, Madison watched as he moved away from her, opting for a seat on the corner chair to her side. They were seated face-to-face.

"I honestly can't believe I got the job after that." Rather than let her emotions run wild, she caught the angst in Alex's face. His expression was twisted. Tortured. She reached over to stroke his chest. "Sorry. I didn't mean to dredge up more."

"No, it's not that." Regret seemed to fill his eyes, and his clenched jaw worried her. Pulling away, he clasped his hands and steepled his fingers toward her. "Madison, remember I asked if you remembered our first encounter?"

Nodding, she hated admitting it. "Yes. And I still don't."

With a hand on her knee and releasing a deep breath, he looked her straight in the eyes. "Seaver didn't spill the coffee on you. I did."

"You did?" Madison wrinkled her nose, hardly believing him, but Alex persisted.

"Yes, me. Me and my dark roast and Woodford."

As more of his explanation spilled out, Madison hung on his every guilty word.

"I was edgy and irritated that morning when my car didn't show up." Stopping himself, he came clean. "But the truth is, I was an asshole of epic proportions because . . ."

"Because what?" Madison wasn't letting the moment slip by without the truth. All of it. "Whatever it is you've been keeping bottled up, it's time. Time to let everything go."

Lacing his fingers, gripping so tightly his knuckles turned white, Alex continued. "I had a hard time dealing with the past, Madison. And sometimes, I —I still have a hard time. There are days when everything crashes in around me, all at once with no warning. I don't handle it well, so I just escape. Get away. As far away from anyone and everyone as I can."

"You self-isolate," Madison said, clarifying with a term she knew all too well.

"Yes," he said quietly. "Anyway, that morning, I could feel it coming on. Taking over. I tried the spiked coffee to take the edge off, and when it didn't work, I tried getting away."

Gently, she reached for his hand to comfort him and he took it, sandwiching it between both of his, as if desperate to keep her there. She dipped her chin, nudging him with her eyes to continue.

"I didn't see you," Alex said softly. "You were right in front of me. And I know this will sound crazy—or crazier—but I kept feeling like you were coming. Like I needed to look out for you. Because maybe we would just, well, bump into each other."

He paused, noticing her playful squint.

Did he really just say that?

"The point is, I had you. Right there under my goddamned nose like you were gift-wrapped and hand delivered by heaven itself, and what did I do? I doused you in coffee and booze, berated you, and stormed off."

Taunting him, she said, "I believe your exact words were 'watch where you're going.'"

Smirking, Alex took the ribbing. "That sounds about right. And I believe you astutely singled me out as a jack-hole. A jack-hole who nearly lost you."

His expression wasn't just apologetic. Madison could see he was more than just sorry. He was tortured.

"And today," he said, "I nearly lost you again, and all because I didn't tell you everything up front. Madison, I'm so sorry. I swear I'll never keep anything from you again."

But she was only half listening, readily forgiving him more than it seemed he might ever forgive himself. Her mind wandering for a moment, she fixated on his words, the ones he'd just said a moment ago.

I called him a jack-hole, but how did he know?

Curiosity piqued, she was ready to pull the curtains all the way back and completely expose this Wizard of Igz. "You know, I've spent a lot of time wondering how a girl like me was lucky enough to land a job like this. I mean, maybe I wasn't exactly *un*qualified, but I was definitely *under*qualified. Gina said as much. And I walked in dressed to audition for office floozy number two. On top of which, I told the VP of human capital that I wanted to shove my heel up her executive butt. And yet I was hired. On the spot. Or technically, on the spot my ass fell on in the lobby. You didn't have something to do with that, did you, Mr. Drake?"

He nodded, giving her a boyish grin that always brought out those sexy dimples.

Serious and businesslike, Madison stood. The consummate gentleman, Alex tried to stand as well, but she placed her hand on his shoulder to urge him to sit and stay.

She didn't release her touch until he relaxed all the way back in his seat. Pacing, Madison pieced together the puzzle. The one hidden in plain sight. The one she'd struggled with for so long was now evident and clear.

"The shoes!" she blurted. "Those gorgeous shoes you bought me. You knew about my broken heel because"—she studied him, eager to see the truth reflect back in his eyes—"you saw my heel break. There's a camera in Gina's office, isn't there?"

"Actually, there are three." When Madison froze her pacing, fidgeting uncomfortably and tugging at her collar, Alex quickly explained. "Gina insisted. We've had a few disgruntled employees in the past, and in case anything happened as a result, she wanted to ensure she could capture everything on video. They're in the corners of the ceiling, in full view."

Mentally sorting through the memories of the day she interviewed at DGI, Madison locked another piece in place. "And when I was making my, well, illustrious escape, Gina's phone rang. I thought it was security, but it was you. *You* hired me."

"I heard you tell Gina off. I heard every word of you describing my deplorable behavior. I had to make it right."

Of all things, that tidbit actually took Madison by surprise. "So, you didn't hire me because I was Jack's sister?"

Alex shook his head. "It wasn't until Gina called out your name after I told her to hire you that I realized you might be Jack's sister. I even asked Paco to check it out, but he literally took forever. Like he was *trying* to blow me off."

Madison turned away, masking any insider knowledge of Paco's guilt.

"He didn't confirm my suspicion until after our first night together, when I asked him to look after you that morning. Madison, from the way you stood up to Gina, and protecting Joe from those thugs, and even standing up to me when you thought I might hurt him, *you* were the woman I've been waiting for, Jack's sister or not. The whole month I was traveling after that, I couldn't stop thinking of you. I've been trying to figure out how to tell you. About the coffee. And the gifts. And Jack. I thought that if you got to know me better, good and bad, you'd have more insight. A better understanding because, well . . ."

Together, they said in unison, "It's complicated."

Nodding, Madison imagined how the awkward conversation might have played out.

Hi, I spilled coffee on you and was a total d-bag about it, so I hired you to make it good. And, by the way, I was in that whole explosion that killed your brother, Jack, but had nothing to do with it. At all. And it has nothing to do with why I'm chasing you.

"Best-case scenario," Alex said, "it would be a remarkable meet-cute story that no one but our closest friends would believe. And worst case, I'd get to hold you a little longer before . . ." He shrugged, unable to finish the sentence, then his eyes met hers.

"But, Madison, before you make up your mind, you have a right to know all of it." White-knuckled again from squeezing his clasped hands, he huffed out a breath. "There are times when I'm not okay. And I don't just get okay. I have a really hard time dealing with things. But I will deal with it. Shield you from all of it."

Her heart swelled, and a wry smile formed at his impossible offer. *He always needs to protect me.*

"Shield me?" she asked. "So you can continue hiding this part of your life and how deeply it affects you, even though it is your life? Is that what you were doing at Jess and Mark's place? Let's pretend nothing was wrong, even though you hurled your phone halfway across the property?" Gently, she exposed him, as if he were a kid denying tasting a chocolate cake, though his lips were slathered in frosting. "Tell me who you were calling, and know that whatever you tell me, this is our safe space. We can tell each other anything."

His lips formed a wry grin. "Mark."

But his calling Mark didn't make any sense. Mark was close by at the time, in the other room. When she frowned at Alex in confusion, he answered her unasked questions.

"I didn't know how bad the attack would be and I couldn't move. If he picked up, all I'd have to say is *get Madison*, and he would've discreetly found a reason to get you out of there. Just until I rode out the wave."

"You mean ride it out alone. You think I don't see it? Don't see you? Alex, you run at midnight. Push paperwork until three a.m. You can't shield me from every side of you, and I wouldn't want you to."

"But, Madison—"

She held up a hand. "Alex, I need you to stop trying to protect me for a moment and listen. After Jack died and my parents divorced, my anxiety was out of control. Everything set me off, so the doctors put me on meds. My mom thought it would help. Help me sleep. And eat. And be around people. And breathe. Because God forbid I deal with what I was feeling. So, I tried to hide it. The meds. The anxiety. *Me*. I became invisible in my own life. I didn't let anyone know, not even my dad, because I figured it was my issue to deal with."

Shutting her eyes, she wrapped her arms around herself. "The only thing that got me off the meds was joining the track team in high school. Running isolated me. Gave me precious seconds away from the unrelenting feelings that were just around every corner, ready to swallow me whole. I found a way to keep up with the heart that always threatened to pound right out of my chest."

With a small smile, she shrugged. "I still break out in hives every now and again, and I still work out when my pulse jumps ahead of me. Is that something you want me to hide from you, Alex? If you're part of my life, should I deal with it all on my own?"

"No. God, no. Madison, I'll always be by your side. I'm not going anywhere."

She moved in front of him, her tone reassuring. "Then why on earth would you expect any different of me? And by the way, *I'm* not going anywhere. You might be the guy who was a total ass to me . . ." Alex turned his head away, but she kept going. "But you're also the guy who gave me a chance at a remarkable job, rescued me from a pretty scary situation from three nutjobs on the street, and cared for me like no one ever has."

Madison leaned over to cup the scruffy angles of his jaw, encouraging his eyes to meet hers. "And you might *not* be the guy who was able to save Jack's life," she said, sniffing back a tear. "But make no mistake, Alex, I know you're the guy who nearly died trying." She pressed a soft kiss on his mouth, whispering to his lips, "Like I said, I'm not going anywhere."

With that, he stood, looking down at her and pulling her near. But an attempt at a tight embrace was stopped by the palm of her hand planted firmly against the solid muscles of his chest.

"Oh, you're not off the hook just yet," she said with a scolding tone, ready to toss him one fiery coal of a question to blaze a trail far away from the past.

Spreading his arms out wide, he waited. "What do you need?" he asked, his deep tone sending heat straight to her core.

Licking her lips, Madison stepped back. "I've been replaying what happened that day. The day we met. Our little meet-cute over coffee."

His posture tense, he stood tall, as if ready for whatever punishment she had ready.

Come on, Alex. Smile.

She kept going. "Something about it is really making me wonder. Tell me something, Mr. Drake . . ."

He swallowed hard. "Anything, Ms. Taylor."

Toe-to-toe, she stared up at him. Businesslike and arms crossed, she gave him just a glimpse of a bewitching smile.

"If you hadn't spilled the coffee on me, and I'd been wearing my button-up-to-my-neck blouse beneath that blazer when I was interviewed by Gina, and had my hair up and away from my face, similar to how it is now, would you have been watching so intently, hanging on my every, um, word?"

Between the arch of Madison's eyebrow and her suggestive tone, he relaxed his stance, finally caving with a boyish grin when he realized she was toying with him, daring him to join her game.

"Why, Ms. Taylor," Alex said with a mild amount of indignity as he took a few leisurely steps behind her. The heat of his hands worked across her shoulders and down her arms. Her shiver was instant.

His hands made their way to her wrists, unlocking her arms. She melted into him as he worked to slide off her robe. "You could have been wearing anything. Blouse. No blouse. Adorable *E.T.* T-shirt."

Carefully, Alex tugged at her scrunchie, releasing her wavy locks. Fingering her tresses free, he loosened her cascade of waves down her neck, laying the tendrils gently across her heaving chest. His tone was low in her ear.

"You could have had your hair in any style. Up, down, French twist, chignon," which he said with a perfect French accent, and turned her in his arms.

She peeked up at him through her eyelashes, welcoming his seduction.

"No matter how you looked, I have every confidence that, like now, I wouldn't have been able to take my eyes off you." His fingers lifted her chin, and his mouth melted over hers, pressing lightly on her lips. "But," he said with a serious and discerning glance, "for the record, the blazer *sans* blouse will forever be a fan favorite."

Smiling, Madison welcomed another kiss, parting her lips and letting Alex explore deeper with sweeps of his tongue. His strong arms embraced her, lifting her so her legs could wrap around his hips and waist. Relaxed in his hold, she rested easily on his hands, and he tightened his hold under each cheek.

His lips never left hers as they made their way to the bedroom. Once there, he set her on the bed, soaking in every bit of her in his hungry gaze, panda slippers and all.

When he reached for his tie, Madison stopped him, letting him loosen the knot but not fully release it. "Hang on. You got my runway best. How about yours?"

Leaning down, Alex rested both hands on the mattress, caging her between them. Growling, he lightly grazed his lips against hers. "And just what did you have in mind?"

Button by button, she unfastened his shirt, then tugged it loose from his slacks as he helped, unclipping the cuffs. Peeling the tailored shirt from his skin, she finished with one final move. Drawing the collar down through the inside of the tie, she managed to slip it off without disturbing anything else. The only thing covering any part of his ripped upper body was his GG bees silk tie.

Suggestively, Madison tightened the knot back up to his neck, slipping a finger along the line of the dip in his collar bone, then leaned back, fully admiring her masterpiece. "There. Now there's a fan favorite."

Not the least bit shy, Alex looked down, impressed with her work. He returned his gaze to hers. "How about I keep on mine if you keep on yours," he said, eyeing a T-shirt that had to be wonderfully tight for the occasion. "I mean, it really is one of my favorite movies. You know, it inspired the song 'Heartlight' by Neil Diamond."

Could he be any more perfect?

"You don't say?" Tugging his tie like a silk leash, she summoned another kiss.

Alex was everything. Tender and sweet. Frisky and fun. And maybe a first for both of them, free. Free of any fears or doubts, there were no walls between them, no secrets holding them back. Together, they could cherish and adore each other for the beautifully imperfect people they were.

"Lie back," Alex said softly, quickly removing the rest of his clothes, then kneeling before her.

He removed her slippers, then slowly massaged his hands up her knees and past her thighs. Hooking his fingers into the waistband, he took off her pajama bottoms, laying a trail of hot kisses across her skin before returning her slippers to her feet. She lifted her head, squinting at him with a look of pure suspicion.

Climbing on top of her, he said quietly, "There. Now you'll be snug and comfy while I get snug and comfy."

Her giggles melted as his mouth crashed onto hers. The slightest parting of her lips willingly invited his tongue in, and her hips began to rock, riding the solid thigh that pressed against her core.

A few hot kisses landed on Madison's neck, open-mouthed ones that grazed along the thin fabric of her shirt as he lifted it to bare her breast. Massaging its weight in his hand, Alex teased her, circling his fingertip along her nipple.

It was agony, and she needed more. Brushing his lips along one nipple, he plucked the other. Her back arched, and his teeth unleashed one terse pull before releasing her breast and inciting a moan.

Lazily, he skimmed a finger across the plane of her stomach before skating it along the inside of her thigh. Madison ached for him. Needed him. Begged with her body as she spread her knees wider, needing him more with each touch.

Alex breezed his fingers softly across her wet pussy, dipping them in just enough to coat his finger with her wetness. He ran the finger across her mouth, then licked. Their kiss was intoxicating. Tasting him as she tasted herself.

With her legs spread wide, his fingers once again painted her slickness across her folds before plunging deep inside, fucking her in long strokes before pulling away. Beneath heavy lids, she watched. Alex sucked each finger clean, enjoying every bit of her flavor.

Desperate, she leaned over, kissing him and pressing him to his back. Swinging her leg over, she climbed on top of him, needing all of him deep inside her. Rubbing herself against the length of his cock, she moaned at the sensation before trying to take him in.

"*Shhh*, not yet." He groaned, reaching for the nightstand to retrieve a condom from the drawer, and tore it open.

Madison snatched it from his hand and tossed it aside, lowering herself. The swollen tip of him held a bead of pre-cum she had to lick. Stroking his shaft, her tongue crossed the head before swallowing him clear to her throat.

Falling back, Alex said, "Yes, Madison. God, yes." He stroked her hair, and she let him move her head in all the ways he needed.

She took her time, sucking him hard, then pulling back to sweep her tongue along the smooth round tip. Her rhythm picked up, sucking and releasing, and she watched as Alex took her in, staring back at her.

"Wait," he said in a low voice, gruff in his plea.

She rocked her head up and down the length of his shaft before taking one last circling lick. Then she took a second to sheath him and take in his size before inching her body in place.

His strong hands grabbed her hips, holding her still as he forced all of himself in at once, stretching her wide. Gripping her ass, he rocked her, watching her body move as he thrust up into her, completely making her his.

Alex's thumb rubbed her mouth, brushing the fullness of her lower lip before sliding inside. "Suck, Madison."

She did, not losing the rhythm of riding him. Slowly, he pulled his thumb from her lips and place the ball of it on her clit, rubbing in circles as she increased her pace. She was on the edge. But watching him, so was he.

"More," she begged.

Still inside her, he flipped her to her back. Wildly bucking, he filled her as she cried out. Slowing, he pulled out only to the tip, then thrust firmly in to the hilt before fucking her hard and senseless.

Panting, Madison cried out, "Please, don't stop."

"Your wish is definitely my command."

Alex did this over and over. Driving her to the brink, slowing, then dragging his length out, only to force himself back in and fuck her until her body exploded in a thousand pulses of pleasure, collapsing on his thickness in crushing waves. Her cries weren't the only ones filling the room, and the climax that ripped her apart was fueled by his, filling her with a heat she could feel deep within.

Dizzy and drained, he dropped his head next to hers, and his lips nuzzled her ear. His breaths were labored and heavy, leaving him fighting to speak. Breathlessly, he said, "I love you, Madison."

Stroking his hair, Madison took in a long, lingering whiff of his scent. "I love you too," she said, tightening her legs around him.

~

Comforted in being spooned by Alex, Madison lay there exhausted but awake. Somehow, the tip of his tie rested on her arm, where his finger lazily stroked. She remained in her T-shirt, not minding the question it raised.

"Madison E. Taylor, right?" he asked.

She grinned but was content to keep her back pressed into him, avoiding his eyes.

"Madison E.T.? Is that why Jack got the shirt for you?"

"Mm-hmm. How did you know my middle initial?"

"Oh, I have my ways." His voice lowered to a whisper. "It's discreetly hidden on the back of your access card. And on your license. And on the employee roster. And listed on your Skype profile." He chuckled into her shoulder, then nibbled it. His voice regained its soft volume. "What's the E stand for?"

Madison gazed into the darkness. "Nothing special. Just a name." She pulled his hand into hers, weaving their fingers together. "Alex, I'd like to take you somewhere tomorrow. Is your calendar really free?"

He pulled her hand up, giving it a long kiss. "Yes," he growled low, letting his lips linger on her knuckles.

She glanced back, craning her neck to look at him. "I ask because it might take the whole day. Maybe even pour into the next one."

He rolled her back toward him and looked down on her, his gaze soft and sincere. "It can take the whole year." His lips found hers. "I'm all yours, Madison Taylor. Completely and forever yours."

They lay there, holding each other for the rest of the night.

Though Alex dozed off, Madison was energized, preoccupied with ideas. She stayed awake most of the night, her feet kicked out just enough from beneath the covers to expose the panda slippers still on her feet. She only nodded off after working out the details of a plan.

CHAPTER 22

ALEX

ALEX AWAKENED, reaching for Madison. Instead, he found a note. He grabbed it, but then slid his hand between the comforter and the bed, finding it just warm enough to mean she'd left about half an hour ago. He rubbed the sleep from his eyes and read the delicate print.

> *Take your time getting up.*
> *Coffee when you're ready.*
> *Big day. No hints.*

He rolled to her side of the bed, pulling in a long breath of her scent. A faint hint of her perfume and shampoo blended with the seductive aroma of her body, and that delicious smell of sex. With another deep inhale, he moaned. Rolling back, he thought of last night.

Before he could get too lost in remembering each of her delectable curves, the faintest whiff of coffee hit him. Alex yawned, then propped up on his elbows.

At the end of the bed, he could see Tom Ford jeans and an Armani navy T-shirt had been laid out. *When was my last casual day?* With nothing at all coming to mind, he savored the thrill of unpredictability.

No hints, huh? I love a challenge.

Strolling through the penthouse wearing nothing but a smile and the gold-accented tie, Alex strutted straight to the kitchen. Straightening his tie, he decided to make himself more presentable. He cleared his throat, then entered.

Madison whirled around, admiring him with a giggle. He let her eyes roam across his head-to-toe fashion statement. Giving her his best *GQ* pose, he adjusted an invisible cuff. "Good morning, Ms. Taylor. I heard coffee was up for grabs. Tell me, is there a dress code?"

Madison, in her white peasant blouse and denim stretch capris, brought her oversize mug of cappuccino to her lips. "Oh, you've met it." She took her sip with another hungry glance up and down. Then, with a whimsical frothy moustache, she asked, "Espresso?"

"Please," Alex said, stepping closer to kiss off the foam.

She started the machine, then straightened his tie before handing him the saucer and cup. He sipped it slowly, leaning a hand on the bright Calacatta marble, enjoying the views that baked in a sun-filled metropolitan morning. He stood every bit as dignified as if fully suited up for work.

"If you entered DGI as is," she said playfully, "would anyone tell the emperor he had no clothes?"

Considering her question, he said, "They might not, but I'm pretty sure their lawyers would." Still gazing at the view, he asked, "No hints, huh?"

"No hints," Madison said, her businesslike tone conveying the staunchness of her position, while mimicking his nonchalant *always the CEO* demeanor. She stared out the window too, enjoying another long sip of her nearly empty drink.

Alex's gaze moved from the window to meet hers, which darted to the arrival of his morning wood. "At least tell me if it's in the city or not."

Setting her cup aside, she went in for a long, tender kiss, welcoming every muscle of his nude embrace. Peering at him through deceptive come-hither lashes, the girl held her ground.

"Not one single hint, Mr. Drake." Madison looked down, admiring the skyscraper nestled longingly between them. "And as much as I'd like you to poke and prod it out of me, I'm sorry to say we really, *really* don't have time for that."

Apologetically, she looked up. "I'll start your shower," she said, giving him one final kiss before heading to the master bath.

With a heavy sigh, Alex leaned over, ready to place his cup in the sink, Yelping, he glared at the Calacatta marble giving him freezer burn as it tried to prove it was harder than him. He scowled at the counter.

This is not a competition.

CHAPTER 23

MADISON

WHILE ALEX ENJOYED A LEISURELY SHOWER, Madison made a call.

"Hello, Miss Madison." The usually upbeat Latin accent sounded ever so slightly annoyed, probably due to her helping herself to his Lambo. "If this is payback for the earrings, I'm pretty sure I did *not* say you could have my car."

Madison played it off. "Are you *sure*? How much can one really remember when they were three sheets to the wind?" His silence was a blaring broadcast of the doubt in his mind. Madison only let it linger a moment before fessing up. "Don't worry. You didn't give me your car. I'm just borrowing it."

"Well, at least you took it to Alex's." When Madison didn't respond, he said, "And no, that's not mind reading. I have a tracker." He paused, then added, "But never mind. Keep it."

Madison's own doubts tapped her shoulder. "That's generous. And crazy. Are you still drinking?"

He chuckled. "No, Miss Madison, I'm not still drinking."

A new set of ringtones announced his request to take the call to FaceTime. Smiling, she accepted.

Paco had his face fill the frame, like ear to ear. Glaring at her, he popped that ridiculously adorable raised eyebrow. The one that always meant he was far from mad.

Bursting with laughter, Madison faked her own knowing squint, and he finally moved the phone to pan out the view.

At first, she assumed he was just proving his sobriety by looking fresh as a daisy, sporting a sharp new suit, pressed pocket square, and those gorgeous diamond earrings. But then his stolid expression melted into an overflowing grin as he swayed just out of the shot. The camera caught the unmistakable logo of a gold-on-black charging bull.

"Pull back," he said to whomever held his phone. His impromptu cameraman did so, showcasing Paco prominently seated on the hood of a Rosso Mars red Aventador. "Like I said, keep it."

Delighted, Madison let out a loud squeal. "Really?"

Paco pulled the letter she'd left him from his interior breast pocket, giving it a pageant wave before the screen. "Really, Miss Madison," he said, his voice low and compelling.

She'd given him a meaningful gift. He was clearly tagging her back. He took his phone back from the attendant, and she heard him request a little privacy.

But she couldn't wait any longer before addressing a serious issue with the man. "Paco, seeing as you're the only brother-in-law I'll ever have, how about you just call me Madison?"

Rather than respond, he simply gaped at her with a beaming grin and a few appreciative blinks.

"Is that a yes?"

He nodded. "Yes," he said, returning the letter to his inside pocket, and patted his blazer at his heart. "Okay, *Madison.* Yes, really. That car is my gift to you. Plus, you need an excuse to wear those badass gloves."

"Well, you giving me this car is kind of fortuitous, and keeps me from having to ask for an extended loan. But I do still need a favor."

"For my favorite *hermanita*, anything."

Hermanita. Madison knew the term of endearment from ninth-grade Spanish. Her heart melted at the word. *Little sister.* It hit her then, how she missed being a sister.

"So, what wicked scheme shall we be partners in crime on?"

CHAPTER 24

ALEX

ALEX STROLLED out from the bedroom, comfortable in his shirt and jeans. Though the lines naturally showcased the prominent cuts and curves of his chiseled build, everything still hung loose enough to make the outfit freeing.

His hair, still damp from the shower, was the extent of the effort he'd make in his appearance, giving it a quick comb-through with his fingers. And his scruff could use an extra day to grow out. Why not? No meetings. No work. His executive staff got the memo he'd sent them, so not a single email or voice mail waited on his phone. Nothing was on fire. No one needed his undivided attention. No one but Madison.

What's she got planned?

He found her packing his things in an overnight bag. "Don't forget my Speedo," he joked.

As he approached her, open-armed and ready for an embrace, she greeted him with, of all things, his portfolio. "I know you're not used to being away from work, so I printed out a few things, just in case you need something to pass the time."

Disappointed, he took it, overstuffed with hours' worth of paperwork. He thumbed through it. "Um, exactly how far are we going?"

"Just far enough. And I'm driving. The rest of the luggage is already in the car."

Alex scanned the documents as the elevator carried them down to the garage, and, of course, several items screamed for his attention. So much so, he barely noticed the car they got into.

A bright stream of daylight hit him as the garage door opened, forcing him to squint. He scanned the car. No sunglasses.

Wait, whose car is this?

"Here," Madison said, handing him a pair.

"Thanks," he said, now even more suspicious as he checked out her instant ease behind the wheel. Ready to give her a few pointers, he was surprised as she powered on, revved the engine, and slammed the pedal to the metal, swiftly carrying them off.

Nothing like pulling some early morning Gs to wake you up.

Her overpowering acceleration whipped him full force back into the seat, bringing a wide smile to his face. "So you like fast cars, beautiful? I'll keep that in mind. Paco's car?"

Demurely, Madison smiled at him. "No."

Alex scanned the interior of the car, then slid his butt around in place, as if waxing the seat with his ass. "Well, I'm pretty sure my butt has a permanent imprint in this seat. It's remarkably molded to my shape."

Shifting his motion to thrust back and forth, his little hump fest pushed Madison's restraint to a full-blown laugh. "I don't know what to tell you. It's not Paco's car."

Dumbfounded at her attempt at deception, Alex decided to turn up the heat. Despite the hard stare he laid on her, her expression remained stoic. Even as he leaned over, growled against her neck, and asked, "Not Paco's car, huh?" she didn't crack.

With his gaze firmly on her, he popped open the glove box he'd opened a time or two before. Without looking, he fished out the contents.

Hooking the fuzzy handcuffs with his finger, he dangled them next to her face. "And these, Ms. Taylor? Are these for later when I've been very, very bad?" His voice was deep and scolding.

Busted, Madison cracked a smile, crumpling under the pressure. "Okay, okay. The car isn't Paco's because he—well, he gave it to me. It's mine now." She then circled a finger at the cuffs on prominent display. "But *those* are not."

Alex slumped a little in his seat, flipping through a wide range of possibilities that could have led to this.

Paco handed over his Big Banana to Madison? Color me impressed and confused. But at least it explains the charge from Paco's favorite Lamborghini dealer.

"Well, you must have given him something *extremely* valuable in return."

Patiently, Alex waited for her to reply, but was met with her tight pouty lips and a poker face fixed diligently on the road ahead. Sure, he could press her further, but instead, he sat and plotted, knowing he'd eventually get to the bottom of it. Hopefully, she'd resist. Handcuffs around her sexy little wrists would be an interrogation well worth the wait.

"All I can say," he said, "is if Paco gave you this car but not these," he clapped the cuffs together before tossing them back into the glove compartment, "then we seriously need to work on your negotiating skills."

Madison's smile widened as she looked over, but he didn't look back, instead opting to bury his nose in an insane pile of work.

Alex pulled up one document, scrutinizing it like a page from the *Wall Street Journal* while using his free hand to take Madison's from the task of steering. Planting a firm kiss on it, he brushed his lips over her knuckles for a second before returning it to the job of handling this beast of a car.

She accelerated a little more, and Alex ignored a small, unsettled voice inside his head that told him something was brewing. Something big. And good or bad, he could sense it. Whatever *it* was, it was present and powerful, and he suspected it would change everything.

CHAPTER 25

ALEX

As the three-hour drive breezed by, Alex couldn't resist a quick dive into DGI's latest quarterly projections. Something about the hum of this car and the portfolio on his lap always flipped him to full-on work mode.

He only asked Madison *where are we going?* and *are we almost there?* a few times before easing back into the passion that kept him sane all those years. Work.

But as the car slowed, Alex looked up and took in the quaint country road they were now traveling. Something seemed familiar. The houses were close enough to each other to be considered a neighborhood, but were far from being on top of each other. The modest homes were spaced out on large, tree-filled lots, where the residents enjoyed privacy but not solitude.

As soon as Madison cut the engine, Alex paid closer attention to one house in particular. It was sweet and alive with spring flowers and a variety of birds flitting to and from feeders in the yard, each hung at the best vantage point from nearby windows to give any onlookers a glimpse at birdwatching.

He remembered. Cardinals. Bluebirds. But mostly sparrows. The little birds that had given him fleeting moments of thinking about something other than his pain. Or the past. Instead, he'd just watched them fly free.

Stunned, he turned to Madison, who'd already exited the car. A small grin emerged as he focused on just one thing. "Dan?" Opening his door, he slowly climbed out of the car. Dazed, he took a few steps forward and grabbed her hand.

"You okay?" she asked, a small trace of worry in her words.

"Madison, how—" He stopped short, realizing the answer. "Paco." He took another look at the house he hadn't seen since . . . "Are you sure you want to do this?"

"Don't worry. I'm sure."

Alex took a single, contemplative breath. Then, without warning, he whisked her away, yanking her hand to tow her around the side of the house. Moving stealthily and damn near in a belly crawl, he led her to the edge of the back porch. She had to think he was a psychopath, but he knew what he was doing.

Looking left, then right, he pressed his back against the wall, and held Madison back as well, as if hiding from an enemy's sights. Poking his head around the corner, he examined the yard. It was well-maintained with several Adirondack chairs, one with a fresh bottle of beer saturated in condensation. It was the perfect cold drink for a warm day, and had only recently been abandoned.

"What are you doing?" she whispered, giving him a concerned look.

Ready to explain his bizarre tactical movements, he froze. The unmistakable cocking of a single-action pistol cracked the air. The barrel was pressed to the side of Alex's head, prompting him to hold up both hands.

"I'll tell you what he's doing," the booming voice announced. "He's making himself at home." The gruff man uncocked the gun and placed it on a nearby table, where two more ice-cold beers waited. "Welcome home, *both* of you."

Madison took Alex's hand, tightly clinging to it while swinging around to give her dad a big bear hug. "So, you two *do* know each other." Spotting the beers, she released Alex and headed over to the waiting bottles.

Dan gave Alex a good once-over. "Well, it's been half a second, but I reckon I'd spot AJ just about anywhere." Her father slapped Alex's open hand, shaking it hard. "How've you been, son?"

"Better," Alex said, pausing as if to add *I think*. He broke their handshake to remove his sunglasses and hang them from the neck of his shirt. Uncertain, he met Dan's gaze. "A lot better since . . ."

Alex hesitated, suddenly concerned how Dan would feel about him and Madison. Dan was one of the few people who knew the shape, size, and weight of every skeleton in Alex's closet. That, and it had been nearly a decade since they'd seen each other. He had to have doubts. What sane man wouldn't have doubts about a loose cannon like Alex Drake dating his daughter?

"Good!" Dan patted his shoulder. "You being better is very good."

His expression was so warm and approving that Alex shook his hand again, at which point Dan pulled him into a bear hug that Alex couldn't help but reciprocate.

"Thanks, Dan."

"No need to thank me. You did all the heavy lifting."

"Well, at least for the beer, if I can pry one away from your girl there."

Madison held it at arm's length, teasing Alex with it while making her way to the chairs on the lawn. Eagerly, she kicked off her shoes so she could wiggle her toes in the freshly trimmed blades of grass. Alex followed suit, unable to remember the last time he'd felt the simple joy of bare feet on the ground.

Madison handed Alex his untouched bottle before plopping her butt in one of the chairs. She was looking at them both with a fascinated smile as her gaze moved from Alex to her father. "I still can't figure out how I had no idea that you two knew each other."

Dan and Alex exchanged glances, silently debating who would start. Finally, Dan jumped in.

"Well, after the divorce, your mom took you away. You needed stability, and I was, well, really messed up after we lost Jack."

An apology clearly on her tongue, Madison grabbed his hand, but her father squeezed it quickly, then waved off what she was about to say.

"No, Frankie, your mom was right. Saying I had a tough time coping is like saying a tornado is a stiff breeze. I needed to deal with my shit without dragging you down with me. I needed to be alone. At least, I thought I did. And then I met AJ. I didn't think anyone could be more messed up than me." He took a swig of the cold beer, giving Alex an unsettled glance. "Boy, was I wrong."

Alex drew in a breath. "I returned to the States with just one thing on my mind. Returning the book and photo. I never felt right about having them. After all, Jack had a family. I figured it was the least I could do."

Dan glared, shaking a finger at Alex before correcting him. "Hey, if you're gonna tell this story, don't gloss over the nitty-gritty details." He turned to Madison. "The guy who showed up on my doorstep wasn't exactly *released* from the hospital."

When Madison glanced at Alex, he shrugged with a guilty smirk. "Okay, okay. I left the hospital a little early, but I hated taking up a bed with all the injured vets around me. I felt like, I don't know . . . a fraud. I wasn't active duty, and I was *technically* stable, so they couldn't keep me. I caught the next plane back. All I knew was that I had to get the book and photo back to all of you. But by the time I got here, I guess I—"

"Collapsed." Dan frowned, pointing an accusatory beer at Alex. "Right in my arms as I opened the door. Like a baby."

Alex shook his head. Of course Dan had to give him crap right in front of Madison.

"I nursed him back to health like Florence-fucking-Nightingale." Dan seemed to be enjoying slipping into gunny sergeant mode, savoring every minute of slinging shit at Alex. Because billionaire or not, in front of Dan's little girl, Alex had no choice but to grin, eat it, and gush, "Mmm, what a chef."

"To set the record straight, I leaned on your shoulder. No one carried me like a baby," Alex said with a scowl, glancing at Madison, and she giggled at his *don't buy the hype* expression.

"Seriously, I wasn't sure what to make of him," Dan said. "He had Jack's book, and the photo, and apparently spent the last few months with Jack. Well, all that, and he probably had one hell of a story."

"Speaking of that," Alex said, suddenly remembering. "When's the last time you saw that photo?"

"Oh, I'm not sure. I mean, it should be in my office. Why?"

Madison leaned in. "Dad, a man gave me that photo and made up a pretty horrible story to go with it. We're trying to figure out how he got it. Alex explained that you gave him Jack's book, but that the photo should be here."

While Madison talked, Alex pulled up Frank Seaver's Google image on his phone, then handed it over to her.

Madison showed Dan. "This guy. Does he look familiar?"

"Oh, him." Dan shrugged at Alex. "The way he was poking around, I figured he was trying to get some dirt on you. The son of a bitch said you used this address, but that was nearly a decade ago, so anyone looking that far back had to be grasping at straws. I tried finding out what he was after, but I guess while I was busy fishing, he netted me. A few questions in, and he asked to use the bathroom. At the same time, I took a call. Telemarketer. Then he came out, thanked me, and left. Makes me wonder if anything else is missing."

Determined, Dan stood and headed into the house with Madison and Alex on his heels. At the creak of the floors and the sunbeams hitting the sofa, Alex froze in midstep.

Maybe Madison had come and gone from here whenever she pleased, but not Alex. The last time he was here, he was barely holding on. Dan called it recovering. Like drawing a fine line between endlessly treading water and slowly drowning.

It hit him all at once.

The books on the bookshelf—he'd read them all. The quilt on the back of the sofa—which was his bed for the better part of a year. The photos on the walls—of the wife and daughter Alex always wondered about, but never prodded or asked. Even the smells—that same musty scent that would sit in his nose and hold him to the smallest shreds of life. Here and now.

His feelings were a mixture of sins and redemption, pain and hope. Alex needed a moment to take it all in, and Madison seemed to be giving it to him with a tight hug from behind, wrapping her arms around his waist and anchoring him to her.

"I'm right here," she said softly.

Alex sucked in a calming breath, easing his exhale and holding tight to her embrace. Somehow, just having her close chased away the ghosts of the past. He pulled her around and kissed her soft lips. "Thanks, beautiful. I needed that."

Dan returned in a huff, moving past them to the kitchen.

"What is it, Dad?"

"Nothing, maybe," he muttered. He opened a drawer, rummaging through it quietly, then shut it. Pensive, he returned to them. "He got the picture, but nothing else. Pisses me off that jackass got something off me."

Madison hugged Alex tighter, then looked up at him. "You might have something for Dad. In your wallet."

Smiling, Alex knew that look. Something in his wallet? No idea. But Madison had something up her sleeve, and Alex complied. Curious, he tugged the wallet from the back pocket of his jeans. Secured in the fold was the photo of him and Jack.

Before handing it over, he re-committed it to memory, ready to give it up to Dan. But Dan waved it away.

"You keep it. I've got another one." He motioned with his chin, pointing toward the bookshelf.

Quizzically, Madison and Alex both looked, not seeing what Dan meant. Then Alex noticed a frame that hadn't been there all those years ago.

Inside was a photo, trimmed with a solid black matting. It was the same as the one on Alex's baby grand piano—a picture of Madison and her dad smiling, holding up a photo. But this one was much bigger, at least twice the size of the one in Alex's place. And the photo of Madison and her dad? They were holding their own photo, and it was crystal clear. So clear, in fact, that Alex and Madison had to do a double-take.

What Madison and her dad were holding up all those years ago was the exact same photo Alex held now, with one unbelievable difference. It was completely intact, with a uniformed Staff Sergeant Paco Robles standing with his arm slung over Jack's shoulders, and Jack's arm tight around his waist. A beautiful snapshot frozen in time, magically recaptured into existence.

"Dad, how did you get this? How is this even possible?" Madison's words were fervent. Astonished. Holding an importance Alex wasn't sure he understood.

"Well, Jack called me from Italy. He wasn't supposed to, but he said he had something he needed to send me. Only . . ."

Alex felt something in his tone. "Only what?" Their trip to Italy was in the weeks before Jack was killed.

"Only, he said I wasn't supposed to have it. I'm guessing you all weren't supposed to have any evidence of your mission. In fact, he told me flat-out that after I saw it, I should print it but put it somewhere safe, and delete the digital copy. No record of the email could exist. Instead, I printed it out and grabbed Madison before she ran out with her friends. We took a quick shot of a picture within a picture. I emailed that back to him. I knew he'd get it, but no one else would understand. Hidden in plain sight. For us to share."

"This is incredible," Madison said softly, admiring it.

Dan pointed back to the bookshelf. "Just like the one I printed for you, Alex. Except I wanted yours to be small enough that you could keep it in your wallet, since neither of us were exactly sure where you'd land after you left."

Madison swooped over and picked up the frame like a precious gift. Her eyes gleamed as she held it reverently in her hands, murmuring, "Hidden in plain sight."

Alex noticed a tear rolling down her cheek and brushed it away with his thumb. "What is it?"

Laughing through her tears, she looked first at Alex, then at her dad. "It's us," she said, then explained. "It's all of us. Our family."

CHAPTER 26

MADISON

UP WELL BEFORE the crack of dawn, Madison looked over at Alex. Waking up before the workaholic mogul gave her a small thrill, and she watched him slumber away. His breathing was deep and restful, as if for the first time ever, he could relax.

Let's keep it that way.

The sound of rustling elsewhere in the house meant the old gunnery sergeant was up and at 'em. Sliding from the curve of Alex's strong arm, she slipped from the bed and out of the room, following the light to the kitchen.

"Coffee, jellybean?" Dan asked with his back to her.

In her warm socks, Madison skated across the kitchen floor and wrapped a warm hug around him. "No sneak attack on you. Coffee sounds great."

Dan handed her a cup as she scrounged through the fridge for anything that would pass as cream. A small carton of two-percent was close enough to its expiration date that it would do. Sugar was permanently planted front and center on the table, with a small stack of pennies for company.

"So, you and AJ," Dan said. "What's going on there?"

Her father wasn't looking at her, but took his seat and patiently waited, stirring a few spoons of sugar into the instant brew. Satisfied with his usual amount of sweetness, he put the spoon down and took the mug in his hands, cupping it close but not taking a sip. He just studied the ripples across the surface as he blew, then watched her through the escaping steam.

360

Madison sat down next to him and scooted her chair close, grabbing his spoon and helping herself to the sugar. "Something, I don't know . . . wonderful." The chance of concealing from her father how head over heels she was for Alex was definitely zero.

With a deep whiff of the coffee that always reminded her of home, she took a long, slow sip and waited for her dad's reaction.

But Dan didn't react, simply resumed his Maxwell House stare-down over the rim of his cup. Her cheesy smile must have been too much. "Does he make you happy? Take care of you?"

His parental squint was unmistakable. Truth serum in a stare. She might as well be ten years old again.

Madison set down her cup to clasp his hands. They were tight around his mug, almost white-knuckled with worry. "Dad, I'm happier than I've ever been in my life. He really does take care of me, and I hope he feels like I take care of him too."

Knowing she was positively glowing, she enjoyed being able to share something wonderful with her dad. Pleased, she released his hands and took another sip.

"Well, you've both been through a lot." He took a gulp and let out a small laugh. "Between the two of you, I couldn't tell you who I've worried about more."

"Hmm, your fiercely independent, introverted, occasional basket case of a daughter falls for a high-profile and intermittently tortured workaholic. I take it you're not worried now, are you?" Her grin ticked up with an air of whimsy.

Sitting back, he relaxed. "Nope, not worried at all. But I guess it's time I let you in on a little secret."

More Alex secrets? I. Am. Listening.

"Remember when I asked you if you if you needed money for anything? Getting settled? Giving college a try? Or if you needed anything before you went to New York?"

Madison nodded.

"But you," he said, reaching out to tap the tip of her nose, "*you* always said no. Why?"

Why? It was Madison's turn to stare down the dark liquid steaming in her cup. "I don't know. I guess I just really wanted to make it on my own. You made your own way, and so did Jack."

"Jack had a scholarship."

"Jack *earned* his scholarship. He was so excited starting his career. I knew it was because he did it all on his own. I wanted that, something I earned all on my own. Because with you, and Jack, and even Mom with her real estate, why should I be any different?" Madison shrugged. "After what happened to Jack, I just felt like exploring my options. Trying new things. Checking out the world. And I loved every job, every journey, and every life-long friend I've made along the way. I'm not sure I'd be the same person without them, and I wouldn't change a thing."

Dan raised a brow at her. "So, you don't regret not taking me up on the money?"

The money. Like there was any. Madison's dad would have given up anything and everything he had for her. Knowing that was enough. It pushed her to work harder than anyone around her so she would never have to ask him for a dime.

"Nope. No regrets."

Dan gave her a big grin. "Why don't you take a look in that drawer over there."

"The junk drawer?"

Sure. Maybe there's a new stash of pens, paper clips, or rubber bands.

Madison opened the first drawer. On top was a *TV Guide* from 1985. "Charlie's Angels?" she asked, holding it up.

Dan scoffed. "Not that drawer. The next one."

The next one was a mystery, filled with letter upon letter. A hundred of them, maybe more. All were addressed to Dan Taylor in a familiar handwriting with sweeping strokes and the smallest tail on the n's.

Alex.

Her fingers walked across the top of them, checking out a few for the date they were postmarked. They went back years. The return addresses varied, but they were all from the same person. *AJ Drake.* As far as she could tell, none had been opened. She grabbed the top handful and turned back to Dan.

"Dad, what is all this?"

Dan looked over. "Jellybean, that was AJ's personal trust fund for you. Well, and me, I guess. He sent these a few times a year. I stopped opening them when they stopped including letters, just checks. But I never cashed one. I *did* keep them, though. as a reminder of AJ."

Madison couldn't help but hold one of the more recent ones up to the light. Then another. And another.

"Dad! This is some serious money."

"Yes, Frankie, it is. But AJ earned it, not me, and I didn't need it. I thought maybe someday you would. Checks are only good for six months, I guess, because he kept upping the amount. Like a running tally. Some crazy, personal lotto, right? I figured I'd have them just in case you ever needed them."

She took a second, then plopped back down on the chair next to Dan, staring in total disbelief at a handful of envelopes that had to contain the equivalent of the net worth of a few countries.

Dan snagged one and waved it in front of her face. "I just needed to let you know. Without knowing you or asking for a single thing in return, AJ's been trying to take care of you since way before now. And I guess a small part of me is glad he finally gets the chance."

Madison looked down at the envelopes fanned out in her hands, thinking of Alex as he lay blissfully asleep. Urgently, she checked the time. "Dad, I need to go out for a while. Can you keep Alex occupied?"

"Good old-fashioned diversionary mission?" He picked up a penny from a small pile on the table and slid it to Madison. "I'm all in."

Madison swiped the penny, palming it tight as she headed over for a rushed hug. "Thanks, Dad."

Grabbing her bag, she slipped out into the dark morning.

CHAPTER 27

ALEX

ALEX'S deep sleep was interrupted by a loud crack and rumble, the distinct rev of the Big Banana, Paco's—*no, Madison's*—yellow Lamborghini.

"Madison?" he mumbled, grogginess clouding his vision as he looked around. He stretched himself awake. Rolling over, he slid a hand over the sheet on her side of the bed. Cool to the touch. The lightweight blanket wouldn't hold the heat in, though, so maybe she hadn't been gone long.

Slipping on a pair of sweats and a T-shirt, he headed out of the room and followed the light emerging from the rustic kitchen. Madison's father was busy fixing a cup of coffee, though there were two on the table.

"Black, right?" Dan asked.

"Right," Alex said with a yawn. He accepted the fresh cup gratefully and sat in a seat that was definitely warm beneath his butt.

Curious, he slipped a hand around what had to be Madison's mug, still half-full. The warmth remained. Dan pursed his lips in amusement, and Alex could feel his scrutiny.

"Well?" Dan said, beginning the test. "What can you tell me?"

Sipping from his own mug, Alex's free hand held Madison's abandoned cup for a moment. "She's been gone a few minutes, which only confirms what I already knew, since she opted to blow out of suburbia revving at a hundred thirty decibels. But, from how Madison indulges in coffee, she must have had a bit of a heart-to-heart with dear old Dad."

Dan smirked, and Alex continued.

"Her cup's warm enough that, even with the ambient coolness of the room, I'd say you two were talking for twenty, maybe twenty-five minutes at the most. On top of which, she decided to leave suddenly. Not a lot of pre-thought. Otherwise, she would have paced herself to either finish her coffee faster, or just pass on it altogether."

He glanced up at Dan, who nodded.

"I love my little girl, but a covert escape in the dark of morning is just not her style," Dan said, and they both chuckled. "Madison had to go do something, but she'll be back a little later."

A sip of the piping-hot coffee warmed Alex from the inside out, the flavor pulling him back to so many mornings past, long ago. Funny how the inexpensive brew always managed to ease him. "You know, I forgot how great your coffee is."

"Good to the last fucking drop." Dan held up his mug in a toast, then drained the last of it before standing again to get a refill. Once he'd poured himself another cup, he lingered at the counter. "AJ, can I ask you something?"

"Anything."

"Do you still have my phone number buried somewhere in that highfalutin phone of yours? Maybe not in the top ten, but somewhere?"

Alex said quickly, "Well, you were number one, but got bumped about three and a half weeks ago."

"That's interesting. See, Frankie and I caught up a little, and it all strikes me as, well, odd. Why didn't you just call me and ask for her number?"

"Because that would have been too easy. And you know me, Dan. It's the hard way or no way."

"Seriously?"

"Seriously." Alex let his head fall back before raking his fingers through his hair. With a long sigh, he sat up straight again. "I guess I didn't feel right about it, with how much you'd helped me. Everything you did for me. I think it would have been, I don't know, rude maybe. Like, *hey, thanks for saving me from myself and all, letting me crash at your place for months on end, and nursing me back from the brink of death. By the way, I'd like a go at your daughter. What's her number?*"

Dan smirked. "Well, good to see that at the very least, you're still so goddamned polite. But with your resources, you could have had her information in a New York minute."

Perplexed with himself, Alex shook his head. "If I couldn't ask you to your face, I sure as hell wasn't going to do surveillance behind your back, no matter how trivial it seemed." He pushed out a long breath. "I wasn't sure I'd be good for anyone, let alone *your* daughter and *Jack's* little sister. And meeting Madison wasn't exactly premeditated. I mean, I didn't set out to do it."

After taking another sip of his coffee, he pushed on. "But I don't know, I couldn't shake this feeling. I just kept getting the sense that we were going to meet, run into each other, almost as if—"

"As if by fate?" It was Dan's turn to be perplexed and shake his head. "Damn, son, are you telling me that under all that hard-charging exterior bullshit, you're a hopeless fucking romantic?"

Alex smiled at the teasing before explaining further.

"The first time I saw her, it was only a hunch. I didn't actually know who she was until after our first, um . . ." He glanced nervously at Dan, careful as he continued. "Our first date. Not fate, exactly, but I don't know, like maybe someone was looking down on us. Lending a hand."

Dan scowled at him. "Jack wouldn't lend you a hand." Then his glare melted into a broad grin. "Jack's style would've been a swift kick in the ass."

Alex laughed out a relieved breath.

"Well, be it fate or friendly forces," Dan said, "I can't think of two people better suited for each other. And I know you'd tear out your own heart before you'd break Frankie's."

"I would." Alex beamed at Dan, grateful for another round of fatherly bonding with him. It had been so long. Too long. But here Dan was, once again appearing in Alex's life at just the right time, being the father he'd never had.

Dawn was breaking in the distance, and a ray of sunlight pierced through the kitchen window, striking a row of pennies along its ledge.

Alex's gaze followed the beam to the table, sparkling against the small copper pile in the center of it. "You know, I forgot about all the pennies around here. They're in Madison's room too."

Grabbing one off the windowsill, Dan tossed it to him.

Catching it easily, Alex smiled as he admired it for a second. "You threw one at me when I left. I guess they're pretty lucky."

"These pennies aren't about luck. They're about loyalty. Risk. Never giving up. Don't you know the saying *in for a penny?*"

Alex downed another sip. "Something like *in for a penny, in for a pound?*"

Dan nodded.

"Okay. So, what does it mean?"

"Back in the day, the Brits coined it, saying if hanging was the punishment regardless of the crime, why not go for broke? If I stole a penny, and it had the same punishment as a larger crime, I might as well steal a pound. But we red-blooded Americans took it to the next level. If I'm gonna risk anything, I might as well risk everything. If I'm going to start something, I'm gonna see it through to the end. In our family, we always used it to show we had each other's back, through thick and thin."

Alex thought of the penny Madison had left on his desk. There was so much meaning behind it, and after just one night together.

Could I love Madison Taylor more?

"That you?" Dan asked, interrupting Alex's faraway stare to alert him to the faint ring of his cell from the bedroom.

He hurried back, picking it up a second too late. It was Gina's office line. And at 6:40 in the morning, it had to be important. Before he could dial back, her devil-horned avatar displayed again. This time, he was quick to accept.

"Hey, Gina. You're up early."

"Not my idea, I assure you. But that's what happens when I hear a competitor's VP is coming in for a meeting."

"It has to be a mistake. I don't have anything on my calendar. Did you check with Paco?"

"That's just it. He's not answering, and Madison Taylor seems to be assigned to meet with the VP. It's an invite from your calendar."

What? "With who?"

"That d-bag Frank Seaver. Are you okay with this?"

Hell no, I'm not okay with this. Madison said she didn't know how that son of a bitch got the contract. And yet here she is meeting with him. While I'm all of a sudden out of town.

"Boss?"

Alex settled down, not wanting to bring Gina into the angst of his love life. As the head of human capital for DGI, plausible deniability was her preferred default. "Yes, I guess I am. Do me a favor. Send me the details, but don't let anyone know I know." Two seconds later, a text pinged his phone with the time and location of the meeting. "Got it."

"Do you need me to get a car to you?"

Calculating the distance, he declined. "There's no time for that." He looked out Madison's bedroom window, noting an open field next to the house. "But I've got a faster ride. Thanks, Gina."

He hung up, sent a quick text, then scrolled to number five in his favorites. He clicked it, and after a few rings, the call was picked up.

"Hey, man," Alex said. "I'm gonna need to call in that favor. I just texted you my location, and bring the baby."

"Everything all right?" Dan was at his door, handing Alex a fresh cup.

With his thumb disconnecting the call, Alex painted on a smile. "Fine. Work stuff," he said, not wanting to involve Dan. Or worry him.

Dan scowled at him. "You really think you can clam up on me and think I won't see right through it?"

"Nope." Alex huffed out a resigned sigh. "You're right. It's just . . ."

Hesitating, he considered what actually weighed on his mind, and what he should share with Dan. The fact that Madison headed back to the city without him? Setting up a meeting from his calendar? Taking a meeting with one of the scuzziest people on the planet without a word to him?

I guess when she said, "I'm not going anywhere," she meant for the night.

Dan didn't need to know all that, so Alex tossed out an obvious comment, sharing his observations but not sounding overly concerned.

"It's just that it doesn't seem like Madison to leave half a cup of coffee behind." He smiled, only half joking about the girl who could nurse a cappuccino for hours.

"No, it doesn't. I'm sure she'll be back soon."

"I wouldn't bet on it." Alex let out a slow, uncertain breath. Dan deserved the truth. Or some of it, at least. "Your little girl's hightailing it back to Manhattan."

"What?" Agitated, Dan flailed his hands, nearly sloshing his coffee beyond the rim. "I've got four pounds of short ribs marinating. I was counting on Frankie to tackle at least a pound of them."

"Well, if she doesn't, I'll eat every last rib because they're amazing. But don't worry. I'm heading that way now. Come hell or high water, I'll be back. With Madison. And a real New York cheesecake."

Alex's adamance must have been apparent because Dan smirked, relaxing with another sip. "Sounds like my little girl's giving you a run for your money."

God, I hope not.

CHAPTER 28

ALEX

ONCE THE HELICOPTER came in for a soft landing in the open field, Alex hurried over and hopped in, waving back to Dan.

Dan called out, and Alex could read his lips. *Don't forget the cheesecake.*

He returned a solid thumbs-up, hoping like hell he could keep the other half of his commitment to Dan. He slipped on the waiting headset and fastened himself in, speaking into the mic. "I owe you, man."

Mark toggled several switches and gave him an annoying grin. "Well, I do like it when Alex Drake owes me. I've had my eye on a yacht . . ."

Running through the lines of the memorized checklist, Alex received clearance from the nearest tower, took over as pilot, and they were off. By the unsteady climb, Alex could see his emotions were a little volatile. Mark noticed too, of course, and placed a steady hand on his own cyclic.

"Easy, partner," Mark said. "Maybe it's been a hot second since you've handled this pristine piece of machinery, but trust me, she likes a gentle touch."

"She?" Alex asked. "Sounds like you and she are getting close."

"Her name is Lola, and yes, we are."

Mark motioned to take back control. Figuring it was in their best interest to arrive as fast as possible but in one piece, Alex gratefully acquiesced.

"Want to take a load off?" Mark asked. "My psychotherapy rates are pretty reasonable."

Alex scoffed. "Liar. You'd take me for every penny I have . . . and Lola too."

"True," Mark said without bothering to argue the point. "Let's begin your session. Should we open with some deep-breathing exercises? I hear Lamaze can get you in a nice, relaxed state."

Alex rolled his eyes, not joining in on Mark's laughter.

For kicks, Mark hung a hard left, taking them down with enough of a drop to feel like a roller coaster. For the first time in an hour, Alex smiled. A genuine smile.

When Mark came to the authorized altitude, he eased into a fast but comfortable speed. "So, what's on your mind?"

"You know your old pal Seaver?"

"Yeah . . ." Mark gave him a wary glance. "Come on, Alex. You don't need to snarl every time you say his name. Frank might be a bastard, but he's damn good at his job."

"Madison is meeting with him. In two and a half hours."

Mark whipped his head around. "Why the fuck is she doing that?"

And there it was. Mark knew it too. There would be no reason for a junior analyst to be meeting with the *damn good at his job* ass-wipe.

"Who knows? All I know is she did it on a whim. Didn't let me know. Didn't let her father know. She headed back to the city without a word. Speaking of her father, you'll be eating with us tonight at his house. We're having ribs."

"You don't have to twist my arm. But don't veer from the subject at hand. Back to Madison."

Uncertain how to inch into the shallow end of a topic that instantly dropped a thousand feet deep, Alex started with an unsettled shrug. "Maybe with Madison, I jumped the gun on our relationship—"

"You?" Mark's feigned look of surprise was met with Alex's glare. "And define *relationship*," he said, stretching out the word for effect. "Are we even at ten weeks yet?"

"As a matter of fact, we are." *If we count from the very first time we met.* "So, go fuck yourself. Anyway, as I was saying and to your point, maybe I need to . . . I don't know . . . back off and let it evolve naturally. Build something based on trust."

"Or lust," Mark said, waggling his brows. "It comes a close second. And it rhymes."

Mark was enjoying this way too much. It was the first time Alex had come anywhere near a serious talk about his first real relationship. Waist deep in uncharted territory, he was grateful for the ear of a man happily married to the love of his life. Ready to receive every bit of wisdom, sarcasm, and judgment this man had, Alex pressed on.

"The thing is, I . . . I have no fucking idea what to do. I'm going out of my goddamn mind wondering what the hell is going on. And . . ." He sucked in a breath, barely able to admit this to himself, let alone to the man he considered a brother. "I might have handed her the keys to my kingdom on nothing more than blind faith."

"What do you mean?" Mark gave him a sharp look.

Alex stared at the view a moment before continuing. "I might have given her full access to my calendar."

"So? Everyone in your inner circle has that. Jess and I have it too."

"Well, she set up the meeting with Seaver by sending him an invitation . . . from my calendar. So now it looks like I've made a meeting with him. On top of which, he apparently had access to private information."

"Information? Like, the sort of information that puts you in a compromising position? Tell me it's not more than your occasional indulgence in chick flicks and romance novels?"

"More like a commitment I made to Madison. In private. I wanted her to get to know me better, and basically swore I'd never lie to her."

"And that's a risk because . . ."

"Because I said that if I ever lied to her . . . and the operative word is *if* . . . she'd be entitled to all my corporate and personal assets."

With a deep chuckle, Mark marveled at his friend. "Wow. Way to make the rest of us look like underachievers. I wouldn't worry about it, though. It's not like you lied. Or put in in writing."

Clearing his throat and rubbing a newly formed ache at his temple, Alex said slowly, "I might have put it in writing. And had Paco witness it."

The somber look on Mark's face reflected every pang of torment Alex was already feeling.

"Oh, it gets worse. According to Madison, she has no idea how he got a hold of it, but it was in her possession. At the penthouse. It's not like she dropped it on the way to work. Seaver is an attorney. He knows what he's got. Maybe they're in it together."

The silence was stifling. Mark didn't say a word, but rather sat quietly, processing it, no doubt mentally pelting Alex with an imaginative assortment of colorful names.

Eventually, Mark made eye contact, looking Alex up and down until a high degree of certainty filled his face. "Well, well, well. Sounds like Alex Drake is in love." Which was immediately followed by Mark singing, "Alex has Madison sitting on his tree . . . "

Alex huffed out a frustrated breath. "I'm serious. What if I was wrong about us? About her? Trusted her when maybe I shouldn't have. And for reasons I don't want to talk about, maybe there's a part of her that can never forgive me for my past. Whether she's calculating and conniving, or just young and naive, it doesn't matter. Either way, I'm fucked. Paco was right. I put not just me, but my whole goddamned corporation at risk. Globally, thousands of jobs. Not to mention everything I owe to the shareholders. It was irresponsible."

"It was decisive."

Frowning, Alex shook his head. "I need to take a step back. Slow down. Maybe put things on pause, at least for the moment. Think more. Feel less."

Mark took an aggressive and dangerous nosedive before pulling up. Gripping a hand strap, Alex forgot the luxury chopper was built for maneuverability as well as speed until Mark's little trick reminded him. Apparently, his friend seemed intent on getting his attention before laying into him.

"I'm not sure at what point you turned eighty-five," Mark said fiercely, "but it looks like shit on you, man. You made billions by shooting from the hip, using the fucking Force, and trusting your gut. And now, because you're not the one in control, you run? Is that what you want? A life that's safe and secure? Empty as fuck and boring as shit? Because I doubt it, and I'm pretty sure those aren't the qualities that drew Madison to you in the first place. And isn't it part of Madison's allure that you can't control the woman? News flash. Women can't be controlled. The sooner you come to grips with that, the better."

Crossing his arms over his chest, Alex didn't respond, pressing his lips into a tight line as he contemplated Mark's words for the next fifteen minutes of their ride. Silently, he lined up a few plays in his head, finally deciding on the best course of action.

It must have been written all over his face, because when Mark glanced at him again, his face broke into a huge grin. "Well? What are we doing? And who's going with you?"

"Going with me?" Alex met Mark's grin with a devious smile. "Oh, I think you and I both know who I'm bringing."

"I had a hunch."

Alex gave them both a critical once-over, running a hand over his own grown-out scruff and taking in how Mark had graduated from burly lumberjack to potential cast member of *Duck Dynasty*. "Well, first things first. Barber, then tailor. There's zero chance I'm barging into a meeting looking like this, and frankly, you could use a makeover."

Mark checked the clock. "Do we have enough time?"

"Trust me, Rip Van Winkle, we're making time."

CHAPTER 29

MADISON

MADISON DECIDED to wear her most serious black-on-black suit, conveying both the gravity of the situation as well as armoring up for what could be one hell of a fight. Though Paco had insisted on joining her, she'd adamantly declined. This was her fight. She'd do it alone.

On her way to DGI's conference room 214, she calmed her nerves by thinking of Alex. He'd walked her through those crazy self-defense moves after rescuing her from the street thugs, patient with her until she nailed each one. The powerful mogul had taken his valuable time to give her a one-on-one self-defense lesson, imparting a few words of advice to make her safer. Stronger. And in the face of danger, a more worthy opponent.

Here goes nothing.

Arriving in the conference room a few minutes early, she took the seat at the head of the table. The power seat. And the perfect vantage point to take in all of Frank Seaver as he strutted through the door a moment later.

"My dear, you look ravishing. So well suited at the head of the table. Exactly where the CEO should be." He strolled up to greet her, leaning over as if to give her a kiss on the cheek.

Because his balls are definitely bigger than his brains.

Madison leaned back, extending a firm arm and insisting on the professionalism of a faraway handshake. Nothing says *back the fuck up* like a stiff arm and a glare.

Seaver smiled, then kissed her hand. The slobbery lip print he left made her wince.

Gross. She pulled her hand back, wiping it on the chair and making a mental note to return with a gallon bottle of bleach.

"Now, my dear, is that any way to treat the man you're getting into bed with?"

Madison managed to swallow the bile rising in her throat. "Oh, I'm not getting into bed with you, Mr. Seaver. Figuratively or otherwise."

Dismissively, she waved her hand, giving him permission to sit. Once he did, she clasped her hands on the conference table, powering up for her play.

"I'm here to tell you that you don't have a deal, and you don't have my vote. I'm sorry you've wasted your time, but there's nothing left for you."

"If that's your position, very well." His words were too easy, and she watched him relax back in his seat. "Let me ask you something, Ms. Taylor. Is it difficult? Living with the guilt."

"What guilt?" *He's baiting me. He has to be.*

"Oh, the guilt that your brother sold out his country for a few measly dollars."

"That's a goddamned lie!" Madison's rage got the better of her before she could reel it in. But tears would be so much worse. She had to bite the inside of her cheek to keep from crying.

How dare he disparage Jack that way?

"Maybe," Seaver said smugly, "but I've got friends that tell me otherwise. Like, that his treason was covered up. Or maybe they'll just say what I want them to say. Who needs proof when there's social media, and a senator or two in your pocket? Wow, I might be sitting on the exposé of the year."

"What do you want?" Madison demanded impatiently, now thoroughly irate. "I told you, I don't have any shares for any proxy vote."

"You don't now, but you will." With a smarmy smile, he took out a contract, placing it before her along with a pen. "I'm going to make this so easy for you. All you have to do is sign. That's it. No muss, no fuss. Just a signature away from being a world-class millionaire."

Confused, Madison took a moment to scan the contract, pretty sure he'd ignored everything she'd said. "This says I'm signing over all my shares to you," she said as she tossed it onto the table. "Shares I don't have."

"It doesn't matter. Between your contract with Drake"—Seaver pulled out the original taped-together contract Alex had given her and laid it next to the contract she'd just thrown down—"and mine with you, it's all I'll need."

"Aren't you forgetting something? Alex Drake would have had to lie to me for his contract with me to be valid. He's never lied. Not once."

Seaver leaned back in his chair with a chuckle. "He doesn't have to. With your signature on that piece of paper, a lie is implied. It's all I need, enough to force him out. Drake will be left with two choices—a scandal or a buyout. My bet's on the buyout. Oh, and your brother can rest in peace. See? One little signature, and it's win, win, win." He nudged the Mont Blanc pen closer to her. "Now, wouldn't you like an ending where everybody wins?"

Madison considered the sleazebag's offer. She thought of what Jack would have wanted. And her father. Then there was Paco, and all the sacrifices he'd already made for Jack.

Finally, she thought of Alex, and his words came back to her. He wanted peace and freedom, and her. He was ready for an exit strategy, ready to take whatever golden parachute buyout was offered and run with it.

Her arm itched like a son of a bitch, but the hives would have to wait.

Glaring at Seaver, she took the pen and held it up. "Mr. Seaver, why don't you shove this pen right up your ass? No matter what you threaten me with, I'm not signing. Do what you will."

Tossing the pen on the table, Madison stood, prepared to leave. But when the door to the conference room opened before she left the table, her jaw dropped.

CHAPTER 30

MADISON

"YOU KIDS TRYING to have a meeting without us?" Alex asked as Madison stared in awe. Alex was bright-eyed with the confidence of a man who'd spent years accustomed to having the upper hand.

"They grow up so darn fast," his companion said, a man sporting an equally impressive suit and demeanor.

Alarmed, Seaver jumped to his feet. "Mr. Donovan, what are you doing here?"

Madison recognized the name, but not the man. Mr. Donovan, also known as *the Sniper*. The hard-charging CEO of Excelsior/Centurion, Frank Seaver's boss, and Alex Drake's most aggressive competitor.

"*Now* the meeting can begin," Donovan said as he and Alex crossed the room.

They made their way to the conference table, but the Sniper went out of his way to walk over to Madison. Rattled, she stepped back from her chair, ready to relinquish her seat to either of the two high-powered CEOs.

He shook her hand, then firmly nudged her back to her seat. She realized as she lowered herself into it that he was slipping something into the palm of her hand. "It's good to see you again, Ms. Taylor."

See me again?

Madison's reaction volleyed between skepticism and irritation . . . at herself. First, she couldn't recall meeting Alex, and now this Manhattan CEO had apparently been met and forgotten too.

Really? her inner voice wailed. *Another one?*

As the gentlemen—and Slimy Seaver—took their seats, she held her hands in her lap, then looked down in bewilderment when she opened her hand. Donovan had given her a shiny new penny. Staring at him, she leaned back in her chair, uncertain where any of this was going.

Eyeing Seaver, Mr. Donovan spoke harshly. "Are we resorting to strong-arming analysts now to force a competitive edge? It's not exactly what we're known for."

Blinking rapidly, Seaver remained silent.

From his blazer pocket, Mr. Donovan retrieved a pair of glasses, slipped them on, then scooped up the contracts on the table. He held them up high to read them, hiding his face from Seaver, but allowing him to privately grace Madison with the assurance of two long wink-winks.

His smile was infectious. And familiar.

Abruptly, he snapped the pages with annoyance and handed them to Alex. With his glasses on, Madison finally realized who he was and gasped.

Add a shaggy beard and a layer of easygoing flannel and he was Jess's husband, Mark, aka "Mr. Bishop." Or, as he was often referred to in headlines in the *New York Times, Marcus* Donovan.

"That sheet of paper's in pretty rough shape," Mark said. "And here I thought your days of dumpster diving were over."

Seaver admitted nothing while Alex reviewed the tattered document, admiring his own work.

"This little baby is well-written, concise, and fairly generous of me. But if someone were thinking of using it, and I'm not being overly critical, there's just one little hiccup. You see, despite the arts-and-crafts way it's been taped back together, it was obviously torn up, crumpled, and discarded. Meaning that the owner at the time, indicated here to be one Ms. Madison Taylor, didn't seem to want it."

Mark raised a brow at his employee. "Seaver, you're slipping. You're an attorney. Don't they teach you anything at law school? To be a binding contract, there are several elements that must be met. The first is offer. And the second is?"

Shifting in his seat, Seaver averted his gaze as he mumbled, "Acceptance."

Mixing his arrogance with fun, Mark rejoiced. "Yes, Seaver, *acceptance.* I knew you'd get there if we dropped enough bread crumbs for you. And a contract that was torn up, crumpled, and discarded seems proof positive that there was no actual *acceptance*. But let's just verify that, shall we? Ms. Taylor, do you accept the terms of this contract?"

All eyes turned to Madison.

She sat up, gripping the penny a little harder as she directed her stern words at Seaver. "No, I don't."

Mark clapped a hand on Seaver's shoulder, grabbing his attention. "There. No acceptance. The contract is not binding. Ms. Taylor is not the owner of any of the shares of DGI." Puzzled, he exchanged a glance with Alex. "But you know what's really bothering me, Mr. Drake?"

"What's that, Mr. Donovan?"

"It's the odd way that Seaver, my senior VP, went about this. Hiding his intentions from me, his boss, the CEO of Excelsior/Centurion. Hmm, makes one wonder."

Alex smirked. "Indeed, it does."

"I'm guessing," Mark said, "it's because this little scheme wasn't about DGI at all. Well, it was a little about DGI, but it was really about E/C. The hostile takeover of your company paved the path to a different scheme. This wasn't about giving E/C the proxy vote, but to giving *Seaver* the proxy. So, why stop there? He would have a license to hunt. If he did that, a merger between DGI and E/C would be imminent, and the next step in Seaver's plan at world domination? I suspect it would be my own golden parachute."

Alex chimed in. "And, no doubt, a less than generous one at that." He gave Mark a consoling pat on the back.

Seaver jumped to his feet. "Mr. Donovan, this is a complete misunderstanding. You can't possibly doubt my loyalty to you."

A deadly smile ticked up Mark's lips. "Seaver, if there's one thing I know, it's that the only loyalty you've got is to yourself. Lucky for me, you've violated several terms of your employment, including misrepresenting the interests of E/C and me. So, with that, I'm pleased to inform you that you are no longer employed by or represent Excelsior/Centurion. At all."

Seaver huffed out, "You can't fire me. I'm on the board of directors."

Alex grinned. "Well, I'm sure they'd love to see how you really operate." He pointed to a corner of the ceiling, where a camera stared down at them. "Smile pretty." Dropping the pretense of cordiality, he gave Seaver a lethal glare that would cower most men. "Let me break it down for you. If anything is leaked to smear any of us, or anyone in Ms. Taylor's family, that little footage is going be the viral video of the year."

Mark pulled a folded piece of paper from his breast pocket and handed it to Seaver. "Now, *I'm* gonna make this easy for *you*. Sign this resignation, and your ass stays out of jail."

The blood drained from Seaver's face, and his hand shook a little as he reached for the pen. Marcus Donovan was infamous for his threats, and just as well known for always backing them up. Seaver steadied his hand, quickly signed, then raced out of the room without another word.

Alex and Mark snickered, amused and pleased as they watched him leave. With him out of the way, they both turned their attention to Madison.

"You okay?" Alex asked.

"I—I think so," she said before turning to Mark. "So, you're Marcus Donovan. CEO of Excelsior/Centurion. The biggest rival of DGI. The Wall Street *Sniper*. Yet, you two are best friends?"

Mark patted her hand. "Well, yes. And yes. Alex and I built our companies, and our friendships, around the same time. We both knew that to get an edge and keep it, we needed to stay sharp. We couldn't do that by coddling each other. We needed to compete. Hard. So, we've kept our friendship low-key, but have always championed each other behind the scenes."

Alex interjected. "It's the same with martial arts. I can't get better if people *let* me win. I have to earn it. Keep pushing, and learning, and growing. Otherwise, my skills atrophy until I'm defenseless. Our fierce competitive streak keeps us on our toes, and ensures our respective companies are always the best of the best."

As Madison listened, it was easy to see why they were close, and how they managed to make it all work without anyone knowing. What wasn't easy to see was how they got to the meeting in time. "I seriously hauled butt to get to the city, change clothes, and prepare for battle. I can't believe you got here so fast."

Pinning her with his dark gaze, Alex leaned closer from across the table. "And I can't believe you tore up that contract."

Despite the heat rising between the two of them, the savage hunger in his eyes and the wetness between her legs, they weren't exactly alone.

Deliberately, Mark cleared his throat to remind them. "It's a piece of cake when I'm the custodian of Alex's sexy new baby, which cruises at a comfortable one hundred seventy-five miles per hour."

Her furrowed brow relaxed, but the wheels in her head still spun like crazy. "And the camera? I was just in this room a few days ago. Conference room 214 doesn't have cameras. Everyone knows it."

Alex weighed in with a broad, boyish grin. "You're right. Everyone knows there's no cameras in this conference room, including Seaver. When I discovered the meeting, I had a small crew install the equipment. Life's good when you're the head of a company renowned for surveillance." He took Madison's closed hand. "You sure you're okay?"

The penny was warm in her palm. Relieved, she smiled at them both, letting out a long breath with her response. "I am now."

Alex stood and pulled her to her feet, wrapping her in a warm embrace. "And for the record, the terms of the contract were never satisfied. I'm sorry, Ms. Taylor, but under the circumstances, there's no way you could get all my assets."

Alarmed, she opened her mouth to protest, but her argument was stopped by his finger against her lips.

"I'm afraid the most I could possibly give you is, well . . . half. And maybe a shredder for Christmas."

Madison's eyes widened, but Alex gave her no chance to respond as he stole a series of soft, warm kisses.

CHAPTER 31

MADISON

A week later

THE BALLROOM WAS alive with music and chatter as Madison and her escort made their way into the reception. Crossing the grand ballroom, she floated past the head table, wearing a gown that luminously trailed her every move. The silvery lace was enhanced with jet-black accents, its elegance perfect for a magical night.

Taking her seat at another table, she practically beamed, an odd contrast to her sulking escort who dropped into the chair next to her. Drumming his fingers on the table, Paco seemed thoroughly annoyed.

"Oh, *hermanita*," he said, seething with suspicion.

"Yes, brother dear?" Madison coyly replied.

His pursed lips unlocked to vent. "I might be okay with bringing you here because, as you said, the RSVP was already sent and the seats were already assigned. *And* I might even be okay with you not taking your proper seat at the head table to hang out with me here, because you're an angel and that's just the person you are. But I'm not—let me repeat—*not* okay with the two of us stuck all alone at a table for five."

Snatching up an elegant place card from the table, he fumed. "Other than yours and mine, the place cards aren't even filled in. *VIP Guest*. What the hell is a

VIP guest? We'd both better damn well be VIP guests, but at least we have names. This is too high school for words. What the hell is going on?"

Madison shrugged, bringing a glass of bubbly at her lips to avoid answering. As she sipped, she caught a glimpse of one of the very, very VIPs in question, and waved him over with glee.

Paco turned, checking out the person Madison was summoning. Noticeably shocked, Paco stood and chugged his full glass of champagne, then reached for hers and downed it as well. "You didn't say your father was coming."

"I didn't? Oh. Well, he's coming." She nudged the bottle of Moët just out of reach. As Paco tried reaching for the bottle to pour himself another glass of courage, she whispered, "Don't be nervous. He hardly ever makes anyone drop and give him twenty anymore."

Madison stood and threw herself into her father's arms for a tight squeeze. "Dad, I'm so glad you could make it. You look amazing."

Dan beamed at her. "Well, AJ hooked me up with this monkey suit, and wearing it to mow the lawn or work on the car seemed a bit much."

Paco couldn't sneak back a few steps without Madison grabbing his arm and yanking him near.

"Dad, I want you to meet someone very special." Madison pushed Paco's hesitant body right in front of her dad. "This," she said ceremoniously, "is Paco. Paco, this is my dad, Dan."

Madison watched Paco snap to attention, as if Gunnery Sergeant Dan were in uniform and on duty.

With Paco nervous and Dan impatient, Madison second-guessed the brilliance of her idea. The lights lowered, and the DJ transitioned the music to a ballad.

Surprising Madison, Dan barked out an assertive demand. "Let's dance."

Figuring anything was better than this, Madison moved in to take her father's elbow and accept.

Dan simply nudged her away, instead yanking Paco by the elbow and whisking him to the center of the dance floor. Dragging his heels, Paco threw a helpless look at Madison, who covered her gaping mouth with one hand and threw him a confident thumbs-up with the other, approving with enthusiastic nodding.

CHAPTER 32

PACO

AMONGST THE COUPLES crowding the dance floor, Paco felt oddly like a wall-flower of a prom queen as Dan took the lead. His steps were remarkably good, though Paco had a hard time relaxing.

"Look," Dan said gruffly. "I'm sort of a cut-to-the-chase kind of guy."

"I respect that, sir," Paco said, nodding solemnly.

"I understand I owe you a debt."

At Dan's disarming words, Paco relaxed his tight shoulders, more confident in his steps. "No, not at all. You don't owe me anything. I was just . . ." Paco chose his words carefully, not sure how much Madison might have shared with her father. "I was just honoring a fellow service member. And a hell of a man."

Dan stared at him, narrowing his eyes as he digested the words. "Interesting," he said, letting the word hang for a second. "True enough, but not exactly the whole truth."

Feeling caught in the semblance of a lie, Paco fumbled to explain. "Sir, I'm—"

"No *sirs* between us." Dan glared back, insulted. "No *sir* or *mister*. You can forget all that shit right now. Call me Dan. Or—" He paused for a moment to pull a small item from his breast pocket and place it in Paco's hand.

Taking a closer look, Paco stared at it in disbelief, trying to make sense of it through suddenly watery eyes. It was the photo. The only one of him, Jack, and Alex—intact and encased in a small silver frame.

Before he could ask, Dan continued. "Or you can also call me Dad."

384

Shocked, Paco had nothing to say.

Dan grunted. "Okay, maybe that's too much. How about you at least let me call you *son*?"

Closing the space between them, Dan swooped in for a hug, a heartfelt squeeze that stole Paco's breath. Overwhelmed with emotion, he hugged back very, very hard.

Before his tears could break free, Madison cut in.

"Hey," she said, wiping a rogue tear from Paco's eye. "I'm sorry to barge in on the moment, but the other members of our party have finally arrived."

After kissing Paco's cheek, she pointed to the double doors, where Alex was leading an elegantly gowned woman into the room.

"Yasmin!" Paco gasped as they approached. "What—"

Alex cut him off. "Don't worry. I've got twelve guards posted throughout. All entrances are covered, and nobody knows she's here. It's been a while since you two caught up," he said, handing her off to the man officially recognized as her husband.

In Yasmin's native tongue, she and Paco began to talk before he pulled her away to the dance floor. She struggled a little with the steps, but as he led her confidently, she relaxed with a smile.

Paco watched as Dan made his way to the bar, and admired Madison cuddled in Alex's arms. He mouthed a small *thank you* their way before the music swept them away as well.

CHAPTER 33

MADISON

M ADISON HAD ENJOYED every minute of the wedding and the reception that followed. Seeing her dad dance with Paco. Meeting the woman who'd saved his life. Soaking in a moment to press against the solid muscles of one Mr. Alex Drake.

Gazing up at him, she was captivated. His handsome features and tender eyes looked back, and she could almost imagine they were alone.

"Isn't that Alex Drake?" she overheard someone say, which ticked up her anxiety to the point she hoped her hives didn't break out, seeing as she was in a sleeveless gown.

Alex pressed his warm cheek to hers. "Hey, how about we get some air?"

Relieved, Madison said, "I'd like that."

With his arm at the small of her back, he led her to an isolated balcony private enough for just the two of them. The brisk evening air chilled her into shivers, and she hugged herself, as the off-the-shoulder gown hardly held in the heat.

The satiny lining of Alex's jacket draped her with warmth as his kiss skimmed her neck. It was still warm with his heat.

"Better?" he asked.

"Mm-hmm," she said, smiling. Redolent of his cologne and his own scent, his jacket gave her all she needed to wrap it closer and soak him in.

"I've got something for you," Alex murmured in her ear, holding her tight from behind.

Madison looked back, noticing his gaze was fixed on the stone railing of the balcony. She turned to look and held her breath. On the railing was a small velvet jewelry box beckoning her with its distinctive blue hue.

Locked in place, Madison could only stare at the unmistakable Tiffany & Co. box. Her heart thundered, threatening to pound clear out of her chest.

This can't be happening.

As if reading her mind, Alex tightened his hold and nuzzled her ear. "It's not what you think," he said with a light peck. When she gave him a skeptical smile, he said, "Go ahead. Open it."

She took a few slow, unsteady steps toward it, as if she might scare it into flight if she moved too fast. Glancing back again, she was reassured by Alex motioning her forward with a nod.

Madison nodded too, if only to herself. Staring down at the velvety casing, she scooped the box into her hands. Prying the lid just a little, she built enough courage to open it.

Alex was indeed telling the truth. It wasn't at all what she thought. It was a hundred times more.

Where a ring could have been, a shiny new penny stood upright with a note tucked in the lid. When she propped the box all the way open, she could read each of the three little words.

I'm all in!

Madison's face blossomed with a huge smile as she took it all in.

After one night together with Alex, she'd made a wish, pouring her hope into the silent message—a shiny penny left behind. A crazy dream of forever being tied to a man who managed to steal her heart. And tonight, he'd wished it right back, promising his heart in return.

She turned back, finding Alex Drake coming as close as he ever had to a lie. There he was, before her on one knee. With a gasp, she covered her open mouth with a hand.

"Madison *Elizabeth* Taylor . . ."

It made her burst out in a sweet giggle, and not just from the amazing setting and proposal to come, but also because it was the first time she'd ever heard her entire name out loud when she wasn't in trouble. Yet somehow, she had the sneaking suspicion she was about to get in a whole lot of trouble. The man before her was the total package, offering her a life filled with risk and adventure, alive with perpetual seduction and unrivaled romance.

Sporting those charming dimples, he kept going. "I never imagined I could find love, or be loved, so fully and completely. From the day our worlds collided, I was forever changed, and I can't imagine a single day of the rest of my life without you." He held up a ring, whose brilliance and size seemed to pale in comparison only to the full moon above. "Please, Madison. Marry me."

Unable to speak or move, she simply nodded, letting the happiest tears stream down her cheeks.

Rising, Alex took her trembling hands with a sparkle in his eyes. "Is that a yes?"

Madison's smile widened, and she nodded as she whispered, "Yes, Alex. Yes."

After placing the ring on her finger, he wiped more tears with his thumbs as his hands cradled her face. His mouth descended on hers with a kiss, making her head swirl and her knees weak.

Is this real? To love and be so incredibly and unconditionally loved back?

But it was real. And she was his.

Several low voices pulled Alex from their kiss, and Madison from her thoughts. She pulled back slightly from his embrace, realizing they were no longer alone. Looking over, she giggled at the small audience of her family and very closest friends standing just inside the doorway.

Sheila leaned against Paco, confused and unsure. "Did my girl say yes?"

Alex nodded, squeezing Madison tighter to him.

At that nod, Paco pulled up his phone and gave Madison a loving look. "She said yes," he shouted into the phone.

A moment later, Madison jumped at the loud booms of fireworks overhead, popping in rapid succession as they lit up the night sky.

Sheila raced over to hug her bestie, handing over her bouquet and meeting Madison's regretful glance.

"I'm sorry," Madison said sincerely, not wanting to take anything away from Sheila's wedding day.

"Don't worry. Everyone thinks the fireworks are for me and Kent. Only we," she swirled her hand around at the gathering on the balcony, "know the truth."

Smiling, Madison accepted the arrangement, lavishly spilling over with roses and peonies.

"And speaking of truth, Little Miss *Curious*," Sheila said, prompting Madison's blush to burn its way up her cheeks. "The truth is, I couldn't be happier. And I get why you kept it on the down low, but I'll forgive it all if you promise me this—I get first crack at your wedding announcement."

"Deal!" Madison said with relief, beaming back at Alex, who tore his gaze away and began waving toward the door.

"Samantha!"

Sexy Samantha?

The woman approaching them was elegant and poised, and beaming with delight. Alex released Madison for a moment to accept Samantha's businesslike hug before handing her off to Madison, who was embraced with one much warmer.

"Well?" Samantha asked impatiently under her breath. Her gaze darted to Alex.

Without a word, Alex swept Madison's hand up in presentation, letting her admire it. "As always, your work is impeccable."

"Your work?" Madison asked.

"Madison, meet Samantha Hayes, the designer of your ring. She owns Hayes Fine Jewelers."

Hayes Fine Jewelers? The same jeweler who designs engagement rings for actresses and influencers? Heads of states and royals?

"You have no idea the lengths Alex went to keep this from the press," Samantha said with a laugh.

I've got some idea.

Alex reclaimed Madison, locking his strong arm around her waist. "I couldn't risk scaring you away. Nothing says *run for the hills* like a dozen reporters asking about an engagement."

They all laughed until Sheila chimed in. "To set the record straight, Madison has never run from this reporter."

Samantha handed a small box to the bride. "You must be Sheila. Congratulations. Sorry to crash your party and run, but when a client requests this, I make it a point to always deliver it personally. Now I'm off to London for the next ten days."

Delighted, Sheila popped the clasp on the hinged velvet box and pried it open. Inside was a golden gift certificate with her name filled in and signed by Alex, but no dollar amount.

"Thank you," she said repeatedly, though her confusion was still clear on her face.

Samantha leaned in, saying softly, "The technical term for that is a blank check."

After nearly taking out everyone's eardrums with her scream, Sheila grabbed Alex in a grateful chokehold he didn't seem to mind.

Eventually, she released him, putting a momentary halt to her gushing to hug Samantha. "You can't go!" Sheila said firmly. "You have to meet my husband. And have cake and champagne."

"Consider my arm twisted," Samantha said with a quick hug to both Alex and Madison.

Sheila followed suit, leaving a kiss on Madison's cheek and a smug comment whispered in her ear. "This certificate proves my point. Samantha *is* sexy."

Giggling, Madison glanced at her ring. "Yes, she is."

Sheila stepped away to lock arms with the sexy jeweler and lead her back inside.

As an endless stream of fireworks exploded in the sky and her heart pounded, Madison melted as Alex gave her another breathtaking kiss. He brushed a strand of hair behind her shoulder as he looked into her eyes.

"I love you, Madison."

Madison let her finger trace his jaw, finding a resting spot in the dimple of his chin. She was ready to expose one last tidbit she knew about Alex Drake—a namesake he shared with another man so very close to her heart. "I love you too, Alexander Jackson Drake."

With that, Madison and Alex shared another kiss—a bond that swept them through the night and into a new life, and adventure, together.

BOOK 3: BURNED

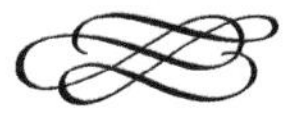

AN ALEX DRAKE NOVEL

BURNED
AN ALEX DRAKE NOVEL
LEXXI JAMES

PART I
THE PRESENT

CHAPTER 1

MADISON

Manhattan

CROUCHED awkwardly in the small space between the watercooler and the wall, Madison couldn't help looking up at the half-filled tank in disbelief.

They're actually gossiping next to the watercooler? How horribly on the nose.

Deflated, she flinched at the sting of each rumor she overheard from her unintended surveillance spot. And the question she mentally kicked herself over wasn't how could this have happened, but how could it not?

Somehow, she'd managed to convince herself that the news of her upcoming nuptials would be barely newsworthy in the engagements section of the *New York Times*.

Ha!

She'd even helped craft the matter-of-fact snippet, certain it would be buried beneath the actual full-blown wedding announcements, not to mention the reports of stock surges and gripping national news.

Her best friend, Sheila—the up and coming reporter Madison had promised the story to—had made every change Madison requested. In the end, the announcement was limited to a single line.

BILLIONAIRE CEO ALEX DRAKE AND DGI ANALYST MADISON TAYLOR TO WED

Sheila had been promised the scoop, and Madison Taylor was a woman of her word. She held tight to her integrity, no matter how uncomfortable it was. And it was definitely uncomfortable . . . hiding in a corner behind the coffee bar in the break room of Drake Global Industries.

Madison sucked in a silent breath, taking in this long, exhausting day had begun well before the crack of dawn. Glancing at row of international clocks on the wall, the one set for New York time hadn't yet hit eleven a.m.

Awesome.

Texts had begun blowing up her cell phone about five a.m., a total of several hundred, because apparently her number was splayed across the Times Square Jumbotron.

How do I get my number unlisted from the world? Just a small-town girl engaged to a billionaire. Nothing to see here, folks. Nothing to see.

Madison wiggled her toes, afraid they were falling asleep. *I should've called in sick.*

Sick. Or freaked out. *Tomayto, tomahto.*

None of this was as bad as she'd imagined. No, it was so horribly, awfully, painfully much worse.

How this should have gone down was with her busting out a magnanimous can of whoop-ass on her slanderous coworkers the moment she heard the first barb. But this was Alex's company, not hers. And temper tantrums at the office from his new fiancée wouldn't be a good look for either of them. Confronting her detractors would create a situation the press would undoubtedly blow completely out of proportion.

Instead, the women's incoming voices with her name on their lips as they approached the break room had rushed her ass to retreat to a corner that, between you and me, it barely managed to squeeze into.

And there she remained, wedged between the wall and the watercooler. In competitive hide and seek, this space would have rated a C+ at best. But if she were very quiet and still, her secret hideaway would work.

"Madison Taylor," one of them said with disdain. "Who would have thought it? All sweet and innocent, and fucking the boss the whole time."

Madison peeked out as best she could, eyeing the trio of women she'd never even met. After all, over a thousand DGI employees worked at the headquarters here in Manhattan.

Who cares what they say?

Annoyed at herself, she stifled a snort. That was a stupid question. She cared. Way more than every brain cell in her ducked-down head said she should.

I don't even know these women.

But if middle school had taught her anything—other than how to use a tampon, that hair gel and eyebrow tweezing should be done sparingly, and that the little boy you crushed on so hard and wished you could marry someday was batting for the other team—it was that where a trail of mean girls started, endless swarms of them followed.

"I'll bet Little Miss Prim and Proper does it every which way. Like a pet on some diamond-studded leash. You know, a girlfriend of mine dated him."

Unimpressed, Mean Girl Number Two responded with another slap in the face. "Who hasn't?"

The third chimed in. "Yeah, he's had more women spread eagle than the American Society of Obstetrics. And does that man have a dark side. Kink to the core. Only one way she's marriage material."

Madison's frustration and anger slid to the back seat as her curiosity called shotgun, with a flutter of hope that the next words spoken would be *true love.*

The third girl snickered. "Ménage."

"Not *à trois,* if that's where you're going."

Madison let out a silent exhale of relief.

"More like *à cinq.*"

Her eyes popped open wide. *Five? Really? Oh, come on. Do I walk like I've been done every which way to Sunday?*

"Now we know why there are so many chairs in the boardroom," one of them said, which drew a titter of cruel laughter from the others.

Madison rolled her eyes. This was too much. With the air ripe with premium roast and vicious gossip, she was losing her cool. It didn't help that these women were taking the longest coffee break ever, lazily drawing out their time—and Madison's as well.

All I wanted was some freaking water.

Her options were dwindling, but she could always confront them. Jump out and defend her honor, slaying them with an accusatory "gotcha" finger pointing straight at their shocked faces as she exclaimed, "Aha! I heard every word."

So what if it lost its impact because she'd been listening way too long?

Jump up and confront them? At this point, standing might be its own challenge. Hiding had been a bad idea from the start, one that grew worse with each minute she stayed put.

No amount of yoga or deep breathing would prevent her cramped legs from falling asleep. And, of course, the women were taking their sweet damn time finishing up, because God forbid they actually get back to work.

Madison said one silent prayer after another that the women would leave before her legs completely gave out. Impatiently, she squatted, waiting out the swarms of prickles running up and down her calves and thighs, willing herself not to fall flat on her ass when her muscles finally gave out.

After about a million years, the gossips collected their coffee cups over-flowing with freshly slung mud before inching their way into the hall, continuing their obnoxiously loud chatter and giving Madison a reprieve.

A much-needed reprieve that would have to wait even longer. It would seem that with all her patience and silent fuming, her wedged-in body was now hopelessly stuck.

Huffing, or semi-hyperventilating, she sucked in a long breath and gripped the watercooler with one hand while resting her other palm on the wall.

Madison's first heave to push herself up seemed promising. At halfway through heave number two, she stopped short to avoid the sloshing tank from tipping completely over. And when another set of footsteps casually strolled into the break room, she did what any self-respecting junior analyst marrying the boss would do in her place. She froze.

"Hello?" the sultry voice called out, undoubtedly noticing the still sloshing tank gurgling, complete with big, blaring bubbles and all.

Shyly, Madison peered around the tank as subtly as she could, watching the slow sashay of a five-foot-ten-inch supermodel with ass-length hair heading straight toward her.

Crap.

The woman who certainly didn't need the five-inch stilettos rocked them like the world was her runway. She moved like magical fairy dust had touched one of *Charlie's Angels*, endowing her with a crazy blend of beauty, boobs, and even maybe the softest touch of badass that Madison admired.

This woman set Madison's nerves on edge as she stooped before her, eyeing her up and down with a grin. "Everything okay?"

"Oh. Yes." Madison nodded, struggling to appear casual and nonchalant. "I just, um, dropped something."

The ruby-red lips of the strange woman widened with intrigue as she barely glanced around the floor. "And then sat on it? Is it an egg? If you're a golden goose, I'm claiming you."

The stranger stood and extended her hand. Madison graciously accepted the hoist of her remarkably strong and effortless pull.

The relief of standing pushed an uncontrollable sigh from Madison's throat. "*Ah*, thank you." She rubbed at the pins and needles in her thighs, pointedly glancing down. "See? No golden egg."

Her rescuer smirked. "Well, I guess I won't be your captor, then."

"Good thing too, as I'm already spoken for."

"So I hear," the woman teased, arching a perfectly shaped brow.

When Madison's face fell and she ducked her head, the stranger tipped her head back up with a couple of soft fingers beneath her chin.

"Yeah, the trio in the hall weren't exactly curbing their enthusiasm." Confidently, she stroked Madison's arm. "Don't let them get to you. Jealousy is *très déclassé*."

Soothed, Madison wasn't sure what to say in response. "Thanks. I appreciate that. Can I treat you to a coffee?" she asked, offering up the selection of coffees displayed next to a dozen Keurig machines.

"Actually, I don't do coffee. I just came to recycle my water bottle." Giving the clear plastic enough of a squeeze to make it crackle, the woman placed the empty Evian in the recycling bin. "And I should really get back."

"Well, thanks again for helping me up." Extending a hand, she introduced herself. "I'm Madison."

The woman clasped it in both of hers, smoothing a thumb against her skin. "I know," she said, leaning close and flashing a knowing grin. "Pretty sure everyone knows."

A short silence hung between them while their eye contact teetered to awkward.

Finally, the woman released Madison's hand, offering her own cryptic introduction. "Just call me *J*."

"Jay?"

"Mm-hmm. You know . . . like J-Lo."

Madison smiled, finding the name fitting, considering the woman carried herself with the confidence and poise of a known triple threat. "Well, *J*, it was nice to meet you."

"You too."

J began a very catwalk departure, pausing only for a moment as Madison called out, "See you around."

With a slow turn and a suggestive grin, *J* gave her a solemn but friendly reassurance. "Definitely."

She then disappeared down the hall, leaving Madison with an unsettled knot in her chest.

Without a doubt, the underbelly of the DGI grapevine would be buzzing with everyone's take on *Junior Analyst Beds the Boss*. Yup, this was the perfect way to grow a budding career built with hard work and integrity, taken seriously at every step for the smart, savvy, growing businesswoman she was.

Riiight, her inner voice said before another thought hit her. *I could leave.*

Leave? For how long . . . a day? A week? It didn't matter. Everyone knew. *Everyone*. And the few people who didn't—like the preppers avoiding the news or the castaways on deserted islands—offered little solace that this would all blow over.

Desperate to shake off her plummet into the freefall of anxiety, Madison weighed her options. Fresh air was always a good call.

Tempted by the bright outdoors peeking through from the lobby exit door, Madison took a determined detour to a street vendor on the corner. Hurried and trying not to make eye contact with anyone, she bought a pre-wrapped salad and a glass bottle of Coke—the kind with real sugar—because it was that kind of a day.

Armed with lunch, Madison slunk back to her office for a little alone time to focus on two side-by-side oversize computer monitors filled with lots and lots and lots of data.

Because data didn't gossip, and data didn't judge. And the mountain of glorious data at her disposal was enough to hide behind for the rest of the day. Alone. Diligently working and not obsessing over the ticking time bomb of an expiration date for this very precious and amazing job.

CHAPTER 2

ALEX

"Five hundred million?" Alex Drake asked, staring at his computer monitor while barely paying attention to the conversation from the speakerphone.

Preoccupied, he wasn't exactly on top of the discussion, but like the CEO he was, responded decisively. "Sounds fine," he muttered, approving who the hell knew what. For all he knew, he'd agreed to bribes, sex toys, and a year's worth of hookers for the Senate.

The email that had snagged his attention sat unopened for several moments, his finger hovering with uncertainty, because approving whatever half a billion dollars was buying was an easier decision than opening that email.

Labeled PRIVATE, it had been sent by a ghost he hadn't heard from in ten years, the only person he'd thought about all that time with the same interest as he'd wondered about his close friend's little sister. Madison had become his fixation. But *J. Stone* had been an unclosed chapter of his past.

With the shame of idiocy settling in and the insistence that there was no fear in reading an email, he finally clicked it open.

Within the email was a video clip taken from the DGI headquarters lobby not ten minutes ago. The *J* from the email was front and center, strolling through the lobby of the headquarters of his multibillion-dollar empire as if she owned the place.

Is there some corner of her misguided mind that thinks she owns me as well?

With thoughtful intensity, Alex studied the footage frame by frame, desperate to analyze the three-minute clip. The statuesque woman made long, stately strides to the security desk. Fife, DGI's chief of security, stood to greet her and pointed to the lobby restroom. She thanked him and stepped away.

In her natural sashay, she made her way to the ladies' room, waving her arm back to the camera and holding up three fingers. She disappeared behind the door.

A sound of gruff irritation left his lips, followed by, "Shit," as he jumped to his feet. The video was done.

"No to the orphanage donation?" his vice president of corporate charities asked, shy surprise in her tone.

"What?" Briefly, Alex focused, mentally flipping through the slides he'd scanned a few hours earlier. Recalling the line in question, he rushed to agree.

"No, no. We're good. Approved for the orphanage, and I've gone through your analysis. Well done. Approved for all charity requests for the next six months, but let's keep a close eye on the burn rate for the food banks. I'd like to revisit in thirty days in case we need to send them more."

Rising to his feet with a finger ready, he said, "I need to cut this short." He blurted out a *thank you* before killing the call and taking his private elevator downstairs to the lobby.

With a quick glance around as he tried to appear nonchalant, Alex swiftly stepped into the ladies' room.

An observant glance at the orthopedic shoes revealed beneath the door of stall one urged him to rush past the closed door, eager to avoid any face-to-face meetings. He ignored the usual sounds commonplace in bathrooms.

At stall three, the closed door he was sure was vacant gave with the slightest push of his fingers. Having said a silent *thank God*, he entered.

Empty.

He took a doubtful look into the pristinely clean bowl, certain no further exploration was necessary, but made a mental note to give bonuses to the cleaning staff.

When the toilet from two stalls over flushed, Alex shut the door. Behind it, he found a note, recognizing the ornate penmanship.

Alex

Tamping down the faintest trace of a sentimental thought or emotion, he snatched down the taped note and flipped it open. One word was carefully scrawled, with a heart over the *i*.

Congratulations

Alex flipped it over, diligent in making sure he hadn't missed more.

J wasn't his past. She was ancient fucking history, returning to taunt him in his own lobby while leaving behind no trace except an email and a cryptic note about his impending nuptials. It didn't make sense.

Dumbfounded, Alex couldn't make heads or tails of it, but was certain this wouldn't be her last word. Slipping the note in his pocket, he stepped out of the stall without checking to be sure he was now alone.

"Oh!" the elegant older woman said in shock. She wore a smart blue suit that matched her wide eyes, and the orthopedic shoes he'd glimpsed beneath the stall door.

Grateful that he didn't recognize her, Alex gave her a shy smile. Clinging to a hope, a prayer, and blind faith that her thick glasses made him indistinguishable in a lineup, he apologized and excused himself, briskly moving past her.

"Ahem." Her expression stern, she cleared her throat and glanced pointedly at his hands, then at the sink.

He took a begrudging step to the sink, not bothering to explain he hadn't actually used the toilet in the women's restroom. He wrapped up as soon as he'd mentally finished his ABCs and headed back to his office, pretending, as Fife did, that he hadn't been spotted.

Between the mysterious note and the uneasy feeling that, as CEO of the company, he might be adding another idiosyncrasy to the growing list of rumored ones he knew of, he welcomed an incoming call from Mark Donovan.

The man might be his evil arch nemesis in public as CEO of Excelsior/Centurion, but to Alex, he was one of only a handful of very close friends.

"Hey, Mark. I see you're calling from your cell, so may I assume bail money isn't required?"

"Not this time." Mark's tone was far from easygoing as he blew out a heavy breath. "Listen, we need to talk. It's a guy thing."

It's a guy thing wasn't a guy thing. It was code. Mark needed Alex's ear, and it had to be somewhere secure and away from both of their offices. In these situations, they met at an off-the-grid secure facility both of them knew the route to by heart.

Frowning, Alex kept his voice even and light as he said, "Sure."

Tonight, they were supposed to be heading out for a weekend getaway. Alex and Madison would be meeting Mark and his wife, Jess, at their luxury cabin hidden deep in the Adirondacks. This would change the plans.

"How about you ask Jess to grab Madison?" Alex said. "I know she would love a girls' drive up." Caution prevented him from saying anything else.

"Perfect," Mark said quickly. "You let Madison know, and I'll tell Jess."

"When do you want to get together?"

"You know. See ya."

From the *see ya*, Alex did know. Those two words translated to a time. *Five thirty*.

CHAPTER 3

MADISON

LIGHTLY MOVING the bits of lettuce and chicken of her barely touched Caesar salad around in its plastic container, Madison couldn't bring herself to eat. The spreadsheets she tried to analyze were blurring together, one nonsensical cell at a time, while the computer's clock seemed to be going painfully in reverse.

She ignored the cream-colored corporate walls as they closed in on her, but couldn't push away the agony of the incessant itch creeping up her arm. A few scratches to ease the small patch of hives was enough for the time being.

How bad will it get? How do I prepare? Can I prepare?

Prepare for what? Whatever *this* was, it wasn't like a Twitter swarm, where people she didn't know trolled her from behind the anonymity of a computer screen.

No, the people letting their voices be heard weren't anonymous. And though she couldn't pick any of them out of a lineup, or even a corporate directory, they were people she'd continue to see, day in and day out. Bump into in the hall. Hide from in the break room. And avoid like the plague.

And what about Alex? Was she his Achilles heel? A DGI liability where corporate gossip became the catalyst for a sharp drop in stock price? If the world at large wanted to look down on her, so be it. But Alex didn't deserve this.

The scrutiny of cavorting with a junior analyst—because obviously, she and Alex had cavorted—should be a non-starter. The truth was that Alex had nearly died trying to save Madison's brother years ago, but it was none of anyone's business. And that type of news wouldn't matter, because stories like that didn't sell. At least, not like a bogus, tantalizingly lurid and horrendously salacious office scandal.

Ménage à cinq, my ass. Wait! That came out wrong.

Defeated, she dropped her head back against the soft leather of the headrest as she closed her eyes and pushed out a heavy breath, wishing she'd stayed in bed.

"Sleeping on the job?" a cheerful Latino voice called out.

Relieved to see the man who was always a friendly face, she lifted her head and gave him a huge grin. Leaning against her door frame was Paco Robles, Alex Drake's right-hand man. An invisible mastermind behind the scenes. And the only man in the world who could earn his way to becoming her brother.

Madison gave him a wry smile. "Just reminiscing about how nice life was yesterday."

Paco took a seat and wheeled his chair next to hers. Making himself comfortable, he leaned back into it, clasping his hands across his Tom Ford-clad abs as he said casually, "Ignore it."

Without a word, Madison handed over her phone, showing him that the notifications and messages were well past a thousand so far.

Completely unconcerned, he waved a manicured hand. "It's just a blip. A little sensationalism. I promise you on all the couture I cherish more than bacon, it will pass. And no matter how beautiful yesterday's sunset seems today, we have to focus on the sunrise ahead."

How can I argue with this man? Seriously, he loves couture and bacon. He's obviously brilliant beyond his years, and it would serve me well to listen to him.

Without asking, he gently gripped her wrist, stretching out her arm and delicately sliding up her sleeve. Clinically, he scrutinized the reddening splotches wrapping her forearm.

Dismayed, he let out a long breath, his expression filling with concern. "That's pretty bad. Want me to take you home? Or at least out of here to get some fresh air for a bit? I know all the people-free secret passages."

"I'll bet you do," she said, hesitant and shrugging away his concern.

Surprising her, he pushed her executive chair aside, letting it wheel away from behind her desk as he took ownership of her keyboard, clicking away as he accessed her calendar. Like any nosy big brother would.

"Wow," he said as he let out a whistle. "An exciting afternoon of South American market analysis." After typing a few keystrokes at lightning speed, he hit ENTER with exaggerated satisfaction. "There."

She pulled herself closer to examine his work. With a playful glare, she asked, "My entire afternoon is now blocked for a last-minute Latin-relations meeting?"

"*With* the ambassador to Puerto Rico. Get your stuff. *Vámanos.* There's nothing the ambassador hates more than waiting."

Heading out of her office and down a hall, they made their way through a door Madison hadn't noticed before. "Puerto Rico is a US territory. There is no ambassador."

With comfortable authority, Paco challenged her. "That just means the title's up for grabs. Called it."

"Yes, Your Excellency," she said, laughing.

They arrived at yet another private elevator, because apparently this place had more of them than floors, bathrooms, or parking spaces combined. Entering, he swiped his access card across the panel, which brightened the blue backlight of all the stainless-steel buttons. He pressed G.

During their descent, Paco focused on texting, and it suddenly dawned on her that she was probably encroaching on his own agenda for the day.

She covered his hand with hers, giving it a gentle squeeze and stopping him mid-text. "Seriously, I appreciate everything you're doing for me, but I can't tear you from your schedule."

The elevator opened. "You're not. This *is* actually a business trip."

Madison smirked. "Oh, I'm sure it is, Ambassador Robles."

Once they arrived at the private garage, Madison's thrill level kicked up a notch as Paco opened the driver's door of his very new and droolworthy Rosso Mars red Aventador and beckoned her to climb in. The man changed Lamborghinis as frequently as he changed boyfriends, and this would be Madison's first time behind the wheel of his new beast.

"What's her name?" Madison asked as she started the engine.

"Hot Cherry."

"Could be sexy. Could need antibiotics."

"Hush your mouth. She'll hear you." Reassuring the car with several long caresses to his side of the dash, Paco said, "Don't listen to her. You're sex on wheels. Easily making men hard from your curves and your purr."

"True."

As Paco was the bossiest navigator ever, Madison drove well beyond the comforts of the speed limit as soon as traffic let up.

"I'm not an old lady," she said with a giggle.

"Seriously, my grandmother would kick your ass from her walker. In a few minutes, we'll have an open stretch. Gun it, girlie."

Nothing weighed on her mind in that moment. Just the roar of the engine, the rumble beneath her seat, and the exhilaration of pushing Paco's Hot Cherry to the point of nearly popping.

In no time, Paco gave her the signal that they were nearing their destination and she could slow down. A few turns later, they arrived at what Madison recognized to be a government building. It was a VA medical center, but one with a satellite building attached. The letters DGI were on the side.

"What is this?" Madison asked as she pulled into the reserved spot he directed her to and parked.

"Drake Robotics works closely with this VA medical center. I thought you'd like a tour."

Madison beamed. This wasn't your run-of-the-mill distraction from a hard day at the office by heading to a mall or a bar. It was an opportunity. A gateway to work closely with cutting-edge science and veterans.

As she and Paco began their tour, the vets they met with were unique, each battling their own mental and physical challenges and conditions.

One man, John, had been the sole survivor from his team. She didn't know why she opened up about the loss of her brother. And she didn't know why he opened up about his guilt. But both were raw and honest, with no expectation to fix or be fixed. Just to listen. And understand. And be. It was a deep, tear-filled connection, and it felt good.

Also, John reminded her of Alex, what he might have been like a month after Jack's death. An Alex she never knew, but somehow connected with now.

Over the course of her visit, she moved on to others. Others who were missing pieces of their bodies, or their minds, or their hearts, or their souls. People who were shadows of the people they once were. And people who might never again be complete, or fulfilled, or happy, or whole.

But being around them gave Madison a glimmer of hope that she could take her own incompleteness, and unfillable emptiness, and never-ending sadness, and use it for something that might be good, even if only in the smallest way.

What each of the veterans she met wanted was as much of a surprise as what they didn't. No one wanted accolades, and they definitely didn't want pity. Madison could relate.

On the want list were ordinary, everyday things. Food items like Girl Scout cookies and a real goddamn drink were popular. Their favorite brand of toiletries and books ranked on the achievable scale, and Madison promised to return with all of them.

On the other end of the spectrum? They wanted their lives back. Their friends alive. Their sanity. Answers. Why?

These were all the things Madison wished for them because that was where they connected with the strongest. She'd wanted all those things too, and to this day, she still did.

Paco had given up his pocket square for her near the beginning of their tour, but it was apparent early on that the big, bad Mr. Robles needed it just as much as she did throughout the day. Though there were tissues at every bedside, sharing the single handkerchief seemed to soothe them both.

Before rejoining the others, Madison stopped Paco to ask, "Does Alex come here?"

Paco shook his head slowly, giving his lips a tight, disconcerting crimp. "It's not for lack of trying. The flashbacks kick in the hardest here. And it's not the men or women. He works with plenty of vets. Something about the smell of a hospital, I suspect. And," he said carefully, "it was the last place he saw Jack."

With a weak shrug, he sucked in a slow breath, cautious before letting her in on more about the man she'd be marrying.

"It knocks him off his game, and not for hours or days, but for months. We all have our triggers, and let's just say Alex Drake has more than his fair share. It took some convincing, but we assured him he was doing enough. More than enough. With Alex, it's like watching him snuff out a raging fire to a smoldering flame, only to douse it with kerosene. We all have our limits, *hermanita*. This isn't for Alex. But perhaps it's the chicken soup tailor-made for your soul."

Smiling, Madison pulled Paco into a tight squeeze, with his strong hug back rocking her gently.

"It's all perspective, Madison. A few hours ago, you were wishing today away." He pulled back, dabbing away her tears while beaming at her through his own glistening eyes. "And now?"

"Now?" She inhaled, not needing to think it through. "Now I think this is one of the most amazing afternoons of my life. And I can't let it be the last. There have to be ways I can help."

He kissed her cheek. "I'm sure there are." A series of short buzzes erupted from his pocket, and he pulled out his phone. "Fife's getting antsy. Must be the new access cards. Ready?"

Madison nodded, naturally wrapping her hands around his arm as he led her back. Heading outside, she couldn't quell the butterflies fluttering in her stomach. Or pinpoint what exactly her future held.

She sensed the winds of change storming about, like a tornado raging across the Oklahoma plains.

Apprehensive yet resolute, she knew she needed to share this with Alex.

But when?

CHAPTER 4

MADISON

Although with a little less tread on Paco's tires, Madison returned both the car and them safe and sound—and scratch-free—to DGI headquarters. There was no hiding his small, relieved breath when she eased Hot Cherry into her assigned space in the garage.

Although she was ready to make a beeline straight to Alex's fifty-second-floor office, Paco yanked her back, directing her to the security desk.

New access cards were ready for beta testing—a highly customizable form created to give unfettered entry to anything and everything in the building. Only a short list of people could perform the test. A very short list.

Other than Alex and Fife, just Paco and Madison, actually.

Fife seemed ready to take their prints and retina scans, modifying the data in the beta cards. But once they arrived, he hopped to his feet, standing at attention as he struggled to stutter out, "G-good afternoon, Ms. Taylor," without an ounce of love for Paco.

Coughing through a laugh, Paco drew her attention to the *New York Times* on the desk, splayed open to the prominent engagement announcement several font sizes larger than the rest.

"Not you too," she said, exasperated as she cringed. Her stern words softened his expression to the helpless look of a scolded puppy, which was ridiculous for the hardened ex-SEAL. It sent her over the edge.

Grabbing his giant shoulders, she pushed the two-hundred-eighty-pound behemoth of pure muscle effortlessly to his seat.

"Fife, I need you to pay very close attention to every word I'm about to say. I. Am. Madison. Your pal Madison. The girl who tosses you chocolate-covered espresso beans when your lunch slump hits. The girl who challenges you on a daily basis for who will come in first and leave last. The same girl you picked up like a rag doll right in the center of that very floor."

He followed the path of her finger as she pointed for effect.

"So, do not—and I repeat—do *not* even begin to look at me and see the CEO of DGI, Mr. Alex Drake, because you and I both know he couldn't carry off these heels to save his life."

Cracking an amused grin, she was relieved to finally see Fife give her one back, at which point she playfully poked his chest. "Is that clear?"

"Yes, ma'am." He saluted sharply, then leaned in. Even from a seated position and with Madison in four-inch-heels, the two were nearly eye-to-eye. "So, which of you decides if we press charges?"

Confused, Madison turned to Paco, then back to Fife. "Press charges?"

Nodding, he explained. "I sent you both an encrypted email."

Paco checked his phone. Frowning, he hesitantly passed the phone to Madison, highlighting the email Fife was referring to.

Urgent and Confidential. We caught a woman with items on her computer that violate her terms of employment. Images of Ms. Madison Taylor in unflattering poses. Doctored images had Ms. Taylor's face superimposed on various women's bodies. All in compromising positions. All retrieved. All recipients identified. Termination procedures in progress. Press charges?

With a loose hold on her skyrocketing anxiety, Madison found herself right back in the mess she'd left before lunch.

Great. And by great, I mean everything about this sucks big fat donkey nads. When, for the love of God, is this day going to end already?

Paco pointed to the center monitor of Fife's computer. "Pull up her badge credentials, and what we've got on her right now."

Fife brought up the DGI-issued ID of one Margaret Cunningham on one screen, while loading several documents across the other screens. Madison let out a gasp of recognition, stealing Paco's attention.

"You know her?"

"Yes. I mean, no. I mean . . . I—I've seen her around," she said with a meek shrug.

Yanking her elbow gently but firmly, Paco pulled her out of earshot of Fife, then unbuttoned his suit and pocketed his hands. "What? Who is she?"

Madison swallowed her embarrassment as best she could, unable to quell the heat rising up her cheeks. In a hushed voice, she explained. "I saw her this morning. Her and a couple of others. I overheard them talking trash about me, but it was just, um, watercooler gossip. Hurtful. Hateful. But nothing to get fired over."

"Well, Fife didn't put everything in the email. The stuff he pulled up is a lot more incriminating than that, and not just about you. Looks like she offered confidential corporate intel to a competitor." He cleared his throat. "Our best competitor."

And by best competitor, Paco had to mean Excelsior/Centurion and its CEO, Mark Donovan. To the outside world, he and Alex were hard-charging, fight-to-the-death competitors. But to those in the know, he was Alex's brotherly BFF.

"So, that's how they caught her?" Madison asked.

"No, actually. Security was tipped off earlier today and called me. Hang on." Paco gestured to Fife waving at them, motioning for their attention. "They're escorting her out now. Here, let's move out of sight."

From their observation point, they watched as Mean Girl Number Two was led away by security, carrying a big box of her belongings. Her eyes were swollen and red-rimmed.

But before she could exit the building, another woman deliberately crossed her path. A woman with high heels, ass-length hair, and that familiar crimson smile.

It was *J*, pausing only momentarily during her casual stroll to find Madison across the room. Dropping her sunglasses, *J* touched the arm of them to her full, flirty lips and shot Madison a very deliberate, very direct wink. Returning her shades to their placement high on the bridge of her nose, she widened her smile as she watched the woman being escorted out.

Urgently, Madison patted Paco's arm. "See that woman?"

Paco looked in the direction Madison pointed with her chin. "The femme fatale? Who could miss her."

"Who is she? Or what department does she work in?"

Paco looked at Madison and spoke carefully. "No idea who she is. She doesn't work here. Why do you ask?"

Adoring the man beside her, Madison gave him a look of disbelief. "Maybe your walking encyclopedia mind of all twenty thousand employees is off, and she hasn't made your radar yet."

"Nobody's off my radar," he said with equal parts confidence and admonishment. "I might not recall random facts, and I'm no contender for *Jeopardy*, but images are my thing. Faces, maps, anything visual. Like a glistening, bare-chested Hemsworth after a long, breathy swim, what has been seen cannot be unseen. It's a blessing and a curse."

Straightening his tie, he added, "And it's twenty thousand, four hundred, and eight people, and that includes the nineteen onboarded this morning. Maybe Nikita was in the building for a meeting or something else. Like a leather convention."

That made Madison stifle a laugh.

"And I didn't vet her, so she wasn't meeting Alex. All I can say is she doesn't work here. Guaranteed."

Madison glanced back to find J, but it was too late. Both she and the now former employee Margaret were both gone.

"Come on," Paco said, ready to head back to Fife's desk.

Fife repeated his question. "Press charges?"

Paco examined the screen. "Let legal take care of it. They'll see if we have enough to press charges."

"Paco," Madison whispered with a pang of paranoia. "Could she have maybe been, oh, I don't know . . . set up?"

Instantly, Paco tugged her away from the desk, emphasizing the importance of his question with a firm hand on her shoulder. Lowering his voice, he asked, "Why would you think that?"

Hesitant, Madison only shrugged. Honestly, she had nothing. And it wasn't like she missed the middle mean girl. *Good riddance.* But she couldn't shake the niggling feeling.

Paco patted her hand reassuringly, giving her a comforting smile. "Look, the information she tried peddling was an attempt to seriously compromise DGI. Legal will investigate it, and TRex will verify all of it." He leaned in. "And we'll wipe whatever she had on you. No matter what, DGI will at least threaten her with criminal charges if she persists with a fake-news smear campaign. According to the law, doctored photos are libel. We can't just sweep it under the rug, Madison, or have it looming over your head like it's your fight alone. Our strongest position is to protect you, because protecting you *is* protecting DGI."

"But . . ." *Damn this nagging feeling.* "Are you sure she did it?"

"No, I'm not." His words were flat and direct. "But Fife is. If you saw her this morning, and she was just escorted out, I know what that timeline means." He lifted a confident eyebrow, holding it high for effect. "Your little gossip girl confessed. Totally cracked under the pressure. Sometimes, one cross look at a person, and they fold like a cheese quesadilla."

It was Madison's turn to check on a buzzing text. "Oh, Jess is almost here, and I wanted a quick chat with Alex before heading out."

With a warm hand pressed to her back, Paco led her to Alex's private elevator, one she knew well. Hidden from sight from any onlookers in the lobby, it would quickly whisk her directly to his office. But even that didn't ease her tension or unfurl her brow.

Paco grabbed both her hands and brushed his thumbs over her knuckles. "Relax, or I'm booking you with my Botox guy, stat."

As if on command, she relaxed and a giggle burst from her lips.

"It's under control, Madison. Don't worry about a thing. And for the love of all things Henry Cavill, and I do mean all things, have fun."

Paco pecked her cheek good-bye and reached in to hit the button for her. It seemed he'd developed an annoying new habit to keep her from doing anything at all for herself.

As the elevator zoomed upward, Madison shot a text to Alex before arriving at his floor.

MADISON: *Free? It'll just take a minute.*

CHAPTER 5

MADISON

ANXIOUSLY, Madison stared at her cell. With no response from Alex by the time she reached the fifty-second floor, uncertainty set in. It might be a bad time to interrupt his day. Meekly, she headed for his office. There, she checked her cell again.

Nothing.

Pacing slowly in front of Alex's closed office door, she stood there, hesitant to knock. Startling her, it flew open, revealing the hardened features of a damn good-looking man as his solid body filled the door frame.

Pretending to be taken aback, Alex gave her a stern look. "Free? Seriously? I'm afraid not."

Without another word, he whisked Madison into his strong arms, lifting her off her feet to his chest in a tight embrace. His lips crushed hers, melting her with a passionate kiss. In seconds, he'd swiftly moved her into his office and against the door as he closed and locked it. His cock was hard against her belly, making her ready for him in that instant.

Whatever she had to get off her chest could wait. Not that she could remember what it was.

Pulling away just enough to lean a hand against the door, Alex drank her in with dark eyes, just a glint of boyish charm behind his devilish gaze.

Alex Drake, CEO of Drake Global Industries, was a corporate hard-ass and a fighting badass. But to her, he was the man who nearly died trying to save her brother from the RPG that took Jack's life.

Alex's magnetic eyes and suggestive smile were permanently laced with naughtiness and sin, but he was her safe place. Her hero. And at some point in the near future, her husband.

Amused, he cupped her cheek, tracing his thumb along her full bottom lip. "I'm not free, Ms. Taylor. I'm engaged. I thought we had an understanding."

She welcomed another kiss and smoothed her hands along his chest. The muscles of his sculpted body were barely a mystery beneath his well-fitted suit, much like his insistent and exceptionally large hard-on.

This man was lust personified, and she'd forever be at his mercy with his lips. His heat. His closeness. His touch. And that deep rumble from his throat that lit a wildfire across her core.

As his tender kisses made their way down her neck, he took a breath, releasing its warmth with his sincere words. "Sorry I didn't text you right away. I needed to cancel my meeting."

His thumb brushed her nipple, gently gliding across it as it peaked beneath her bra and blouse.

Her breath hitched. "You . . . canceled a meeting?"

His hand slid over the curve of her breast, down her waist, until he palmed her ass and pulled her in. "That's what happens when something comes up." He rocked his erection against her. "Change of plans, beautiful. Jess will be here in twenty minutes to pick you up, which doesn't leave much time. And you know how I like to take my time."

Do I.

His words were insistent and demanding as he growled, "Undo my pants," leaving no room for negotiation.

Lowering her hand, she lightly traced his abs beneath his shirt before moving to his slacks. She unfastened his belt, undid his zipper, and let the weight of his cock jut free and fall into her caressing hands.

His deep rumble of approval made her wet, and the bead on his tip begged for her tongue. Before she could lower herself, he said, "Take off your panties. I have to see your pussy."

Madison obeyed, sliding down the soaked panties from beneath her skirt and placing them in his hand. He pocketed them.

"Now, take off your skirt."

Biting her lip, she did, inching it slowly enough to bring a moan to his lips.

She slid the soft fabric down her legs, then stepped out of it, bare from the waist down except for her peekaboo-toe heels.

"You're so wet," he said, brushing his hot mouth against hers. "Stroke yourself and give me a taste."

Madison moved two fingers down, slipping them in and out across her folds. His large hand wrapped her wrist, pulling those soaked fingers to his lips. He sucked them in and pinned her with a hungry, desperate gaze.

"I need you," she said, barely able to breathe.

"And I need you. Against the window. Facing out."

She stifled a gasp. It was broad daylight, and Alex Drake was telling her to flash the world.

Taking in the floor-to-ceiling wall of windows, she then turned back to him with a questioning glance that was met with his nod. Madison's lips lifted into a shy smile as she did what he asked.

Slowly and unsure, she stepped to the window overlooking the panoramic views of Manhattan's Central Park. She scanned about. DGI was one of the taller buildings along the skyline, but not the tallest. Most buildings were a good enough distance away that anyone looking out their window shouldn't be able to see what was going on.

Hopefully.

His hands gripped her waist, and his lips warmed her neck. "Give me another taste of you."

In the spotlight of a bright day, Madison slid her finger between the lips of her pussy, coating them with the sweetness of her dew. She tensed as he slid his hands higher to release the buttons of her blouse.

"*Shh,*" he whispered, and even with her heart thundering, she relaxed. "Let me have this. Have you."

Closing her eyes, Madison moved her soaked fingers over her shoulder and waited. Button after button, he undid her blouse, exposing her to the world as he sucked those glazed fingers into his mouth.

The front clasp of her bra released with a snap. Her nervous body jolted, calming as his hands took their time caressing the weight of her breasts. Feeling her. Freeing her. Keeping her body on unforgiving display.

Alex released her, letting her stand for a long minute as he removed a condom and sheathed himself. The tip of his cock barely touched her aching entrance.

Her body bucked back, a reflex of raw desire and need. He took her hips, holding them tightly to control everything. What she received. How she received it. Her pulse. Her breathing. Her wetness. Her want.

"Rub yourself," he said, the low rumble of his voice cascading from his chest down her spine. "That's it. Fuck yourself for me, Madison."

And she did, over and over, showing the world her dirtiest desires. Peeling back her private, most secret needs.

His powerful hands moved up again, gentle as he took her nipples into a pinch, guiding her to lean her body flush against the glass. The heat of his body pressed hard against her back. She cried out, the icy sensation flashing across her body in a wave of heat.

"I'm going to fuck you, Madison. Fuck you hard and make you mine for all the world to see. Would you like that?"

God, yes.

His lips sizzled against the nape of her neck, and she shivered. Her lips trembled as she admitted it, as much to herself as to him.

"Yes," she said softly.

"Yes," he growled against her temple.

In one full thrust, he pinned her against the glass, pumping her hard. It was frightening. And exhilarating. She shuddered, feeling herself start to tumble under his merciless pounding, forcing her climax before the world.

"Alex . . ."

She panted out his name, growing dizzy and delirious as he buried himself with each hardened thrust. Over and over, Alex Drake staked his claim on Madison and Manhattan at the same time.

God, that's hot.

"Come for me," he said, picking up speed until his thighs tightened, riding her to his own peak. His low words were at her ear, their tenderness a contrast to his raw, carnal plunder. "Now, Madison. *Now.*"

She did, falling hard and free, giving herself over effortlessly and completely. She was his. All his.

Madison smiled, feeling weightless and light as Alex reluctantly replaced her clothes before seating her on his lap. He held her, leaving kiss after kiss along her lips and cheeks.

Checking his watch, he blew out a breath of resignation. "You two will have a head start, but Mark and I will catch up as soon as we can."

Madison's cell pinged with an incoming text, and she checked it. "Jess is here."

Her pout was met with his smiling kiss. "Come on. I'll head down with you and say hi to Jess. Fife sent someone to your office to pick up your bag and purse and take them downstairs."

Their short walk to the elevator was quiet, and Madison grew more unsettled as they entered the car that would carry them down. Uncertain if this was the best time to spoil the mood, she stayed silent and still. Like there was any way that would fly in the face of Alex Drake.

Cupping both her cheeks in his warm hands, he took a long look into her eyes before asking, "What?"

It was no use denying it. "Alex, I'm . . ." She tried looking away, but his thumbs gave the gentlest nudge, softly stroking her cheek.

"You're what?"

He smiled, inviting more of whatever she had to say. He could see right through her and melt her with his gaze. Denial wouldn't work.

She clasped his hands tightly to her cheeks, nuzzling her face in the warmth of his palm. Stalling for a second, she took a breath and let it out slowly. "I'm leaving DGI."

Contemplative, he took in her words before strengthening his smile and softening his response. "You know I want you to stay. But I want something more than that. I want to talk about whatever's on your beautiful mind. Because no matter what, I want you to be happy. I *need* you to be happy."

His lips pressed hers, then again. And again. "Your happiness is about to be part of my legal obligation," he said, dropping his forehead to hers. "And I take my obligations very seriously."

She let her body mold to his, secure in his hold. It was always easy losing herself in the heat of his touch, the rise and fall of his chest and the pounding beats of his tender heart.

Another lasting kiss burned deeper between them, locking them in a moment undisturbed by the ping of their arriving floor, or the opening of elevator doors to the hidden entrance off the side of the building.

"Hey, if y'all want to head back up for a quickie, I can wait."

The sweet mountain twang of a mischievous voice rang out from the curb.

Jess was a definite New Yorker, completely uninhibited in letting the passing pedestrians know what she was thinking.

Alex pulled away from the kiss but placed a loving peck on Madison's head as she waved to Jess.

As Madison took several steps to the Land Rover, Alex scooped her back against his chest. "Just where do you think you're going? You heard the lady. Jess said she can wait."

With a stern lift of her brow, Madison gave the man she loved an adoring scowl, tapping his watch as a reminder. Sinking his shoulders in response, he let out a frustrated grunt, giving in to the demands of his unrelenting schedule.

Hand in hand, they made their way to the SUV.

"Fine," he grumbled, "but you'd better make it up to me. Speaking of up . . ."

Alex tilted her chin, encouraging her to take in the full view of the sweeping building behind them. DGI was a solid wall of reflective glass, holding every secret tight within. Her shocked smile was met with his words.

"You're mine, Madison. And mine alone."

"Yours," she said softly, beaming.

Before she could move, he opened the car door with enough reluctance, she soothed his pout with another peck, then hopped in.

"Drive safe, Jess," he said before giving Madison a last kiss good-bye. He shut her door, giving the roof two taps, then stood back as he sent them off.

Madison thrust her arm out the open window, letting her hand slide across his sleeve as Jess pulled away.

CHAPTER 6

MADISON

As Jess drove away from the city, Madison took a relaxed breath, ready to be done with the drama of the day. A long, winding drive with Jess was just what the doctor ordered.

Jess Bishop wasn't just a friend. She understood in ways no one could, having married her own tycoon despite her repeated attempts to push him off.

Feeling free at last, Madison kicked off her shoes and told Jess about what had happened that day, purging her pent-up emotions, knowing she could count on Jess for something no one else could give her on the topic. Perspective.

"So, the way I see it, you've got three options," Jess said matter-of-factly once Madison was done. "Option number one, you can stay at DGI and ignore the gossip girls until the rumors die down. Even if that never happens."

Unimpressed, Madison folded her arms over her chest with a frown.

"Or two," Jess said pragmatically, "you ditch that whole work bullshit and become Alex Drake's little woman, never to lift a finger again in the service of others. Well, except for Alex, of course."

"Of course," Madison said. "But I like working."

"You don't have to convince me." Jess gave her a chagrined smile. "I drove hours to come to the city for a one-hour meeting with a select group of donors. Trust me, I feel you on this. I'm not here to make up your mind for you, missy. I'm doing my duty as your friend and pointing out your options."

"Fair enough. It's an interesting suggestion. But I'm not sure I could convincingly pull off a life of leisure."

Jess gave her a side glance. "From one working girl to another—and not in the lady-of-the-evening sort of way—neither do I."

Their kindred connection was just the boost Madison needed. It was wonderful not to be judged for wanting to be comfortable in her own skin.

And with Jess, explanations were never necessary. She understood Madison's need to contribute to something bigger than herself. Jess got it because she'd made her own career a priority long before her marriage.

From what Madison could glean, marrying Mark Donovan hadn't changed Jess. From everything Mark said, Jess was still the same small-town mountain girl who held her own and stood her ground. Something Madison suspected she did long before any man appeared. Not that Mark Donovan was any man. He was, after all, a billionaire.

"So, what's behind door number three?" Madison asked.

With a mischievous grin, Jess exhaled a long breath. "Three? Three would be where your give-a-fuck factor flies out the window, and you do whatever the hell you really want. Whatever makes you happy."

Madison smiled. "Alex sort of said the same thing."

"Well, I've known Alex a good long time. If anyone's a fan of the zero-fucks-given strategy, it's him. He and Mark definitely have that in common."

Madison let her gaze float out the window, following the thick evergreen tree line as Jess continued.

"You and I are cut from the same cloth, Madison. Our paths will always be paved by passion, regardless of what we do. Or where we go. Or how many men we're reputed to pleasure at once in a corporate conference room. Four, was it?"

A burst of giggles filled the SUV, and any remaining frustration Madison held on the topic evaporated. Laughing over the same situation that only a few hours ago had her backed into a corner between a watercooler and a panic attack was a welcome relief.

"Five is the word on the street," she said proudly with a shake of the head. "Yup, Madison's my name, and passion's my game. I'm gonna need a website, and I'll have to check to see if one-eight-hundred-P-A-S-S-I-O-N is available. Let the Kickstarter campaign commence!"

Madison's laughter rang out, then faded, replaced by curiosity and possibilities. "Jess, what did it take for you to start your charity? I mean, other than your passion?"

"Let's see." Jess drummed her fingers on the steering wheel. "Well, there was —and is—a whole lotta begging for money. Donations, both in financial backing and for things like supplies and office space."

"Really? Office space?"

"Sure. People who might pass on donating cash will be all in on surplus items, including unused real estate. It's a tax write-off for them and the foundation of a nonprofit for us."

Jess paused, swerving just enough to avoid the squirrel on a suicide mission, before casually proceeding.

"And that kind of door-to-door soliciting meant I had to get over my awkward shyness. Never hold back. Ask donors for exactly what I want. I put the needs of the nonprofit over my own comfort zone, and I had to recruit an army of volunteers. But at the end of the day, I'm driven, believing that if I didn't do it, no one else would."

"Do you love it?"

"Madison, I live for helping others. It's incredibly rewarding. Not a week goes by that I don't hear how I've made a difference in someone's life, straight from the mouth of the person whose life I helped change. It's not about money. I'm making a difference. And it's all I've ever wanted to do."

The road stretched on, leaving behind the noises of the city and high-rise buildings, unspooling to reveal thick dark green pines, fresh air, and the blue skies of a brightly lit, late summer's afternoon.

Jess meandered along memory lane, sharing the origins of her nonprofit work and the stories of the people her charity impacted. Tucking a leg beneath her, Madison relaxed into her seat, attentively hanging on to every one of Jess's heartwarming words for the duration of the ride.

CHAPTER 7

ALEX

HALF AN HOUR behind Jess and Madison, a black diamond Rolls Royce Phantom made its way into a different area of the countryside north of New York City. Alex was pushing the speed and agility of the vehicle well beyond that of a leisurely drive.

Usually, the car provided a luxurious yet carefree escape, an indulgent respite while moving from point A to point B. But now, its use was much more utilitarian. And frankly, would far exceed the preferences of anyone riding with him, except perhaps Paco.

It couldn't be helped. Adrenaline was slamming the gas, and Alex could only hold on for the ride. Maybe his past was catching up to him, the remnants of the former civilian operative who often lurked just below his polished surface, materializing whenever needed.

Most days, Alex was a work-hard, play-hard multibillionaire in a $12,000 suit. But not today. Now he was back into trained operative mode, observing a myriad of subtle signs that triggered his intuition to levels long ago suppressed, but never fully abandoned.

The excessive speed only spiked his pulse and heightened his instincts, but some level of solace would await him at his destination. He was needed, and whatever wisdom he could impart would be well received by Mark. Perhaps in return, the man could reciprocate with some sage advice on Alex's own perplexing issues at hand.

Not quite two hours outside of Manhattan and closing in on the Hudson, Alex veered off onto a nondescript wooded country road with no street signs and no asphalt.

The road slowly narrowed to a rugged dirt trail, intentionally giving the *you must be fucking lost* vibe to anyone who happened upon it.

But Alex was far from lost. On the contrary, he was safe and sound, and in a strange way felt as if he were heading home.

The road came to a dead end at a cinder-block wall twelve feet high with an intimidating towering metal gate. A DGI swipe panel greeted him, and Alex was ready, hovering his access card across it.

The gate opened, letting his car proceed through before closing behind. A short distance away was a plain building in the middle of a field. At the side of the building, another panel awaited him, and his swipe opened a steel garage door easily two cars wide.

The garage was empty at the moment, but the high shine of Mark's familiar dark-sapphire Bentley would be there soon. Alex parked and then headed inside, unconcerned at leaving his cell phone behind in his car.

The highly customized Sensitive Compartmented Information Facility, or SCIF, would block all cell phone service and any other radio frequencies. The only phone or internet access was completely reliant on a web of long-line communication cables buried deep within the ground below.

With the building impenetrable to electronic surveillance and data leaks, bringing his phone inside would be pointless unless he wanted to snap a selfie.

Again, Alex swiped his access card along a panel in the wall, and the heavy military-grade security door gave a loud clank as it unbolted, then swung open to the interior of the building. A smile formed as he stepped through. Once he reached the main control room, he made the necessary preparations—turning on the lights, setting up controls for the ready, and unpacking a well-used deck of cards.

He took a seat, and within minutes, the door opened again.

Lounging comfortably in a luxurious chair at a small round executive table as Mark walked in, Alex said, "Good to know your memory isn't slipping. Or did you have to make a few U-turns?"

Expertly, he shuffled, then flipped a few cards in succession. Mark took his own seat as Alex silently lipped the face value of each card before revealing it—a parlor trick they shared in common. Playing cards helped pass the time during extended surveillance missions or while stuck in a no-cell zone.

Mark scooted his executive leather chair closer. "No U-turns. I might occasionally misplace my key fob, but I could drive here blindfolded."

Mark had called this meeting, but without words, Alex understood. Something was weighing on his friend's mind. Something heavy. Something that required a secure facility away from the office and couldn't be discussed by phone.

Conclusion? Cards would be needed.

The game was perfect. They could talk through anything while playing, letting their right-brain thinking work effortlessly in the background and in tandem with their left-brain rationale.

Blackjack was out. They were both so adept at counting cards, a game of twenty-one might as well be played with the cards facing up.

Alex dealt, skillfully flicking two cards to each of them before laying several between them, face up, to commence the game. Each had small stacks of chips ready and waiting, and the men scooped up their hands, wearing their game faces with knowing grins.

"And don't forget about the pantry," Alex said. "The prepper stash has plenty of Jefferson's Ocean and those wasabi almonds you love."

Without warning, Mark slapped his cards on the table. "I can't possibly play on an empty stomach."

Grinning, both men abandoned their cards to free up their hands for whatever booty they would bring back with them. Briskly, they made their way down the hall.

Both walls were lined with handguns, rifles, an occasional semi-automatic, and an assortment of knives, all neatly held in place with custom-fitted fasteners that not only kept the items secured, but managed to provide an elegant display of the lethal weapons.

The hall ended at an expansive walk-in pantry, filled with chrome shelves stocked with a balanced assortment of fine and junk foods, sodas, liquor, and glass tanks of water.

Looting through the pretzels and chips, Alex checked his watch. "Madison and Jess should be at your cabin in about two and a half hours. We won't be far behind with the baby out back."

The *baby* referred to Alex's Sikorsky S76-D executive helicopter, whose custody he and Mark enthusiastically shared.

With his stash pocketed, Alex poured two bourbons, then handed a lowball to Mark.

"To marriage," Mark said, holding his own glass high.

"To marriage." Alex gave the waiting glass a clink and took a sip from his, breathing out the warmth of the smooth spirits in a long *ahh* of a breath.

Once Mark crammed wasabi almonds in one pocket and M&Ms in another, they were set. Nearly set. Both men snagged a Snickers, and Alex grabbed the bottle of Jefferson's before they headed back to the cards. At the table, they settled again into their chairs and refocused on the game.

"What's on your mind?" Alex asked, peering over the cards he held.

Mark tossed a few chips to the center of the table before answering. "I've landed this deal. A hundred-million-dollar deal."

Alex let out a long, impressed whistle but didn't say a word.

"They even wired me a million bucks up front just to sit down and chat."

"Well, we're sitting and chatting. Where the hell's my cool mil?"

Even with Alex's smartass remark, Mark would only return an unenthusiastic smirk. Staring blankly, he folded, giving up that round to free up his hands to grip the half-filled glass. Mark studied it but didn't sip. Instead, he swirled the glass, coating the amber liquid up its walls, watching the lazy legs trail down the sides.

"It's the perfect deal. Perfect," he said with a frown. Huffing, he took a sip. "Too perfect. And I feel crazy questioning it, but my hackles are up. I'm right back in full-on operative mode, and I have no idea why."

With a slow shake of his head, Mark seemed to be wrestling for the right words. He sipped again as if it was his only option. Or possibly because it couldn't hurt.

Alex reshuffled the deck but didn't deal another hand. Patiently, he bided his time.

Finally, Mark met his eyes. "Just to satisfy my own curiosity, I tried tracing that million-dollar direct deposit. And . . ." He paused with an unsettled look. "I couldn't. And this is me saying that." The man who built a global empire by tracing the untraceable.

"How's that possible?" Alex asked aloud but almost to himself.

It was impossible. Mark's company wasn't one of the best. It was *the* best at tracking money movements for a range of government agencies and private corporations. And when they were sure no one would else would ever know it, they tracked money at DGI's request as well.

Excelsior/Centurion didn't stop there. They could discover the real sponsors behind suspicious activities of any funds movements imaginable. And yet, here sat a genius, thrown off by a million dollars that had materialized out of thin air.

Alex set the cards aside, opting to wrap his hand around his own bourbon. "Sounds like someone knows how to cover their tracks. Let's start at the beginning. What do they want?"

"That's just it. All they want is to meet. One-on-one. And when I say one-on-one, I don't mean company to company. I mean just me and one of them—whoever *them* is."

"I see why you're nervous. It feels like—"

"A setup. Or an execution. God knows, I've got just as many enemies as friends."

"Don't be ridiculous." Alex scoffed. "We all know I'm your only friend."

Mark ignored Alex's grin and pressed on. "On a deal this big, I'd expect a small entourage on both sides, with lawyers and accountants up the ying-yang. Nondisclosure agreements as thick as the Bible."

"So would I."

"The money was wired specifically for a meeting with me. Just me. Anywhere I want. Literally anywhere in the world. They just need a location before midnight, and the meeting will happen at two p.m. local time wherever I select, the next day."

Alex lifted an intrigued brow. "So you're skeptical, yet interested."

Mark nodded. "Skeptical? Yes. And idiotically interested? Of course. How could I not be? A hundred million dollars is a big fucking carrot. What do I say . . . a date sounds fun but I'm washing my hair?"

Alex speculated aloud. "You told them you'd think about it?"

Mark lowered his gaze.

"Ah. You agreed to meet."

Mark pointed an accusatory finger his way. "You would too!"

Nodding, Alex agreed. "I would."

"On top of everything else, they only send emails. No calls."

"Smart. Phones are too easy to trace."

"Exactly. With email, each transmission is hitting false nodes, and not just a few. Literally hundreds upon hundreds. The emails could be coming from anywhere. From anyone. I don't know if I'm dealing with a head of state, someone on the dark web, or a crazy-genius twelve-year-old in his mama's basement." Mark popped a few almonds into his mouth, deep in thought as he chewed. "I know I'm being played, but with that much money on the table, I'd be insane to turn down a meeting."

"Look, your paranoia might be wrapped up in a conspiracy deep-fried in insanity, but your instincts are solid. They've saved your ass and the asses of your teammates too many times to discount them. They're always spot-on, like a sixth fucking sense." Unwrapping his chocolate bar, Alex pointed it at Mark. "Got anything else?"

"Yeah, their name. But a name that's absolutely clean of any cyber footprint. Not even the pretense of a backstory. A ghost."

Mark downed the rest of his drink and helped himself to another pour as Alex sat up, giving Mark a curious look as he ripped open his bag of M&Ms.

With a sufficient amount of suspense between them, Alex asked, "So . . . what's the name?"

"Jordan Stone." Mark tossed out the name and refreshed both drinks. It wasn't until he looked up that he found Alex's expression had dropped. "What? You know this guy?"

Suddenly cold, Alex felt the blood drain from his face. "Maybe," he muttered, clenching his jaw.

He didn't sip this time. He tossed back the contents of his glass and stared off. Mark let him go for a minute.

When warmth returned to his cheeks, Alex filled with a spark, springing back from his thoughts with a vengeance.

"You're taking the meeting," he said firmly.

Mark sat up straighter. "I am?"

"You are. Send them an email." Pointing to the console at the other end of the room, Alex nudged Mark to grab a computer where communications were enabled through a deeply buried land line. "They want to see an untraceable email, they've come to the right fucking spot."

Both men stood and moved to their own systems, each set up at either side of the room, logging on with an insert of their access cards.

Mark opened an email, posturing his fingers, ready to type. "Okay, what do I say?"

Smiling, but not looking at him, Alex began his own feverish typing. "Tell them you're ready to meet. Right here. Give them our coordinates. Tell them they've got one hour, or you're gone. Let's see just how close this ghost is."

But Mark didn't type a word. Waiting for an explanation, he did nothing but sit quietly and level Alex with a heavy stare. His reticence wasn't surprising.

Alex knew that what he was saying was madness. Giving up the position of a secured facility that had for the better part of a decade remained off the grid? Absolute fucking madness.

Without otherwise acknowledging his friend, Alex began to speak. "You know my history. My loss."

Mark nodded as he sat back in his chair. "Yes," he said solemnly, his voice soft. "Madison's brother, Jack."

Instantly, Alex stopped typing. "It wasn't about the mission. There was something about it that was . . . different. Strange."

"Strange how?"

Struggling for the right words, Alex finally blew out a frustrated breath. "I don't know. The way I was . . . recruited. And the way you're being lured. It's familiar. Has the same look and feel as . . ."

"As what?"

"As the person who recruited me. The same one who vanished without a fucking trace. The person at the bottom of everything." Alex resumed typing as he let out a huff. "Jordan Stone."

PART II
THE PAST

CHAPTER 8

JORDAN

Over ten years earlier – Southern California

JORDAN STONE PULLED her brand-new Mercedes convertible to the curb in front of a run-down two-story house. The custom red paint of her car bore a striking resemblance to her favorite shade of lipstick, making her car stand out like a sore thumb in the neighborhood that wished with all its might it could be considered middle class.

The dilapidated home looked like a frat house in the middle of an otherwise quaint street in the suburban neighborhood. Blinking through her disbelief, Jordan flipped open her moleskin notepad to double-check the address, disappointed to find the street name and number were indeed correct.

Drake Cable and Comm had all the sophistication and grandeur of a heaping pile of horseshit. At least most garage startups could mow their lawns.

Fuck me.

Once again, Jordan had managed to draw the shortest goddamn straw, though she never actually held the power to pull the straws herself. But at the end of the day, it didn't matter. She had one job to do, and just like FedEx, she'd deliver.

Her assignments were strategic and precise. The recruiters, much like the recruits, were never random. If Jordan had been selected, she knew what it meant.

The targeted recruit had to be male, under thirty, hardworking, unattached, and with enough *fuck authority* in him to make waves but never attract the wrong kind of attention.

Bribes were easy, but they were out. MICE incentives would go nowhere with a man like this because *money, ideology, coercion,* and *ego* couldn't lure this man. The only way her handlers could know that for sure was if they'd already tried.

But with her ass parked on his street, she had enough presence of mind to know the man met the two must-haves warranting a visit from Jordan Stone.

First, he was critical. An essential cog in some game-changing mission's wheel, and nobody else would do.

And second, he had a hard-core vice—sex—which just happened to be Jordan's specialty. She could set a honey trap like no other, with an impressive and disturbingly high track record for sealing the deal by tapping into a man's filthy desires and giving him everything he craved. For a price.

With a quick flip of the visor, she examined her reflection, taking in her dark hair and big, dark eyes that could come from anywhere. Men loved an exotic look they couldn't exactly pin down.

Jordan's fluency spanned seven languages, with enough of an understanding of a dozen others that she could blend into the woodwork wherever she went.

Time and time again, men called her striking, and she could pass for any range of ethnicities. Latin or Middle Eastern. With the right makeup, some blend of Asian or Indian. And all too frequently, Eastern Bloc.

With all that goodness wrapped up in a body that wouldn't quit and a nonexistent gag reflex, she'd managed to find her perfect line of work, commanding an under-the-table salary that kept her deliriously comfortable in the lifestyle she'd very much become accustomed to.

On days like this without knowing exactly what to expect, she kept her hair pulled back, protectively secured in a bun at her nape. Today, her eye makeup was smoky, but not overdone, but her lips needed refreshing.

From the center console, she reached past the subcompact Glock to grab her signature dark-cherry lip gloss, smearing the line just a smidge over the rim of her DSLs. The look exaggerated their fullness, like she'd just sucked a man dry and was hungry for more. Admiring her *fuck me at will* glamour shot, she flipped the visor closed and sighed before she climbed out of the car.

The cobblestone path to the front door was a bitch on her thousand-dollar heels, but she donned a smile, nonetheless. With her hand postured to knock, she lowered it, hearing loud voices and high-pitched giggling coming from somewhere around the side of the house.

After picking her way through the unkempt grass around the house, she found her day was looking up. The apparent sorority kegger by the pool was abundant with beer, string-bikini butts, and too many bouncing breasts to accurately count. Some were covered but most were not, with the gorgeous women opting to go *au naturel* in the glowing California sun.

Always a fan of the water, Jordan found herself perking up at the idea of a party by the pool.

When someone slapped a cold beer in her hand, she accepted graciously, enjoying a long, slow sip. Her semi-sheer white blouse and skin-tight black pencil skirt didn't exactly help her blend in, but it wasn't like anyone was enforcing a dress code.

She took her time heading into the house through the open sliding glass door. Whatever douchebag she needed to recruit could wait. Jordan was too busy soaking in the semi-nude bodies of every woman around her.

Eventually, and only after letting a topless woman lead the way, she finally entered the home of what had to be the hero of frat houses across America. His round-the-clock partying explained the empty bottles of booze, candy dishes of condoms, and strategically placed dildos. Apparently, dinner around here came with a floor show.

An attractive blonde, adjusting her string bikini top, teased Jordan with a smile. It was enough of an invitation for Jordan to slide a hand along the woman's shoulder. And the loud music gave Jordan the perfect excuse to lean close to the buxom blonde's ear.

"I'm looking for Jack."

Blankly, the woman stared back, so Jordan smoothed her hand to a more attentive caress.

"The guy who lives here."

"Upstairs," the blonde replied, disappointment dragging down her smile. "But if you change your mind about him, I'll be right here."

Softly, Jordan's lips brushed the woman's ear. "I'll be back," she said, giving her earlobe a seductive suck before leaving it with a terse bite.

Satisfied at her new playmate's peaked nipples, she brushed the nearest breast with the cold bottle of beer, then handed it to her before heading upstairs.

Jordan found most of the bedrooms wide open, despite the sleeping or debauchery going on inside. But it was the double doors of what had to be the master bedroom down the hall that caught her interest.

Target acquired.

Trying the handle, she found the door was locked. She examined the builder-grade hardware, recognizing the miniscule hole in the center of the knob.

Whisking a thin bobby pin from her bun, she shoved it in, easily releasing the lock. Silently, she slipped inside, enjoying what had to be the matinee.

Two women, easily mistaken for twins, had apparently flipped a coin to decide which end of the man each would be riding.

The first—the one Jordan mentally nicknamed Reverse Cowgirl—got tails and was thrusting vigorously across the naked man's cock. The other—not doing anything particularly worthy of a nickname—held a steady pace grinding across the man's mouth.

With her eyes wide and her panties soaked, Jordan leaned against the now closed door. Joining the ménage was enticing. And the surest way to lose a new recruit.

Putting out before the ink was dry was the fastest way to tank a deal. When men couldn't get what they wanted, they were attentive. Obsessive. Willing.

Appetizers were totally on the table. But a full meal of Jordan Stone? That would remain a promise for the future, and the surest way to keep her marks so very hungry for more.

With Cowgirl picking up her pace, things seemed to be wrapping up. Or so Jordan thought. Not missing a beat, the woman stretched toward the nightstand, reaching for the leather wallet resting there.

Seems a bit late for a condom.

Amused, Jordan watched as the woman tugged out a thick wad of cash. Sweetly, Jordan spoke. "I'm not sure that belongs to you."

Both women jumped from their respective positions, quickly slipping on their ridiculously small bikinis in a misguided effort to escape with a modicum of decency. But just barely.

The man, still rock hard, wiped his face before propping up on his elbow.

"I'm not sure what's going on, but looks like a seat just opened up." His voice was groggy and deep, and he looked Jordan up and down with a decidedly diabolical grin. The kind that had *sucker* written all over it.

Jordan opened the door wide, letting the uninteresting one escape. But as Cowgirl tried following, Jordan slammed it shut, slinking back to lean against it.

"Bitch, get out of my way."

Jordan took a moment, looking the girl up and down. "Like I said, I'm not sure that belongs to you."

They both eyed the wad of twenties held tight in her hand.

Snarling, the blonde fisted the money in front of her. "Yeah? Well, it's mine now."

Her feeble swing at Jordan backfired, giving her the opportunity to grab the girl's arm and flip her around, pinning her hand high against her back.

"Fucking bitch, get off me!"

Impressed, Jordan smiled to find her still clinging to the wad of cash. In an unchallenged move, she forced Cowgirl forward onto the bed.

With her target enjoying the action, Jordan took center stage in the girl-on-girl show. As she pouted her plump lips, she dragged the girl's fist down to the top of her ass, taking a second to imagine sliding her tongue through the crevice encasing the thong.

Captured in Jordan's grip, Cowgirl tried to struggle as Jordan skimmed her fingernail down her spine. At the base of her butt, Jordan playfully snapped the thong, causing her captive to squeal. A few moves later, she'd lassoed the stretchy bikini bottom around the woman's wrists like a scrunchy, immobilizing her on the spot.

"Goddammit, let me out of this!"

It took a small amount of effort for Jordan to wiggle the cash free. With it, she took a seat on the opposite side of the bed, setting the cash on her thigh.

"I believe this is yours." She took his hand and placed it on the small stack of twenties, pressing his grip firmly to her thigh. Directing his eyes, she glanced at the open wallet discarded on the floor.

He inched his fingers around the money, slowly pulling his hand from her leg. "Thanks," he said, hopping off the bed but not bothering to get dressed. He took a look at the woman hogtied in place.

Jordan smiled. "The trick is in the knot. If the little thief moves too much, she'll feel the excruciating sting of one hell of a stem-to-stern wedgie."

Straining to turn her head, Cowgirl sweetened her tone from minutes ago, doing her piss-poor best at being persuasive. "Look, you had a great time. I didn't think you'd miss it. J-just let me outta here, okay?"

"Jesus," the muscular man said, blowing out a breath. He couldn't take his eyes off the knot. "How the fuck do I undo this?" In an innocent move for such a sexy man, he scratched his head, with an inquisitive helplessness to his almost boyish gaze.

He's sweet.

Taunting him, Jordan handed him a challenge. "Well, if you must. You'll probably have to cut it." Then more deviously, she said, "Or tear it . . . if you can."

Her dare was enough. Smacking the jiggliest part of Cowgirl's ass, he scolded her.

"Now, I'm going to let you go, but only so you can get on the straight and narrow. Hmm . . ." Looking down at his wilting shaft, he smiled. "Well, at least get on the straight, because I'm far from narrow."

Leaning down, he softly suggested, "Hold still."

It was good advice, and she sucked in a breath. With the bikini bottom in both hands, he ripped it apart and tossed it away.

Free, Cowgirl jumped up and scurried out of the room, slamming the door as hard as possible behind her. Alex moved his attention back to Jordan, now splayed across his bed.

Grinning seductively, Jordan said, "She seems nice."

CHAPTER 9

ALEX

WITHOUT A WAY of knowing who this woman was or why she was making herself comfortable on his bed, the man stood, his willy flying free as he smiled, patiently waiting for an explanation.

"You must be Jack."

Fuck me.

And just like that, the party was over. It didn't matter that her giggle was spellbinding, and her lips were everything his cock ever wanted. Whoever she was, he wasn't interested.

He huffed out an irritated laugh. "And you must not know me at all if you're calling me that. What are you, some sort of banker or site inspector or something? Did I miss dotting an *i* on the three-hundred-page document where I signed away my house, car, and firstborn to the bank?"

Pulling on his jeans, he instantly regretted his tone as she shifted just enough to give him a glimpse of something enticingly red beneath her skirt.

His irritation wasn't about his name. Sure, he hated it. His easy-breezy middle name was convenient, often the focus of telemarketers, a few members of his deliberately distant family, and a revolving door of apathetic attorneys.

The name had also been his dad's, which was the extent he knew about the man, other than the guy's credit was good. It served its purpose, giving him enough of a start in the absence of an actual father.

The name was good enough for business documents and legal representation, but being called it was never preferred. Ever. For all the pomp and circumstance of his given name, Alexander Jackson Drake went by a simple moniker.

"My apologies, Mr. Drake," she said, diplomatically backpedaling as she licked her lips. "From the looks of this place, perhaps you prefer Big Daddy Plumber."

He couldn't hold back a small grin.

"What do you prefer I call you?" she asked, her tone alluring and hypnotic.

Everything in his body said he was being played. Well, everything but his cock. As much as he wanted to tell her to fuck off, his dick had other plans.

"AJ." He turned away, scanning the mirror to check his appearance. Clean shaven but disheveled, he figured it would do. Catching her eye in the reflection, he asked, "And you are?"

"Jordan. Jordan Stone. And I'll only take an hour of your time."

Sales talk. Best dick deflater ever.

"Well, Jordan, Jordan Stone, did we have an appointment? If so, we'll have to reschedule because I'm fully committed today."

Impatient, he headed for the door, opening it wide and waiting. Yet, there she sat, far from deterred. Unconcerned, she slipped off her shoes, letting the stilettos fall to the floor.

"No, you're not. They left." Stretching across the bed, she looked up at him through the thick lashes of a smoking-hot woman in heat. "You're all mine."

He stayed close to the door, not entirely trusting himself with the woman eyeing him like a juicy steak. "Look, whatever it is you're selling, I'm not interested."

With effortless ease, she removed the remaining pins from her hair, letting the lush locks cascade freely down her shoulder and across her breast. "Oh, I'm not selling, AJ. I'm buying. Your products. Your services. You."

"Me?" he asked, covering his curiosity with a weak attempt at indignity.

"Only in the dirtiest way possible," she said with a promising tone that charged straight to his dick. "Why don't you close the door and see if my lips can . . . convince you?"

Not needing any more convincing, Alex was sure and decisive as he slammed the door shut.

CHAPTER 10

JACK

The same day – Newburgh, New York

As approaching footsteps echoed from every wall of the vast room, Jack Taylor heard the voice that went with them booming with a confident authority that was warm and friendly as he chatted with his escort. A lowly cadet, Jack remained locked in place, used to the perpetual state of standing at attention. It had become second nature over the past four years.

His West Point training ensured his eyes didn't move, remaining fixed on an imagined point far away. It was tempting to take in the view overlooking the blue Hudson River, or the vintage military paintings that lined the walls. Or to glance at whomever happened to be commanding his attention. But he waited, not meeting the man's gaze, whoever he might be.

"You must be Jack." A tall man with salt-and-pepper hair came to a halt in front of the first-class cadet, a senior by civilian university standards.

"Yes, sir. Jack Taylor. Nice to meet you, sir."

Remaining at attention, he waited for an *at ease* before relaxing his lifted chest or locked arms. After all this time, old habits would die hard.

Apparently knowing this, the gentleman went ahead and gave him permission to relax. "At ease, young man."

"Thank you, sir."

Jack understood the visitor to be retired, but a lieutenant general, nonetheless. And once such upper-echelon titles are achieved, retired or not, they're never willingly relinquished, even after retirement from the military.

Why a man of his stature would be meeting with him, Jack didn't know. But the reason had to be good. Visits like this were unheard of unless the parties happened to be related. With his father being a retired gunnery sergeant, Jack knew his own relations were definitely on the opposite end of the social spectrum.

"Great to meet you, Jack. My name is Jordan Stone, and I've heard a hell of a lot about you."

Though the statement took Jack by surprise, he didn't ask any of the many questions running through his mind. What he was meant to know, Mr. Stone would undoubtedly get to.

Jordan Stone took a chair at a round table kitty-corner from where Jack stood and offered him a seat. The table that normally seated six instantly became cozy and comfortable. Somehow, Jack suspected this man harnessed that power naturally, making everyone he met feel vital and appreciated.

"I'm glad we could make this meeting happen, since I'll be returning to the Pentagon this evening."

Attentive, Jack found himself admiring the man. His well-fitted dark gray suit was perfectly rounded out with a red, blue, and silver regimental tie. The pin on his lapel featured a compass rose, adding a handsome elegance to his outfit.

The man could be a congressman. Or a multimillionaire. The strength and power emanating from him was enough to make or break people, armies, or whole countries, yet he kept it wrapped tightly in a quiet commanding presence and easy smile.

"Yes, sir. I appreciate that you have a very busy schedule. The commandant said you needed to speak with me about my future." Jack's questioning tone was deliberate, as he was dying to know what an important man like this might want.

"Jack, I'm gonna cut to the chase. We've been watching you since you arrived at the academy. Top scores in every subject. Impressive performance with weapons and hand-to-hand combat. But what really got our attention is the paper you presented."

"My paper? The one on securing a tactical advantage on the war front?" It wasn't rocket science. To Jack, his conclusions were simple and obvious.

"What can I say? Your idea has a fan base, and we'd like to put it to the test."

Surprised, Jack lifted a brow. "A live mission? With my strategy?"

"Well, there's a little more to it than that. But everything we're going to discuss will be strictly *need to know*. We can discuss the details once we've upgraded your security clearance, but nothing about this can be disclosed. Not to family or friends. And by your looks, I'm sure you're popular with the ladies, but no pillow talk to impress. Can we count on you?"

Despite a pitch that felt a little too "ask not what your country can do for you," it tugged at every sense of military loyalty and patriotism in Jack's soul.

Not needing to think it over, he simply said, "Yes, sir."

The hand Mr. Stone laid on his shoulder felt proud. Paternal. "I'm not just asking if we can use your idea or if you'd like to play along, Jack. I'm talking about a covert mission with you leading the charge. American lives are depending on this. Depending on you. If you have any reservations, you can turn me down. But we have a mission that can't wait, and I need your answer now. Jack, are you in?"

There was no hesitation. No need for a second thought. Nothing would keep him from this once-in-a-lifetime opportunity. It would forever change the course of his life—Jack could feel it.

"Absolutely, sir. I'm all in."

CHAPTER 11

PACO

The same day – US Territory of Puerto Rico

STAFF SERGEANT PACO ROBLES strolled out of the Fort Buchanan Education Center into a wall of hot, humid air that always took a second to adjust to after the comfort of an air-conditioned room.

Having grown up on the sun-drenched island, Paco was used to the conditions. With the exception of boot camp, he'd spent every day enjoying an ocean-front life close to the equator.

One step out the door and intense sunlight flooded his face, causing him to squint as he adjusted to the brightness of the day. And despite his thick battle-dress uniform smothering his skin, his two-percent body fat prevented him from ever breaking a sweat. To him, ninety-eight degrees was nothing. Just another day in the life on an island.

Today, he'd taken his second crack at the Defense Language Aptitude Battery, or DLAB, but he didn't consider it a second chance.

The ninety-minute assessment gauged one's aptitude for picking up languages. In theory, with a higher score came greater potential for the test taker to master increasingly complex languages. For a man seeking action and adventure away from his island home, only the highest of scores would do.

The Department of Defense's home-grown test was a web of complete insanity, comprised entirely of made-up words, nonexistent phrases, and strings of noises that made no sense at all. Arrogant as ever, Paco considered the challenge a piece of cake.

He wasn't discounting the importance of the results. Quite the opposite. This test would be the determining factor for coveted opportunities in a high-paced linguistic training program, and Paco wanted in.

He understood the expectations. Training in romance languages like the Spanish he grew up with required the lowest marks. Russian, Punjabi, and Croatian needed scores in the mid-level range. For three types of Arabic, as well as Chinese and Korean, the assignments were a golden ticket to a new life and would require the highest of grades.

When Paco completed his first test, he knew his results would be high, but a perfect score was unexpected. Prideful and arrogant, he accepted the news without a lick of modesty. His superiors rejected the score and demanded a retake.

Ecstatic at another chance to show off his instant mastery of nonexistent languages, Paco welcomed the challenge. That wasn't just his ego leading the charge. He knew what they all knew. He was getting all the right sorts of attention to change the trajectory of his life.

Today was the retest. He'd bet his last ten dollars before payday, his well-earned stripes, and his left nut, that he'd aced it once again.

Knowing round two was in the bag should have eased him into a leisurely rest of the day. His future was shaping up. Promise was in the air. But so was something else. An unnerving feeling. A sense he couldn't shake. A tension in the air.

Street-fighter instincts that shaped him in his youth had molded him into a deft predator. As such, he was rarely the target. So, why the fuck were his hackles up and his heart pounding out of his chest, like some goddamned bunny about to be snatched up by a hawk?

He knew why.

He was the prey. Or, at least, he was being watched like one.

Surrounded by several buildings, he scanned the perimeter, but no one was keeping an eye on him from any of the industrial windows.

Several cars were parked close by, all without occupants. At this time of day, the lunch-goers were already back in their offices, and the early birds would start heading out in another two hours or so. So, why in the ninety-eight-degree heat with ninety percent humidity was there a man standing on the sidewalk, wearing a bright linen suit?

The man wasn't doing anything particularly suspicious. Just standing there wearing some expensive-looking glasses and a baby-blue tie knotted at his neck. As he was, holding a casual pose with his hands pocketed, anyone walking by might think he wasn't doing anything at all.

But that was just it. On a military installation in this unforgiving heat, who just stands? Stands and stares?

Not one to run from his shadow, Paco took a keen interest in testing his theory.

The staff sergeant secured his government-issued cap and straightened his battle-dress uniform, then headed a few buildings over. In a move that felt strange even to him, he walked around a corner, then ducked behind it, crouching down.

Slowly, he moved his head enough to peek past the corner at where he'd just come from, but there was no one in sight. Wondering how the man had disappeared so quickly, Paco remained where he was, waiting.

With nothing happening and the guy gone, why did he need to keep his position? Hell, even if no one was watching him before, anyone who saw him now would sure as hell be watching him.

He set aside his doubt. *I'm never wrong.*

Eager to enjoy the few remaining hours of the rest of his day to hit the beach before sunset for once, he glanced about.

Nada. Not a fucking thing going on other than him getting dangerously close to failing to report for duty because he needed to waste more time playing chase with a goddamned ghost.

Lamest game of hide and seek ever.

Finally fed up with skulking about and feeling like the village idiot, Paco stood up, dusted off his uniform, and took several steps out in the open, ready to get back to work.

"Staff Sergeant Robles?"

The man's voice wasn't exactly booming. More like blithe and playful.

Paco whipped to the right, now facing the suited man, who seemed to have made himself comfortable leaning against the wall. Just around the corner from where Paco had been crouching. Had he peeked his head around the corner just a bit more, he would have seen him.

Eyeing the guy, Paco had the unsettling suspicion that this man, whoever he was, had known Paco was there the entire time. Hiding behind the corner. In all his idiotic glory.

Shit.

Despite the wave of irritation that nearly forced a *fuck* from his lips, he kept his mouth buttoned up, not knowing exactly who he was dealing with.

With a second and much closer glance at the man, Paco took him all in. From the bright white of his cocky smile to the sunglasses Paco imagined would cost two months' of his salary, the man was everything Paco wanted to be when he grew up. *This* was his vision of the future.

Hopefully, this wasn't some guy about to snuff out his dreams, relaying some trumped-up bullshit message like *we don't care how high you score or how many times you test, you're not getting in.*

Arguing with the voices in his head, Paco stood nearly at attention. "Yes, sir, that's me." *As if he couldn't read my nametag now that he's three feet away.* "And you're following me, so what do you want?"

"I wasn't following you." The man dropped the facade and chuckled. "Well, not at first. I was waiting to speak to you, but when you raced around this building, you piqued my curiosity."

The man's smile was absolutely perfect. Too perfect.

That did it. Whatever extra money Paco managed to scrounge together was now earmarked for a set of bright white and perfectly straight veneers.

The man slid the impressive glasses off his nose, then twirled them with casual indifference by one hand. "And it's not about what I want. It's what I want to give you. A career proposition. Come on, I've got a car waiting, and the garrison commander has already approved your indefinite leave so long as you're with me."

It was Paco's turn to laugh, breaking form and folding his arms tightly over his chest. "Indefinite leave? Sure, because that's a thing. Is that why they slapped these stripes on my arm? To let me leisurely stroll away from my duties on a whim?"

Whatever his game was, Paco was done buying this guy's bullshit. Breezing past him and walking away, Paco felt the man's deceptively strong hand yank him back.

Paco's instinct was to fight, but when he whipped back, punch pulled, the man merely held up an envelope.

Paco's name was typed across the front, with the base commander's return address in the top left corner. He ripped through the sealed flap, unfolding the letter inside to read it.

Was his linguistic mastery suddenly deceiving him?

Not completely sure, he had to read the letter again. On the commander's letterhead, and with his barely dry signature, the message confirmed everything this stylish, albeit mysterious man had said.

Before Paco could respond, the man was briskly walking away. "Hey! Wait up." He hurried after the guy who moved remarkably fast, yet gave every appearance of maintaining the pace of a casual stroll.

"Come on, Robles. Move your ass." Again, the man flaunted the sunglasses Paco lusted after, sliding them down just enough to give him a scandalous wink.

When Paco caught up, he slowed his pace, mimicking the man's mannerisms by standing taller as he stepped. "Are you gonna tell me what this is about?"

"Eventually."

Paco's pout must have caught the man's eye, moving him to nudge his elbow lightly at Paco's side.

"Hey, I promise, I'm about to put a whole new life at your fingertips. It'll be up to you if you take it."

"So, you grant wishes?"

"Not exactly. You only get one wish out of me."

Confident, Paco said, "One's all I need."

They arrived at a Jaguar convertible far too upscale for most workers at the base. It had been left running, assuring Paco of a sweet, air-conditioned ride to wherever the hell they were going.

The man removed his glasses. "Here," he said, handing them over. "I saw the way you looked at them. I've got another pair in the car."

Whatever hesitation Paco had about accepting the lavish gift was fully ignored as he snatched them up. He put them on, posing just enough to get a few claps on the back from his new best friend. "Thanks."

"You got it."

"Since you know me and my commander, and I have no idea who you are, what should I call you?"

"You can call me Stone. Jordan Stone."

CHAPTER 12

ALEX

Three days later – Denver, Colorado

BETWEEN HIS FLAT tire on the way to the airport and then a flight delay, AJ still managed to arrive at the two-bedroom penthouse suite of the Four Seasons Denver a little ahead of the requested time. Hopefully, that was fine.

From his first-class flight to the awaiting chauffeured town car, his travels since leaving California had been extremely comfortable, despite his uneasiness. First flight. First real trip away from home. First deep-throat blow job that landed him here today.

Fuck, that was amazing. His jeans tightened at the thought of it.

As he walked through the expensive hotel, he assumed yanking at the front of his pants would be a no-no. Letting out a frustrated huff, he refrained from publicly adjusting himself.

His throbbing cock wasn't his fault. It's one thing for a man to press into a woman's mouth and come down her throat. It's a whole other thing to push past her tonsils while her tongue tickles your balls.

The furthest thing from AJ's mind was a business deal, no matter what he might have said in the throes of her sword-swallowing trick. No, AJ was here for one reason and one reason alone—to get to know this woman's God-given talents better.

But had it not been for her attempt at a Guinness world record, he'd have passed, and not so politely. And that went for whatever she wanted, because it was a little vague.

Or maybe she'd laid out everything in extraordinary detail that he just hadn't heard in the afterglow of being balls deep in her mouth.

What he did hear was Four Seasons, Denver, today at six thirty p.m. And *all expenses paid*. What he didn't hear was *dress code*, realizing way too late—as in now—that he might be underdressed.

Wearing well-worn jeans, a Gap pullover, beat-up loafers, and carrying a cheap overnight bag with a few moth holes, everything about him screamed *does not belong*. AJ half expected hotel security to escort him out.

But they didn't. Hell, they even called him *sir*. Because they obviously mistook him for the sort of man who would frequent an upscale joint like this.

The sort who wore suits from William Hunt on Saville Row and custom Antonio Meccariello shoes made in Italy, and wrote big fat fucking checks to charities, and tipped well. Bummer for them that they didn't get the memo, because it sure as hell wasn't him.

AJ was, however, a fast learner. And Jordan had seemed sure that she could teach him everything she knew in a few hours, so here he was.

Cautious, he checked and rechecked the number on the wall, ensuring he had the right room before he let himself in. He pulled the keycard from the overnight envelope. It had been sent to him with instructions on accessing his airline ticket, and a note on how to get to the hotel, as well as the room.

He swiped the keycard, surprised when the door unlocked. Still, he knocked as he slowly opened it.

"Hello?" he called out, taking a slow step inside, but there was no response. He set his bag down near the entrance, gaining the confidence to walk further in.

The lavish suite was unlike anything he'd ever seen, staged with contemporary furnishings and dozens of fresh roses the color of buttercream frosting. For reasons he couldn't fathom, he leaned in and took a long sniff, appreciating their sweet perfume. They brightened the room and made him feel cozy and at home. Not at *his* home, but at home, nonetheless.

For a few minutes, he took in the view, then headed toward what he presumed was the master bedroom, practically tiptoeing across the suite wherever he moved. In the center of the biggest bed he'd ever seen was a note, weighed down by a black leather riding crop.

A wide smile spread across his face. *Fuck, she's sexy.* He unfolded it.

Take a shower.
I'll be back.

As she instructed, he made his way to the master bath, stripped, and show-ered, washing away the grime of the day as well as the life he'd known.

The luxurious bathroom was aglow with the natural light of early evening in Colorado, casting the walls in crisp golds and rich oranges. Glass and stone fixtures gave way to the Rocky Mountain sunset flooding through the floor-to-ceiling windows on the sixteenth-floor.

The experience was alluring and exquisite, as much as it had to be temporary and fleeting. This sure as hell hadn't been his life—where bathrooms came with nicer toiletries than he'd ever seen, plush robes, and fuzzy slippers, where hot water somehow managed to feel and taste soothing and soft . . . and expensive—but it was the life AJ wanted. And in the deepest part of his soul, this was the life he vowed to have.

AJ lost himself in the view. If the sun never set, he'd probably stare at it forever.

I could get used to this.

He soaked it all in, ignoring the Debbie Downer voice in his head that told him none of this was real. Once-in-a-lifetime deals didn't exist, and even if they did, they wouldn't for a guy like him.

Shower done and feeling refreshed, he grabbed a towel, bringing its fluffi-ness to his nose for a whiff. It was then that he realized his pile of clothes seemed to have vanished.

What the . . .

Still wet with water dripping from his hair and chest, he wrapped the over-size towel around his waist and opened the door.

There lay Jordan, lusciously long-legged Jordan, sprawled in the center of the bed. Which seemed to be her natural habitat.

No complaints.

Her lacy black bra left absolutely nothing to the imagination, and her matching G-string was barely there. But what stood out for AJ was her bright red stilettos. They were the hottest shoes he'd ever seen, and he'd be damned if those weren't staying on the entire time.

"AJ. So good to see you again."

Her raspy voice was like a vise grip to his cock, which tented the soft cotton bath sheet as he stood before her.

"Hi," he said like an adolescent idiot, unable to think of another thing to say to this goddess before him. His attempt at a predatory stroll toward her was juvenile and awkward. When he neared, he bent a knee, ready to set it on the side of the bed.

"No." Her voice was commanding, stopping him in his tracks. "You're not ready."

Uncomfortable and uncertain, he paused. Her gaze washed over his body, as if memorizing every line. No woman had ever studied him like that. Like she was measuring him up. Taking a tally. Making decisions.

Opting to follow the instincts of a man in his early twenties, he flexed a muscle or two. It spurred her smile . . . maybe in approval. Maybe not. He smiled warmly in return.

Did he need her approval? The longer she looked, the more he did. In the long moments filled with the distance between them, he became consumed. He had to please her—give in to anything and everything she desired.

"We have a deal, AJ, and I plan to deliver."

Fuck yeah, they had a deal. A truck filled with cash. Being his own boss. A clothing allowance. Topped by the delectable Jordan Stone promising him the lesson of a lifetime.

In one night, she'd guaranteed to teach him how to never be manipulated by a woman again.

Jordan Stone had managed to nail his Achilles heel. He'd nearly been taken for three hundred bucks a few days ago. It was a weakness, one he intended to shield in chain mail.

And it was important to him. How she knew that, he didn't know, but she did. And he was game. Having his cake and eating her too? It was a win-fuck-ing-win.

So, here he stood, right next to the bed. Waiting. Eager. And ten seconds from humping the bedpost if she didn't get on with it.

"Remove your towel and hand me my crop."

He took a moment before complying. The crop was seductive in her hand. She licked her lips, then let the tip of the crop barely touch his sensitive balls.

His head dropped back as he let out a breathy, *"Ahhhh."*

A low moan erupted from deep within his chest as the crop continued upward, tracing a lazy line around his shaft. When it reached the tip, it moved away. Without warning, she struck his outer thigh.

"Ow, fuck," he said, scowling as he jumped back out of reach.

"Now that I have your attention, here's how this works. You're going to listen to me and do exactly as I ask. If you don't, I'll—" She lifted the crop to her lips, tugging it with her teeth before releasing it. "Redirect you."

AJ looked down at the bright red welt forming, then noticed his rigid cock was throbbing too. It was another surprise.

The tip of the crop found his chin, drawing his eyes to the intensity of her gaze.

"If you can't follow simple directions, you'll have a few more of those little love taps, and neither of us will be satisfied. But . . ." Her smile ticked up, and she bit her pouty lower lip. "If you're a quick learner, and I have faith you are, then we'll both enjoy your lesson. Oh, and just so we're crystal clear, you have just under two hours to learn all you can."

Pointing the crop toward the door, she said, "You'll notice we're in a two-room suite. When we're done, I'll need my privacy."

She tapped the crop to his shoulder, and he sucked in a flinch.

"Ready for your lesson, Mr. Drake?"

He tried maintaining eye contact, but the leather circling his shaft again made his eyes slam shut. "Y-yes."

His dick stiffened like granite. Opening his heavy eyes, he watched as she wiped the bead of precum that had formed, giving the leather a glossy coat, before laying the crop at her side.

"Look at my breasts." She plucked her nipples, then caressed the weight of her breasts in each hand. "Don't be fooled by headlights. High beams don't mean I'm into you. Maybe they're always like this. Or maybe it's cold. Maybe I'm fantasizing about all the money I'm stealing from you."

Instantly, he frowned, and she continued.

"My point is even if I'm not into you, you can get me into you." She scooted away from the center of the bed to make room. "Now, sit."

As was becoming their custom, he obeyed, taking a seat next to her. As soon as he rested back, she straddled him. Every part of him paid attention.

"For the next few minutes, I'm going to enjoy myself, and you're not going to move a muscle. Understand?"

"Y-y-yes," he stuttered, barely able to speak as she rested her weight on his rod.

He could feel her dampness, and wetness like that couldn't be faked. She was into him. She had to be. Didn't she? As her hips swayed, he moved his hands, palming her perfectly round ass.

Crack!

"Fuck!"

Her smile widened with diabolical delight. "I'll repeat myself, so you don't make this mistake again. You're. Not. Going. To. Move. To ensure we're clear, I'm going to ask you again." Her cleavage spilled against his chest as she spoke into his ear. "Do you understand?"

"Yes," he muttered through clenched teeth, accepting that his hardened dick couldn't deny that he enjoyed the pain.

With two fingers, she pulled her panties to the side and slid her weeping pussy up and down him. "Feel me gliding against you?" she asked, nipping his ear with her teeth. "Do you want me?"

Must not move. "Yes."

"Right now? Can you think of anything other than pounding me senseless?"

"God, no. I can't. Jordan, please, I need you." He squirmed through her excruciatingly slow, torturous rhythm.

Must not move. Must not move.

Must. Not. Move.

Holding his breath, he fisted the comforter in frustration, not minding another lash necessarily, but holding out for whatever he should be learning. Because he was, after all, a fast learner.

"So, tell me something, AJ." Her mouth brushed his wanting lips, and for the first time in his life, they trembled. "In this condition, could you possibly steal from me?"

His body stiffened, snapping his mind back to the game.

"No," he huffed out, realizing what she'd been doing. Luring him. It was just a distraction. A sweet, hot, soaking-wet distraction that coated his dick in her heavenly juices, and one he now understood.

With barely a kiss on the lips, she lifted off him, rolling onto her back. "Now, my turn."

God, yes. Her turn.

She slid two fingers through the string of her panties, releasing a breathy gasp as she pushed in, pumped a few times, then pulled out her coated fingers. He could feel an orgasm just out of reach, and all he could do was watch.

Touching his lips, she rubbed her fingers back and forth, glazing them before pushing through. Once he'd sucked them clean, she said, "Remove my panties."

The second he made a grab for them, she raised the crop. He froze, staying very still, anticipating the sting. But it didn't come.

"With your teeth," she said.

Headfirst, he dove down. As soon as his breath hit her skin, she fisted his hair, forcing his uncertain eyes to lock with hers.

"Do it slowly. So much so, you're sure you're going too slow. Your primitive little caveman mind will be in a perpetual state of feeding impulses. Fight that. It's not about you. It's about stoking the flames. Mine. Teasing and tantalizing my pussy so it aches for your touch."

She let go. "Do it, AJ . . . make me desperate for you."

Nodding but not taking in a word of what she said, he moved too quickly.

Crack!

Fuck, I can't believe how much I like that.

Still, he got the point. Slowly, he nibbled, kissed, and licked her soft skin as he traveled from one side of her hips to the other.

Though her body wasn't much more than a foot wide, it may as well have been the George Washington Bridge for how long it was taking him to cross from one side of her to the other. At one point, her breathing became so still, he wondered if his snail's pace had actually lulled her to sleep.

But then, like a light at the end of the tunnel, her body shifted. Her moan was the siren's song he'd been waiting for. Daring a look at her face, he noted her heavy eyes sparkled with a hint of lust.

Finally.

This well-earned victory almost got the better of him, but he was patient as a greater conquest lay ahead. He considered a brazen reposition, then inched his way down until his mouth was directly over her center. Gingerly, his teeth tugged the stretchy scrap of lace down, bit by itsy-bitsy bit.

He let his lips graze her clit but didn't lick it like he wanted. Half expecting the crack of the crop, he enjoyed her hips rocking against his mouth. She was moving to let him pull the panties out from under her ass.

"*Mmm.*" She moaned, but he ignored it.

Not yet. Focus. He forged onward and downward.

Continuing his path, he brushed his lips down the length of her legs, breathing, kissing, and nibbling throughout his passage. When he reached her strappy shoes, his teeth took care, delicately taking the dainty lace past her cherry-red stilettos.

She spread her legs, inviting him. The clear shot of her soaked pussy nearly reeled him in, stopped only by the slice of her six-inch heel digging into the center of his chest.

"No." Her tone was commanding and unapologetic.

He felt a crack, but it wasn't the whip. It was his spirit breaking beneath the weight of sexual frustration.

"Remove my shoes," she softly commanded, "and massage my feet."

Massage your feet? Now? What the—

His nearly begrudging pout was stopped. Somehow, between his devastating disappointment and her sly vixen smile, the rules of the game revealed themselves. He understood.

Instant gratification was the root of all evil. Predictable. Anticlimactic. All the power he coveted was in the delay itself, obliterating every calculated brain wave with a heavy dose of lust.

This was the promised land. The holy grail. The ultimate power of the *P*, and his priceless prize on the merry mount to orgasm.

He might have been at the brink of insanity, but so was she. Plump lips. Bedroom eyes. Heavy breaths. Nipples that could cut glass, and a river running through her pussy. How long could she deny herself?

Game on, baby. Game fucking on!

Unhurried, he uncinched the thin leather strap on her shoe with its bright red sole, and pressed soft, tender kisses along every inch of her ankle and lower leg.

Devoting the power of his strong hands to the arch of her foot, he was pleased to hear her pleasurable moan. Attentively, he caressed her ankle and kneaded her calf. Only after an *ahh* escaped her lips did he remove her other shoe.

"I knew you were a fast learner."

"Mm-hmm." Tamping down his ego, he accepted the compliment without getting arrogant. But she was changing, and it was undeniable.

Her muscles relaxed. Her body responded. And fuck if her pussy wasn't getting wetter by the second.

With a single finger, he stroked the inside of her thighs, and she spread her knees, blooming like a naughty little flower. A taste was tempting, but he'd give anything to hear this woman beg.

Moving up her body, he teased her, laying tender kisses in a solid perimeter around her weeping folds, but not getting near them. Her body writhed, and he smiled.

It would barely test his strength to rip off her bra, and probably result in a whip-worthy offense. He staved off that temptation by tracing a single finger down one bra strap at a time, tugging it low enough to set her weighty girls free. He teased her nipples, coming close, but staying just far enough away to avoid them.

Like the temptress she was, Jordan breathed hard, her breaths raising and lowering her chest, closing the distance between her nipple and his mouth.

His eyes met hers, as if to ask permission before a featherlight lick. It was enough that she arched her back. His hungry lips took her in his mouth as her core found his staff. He pulled away, and this woman who held so much control released a whimper.

That's it, baby. Let's hear you beg.

Her expression transformed, swinging from seduction to desire. No longer the lion tamer, she wanted to be taken. Tamed. Maybe it was his turn to take the whip.

When he reached for it, she shoved it away. As her sex chased his rod, he held it just out of reach.

"No," he said with gruff insistence. "Not yet." It was his turn to fist her hair, sear her skin with his touch, and take control.

He moved two fingers across her clit. Her legs fell open as her eyes fluttered shut. But he wasn't crossing the River Jordan until her pretty pouty lips actually begged.

"Lick me," she said on a sigh that sounded like a beg.

Her two little words were pure caffeine, and his tongue surged in for the taste he'd waited for. Jordan Stone, this mouthwatering rush of a woman, had all the makings of his new favorite meal. He ignored the nagging suspicion that his first taste would be his last.

He nearly came when her hand unexpectedly groped for his cock. With a growl, he stopped mid-thrust and steadied his breathing, but it took every bit of trembling willpower he could muster.

"What's the matter, baby?" Her question was torture. "Are you coming in my hand instead of deep inside the hungry walls of my tight, wet cunt?"

She was playing dirty. Dirty words. Dirty ways. It nearly sent him over the edge. His mantra shifted to *must not come.*

"Don't you want to fuck me?" she asked, adding sweetness to her tease.

He froze, so ready to flip her like a coin toss, not caring which hole he sank his desperate cock into.

I've got to calm down. Think of anything. Paying bills. Closing sales. Haven't been to church in a while. Catholic school. Itchy uniforms. God, and girl-gone-bad Jordan bent over the desk. Skirt hiked up. Ready for the ruler.

Shit! This isn't working.

"I give," she said, and he didn't care that it was a lie. "Make me come. Then shove every inch of that monster dick inside and ride me until you blow so hard, you forget your fucking name."

After several long licks across her swollen folds, he found her clit, nibbling the little nub before sucking hard.

Certain his tutor was far from a delicate flower, he shoved three fingers inside and gave her several deep thrusts. Instantly, she came, clamping his hand to a stop as she screamed several instances of *fuck, oh God,* and of all things, his name.

Hearing it come from her devilish red lips was everything. Sweet. Satisfying. Intoxicating. Something deep inside told him he'd never forget it. And for a woman who reeked of manipulation and a fake name, he couldn't help wondering if he could ever live without it.

"Don't stop."

AJ came up for air. "So demanding," he said, cocky and certain that in the afterglow of a jarringly strong orgasm, the last thing she'd want is to lift a finger toward the crop.

"Not just yet." Her tone was breathy as she struggled to lift her heavy lids. Still, that demand for compliance was very much present behind her dark eyes.

Nestling his face back between her legs, he nibbled and licked, eager to give her anything and everything she needed.

The condom she laid on her thigh gave him enough permission to slip it on. *About fucking time.* He sheathed himself and returned his eager body over her sweat-drenched one.

Panting, Jordan shared one last lesson. "After an orgasm, every square inch of my skin is hypersensitive. Any touch will only enhance the already exploded sensation. Use that little tidbit for all it's worth. But keep in mind your time's almost up." She chided him through panting breaths. "Not that you'll need all that much."

The base of his cock rubbed up and down. He savored the feel of her as he dipped in. Like tiptoeing into uncertain waters, he'd barely breached her slick entry before Jordan pulled him into the deep end. Both of her deceptively strong legs wrapped around him, heaving him hard and driving him to the hilt in one fell swoop.

It was pure ecstasy. "Fuck, that's good."

"I thought you'd like it."

"Demanding and impatient. A lethal combination."

"You have no idea."

Whatever she said next was lost. Reclaiming his thrusts, he slowed his achingly painful pace, but it couldn't end. Not yet.

It was his turn. To take his time. To tear down her walls. To top her.

He licked her nipple, letting his teeth graze it. Again, she tightened her legs around him, driving his ass forward. But despite what must be five hours a day in the gym, her slender frame was no match for his blockade of brute strength.

Easily, he held off, deciding to take a thumb to her clit. "What's the matter, baby? I've still got a few minutes on the clock."

"That's what you think."

Without warning, she gripped his hair, drawing his face to hers. Her fist tightened, enticing his lips apart. Her licks were that of a kitten, luring his tongue, enticing his mouth. Taking him one controlled suck at a time. His rhythm wasn't his own. Much like his mind. Or his cock. Or maybe, his heart.

Then he felt it.

Sliding slowly through the walls of his ass, the woven cane of the crop flossed through his cheeks, grazing his delicate hole. She rubbed away every one of his senses, until all that was left was a mindless thrusting machine.

Surrendering, he forgot himself in the depths of her body and the heat of her core. Erupting, he filled her until nothing was left. Just an empty, heaving, collapsing shell of a man who'd pretty much do anything for her.

Drained, their bodies stayed connected even after she rolled him back. She straddled him as every strained muscle in his body melted away and relaxed.

He looked up, seeing her body aglow with the sheen of satisfaction. Her smile was sweet and sexy and everything as she peered down at him through a thick cascade of tousled locks.

Captured in the moment, he lay there, content to live in the warmth of the moment and the softness of her gaze, not to mention the wet heat of her crotch.

Unguarded, he pinned her with a sentimental gaze that she seemed to return. Her fingers lowered to his ribs, lightly, almost lovingly, brushing his skin. When her nails unexpectedly raked up his sides, digging in mercilessly, his back snapped into an arch. Hissing, he buried his fists in the soft down comforter.

"AJ?" she said almost casually and to herself. "No. I don't care for the name at all. On you, AJ sounds like a handyman. Or a garbage collector."

"You're renaming me?" He forced out the words, still tightening his jaw.

"Let's call it branding." Her nails sliced his obliques, digging in until a moan shot from his lips. "And I know how you feel about the name Jack."

Her hands left him, but it was a temporary relief. His pulse spiked when again she handled the crop, swirling the leather tip to his sensitive balls. With an uncontrolled gasp, he stiffened.

"What does the *A* stand for?"

"Alexander," he huffed out with near certainty.

Slowly, she dismounted and stood at the side of the bed. "I'm going to call you Alex."

He felt the leather move from his balls and wilted shaft, up his abs and chest, then to his chin. Swallowing, he waited for round two.

"Rest for a few minutes, but head to your own room before I'm done showering." Her sumptuous curves made their way to the bathroom, not bothering to turn back. "This is good-bye, Alex. It's been a pleasure."

With that, she shut the door. The water turned on, alerting him that her shower was ready and the stopwatch had started.

In his own bedroom of the suite, Alex lay in the darkness, sinking into the luxury of the king-size bed. It felt a million miles from hers, though her scent was everywhere.

With his eyes closed, he could see every peak and valley of her naked body. Every soft, velvety angle of her smooth skin. The endless darkness of her eyes. The poisonous pout of those full red lips.

Erotic. Mesmerizing. *Jordan.*

It couldn't be over. Not yet.

Aimlessly, he scanned the room, finally looking over at the digital clock on the nightstand. *Midnight.* Three hours since his time with her. Since she climbed off him and bid him an ominous and final farewell.

Whatever fleeting moment they'd shared, it was real. He had to see her. Now.

Unable to find a light switch, he made his way across the dark penthouse, only stubbing his toe once before finding her bedroom. Noticing the bright light beaming from beneath the bottom of the door, he prepared to knock.

The tightened skin of his fist aggravated the welt on it, making it sting again.

Fuck. What sort of smack awaited him for disturbing her beauty rest? Freezing for only a moment, he braced himself for the whip ahead and gave the door a few light knocks.

"Jordan?" His voice was hoarse, and he cleared his throat. "Listen, I'm sorry to disturb you, but I, well, I—I have to talk to you."

Silence.

Slowly, he checked the handle, relieved when it moved freely. It was unlocked. He pushed the door open a crack before entering.

"Jordan?" Opening the door wide, he found the room bright, with every lamp on in the space, and he took a few steps inside.

Deflated, he understood. Everything was quiet. Bed made. Bathroom wiped. Closet emptied. All that remained was a large manila envelope in the center of the bed with *Alex* scrolled across it.

On the very bed that had changed so much in him, he plopped down, unbothered by his naked body making a fresh set of imprints in the fluffy down comforter.

Pulling in a deep breath, he picked up the envelope, checking the contents before spilling them out. Instead of a long, intimate note he'd briefly hoped for from the addictive Jordan Stone were several impersonal items . . . the makings of a new life.

The hotel bill showed the room was paid in full for the next five days. There was a pending offer on his home for way over market value. A first-class ticket for that fifth day would take him from Colorado to Dulles International Airport.

That's Washington, DC, I think.

An elegantly typed itinerary laid out locations and plans, including the town car service that would await him at the airport.

In a smaller envelope was an American Express Platinum Card and a letter granting him $20,000. Not a line of credit, but a pre-loaded amount he could spend recklessly and at will. And maybe use to tip well.

But to his dismay, there was nothing else. The mysterious Jordan Stone had vanished like a thief in the night.

CHAPTER 13

JACK

Five months later – Southern Italy

Sipping a house red, Second Lieutenant Jack Taylor was ready for some well-deserved R&R. The mission was taking its toll, dragging on endlessly for the three-man team. Permission had been granted for shore leave to nearby Italy. At least, that's what two of them assumed, but only Jack knew the truth.

The local cantina should have been laid-back and enjoyable as he and his teammates relaxed and forgot about the Middle East. Their work had been methodical and intense, without the luxuries of reliable electricity or running water. Or for that matter, actual beds.

Italy was a blissful world away, and with the money they'd all saved, it was easy to live it up. But their world-class, week-long getaway was taking an inconvenient turn for the worse, because, as usual, AJ was being his cocky self and stirring up shit.

A small but intimidating mob began circling AJ in the loud cantina while Jack and Paco kept their distance, remaining quiet but standing by. Unsure of his next move, Jack watched from the bar, thinking through the consequences of each possible reaction to the fight brewing. How would it impact their mission? Because any impact would risk too much.

Neither he nor Paco were in uniform, so nobody would suspect they were active-duty military, but the last thing their team needed was unwanted attention. As usual, AJ had missed the memo.

"*Scusami, signori.*" AJ held up his palms to the men as he fumbled through his pleas in broken Italian, not realizing he was being backed into a corner. "Um, the women, *le donne*, they approached me. Uh, *mi ha chiesto di uscire a cena . . .* they asked me to eat. To have dinner."

As if the angry mob gave a fuck. And the more he begged in his butchered Italian, the more irritated the already pissed-off men surrounding him became.

"He's gonna get his ass kicked," Paco quietly sang to Jack, not holding back a sexy smirk. "Perhaps we should just order another carafe and enjoy the show."

But Jack couldn't let that happen. Lowering his voice, he said, "We fucking need him."

"Fine."

They shared a knowing glance and an exaggerated eye roll before heading in to rescue their single biggest pain in the ass, but they were a minute too late.

When the first swing barely grazed AJ's jaw and the second landed solidly on his abs, fair play seemed to be drawing to a close. With AJ's arms wrestled behind his back, the tallest of the group was poised to punch. Jack managed to grab the man's arm in mid-swing.

Paco, who easily passed for a local, gave diplomacy a go in perfect Italian. "*Non è necessario. Porteremo questo turista a casa?*"

None of this is necessary, Jack translated in his head. *How about we take the tourist home?*

No one cared. And this show of testosterone was about to go from a few jabs to a full-throttle MMA match. AJ had broken the cardinal rule—*thou shalt not hit on the women other men called dibs on*—and an ass-kicking was in the cards.

A third man took a cheap shot at AJ, the blow to his gut sending him to his knees. It was enough to launch Jack and Paco into the line of fire.

Five against two. Jack wasn't sure about the odds. He hoped Paco's hand-to-hand combat moves would do better than his botched attempt at diplomatic relations.

Immediately, Paco held up his hands in surrender.

We're so fucked.

A towering man lurched at Paco but Jack couldn't help, caged inside his own cluster of three men. When the biggest threw a punch his way, Jack's adrenaline reinforced his training. The swing was hasty, and he ducked before sending his boot straight at the angry man's nuts.

One down. The two others were no match for him, and he easily subdued them.

Paco.

He whirled around, ready to rush to Paco's aid, but there was no need. Jack found his teammate smiling as he stood over both his opponents, rolling and moaning on the floor. Not only had Paco overpowered two massive attackers single-handedly, but he looked hot in the aftermath. *Damn hot.*

Jack refocused, scanning his surroundings for emerging threats. Everyone seemed to be settling down, with the latest commotion being the matronly owner, yelling at the instigators like hooligans and berating them for fighting with people who actually paid for their food.

For the moment, he could relax, but he didn't. Instead, he locked his body, avoided Paco's eyes, and desperately tried to ignore the tight throbbing in his jeans.

Just the thought of Paco taking on two goliaths alone—Jack couldn't get it out of his mind. The man was a lean, mean, fighting machine with the smile of a saint and a body made for ungodly sin.

"You all right?" Paco laid a hand on his shoulder. Without intending it, their eyes met and locked. For just a second. Maybe two.

Maybe—

AJ moaned, looking like hell. Jack and Paco each held out a hand, hoisting him back to his feet.

Holding his ribs, he mumbled, "Thanks. I really owe you both. I'll make it up to you someday, I swe—"

"Oh, you poor man," a buxom brunette purred in her native Italian. Nestling against him, she held him up, wrapping a hand around his waist.

"So courageous," a blonde said, also speaking Italian. Alex beamed at his understanding. The roll of her Rs was a universal mating call.

He was so brave?

AJ smiled, suddenly oblivious to how he got in this mess to begin with. The women moved to his sides, creating a lusty set of human crutches.

"Oh, uh, it was nothing," AJ said, playing it cool in an obnoxious and ridiculous sort of way.

Unnerved, Jack pinched the bridge of his nose, holding back his own urge to kick his teammate's ass. Without a doubt, Paco would be in.

Irritated, Paco shot AJ a glare and motioned him over.

"*Scusi*, ladies," AJ said, excusing himself while exaggerating the pain of moving away from them.

"Hey, Casanova, those two have just one thing on their minds," Paco said softly, and AJ waggled his brows. "No, dumbass. They're trying to steal your wallet."

AJ smiled with a nauseating degree of confidence. "God, I hope so," he said with a grin. He patted Paco's shoulder, then Jack's. "Thanks again, and don't wait up."

Jack watched as AJ welcomed the bodies of the women, exaggerating his stagger with every step. With a quick glance back, AJ winked. Jack looked blankly at him in disbelief while Paco simply shook his head.

"The fucker just won't learn," Jack said.

Paco nodded. "Buttheads never do."

CHAPTER 14

ALEX

THE WOMEN LED AJ to a quaint hotel a few blocks away.

Their room was rustic with amber-hued walls cracked and pitted from poor construction and age. The queen-size mattress seemed well worn, and he wondered if it would buckle under the weight of the three of them. A small floral scarf draped the only lamp in the room, giving AJ barely enough light to see the surroundings or the bed.

Smart choice.

The women wasted no time peeling off their clothes, down to their frilly undergarments. Eagerly, they began removing his.

"*Come ti chiami, caro?*" one asked as she looked him up and down, licking her lips.

"My name? AJ." With Jordan's voice echoing from the dirtiest crevices of his mind, he reconsidered and changed his response. "But, um, call me Alex."

"*Buono,* Alex."

He waited for their names. The brunette leaned in, speaking for them both. She introduced herself as Sofia and the other as Bianca. Bianca the blonde slipped her tongue into his mouth and her fingers into his pocket—a slick attempt to rid him of his wallet.

Perfect. Time for my field test.

With an excited grin, he tugged out the new leather wallet, holding the prize before them. Their wide smiles were just shy of a drool.

He gave the wallet a carefree toss to the seat of the only chair in the room, leaving it there for them to admire. As if hypnotized by it, the women needed a moment to remember he was even in the room.

Alex smiled wide. *Game on.*

Attentively, they massaged his arms and chest, steadily making their way to his cock. But Alex was ready to take his sweet time.

"Uh-uh-uh," he said softly, shaking his head playfully.

Pulling the brunette to his body, he laid a kiss on her pouting smile, while taking the other by the hand and caressing her skin. One kiss later, he moved his focus to the other and groaned out her name.

Bianca leaned in for a kiss, but he didn't give it to her. Instead, he lightly brushed his mouth to hers with barely a nibble of her ready lips.

"*Mmm.*" She moaned, enjoying the sensation of being gently tasted.

Maybe a man had never bothered taking his time with her. Hell, it was just as new to Alex too. He repeated the featherlight kiss with Sofia and elicited another moan.

A small step for Alex. A huge step for Neanderthals worldwide.

"Now, ladies," he said low, "I hope you're not in too much of a hurry, because I intend to take my time."

Ignoring him and ready to get things underway, they started removing their lacy bras.

"*Lentamente, mia preziosas,*" he demanded with a low grumble.

His request to go slower baffled them at first. Intrigued, they complied as he lined them up, one behind the other in his own sexy conga line. He began a very precise demonstration, making certain they understood there were rules to this game, and he was in charge.

Alex traced a figure eight on Sofia's shoulder, insisting she mimic his actions on the same spot on her friend. "*Fai come faccio io, capisci?*"

Sofia nodded, understanding they were to mirror everything he did, and transferred the sensation to Bianca.

He started with the smallest of tasks. Very slowly, his slipped off Sofia's bra strap. When she did it too quickly to Bianca, Alex corrected Sofia, taking her hand and showing that the move should be slower. Like Alex, she was a fast learner. He rewarded her with a peck on the neck, and she repeated the move on Bianca.

Damn fast learner.

He slid a finger down her spine, forcing her neck back with a shiver. *"Fallo, mia bella,"* he insisted, coaxing her to stimulate her friend likewise.

With the same softness, she complied. Bianca's response equaled Sofia's, though she added an uncontrolled whimper.

Satisfied they understood the rules, he mentally started the clock. "Now, let's have some fun."

For the first time in his life, there was power at his fingertips, and Alex relished it. Sure, it was sexual power, but as powers went, he'd take it.

His hard-on was like solid granite—partially fueled by that aforementioned surge of power—but it would have to wait. Stoking their desires was, it its own way, exciting. He hungered for more.

In the end, Jordan Stone had kept her word and then some. *She gave me a superpower.* With a single touch, he'd made not one, but two women writhe and moan.

Should I use this power for good or evil? he thought, then chuckled to himself. *Tonight? Fucking evil.*

His lazy finger traced around Sofia's ass to the front of her upper thigh, then slipped into her panties and down her hot, wet center. Breathless, she gasped, dropping her hand. Succumbing to her own pleasure, she failed to repeat the move.

Gruffly, he murmured a tender instruction in her ear. *"Si, mia bella.* Go on."

She sucked in a breath, then did as he asked. Mimicking him, she pressed her finger past Bianca's panties and to the center of her core, forcing a gasp.

"Mmm, molto buona. Very, very good," he said on a groan.

In and out he moved, satisfying both women at once. The rush was euphoric.

Next, he unclasped Sofia's bra and discarded it to the floor. Pleased, he watched as his actions were willingly repeated. Moving through a series of activities his naughty mind made up on the fly, Alex pulled Sofia back to his chest, wrapping an arm around her and teasing the outer rim of her nipple. His other hand once again played with her pussy, which soaked the scrap of lace.

She was hot, but her responsive little friend was so much hotter, squealing from the lightest touch that cascaded across one desirable Italian woman to the other. Again, he kissed Sofia's shoulder, and she repeated the movement.

How far can I take them? How far will they go?

When he pushed two fingers inside, Sofia was in heaven, but there was no response from her friend. Sofia was hesitating.

Murmuring impatiently, he said, "Now, *bella*," maintaining a slow rhythm between her legs.

Finally, Sofia did it, and Bianca nearly burst his eardrum with her cry. Outwardly, he worried that their landlord might be heading up to their room. Inwardly, he ate up every decibel.

Best superpower ever.

He upped the ante, getting on his knees behind Sofia, enjoying her shiver as he dragged her soaked panties to the floor. As she was about to do the same, he halted her with a silent *shhh*. Pressing a finger to his lips, he motioned her to the bed, giving her enough unspoken commands that she tiptoed over and sat quietly on the side of it.

To Bianca, he tugged down her panties as well, relishing the tremble it gave her. Kneeling behind her, his warm, strong hands grabbed the front of both her thighs, yanking her back to the surprise of his ready tongue, penetrating her ripe pussy.

Her scream was twice as loud as the first, but he imagined if no one came rushing to her aid before, he was probably in the clear. Her raw cry was a wild mix of shock and joy, and she nearly came on his mouth as she fought to steady herself.

Delighted, Sofia laughed, grabbing her friend and pulling her to the bed. Standing before them, he motioned for them to scoot forward, just enough so their butts were at the edge. Eagerly, they did as he asked.

Alex retrieved a condom from the wallet they'd been so enthralled with, taking his time to flash it so they could see the cash inside. Instead of holding their attention, his dawdling seemed to irritate them.

"Hurry," Bianca said, for the first time giving any impression that she spoke English, and very well, he might add.

Casually, he stripped off his clothes, drawing their gazes, and hearing, of all things, Jordan Stone echoing in his ears. *In this condition, could you possibly steal from me?* He couldn't then, and they couldn't now.

Sex wasn't the superpower. Desire was, and it made him wonder.

What else do people desire?

Smiling, he stepped before them and tossed the condom to the top of the bed. "Whichever of you gorgeous *donne* comes first will get a trophy. A big, hard trophy."

Longing painted their expressions, but they sat obediently, waiting for his next command.

He took the hand of each, overlapped one over the other, and delicately placed them suggestively at the source of each other's heat. Either from the lust he'd stoked in them, or genuine interest or instinct, their fingers began to sink in. Sink in and stroke, like two naughty little playmates exploring each other for the first time.

With the momentary loss of his damn mind, he watched as they closed their eyes and began exploring, rubbing each other as if rubbing themselves.

Fuck, that's hot.

If he let them keep going, they'd be done, and he couldn't have that. With their growing moans, they were seconds from simultaneous orgasms. He cut in. This was his time to shine.

When he moved their hands away from each other, an audible *aww* came from both women. They squirmed until he pumped two fingers inside each of them, sending them closer to that climax they so desperately desired.

It was a race for the history books. AJ Drake, two hot Italian women, and a neck-and-neck race to the *fucking* finish line. Nothing was more disappointing than a moment like this without a photo finish.

He couldn't predict it, but Bianca went over first, seconds from Sofia surrendering to her own wild orgasm. That Alex hadn't come just from watching was also, he presumed, another superpower.

Huffing and sweating, the ladies wove their hands together, connected in ecstasy as their breathing steadied and slowed.

"It was close," he said in a deep, rumbling tone. "But we do indeed have a winner."

He slid his fingers out of them and both whimpered from the loss, but Bianca spread her legs in anticipation.

Firmly, he said, "Put it on me."

Bianca grabbed the condom and tore the package open with her teeth. Before rolling it on, though, she took him in her mouth, sucking him hard until he felt the sensation clear to his toes.

"Yes," he said on a moan, checking his ego and realizing he might have lost this battle had they gone first.

He fisted her hair, pulling her away as he watched her bite her smiling lip. "Now, *bella.*"

Obeying, she wrapped him and then returned to her comfortable recline, letting her knees drop wide with her wet pussy waiting.

"*Tsk, tsk, tsk.*" Alex shook his head. "And what about poor Sofia?"

Obediently, Bianca moved her hand back to Sofia, pumping her fingers softly inside her swollen folds. He swiped the tip of his cock against Bianca's entrance, and she matched his pace with her friend.

In one, hard, forceful thrust, Alex was deep inside Bianca, and she was three fingers deep inside Sofia.

"That's right," he said, guiding her. "Fuck sweet Sofia just like I'm fucking you."

Again and again, he forced his way in to the hilt, keeping a rhythm Bianca easily matched, letting him please both of them at once. Letting him get lost in the moment. Having all the attention of two women at once.

A second later, he felt Bianca's walls crash around him, milking him hard. It sent the sensation through every square inch of him until his balls tightened, his thighs bore in deep, and every last inch of him was squeezed deep inside this beautiful blonde.

An uncontrollable shudder hit him, and he fell forward, deafened this time by his own rough screams. His arms braced, saving the beauty beneath him from being crushed. She let out a breathy giggle of relief, and he kissed each of her nipples before placing a gentle kiss on her lips.

He looked over at Sofia, her face glowing and radiant, and her heavy lids sleepy. They kissed as well before he lifted off the bed.

Catching his breath in the warm room, he watched as the two sweat-drenched women began to shiver. In a caring way he didn't understand, he moved each woman higher on the bed, covering their spent bodies with the tattered blanket. Looking down, he loved how beautiful they were—giving themselves so completely to him, and now cuddling with each other.

Sweetly, he kissed each on the forehead as he tucked them in. Heading to their bathroom, he passed the small chair still holding his unfolded wallet. Not meaning to, he'd left a lot of money in it—some of the spoils of his own breathless night not so long ago.

He moved past it, making his way to the tiny bathroom that seemed cramped by Western standards, but fared well compared to the accommodations of the desert home awaiting him.

Decidedly he shut the door, letting his performance determine the fate of his cash. AJ took his time, uncommon to his carefree nature, but at a pace that he seemed to enjoy.

Tending to his grooming, he cleaned up a bit, helping himself to their soap, comb, floral lotions, and something that might have been mouthwash. He couldn't be sure.

He took inventory of all their toiletries, uncapping them and taking intrigued sniffs of the local brands. He practiced his Italian, patiently sounding out each Italian word of the long list of ingredients on the label.

Through a small window, he breathed in some fresh air and admired a few passersby, talking, laughing, and eating whatever they must have picked up along the way.

After wasting as much time as he possibly could in the small space, unless he wanted to grab some spackle and start repairing and painting the cramped room, he'd exhausted all options for putting off his return.

Slowly, he opened the door. It brought a proud smile to his face that the two women were very much where he'd left them, curled up side by side, spent and asleep. The wallet seemed untouched, but that was just icing on the cake.

Silently, he dressed, taking in what had to be an A+ in his Jordan Stone lesson, and the vision of two women he'd never forget. And not for the women themselves as gorgeous as they were, but more for the bragging rights.

If only I had someone to brag to.

Finally, he snatched up his wallet and counted the bills inside, heaving out a satisfied sigh. Pleased, he flipped the wallet, pocketed it in the back of his pants, and slipped out of the room. With an amused grin, he headed back to the hotel.

Good-bye, AJ.

Hello, Alex.

CHAPTER 15

JACK

THE SHRIEK of sirens echoing off the stone-faced buildings on the narrow streets grew louder as they approached.

Out of habit, Jack barked out an order, immediately regretting his tone. "Let's go." He headed toward the cantina's front entrance, but was yanked back by Paco's strong grip.

"This way." Paco led him through the kitchen, and when they burst through the back door into an alley, Paco headed to the right. "Come on, I know a shortcut back to the hotel."

"How do you know that? I thought this was your first time in Italy."

"It is. But I looked over the maps you had."

Hurrying, they picked up the pace, falling into the comfortable stride of a military run.

"You only looked at them for a second," Jack said, remembering Paco had barely scanned them.

"Yeah, I've got this weird way with things like that. Languages. Images. Faces. Not everything, but those seem to stick in my brain."

"I guess you're stuck remembering my face." *Did I just say that?* Quickly, Jack added, "Mine and AJ's."

Paying more attention to the direction of their run, Paco said, "I guess so."

They maneuvered up and down the winding cobblestone streets until they reached the dim lighting of the back of their hotel. The door was unlocked, and they managed to get through the lobby and up the stairs without passing anyone.

Slowly, they approached the doors to their rooms, but Jack was still on a high from the events of the night. Looking over at Paco, he realized he didn't want the night, or vacation, to end.

"Hey, I'm still a little wired. Want a drink?"

"I've got plenty," Paco said, opening his door and gesturing inside with an easygoing grin that could melt a man from a mile away.

Jack took a few steps inside, feeling the heat of Paco's body follow him. With a gracious wave, he invited Jack to help himself to the small refrigerator, stocked with an assortment of minis, presumably identical to the one in Jack's own room.

"Help yourself."

"Thanks," Jack said, rummaging through the stash.

"I also bought some vodka. It's on the counter if you prefer something harder."

Harder? God, do I. Jack swallowed, unable to stop the heat rising in his cheeks.

"Perfect," he said, taking one for himself and tossing another to Paco's waiting hand. With the caps twisted off and each taking a sip, an unsettling silence fell between them.

They say people get close in combat. Well, Jack got close, all right. Too close, perhaps. With temptation sitting a few feet from him as they guzzled the booze, hiding his feelings was taking an exhausting toll. And hiding in plain sight seemed to be catching up with Jack Taylor. Another mini was in order.

"You okay?" Paco asked.

Jack took a deep breath. "I, um . . ." He turned to face Paco. "No, I'm not."

"Want to talk about it?"

Deflated, Jack shook his head and downed another drink. "Look, I'm about to say something . . . and it's something I don't *want* to say. It's something I *have* to say. It could . . . it could change everything."

"Could change everything?" Paco repeated each word deliberately.

"Actually, no. It *will* change everything. And I'll just leave once I've said it. I'm not trying to make things difficult. I just . . . I can't *not* tell you . . ."

Paco sat up straighter in his seat on the worn vintage sofa. "Shit, what is it?" he asked, concern growing in his tone. "Look, Lieutenant, whatever it is, I can take it."

Jack's wry smile faded. "Fuck, I don't even know how to say this. I mean, I've never said anything like this. I—"

"Just spit it out. It'll be fine. Things always seem worse in our heads. Just say it."

Jack's tortured glance met a flood of admiration from Paco's eyes. Respect. Honor. Suddenly, it all seemed so undeserved. It was a look Jack would never forget, knowing that any second now, it would vanish.

I can't keep living a lie.

Jack sucked in a breath, holding the air for a short eternity before letting it all spill out. "We've been working together for a few months now. And every day I get to know you better, but . . ." Again, he trailed off.

Despite the dangerous threats that were part of the daily lives of their mission, this moment was a thousand times scarier. But what if he let it pass and said nothing? What if they went back into the heart of enemy territory, and he never said a damn thing? What if something happened to him? To Paco?

It's now or never.

"I've never met anyone like you, Paco," he said, sinking into the truth of his words.

"Like me?" Paco gave Jack a squint that demanded he clarify. "What the hell is that supposed to mean—*like me?*"

"No, not like that. Not in a bad way. I mean . . . fuck." He huffed under his breath. "Look, it's just . . ." *Now. Or Never.* "You look, um, good. No, not good. You look great."

"Yeah?" Paco drew out the word, fully convinced of the truth in that statement, and seeming to wonder why that would be an issue.

Trying to ignore Paco's charm, Jack refocused. "I mean, *really* great."

"Still with you," Paco said proudly. "You look great too. But I'm totally lost on why this is an issue."

Stop smiling. Say it!

"It's not an issue. But it is an issue. I guess what I'm trying to say is . . . you're the sexiest man I've ever seen, and I . . ." He met Paco's gaze. "I'm in love with you."

His last words slipped out, quiet and soft. Unintentional. Apologetic.

As Paco stared at him, wide-eyed, his mouth agape, Jack found it unbearable. His gaze fell to the floor. "Like I said, I couldn't not say it. If you want to leave or be reassigned, I understand."

"You do?"

Jack paced the small room, suddenly cold and embarrassed, and uncomfortable in his own skin. "What the hell am I saying? *You* don't have to do anything. Not leave the team. Not be reassigned. I should be the one to be reassigned."

"Really, because isn't this your mission? Your play? But to avoid my discomfort, you'd be reassigned."

"Sorry, Paco. I should go. I just, I don't want to—"

His babbling was shut down by Paco's sudden closeness, his body blocking his path. Jack hadn't noticed the man silently stand and stalk over, but here he was. Meeting his gaze. Caressing his cheek. Smothering Jack's lips with a blazing-hot kiss.

Holy fuck.

Jack couldn't think or move. The moment was everything. The decadent kiss was what he'd craved on a semi-daily basis. The sensation burned through his body, branding his soul while setting the rest of him on fire.

In moments, they'd ripped their clothes away. Jack dropped to his knees, wasting no time taking hold of exactly what he wanted.

"W-wait!" Paco panted out.

Jack looked up, releasing an exasperated breath but keeping a warm smile on his lips. "Look, I'm ready to take this at whatever pace you want, but I'm buck naked, kneeling before you with your gorgeous rock-hard dick in my hand. If you're having doubts, *now* is the time to say so."

Jack's chuckle quickly faded as Paco slowly shook his head.

"I'm not having doubts, Lieutena—I mean Jack. I just . . ."

Jack stood, not touching him but meeting his eyes. "Hey, we don't have to do anything. At all. That kiss was more than I could have ever dreamed of. Well, I mean I *did* dream of it."

Despite his smile, Paco's brow was creased, and he squeezed Jack's hand before lacing their fingers in a tender hold. "You could lose your commission. We're inches from fraternization."

Glancing down, Jack grinned. "Yeah, I'd say roughly eight inches. Hell, maybe nine." He reassured Paco with a kiss. "I wasn't bullshitting. I'm head over heels in love with you. You're kind, considerate, smart, brave, funny as hell, and hotter than fuck. I'd be crazy not to grab you and never let you go. If this is my last mission, I'm at peace with that. It is what it is. I want a shot with you—a real, wildly romantic, happily-ever-after shot with you. I've never felt anything even close to what I feel for you."

They kissed until Paco's warm lips relaxed.

Jack gave Paco's cheek a tender rub. "I've got another gig already lined up after this mission. So, the only way this stops is if you want it to . . . because I know what I want."

"Are you sure?"

"Yes," Jack said firmly, "but this isn't all about me. What do you want?"

Paco didn't speak. He didn't need to. And there were no more words between them that night.

Words, or anything else.

CHAPTER 16

PACO

The next day

PACO AWOKE and stretched in bed, quickly realizing his companion was MIA. The beams of sunlight peeking through the curtains meant he'd slept much later than normal, bringing a sly smile to his face.

His reminiscing about the amazing night before and his morning wood were interrupted by a strange noise from the hotel's hallway, drawing both his attention and suspicion. Maybe it was Jack.

Paco leaped up, cracking the door open enough to poke his head out, but keeping his nude body concealed.

He and his across-the-hall neighbor, AJ, opened their doors simultaneously. They questioned each other in silence, quizzically cocking their heads before realizing neither was the culprit.

Another set of noises drew their attention down the hall. A man wearing a hat was struggling to gain access to Jack's room.

"Hey!" Paco and Alex called out in unison, neither moving to catch him.

The man shoved something beneath the door before making a hasty escape.

Frustrated, Paco gave Alex a dirty look before instinctively understanding the reason Alex wasn't chasing the man down. Apparently, he, too, was buck naked.

They both shut their doors. Paco jumped into his pants and returned to the hall, practically racing AJ to Jack's room. They knocked.

"Jack?"

"Jack!"

"Yeah?" he answered from behind them.

They both turned. It seemed that Jack was up bright and early, and had returned bearing gifts not only for Paco but for AJ as well. In his hands were three small coffees on a rickety tray with an attractive assortment of local pastries.

Frowning, Jack narrowed his concerned eyes on Paco, transparent in wondering if the cat was now out of the bag. Paco returned a subtle shake of the head, noticing what might be relief pouring through Jack's silent exhale.

Oblivious as usual, AJ disregarded the silent conversation transpiring before him and crammed a pastry in his mouth. "Thanks," he mumbled, barely managing his mouthful as he grabbed a cup.

"We caught some guy trying to break into your room," Paco said low, keeping his alarm quiet from the neighbors. "He slid something under the door."

Jack handed Paco the tray. "Oh, uh, good. I was expecting a delivery. He left it. Great." He dug a tarnished brass key from his jeans pocket and unlocked his door before opening it.

Before Alex could make a grab at another pastry, Paco shoved the tray into his hands, giving himself the freedom to pop his freed hands staunchly to his hips.

"The guy was trying to get into your room," Paco said firmly to Jack, barely masking his concern.

Jack turned to Paco and gripped his shoulder. It felt condescending.

"I said he could if I wasn't here. Hey, um, why don't we all get together in about an hour to head back?" Jack snagged a coffee off the tray and slipped into his room, shutting the door behind him without another glance.

Dumbfounded, Paco stood, blinking in disbelief at the rustic wooden door. He glanced at AJ, still carrying the tray, who gave him a cheesy grin.

"Coffee?" AJ said, bringing yet another pastry to his lips. Paco's glare prompted him to add, "Sorry, it's just that I'm starving. I worked up quite the appetite with those girls las—"

Avoiding landing his fist on AJ's throat, Paco brushed by him and returned to his room. With the door shut, he leaned against it.

Well, fuck. Welcome to the morning after.

Hanging his head, he startled as a large envelope flew from beneath the door, knocking against his feet. As soon as he moved to pick it up, he noticed the shadow. Whoever pushed it through was still there. *The guy from Jack's room.*

Without the convenience of a peephole, Paco yanked open the door to check. But it wasn't the man in the hat at his door. It was Jack, carrying the tray with the last coffee and a single pastry left on it.

Grinning, he said, "I nearly lost a hand tearing these from AJ."

Unamused, Paco gave Jack a death glare harsh enough that it wiped the dimples right off his cheeks. *Curse those dimples.*

"Can I come in?" Jack asked. "I'll only stay a minute."

Reluctantly, Paco stepped back, letting Jack enter for the second time. And cursing the first.

Jack set down the tray and swooped the envelope from the floor. It had a slight bump in it that he fiddled with, thumbing it over and over again. "I know how that must have looked back there, but—"

"Don't worry, Lieutenant. Your secret's safe with me. If that's all, sir, I've got to get ready to leave."

The sadness in Jack's eyes made Paco turn away.

But Jack didn't leave. Softly, he said, "I see. We're back to *lieutenant* and *sir* again. I understand."

"Yes, sir, we are."

Undeterred, Jack tapped the corner of the envelope against the palm of his hand. "Well, speaking as your superior, Staff Sergeant Robles, I actually came here because I need you to hang on to this. For safekeeping."

With an air of gravity, Jack handed over the envelope, and Paco stood almost at attention as he accepted it.

"Open it," Jack said. "I need to confirm you're up for the task."

Carefully, Paco peeled open the flap of the brown envelope. He looked inside before tipping it to pour its contents into his hand. It was a ring. Golden, though it couldn't be gold. An embossed signet ring with a thick, plain band.

Paco held it to the light, studying it, not noticing anything but a cheap piece of jewelry whose value couldn't exceed five bucks.

Jack snatched it back from Paco, tossing it in the air and catching it again. "You can get a closer look later. But only if you're up for everything this task entails. And I hope you are. Just so you don't get the wrong idea, this isn't yours to keep. Think of it as a placeholder."

Paco set himself up for operative mode, remaining professional as he listened intently, ready to receive his orders. When Jack shifted, professional flew out the window, and all Paco could do was listen to the deafening beats of his own heart.

Before him, Jack lowered to one knee, lifting the ring high. Paco held his breath as Jack began to speak.

"I know we haven't known each other that long, and this might seem, I don't know, hasty. Impetuous. Fucking nuts. But I can't imagine the rest of my life without you, and I don't want to try. I love you, Paco." Jack filled his lungs with a nervous breath, then continued. "Will you do me the unbelievable honor of marrying me? I don't have much to offer, but I swear I'll spend every hour of every day of the rest of my life making you happy."

For one of the first times in Paco's life, he was speechless. He looked down on the man smiling up at him. A man who led with his heart and was too gorgeous for words. A man he'd laughed with until dawn and shared every last one of his secrets with. The man asking him to take a leap of faith.

Shutting his eyes, he nodded without a word. Jack stood, wiping the tear Paco hadn't noticed, and gave him several sweet, soft kisses that he eagerly returned.

Jack broke away with an unmistakable sigh of relief. "And if you keep calling me *lieutenant* when we're alone, it's gonna start to turn me on."

Paco let a wide smile burst out for the first time that morning. Slowly, and somewhat ceremoniously, Jack lifted Paco's hand and slid the ring onto his finger.

Small problem. It didn't fit.

Paco's raised brow met Jack's determined eyes. For a moment, Paco allowed his finger to be nervously twisted and turned, while the ring continued to ram his thick knuckle.

Clearing his throat, Paco took back his hand and slipped the band from his ring finger to his pinky, adoring it proudly. "As usual, officers give the orders, while we enlisted men execute the mission."

With a chuckle, Jack kissed him softly. "I'm too happy to argue." He clasped Paco's hand, then almost apologetically said, "It's just an IOU until we get back. But I had to get you something. So I know you're mine."

"I'm yours."

Jack pressed a long kiss to the back of Paco's hand, then wiggled the ring to ensure its fit. "Keep it safe. You'll get to exchange it for something perfect in a few weeks."

"You're perfect," Paco said, stepping into his embrace, but Jack pulled himself free.

"Hang on." He grabbed the corded phone from the desk and dialed a room extension. "Hey, AJ, I need a bit longer. How about we all circle back in two hours instead of one. Yeah, I just want to do some quick sightseeing before we go. Great, thanks."

Paco smirked as Jack replaced the receiver, then forcefully tugged his lover by the waistband. "Well, I'm happy to show you my Tower of Pisa, but I can assure you, it won't be leaning."

CHAPTER 17

ALEX

Three weeks later
An undisclosed location in the Middle East

"Hᴇ'ᴛ ᴀᴛ ᴛ ᴀɢᴀɪɴ," Alex heard an exasperated Paco exclaim.

It was well deserved. Alex couldn't help his pacing or muttering as he tested and retested the technology he'd created on the fly. So much was riding on this operation, and as the lone civilian on the team, his insecurities had set in hard. Nothing could go wrong.

"Well, I guess that's why he gets the big bucks," Jack said, trying to squelch Paco's irritation. The guy was a natural-born leader, always commanding, yet warm. "AJ," he called out.

Alex strolled over, fiddling with a small gadget in his hand. "I'm thinking of going by Alex. What do you think?" he asked, genuinely wanting Jack's perspective but feeling unusually vulnerable.

Jack studied him, thoughtful as he considered the question. "Alex Drake?" He nodded. "Hmm. Actually, I like it. Sounds like a name you could build a high-tech empire with," he said, teasing him with a smile.

"Good. Settled. I'm Alex from here on out." Decisive and confident, he stood taller, straightening his collar and returning Jack's nod.

"Okay, *Alex*, we're gonna take a quick picture before our mission officially comes to an end."

487

Alex pocketed his tools and reached for the camera, but Jack grabbed his arm. "All of us. I'll set the timer so we'll all be in the shot."

Jack was the things great men were made of. And Alex was a lone and often lonely wolf hiding behind his Mister Life-of-the-Party persona. As was often the case, Jack eased Alex's insecurities, determined to show him he was part of the team. And each time he did it, it was appreciated.

Deep down, Alex knew he was annoying as shit. Sometimes intentionally. Often, more precautionary than anything else. His OCD was unrelenting. Incessant. He might have already checked and rechecked absolutely every fucking thing, but he had to.

Okay, maybe he didn't have to. He was a perfectionist intent on covering for all that was imperfect in his life. A facade for all that was missing. And Alex could sense that Jack had his own mask on too.

Alex wasn't sure if Paco knew about Jack's feelings. The man was obviously in love. Certain he himself was too arrogant or vain for love—or jaded in the wake of Jordan Stone—but Alex enjoyed being a spectator. Deep down, he wished Jack all the luck in the world. A world he suspected would always be just out of his reach.

"You sure?" Alex asked.

Their orders had been unequivocal. There was to be no evidence of their time overseas. But Alex wasn't making waves. Far from it. Of all things, he had this strange polite streak he just couldn't shake.

There were more reasons than one not to intrude on the photo op. The unlikeliness of their blossoming relationship was just the start. Both Jack and Paco were military. Alex hadn't earned a part in that. If anything, Alex had been the *I don't work for you* guy a time too many and should have been permanently iced out.

Alex hoped his precision and tech savviness would guarantee his permanence as part of the team. His devices were an undeniable reflection of himself —tailor-made to hide in plain sight. He was as camouflaged as any of his products, and as closed off as they came. But Jack always managed to break through with his genuine caring and directness.

Jack punched his shoulder. "Don't be an asshole. Of course I'm sure. Robles, come on."

Once Jack set up the camera and timer, they all stood, nearly at attention, professional to a fault. As the timer counted down, Jack huffed out a breath as he shook his head.

"Oh, this isn't the shot we're taking. This isn't a mug shot . . . it's something we'll look back on for years. The beginning of our bond. Come on," he said, grabbing their waists and drawing them in.

Both men threw their arms around his shoulders, all laughing with smiles wide. That precious moment was captured with the countdown.

In three . . . two . . . one.

PART III
THE PRESENT

CHAPTER 18

ALEX

Upstate New York

Lost in his memories, Alex stared at the photo from his wallet. The one of the three of them together the day before the attack. Before Jack's death.

Why did Jack have to die?

Unsettled, Alex shut his eyes, but a ping from his computer there in the bunker brought him back to the present, alerting him to an incoming email from an anonymous sender. Mark Donovan's one-hour ultimatum had worked.

Controlling his reaction, Alex calmly said, "Received," before making what he knew would be a fruitless attempt at tracing the transmission.

Jordan Stone was returning to his life, and he had to know why. Alex's gaze fell to his wrist, checking his watch to verify the rendezvous time.

A nervous energy filled the room as Alex read aloud the confirmation, which said nothing more than, "Give me ten."

"Ten hours?" Mark asked. "Is he negotiating?"

"No," Alex said, not bothering to correct Mark's continued presumption on gender. "I'm pretty sure Jordan means ten minutes."

"That's impossible," Mark said, but Alex only gave him a knowing glance.

Cat and mouse just took on a whole new meaning.

Without a clue what to anticipate, they were ready for anything. The secured bunker was equipped with state-of-the-art surveillance equipment that should alert them to an approaching vehicle a full mile out, but no alerts were set off.

Five minutes.

"What are you doing?" Mark asked, sounding a little panicked as he watched Alex deactivate the audio alerts and ensure the surveillance was set to record.

"Trust me," he said, half wondering if he should trust himself.

The bunker also had a weakness—an area that could be penetrated. It was ingenious and barely discernable, but Alex had discovered and secured it years ago, wondering about it time and again. Early on, he'd chalked it up to a design flaw. But today, he suspected he was about to find out the purpose of its well-constructed design.

Electronically, he disabled the locks securing it. This wasn't about preparing for war as much as staging a welcome. Well, a welcome with weapons in hand.

Not overly concerned, but better safe than sorry, Alex and Mark geared up in the armory. Of course, Mark couldn't help but select the most outlandish weapon from the high-end arsenal, a Heckler and Koch MP7.

"Seriously?" Alex asked.

Mark embellished his ensemble by loosening his tie and slipping the silk to his forehead. He re-cinched it at the temple in an impromptu Rambo impersonation. "What?"

When Alex lifted an agreeable HK45 from the wall, a noticeable *aww* came from his BFF.

Grabbing an assault rifle, Mark said playfully, "How about I go with 'I'll give you a war you won't believe,' and you do, 'say hello to my little friend.'"

Returning the heavy weapon to its setting, Alex held up his moderate weapon. "I'm good."

Without warning, the lights died. The backup generator kicked on, flooding the corridor with the red hue of emergency system lights. Within seconds, the standard power returned.

"Showtime," he said to Mark.

Unsurprised, Alex added this incident to his running mental checklist of unexpected/expected events. And instinctively, he knew. They were no longer alone. His natural intuition was confirmed by a voice penetrating the air from within an impenetrable facility.

"I'm in your pantry." The voice was distinctly male, and a surprise.

They took hurried but deliberate steps down the corridor, Mark with a submachine gun, and Alex holding the familiar and comfortable grip of the reliable semiautomatic handgun.

Unthreatening, the man they came upon seemed to be preoccupied with pilfering liquor, leaning over to help himself to their bourbon. With his back to them, he stood.

The tall man's gray-white hair was neatly trimmed in trademark military fashion. Spreading his arms wide, he revealed that his only weapons were a bottle of Jefferson's in one hand and a lowball in the other. Still, he knew the drill, holding his arms out wide but not letting go.

It was a charming attempt to show he was unarmed, content to hold his stance. Calm and confident, he seemed to know they'd refrain from riddling him with bullets if only to prevent spilling a drop of some of their favorite booze.

"Relax, boys, I come in peace," he said evenly, chiding them as he slowly turned in a circle. "Sorry, I tend to have a flair for the dramatic." Completing his rotation, he took a long look at Mark. "Ah, I see I'm not the only one."

Alex darted a glance at his *First Blood* friend.

"Fuck," Mark huffed out as he yanked the tie from his head.

"An interesting trick," Alex said to their uninvited guest. "You mind telling us who you are and how the hell you got in here?"

Mark frisked the intruder, who kept his arms high, still firmly holding the bottle and glass. Deep in analysis, Alex gave him a once-over.

Considering the man's expensive slacks, pullover, and sedately casual demeanor, he had to be some form of senior operative, and of an age that suggested he might be retired. Possibly a free agent, which would always be a concern. But the intruder seemed to have no intention of reaching for a weapon, so on some level, Alex could relax.

"He's clean," Mark said, surprise returning as his statement sounded like more of a question. Unlike Alex, Mark was taking no chances, and when he stepped to Alex's side, he centered the semi-automatic straight on the man's chest.

"Who are you?" Alex asked.

"I'm Jordan Stone."

Squinting, Alex cocked his head as the answer lingered between them.

The man smiled. "Yes, I can tell by the look on your face that my name might have led you to expect someone else." When Alex didn't react, the man shrugged and continued. "True, I'm not *your* Jordan Stone. Let's just say I'm the senior Jordan Stone, both in age and hierarchy. You can just call me Stone."

But he does know Jordan.

"How about I call you Houdini? You wanna tell us how the fuck you got in here?" Alex maintained a calm tone with loosely masked comical inflections. He didn't exactly need answers, but he wanted them.

Never one to tip his cards, Alex preferred all would-be adversaries feel warm and secure in thinking they held the advantage. The subtle tactic always preserved the upper hand of knowing more than he ever disclosed. Unfortunately, he was sure the man before him was very much the same.

At a glance, Alex pieced together more about his opponent. With his thousand-dollar shoes and Mister Rogers sweater, before him stood a man who had no fear, least of all from the fashion police.

No amount of scare tactics would faze this guy. Threats and intimidation were out. Any attempts to retrieve his intel by force wouldn't go far and wouldn't be necessary. Alex didn't need to waste his time.

This man was here for a game. And on a completely instinctual level, Alex knew Stone would willingly bear it all. He was here to play.

"May I?" Stone asked, exaggerating his movements to set down the contents of his hands.

The show was slow and anticlimactic, but Alex noticed that Mark tightened the grip on the weapon anyway.

Once he set down the bottle and glass, Stone carefully pulled his wallet from his back pocket. He opened it, pulling out a business card, but didn't immediately hand it over.

"When this facility was built," he said, "you were given a phone number you could call for both rudimentary maintenance as well as emergencies. You were instructed to memorize that number, and to set up a password and access code that you'd need to give to any operator who answered, confirming your identity."

"Yes," Alex said slowly, skeptical.

Stone passed him the card, giving him a moment to review the information. The card simply said *Stone* for his name, followed by a phone number. It was the same number Alex had committed to memory years ago. Intrigued, he looked up from the card, permitting Stone to continue.

"Your password is Cristo, and your code is 1220," Stone said, and Alex lowered his weapon. "Jack Taylor's birthday, December twentieth."

No one could know that. It meant this man was probably knew more and was more threatening that Alex could have imagined. It also meant training a weapon on him was pointless. And perhaps a little rude.

Securing the safety, Alex stood down and pocketed his pistol. It was a noticeable contrast to Mark, who refused to drop his defenses, holding tight to his former sniper life. Hospitality be damned.

"Mr. Drake, I know all this because I was the contractor you hired to build this SCIF a decade ago. I've been in and out of your life for a very long time."

To that, Alex said nothing, preferring to listen.

Casually, Stone poured a healthy serving of bourbon into his glass. "I needed to keep tabs on you. Make sure you were, well, all right. I orchestrated this, just as I paved the way for your first few major defense contracts."

Alex let the words sink in before asking, "Why?" Unworried, he stepped over to Stone, studying his eyes as he thought back to the beginnings of his business. His life after Jack. "Why would you, or anyone, go to the trouble? I was a nobody."

Stone took a sip before blowing out a long breath of resignation. "Because I was also the mastermind behind Jack Taylor's last mission."

ALEX

ALEX LED them back to the main control room, which was ideal for lengthy conversations. Stone's statement seemed to promise just that.

They offered Stone his choice of seat. He took the one Mark had used and picked up the cards lying on the table in front of it. Mark sat across from him, giving him the cleanest shot . . . just in case. Alex was sure that for Stone, distrust would only garner his respect.

With the comfortable club chairs and the conference table still set up for playing cards, the awkward circumstances seemed somehow laid-back and natural. Just a few guys hanging out, drinking, chatting it up, with near disregard for the locked and loaded weapons at the ready.

Stone slid two cards to the center, face down, inviting Alex to what just became his game. Alex gave in, abandoning his firearm to Mark, who set aside the machine gun and rested Alex's handgun on his lap. Alex had a clear view of it still trained on Stone, undoubtedly with the safety switched off.

Stone sized up his cards, then seemed to do the same thing with Alex. "You know, you've grown so much."

Alex engaged him, imagining for the moment that the older man was a long-lost uncle and not a potential evil mastermind. Skillfully, Stone walked a tightrope of sharing just enough to keep him intrigued, while not giving away his hand.

"You're not the same kid we found all those years ago, wet behind the ears and hungry for a deal. No, the man sitting before me has a penchant for finding the truth."

"Is that why you're here? To give me the truth?" Alex asked. Stone's words reeked of bullshit, and yet held to something sincere.

"I am. And not just because you've got the bottomless resources to bankroll what could be a costly mission, but that you aren't afraid of a little danger. For a man like you, it's less of a deterrent and more of an aphrodisiac."

"We all have our vices," Alex said, picking up his abandoned lowball and sipping in agreement.

Stone raised an eyebrow his way. "I'll give you two choices, Alex Drake. Call it an initiation. I want to see where your allegiance lies. And for the rest of your life and mine, you'll only ever get the answer to one. Ready?"

"Sure," Alex said without the faintest trace of concern.

"I have two different people I could tell you about. And I swear to tell you everything I know about one of them. No matter which path you choose, I'll still end this meeting by asking you for one favor. The same favor, no matter which way you go."

"Okay." Intrigued, Alex set down his glass and clasped his hands on the table in front of him.

"Tell me who you want to know about. Madison's brother, Jack Taylor, and his mission? Or your Jordan Stone and hers?"

Calmly, Alex said, " She's not my Jordan Stone."

And she never was.

For Alex, choosing between the two—the woman who gave him his name, and Madison's dead brother—didn't require any thought.

"Jack," he said firmly, then reminded Stone, "Everything you know."

Agreeing with an approving nod, Stone continued. "Jack wasn't just any recruit. He was my recruit." Averting his eyes, he said, "He was special. The whole reason I agreed to come in."

"Special how?" Alex pressed, annoyed by how Stone chose his words with caution. "Look, either you come clean or this meeting is over."

"Fold." Stone tossed in his hand, not bothering to acknowledge Alex's ready dismissal.

Coolly and without missing a beat, Alex dealt again.

After picking up his new cards, Stone pressed on. "Jack was special in the same way you were special, and Mr. Robles was special. In such a unique way, it's hard to nail it down in words. And Jack wasn't recruited for your mission. He was recruited for mine. Yours was his cover."

Alex snapped his gaze up from his cards. "Living in BFE for months on end was a cover?"

Stone nodded. "His real task was to get a list of names. Double agents. He was my hand-selected operative, and as soon as he'd finished the job, he would have been permanently assigned to my team—to me." He swirled his bourbon, watching the caramel-colored liquid glaze the inner walls of the crystal lowball. "I saw in Jack what someone saw in me a very long time ago. So much so, I planned to bring him up in the ranks."

"You made him a promise?" Alex asked, leery of a line.

"No. Just the hopes and dreams of an aging man with no children. Wanting to pass on my secrets and wisdom to an amazing young man who'd most likely succeed me."

Mark finally chimed in. "So, you were Merlin to Jack's King Arthur?"

With a sad grin, Stone looked suddenly older as he replied. "If you consider the tragedy of both endings, yes."

Alex noticed something unexpected about Stone in that moment, that the loss of Jack was his loss too. Needing the rest of the story, he said softly, "Go on."

"Jack spent months grooming the informant, securing the intel, and assured us he had everything. We were about to pull the team back. Then, out of the blue, the contact had more. Something new. Something important. I didn't approve the continued mission, and yet Jack received word that he was cleared to proceed. But," Stone sighed, "he was burned. You all were."

Mark interjected. "Hang on. An elite team is sent in, one in deep cover, and you're saying their mission was compromised? Missions like that don't just get burned. Sounds like an inside job amongst you puppeteers."

Mark gripped the gun tighter, but Alex calmed him with a gentle tap on the arm.

Remorseful, Stone looked at Alex. And without the need for words, Alex understood. This was more than a mission mishap. Stone had been deeply affected by it, leaving him something that both he and Alex had in common.

Guilt.

"*We* weren't burned." Alex leaned in. "Jack was. And like Mark said, sounds like his mission—his real mission—was compromised by someone on the inside. Pretty high up. Even higher than you."

Stone slumped back, nodding as he tightened his jaw. "I've always felt the same, but never knew for sure. Above me or below me, whoever it was, they covered their tracks like a pro. Within a few months, I was so upset and pissed off, I couldn't think straight. In the midst of the blowback, I left. I wasn't to blame, but took the hit nonetheless."

Stone pointed a finger, then tapped it hard on the table. "I made every effort to unravel the truth, tugged every thread, grasped every straw, and spent the better part of a decade digging for any clue to what really happened. But a few weeks ago, a glimmer emerged, and I jumped on it."

"So, you're here for the big reveal?" Alex asked. "Like, why not just call if you wanted to talk?"

Adamant, Stone shook his head. "No one can know you and I have talked. We didn't have a middleman. We knew, with the right staging, that Mark would bring you in. Even after all these years, I never know who might be listening. Waiting. Meetings can't go through your admin support or be on your calendar."

Stone polished off the remainder of his bourbon and set the glass aside. "And I don't have a big reveal. Not yet. I'm here because, as I told you up front, I need a favor." He clasped his hands tightly on the table, returning his desperate eyes to Alex's. "I need your help."

CHAPTER 20

ALEX

FOR MOST OF the helicopter ride to the Adirondacks after the meeting concluded, Alex remained silent, deep in thought. And Mark did what he always did when Alex needed to process things. He gave him the room to think.

The time passed quickly, and then Mark's lavish cabin emerged in the clearing past the green spikes of lush pines. The tension that had built in Alex's neck and shoulders released as he made out Madison, waving to them from below on her stroll along the lake. Deliberately, he lifted his mood, determined not to tear his fiancée from what was left of her lighthearted and carefree day.

After a soft landing on the grass, Alex hopped out to head in the direction she'd been walking. The heat and humidity gave him all the incentive he needed to shrug off his blazer and tug off his tie.

"Madison?" he called out, searching up and down the lakefront, unsure of which way she might have gone. When he nearly tripped over her pile of discarded clothing, he smiled.

Squinting, he looked across the brightly shimmering lake. The flickering sparkles masqueraded her, hiding her in a sea of glittering light. With a kidlike splash, she teased him, swimming out further.

"Hey, beautiful. Want some company?"

"You're a little overdressed for the occasion," she called out, the only woman who could pull him from his dark thoughts and entice him to come out and play.

And just like that, Alex began ripping off his clothes, certain his stripping would give him high marks in both technique and speed.

When there was little left to reveal, Madison shouted, "Alex, wait!"

"Wait? While a sea nymph skinny-dips before me? Like hell I'll wait." Defiant, Alex grabbed the waist of his pants, shoving the last of his clothes proudly to his feet.

A two-tone whistle broke through the air. It would have been welcome from Madison—not so much from Jess.

Fuck!

"Jeez," he said, hurrying to scoop up his clothes to cover himself. "Um, hi, Jess."

"Hey, hot stuff," Jess said with a wink, giggling as she laid down a fresh towel on the grass for Madison. Delighted but careful to maintain eye contact, she turned, meeting Alex face-to-face. "Just came down to bring Madison a towel. Oh, I didn't bring two. Shall I . . ."

As nonchalant as a man could be when mostly naked with his best friend's wife, Alex said, "No, I think Madison and I can make do."

Jess slowly sauntered away, stopping to whirl back around with juvenile enthusiasm. "Only if you're sure," she said, smiling as she waited out his response. Hearing Madison's giggles, Jess was no doubt enjoying his discomfort as much as his full moon.

Stoically, he faced Jess, replying under his huffed and embarrassed breath. "I'm sure, Jess." When she opened her mouth to reply, he shot back, "Positive!"

"Well, as long as you're sure." Jess gave Madison a very drawn-out wave and giggled her way back to the house, Madison's laughter echoing hers.

With the coast clear, Alex dropped the bundle and streaked into the water. "Time to take care of you, Ms. Taylor."

Squealing with delight, she swam out further but couldn't outpace him.

Stroke after stroke, his body pushed effortlessly through the water. Once he caught her, he paused, soaking in the amber shimmers and afternoon glow surrounding her. She was his angel.

As the sun began its descent, she floated, skimming her fingers along the surface, sending out soft ripples of the water with every pass.

Alex moved in, closing the distance between them, but stopped shy of a kiss. "Do you know one of the biggest advantages of meditation?"

Grinning, she gave him a quizzical look as she shook her head. "What?" The word whispered off her lips, daring him to kiss her.

He gazed at their fullness but pulled back. "It teaches the mastery of . . . certain things."

"Hmm, like what?" she asked, her eyes wide with interest as she treaded water before him, naked.

A foot taller than she, he was able to plant his feet firmly on the lake bottom. It took nothing to prowl up to her. He kept enough of a distance so there would be no touching. It was a small punishment for her sweet giggles, but it would do.

His gaze met hers before his mouth descended to her ear. "Like, breathing," he said low, then licked down her neck before submerging his head beneath the surface.

Her body was cool to the touch, and he enjoyed warming her with his hands, caressing her waist and hips beneath the water. Her shiver was delicious, and he kissed her belly, feeling her soft panting as he worked his way down.

He placed the heat of his palms around the soft mounds of her ass, pulling her toward him and spearing her with his tongue. Hearing her muffled shriek above the surface, he lapped at her as her body went limp.

In the last few seconds of his held breath, he tickled her with a few bubbles, then stood.

Sliding a hand between her thighs, he laid her on her back, supporting her beautiful body as it floated on the surface. With his head between her legs and her thighs draped over his shoulders, Alex feasted on her, lapping her with his tongue as he enjoyed the scene. The sunset and her breasts. Her wet pussy against the surface of the lake. The two of them. Alone.

The water was cool and sweet as his tongue sliced delicately across her folds. Her own honey was decadent, and her swollen pussy was so soft and ready.

As he teased a finger to her entrance, his mouth found her clit and sucked. She moaned. Back and forth, he worked two fingers in, penetrating her deep, then deeper with each thrust.

When he found that sweet, precious spot, her walls clamped around him as she came hard, crying out in ecstasy. Waiting patiently as she came down, he removed his fingers and wrapped his arms around her, embracing her into his chest. She panted as he cradled her body close to his.

He gave her kiss after kiss as he carried her shivering body toward the bank.

"And where do you think you're taking me?" she asked, kissing his neck. Her fingers suggestively traced figure eights across the scars of his chest as she pressed delicate kisses here and there.

"The sun is setting and you're cold. I don't want you getting sick."

"Then warm me up," she said. The double dare behind her eyes was tempting, and it made Alex stall.

Indecisive, he paused in the shallower water as he weighed his options. Did he have the willpower to pull out when the time came? He considered it, taking in every inch of her voluptuous body as she lay in his arms.

Not a fucking chance in hell.

His angst made her giggle. "What's wrong? Can't whip out a condom from here?"

"Must you mock the misfortunes of others?"

"Alex, we're engaged, and I get my shot regularly. It's ninety-nine percent effective."

"I like those odds," he said, easily swayed to bareback it.

In one of her most persuasive moves yet, she nibbled his neck as she whispered, *"Please."*

God, she's good.

"So, are you just going to stand there all night, letting me freeze?"

"We are indeed engaged." He reached for her left hand, alarmed to find her ring finger bare. Concerned, he scanned the lake. *It would take a dozen divers to find it. Maybe two dozen.*

"I didn't lose it," she said to put him at ease. "I left it in my jacket pocket so it wouldn't slip off during my swim."

Relieved, he kissed the spot where her ring normally rested.

"Well, then, I won't let you freeze . . . but only because I'm a gentleman. And a gentleman would never let a luscious, wet, naked, breathtakingly gorgeous lady needlessly shiver."

"Thank God you're a gentleman," Madison said, either acknowledging his status or in relief, he wasn't sure which.

In waist-deep water, he released her body just enough to move himself between her legs, which instantly wrapped around him. "Especially for a water nymph who is so exceptionally . . ." He slid his fingers through her still plump, hot folds. "Aroused."

This would be a first. His bare skin inside her. He imagined it, fisting himself before moving his throbbing cock back and forth along her slick sex. Biting the fullness of her lower lip, she tightened her thighs around him.

"So impatient," he murmured.

"Yes," she said, pulling again.

It wasn't her strength that drew him into her, but the magnetic pull of her gorgeous cunt that readily swallowed every inch of his dick in a single, hard thrust. Her tight walls were heaven, encouraging his thrusts and drawing up his balls.

Too fast, he thought, and forced himself to slow down.

Trying, and failing, to take hold of his slick body, she whimpered as her nails clawed along the muscles of his arms.

"Yes," he said, urging her to dig into his skin harder.

All those practiced meditative breaths could help him hold out a few minutes, but not much more than that. "God, Madison, you feel so good."

As he steadied himself, looking down at this woman who was everything to him, his thrusts took on a new and different rhythm. It was beautiful. She was beautiful.

He memorized every curve and every movement. Every pleasure he could bring her. Then he stopped.

"What is it?" she asked, concern flashing across her flushed face as she panted.

As he breathed hard, he could feel his expression contorting. Her serious glance and wrinkled brow forced him to return a breathy laugh.

"I'm fine. I just need a moment." He was solemn, but sweet. "I've never been this close without reaching for a condom. Ever. And, God, you're squeezing me within an inch of my life. I never want it to end. I need to make it last."

Madison wrapped her arms around his neck, beginning her own slow thrusts. "You say that like it'll never happen again. And that might be a problem because I'm getting cold."

Wrapping both arms around her waist, he slid his thumb to her firm little clit.

"Then I'll warm you up," he said, circling his thumb and controlling the pace of their ride in the water. "But I *will* take my time."

Moving his mouth down to her breast, he sucked in her pert nipple, teasing it with his teeth before sucking it hard. She muffled her sounds.

"No." His command was dissatisfied and low. "No holding back. Not now. I need to hear you."

He felt the tiniest tremors building along the length of his dick. God, he wanted it too. Slamming himself deep inside, he forced those throaty screams out of her, satisfied as they echoed across the lake.

"Now, baby. Come for me, Madison."

His hoarse demand drove them over the edge together. The walls of her pussy clamped hard around his staff, milking him as he erupted. His legs buckled beneath the intensity of his own climax.

Alex tumbled backward, taking Madison with him as they dropped with a large splash into the water, letting their loud climaxes spill over into laughter.

~

Sharing the plush bath sheet made way for more cuddling and less drying. Their hair stayed damp and dripping as they helped each other dress. Alex worried as the evening chill rolled in.

He snagged her jacket off the ground, anxious to retrieve the ring before sliding her jacket on her. His hand dove into the first pocket. Empty. In the second pocket, he could feel two items in his grip. When he withdrew and unclasped his hand, alarm set in.

"Shit!"

"What? Did it slip out?" Madison asked. But seeing his palm spread wide, it was obvious the ring was there. Next to it was a small blinking bead. "What's that?"

"It's a tracker," a sultry voice said from behind them.

The woman's footsteps were slow as she took her time approaching them. The deepening darkness didn't help, but even as a silhouette, her tall legs and long hair were unmistakable. And deliberately walking toward them.

"Hello, Alex."

It was her. The seductive ghost from his past suddenly hell-bent on a haunting. An inferno's flame who never took *no* for an answer.

Sure, he might have hungered for her over the years. Even craved her touch in the best and worst ways. But he'd long ago abandoned the thought of it.

Alex held his ground between the angel of his future and the devil from his past. His step was deliberate toward the insistent intruder.

Now, faced with her smoldering gaze and bright red lips, the raw reality of his needs and wants stripped away every thought at all. All but one.

Madison.

CHAPTER 21

MADISON

MADISON WATCHED as Alex drew away from her in an obviously calculated move.

His full-body block was her fortress, and Madison's heart raced as she recognized it. He'd done it once before, in a street brawl right outside his office building. Three against one. But pitted against Alex, those thugs hadn't stood a chance.

Would she?

The woman who approached was unmistakable, despite blending into the twilight. The voluptuous, shadowy figure emerged in a body-hugging leather jacket and skintight jeans, every inch a predator on the prowl.

It was the woman who'd helped Madison collect herself in the break room. And, she suspected, might have done more. *J*, who'd given Madison no more than a letter for her name and a promise they would meet again.

Big surprise. She kept her word.

By the purr of her painted lips and the lust in her eyes, it was easy to see *J* and Alex had a past. No doubt an intimate one.

Well, you and a few hundred others, lady.

But why was she here, hunting them down like an alligator Birkin? A stalker?

What kind of deranged stalker hikes across twenty-five miles of wilderness in wedge boots?

Madison watched the standoff between this woman and Alex, anxious for him to make his move. By his hard eyes and ready stance, it was clear that whatever past he and J shared, they were far from cordial now.

"Hello, Jordan." His voice was cold and hard, slicing the air with a harsh tone that was unrecognizable to Madison.

Jordan. So that's what the J stands for.

With his finger and thumb, Alex crushed the blinking beacon, killing it before he hurled it into the lake. "What do you want?"

"I needed to see you. To talk with you. Alone."

Alex only chuckled, clearly unamused. Casually, he pocketed his hands and turned his face to the mansion behind Jordan. There, a red beam twinkled from the roof.

"Well, I'm not alone. And I don't just mean Madison. Turn around," he said.

Cutesy and spry, Jordan did a little dance as she turned in that direction. She gave no reaction to the sight except the lightest chirp from her lips. The bright red laser beam shot down the grassy slope from the mountaintop manor, disappearing into her chest.

Madison held her breath, realizing Jordan had just become a target.

"And now back," Alex said sternly.

Just as she did the first time, Jordan moved seductively to complete the turn, to find a new beam hitting her from across the lake.

Out of nowhere, two separate snipers were in position and ready, prepared to shoot a woman who apparently needed no introduction.

"As you can see, I'm not alone," Alex said, but if Jordan had a care in the world, she masked it well and simply smiled.

Pressing a hand to Alex's back, Madison softly said, "Alex." It was a worthless plea—not saying more to help a woman who seemed to have gone out of her way to help her.

"You misunderstand, Alex. I didn't mean you. I don't need to see *you*. I need to speak with your beautiful bride-to-be." Jordan raised her voice, hurling it past Alex to its intended recipient. "I need to talk with you, Madison. Alone."

"Me?" Curious, Madison tried to move forward, but Alex held her back with a protective hand, preventing her from stepping any further into the volatile area.

"That's not going to happen, Jordan." Alex's words were final, and perhaps not just to Jordan. "You want to talk, make an appointment."

"Stone already explained why we can't do that."

Before her eyes, Madison watched as the battle to gain the upper hand unfolded.

Alex crossed his arms over his chest. "Well, if you two are together, there's an appointment already set up. We'll see you then."

Without explanation, Alex whisked Madison to his side, keeping her from the gunmen's line of sight as he steered them both toward the house.

Jordan stayed in place, lifting her voice high. "Don't you want to know why Jack was killed?"

Madison stopped short, and Alex did too. She glanced at him, and based on his pensive expression, he knew more than he could share at that moment.

Dismissing his warning glance, Madison did what she knew she shouldn't do. Pulling from Alex's protective embrace, she stepped forward, stopping just shy of the potential line of fire. Cautiously, she closed in just enough to say what she needed to, knowing Jordan was an absolute temptress. A cunning wolf in skintight sheep's clothing.

For a moment, Madison stayed locked in Jordan's gaze, doing her best to shake off her power stare and intimidation. Still, Jordan's provocative allure and unmistakable badass vibe were harder to ignore.

The tension was obvious. Standing before some lethal supermodel from Alex's past, Madison was grateful to be cloaked in enough darkness that how wretched she must look after their swim might be missed.

Despite her makeup-free face and dripping hair, Madison spread her feet and crossed her arms over her chest, desperate to come off more as Cujo and less as a soaking-wet kitten. Because this woman, whoever she was, just brought up Jack as if he were bait.

Unsettled, Madison stayed calm and lifted a brow. "Our position is clear. See you at the appointment." With that said, she turned and hurried past Alex to head back to the house.

"I'm sure you can find your way back," Alex said to Jordan over his shoulder before catching up to Madison.

They walked quietly. Sedately. A few steps in, his arm wrapped around her. It would almost be romantic if not for the disturbing intrusion by a likely old flame of Alex, and a new stalker for Madison.

Lucky me.

Madison broke the uncomfortable silence as they traversed the grass. "Alex?"

He cleared his throat. "Yes?"

"So, that woman. Jordan. I met her today."

"What?" His voice was noticeably strained but remained low as his grip on her tightened.

"I thought it was just happenstance that she found me."

"Found you? Where?"

Oh, you know. Wedged between a watercooler and the wall, eavesdropping on my coworkers speculating that the conference room is where the reverse-harem magic happens.

Madison shrugged. "Around the office."

"She made it past the lobby of DGI?" Alex stopped, but her arm around his waist urged him on, keeping him moving.

"Yes. And now this woman has tracked me down to the middle of the Adirondacks. Where, come to find out, you hired two sharpshooters and had them at the ready."

"I didn't hire them," Alex said, adding to the mystery.

Sensing the tension in him, she said, "There's something I have to know," as they took the back patio steps to the house.

Alex leaned in to open the door, ushering her through. "Anything you want to know, I'll tell you," he said, assuring her as he secured the door and shut the curtains.

Once inside, she clung to him, letting his arms wrap around her. His comfort let her breathe.

Wide-eyed, she looked up at him. "Exactly how many people were watching us during our, um, wet-and-wild water sports?"

"My guess? At least three," he said with a shrug and an innocent smile. He stroked her hair, then tenderly cupped her cheek. "I swear, this wasn't as orchestrated as it seemed. I had no idea anyone was around until I saw the sniper laser. But it's probably a good idea to ratchet up the protection."

Holding her tightly, he smoothed his hands across her back and kissed her tenderly on the forehead. His words were soft. "Let's just say that from now on, I'll be treating you like royalty. Better, even. I'll have more security around you than a princess."

Madison's protest was weak. "Just for a while."

His mouth soothed her pouting lips with a kiss. "Promise."

She kissed him back before being hit by a wave of panic. "What about Jess and Mark?"

Alex glanced away, scrunching his face. "Well, the sniper on the roof was probably Mark."

Madison gasped as she sank against him, realizing Mark must have gotten an eyeful. Mortified, she buried her face in Alex's solid chest.

"He wasn't alone," Jess called out, waltzing down the stairs with binoculars strapped around her neck and a large bowl in her hands. "Someone had to bring the popcorn."

Madison shook her head with an embarrassed whimper.

"Hey," Jess said, "I made sure Mark covered his eyes the whole time." Her chuckle was light as she laid a hand on Madison's shoulder. "Don't worry, you both were dressed by the time Mark got into position. Seriously, are you all right?"

Madison grabbed a few pieces of popcorn. "Yes. No. Maybe? Who's Jordan? Why was she tracking me? And who was the other sniper?"

"*Snipers,*" Jess said, stressing the last *s*. "My brothers live on a few of the acres, tending the land. They're vets, and do everything from forestry to basic bodyguard work when needed. And if there's one thing Bishop men like, it's getting back in the action. The shorter the notice, the better. I texted them when Mark picked up your friend," she said to Alex.

Alex scoffed. "She's not my friend."

Worried, Madison asked, "Should we go somewhere safe?"

"Nowhere's safer than here," Mark said, double-stepping it down the stairs, one hell of a scoped rifle hanging from a strap over his shoulder. He pointed to the windows. "The glass isn't just bulletproof. It can withstand the blast from standard-issue grenades."

"For the record, you were right about our need for security upgrades," Jess said, tossing a kernel of popcorn into his mouth before giving him a peck on the lips.

Mark lifted a brow to Alex. "Whoever that was, she triggered the detectors a few miles back. That crazy cat woman moves fucking fast, and the proximity detectors lost her as she closed in on the lake. But I had your six. Friend of yours?"

Clearly exasperated, Alex shot back, "For the love of God, she's not my friend."

The three of them blinked at him in disbelief.

"Fine. But if she's my friend, she's just become yours too, Mark. *That* would be Jordan Stone."

"Another one?"

"And those are just the ones we know about."

Alex corralled them all to the oversized couches, promising to tell them everything.

But Madison guessed he would probably leave out a thing or two.

CHAPTER 22

MADISON

LATER THAT EVENING, Madison watched from the bed as Alex sent a few quick texts. Once he finished, he painted on a smile as he slid in under the covers. His body moved to hers, and he pulled her back against his chest. Curled up in the solid arms of the man she loved, Madison could only think of him.

Despite quietly holding her, he was stiff, tension filling every muscle of his frame. He was preoccupied, which meant he must be strategizing.

"Mind if I interrupt?" she asked with a smile, tilting her head back toward his.

Alex let out a light laugh. "Was I thinking that loudly?" He kissed her lips.

She skated her fingers across his cradling arm. "Oh, I can feel every bit of your restless energy. I know when there's a disturbance in the force. And," she said carefully, tiptoeing into her next words, "it's obvious you and Jordan have a past."

"Madison—"

"*Shh*, let me finish," she said gently. "I know you two were more than casual acquaintances, but that doesn't matter. Not a bit."

With that, he moved back, turning Madison to face him. He studied her eyes, analyzing the truth in her words.

"Come on. I'm with the legendary Alex Drake. I'm far from the first woman you've bedded. Light years away, maybe." When an amused and exaggerated smile emerged from his lips, she added, "And it's not exactly like you were my first."

His proud grin soured to an instant sulk. Madison felt the vibration of his growl ripple through her, forcing a giggle as she nuzzled into him.

"Let's imagine I am," he said with a playful grin.

"And maybe we could imagine I'm friends with Jordan." Madison's fingers pressed against his lips, quieting him before he could speak. "I need to be ready to deal with her. It's obvious she wants to speak with me. *Alone*, as she put it in her ridiculously sultry way, and I have a sneaking suspicion she's the kind of girl who gets what she wants."

"So are you," he said matter-of-factly. "What do you need?"

"To know what to expect. Tell me about her."

His expression uneasy, Alex ran his fingers through her hair. "I don't know her as well as you might think. And even then, I don't know much. Our encounter was . . . brief." He swallowed hard at the last word, but Madison urged him on with a nod. "I know she'll use her sexuality when she can."

"Who could blame her? I would too, if I had it in spades the way she does."

Alex's lips descended on hers. "You do," he whispered, lightly rubbing his nose against her cheek.

Her head returned to his chest. "Okay, so she's sexy and she knows it. Anything else?"

"Yes." His hand trailed down her back, pulling her in. "She'll try to lure you. With something that, no matter how trivial it may seem to others, will be important to you." He blew out a long breath. "Dammit, Madison, I don't like it."

"Like what?" she asked, feigning innocence.

"That you're going to see her. But you are, aren't you?"

She stroked his chest. "Not exactly. I'm just not going to stop her from seeing me, but I can't make it seem too easy for her to get me alone. I'll have more of an advantage if she underestimates me. Gives me a chance to learn how she operates. Especially since she may have tipped off Fife's team about some corporate espionage."

"What?" Alex exclaimed, practically sitting up.

Patting his chest, Madison urged him to lie back down. "I'm not sure about it. It's just a hunch. But I can't figure out she would do that. Is she trying to sway me? Make me feel like I owe her? I need to let her closer, in a way that makes her think she holds all the cards."

Alex pulled her hand to his lips, kissing her knuckles sweetly, and softly wiggled the ring hugging her finger. He clasped her hand to his chest. "Well, those who underestimate you tend to get burned. And in this world of burn or be burned, my money's on you. Fortune favors a bold, brave beauty with fire in her soul."

"Might you be *fortune* in this scenario?" she whimsically mused.

"I am . . . and I'd love to feel the heat of your fire."

They kissed, and she welcomed his body between her legs, his hard cock firm against her core.

"Oh, one more thing," she whispered, adjusting her hips to the perfect position.

"And what would that be?" he murmured as his lips nibbled across her neck.

"Remember how we said no more secrets?"

Halting mid-kiss, he said warily, "Yeah?"

"Until this is all over, that's off the table. I don't want to risk inadvertently tipping your hand. Whatever it is you're planning, you can't let me know."

"What makes you think I'm planning anything?"

Sweetly, she brushed his lips with hers until they kissed.

Without questioning her further, he whispered, "I'll make you a deal, Ms. Taylor. After tonight, I promise to keep you in the dark, but only on one condition."

"What's that?" she said softly, enjoying the weight of his body on hers.

"Tonight, you have to keep me somewhere dark. And preferably deep."

The head of his cock slid to the entrance of her heat while he trailed hot, open-mouthed kisses delicately across her shoulder.

"Deal," she gasped, barely getting the word out before Alex forced upon her the firmness of his position.

CHAPTER 23

ALEX

Manhattan

By late Monday afternoon, Alex had taken every precaution, making the necessary arrangements to receive one—or more than one—Jordan Stone. As the CEO of a company specializing in next-generation surveillance and reconnaissance equipment, he used every technology available, all of which were at his fingertips.

The appointment booked in his calendar for him and Madison was simply marked PRIVATE. Jordan Stone would not be meeting them. Instead, the fake name of J. Slate would. Fife understood the VIP guest would arrive through a back entry of DGI's Manhattan headquarters, with him being the one and only gatekeeper.

Alex couldn't risk entry into his office, or any of his executive suites or conference rooms. Who knew what sorts of devious devices would be planted by these operatives?

Oh, that's right. He would.

Microscopic monitoring, retractable recording devices, and nano-tracking equipment the size of pinheads were par for the course. He'd grown a multibillion-dollar empire by developing and selling these covert gems to corporate giants and nation states. Today, he needed to ensure they weren't used against *him*.

With new cameras on every floor, he now had visuals on everyone who entered. Even the very persistent Jordan herself. And a sweeper crew, so that wherever any Jordan Stone went, the team would follow, ensuring a full scan and cleanup.

A few small conference rooms were scheduled for renovation on the second floor. The pre-demolition site was perfect for such a meeting. They only needed Stone and Jordan to arrive, and Operation Shadow would commence.

Alex sent a text.

ALEX: Anything?
PACO: Already tracking. Shouldn't we warn Madison?
ALEX: No. Per her instructions.
PACO: Surveillance mode?
ALEX: Hell yes. And we'll interrupt if she looks distressed.

With that, the ping of his cell phone alerted him that his visitor had arrived. Alex scrolled to the highest favorite on his phone and clicked it.

"Madison, Fife texted me. He's here, and he's alone."

"*He* this time?" Madison asked. "It's like we're dealing with a shape-shifter. Okay, I'll meet you down there."

"Love you."

"Love you too."

But before the call with Madison ended, he heard the words repeated again through the phone in a familiar sultry voice.

"Love you too," Jordan said.

The line disconnected.

CHAPTER 24

MADISON

MADISON GLANCED up to find Jordan Stone standing in the doorway to her office. In her pencil skirt, high ponytail, and black-rimmed reading glasses, she looked like an executive. A very hot, strips-on-the-side-to-afford-her-Ferrari executive, but one, nonetheless.

"Mind if I have a seat?" Jordan entered the office, closing and then locking the door behind her.

"Please do. You must be tired after that hike." Madison hoped her tone came off less cocky and more campy. Based on Jordan's smirk, who could say?

Overall, she wasn't sure if Jordan was there to recruit her, seduce her, or skin her and make herself a Madison suit, perfect for walking down the aisle in the hopes of marrying Alex.

Seriously, it was hard to tell.

Jordan took several long strides into the office, rounding Madison's desk and making herself comfortable on the edge of it. She pulled something small from her cleavage, then slightly hiked up her skirt, allowing her butt to glide further back on the desk.

Relieved, Madison watched as Jordan crossed her toned, bare legs, grateful for the lack of a money shot. The little device was pressed. When it clicked, Jordan explained.

"I just need to ensure we're really alone. This will jam any pesky listening devices."

Madison rested back in her chair. "You're sure determined to see me. What do you want?"

"It's not what I want, Madison. It's what *we* want. And when I say we, I'm not talking the royal *we*, like I'm tight with Queen Elizabeth or part of the mob. I'm talking about you and me."

Stretching her leg forward, Jordan slid the side of her six-inch stiletto against Madison's outer thigh. The move was playful. They could have been lounging at the pool, chatting about the cute guys at the bar.

Prepared, Madison didn't stop Jordan. Instead, she analyzed her. Her approach, her mannerisms, even her shade of lipstick. She understood why Alex changed when he briefly discussed her.

Jordan was different. For Alex, Madison imagined she'd have to be. But her mystique was so unusual. And disarming. Captivated, Madison listened attentively.

"At the end of the day," Jordan said, "you and I want the same thing, but this only works if you're in. If you're not, no skin off my nose. I'll be on my merry way, never to darken your door again."

Letting her intrigue lead the discussion, Madison leaned in, equally coquettish in her question. "And what exactly is it *we* want?"

Jordan's smile grew as she bent down, her nearly pitch-black eyes dancing with delight as she took a long peek down Madison's blouse. "For starters, a chance to work very closely together."

Holding out her hands, Jordan urged Madison to take them. She did. Jordan's thumbs brushed the top of Madison's knuckles, soothing in a femme Nikita sort of way.

"Your ring is stunning," Jordan said, admiring it. "Jewelry can be so personal. So intimate. Really sends a message. Now, Alex could have bought you anything . . . a rock as big as your face. But he kept it to a size and style that would suit you. It's undoubtedly flawless, unrivaled in its brilliance. But I have a sneaking suspicion the real statement isn't about the diamond at all. Right? It's inscribed, isn't it?"

Surprised, Madison nodded, trying not to look overly impressed under Jordan's observant eyes.

"Something small, obviously, and highly meaningful to the two of you. For sure, it's less than five words . . . maybe three."

Madison held her breath, wondering if Jordan could actually recite the inscription, *I'm all in*. But she quickly lost interest, moving on to the bracelet on

Madison's other wrist. Slowly, Jordan turned it, letting the exquisite tennis bracelet catch the light. The diamonds twinkled like fire.

"Now, this one puzzles me. Granted, it's utterly amazing. But it doesn't seem to suit you like the ring. Like he got it before he really knew you. Or maybe he didn't buy it at all, letting some lackey do his bidding. Am I close?"

Madison said nothing.

"Hmm, you hardly strike me as someone who wears things for flash, and I'm not even sure you'd wear it just because Alex gave it to you. Knowing Alex Drake, he's given you a warehouse full of precious jewels. But deep down, your nouveau riche status doesn't hold your interest. Somehow, your personality seems a little, I don't know, meeker, perhaps. A bit less ball-busting and slightly more Stepford wife."

Jordan's eyes were bright with mischief as they met Madison's. "Why are you wearing it?"

As Madison looked down and stammered to speak, ready to make up something on the fly, Jordan squeezed her hands firmly.

"Oh, no need for that. Teeing up a deception? Don't bother. It won't work on me. You're too transparent. Keep me guessing, if you must, but don't lie. Much like the bracelet, it doesn't quite suit you."

With a brush of her fingers against a specific area of Madison's arm, Jordan reassured her with a grin. "No hives. Good. I won't worry I'm making you uncomfortable."

Madison had no idea how Jordan could know about that, but she did, and she was right. Madison wasn't nervous around her. The shock of that alone should have triggered a full-body breakout. There was a strange kinship between them that Madison prayed didn't remotely come close to romantic.

Jordan smiled. "Besides, your sweetly innocent inability to lie is exactly why I'm here."

CHAPTER 25

ALEX

ALEX KEPT STONE WAITING, preoccupied with watching the monitor and trying to figure out what the hell was going on between Jordan and Madison. By the looks of it, Jordan was making a move on his girl.

Which is bullshit, fucked up, and wrong.

Hot, but wrong.

The disrupter Jordan brought was anticipated. Its strength, however, was not, and seriously blew his tech out of the water. Attentive, he watched from the old-school coaxial-cable video feed. When high tech failed you, low tech was the ace in the hole. Every time.

A mic with any real range would be easily blocked. He tried anyway. Of course, it was jammed by Jordan's little toy.

Helplessly, he clenched his teeth and analyzed the feed. Per Madison's instructions, she had no idea about their surveillance. It prevented her from tipping their hand.

After an unusual amount of talking and touching, Jordan finally left. Madison also left her office. She was running late for their meeting with Stone and would likely rush to get there.

Alex sent a text as he raced after her.

ALEX: *She's on the move.*
PACO: *Got her. I'll keep you posted.*

Alex caught up with Madison as she arrived at the conference room door. Tightly, he pulled her close. "You all right?"

Frowning, she searched his eyes. "I don't know." She looked away. "Will she keep her word?"

His hands cupped her jaw, forcing her eyes back to his. "What did she offer you?"

"I . . . it's just . . . just tell me. Will she keep her word?"

Uncertain, Alex shrugged, shaking his head with a sigh. "I don't know. Probably. She did with me."

Opening her mouth, Madison seemed ready to share the details of Jordan's tempting offer when the door to the conference room flew open. Stone's impatience at their lateness melted before their eyes as his sincere gaze fell on Madison.

"Madison Taylor," he both asked and said at once, as if finding it hard to believe the woman was actually standing before him. Wrapping her hand in both of his, he smiled. "It's very nice to finally meet you. You're as beautiful as your brother always said."

Keeping her hand in his, he led her into the room, followed by Alex. "I'd always hoped we'd meet one day." His eyes still searching hers, he asked Alex, "Did you tell her who I am?"

Madison answered. "You're the handler that recruited my brother for his mission."

Reverently, Stone nodded. "I promised Jack I'd make it up to him someday."

"So, Jordan was telling the truth?"

There was no hiding his reaction. "Jordan? She was here?"

Alex chimed in. "That's why we're late."

Stone huffed before he smiled, turning sheepish between the two.

"I swear that woman has serious control issues. I told her I was meeting with you. Never mind. It doesn't matter." Straightening to his full height, he could easily pass for a senator or a diplomat. There was elegance in his plea as he asked, "Will you, Madison?"

Protective, Alex laid his hands softly on her shoulders as he gritted out, "Will she what?"

"Give us a minute, Mr. Stone," she said, taking Alex's arm and leading him out of the room. They crossed the hall, entering another conference room under renovation.

Seeing the construction crew, Alex made an announcement. "Gentlemen," he boomed above the noise, and the clamor quieted. "Why don't you take off for a bit. Enjoy the break room at the end of the hall. Come back in twenty."

The men filed through the door, leaving Alex and Madison to their privacy. Making her way past the pieces of metal, drywall, and debris, Madison crossed the room to stand at the large window overlooking the bustling street below. Alex let her wander, pocketing his hands. Though always protective, he remained patient.

"It's ironic, really. This room is in the swirl of a storm and looks exactly how I feel inside. And yet the outside world always goes on." A look of longing filled her face. "I love people watching. I get glimpses into what life could be like for me someday. If I could move on." Wiping away a tear, she glanced back. "But maybe if I had real closure. Maybe . . ."

Alex's patience was fleeting. In three steps, he had her in his arms.

"You were right," she said. "Jordan lured me with something important. Something meaningful, maybe to no one other than me. Even just the possibility . . . I have to do it."

"Do what?"

"Oh, not much. Just enter an ultra-secure intelligence agency with no cover to speak of, retrieve an item, or items, or documents, and possibly data, because they're not actually sure what I'm specifically looking for. After that, I hand over whatever we find to the Stone twins, and cross my fingers in the hope that they keep their word."

Alex sucked in a breath. "Is that all?"

"I have to do it."

"*You?*" Alex asked softly. "I think you mean *we.*"

"No, me. It has to be *me.*"

After a soft kiss, he lowered his forehead to hers. "Not happening. Not without me." When she shook her head, he opted to switch gears to avoid an argument. Brushing an errant strand of hair behind her ear, he asked softly, "And what would you get out of all this?"

Filled with hope, her eyes were pleading. "If Jordan keeps her word, and you said she probably would, somehow they'll reinstate Jack's record. He'll be honored for the military hero he was."

Madison held her breath as she stared at Alex, hoping that as they discussed it, he would come to the same conclusion she already had.

CHAPTER 26

MADISON

WHEN MADISON and Alex returned to the conference room where Stone waited, they found he was gone, leaving a small note behind. Alex read it aloud.

J said it's a go.
We'll be in touch.

"Why does Jordan think it's a go?" Alex asked.

Madison cradled the hard line of his stubbled jaw, soothing him with a kiss. "She needed an answer. I told her yes."

"It's not a go." When she looked up, puppy-dog eyes to the max, Alex sighed before tucking her into a reassuring embrace, muttering gruffly, "Fine. Maybe it's a go, but you're not going alone, and not without training."

"Training?" she asked. Not that it was a bad idea, but training—at least the type she imagined—would take a hell of a lot longer than they had. "Is there time?"

He picked up the note and slipped it into the pocket of his blazer. "Twenty-four hours is plenty. And I know just the right secret weapon to help us out. Someone else who's had a run-in or two with Jordan."

"So, you weren't the only man in her life?" Madison teased.

He laughed. "Not by a long shot, and it's not a man."

525

Madison let out a little huff. "Of course, another woman from your past. Another supermodel, no doubt."

Alex smiled and shrugged in shy agreement.

"And exactly how many more of your bed-post notches will be walking the halls of DGI before our wedding? At this rate, I'll have to get with the guys in PR to issue nametags and hand out swag bags. And we'll need to rush the ad for the yearbook committee. Hell, if every woman from your past shows up to the 'Alex Drake Bon Voyage' to puss-prowling, it'll be the social media event of the year."

"Hey, don't forget we're gonna need lots of velvet ropes and an extra-long red carpet," he threw out before sweeping her into a long kiss and a wonderfully tight embrace. "And for the record, Ms. Taylor, I never bedded Crystal. Let's just say I'm not her type. But Crystal is good, tough, and the only other person I know who has had any connection with Jordan. I've tried to get as much intel as possible about Jordan from her, but Crystal seemed a little tight-lipped."

A fresh grin appeared on Madison's face. *Alex couldn't pry open some tight lips? That's gotta be a first for him.* "So, anything useful?"

"Not much. From what I gather, Crystal wasn't a recruit. At least, not like I was. Sounds like their paths tended to cross. Perhaps still do."

"Cross how? Like, they're friends?"

"My gut tells me they're definitely not cozy BFFs. Maybe they just run in the same circles now and again. Seems like they both stay in their swim lanes and maintain boundaries."

"Well, that's reassuring," Madison drawled, paper-thin sarcasm at its finest.

"Don't worry about Crystal. She's been our best-of-the-best for years. We bring her in when the situation calls for something unconventional. Where, frankly, we're not really sure what the hell we're up against. She always comes through. But . . ."

Alex checked his watch, reconsidering. "You won't get to meet her until tomorrow morning. We have to fly her in. In the meantime, you and I can work on some basic tactics and training."

He kissed Madison's hand and kept it in his, leading her out. She stopped, holding him back by the elbow.

"Alex, before we do any of that, I need to ask you something, and I need you to be completely honest with me."

"Always," he assured her.

With a sigh, she flung her arm at him. "Does this bracelet suit me?"

He glanced at the bracelet, then with confidence, back at her. "Don't diamonds suit everyone?"

"Just tell me, does it?"

"They're diamonds. Both Marilyn Monroe and Paco Robles swear by them. Why? Is something wrong?"

Avoiding the scrutiny of his gaze, she looked back at the bracelet she adored. Deflated, she agonized about what to say. Madison loved everything about the bracelet—from Alex offering it to her more than once, to Paco insistently wrapping it around her wrist.

It was precious beyond the jewels it held. But her sentiments were now tainted by the doubt Jordan had planted in her mind.

"Here, give it to me," Alex said, holding out his hand.

"Why?" she asked, holding her arm to her chest, suddenly protective of the bracelet at his suggestion.

"Well, if you don't want it, I'll take it. I've actually been eyeing it for something. By the size of it, I'd say it might actually be perfect."

"Perfect for . . ."

"A Tiffany and Co. ten-and-a-half-carat cock ring. Nothing says *my girl's getting it good all night long* like a blinged-out D, keeping me erect for hours on end by a band of brilliant square-cut diamonds encased in eighteen-karat white gold."

He took her wrist, gently turning it back and forth, studying the bracelet closely. "But by the way it's dangling, I just need to make sure it's not going to be too tight . . ."

He rushed to undo his pants.

"Alex!" Madison shouted with an innocent swat to his chest.

He whisked her into his embrace, kissing her growing smile.

Taking a breath, he dropped his lighthearted demeanor. "Look, there's something I need to tell you about Jordan. About how she's the best at what she does. Maybe the best in the world."

Madison frowned, not liking where this was going. *We went from his bedazzled shaft to scorching-hot Jordan? God, do I want to hear this?*

Cupping her face in both of his large hands, he softly stroked her cheeks with his thumbs. "Nobody, and I mean nobody, can top her at the mindfuck. She's messing with your head. Don't let her in," he whispered into Madison's mouth, soothing her with a warm kiss.

He scooped up her hand, adding more advice. "And no matter what anyone says, this ring is definitely you," he told her while pressing his loving lips to her fingers.

Madison smiled. Ring or no ring, cock ring or no cock ring, the one thing that suited her perfectly and without a doubt was Alex.

CHAPTER 27

CRYSTAL

Seattle, Washington

TAKING in the views and the fresh air from her penthouse balcony atop Seattle's Loews Hotel, Crystal could finally breathe. Her assignments always took her far from home, placing her in the line of fire more often than not.

Here, high above Elliott Bay, the world faded away and she could relax. With a vodka lemon drop in her hand, she enjoyed her sip along with the sweeping views spanning from the Space Needle to the Seattle Great Wheel.

As her purring fur baby, George, twined between her legs, she reached down to pet him, looking forward to an evening of easing into her favorite pastime—her passion. Corey.

Corey was taking his time in the shower, washing away both the grime and tension from his day. He was often tense, and her role was to ensure he had a night of unadulterated stress relief—which would be her relief too.

The quiet was broken by a distinctive chime from her phone, a unique notification tone that meant an evening filled with pleasure and pain would be cut short.

Alex Drake?

Crystal took another sip before dealing with the message.

ALEX: *Jet picking you up tonight. Usual time. SeaTac.*

Shit. That meant she'd need to be at the Seattle–Tacoma International Airport in just a few hours.

At least she'd be flying in style. If there was one thing Alex Drake was good for, it was rolling out the red carpet. A luxury jet was just the beginning.

They'd talk money after the job was done. If anything, he'd be generous. Cash and cars were givens. This penthouse had her name on the deed as a bonus from her last DGI gig. Crystal could count on another big windfall. That is, if she delivered.

After another sip of her drink, Crystal slowly lowered her martini glass, revealing her soaking-wet and very built husband emerging from the bathroom. The towel wrapping his chiseled waist was disappointing, though the droplets of water still clinging to his damp hair, chiseled chest, and muscular arms weren't. Corey was a soaking-wet masterpiece.

His scowl drew her attention away from her ogling and would need to be dealt with. When he crossed those lickable arms tight across his rugged chest, she gave him her undivided attention.

"What?" she asked, but she knew what.

"Phone in your hand. Drink finished. I'm guessing our night together is off."

His terse tone was deserved. Despite the ring on her finger, he'd been without her and her attentive ways for nearly a month. She'd promised her time to him, but it was a promise she'd have to break.

After setting aside the glass, Crystal slinked over to him. Lightly, her fingers brushed his burly chest, tracing down its center to his ripped abs before nestling in the tight edge of the towel. "It is what it is, babe. But—"

Watching his eyes and testing his reaction, she slid her fingers deeper. Her body pressed against his, and despite his fevered breaths and pounding pulse, he held to his training and remained still.

"Good boy," she said, letting her raspy words heat his neck. She licked several drops of water along his collarbone, content that it lifted his scowl.

"But you're leaving."

His out-of-turn comment was barely excusable. She sliced her fingernail into the tight skin beneath his towel, signaling a beginning to the night. If he made that mistake again, he'd suffer the consequences, ten o'clock flight be damned.

"Mmm. I've got a few hours," she whispered, giving his neck a terse nip.

His moan released. His abs tensed. And his cock tented the thick plush towel.

Looking down, it was clear he'd missed her a lot. She'd need to take her time. A slow burn was required. Otherwise, he'd be climaxing in a few minutes.

Tightening her grip on the edge of the towel, she yanked it from him, exposing that hard, throbbing cock she could practically taste. Licking her lips, she worked her fingernails along the lines of his torso, down to the muscles of his upper thighs. Careful to avoid the eager hard-on demanding her touch, she painted featherlight strokes along his skin.

By the agony of his expression, she was doing it right. His eyes slammed shut as he fought to maintain control.

"What do you want?" she asked, allowing him to speak.

He struggled a little, formulating his words as her finger began a long spiral at the base of his cock, twirling around and up until it grazed the head. With the other hand, she gripped him hard, forcing a gasp as his hands remained in their locked position behind his back. He tried to stay still.

With a single finger, she wiped the bead of precum from the choked head of his cock. "Watch me, Corey."

He did, opening his eyes to catch her opening her mouth and tasting him as she moved her finger to the back of her throat.

"I asked you what you want. Don't make me ask again."

The dark gray of his eyes pinned her. "To . . . give you a massage."

Her lips curled up, then brushed his. "Are you sure?"

Several items awaited her on the table. She grabbed one of her favorite clamps, not only because the pinch was hard, but Corey was especially responsive to this one.

"I like a long massage."

The flash of self-control behind his eyes appeared as it often did. His low tone and direct answer sent lightning to her core. "I'm sure," he said insistently.

Corey was there for her pleasure too. Neither of them knew how long she'd be gone. It would be torture—rubbing his hands across her as she groped and licked at his dick. Each of them knowing that until she allowed it, he wouldn't come.

Skillfully, she clamped him, and he let out a hiss.

"Remove my clothes," she demanded sweetly.

"Yes, Mistress."

CHAPTER 28

PACO

Manhattan

PACO FROWNED at the twinkling lights of the approaching jet far in the distance. He looked down at his phone, rereading the untimely texts that had summoned him here to DGI's private landing strip.

> ALEX: *Jet picking you up tonight.*
> ALEX: *90 minutes. Need you back.*
> ALEX: *More to come.*

Never mind that Paco had been in the middle of a world-class charity event in Dallas. At Alex's summons, he'd dropped everything. It wasn't the abrupt words that caught his attention. Or that Alex was asking. It was the last line. *More to come.*

More to come meant it was both important and classified. *More to come* meant time was of the essence. But what really grabbed his attention was that *more to come* was often code for *you're not going to love it, Paco, so don't ask.*

Fucker.

There he was just a couple of hours later, still in his tux, in the heart of the Big Apple. Who cared that he was the master of ceremonies for the premier affair? Or that he had been moments away from his favorite role—playing Cupid to what promised to be another power couple of the century?

Nooo. Instead, he was once again at Alex Drake's beck and call. Hauling his ass back to New York, only to be the welcoming committee for some unnamed big deal arriving that night.

Dammit, Alex.

Paco didn't know exactly what was up, but something. Something big. Alex wouldn't have one of his top fleet jets landing now if it weren't carrying one of his biggest fucking guns.

To prepare for the landing, Paco opened both winged doors of his Lamborghini and popped the trunk. He stepped back, unsettled as he glanced up at the cockpit windows as the plane came to a stop nearby.

Alarmed, he took a closer look. With the pilot slumped over and clearly unconscious, it was clear Paco's night had just begun.

Fuck! I am so not dressed for this.

Peeling away his bespoke tuxedo jacket, he carefully set it inside the car, then rolled up his shirtsleeves. He narrowed his eyes on the jet's automatic door as it opened, cascading into steps.

Cautiously, he approached. "Let's get this over with, Crys—"

Flying at his head was a fifty-pound Louis Vuitton duffel, and it was flying fast.

"Shit!" He jumped back, catching it solidly in his chest. With an annoyed huff, he set it in the trunk.

Her silhouette seemed to appear out of nowhere, backlit by the lights of the jet.

"Miss me, boo?" Crystal said, her sweet and sassy voice a precursor to her attempt at a hellacious punch.

Paco weaved, avoiding the blow. "Hey, not around the car!"

When he stepped away, she followed suit.

"With all that worry, it must be new. Damn, you change cars more than most men change underwear." She spun, gaining a burst of momentum for the kick she aimed at his face. Once again, a miss.

"Oh, come on, Crystal. We both know the man in your life isn't permitted the indulgence of underwear." Attack mode high, Paco threw several hard punches toward her. "How is Corey?"

"Great," she said, effortless in deflecting his blows. "Besides, I make it up to him in other ways." She threw out three punches in rapid succession, but Paco avoided them all.

He was ready for her fourth punch, catching it in the power of his grip. "I'd hardly call getting my ass cracked with a bullwhip a luxury."

With unrivaled momentum, he yanked her in, spinning her around and thrusting her arm up into her back, a measure to thwart any further resistance. Just in case, he followed up with a chokehold. With Crystal, it was best to be safe.

Summoning her unusual strength, she bounced back against him, springing forward to run up the side of his car. Crystal propelled herself high into the air, clearing his entire body as she flipped. As expected, her landing was Olympic caliber, a testament to her years of devotion to parkour.

Cursing under his breath, Paco raced to his car, kneeling at its side. Carefully, he examined the paint, softly running his finger over the area in question. "Dammit, if you scratched her . . ."

Crystal pulled a penlight from her pocket and crouched beside him, flooding the tight area in several passes. "Looks fine," she said, patting his back. "Despite their sex appeal, all my shoes are reinforced with silicone skids. No marks. No noise. They let me sneak up on all my favorite peeps."

Appeased, he nodded, and they stood.

"Are we done?" he asked.

She dusted off her sleeves. "Not quite," she said, grabbing him around the neck. For the moment, they hugged, patting each other briskly on the back. "Okay, we're done. For now," she warned with a smile, pulling away.

"Should I ask what happened to the pilot?"

"Oh, him? Some bullshit about why I couldn't land the plane."

"Tell me you didn't leave a mark."

"No. The technique I used on him was much more subtle. And I barely knew the guy. To be branded by me means you're someone extra special," she said with a wink.

Paco strolled to the passenger side of his Lamborghini, the gentleman in him ready to help her in. That was a mistake.

Crystal seized the opportunity to plant her ass in the driver's seat. He leaned in, unamused and glaring. Before he could do anything, her door was closed, and she was already firing up Hot Cherry.

"Come on, live a little. Besides, who taught you to drive?"

Paco gave it half a thought, irritated that he was now beginning to perspire.

Prying Crystal from his seat would lead to MMA round number two, and his chances of success were fifty-fifty at best. Stewing, he reluctantly took the passenger seat.

"Hey, that fancy sky cab didn't have much to eat," Crystal said. "I'm starving." Her words were just the straw to break the camel's back.

Shouting, Paco lost his cool. "Crystal, you are *not* taking my half-million-dollar Lambo to a drive-thru."

She sweetened her tone. "Now, I can see from your best Ken-doll getup that you were torn from a fancy-schmancy night with nothing but teaspoon-sized appetizers. You *nearly* worked up a sweat, and you've got a wicked case of the grumps. You and I both know nothing will hit the spot like a Big Mac meal."

"I'm not grumpy," he sulked under his breath.

She tapped a couple of buttons, closing the trunk and his door.

Lips crimped and scowl in full swing, Paco drummed his fingers in an irritated rhythm along his leg before he picked off an invisible piece of lint. "Fine," he said warily as he acquiesced. "Make it a number one. Large. With a Coke."

"That's more like it. Speaking of Coke, where the hell are the cup holders in this beast?" she teased.

Despite his glare, Paco enjoyed the moment she peeled out, looking forward to the sight of the nearest golden arches.

CHAPTER 29

MADISON

MADISON'S SLEEP the night before was restless, leaving her agitated for the day's training ahead.

Although Alex spent some time in the morning sharing what Madison now thought of as *Fundamentals of the Mindfuck*—that, along with a few basic moves did not an operative make. Madison was no more an agent than Alex was a showgirl or Paco was eight months pregnant.

From what Alex told her, the people she'd be dealing with—aka the two Jordan Stones and their ilk—weren't your garden-variety ex-spies. Those types were more like machines. Kill. Wipe for prints. Meet the next mark for a martini at Club Macanudo before a Broadway show.

Instead, she was working with an entirely different caliber of niche operative whose work was subtle and sophisticated. Their goal? Get what they needed and then vanish into thin air. No one would see them coming, and they wouldn't leave a trace.

Essentially, they were ghosts.

Alex seemed to have some insight into their standard operating procedure, an advantage he hoped to exploit. "We have to keep them from vanishing too soon," he said, reminding her of their usual disappearing act.

Correcting Jack's military record was purportedly their only objective. But Alex wanted to know more. Jordan hadn't emerged on the scene out of pure altruism. His goal was to find out why.

They, and Madison in particular, needed a tactical advantage.

Enter Crystal. Elegant. Strong. Smart. And most importantly, she had no prior sexual history with Madison's man.

In a private Defense and Tactical Training room at DGI headquarters, Madison greeted Crystal with open arms. Without tables or chairs in the space, they both stood. Crystal leaned along the wall of mirrors while Madison stood ready.

"I know a few moves," Madison said shyly, a little nervous. "But I'm worried if it really comes to a knock-down-drag-out girl fight, I'm gonna get my ass handed to me on a platter."

"Nah," Crystal said, her lips curled up in amusement. "Just to get some perspective, do you think I'm here to teach you to fight?"

Madison shrugged, giving her a timid "Uh-huh," and an uncertain nod.

"Well, you can relax. My reputation as a badass might precede me, but fighting is more of a hobby."

Crap. If this lesson required rote memory, Madison was screwed.

"Fighting is fun, but skills like that aren't learned overnight. We've got to find something you're good at and hone it. I promise you, whatever it is, we'll find it, and it's usually not what you think. Give me a little blind faith, and let's see where it goes. Okay?"

"Okay," Madison said, nodding firmly.

"Tell me what you're most worried about going into this."

Exasperated, Madison shrugged. "I feel like an average Jane at a superhero convention. I have nothing useful to add, and I'm terrified I'm going to let everyone down. I can't even lie with the least bit of conviction."

"Hmm," Crystal said, then moved the discussion along. "I hear you play poker?"

Cards, yes. Definitely. I'll bring a deck, and I can righteously spank Jordan with my wicked game of poker.

Weakly, Madison nodded.

Crystal took a step forward, stopping mere inches from Madison's face. "Your poker game is good, from what I hear."

Shy but proud, Madison agreed. "It's not terrible."

"So, there are two sides to Madison Taylor. On the one side, you dislike lying. If I strapped you to a lie detector, you'd fail. Your hands are probably sweating at just the thought of it."

"Yes," she said, hoping Crystal wasn't about to start an interrogation exercise.

Can I call a time out at waterboarding?

"And on the other hand," Crystal said, "your deception game is on point so long as it's for sport and not for real. Not for keeps."

"If I tee up a lie," Madison blurted, "I'll let everyone down. Even Jordan knew."

"Jordan Stone?" Crystal raised a brow.

Madison nodded, not realizing Alex hadn't told Crystal about their meeting. "And I've probably just let the cat out of the bag. Alex didn't tell you?"

Crystal shook her head. "Probably slipped his mind."

She took a good, long look at Madison, studying her from head to toe. It was unnerving, but for some reason, Madison stood still despite the heat rising in her cheeks.

Finally, Crystal again met her eyes and smiled. "I've got it. Work with me. We're going to play a little trick on your mind. Everything's a game, and at the same time, everything's for keeps."

"I'm not sure I understand."

"Don't worry. You won't, but your body will. You're very responsive, Madison. Your body is eager to express every thought and emotion."

Embarrassed, Madison tried to turn away, but Crystal spun her toward the mirror.

"It's a skill we can use," Crystal told her. "Allow your body to respond rather than react. You control what you share with the outside world. Give people only what you intend to. I'm going to give you a lesson, one I teach to very few people."

"Because it's remedial?" Madison joked.

"Because it requires a person who's highly responsive. That's something that can't be taught. You're the perfect candidate . . . and I'm sure Alex Drake thanks his lucky stars."

Flushed, Madison dropped her gaze.

"No." It was a command, not a request.

Instantly, Madison held her head high.

"Good. Look at yourself, Madison. You think your body betrays you with something as natural as a blush. You're worried it makes you vulnerable. But in your case, this vulnerability is pure gold. Exactly what we need."

Madison's breath hitched as Crystal stood behind her, moving her hands from the small of Madison's back, up to her shoulders, then down her arms.

"Breathe," she said low. "Relax."

Madison did her best as Crystal squeezed both of her wrists. The pressure wasn't painful, merely calming as it held her still.

Her breath tickled Madison's ear. "And you're going to learn to use that vulnerability because this is your strength. Your superpower. The most honest part of you. I'm going to take you through some exercises. No matter how uncomfortable you get, keep repeating these three words. Don't react. Respond."

Don't react.

Respond.

CHAPTER 30

ALEX

"WHAT DO YOU MEAN, she's gone?" he shouted.

It had been a long time since Alex Drake had flown into a rage. And by the looks on everyone's faces, it wasn't exactly unexpected.

Swallowing a mouthful of fries, Crystal shrugged. "You said teach her a skill, not hog-tie her to a chair. Which, for the record, I could have easily done."

Paco jumped on the Crystal-bashing bandwagon. "If his head explodes, you're cleaning it up."

Unconcerned, she gave him an eye roll.

Flipping the tails of his blazer behind him, Alex propped his hands on his hips. "Any idea where she went?"

After slurping the last of her Coke for an obnoxiously loud and drawn-out moment, Crystal said, "To meet Jordan."

Pacing, Alex flashed Paco a look, telepathically shouting *Save me before I kill her.* To his dismay, Paco simply nodded and grinned.

Crystal pointed a crisp fry his way. "All I know is she got a text from Jordan, and she was gone. But now you've got me all panicked about my Yelp rating, so how about I help you negotiate an arrangement with Stone?"

Alex froze mid-step. "You know Stone."

Chewing her fry, she answered. "Duh. I know everyone. Tell me you have his number. Because if you don't, I can't give it to you."

He knew Crystal wasn't being annoying. That would be a line she couldn't cross. Even for Alex Drake.

Fuck. Alex didn't have the number.

Wait. Maybe, he did.

From his wallet, he fished out the business card Stone had given him when they were in the bunker. Alex dialed the number listed on it, then pressed the button for speakerphone.

"Insurance Services," a man answered. It was Stone.

Crystal rolled her hand, mouthing the words *play along.*

"Yes, I need to check on my coverage for . . . stolen property," Alex said, keeping the conversation vague.

"Stolen property?" There was a momentary pause. "Of course, sir. I can have an adjustor at your place in an hour."

"He's got fifteen minutes," Alex said, insisting with the lethal calmness of a viper.

After a long silence that would have only been made worse with elevator music, Stone finally agreed. "Fifteen minutes."

"See you then." Alex disconnected the call.

Alex was unsurprised that Stone had managed to find his own way into the DGI building, bypassing security, but was relieved to see Mark on the man's heels.

"Where's Madison," Alex snapped at Stone.

"Your guess is as good as mine. Probably playing with Jordan."

Obviously, Stone was saying it to get a rise out of Alex. Throw him off his game.

Letting it slide, Alex demanded, "Call them back."

Stone shook his head. "Out of the question. At this point, it could compromise them both."

"Mark?" Alex asked.

Mark had already moved to the console, pulling up information and maps. "They're driving. If you're sending them where I think you are, they're en route."

"I don't control Jordan," Stone protested.

Alex snorted. "And I love how you think you can bullshit me. If anyone's the captain of the *S.S. Jordan Stone*, you are. Leave Madison out of it. I'll go in."

"Fine," Stone said with a sigh. "May I?" He headed to the console Mark had fired up. "But you'll only delay it, not stop it. Jordan would never take Madison against her will. She agreed."

Mark jumped in. "What is she, the devil?"

"The devil isn't nearly this manipulative," Alex said with a growl.

Stone sent his message and turned back around. "This play doesn't work without Madison. She has to be in."

"Well, that's not fucking happening," Alex said, ready to grab his fiancée the second she stepped through the door and lock her away.

Maybe I'll take her to Paris. She'll be mad, but a chocolate croissant will settle her down.

Seeming to read his mind, Stone said softly, "You can't control her, Alex."

"I can try."

Stone gave him a wry smile. "Like I can control Jordan? As we speak, Jordan is no doubt whispering sweet nothings in Madison's ear, promising she's the only one who can discover the truth and save Jack's honor. And much to my chagrin, she isn't wrong."

"You all should work together," Crystal said nonchalantly as she sat back and filed her nails.

Before Alex could ring her neck and use her head as a bowling ball, the phone rang. It was an incoming call to the landline phone that might be a dinosaur, but it still had a speakerphone.

"I believe that's for you," Stone said to Alex.

With the press of a button, Alex activated the speaker, not knowing if he'd be speaking to Jordan or Madison. "Hello?"

"Alex, listen to me. We don't have much time." It was Madison. Her voice was rushed, but not alarmed.

"Yes, I'm here."

"I need you to let me do this. Let *us* do this. Remember how I said all bets were off? On us keeping secrets?" What Madison meant was that she'd consented to Alex keeping secrets during this op, a ploy so she wouldn't inadvertently tip his hand.

"Yes," he said slowly.

"Well, it's a two-way street. I trust you. Trust me."

What the hell is she saying. Trust her? "I do. I'm just a little distrustful about the company you keep."

The sultry voice shouting, "I heard that!" in the background was quickly followed by, "Trust me too."

Alex ignored Jordan.

"I told them they should work together," Crystal said because Alex had already missed his chance to wring her neck.

"I agree," Paco said, siding with Crystal for the first time in forever.

"Please," Madison said softly, and her sweet voice was his undoing.

After a long moment, Alex agreed. "But new rules. You'll be taken by helicopter, and Paco will join you. Once you arrive, Paco will drive you in a DC-Metro DGI van. We'll be monitoring you. All of us."

"Deal," Madison and Jordan said in unison.

"And I want the play-by-play," Alex said quickly, negotiating on the fly.

"No," came from the phone, this time from Jordan. "You'll just second-guess me. Me and Madison."

Holy fuck, he was going to bludgeon Jordan. Bludgeon her, bread her, deep-fry her, and feed her to the monkeys at the zoo.

"Fine," he forced out through gritted teeth.

"Excellent," Stone said, clapping his hands once, and Alex glared at him.

"Oh, and Alex," Jordan sang. "We won't be able to stay and chat. We're under a terrible time crunch."

Madison said, "I'm sorry, Alex, she's right. From the looks of the map Jordan has up, we'll be somewhere in the middle of nowhere in about fifteen minutes."

Alex pulled in a deep breath. "We'll be here. Paco will have the van ready to go. But I need you to listen to me very carefully, Madison. I have an idea where you're going. It could be dangerous. You're not just jumping in the van and taking off. At the very least, I deserve a kiss."

He could feel Madison's smile through the phone. "Yes, Alex Drake, you deserve a kiss."

"What about my kiss?" Jordan teased, dancing dangerously close to getting it from his ass.

"How about you focus on the road? And keeping my fiancée in one piece?"

"Anything for you, Alex."

The call disconnected on their end, most likely by Jordan.

CHAPTER 31

ALEX

VIA HELICOPTER, Alex had moved their small team consisting of Mark, Crystal, and Stone to the secure bunker north of the city, as another helicopter had carried Paco to rendezvous with Madison and Jordan, and then drive them to Washington, DC.

As Alex's team gathered in the bunker's main control room, he heard Paco saying over the comm, "Just punching in the next directions. Taking off in a minute."

Alex and the others said nothing in acknowledgment. All communication was monitored, and the transmission was used to keep the signal steady.

In the driver's seat with the engine idling, Paco waited for the women to exit the DGI van as Alex, Mark, Crystal, and Stone watched the video of their every move projected by the discreet surveillance camera. There was no wiggle room. No forgiveness for a misstep. They were at entrance to the premier spy stronghold of the United States, about to flip the script on the puppeteers themselves. A clean entry was just the first in a long maze of obstacles ahead.

Alex's heart thundered and he could barely blink as he watched Madison step out of the van. He'd seen her for barely a moment as she got into the van before Paco had raced her and Jordan away.

But now it was different. He could drink in her image and take half a second to enjoy what he was seeing. Wonder if what he was watching wasn't Madison Taylor, but the soon-to-be Madison Drake.

Jordan barely drew his attention, blending in seamlessly with the crowd. Her nondescript pantsuit was the blah blue-gray preferred by too many women in the field. She kept her hair in a low braid that was too boring for words, and wore heels that were high, but not too high. She must have hit a thrift shop on her way in.

The lanyard she sported held her identification badge, no doubt one that was actually earned. Jordan Stone was a mystery. It came as no surprise that she might, on some level, still belong to the Company.

But it was Madison who captured his heart, eyes, and cock. The outfit she wore wasn't anything she'd normally select, making her look as if she'd stepped off the cover of *Vogue*.

The glossy black Louboutins showed off a peekaboo toe and a splash of red. His gaze traveled up her toned, bare calves to her thighs. The short black fitted skirt stretched in ways that were absolute sin as she moved, and the matching custom-tailored blazer hugged her breasts in a way that was the perfect blend of *nice to meet you* and naughty. Her hair was pulled back in a low, thick bun at the nape, and her black-rimmed glasses completed the sophisticated *sex on demand* look.

Madison turned back, waving good-bye to Paco and everyone else who watched the feed from the van, with her breasts spilling out and her pouty nude lips so ready for the taking.

Alex sucked in a breath and yanked Crystal aside. "Is there a reason my fiancée got the memo to wear *business scandalous*?"

"Mm-hmm." Despite his hard glare at her, Crystal kept her gaze fixed on the screen, watching the ladies as they headed away. "You said give her an advantage." Lightly, she laughed under her breath. "Trust me, she's got one."

Alex reined in his temper. *Suddenly, everyone wants me to trust them.*

With Stone turning toward them, Alex returned to the others, now wanting to discuss it.

"Paco, we've got her," Mark said into the mic.

With no more to see on Paco's end, and Madison's link confirmed, he would depart. Lingering would draw suspicion, and his access was restricted to a very short window of time relegated to drivers of VIPs. He drove the van out of the compound toward a satellite DGI stronghold a few miles away.

Alex flipped the monitors to a new channel, picking up the micro camera transmitting from Madison's glasses. Jordan held open the heavy glass doors, allowing Madison to enter.

From the console, Alex pressed a button. "We've got you. Clear your throat if you can hear me."

Madison did so just as she stepped through.

"What's the play?" Alex asked, realizing that never in a million years could Jordan manipulate Stone. This wasn't her idea, after all. It was his.

Not denying it, Stone said, "Madison was the key, the key to a coverup buried somewhere in that building. Her loss was genuine. And all good covers start with the truth."

CHAPTER 32

MADISON

Langley, Virginia

CLEARING HER THROAT, Madison anxiously eyed the larger-than-life seal inlaid in the floor. Along its border, it read CENTRAL INTELLIGENCE AGENCY. She stepped deliberately across the seal, determined not to be afraid, as she and Jordan walked through the large lobby.

Seeing the guard, she froze. Jordan had to brush her elbow, nudging her to move. She did, letting Jordan escort her to the security desk.

There, Jordan flashed the identification dangling from her neck. "I believe you have a badge for Ms. Taylor." She looked at him through her lashes, laying on the sultriness extra thick.

The young security guard thumbed through a set of folders standing in a desk organizer. Finding the correct envelope, he opened it and fished out the badge. Pointing to his clipboard, he didn't bother smiling as he said, "Yes. Sign here."

As instructed, Madison quickly scanned the entries. She found the skipped-over space on the sign-in sheet that Jordan was certain would be there. By signing there, rather than at the bottom, she avoided leaving any documentation that she'd been the last one to sign in.

Their end-of-the-day appointment was deliberate. It ensured the building would quickly empty as the civil servants left the office, either heading home or to happy hour. It also made her arrival time appear much earlier, and that by the end of the day, it would appear Madison Taylor should be long gone.

In the event of an overzealous end-of-day security check, they'd only follow up with the last entry or two to ensure all appointments were concluded and that security could lock up. As it was, Madison's sign-in placed her at the headquarters hours before.

To avoid the guard noticing, Jordan tossed out possibly the oldest distraction in the book. "So, you got big plans tonight, Officer?"

Predictably, her inviting tone snagged his attention. "Um, nothing special."

"Really?" she purred. "Well, if you need a hand doing nothing special, give me a call." Jordan slid him what Madison was sure was a real number—even if it was to a burner phone—and it did its job to draw his attention from Madison.

"I'll do that," he said, lowering his voice and palming the card discreetly.

From the corner of her eye, Madison noticed as Jordan swept her finger back and forth across his thumb. Madison's eye roll was uncontrollable.

Don't react, respond? I'm ready to respond, all right. Fingers crossed we get out of here before I throw up all over the security desk of the CIA.

Madison stalled for only a moment at PURPOSE OF THE VISIT, filling in that block with four letters: F-O-I-A.

FOIA, or the Freedom of Information Act, had been America's check-and-balance system since July 4, 1966, giving every citizen the right to access information from the United States government.

The government had always been cagey in complying with FOIA, which was why documents for Area 51 and Kennedy's assassination had never been fully released despite millions of FOIA requests.

If Madison's own request from years earlier had been received, it was left unacknowledged. The death of a no-name, average American citizen should have been inconsequential to the powers that be. But one of the Jordan Stones had worked a miracle.

All the right people had been convinced that Madison would need a face-to-face discussion about her brother's death, or she was going to the press. And no one wanted to risk a future billionaire's wife inadvertently digging up information that could compromise new and ongoing missions.

Distracted, the guard didn't even glance at the clipboard as he handed Madison a numbered ESCORT REQUIRED visitor badge. This was anticipated. Jordan's escort privileges, as remarkable as that sounded, remained intact.

"This way, Ms. Taylor," Jordan said, motioning her down the corridor. Each passage led to a maze of lookalike halls, cubicle farms, and walls lined with offices.

Scanning the wall plaques, they found who they were looking for. Mr. Jeff Lowell, a low-level analyst who would diligently give Madison some bullshit story about how the records were misplaced, or lost, or whatever he had to say to end the meeting and move her along.

Keeping him occupied for at least twenty minutes was their goal. It would take that long for Jordan to hack his computer and download the information they needed for the next step of their plan.

Anyone more senior to Jeff would immediately recognize Jordan's attempt. Someone junior to Jeff wouldn't have the accesses required. And the physical position of his office, optimally located a hall or two from their ultimate destination, made him a perfect match.

Madison had no idea how that was pulled off, but it was. And it would give Jordan enough time to pinpoint the exact location of the files they needed.

Jordan gave Jeff's door a brisk knock but opened it before he could. It was a quick way to check their security protocols. Apparently, its cypher lock was just for show.

Swinging the door open wide, Jordan breezed in. "Hi, Jeff. I'm Jordan, the escort for our visitor. I believe you were expecting us."

Fumbling to put away his late lunch, he swept the half-eaten sandwich and scattered potato chips into the top desk drawer. *Gross.*

After dusting off his rumpled shirt and slacks, he straightened the knot in his stained tie. "Sure, come in."

"This is Ms. Taylor. She sent in the FOIA request."

"Of course. Please, have a seat." He stood but didn't extend his hand for a shake, and Madison breathed a sigh of relief.

When he motioned for them to have a seat at the small table with four chairs, only Madison sat down with him. Jordan remained standing.

"I've been sitting all day," she said. Obviously, he could relate and nodded.

"First," he said solemnly to Madison, "let me say how sorry I am for your loss."

As he proceeded with the canned pleasantries, Madison watched Jordan, studying her moves. Casually, she leaned back on the edge of his desk, using her body to block his view as she attached a high-tech extractor to his laptop. Jeff was about to look over as Madison created a distraction.

Abruptly, she slammed her hand hard on the table. *Ow.* "Look, I have a right to see my brother's records. All of them."

It worked. Jordan stepped over to the dirtiest window known to man. She needed a clean cell signal. With the grime across it, Madison wasn't sure that was happening. But even a weak signal would make it possible. The stronger the signal, the faster this would go.

"Ms. Taylor," Jeff said, "I understand your need for closure. But it's been ten years. Maybe it's just time to let it go."

"What did you say?" she snapped as heat traveled to her cheeks in record time. She was genuinely about to blow.

Jordan didn't move. Instead, she stood there and watched, an intrigued spectator with her narrowed eyes and lifted brow. She wasn't about to intervene. Or help. Jordan Stone was too busy staring, seeming to wonder what Madison was going to do.

In the moment, it was something Madison wondered too. Her emotions were all over the place, and between her strong urges to cry hysterically or hit this guy with a full-on freak-out, she sat there, wrestling for her self-control.

Shit. What do I do?

It was Crystal's voice she could hear in her head. Or more precisely, from the tiny audio feed coming from the arm of the glasses she wore.

"Madison, this kid is young and naive, and that's why we targeted him. You're still in the game. If you push him, he might grab a supervisor. Think of our discussion. Let him see what you want him to see."

Mark cut in. "Jordan's working fast. She's close. She needs another six or seven minutes, tops. Keep this guy distracted. Chat about anything. How about this? He's completely obsessed with getting swole."

Madison's eyes popped. *Uh, what?* Her continued silence prompted Alex to pipe up.

"Mark means he's into extreme fitness. He's aiming to someday be the next American Ninja Warrior. He seems to do anything and everything to build endurance."

That wasn't exactly news. Behind him was an impressive display of medals and trophies for everything from triathlons to warrior competitions, but primarily 10Ks and marathons.

"Yeah, I know," she said aloud, cutting herself short, realizing she'd just replied to Alex.

I can't keep all these conversations straight. Where did Jeff and I leave off?

"You know . . . what?" Jeff asked, staring at her. When she stared back blankly, he began to stand and turn toward Jordan. "I'm sorry I can't be of further assistance—"

"I mean . . ." Madison gently motioned him back to his seat. "Yeah, I know. As in, I hear what you're saying. You're right. It has been a long time, and I should let it go. But it's hard. So very, very hard."

Licking her lips, she took an exaggerated deep breath. Predictably, his gaze fell to her chest and he slowly returned to his seat.

Pointing to the *I love me* wall behind him, she continued. "Especially this time of year, with folks ramping up for our hometown run."

That got his attention, though his eyes remained fixed. "Oh, your brother was a runner?"

"Yes," she said, enthusiastic to bring up something about the brother that she actually knew.

I might not have known everything about the secret life of Jack Taylor, but I've got this covered.

"Jack loved to run. I run too, but I could never keep up. Jack always said I needed to work on my breathing if I was going to get serious about long-distance running."

She followed with another deep chest-popping inhale for effect.

Eager to impress, Jeff launched into a full-fledged lecture on breathing techniques, how he built his cardiovascular stamina, and who knows what the hell else, because Madison zoned out almost immediately. In the eternity it took for Jordan to wrap up, Madison smothered several yawns.

"Well, I think we've taken up enough of your time," Jordan finally said.

Oh, thank God.

Madison leaped up on cue, reluctantly taking Jeff's icky hand. She used the move to pull his attention away as Jordan retrieved her device. All evidence of her hack into the impenetrable system had been removed.

Jeff swallowed Madison's hand in both of his. *Yuck.*

"Listen, if you ever want some running tips, I could meet you sometime. You know, to do a run and," his gaze drifted down again, "work on your breathing."

Eventually, his gaze caught the sparkling from her ginormous ring. "Oh, you're engaged?" He gaped at her as he dropped her hands.

"Yes," Jordan gleefully answered for Madison. "To a powerful tycoon with the thrusting power of a SpaceX rocket."

After a brisk clap on Jeff's back, Jordan scooted Madison out of the room. "This way," she said, rushing Madison down the corridor.

They cut right, stopping at a door devoid of any markings save for a small metal plaque engraved with ARCHIVE 5. Jordan attempted the handle. Like Jeff's, it was reinforced with a cypher lock, also non-working. She opened the door and they scurried inside.

Along the wall, Jordan found a light switch and flipped it, flooding the pitch-black room with bright fluorescent light. A small desk and chair next to the door held an incredibly old computer that seemed eerily undisturbed for some time.

In front of them, the vast space held row upon row of industrial metal shelving about six feet high, filled to capacity with boxes and binders. The rhyme and reason to their order could have been the eighth wonder of the world.

Madison deflated. "How are we going to find anything in here?"

Immersed in her phone, Jordan said, "Looks like the only items here are those that haven't made it to being digitally preserved. Budget cuts. Everything here is from the year of Jack's mission. The oldest records will be at the end, and the newest here up front."

"But what if Jack's were stored electronically?"

"They weren't," Jordan said. "There are some missions they'll never store digitally. Too many old-schoolers in senior leadership positions believe the best way to keep something safe is by keeping it far away from technology. Hard copies only. We can only hope they didn't destroy them. But our chances are good they didn't, because Stone is positive the mission was never completely closed out."

Jordan headed down the long expanse of a warehouse with Madison on her heels, glancing at the never-ending rows of shelves.

"You think they'd rather keep everything in an unlocked room than store them digitally?"

Jordan slowed down, studying the boxes. "You've heard that military intelligence is an oxymoron, right? Well, you're smack dab in the heart of the proof. Since the building itself is secure, folks get lazy. Securing each office gets old fast. And a lot of historians and archivists were never operatives or active duty. Having to unlock the door every time they return from taking a leak is too much of a hassle."

"Could the archivist be back at any moment?" Madison asked, worrying aloud.

Jordan sneered. "No. He's out today. Sudden case of stomach flu."

Finally, Jordan stopped somewhere in the middle of the room. She grabbed a box off the shelf and plopped it onto the floor. "Jackpot. Operation Firefly."

"Firefly?"

"Jack's last mission," Jordan said, flipping off the lid.

Her fingers flew through the contents, pulling out a file and checking the documents within, then tapping it back down only to move on. A bright blue one caught her eye, and she opened it wide on top of the box.

"Alex," she said, speaking to him through the mic in Madison's glasses. "In your statement, you mentioned that someone tried to enter Jack's hotel room, then left an envelope. Is this the guy?" She pointed to a small black-and-white photo paper-clipped to the corner of the file.

"Yes," Madison heard in her earpiece.

"Yes," she repeated aloud to Jordan.

"Hmm." Jordan hastily flipped through the papers. "The man you saw goes by the code name Roberto, as well as a half dozen other names, but little information is here other than that he owned a small jewelry shop and was a mule for the letterbox."

"Letterbox?" Madison asked.

Alex translated the reference. "A letterbox is a liaison. Receiving and passing messages, or items. It means Roberto was just another cog in the wheel. The real guy passing the info back and forth, the letterbox, remained anonymous."

"There's little else here," Jordan muttered under her breath, "except Jack did receive the package."

Madison reviewed the pages as Jordan rummaged through the box. "There's something else. Whatever he received was small. Very, very small. And platinum."

Jordan didn't break from her work. "Yes, but that makes it even more of an issue because it could be anywhere. Or long gone, perhaps. Whatever it was, it was extraordinarily valuable. A key of some sort. Perhaps to a code."

"How do you know that?" Madison asked.

"Here . . ." Jordan pulled open an envelope. She slid a few index cards out into her hand. "This is coder talk. What they were doing not only required the decoder, but also the item that needed to be decoded."

Jordan flipped them slowly, one by one, ensuring Madison's glasses recorded every piece. "It could be the access codes for major power grids, or nuclear launch sequences. Without a decoder, it might as well be your nana's recipe for caramel apple strudel."

How does she know about Nana's apple strudel?

"Practically worthless," Jordan said, for the first time showing signs of frustration. "But there is this . . ."

From the folder, she removed a single sheet of paper. It was Jack's military orders. Madison had never seen them before. The form was covered in blocks, each filled in with various bits of information on Jack, including his name, social security number, location of each assignment, and its duration.

Jordan pointed to the paper. "You're gonna want to hang on to that."

Madison's spy wardrobe seemed to be missing pockets, though Jordan's pantsuit had several, on both the blazer and the slacks. She handed it back to Jordan. "Do you mind?"

Jordan's eyes danced with delight. "Not at all," she said, neatly folding the page to the size of a credit card. With a single finger, she pulled open Madison's blazer and inched the folded paper between her breasts.

Transfixed, Madison watched and then winced, drawing in a sharp breath. *Oh. My. God.*

The issue wasn't Jordan's little move. It was that Madison couldn't help but watch. Meaning, so did everyone else in the team, via a close-up view of her cleavage captured by the microscopic camera in her eyeglass frames.

As she stammered, not sure what to say, Jordan smothered her mouth with her hand. From the faraway entrance, someone had just opened the door.

CHAPTER 33

MADISON

"Hello," a male voice bellowed.

Madison sprang to her feet and peeked through the small openings between the boxes on the shelf. The guard might be older, but by his large build and impressive height, he looked intimidating as hell.

Silently, Jordan reassembled the contents of the box and returned it to the shelf. Despite her swift moves, Madison managed to catch sight of Jordan's annoying little fingers snagging something from the box. Whatever she'd pulled out, she pocketed. But with the man's shoes tapping toward them, there was no time to say anything.

In a heartbeat, he was a few shelves away, hot on their invisible trail. Any second now, they'd be discovered. Frantic, she looked to Jordan for a solution.

Nothing.

Jordan stood there, completely relaxed, smiling as if she had no intention of moving from their spot. Bug-eyed, Madison shrugged, gesturing wildly for a response.

Not a one.

Maybe Jordan was planning to wield a kick-ass martial-arts move on the man.

Should we bolt? Sneak away or outright run? Was this what Alex worried about? Would Jordan ditch me? Or worse, pin this on me?

Jordan was wearing a badge. For all they knew, she belonged here. What was

Madison's excuse? Madison was the one to sign in, not Jordan. And it was Madison who had met with Jeff.

This is bad. Very, very bad.

Resolved to accept the number of ways this could go down, Madison was ready for anything.

Correction. Almost anything.

Jordan removed Madison's glasses and placed them high on the shelf. Unclipping Madison's hair, she fingered through to fluff the strands, laying them loosely about her shoulders, then mouthed the word *perfect.*

She can't seriously think I'm gonna seduce this guy. Not only is he fully armed, but he's also older than my dad. How about this? I'll bat my eyes, heave my breasts, and hand him Jordan's business card. I hear it's guard night at her place.

As the footsteps rounded the corner, Jordan grabbed Madison's shoulders and pinned her against the shelving. Madison's slight squeal was muffled by Jordan's full lips, and her body was smothered in a dizzying touchy-feely embrace.

Of all things, Jordan moaned, freely sliding her hands over the curves of Madison's butt. Shocked, Madison gasped.

Jordan's hand yanked her thigh up and around, wrapping herself in Madison's leg. Footsteps louder, the guard closed in.

Breast to breast, Madison couldn't think, and began echoing the seductive sounds of her impromptu lover, letting her hands wander Jordan's body in return, though much more innocently.

The guard's shocked gasp was loud and distinct, and Madison nearly laughed out loud as she heard him stumble backward and release a *good Lord* under his breath.

Determined, she maintained her calm . . . even as Jordan touched her warm tongue to hers, invading her through her parted lips. Finally, the guard tiptoed away.

In the distance, the door clicked open and slammed closed, but neither she nor Jordan broke from the kiss. Her breath hitched again when Jordan rounded first base and headed for second.

Unless she stopped it, Jordan's hand was sliding its way across her thigh and up the back of her skirt. Even as Jordan filled her hand with the fullness of Madison's tense ass, she didn't pull away.

Instead, she replayed Crystal's words. Over and over and over again.

Don't react. Respond.

Don't. React.

Respond. Respond.

Respond.

For the moment, Madison allowed her body to be swept through a tidal wave of touching and kissing. And feeling.

Her mind cleared, allowing her to focus. A minute later, a single thought broke through.

Yes.

CHAPTER 34

ALEX

Alex could only sit and breathe as the group remained glued to the uneventful screen. The micro camera seemed to be sitting upside-down on a shelf, abandoned where Jordan had placed it, diligently recording every second of the boring wall across from it.

The microphone? That was another story. Thanks to the latest technology for unrivaled surveillance, the audio was crystal clear. It captured every moan and whimper, long after the footsteps of the guard had moved on.

Like his companions, Alex watched nothing but a blank screen, eager for a continuation of the video. Though certainly not for all the same reasons.

Crystal broke the almost silence. "I need a snack. Anyone else?"

Quickly, Mark and Stone followed, none making eye contact with Alex, who was too preoccupied to glance back at any of them.

He barely heard them leave. With his head swirling, heart racing, and cock standing tall like a redwood, he sat frozen. Settling his breaths, he waited. And waited. *And* waited.

After what could have been seconds, hours, or days, the trio returned with snacks in hand. The screen hadn't changed, and Alex hadn't moved.

No doubt, it was awkward as shit for them all. But he didn't care.

Eventually, the glasses were yanked from their spot and clasped in the ringed hand of Madison. After several steps, the glasses were flipped, staring up at Madison's face.

"I need a word with Jordan. Alone."

What the fuck?

Before Alex could say a word, the video was capturing the inside of a desk drawer, letting them all stare at a few paper clips and dust. Muffled voices could be heard, but not made out.

"I'm sure you can clean up the audio," Stone said helpfully.

Mark didn't make a move. As a happily married man, he knew the drill.

"No," Alex said calmly. His response was blunt. "Madison requested privacy, and we're giving it to her."

Madison had asked for his trust, and by God, he was giving it to her. But at the moment, his issue wasn't trust.

Madison had crossed a line. With her moans fresh in his ears, and that smudge of Jordan's signature red lipstick visible on her kiss-swollen lips, one thing was clear.

He'd be seeing her.

Soon.

But not fucking soon enough.

CHAPTER 35

MADISON

WITH THE GLASSES secured deep in the desk drawer, Madison steeled her resolve, casting a nervous smile at Jordan.

"Look," she said softly, "I need to make one thing clear. Yes, you're beautiful and sexy, and can undoubtedly teach me a thing or two. Things that would probably make my head spin, and might be illegal in at least a dozen states. But just as Alex belongs to me, I belong to him. I'm completely his—mind, body, and soul."

Jordan cozied up to her. Locking a strand of Madison's hair around her finger, she let it slip though as she traced Madison's jaw and pulled her chin up. Her lips remained a whisper away.

"Maybe, just maybe, the bracelet does suit you."

They both smiled as Jordan took a step back, opened the desk drawer, and retrieved the glasses. She licked her lips as she slid them up the bridge of Madison's nose.

"She's all yours," Jordan sang to the audience, and sauntered out of the room as Madison trailed behind her.

Upstate New York
Madison was exhausted, grateful to have Paco once again perform the work

of driver as they returned to the rendezvous point. The ride was quiet, leaving Madison to her spinning thoughts.

As the van pulled into the garage of the DGI bunker, the headlights flooded a very serious-looking Alex. Paco quickly killed the lights, but it was long enough for Madison to read Alex's face. His eyes held a hardness she was unfamiliar with, and that made her squirm.

They all exited the vehicle. Madison was last. Even with his arms uncrossed, she couldn't avoid the heavy weight of his stare. She could feel it. Feel him. Her heart pounded and her breath hitched as he held open the large metal door.

Jordan breezed by him, exiting the garage without a word, and Paco quickly followed. Madison tried making her way toward it, but he let the solid sound-proof door close behind the others, clanking loudly as it shut.

They were alone.

"Not so fast, Ms. Taylor," he rumbled low, stepping closer.

The warmth of his body was like the heat of the sun, and his dark stare stole her breath. The space between them was charged and electric. With barely a touch, she was backed against the door. In another step, his hard body pressed against hers.

Madison bit her lip, feeling the pressure of his solid dick. It made her grow wet.

The ball of his thumb pressed against her full lower lip. "I'm not sure this shade suits you."

After one hard swipe of his thumb, he replaced the missing lipstick with a rough, hungry kiss. She knew what he wanted. A taste. A taste of something he'd never known, and he'd never taste again.

With her lips parted, his tongue forced through, exploring in long, sweeping licks. Taking back the mouth that was his.

He unclasped the button of her jacket and her breasts spilled out. His desire was rough and raw. Commanding. Desperate. It left her soaking with need.

Every sensation was different. This wasn't the Alex she knew, but it was the Alex she wanted. Here. Now. Sexy as fuck and hotter than hell.

A *don't react* reminder was the last thing she needed. Her body was giving in, letting go, and responding all over the place. Big-time.

As his hands smoothed over all of her, he didn't miss an inch, careful in tracing and retracing every one of her curves. Only after several complete passes over every square inch of covered skin did he pause, letting his hand settle on the full weight of her breast.

He trailed hot kisses along her neck, across her cleavage, then back up to her ear. Sliding his fingers through her hair, he fisted it, tilting her head slowly to the side.

There, his hot breath cascaded across her neck. Her whole body shivered as he whispered, "If you did what I think you did, your hotness factor just flew off the charts."

He lifted her, and her legs wrapped around. Her arms held tight to his shoulders and neck, and he boosted her higher to hike up her skirt. Easily, his large hands cradled her ass, nudging her to spread wider.

Panting, she asked, "And what is it that you think I did, Mr. Drake?"

Reaching down, she yanked open his pants, releasing his stifled erection. Madison took him in both hands, gripping and stroking him lovingly.

He let out a pleasurable moan. Resting on the seat of his hands, she slid her panties aside, rubbing her aching core with his tip, getting his hardness ready and wet.

"What do I think?" Alex asked, and she whimpered as the tip of his cock teased its way in. "I think you planted a nano-tracker on Jordan."

Sharply, his teeth tugged her ear, forcing her to arch back and take all of him at once.

"Yes!" Madison screamed, riding his length as he slammed himself hard and deep.

There, in the aftermath of her first deep-cover work, Alex staked his unyielding claim on her over, and over, and over again.

CHAPTER 36

MADISON

HAVING BEEN FULLY FRISKED by her fiancé, ensuring every crevice and cavity was bug- and tracker-free, Madison walked inside with him. If Alex Drake was anything, he was damn thorough.

Jordan slinked over to Madison's side. "Your lip color seems to have vanished. Care for some of mine?"

Madison smiled, proudly wearing the rising blush of her cheeks as she huddled with the others around the small conference table. Dozens of printouts were strewn about, displaying the images captured by Madison's glasses. Her gaze traveled from sheet to sheet, studying the information on each page.

Stone shuffled a few around. "We're looking for two pieces—a lock and a key. From the way it looks, we have neither."

"Bullshit," Mark shot back. "My guess is you have one, and you need both."

Unconvincingly, Stone tried to object. "The operation was compartmentalized. I recruited Jack and gave him a broad-brush overview of the mission. But someone else, someone deep in the shadows, pulled him into whatever else he got caught up in. It eluded me then, and it's continued to elude me for the past ten years."

Exchanging glances with Alex and Mark, Stone sighed as his face filled with regret. "All I know is he was sent out to find something—find it and return it. But maybe . . ."

"Maybe what?" Madison latched onto Stone's hesitation.

He barely made eye contact. "Maybe he had different plans. Perhaps he was going to hold on to it."

Angry, Madison snapped, "Jack wasn't a traitor." Exhausted from the day and an inch from losing her shit on the man, she was relieved when Alex rushed over and caressed her shoulders. The gesture calmed her.

Stone waved a hand in apology. "No, of course not. I didn't mean that. I meant maybe he wanted to keep it out of harm's way. Like, he didn't trust the person he was supposed to retrieve it for. But Jack must have inadvertently tipped his hand. Asked a wrong question. Wondered aloud and made someone nervous."

"Finders keepers." Paco huffed, crossing his arms and shaking his head.

"Finders keepers?" Madison asked.

"A fairy tale," Jordan said, casually brushing it off. "A legend. A group of spy vigilantes who find and hold precious information, even from their own superiors and handlers, to prevent an uneven shift of power in the wrong direction. But trust me, government-issued spies aren't in it to break the sanctimonious bonds of big brotherhood. They have neither the financial resources nor the sponsorship to go it alone. It's all a bunch of glorified PR that makes espionage out to be altruistic."

Paco leaned to Madison with a mocking glance at Jordan. "Well, there have been cases of things miraculously turning up at just the right time, and in just the right hands."

Jordan glared his way. "Spies steal. That doesn't make them Robin Hood. Just like finding a few coins under a pillow doesn't mean there's a tooth fairy."

"No," Stone said, refocusing the group. "What this means is we need to focus and find the missing piece. The piece Jack had. And I'm quite confident it's not a tooth. It's either the lock . . . or the key."

Madison countered with a different possibility. "No, at some point, he would've had to have both. Known what he was in possession of. That's what made him dangerous. Otherwise, he wouldn't have been a threat."

Jordan glanced at Alex, then Paco. "You two were around him. Did he show you anything? Give you any hint of what he might be transporting, or perhaps how?"

Alex and Paco looked at each other and shrugged. "No," Alex said. "Nothing at all."

Next to Madison, Paco crossed his arms tight across his chest, no doubt memorizing the photos. He drummed the fingers of his left hand against his arm, a habit that let her know he was deep in thought. Again and again, his fingers rolled. Turning, he blew out an exasperated breath as she held hers in.

"What?" he asked as she stared at him.

Come on, Paco. Read my mind.

Giving her a concerned look, he said, "You look tired."

What? No. That's realization, not exhaustion.

Paco turned to the others. "Hey, I'm going to take Madison home. I'll come back after I drop her off."

"I can take her," Crystal said.

"No, I'll do it. I need some air," Paco said, his voice casual but insistent. Without saying more, he placed his hand on her back as he pushed her toward the door.

"Wait!" Madison stopped in her tracks, determined to explain. "No. I'm not tired." Her tone cracked a bit more than she'd intended. "I'm—"

Alex slipped his arm around her and turned them to walk her out.

"Hey," he said with reassurance. "No shame in it. Look, we've got a few hours of work to do here, and we get it. The day you've had would make anyone tense. It's completely understandable that you're emotional. Let Paco take you home. We'll just be a few hours longer."

With that, he scooted her out the door, placed barely a peck on her stammering lips, and handed her off to Paco. When the door shut, the clank of it locking behind them was just enough to raise her blood to a rolling boil, and she whirled on Paco.

"Paco!"

He drew in a sharp breath, hardening his expression. "Madison, do as you're told and get your ass in the car."

Furious, she marched to his Lambo. Paco's attempt to open her door was met with a *fuck you* glare.

She made a hasty grab for the door. "I can open it myself."

He held both hands high in defeat and moved around the car to take his place again as her driver. With a thunderous roar, he drove out of the garage, his smirk breaking into a full-blown belly laugh.

"What's wrong, *hermanita*? Don't you like it when Alex and I make you out to be the erratic, emotional little woman?"

Her irritation melted. It was all for show. "So, you know?"

"All I know is whatever you were thinking, you were about to let the cat out of the bag, and that's the last thing we want with these folks. Their entire livelihood revolves around how good they are at lying and stealing. Whatever you have, we need to keep it under wraps until they come through with their end of the bargain and restore Jack's military record. It's what you were promised, and what he deserves."

Despite her seat belt, Madison pulled herself over, hugging Paco's neck and giving him a hard kiss on his cheek. "So, now what? I mean, I might be wrong. It's really just a hunch."

Paco waved a dismissive hand. "I trust your instincts, and so does Alex. Whatever it is, you're probably spot on."

Thoughtfully, she considered how best to share her thoughts. "I'd like to wait until Alex is with us to discuss it."

"Okay, we'll wait a few hours. But I'm dying to know what you've got."

I seriously doubt that.

CHAPTER 37

MADISON

Manhattan

ALTHOUGH GLAD TO BE BACK AT the penthouse, Madison wished this weren't weighing on her. Alex and Paco stood before her as she sat on the sofa, hugging a pillow tight to her chest as she stared at them. The men looked at each other, then back to her, their concern growing.

"Madison," Alex said, "whatever it is, we're in it together."

Sucking in a breath, she nodded. "You two should sit down."

They dropped onto the sofa on either side of her, squeezing her in just enough to make her smile. It worked.

"Go ahead," Alex said, nudging her gently.

"Jordan mentioned that Jack had been working with a very small amount of platinum."

Paco placed his hand atop hers. "Something that small could be anywhere. Mailed. Buried. Lost."

"Hidden," she said pointedly. "Hidden in plain sight."

"That sounds like Jack," Alex said, and Paco nodded.

Madison pulled in a ragged breath. "I think I know where it is."

Paco sat up. "Did Jack give it to you? Or to Dan?" If Jack was going to give it to anyone, their father would have been as likely as Madison.

"No." With all the care, warmth, and love she could muster, Madison gazed at Paco. The man who should have been her brother-in-law, but she had to settle for thinking of him as a brother. "I think he gave it to you."

Perplexed, Paco frowned. "Madison, I'm sorry. He didn't."

Gingerly, she brushed the ring on his pinky. "Did Jack ever mention James Zaharee?"

Paco exchanged a blank stare with Alex, and they both shook their heads. Considering Paco never forgot a name or a face, it was obvious he hadn't.

Softly, Madison continued. "Jack was obsessed with Zaharee since he was a child, marveling at his mastery of miniature writing." She lightly rocked Paco's pinky ring back and forth.

Paco pulled off the ring, lifting it before them in his palm. "I see where you're going with this, but I've checked. I've studied this ring every day since he gave it to me. The design is common. There are millions of rings with the identical insignia. And there's nothing engraved on it."

Smiling, Madison clasped her hand around his, enclosing the ring delicately within his fist. Shaking her head, she said, "Jordan said Roberto had a jewelry shop. That makes sense with the ring, but jewelers are also skilled engravers. And whatever he was supposed to deliver was platinum and small. Really small."

She rubbed Paco's hand. "The reason Jack was obsessed with James Zaharee is because he loved the Declaration of Independence. And, well, Zaharee was most famous for writing the entire Declaration of Independence," she pushed out a breath, "on a grain of rice."

Alex wrapped his arm around her. "You think Jack had the ring engraved with the information? On something that small?"

She nodded. "I'm positive he did and kept it somewhere he was sure it would be safe, even if he couldn't keep it secure himself. He could have had it laser engraved on platinum, and then encapsulated into, well, pot metal. Because the melting point for platinum is much higher than that of pot metal, or even gold, it could be heated later, like melting the chocolate away from the macadamia nut. The nut stays perfectly intact, with all its ridges preserved. Then, when he needed to retrieve it—"

Paco yanked his hand back from her before jumping to his feet. "No. Hell no. Madison, it's the only gift I have from Jack. It's my engagement ring, and all I have left of him."

Pacing, Paco slid the ring back on, clasping his hand protectively to his chest. He looked back at both of them. "If you think I'm melting it down in the insane hope that there's a piece of engraved platinum in it, you've lost your damn minds."

Alex stood to meet him, placing a reassuring hand on his shoulder. "Hey, we're not forcing you to do anything you're not ready for. Not at all. But Jack was killed because of it. And you know better than anyone that we can have it replicated exactly, to the tiniest detail. We can even duplicate whatever's in it, so it has the identical weight and feel."

Gently, Madison squeezed Paco's hand. "But there's no hurry. None. Not as far as I'm concerned." She stood and wrapped her arms around him, hugging him hard.

"But . . ." Alex pocketed his hands. "You know none of us will get a moment of sleep until we find out what this is all about. Which is no skin off my nose, because I don't sleep anyway."

With a heavy sigh, Paco returned Madison's squeeze. "And it's the only ticket to Jack's status being fully reinstated." He yanked Alex over as well, linking them all in the tightness of a family bear hug.

Alex said, "Well, that and perhaps Jack's orders that Jordan slid into Madison's ample bosom."

They held the hug and chuckled as Madison lightly swatted him on the ass.

CHAPTER 38

MADISON

Three days later

IN THE COMFORT of Alex's office, Madison watched as Paco studied his ring in the light, seeing its brilliant gleam. "It's too shiny," he said, disapproving of its sheen. It was the first time he'd tried on the remade ring.

For a moment, Paco twisted the band, scrutinizing it as it moved. Though the identical combinations of nickel, copper, and brass had been used, remolded, and stamped to exacting detail, it was clear the patina of age was gone, making the ring look shinier and new.

"Well, a few days of cheap bar soap should dull it down," he said, slipping it back on, flexing his finger as he admired the fit.

Madison looked lovingly at the way it molded to his skin, and smiled at him. Smiling back, he adjusted his tie, signaling he was ready to move on.

"Well?" Madison linked her arm through his, glancing at the ring as she laid her head on his shoulder.

He sucked in a deep breath. "Yes, *hermanita*. It feels right. It's still the ring from Jack."

"Good," she said.

With a kiss to her forehead, he asked, "How's the decoding going?"

"Slow," she said with a frustrated frown.

"Hey." Alex waved them over to his desk, where he'd been painstakingly capturing the inscriptions from the platinum bead that sat in his palm.

No one could know about this, so Alex decided to handle the work himself. With several specialized instruments, he had the code. But it was still no good without the decoder.

"I think I've got an idea," Alex said. "We're not going to give Jordan or Stone the original. Like Paco's ring, we'll replicate it, but with just the slightest tweak to the code."

"How?" Paco asked. "How would you do it without them knowing?"

"Code breaking is my next favorite pastime next to Madison." The man was born to make her blush. "There are repeaters within the code. Like anywhere I see something that resembles an *a*, I replace it with maybe an *m*, but the rest of the code stays intact. It's subtle, in case they've seen this code before, but they won't be able to crack it. Whatever this is supposed to unlock, it won't work."

"Why would we want to do that?" Madison asked.

Alex smiled. "Because we can't just hand them the real one. Until we know what it unlocks, we hand over a dummy."

"But they said they don't have whatever it is this will decode," Madison said, feeling a little silly reminding him.

"Bald-faced lying at its finest," Paco said, replying for both himself and Alex.

Alex set the little bead of platinum in a specially designed box, closed it, and set it down. "You were right, Madison. Jack must have had both pieces at some point. I'm betting Stone has the other one. Smart people don't devote this kind of time and energy when the odds aren't stacked in their favor."

Madison thought about Jordan. "What about the images from my glasses? Jordan took something out of that box when she thought I wasn't looking."

Alex agreed. "Oh. You mean this?" He handed her a printout. In the image, Jordan was clearly holding an access card, one Madison had never seen.

"What's that?" Madison pointed to a small fleck of gold along the bottom of the card. The head looked like a lion. But somehow the image was blurred, with the bottom strangely resembling a fish tail.

"That's definitely a Merlion," Paco said, having sufficiently squinted and leaned in for a look.

He seriously needs to just rip off the Band-Aid and buy a pair of reading glasses already.

Alex raised a brow. "It's the official symbol of Singapore. And I know that access card."

Madison suspected he not only knew it, but probably had a hand in making it.

Smiling, Alex took her hand and squeezed. "Well, beautiful . . . ready to make a deal?"

Taking Paco's hand with her other, she held her breath and nodded. "Yes," she quietly blew out.

Alex grabbed his cell, again dialing the number.

"Insurance services." A man's voice answered, one it seemed Alex didn't readily recognize, though traces of a Latin or French accent could be distinguished from just the two words.

"Yes," Alex said, smiling at Madison's noticeable confusion. "I'm interested in getting an appraisal on something valuable. Some might say it's priceless."

"Hold, please."

The elevator rendition of "Moon River" had Alex and Paco singing along. Madison giggled until the line reconnected. In an instant, they were silent.

"We can have an adjustor at your property in fifteen minutes."

Whispering to Madison, Paco asked, "What's with them and the fifteen minutes?"

"Actually," Alex said, "I'm at my place of work. DGI headquarters in Manhattan. My suite."

Both Madison and Paco flashed him a silent *Are you sure?* Smiling, he nodded.

After only a moment of silence, the man replied. "Yes, sir. Fifteen minutes. DGI. See you there."

Once the call disconnected, Alex explained. "They're done with their games. Once they have what we give them, I doubt they'll stick around. You know what that means?"

Paco grinned. "Operation Shadow commences."

CHAPTER 39

MADISON

STANDING in front of the floor-to-ceiling window of the isolated DGI conference room, Madison lost herself in staring at the clouds in the sky, haloed with
shards of sunlight breaking through.

Is real closure possible?

Before she could tackle the itchy hives working their way up her arm, she
stalled with the approach of steps.

"They've arrived." Alex squeezed her shoulders. "Ready?"

She turned toward him with the slightest nod. "Ready," she whispered, then
headed to the conference table, about to take a seat.

"What are you doing?" he asked.

"I'm—"

"Sitting in the wrong seat. Remember? Jordan was intent on speaking with
you. This is your meeting." He urged her toward the leather executive chair at
the head of the table, holding it out for her. "This is your seat. Mark and I are
just eye candy."

Sitting, she looked over at Mark, who shot her a calming wink. "Well, one of
us is," he teased before slipping on his glasses. He picked up the small box on the
table that held the grain-sized bead of platinum. "You think they'll come
through?"

Bearing his weight on his hands, Alex leaned on the table. "I'm betting they
already have."

"And what about us?" Madison couldn't help wondering if skirting their end of the deal would only leave them burned.

"I promise you we will, but only after we know what the real intent and impact is. We have to make sure the information Jack gave his life for is in the right hands."

A knock at the door pulled Mark to his feet, joining Alex in standing. Madison moved to hop up as well, but Alex gently pressed her shoulder, urging her to remain in her seat.

Jordan entered first, making her way past Alex and barely acknowledging him. Her sights were set on Madison.

Stone, on the other hand, didn't seem to care where he sat. He took the first open seat next to Mark.

Jordan's piercing stare met Madison's bashful eyes. A flash of heat was already climbing Madison's neck, but she played it cool, not hiding or acknowledging it at all.

Don't react. Respond.

She embraced the blush, which seemed to satisfy Jordan.

"So," Jordan said, "you have something for us?"

In a sense, Madison had come to understand Jordan. Her fervent gaze wasn't infatuation, and it wasn't a game. Madison had become her new object of interest, and she was studying her. Trying to catch a tell—a deception. Trying to see if Madison would slip her a fake.

Instead, Madison focused on Jordan's lips. Replaying images of their encounter, she let raw emotions flood her thoughts, turning her deception to desire.

Her body responded quickly. Her pulse spiked. Her breathing became erratic and quick. Her lips felt full, needing the swipe of a lick.

"No," Madison said, her voice slightly above a whisper, yet housing all the power. All the control. "First, you have something for me."

Jordan nodded, pulling a large manila envelope from her Hermès messenger bag. Along the top, *Madison* was scrolled with a lavish heart over the *i*.

Thankful, Madison gave her an appreciative nod and opened it, reading the paper inside once and then again. The letter was from the Human Resources Command, United States Army, and stated the following:

Ms. Taylor,

It has come to our attention that the military records for Jack Taylor may be erroneous, based on information we have received from a third party. To expedite the correc-

tion, please send a copy of any documents you may have to substantiate his military service to the address below. Once received, we will provide written confirmation of the correction.

The mild lift to Jordan's lips was so slight, only Madison could read the subtle smile. It surprised her how disarming this vixen could choose to be. It felt sincere.

Jordan didn't have to give her Jack's orders when she found them in the archives. But she did. Appreciation welled in Madison's eyes, and she let Jordan wipe away a tear that escaped.

Unable to speak, Madison mouthed *thank you.*

"Anytime," Jordan said, enigmatic to the end.

Madison gave Mark a nod, who handed the small box to Stone. Not bothering to open it, he placed it in his pocket, then stood.

"Gentlemen, and Madison, perhaps we'll have the pleasure of working together again. Someday."

They all stood, and Alex gave him a confident reply. "I'm sure we will. It's a small world."

Before Madison could move to the comfort of Alex's arms, Jordan cut in between them, her trademark wicked expression in place. The vixen was back.

Flipping a card between her fingers, she said, "In case you ever need me."

Now used to Jordan's touch, not that she had ever imagined that reality, Madison remained still as Jordan dragged the card across her collar and down her blouse.

Enjoying herself, Jordan took her sweet time tucking it into what seemed to be her favorite hiding spot. She pulled Madison in for a hug, whispering in her ear. "See Alex?"

Madison caught the intensity of Alex's expression, and glanced down at his pants. She murmured back, "Mm-hmm."

"Are his pupils dilated?"

She let out a long *yes,* unable to contain her own devilish grin.

"You're welcome." Jordan softly sighed with a cheek-to-cheek kiss. Releasing Madison, Jordan made her way to Stone, taking his arm as they headed out the door.

Shifting on his feet, Mark said, "I'll see them both out." They left, and he shut the door behind him.

Alex stalked closer, sweeping his darkening gaze over her. Hiding her smile, she bit her lip and coyly averted her eyes.

"You know," he said as his fingers dipped into her blouse. They lingered, brushing her nipple before capturing the small piece of cardstock. Slowly, he fished it out, tracing it up her neck to her chin, lifting her beautifully blushing face and summoning her gaze to his. Disappointed, he grumbled, "I never got Jordan's digits."

Madison's giggles stretched on and on as she melted into the warmth of his tender kiss.

CHAPTER 40

MARK

MARK WATCHED as the waiting driver held open the back door of the black Bentley sedan for Jordan and Stone. Once they were seated, he shut it and moved quickly to the driver's door.

He diligently tried to avoid Mark's scrutiny, keeping his chauffeur hat low and his dark glasses high in an obvious effort to conceal his face. But he couldn't hide everything.

For example, Mark noticed the sunglasses the chauffeur sported were $3,000 Ray-Ban Aviators in 18-karat gold. He often wore a pair himself. As the man's hands locked around the steering wheel, Mark was thankful he didn't wear gloves. It gave him so much more insight into who he was dealing with.

On his right hand was no ordinary ring. The emerald-eyed golden panther was the talk of social media and celebrities, a signature piece of the internationally renowned jewelers Cartier.

Before Mark could catch too many more glimpses into the Jordan Stones and their "chauffeur," the car rolled away.

He made a call. "Over to you."

CHAPTER 41

STONE

ONCE INSIDE THE CAR, Stone sat back as the driver carefully removed his sunglasses. Unamused, the man turned back, digging his elbow into the armrest. "Why am I always the fucking chauffeur?"

Behind him, Jordan leaned forward, wrapping her arms around the leather seat until she connected her hands across his chest. "Because I love seeing you in this outfit."

"Don't sweet-talk me, Jordan. The two of you deliberately kept me out of this one. I'm still pissed."

As well he should have been. He was, after all, the third to round out the team. He had been the man in the suit in Puerto Rico, the reason Paco Robles joined that mission in Italy. And why, to this day, Paco remained by Alex Drake's side.

"We all have our weaknesses," Stone said, hoping he came off more patriarchal and less condescending.

"It was for your own good," Jordan softly added, her tone sincere.

"And for the good of the mission," Stone said, which earned him a huff. It was cause enough to remove the small box from his jacket pocket. "Fear not, *P*, your luck's looking up. We're heading east, and you and Jordan will be the happy couple this go-round."

Pierre Roca, or *P*, adjusted the rearview mirror to speak with Stone more directly, though he seemed content enough to keep Jordan's arms wrapped against him. "And what will you be?" he asked, lifting his voice with hope and the thrill of possibility.

Stone didn't mind that it was annoying. *P* needed a break. "I'll, um, be your butler," he said, at which point *P* and Jordan laughed with delight.

Stone was happy too, but inwardly. He loved having them this close. Outwardly, he ignored them, prying open the box and studying it.

"And that?" Jordan asked, curious about the fate of their recent acquisition.

Stone thoughtfully considered the miniscule chunk of metal, gliding the tip of his finger over it carefully, even reverently.

"I don't know yet. We'll keep it, perhaps. I won't decide until after this trip. It will give us an opportunity to revisit an old acquaintance . . ." His tone tensed. "One who obviously knew more than he ever let on." Frowning, he snapped the box shut and slid it back into his pocket.

Jordan released *P* to sit back and take Stone's arm. "And that's why you'll forever be the King of the Keepers."

Loosely, he concealed the sense of pride that welled within him.

Jordan returned her attention to *P*, wrapping her arms around him again before sliding her tongue to the tip of his ear. Stone pretended not to watch as she gave it a sharp bite. Letting out a deep moan, *P* followed it with a naughty chuckle.

At the very least, they should get a room.

Stone settled back, pulling a pair of reading glasses from his breast pocket as he scrolled through his phone in a weak attempt to mask his irritation. But the woman was half a second from jerking *P* off. Even Stone had his limits.

"Jordan," Stone said coldly, "you never seem this giddy when you play my wife. Why is that?"

"I'll tell you why," *P* said as he kissed her hand, then started the car. "Because you can't truly appreciate her remarkable talent for repeatedly ramming an eight-inch strap-on up your ass."

P and Jordan held their breath, awaiting his response.

Without skipping a beat, Stone sat back and scrolled through his phone, simply acknowledging the statement with a weak, "Touché."

They roared with laughter until Jordan slid back in her seat as well, buckling up and preparing for the ride. Legs crossed, she slid off one shoe and turned to Stone, rubbing her foot softly against his shin. "So, what are you so engrossed in?"

He turned his phone to show her Madison's image lighting up his screen.

"A little young for you, isn't she?"

"And a little sweet for you." Stone pursed his lips before catching Jordan's eye. "Do you think she deceived us?"

Jordan considered it, slumping back in her seat. It took a moment for a smile to warm her face. "I don't know," she mused curiously.

Stone stared at the phone, memorizing her image. "Neither do I. But she's interesting. And," he took a breath, "she reminds me of Jack. Confident. Sincere. Barely on the brink of realizing her true potential. With the soul of a Finder . . ."

When his despondent words trailed off, Jordan placed her hand over his, giving it a tender squeeze. "I like her," she said, unusually sentimental in that moment.

Stone looked at her, then at *P*'s reflection glancing back, his eyebrow raised.

"So do I," Stone admitted quietly.

He took one last look before clicking off the phone and putting it away.

"Perhaps our paths *will* cross again." After a contemplative moment, he added, "I'll have someone keep an eye on her, because you never know."

CHAPTER 42

PIERRE

P READJUSTED the rearview mirror to its original position, again able to see the traffic behind him as he prepared to pull away. Taking another glance in it, he smiled.

The quiet flash of gray should have remained camouflaged in the distance, but to *P*, it was the beacon he'd been waiting for. Despite the drab dot of a helmet well masked amongst the vibrant Manhattan backdrop, nothing could hide it.

Or him.

P chuckled under his breath, finding the disguise as effective as using a busy Parisian street to hide the Eifel Tower.

Taking in an energized breath, he smiled. His faith was renewed. No matter how Stone and Jordan discouraged him, his carpe diem had finally arrived, and this time, he would sure as hell be seizing it.

Come on, Robles. Move your ass.

CHAPTER 43

PACO

PACO KEPT a sharp eye on the darkly tinted Bentley as it pulled away from DGI. His Ducati 1299 Superleggera would easily catch up. Though not a showpiece like its Panigale V4R cousin, the Ducati was exactly the high-performance motorcycle for this job. Anything else would draw too much attention, and the last thing he needed was attention.

Unlike the brightly painted showstopper that suited the average collector, this bike had been superbly converted. Carbon fiber subdued its color to a bland tone, and the added exhaust cutout valve quieted its telltale rumble. The fifty-thousand-dollar piece of stellar machinery was sure to be unnoticed by all.

He slipped on the high-tech helmet, switching on the heads-up display. He could clearly see the location of the Bentley moving along a 3-D city grid, but the display didn't obstruct his view. If anything, it enhanced it.

The tracker Madison had placed on Jordan would signal for a full ten miles, letting him seamlessly fall back to avoid detection.

"Call Alex," he said aloud. The auto-system placed the call.

"Got them?" Alex asked without even saying *hello*.

"Yup. Tracker active. Signal strong. I'll let you know what I find out. And tell Black this new helmet of his kicks ass."

Black would be Davis R. Black, or Richard to his friends. Alex loved every opportunity to collaborate with the CEO of Black Technologies on cutting-edge work.

"I thought you'd like it. Test it to the max so we can let him know what enhancements we need, but for the love of God, be careful. Don't crash." They both knew Paco's penchant for high-speed maneuvers.

"Worried about me? Aw, old age is making you soft."

"Well, I'm worried, all right. That helmet's worth a small fortune."

Underwhelmed, Paco let out a light laugh. "Thanks. I'll keep that in mind. Asshole," he grumbled in jest.

Alex shifted his tone. "Seriously, take care. Keep me posted."

"Will do."

Alex ended the call, and Paco keyed up his playlist before merging into traffic. Nothing like a little "Don't Stop Me Now" by Queen to set this chase in motion.

CHAPTER 44

ALEX

ALEX ARRIVED at their penthouse apartment a few hours after Madison, a little apprehensive about the discussion to come. She'd seemed intent on leaving DGI, though it seemed like a lifetime since she brought it up.

At the depressing thought of not seeing her every day at work, he missed her already. But it wasn't a line. Her happiness was his obligation, and his daily vow to a departed friend.

Ping. It was a text alert from Paco.

PACO: *They're on a Gulfstream. First stop Paris. Drum roll for the final stop.*

ALEX: *Singapore.*

PACO: *Bingo. We lucked out. They left their entire manifest with their final destination.*

ALEX: *Have our folks in Singapore keep an eye on them until you can catch up.*

PACO: *I'll head out first thing tomorrow. I've got the 787 lined up. If they lollygag in France, I'll beat them. Worst case, I'll trail them by a few hours. If nothing exciting happens, I'll be home in a week.*

ALEX: Sounds good. And let me know how the master suite of that new Dreamliner is. At nearly three hundred million, the toilet in that jet better be solid gold and self-wiping.

PACO: If you're asking for shit pics, I'm gonna need a raise.

ALEX: Hey, this is a professional corporate text, not Snapchat. Peddle your fetish photos elsewhere.

PACO: And let me know how it goes with Madison.

ALEX: I will. Be safe.

Alex set down his phone and headed into the living room. A long silver box was set on the soft chaise with an inviting red ribbon that caught his eye. "Madison? What's this?"

She called out from the bedroom. "A gift from Jordan. For me. She left it in my office."

Suspicious and alarmed, Alex was on it in two quick strides. Narrowing his eyes on the box with the hinged top, he couldn't tell if it had been opened.

Inspecting its size and weight, he determined it was just about right for a long-stemmed rose, but could contain anything. Even, in a worst-case scenario of epic proportion, explosives. He handled it with care.

"Madison, I'll be back. Before we open it, I need to have it checked out."

Box in hand, he prepared to head back to DGI to get a good look at its x-rayed contents, but Madison blocked his path.

"Too late," she said as she stepped toward him. With her long legs encased in a scandalous pair of fishnet stockings tucked into glossy high-heeled riding boots, it was clear he wasn't going anywhere.

Beneath her buttoned competition riding blazer was a braless goddess whose gorgeous breasts were taut against the stretchy fabric, begging to be released. She'd finished the look with a pair of black lace panties, a glimpse of them teasing him from beneath.

When Madison took a few steps closer, he completely forgot about the potentially hazardous box that might hold dangerous explosives that could wipe them all from the face of the earth. In this moment, it was the last thing on his mind. He dropped it, letting it slip from his fingers to land carelessly at his feet.

He took a quick look down to notice it had flipped open. The empty box was neither a threat, nor his immediate concern.

Alex recognized the item in Madison's hand. The gift. A braided black leather riding crop that would probably need a few baths in bleach before Madison's delicate fingers should have handled it. He breathed out a small sigh when he saw the tiny gold sticker and realized it must be new.

Delighted, Madison tapped the tip of the crop against the palm of her hand. "I believe you dropped the box, Mr. Drake."

"God, please tell me I'm getting punished for it," he said as he loosened his tie.

Her giggle was light and carefree, and eased his tight lips to a playful grin.

Half joking, he asked, "Did Jordan just become your new best friend, or mine?"

Madison prowled toward him, pressing against him as he sat on the chaise. Sliding herself onto his lap, she teased his mouth with the tip of the leather. He could only lose himself in the moment for so long before reminding himself of the gift giver.

Madison, this could be bugged, he mouthed.

She giggled, leaving him with a smile and a suggestive dismount. "It's not," she said with pure glee.

He stood too, letting his own half smile meet hers. "How do you know?"

Madison brushed his lips, conjuring his moan. She retrieved a small silver card from her pocket and placed it in his hand.

Recognizing the handwriting, he read the note out loud. "It's not bugged. Have fun, *J*."

"Satisfied?" Madison whispered.

He grumbled low. "Not half as satisfied as I'm about to be."

Alex cradled her cheeks, nibbled her lips, and took his time taking long, sweeping tastes of her before tearing himself away.

Resting his forehead on hers, he said, "You're the only woman for me, Madison Taylor."

"And you, Alex Drake, have an appointment."

"An appointment?" He pocketed the card, captivated and curious.

Her lips were a whisper from his, and she had a naughty glint in her eye that spiked his pulse. His gaze washed over her as he returned her grin.

"I believe it's time for my riding lesson," she said softly, handing him the crop. She turned away, sashaying down the hall. "Come along, Mr. Drake."

The braid of the crop felt natural in his grip. Different. New.

His hungry gaze followed her, enjoying every step of her walking away. His ninety-nine percent angel was showing off every bit of her sizzling-hot one percent, plunging a flaming red arrow deep inside his heart. The devil in him longed for her heat.

"Indeed, it is, Ms. Taylor." Briskly, he smacked the crop against the palm of his hand and chased after her.

In their bedroom, Madison waited, leaning against the bed. His glance floated down her body, taking in every arc and angle, finally landing at her shiny black boots. "Are those comfortable?"

She nodded. "Mm-hmm."

He arched a brow. Decisive, he said, "Good, because you'll be keeping them on." He traced the end of the crop along her inner thigh, commanding her. "Turn around."

Once she obeyed, he bent her forward on the bed.

He ran the tip of the crop on a lazy trail up the back of her leg, gliding along the underside of her ass and swiping her core. She moaned. He tore off his clothes and removed his tie. It felt like an eternity since he'd been inside her. The last time was too rushed.

At the sight of her—bent over, wanting, waiting—he pumped himself hard, dredging up every bit of his self-control. As much as he wanted to bury himself balls deep in her tight walls, tonight was for her. If he had his way, every night would be for her.

He placed the length of his thickness along the crack of her soft, round ass before leaning to her ear. "You're beautiful, Madison. You have no idea what you're doing to me."

"Then show me," she begged.

"In my own time," he said, giving her ear a terse nip. Her sexy squeal went straight to his cock.

He caressed the firm flesh of her butt before slowly tugging her panties off as he whispered, "Perfect."

Admiring her firm ass and slick core beneath, he slid the crop against her hip, then let the rod rest along the small of her back.

"Give me your hands," he growled.

Obeying, she lowered her hands down the sides of her body, presenting them to him. He moved them into position, palms against her butt. Stretching the elastic lace of her undies wide, he secured her wrists by looping each end to the waiting crop.

Satisfied with her restraints, he told her, "Don't move. Not a muscle."

With that, he moved her hands, using her own fingers to spread herself for him. Expose herself so he could take in her round ass, soaked lips, and tight hold in a glance. Giving herself over completely, just as he'd always do for her.

He dragged two fingers along her, painting her pretty pussy with her own sweet dew. As soon as she bucked back, craving more, he gave her ass a smack.

"You're not going to move until I tell you to come. Understand, Madison?"

"Yes." She breathed out the word, panting hard.

Alex dropped to his knees with soft, sensual kisses along her cheeks, letting his stubble graze against her thighs, and enjoying each tortured whimper she released.

But she obeyed. She didn't move.

"Good," he said before slicing his hot tongue through the plump folds of her core.

He forced a thick finger inside, and her shudder was instant.

He gave her ass another smack. "Not yet, beautiful."

Moaning, Madison writhed in place.

"Is this what you want?" Alex asked, circling her clit with the pad of his finger. "Do you want me to make you come?"

"Yes," she begged. Her body quivered, and she cried out, "Please."

Fisting his cock, he invaded her with his tongue, feeding on her cunt, lapping up her wetness and fingering her with his other hand. The walls of her sex shuddered with need.

He pressed a second finger in her soaked pussy, and she rocked with him. "Now, Madison. Come for me now."

Alex let her ride out the wave against his hand, slowing his pace as she peaked and floated down. He wasn't done, but he was finished with her restraints. He released her wrists, giving each a tender kiss.

Lying beside her, he moved her on top so she could mount him, because her outfit was perfect for it. His dick was hard against the heat of her wet center. Unconstrained, he shoved every inch of his thick length in to the hilt.

"Yes," she cried. Rocking with his thrusts, she adjusted to his size, sliding herself from the tip of his shaft clear to the base. Owning him as much as he owned her.

"Fuck, Madison, you're so tight."

He reached for her blazer, releasing the buttons one by one, letting it fall from her shoulders and drape along her arms. He pinched her nipples and caressed her breasts. She was breathtaking.

The soft waves of her hair were silky against his hands, and more of her softness brushed against his touch. As her head fell back, her body arched, and her mouth parted to take in deeper breaths with each penetrating thrust.

"Just like that, Madison. Just like that," he said, losing himself in the glory of her, watching as she chased her climax faster, spreading her thighs wider to take in more as he bucked back.

He gripped her hips, driving himself further. Deeper. Madison leaned back, gripping the solid muscles of his thighs, barely grazing his skin with the tips of her nails before timidly shying away.

"No," he said, his voice gruff and stern.

Grabbing the crop, he placed the tip of it to her chin, coercing her eyes to his. She nearly stopped, like that was fucking happening. He gripped her ass, driving himself in, forcing her against his seeping cock, working her back to his pace.

"Never hide what you want from me, Madison." His dark eyes and hoarse timbre commanded her. His hips reignited, ramming her mercilessly. "Do it."

Madison skimmed her fingers along his thighs, sucked in a breath, and raked her nails against his skin.

Alex hissed, arching his back. It was everything. Everything he needed. Everything he wanted. This was Madison. She was his, and he was hers.

"Now," he said, splitting her wide, filling her, and pumping all he had deep inside. She collapsed upon him, crying out as her body shook and her tight core milked him hard.

As their breathing calmed, Madison nestled in his arms, laying her head on his pounding chest. Tenderly, he brushed his fingers across her shoulder, through the long, lush strands of her hair and down to the small of her back.

Disappointed, he found her tension still there, in tight knots along the softness of her back.

"Penny for your thoughts?" he asked, his voice gentle.

"Hmm . . ." She trailed a finger across his chest, lazily drifting it back and forth. "I was just wondering when I might be able to take these off." She bent her knees, casually swinging her boot-laden legs in the air.

He laughed. "In three days." When her skeptical glare challenged his playful expression, he looked down at them again, reconsidering. "Two and a half?"

Rolling her to her back, he made his way down her body one tender kiss at a time. He unzipped the first boot, sliding it off along with its stocking, and worked his massaging fingers into her tight calf.

"Anything else on your mind?" he asked.

Her gaze broke away, staring across the room. Moving from Swedish to shiatsu, he worked her muscles harder, and she moaned with relief. "Your hands are unbelievable. If this whole billionaire CEO thing loses its luster, you've definitely got options."

He caught her playful glance as he kissed the inside of her thigh. "So do you, beautiful. Lots of options at your sexy little fingertips. Listen, if you're worried about leaving DGI . . ." Her wide eyes met his, her angst apparent. "Don't."

Alex removed the other boot and stocking, repeating the process along her leg. "How about this? Stay. Just until you decide on your next move. You'll know the right opportunity when it comes along. And there's a lot more to know about DGI. We do a lot of work with vets. Our robotics center is located next to a VA medical center. I'd love to introduce you around. It's . . . been a while since I've been there."

He drew in a deep breath, ready to battle another demon or two for the woman he loved.

She cupped his cheek, sweetly laughing as she caressed his jaw. "Well, I'd say that sounds right up my alley." Her fingers combed through his hair. "You're the love of my life, Alex."

"And you, Madison, are the love I never thought would happen. The happiness I never imagined, or even thought I deserved."

He pulled her hand to his lips.

"Other than you and me being together, nothing else matters. If you want to be part of DGI, then you're going to be a fucking part of it. I didn't build this company by giving a rat's ass about the court of public opinion, and I'm not about to start. But," he gingerly caressed the small of her back, holding her close, "if your dreams are taking you down a different path, I'll still be the man by your side, every step of the way. You've given me a gift, a life far beyond what I dared to even hope was possible. So, mark my words, Ms. Taylor. I won't settle for anything less than you being over-the-moon ecstatic on a goddamn daily basis."

He kissed her again, taking in a deep breath and loving the smile his lips left on hers.

CHAPTER 45

Three weeks later

MADISON TAPPED HER FINGERS, eager as her phone attempted the FaceTime call. It was more than a little frustrating to watch it click over to voice mail.

Unavailable?

She checked the time and did the math in her head. Five in the morning in New York should be five in the evening in Singapore. Scrolling through her text messages, Madison verified the time and date. And she had accounted for the shift in time zone.

As she reread his last text, she squealed with the announcement of an incoming call. Eagerly, she tapped to accept it.

"I'm sure you have an excellent reason for refusing to FaceTime me, Mr. Robles."

"Well," Paco said, keeping his tone casual. "I can't FaceTime right now because I'm . . . um . . . sunbathing."

"And?" Madison drew out the word.

"And let's just say I don't like tan lines."

Slapping a hand over her open mouth, she couldn't mask all her girlish giggles.

"Well, then don't pan down," she said. "Come on, I need to see your face. You were only supposed to be gone a week. For those of you playing along at home, that's seven days. We're now blazing past three weeks and heading for four, and a month without Paco is a month without sunshine and Starbucks. Seriously, I need my Paco fix!"

In the small span of silence, it was obvious her pleas were falling on his diamond-studded deaf ears.

"Don't worry. I promise you'll see me soon, *hermanita*. But what's going on today? How's it been working with the VA and the robotics team?"

She didn't mean to sigh. Especially in the face of him calling her his little sister.

Paco picked up on her angst. "Let me guess, Goldilocks. That bed's nice and all, but your frisky little feet are dangling over the edge and anxious to move along. And quit giving me that look. Seriously, those wrinkles aren't going to Botox themselves."

Even though he couldn't see them, her furrows melted, but it didn't wipe away all of her gloom. "God, what's wrong with me? I'm being handed one silver platter after another, and all I'm dying for is a plastic tray of all-you-can-eat from Golden Corral."

"Girlie, I've got you. We'll meet up at the chocolate fountain. And don't call me God. Your Royal Highness is my absolute limit. I'm not a deity. I just look like one."

"I'll bet you do with all that *au naturel* exposure."

"But if we're heading to a buffet when I return, I'd better hit the gym. Actually, I could head there now."

Cutting the call short? Already?

"Wait. Before you go." She quieted for a moment, hesitant to make her request. But Paco's quirky mind reading was as sharp as ever. As she struggled for words, a text popped up.

As always, he made her grin. It was a picture of Paco wearing a traditional *baju melayu* suit. The buttercream silk suited him perfectly, and it draped him like a second skin, custom tailored to perfection. His smile was brilliant, and he looked as though he was posing for the cover of *GQ Singapore*. Behind him was a giant stone sculpture of what he'd called a Merlion. Its surroundings looked like an oasis across the globe.

"There," he said. "Is that what you need? Now you're seeing me."

"Worst loophole ever." She held the phone a little tighter as she fawned over the shot.

"I promise, I will see you very, very soon. Listen, I'm running late. I've got a big night ahead—"

"Of course you do," she teased. "New York nightclubs are in their twenty-third day of mourning your departure. Their vigil continues."

"As it should. And I know you have a big day ahead." His tone was knowing and suggestive.

"I shouldn't be surprised that you know about the meeting, but just how much do you know? Alex won't tell me a thing except to show up in his office at four sharp."

"Well, I would tell you, but it will take more time that I have. I really have to run. My sunblock has faded in all the wrong spots."

"How inconveniently convenient."

But she couldn't end the call just yet. Not like that. And if there was one thing Madison Taylor could count on, it was that Paco would burn and blister to a disturbing degree before he'd hang up on her.

Softly, she said, "This thing today. Whatever it is, I feel like it's important. To us. To our family. And I don't want to do it without you. I know the time difference, but can I FaceTime you from the meeting, so I can see you? Really see you? I mean, it'll definitely cut into your beauty sleep—"

"I promise you, no matter what, you'll see me." His words were tender and sincere. "But I really have to go. Talk soon. Love you, *hermanita*."

"Love you too."

Though her days were now filled with learning the ins and outs of Drake Robotics, today was different. Madison had called it quits early with the prosthetics team to hurry back to DGI.

Setting foot in the skyscraper was vibrant. Thrilling. Like coming home. It was nothing like when she'd left all those weeks ago.

Her early arrival was intentional. The meeting with Alex wasn't for another half hour, but it gave her a chance to revisit her old digs. Her first real office. Her energy was off the charts, and she bubbled over with exhilaration.

Smiling, Madison hopped into her familiar leather desk chair and fired up her computer. Immediately, a message popped up, making her grin from ear to ear.

ANONYMOUS: *Hi.*

She let out a little sigh at the nostalgia the message evoked. *I'm so head over heels in love with you.*

MADISON: *Hi back at ya.*

ANONYMOUS: *I'm taking an employee morale survey.*

MADISON: *Really? Because the president of the morale committee used that line on me months ago.*

ANONYMOUS: *You don't say? How'd that turn out?*

MADISON: *Oh, you know. Totally marrying the man.*

ANONYMOUS: *So, you're saying it works. Then I'd better get back to business. What Starbucks beverage would make you happiest right now?*

His question made her smile. *Hmm, an extra creamy Alex Frappuccino would sure hit the spot.*

MADISON: *I'm going with an oldie but a goodie. Iced matcha latte with almond milk.*

ANONYMOUS: *You sure? They've got a ton of coffees. And an exotic collection of iced teas.*

MADISON: *Iced matcha. I'm positive.*

I may not be able to make a career choice, she thought, *but the least I can do is pick a drink.*
Madison glanced at the clock on her desktop as footsteps approached. *That can't be the matcha. It's only been a minute.*

MADISON: *Gotta go. Someone's coming. I feel like a kid waiting for the ice cream truck, with the sweet sound of tinkling music miles away. #waiting4matcha.*

Love you.

The footsteps stopped as she finished typing.

"I love you too," Alex said with his captivating voice and charming grin. In he strolled, carrying a tall green cup of her favorite drink. "One iced matcha latte with almond milk coming up."

He set the drink on her desk and leaned in for a kiss. She locked her arms around his shoulders and pulled him in.

"Now that's one hell of a kiss," he said, stealing another one.

Suspicious of his remarkable accomplishment, she eyed the drink. "Wait, how's that possible? You messaged me, and I only just said what I wanted."

He whipped out his phone. "DGI app. And Paco's not the only one who can read your mind. I am about to marry you, after all. I'd like to think I know you on a deeply intimate level."

"And what would have happened if I'd decided on something more spontaneous?" Her eyes lit with the challenge.

Alex sat back on her desk, casually crossing his arms as his brows lifted. "Well, it's all very logical. There are technically over eighty thousand combinations of Starbucks drinks."

Intrigued, Madison sat taller.

"Now, you prefer almond milk, so that narrows the field. And you only drink hot beverages first thing in the morning . . . basically, nursing them until they turn into cold beverages. Field further narrowed."

Her subtle smile transformed to a wide grin as he continued.

"And although they can do any number of custom drinks, you pretty much stick to basic menu offerings, especially with iced drinks. So, after all is said and done, we're really down to about thirty-one possibilities."

Madison drew the straw to her lips and sipped, waiting for the rest of his deductive reasoning, but he stopped. "Okay, so we're at thirty-one. How did you get from thirty-one to one insanely perfect iced matcha latte?"

"Telepathy?" he said.

"If it were telepathy, you'd be naked." Suggestively, she sucked the straw between her lips.

"Hey, I have to have some trade secrets up my sleeve." He kissed her forehead. "So, four o'clock sharp. My office. Not a second early or late."

Sure. Nothing ominous about that.

"Four o'clock sharp," she whispered in agreement as he leaned over for a sweet farewell kiss. "And I thought we said no more secrets?"

He headed out, saying over his shoulder, "Trade secrets don't count."

Watching that man walk away, Madison sipped her drink and smiled as she imagined him naked.

And in slow motion.

She'd just returned to her screen when another alert popped up. She clicked the message. It was from Fred, the head of IT.

FRED: *Hey, you're online. You need to get to the break room a floor down ASAP! Someone left THIRTY iced coffees in assorted flavors. If you can't, let me know what you like, and I'll grab it before the masses gets wind of this manna from heaven.*

Madison calmed herself, preventing the consequential creamy matcha goodness from spraying out her nose.

MADISON: *You're such a sweetie, but I'm good. The manna delivery man hit me up earlier.*

FRED: *As long as you're covered.*

She passed the remaining time catching up on emails, clearing out a few tasks, and soaking up every minute of being in the moment. Her smile re-emerged with every scrumptious sip.

Trade secrets, indeed.

Madison eventually made her way to Alex's office, careful to check the time. Sucking in a deep breath, she was ready to FaceTime Paco.

At the exact time—not a minute early or late—she knocked.

Someone knocked back. Before she could knock again or try the door, her phone rang.

Paco!

She accepted his FaceTime request. His face filled the frame as he waggled his brows, and she burst out laughing.

"It's two minutes after four your time," he said. "Why aren't you in Alex's office yet?"

Madison hushed her laughter as his fabulous eyebrows launched its own little variety show, dancing with wild exaggeration. "I can't believe how happy I am to see you, Paco. And I tried, but it sounded like a bizarre game of knock-knock."

Paco stayed in the frame when a voice boomed from behind him.

"Did you try the password?" the man shouted.

Dad?

Wait. Dad's in Singapore?

A round of raucous laughter broke out from behind Alex's office door. Without knocking, Madison opened it. As soon as she did, she froze, captured in that state of over-the-moon ecstasy that Alex had raved about.

CHAPTER 46

MADISON

Stunned, Madison couldn't believe it. There they all were, laughing from their seats around the conference table. As soon as they saw her, they stood.

Her father, Paco, and Alex were on the far side, with Mark and Jess on the other with a man she didn't recognize nearest. The stranger was seated next to the head of the table, a seat, she guessed, that had been saved for her.

Madison quickly made the rounds of hugs and kisses, while holding on to her confusion as much as her joy. Paco was her first hug.

"Sunbathing, huh?" she asked with a grin.

He gave her a coy shrug. "I was technically in the sun."

"Where?" she asked, drawing out the word.

"Basel. I needed a quick stop before New York to pick up some goodies for everyone."

Dan proudly displayed the watch on his wrist. "See what I got?"

Paco lifted his wrist as well. "Matching Patek Philippe watches."

Her loving gaze locked on her dad, who was tickled pink to have a twin adornment to Paco's. Without a doubt, he hadn't the slightest clue that it probably cost more than his house. He and Paco were together. Nothing filled her heart more.

Having greeted all but one, she pulled away to meet the mystery member of the party. The silver-fox Patrick Dempsey lookalike sported a deep blue suit and golden two-toned tie. She couldn't help but think he looked familiar.

Unworried, she wrapped her arms around him. "I don't know who you are, but you're in such good company, I have to give you a hug," she said firmly.

He laughed as he returned the gesture. "Well, I'll take it, young lady. I'd say it was icing on the cake for today, but I think that's still to come." He motioned for her to take her seat, and they all sat. "It's great to meet you, Madison. I'm Bill Charles—"

Congressman Charles?

"—and Alex and I go back quite a few years. Before this whole DGI world-domination bit, for sure. We met when I was using my GI Bill to get a law degree. Alex willingly took the aid of a struggling law student to help with some contract writing."

Alex chimed in. "A stellar lawyer who would work for a few bucks and some home-cooked meals. Let's just say it was definitely the Casablanca beginning of a beautiful friendship."

Bill placed a hand on hers, giving it a gentle squeeze before proceeding. "Alex reached out to me and shared with me what happened with your brother. I'm so sorry for your loss, but I'm just as sorry for his. He was stripped of a status he was entitled to, and as a vet, that just . . . well, I won't pelt you with expletives, but let's just say it didn't sit well with me. So, while you were working with Army Records, I was digging into a few other things."

He released her hand, reaching for the glossy black folder on the table before them, and slid it to her. Flipping it open, she saw it had a few documents on one side, and a small envelope tucked into the pocket on the other.

Madison reached for her father's hand, and he scooted closer to take it. They exchanged a teary gaze before carefully studying the contents.

The first letter acknowledged Jack's length of service at the time of his death, reinstating his active-duty status posthumously. But it was the second that brought on the rush of tears.

She handed the fancy document to her father, who shared it with Paco. This was no letter. It was a certificate.

To all who shall see these presents, greeting:
This is to certify that
The President of the United States of America
has awarded the
PURPLE HEART
Established by General George Washington

at Newburgh, New York, August 7, 1782
to
Second Lieutenant Jackson D. Taylor
United States Army

Dan's face dropped to his hands, and Paco squeezed his shoulder for support. Everyone understood, and each and every one was a mess of tears.

Madison swiped helplessly at her cheeks. *For all their planning, no one thought to bring a box of tissues?*

Mark found one quickly and passed it around.

It was then that Madison noticed the boxes. Medals undoubtedly filled them, but no one reached for them. They couldn't. Instead, they just focused blurry eyes on the certificate.

Madison took a deep breath and tried to move on. Again, she took to the folder, but seemed to be staring at an identical certificate. She removed it, her blurry eyes struggling to see the words, then she gasped aloud. This was no copy.

"Oh my God," she blurted, and shot a glance to Paco. She jumped up and hugged him. Hugged him hard but couldn't speak.

Dan grabbed the certificate. In half a second, he was doing the same thing, wrapping his arms around Paco and blubbering like a baby.

Not knowing what was going on, Paco caressed Madison's back tenderly. "Hey, there now. What is it?"

She pointed, and Paco looked down to see the second certificate lying next to Jack's. They were virtually the same, with the distinctive difference in two lines, indicating who it was issued to.

Staff Sergeant Paco J. Robles
United States Air Force

Madison wiped his cheeks, tending to the slow stream of tears Paco hadn't noticed.

"There has to be a mistake," he said. "I didn't lose my life in combat."

The congressman spoke up. "That's not the only reason the Purple Heart is awarded."

Alex nudged Madison and Dan back, letting Bill take center stage for the moment ahead.

"Your wounds and concussion were the result of a terrorist attack—one that happened while you were part of a military mission. There's no mistake. You're a deserving recipient."

Congressman Charles stood and opened one of the boxes on the table before him before removing its contents. "I am honored to formally present you with this Purple Heart for your bravery in service to our country." He held the medal as Paco stood, then pinned it to his lapel. As he shook Paco's hand, Paco blinked silently in amazement as tears streamed down his cheeks. "Thank you for your heroism, Staff Sergeant Robles."

When the congressman stepped back, Madison and Dan immediately rushed over to envelop Paco in hard hugs. They held each other for several minutes, finally releasing him to let Alex give him a handshake and a hug. Paco wrapped his arms around Alex, resulting in both men exchanging pats on the back.

Soon, they all returned to their seats, and the congressman rested his clasped hands on the table. "But it doesn't end there."

He tapped at the last of the contents. A small envelope still in the folder. With trembling hands, Madison removed it and emptied its contents. In her hands was a check.

"I don't understand," she said, dabbing at her nose and eyes with the fresh tissue Alex handed her. She searched Congressman Charles's face for the answer, and he began to explain.

"Because Jack died on active duty and in combat, he was entitled to certain benefits that were never paid out. These are those benefits, with a small amount of interest."

Madison looked at it again. Though far from a million dollars, it was still a whole lot of money. Much more than she'd ever expected, though she never really expected anything. She handed the check to her father, who shoved it back.

"Dad, this is yours," she insisted.

"No, jellybean, it's yours. In case you hadn't noticed the last time you were home, *somebody* has been keeping me swimming in checks."

Madison smiled at the inside joke. All these years, her father had been sitting on millions of dollars in uncashed checks, every last one of them signed by Alex Drake.

Thoughtfully, she studied the check, then considered Paco. Jack and Paco might as well have been married, and the money should rightfully go to his spouse.

"Don't even give me those puppy-dog eyes, girlie. I've got more than enough for the rest of my life."

The last thing Paco meant was money, though the man had enough to buy a small island or two. Or eight. She heard his meaningful words loud and clear and followed his fingers as they brushed the Purple Heart on his chest.

"You don't have to decide this minute," Jess said, her words full of wisdom and promise.

"Still not giving me the answers, huh?" Madison asked, recalling their conversation on the road trip to the Adirondacks.

"Nope." Jess grinned. "Although, I'll bet that would make a nice little bit of seed money for a certain one-eight-hundred-passion project."

The others didn't understand the inside joke, but waited as Jess and Madison enjoyed a tear-filled moment.

"Actually," Madison said, "I think that's probably perfect."

"What is?" Dan asked, wrapping her in his arms.

Madison faced him with a big grin, glistening eyes, and for the first time in a decade, a surge of hope. The hope that she could finally move past her grief. Take her love for Jack and catapult it to a whole new level.

"This," she waved the check back and forth, "is perfect. It's Jack's past and my future. And our legacy," she said with a tender glance at Paco and her dad.

"This is the beginning of a new nonprofit to help families of fallen service members." She took the check in both hands, seeing all the boundless potential in the small piece of paper. "The Jack Taylor Foundation."

The words had barely escaped her lips before the congressman chimed in. "I'd like to match that amount."

"Me too," Mark said.

Alex jumped in. "Me three."

"Nope. No check writing from you, Mr. Drake," Madison said.

"Why not? I swear, my check will clear," he joked.

"Because you've been writing checks to the Taylors for long enough."

Alex scrunched his face with exaggerated offense. "Seriously, my money's no good here?"

"Your money? No. Well, at least not now," Madison said, adding, "But your *here* is good here."

Alex's indignation transformed to confusion. "Huh?"

"Your *here* is good here. Here. DGI headquarters. I'm gonna need an office, and this might be the perfect place. You've got a lot of unused resources in these sky-scraping digs. Perhaps you could donate a small piece of the DGI pie? An office or two for me and whomever else I can rustle up to volunteer?"

She gave her father an adoring look, and he shot back a wink of approval. "And supplies," she said to Alex. "Seriously, your supply room could use a bit of a cleanup."

Frowning, Alex maintained his pout. "You've got it. Anything you need. But I'd still like to donate a few bucks to this foundation."

In Alex Drake terms, a few dollars could easily mean a few hundred thousand or a few million.

"Not a cent. At least, not until I figure out what I'm doing. And as for the two of you," her gaze darted between Mark and the congressman, "you have my sincere thanks, but I'll hold your IOUs for the moment."

She snapped the check between her hands. "First, let's just see what I can do with this. This is where it will start. This way, Jack is the *foundation* of the Jack Taylor Foundation."

"And you have one hell of a kickass mentor to help ensure that goes as far as it possibly can," Jess said.

Madison nodded at Jess. "That I do."

Congressman Charles checked his watch. "Unfortunately, I'm needed across town." He stood and extended his hand to Madison, who took it in both of hers. "And my IOU can be collected anytime, Madison. Anytime at all."

She jumped up to wrap another hug around his neck, this one much tighter than the first, before returning to her seat. The door closed behind the congressman, and Madison smiled at her friends and loved ones left around the table.

"Okay," Paco said, "I don't know about you all, but my oncoming jet lag is only slightly offset by being absolutely famished. And if you don't figure something out quickly, I'm taking Madison up on her offer for some chocolate-fountain fun."

Confused, Mark and Alex squinted at each other.

Madison and Jess watched with excitement, shouting in unison, "Food challenge!"

The air filled with chatter about themes and menu items. Soon, they agreed that Paco's place was centrally located and should host the festivities. It was even better that he'd become the B&B for Dan.

They paired up, with Paco and Dan agreeing to get the charcuterie and champagne ready for everyone's arrival. Mark and Jess would head to a different store than Alex and Madison, and all would meet back at Paco's in an hour.

~

As the elevator opened to the DGI garage, Alex and Madison strolled toward the lone luxury car left in the empty subterranean space. His fingers wove through hers.

"Madison, I want to give you something. An engagement gift. And . . . it's a little fancy," he said with a pre-emptive apology as he let her into the car. He made his way to the driver's side and sat but didn't start the engine.

"Alex, you've already given me more than the Publisher's Clearinghouse."

"Then one more piece on the pile won't make much difference," he said in that adorable tone that absolutely melted her.

Watching her, he waited for the smallest inkling of approval. She gave it in a big, beautiful kiss.

"Good." Stealing another kiss, he whispered, "Close your eyes."

He slipped a velvety box into her hand. Even with her eyes shut, she knew it had to be a particular familiar shade of blue. "Okay, take a look."

Opening her eyes, she opened the elegant box. Her sharp gasp filled the air. "Alex . . . I don't know what to say."

The box was brilliant with the sparkle of diamond earrings, their light dancing with every subtle shift of her hand. They perfectly matched her engagement ring.

"I wanted you to have a pair since your last ones were swiped from under your nose by a dastardly thief."

"Hey, that's my brother you're talking about. And technically, I gave them to him."

Madison loved that Paco conned them from her right off the bat. Since that day, she'd never seen him without them. She flipped down the visor, admiring her reflection as she put them on.

Alex stroked her cheek. "Well, I'm hoping these are very much to your liking. That you feel like they're truly *you*, because, and I say this with all the love in the world . . ."

She turned to him, suddenly concerned. "Because what?"

He took her face in his hands, caressing her cheeks with his thumbs.

"Madison, in all seriousness, if for whatever reason you don't like them . . ."

His eyes tracked hers as he took a deep breath. Solemnly, he shook his head before whispering, "I'm not taking one for the team. A diamond-studded cock-ring is one thing. But I am absolutely, positively not getting anything pierced."

Madison watched this handsome man with the lickable dimple return to the task of starting the car. "So, now there are conditions on our love?"

"Damn straight. I draw the line at piercings. Besides, you have conditions too, with the whole 'no check writing from you, Alex,'" he said, mimicking her in his best falsetto.

She threw back her head with a laugh. "Not forever. Just not now. Which is more than you're giving me, since, apparently, piercings have made its way to your hard-limit list."

"Trust me, you don't want anything to snag on the way out. Speaking of lists, we need to figure out what we're picking up at the store. I'm in the mood to kick some best-friend butt tonight. Team Drake's taking home the trophy." He gave her a naughty glance. "And speaking of trophy . . ."

"Let me guess. If you win big, I'll win big too?"

"Without a doubt, you'll be taking first. Repeatedly."

"Why do I have a feeling I'm going to see your trophy either way?"

"Because you, my determined little sex kitten, have a remarkable way of keeping your eyes on the prize."

He took her hand to his lips, giving it a reverent kiss. He wove their fingers together and rested their joined hands on his thigh.

As they drove off into the sunset, Madison marveled at the prize of a man sitting next to her. He did more than restore her brother's military record. He had Jack and Paco officially recognized as the heroes they always were.

And all this time, Alex Drake had been like a son to her father, generously giving what he had and asking for nothing in return.

True, the earrings, like the bracelet and ring before them, were masterpieces. But they paled in comparison to Alex Drake himself—the man who'd blown into her life with a snide remark and a splash of spiked coffee. The man who'd lovingly labored every day since then to slay his demons and steal her heart.

Next to her sat the man she was destined to love forever. The man she was going to marry.

As they took off into the glowing kaleidoscope of a bustling New York evening, Madison knew that together, they could take on whatever life threw at them.

They'd thwarted a building full of occasional busybodies. Danced with a dangerous group of ex-spies. And in the midst of it all, they treaded dangerously close to what was sure to become Manhattan's event of the century—their wedding. And let's not forget the spur-of-the-moment pop-up food competition.

Life was throwing Madison and Alex one racy adventure after the other, and they were ready to face it all. Her smile spread wide as she admired their interlaced fingers and squeezed a little tighter.

Bring it on!

Because hand in hand, they could tackle anything. Together, they could take on the world.

BOOK 4: FINDERS KEEPERS

AN ALEX DRAKE NOVEL

FINDERS KEEPERS

LEXXI JAMES

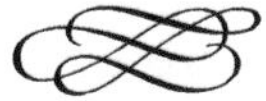

ALEX

ALEX DRAKE STOOD before a full-length mirror, eyeing every detail of his new three-piece suit. Normally, his custom tailoring would be done in the comfort of his penthouse home. Today, Alex and his best friend were meeting with his tailor in his office—a grand executive suite at the top of his skyscraper in the midst of Manhattan.

The look was flawless. A tad more formal than he preferred, but with a reluctant nod, he approved. This wasn't just a suit. Frowning, Alex lifted the lapels of his suit jacket to inspect the vest.

Though comfortable, the weight was much heavier than any normal vest. *It's battle armor.*

When Paco stepped beside him, Alex admired his friend, who was wearing a new suit of his own. "Looks good."

"Good?" Paco huffed. "No, not good. Good is professional and worldly. Boring as shit. We're totally rocking it like James fucking Bond. You killed it again, Josh."

Satisfied, the tailor happily took the compliment and gave them a smile before departing.

Alex's throat tightened by a heavy knot of nerves. He nodded again, sighing to himself.

"A three-piece suit is perfect." Paco caught his gaze in the mirror, his tone confident and reassuring. "Don't worry. Good things come in threes. The number is mystical, magical, hence the rule of threes. It amplifies the intensity of everything. Luck. Power. The Jonas Brothers."

"I'll settle for luck."

Paco lifted a brow. "I'll settle for the Jonas Brothers."

A soft ping sounded from Alex's phone, but he ignored it.

"Not getting that?" Paco asked, a curious smile on his face, but Alex's only answer was a shake of his head. "It could be important."

"It can wait."

Paco didn't ask more, and Alex sure as hell wasn't getting into it. Obviously, Paco recognized the assigned ring tone. *Jordan Stone.*

Talk about a mystical enigma. With legs up to her eyeballs and a penchant for sin and seduction, Jordan Stone was in a class all her own. Alex never knew where he stood with her. *Or with Madison.*

Coming on strong with Alex was one thing. But when it came to his fiancée, nothing was off limits for Jordan, and she made no pretense about it. She liked Madison and would take any and every chance to cop a feel or steal a kiss. *But why?*

And why the three of them to begin with? The three Jordan Stones.

A decade ago, his Jordan Stone, aka *Jordan*, lured him with her wicked ways. And her tongue. Resisting her would have been pointless, but giving in was his undoing.

At the same time, Madison's brother, Jack, was meeting with a much older and supremely powerful man—Jordan Stone, or simply *Stone*. The mastermind recruited the sharp West Point grad with a patriotic song and dance, seducing the all-American guy to do more for his country than his country could do for him.

It cost Jack his life. And left everyone who cared for him devastated in the aftermath.

And then there was the third Jordan Stone—Paco's recruiter, and perhaps the biggest mystery of them all. Where that man with no alias was concerned, Paco left no *stone* unturned. Literally.

On paper, the operative didn't exist. All Paco ever learned about him was that the man died on a mission years ago. Unsettled, Paco continued investigating.

It was one of many things Alex and Paco had in common. If there was an unsolved puzzle, leave it to them to obsess over it.

"Hey. Where'd you go?"

Seeing the worry in his best friend's eyes, Alex forced a smile. "Nothing. Just thinking about threes."

Nodding, Paco gave him a bigger smile. "I know what you mean. Siri," he boomed.

"Siri here."

"Play *Sucker*." Singing along, Paco hip-bumped his boss before busting out all his club moves.

Embarrassed, Alex pinched the bridge of his nose. Sternly, he said, "Paco?"

"What?" Paco gave him an innocent look. "You've got to get out of your own head for a hot second. Nothing does that like letting loose with Kevin, Joe, and Nick."

Shaking his head with an inescapable laugh, Alex avoided the next butt bump by checking his watch. "Oh, look at the time. Airport in two hours."

The reminder was hardly necessary.

Paco killed the music, rubbing his hands together enthusiastically. "When the real party starts!"

CHAPTER 1

MADISON

MADISON GLARED at the sexy stud of a man standing before her. With his arms crossed, he blocked the steps to his transatlantic jet with his solid build.

"No girls allowed." Alex Drake was standing his ground, scoffing at the conventions of political correctness despite his high-profile position. His defiant eyes let her know he meant business. And his telltale smirk showed just how much he loved it.

Hands on her hips, she pushed back. "Is that so?"

An immediate divide was occurring right there on the tarmac of Teterboro Airport. The blurred lines of beauty versus billionaire became irrefutably clear. Men versus women.

Standing on one side was Alex Drake, founder of Drake Global Industries, or DGI. But he stood alone as the other men chuckled, abandoning him as they boarded the jet.

His best friend and cutthroat rival, Mark Donovan of Excelsior/Centurion, was the first to ditch his bestie. And then there was Davis "Richard" Black, CEO of Black Technologies. He threw an apologetic glance at his new fiancée, Jaclyn, who stood in solidarity with Madison.

Alex stepped closer.

Confused, amused, and throwing him the prettiest pouts in all the state, the women stood aligned. Jess Bishop, the sassy, no-holds-barred wife of Mark, might have married the man, but never took his name. She locked arms with Madison as she'd done dozens of times.

Apparently comfortable in the immediate girl power they shared, Jaclyn Long, COO of billion-dollar conglomerate Long Multinational, took Madison's other arm. Though she and Madison had only just met, their obvious alliance was unflinching.

Take that, Alex Drake.

Rounding out the bonds of sisterhood was Paco Robles. A politically astute man who could easily dissuade a take-no-prisoners battle of the sexes, he held his ground with the women. His stance clearly screamed, "I'm not Switzerland."

"That's so." Alex checked his watch. "And it's time to say good-bye." Possessively, he swept Madison from the arms of her comrades and kissed her until her body practically melted into his.

"Wait." Alarmed, she lowered her voice. "You're seriously ditching us?"

"Yes. The boys are heading to Singapore without you." Postponing an explanation, he kissed her again.

"What?" Her brows knitted in disbelief. "I can handle the risks, if that's what you're worried about. I know what to expect, and I'm ready for it."

"Are you?" he asked. In an instant, worry crossed his face.

The question had been asked and answered dozens of times. But as much as nobody wanted Madison that close to certain danger, there was no way they were going to Singapore without her.

"Yes," she said firmly, reassuring Alex as best she could. Impatient, she asked, "And why did we all pack if you were ditching us?"

Paco stepped closer. "Because I wanted to surprise you, and this was the perfect cover. Ladies, our jet is right over there."

"*Our* jet?" Madison turned to him with a worried frown. "So the big macho men are heading into the storm, and we're relegated to the sidelines?"

Et tu, Paco? Et tu?

Looking back at Alex, she asked, "And where exactly are *we* going?"

Her fiancé released a frustrated huff as he gently stroked the pout of her lower lip with his thumb. "Look, this wasn't my idea. Begrudgingly, I support Paco's wishes. Besides, it gives the team time to get everything set up before you all join us. And I'm sure as hell not forcing this on you. I know Jess wants time with Mark, and we all know that Richard and Jaclyn would like a few days to get, uh, reacquainted. So I'll leave it up to you. You're all welcome to join us as we head to Singapore. Or . . ."

"Or . . ." Paco drew out the word for effect, aiming his enthusiastic charm at Madison. "We can head to Paris where a dozen of your girlfriends are already waiting to kick off your bachelorette party."

Wide-eyed and squealing, Madison looked at the ladies who were now as excited as she was.

"I'm always down for a chocolate croissant," Jaclyn said.

Jess grinned. "Being constantly surrounded by Mark and all my brothers, I'll never turn down a girls' getaway."

Inwardly delighted, Madison conceded. "I guess the big macho men *are* leaving without us."

Without another word, Jess and Jaclyn hurried across the tarmac to the luxurious France-bound jet, chattering excitedly about what they wanted to do first when they arrived.

Madison would have bolted too, but Alex wrapped a tight arm around her as he walked her to the jet at a leisurely stroll.

"Hey now," he said, "let's get a few things straight. This is going to be a very calm, sophisticated, sedate girls' getaway. Maybe some spa time and pampering. A glass or two of wine." As they stopped at the bottom of the stairs to the jet, he kissed her hard and ended with a stern warning. "And no exotic dancers."

Smiling, Alex released her, swatting her playfully on the butt as she booked it up the stairs.

Paco joined her at the cabin doorway and called out to Alex with a big grin. "Spa time. Overflowing booze. Strippers galore. Got it!" He saluted sharply.

Narrowing his eyes, Alex shouted back over the roar of the engines. "It's mighty convenient that you're one of the girls when we could really use you."

Madison and Paco exchanged a devilish look before he shouted back.

"The lines have been drawn. Queens rule!"

With that, they ducked inside and the stairs closed behind them. The jet bound for fun and excitement in the City of Light taxied, and from her buttery-soft leather seat, Madison watched Alex through the small window until the plane took off.

CHAPTER 2

ALEX

Drake Global Industries
Singapore Headquarters

DESPITE THE OVERSIZED CONFERENCE TABLE, **Alex** sat just one chair from Mr. Chang, whose first name was nearly impossible for most Westerners to pronounce, a consequence of one too many *x*'s in the mix. So for most, he went by the easier moniker *Jeff*.

Unchallenged by Mandarin, Alex never had an issue with Chang's first name, but both men naturally gravitated to calling each other by their last names. They shared an easy camaraderie, two men who'd separately climbed the ranks of wealth and status through the valley of corporate warfare, one low crawl at a time.

Their respect was instant, and to this day, was very much shared. Which made an adversarial spin on their relationship impossible. But it was fun to try.

Alex tapped a finger to the polished mahogany table. "You've been keeping secrets, Chang."

Chang's humble grin was always endearing, but he didn't disagree. "We all do, Drake."

Casually, Chang poured the tea into traditional undersized cups. They each admired the swirl of steam lifting from their oolong before taking a sip.

Giving Alex an inscrutable look, Chang said, "You'll have to be more specific."

Smiling, Alex enjoyed this. Mirroring his expression, so did Chang. The game was well understood. Love was love, but business was business. Chang nailed it. Their livelihood and security were only as good as the secrets they locked away.

From his inside breast pocket, Alex extracted a small plastic card. The crest on the bottom made the random, ordinary keycard distinctive and specific—a golden Merlion, the symbol of Singapore.

With an indifferent glance, Chang shrugged. Undeterred, Alex slid it closer to his counterpart.

Picking it up, Chang flipped it back and forth. "It's an access card. The design is still widely used today across a vast range of companies. Corporate empires. Hotels. We've even used it, I don't know, ten . . . twelve years ago, perhaps."

"That's the right time frame," Alex said under his breath.

Chang's company, now known as DGI Singapore, wasn't new when it entered the DGI fold. It was an acquisition, the first of many that had grown Alex's corporation worldwide.

Grasping at straws, Alex asked, "Back then, was it connected with any special project? Military, or something covert? Dangerous?"

The uncertain fog in Chang's eyes lifted, replaced with a glint of recollection. "Ah." Clasping his hands, he leaned in. "Do you believe in ghost stories, Drake?"

Assuming Chang was referring to the mystery surrounding Jack's mission-related murder a decade ago, Alex schooled his features and relaxed in his chair, crossing an ankle over his other knee.

Jack being Madison's brother wasn't the only reason Alex was deeply invested in this conversation. The attack had nearly cost him and Paco their lives, and devastated the Taylor family in the aftermath. They all needed answers, and he prayed that Chang had something of substance to offer.

"Well, my life's been haunted by this mystery for a decade, so let's go with yes."

Nodding, Chang lowered his voice, unusually careful with it being just the two of them in the room. "I think you're looking for *Yōulíng Láng*."

"*Yōulíng Láng*." Alex repeated Chang's pronunciation perfectly. The phrase barely challenged his repertoire. Aloud, he translated the meaning of the two words. "Ghost wolf?"

With a somber nod, Chang looked on with regret. "I don't know much. We don't keep records . . . intentionally. My first encounter was as a soldier. My team was deployed to find an operative that had gone missing." His head dropped. "And we did. We found our man."

Alex poured him more tea, empathizing with the pain his friend was dredging up. "You don't have to—"

"You need to know what lies ahead." Taking a breath, Chang continued. "The torture our man went through was extensive. Unnecessarily so. This wasn't a matter of mere information extraction." Chang's eyes locked with Alex's in somber understanding. "And it was only a few miles outside the city. How do you say it? The bastard had balls."

Retrieving the card and tapping it on the table, Alex asked, "Why does this card make you think it was the Ghost Wolf?"

"Over the years, I've seen his handiwork. I've chased him the way people chase Bigfoot or the Loch Ness Monster, in my spare time, and very careful about the resources I throw at the search. Because . . ."

Prodding him, Alex asked gently, "Because?"

Chang blew out a long breath. "Because people who look too hard become the next victim. I don't believe in ghosts, but I believe in the Ghost Wolf. I can tell you this much—his attacks happen all over the world, usually targeting operatives moving very valuable information. And there's always an access card, one you can't trace, wiped down and left with the body. Be careful, *tóngzhì*." *Comrade*. Warning punctuated his words. "To the Ghost Wolf, it's a game. A deadly one."

Thinking of Madison, Alex took a calming breath, hiding his anxiety. "Thank you, my friend."

CHAPTER 3

MADISON

Paris, France
The Eiffel Tower

MADISON STARED down at the note. Strangely, the penmanship had become familiar.

EIFFEL TOWER

NOON

ALONE

PS: I KNOW THE COLOR OF YOUR PANTIES

Grimacing at the last line, she stuffed the note back in her purse. *No, she doesn't. Does she?*

With each passing minute, Madison's apprehension ticked higher. Over and over, she scanned the crowds. Nothing. Then she tilted her head back, viewing the metal weaving of the iconic structure in front of her up to the sky.

Should I go up? Hang out down here? Wave my hands in the air and holler like I just don't care?

Frustrated, she checked her phone. Fifteen minutes after twelve. *She's late, and I'm out of here.*

Determined, Madison hailed an approaching cab. When it stopped at the curb , she quickly hopped in. Not knowing a bit of French, she fished through her bag for the business card to the hotel. The car rolled away before she could find it.

"Don't worry, Madison. I know where you're going." The sultry voice was as taunting as ever.

A dramatic entrance. Of course.

Madison looked up, meeting the driver's eyes in the rearview mirror. "Jordan. If you wanted me to hop in a taxi, why not put it in the note?"

"Because if I take the mystery out of our relationship, how would I ever steal your attention?" Jordan's words were laced with suggestion. "Besides, I had to do some dry cleaning for both our sakes."

Confused, Madison checked her outfit, but then caught sight of Jordan rolling her eyes in exasperation in the rearview mirror.

"Civilian translation? I needed to make sure nobody was following either of us. If someone were following you, watching you adorably check the time with a frantic glance about, they'd realize you'd been stood up. Hailing a cab to head back to the hotel would be a natural response. Further watching would be a waste of their time."

Madison eased back into her seat. "Whose time? Other than you, who's following me?"

Jordan gave her a small smirk. "Someone who's about to make your life a whole lot harder."

Madison didn't respond, hoping her silence would encourage Jordan to disclose more.

"No." Jordan slowly blew out a breath, somehow reading Madison's mind. "We need to convince the puppet masters that you're a pawn, and you play that part so much better when you're in the dark."

Mindful, Madison kept her tone steady and cool. "Then why warn me at all? Won't that ruin your element of surprise?" Her added jazz hands for effect came out ineffective, as Jordan didn't even look.

Without acknowledging the question, Jordan changed the subject, her tone now uncharacteristically serious. "Your party's this evening, but when will someone start missing you? Calling to check on you?"

Of course Jordan knows about the party. If she knows about my panties, details about my party are hardly a national secret.

Madison shrugged. "I don't know. Everyone's busy prepping for tonight. I slipped away because they think I'm at a spa."

"You're not far off. My company can be very relaxing. Just give me a chance." Playtime apparently over, Jordan refocused and continued. "So that leaves the ever-protective Mr. Robles. It should take him about ninety minutes to miss you, and that gives us plenty of time. I'll need your phone."

Not bothering to protest, Madison handed it over. If Jordan wanted to hurt her, nothing was stopping her. As they sped away from the city, Madison decided to sit back and enjoy the ride.

I wonder if she'll kill me if I pester her with "How much longer till we get there?"

Hopefully soon.

Not killing me. Getting there.

Huffing, Madison pouted in silence. *Phoneless rides are boring and inhumane.*

CHAPTER 4

MADISON

Le Port-Marly, France

"It's breathtaking." Madison walked alongside Jordan, admiring the building against a backdrop of picturesque French countryside. An architectural wonder loomed ahead as they ambled along the pebbled path from the car. Secluded within a cluster of trees was an elegant mansion three stories high.

"Where are we?" she asked, gazing ahead in awe.

With a convincing French accent, Jordan said, *"Le Chateau de Monte-Cristo.* The historic home of Alexandre Dumas. You love his book, right?"

Suspicious, Madison answered slowly. "Right."

"It's normally a tourist museum, but I've arranged for us to have lunch in a private room where we can talk."

You know when talking would have been nice? During a cozy car ride with just the two of us . . . while I had no phone.

"Jordan, I know there's a reason you didn't want me to have my phone, but I'm an American in Paris. I'd really love just a few shots of this place."

"Oh, you'll get your photos. But your phone stays in the car."

Entering the chateau, Jordan led the way past stone walls and vintage furnishings to an elegant room with a generous setup of an assortment of wines, cheeses, breads, and dessert pastries. Grabbing a bottle of pre-opened and chilled Moët, Jordan poured two glasses.

Placing a glass in Madison's hand, she clinked hers to it. "To the bride-to-be."

With a wry smile, Madison took a tiny sip. "Are you drugging my drink to put me in a compromising position?"

Jordan's red lips curled to a salacious smile. "Really, Madison? I thought you knew me better than that. I only put willing participants in compromising positions."

Madison smiled back before swallowing a mouthful. "Then what's this all about?"

Deciding a snack would calm her nerves, she set her champagne flute on the linen-topped round table and headed straight for the buffet holding the food.

With a light stroke to Madison's cheek, Jordan sat down in a gilded velvet-tufted chair. "It's about history. You know the story behind Pearl Harbor, right?"

Carrying her plateful of appetizers, Madison sat down and nodded, reciting the highlights she could recollect. *Tora tora tora*," she recalled from the movie. "We knew the attack was coming and let everyone die to protect the secret that we'd tapped into Japanese communications."

Jordan poured more champagne for herself. "And what's the moral of that story?"

Thoughtfully, Madison considered her question. Unstopped by her uncertainty, she tossed out a few possibilities, hoping one might hit the mark. "National security is paramount? Strategic goals outweigh tactical needs? The needs of the many outweigh the needs of the few?"

She recalled that gem from a *Star Trek* movie. But then she paused, noticing the patronizing shake of her companion's head.

"Wrong, wrong, and wrong," Jordan said softly, beautifully walking the line between sarcastic and sultry. "That's your allegiance to duty and country talking. Let's take it closer to home. Why did your brother die?"

Madison stared at the champagne glass she'd been clinging to, but barely drinking from. It remained practically full. Forcing a nonchalant shrug, she said, "Because he had something that was more valuable destroyed than discovered?"

"Collateral damage?" Jordan asked, almost as a confirmation. Clasping her hands neatly on the table, the playful glint usually dancing in her eyes vanished. "Try this one on for size. People are expendable."

True or not, hearing Jack's death described so bluntly made Madison sick to her stomach. Fighting the bile that threatened, she set down her nearly untouched champagne.

Let's see. I could tell her to kiss my ass. But I'm in a foreign country. She's my ride. And she's got my phone.

She's probably paid off the staff for whatever she needs. Setting up the lunch. Chilling the champagne.

Digging a grave?

With a deep breath, Madison hid her pain and kept her response brief. "Fine. Jack was expendable to you."

Jordan took an extra-long sip, seeming to study Madison. A grin appeared, but it didn't reach her eyes. "Remind me, there's a second moral of that story I need to share, but we'll circle back to that later. Like I said, your life is about to get very . . . *je ne sais quoi.*" Jordan paused and pondered, finally settling on the word, "Uncomfortable."

Weary of the games, Madison said flatly, "It's strange. Moët . . . hors d'oeuvres . . . the most exquisite pastries in the world. You don't act like you're threatening my life."

"Obviously, I'm not. Quite the opposite. I'm proposing that you and I become unlikely bedfellows, so to speak." Jordan leaned forward, her finger lightly tracing a line across the back of Madison's hand.

Undaunted by the sensual attention, Madison held her hand in place. "How so?"

"I'll tell you, but I need your every assurance that this stays between you and me. No Paco. And absolutely, unconditionally no Alex."

Lying to Jordan wasn't nearly as hard as it had once been, but Madison decided to hit her head-on. "I love Paco. What I love most about him is that he respects me and will understand my decision to keep something private. Alex is another story. Pet me all you want, Jordan, but if Alex is out, so am I."

Slowly, Jordan lifted herself from the chair and sauntered around the table. Her expression was scheming as her finger brushed Madison's full lower lip. "Sure about that?"

Stern, Madison gave her a flat and determined, "Yes."

Leaning in, Jordan brought her ruby lips a mere whisper from Madison's. "You know what I love more than anything?"

Madison quelled her breathing but maintained her gaze. *She can't possibly mean she loves me. And I, for one, am sure as hell not throwing that into the universe.*

Perhaps Madison's lack of a poker face and likely appalled stare deterred Jordan. She turned and headed for the door.

I guess we're leaving.

Confused, Madison stood and called out, "Are you at least going to tell me what you love more than anything before we go?"

Jordan whirled around but kept her fingers on the vintage glass doorknob. "Winning." The sadistic curl of her mouth broke into a wide smile as she opened the door, revealing a surprise.

CHAPTER 5

MADISON

SHOCKED, Madison quickly crossed the room, leaping straight into the man's arms. "Alex, why didn't you tell me you were coming?"

After a warm kiss, interrupted by Jordan's foot tapping, he answered. "Because no one can know I'm here." Shifting his gaze to Jordan, he raised a brow. "And you didn't win the bet. I told you she wouldn't keep secrets from me."

"*Au contraire, mon ami.* You said she wouldn't keep secrets from you *and* Paco. I call it a win. In my favor." In traditional seductress fashion, Jordan stepped close and cozied up to Alex's back, bringing her lips close to his ear. "Did you bring me my prize?"

Keeping his focus and hold on Madison, he said, "I did." With one arm wrapped tightly around his fiancée, he removed his watch and dropped it in Jordan's waiting hand. "One Omega Seamaster dive watch. As requested."

Unimpressed, Jordan dangled it before them. "A cheap one."

Alex laughed. "You weren't specific, and I was rushed. It's brand-new and works perfectly."

Fastening the man's watch to her wrist, Jordan let it dangle as she fiddled with the dial. Satisfied, she moved from Alex to behind Madison, sandwiching her snugly between the two of them.

"Take a good look at me, Alex Drake. This is me compromising. And it'll never happen again." Kissing Madison hard enough to burn the cherry lipstick into her cheek, Jordan asked, "Now, are we getting down to business, or are we having a three-way?"

❧

A strange feeling swept over Madison at the way Jordan carried herself. *Why is she helping us?*

Alex cut to the chase, prompting Jordan with the obvious. "You have our undivided attention."

Jordan grabbed a chair, flipping it to lower herself to a straddle. In slow motion, of course.

I really hope she doesn't hump it right in front of us.

Wetting her lips, Jordan began. "I'm in a unique position. I'm not clairvoyant, but I come across enough bits and pieces of information to know what's coming. You've been rattling all the worst cages, Alex Drake. Whatever's about to happen, it's about to get personal."

Madison squeezed his hand tightly.

Stroking his thumb along the back of her hand, Alex made light of the situation. "That's me," he joked. "Making friends wherever I go."

"Personal how?" Madison asked, desperate for more details.

With nothing more than a knowing shrug, Jordan smiled.

More seriously than before, Alex asked, "How bad?"

Annoyingly cheerful, she answered. "I believe the word *annihilate* was mentioned."

Even through his suit, Madison could sense the muscles in Alex's body tense. Still, his smile remained stubbornly in place.

"Is that it? Someone rich and powerful is ready to take me down and make it personal? I'm happy to direct them to the end of the line."

Jordan's eyes turned cold. "My dear Alex, when are you ever going to learn that the world doesn't revolve around you?" With that, her somber gaze shifted to Madison. "We always hurt the ones closest to us, don't we? And she's already a bundle of nerves. Barely touched her lunch."

Without waiting for a response, Jordan downed the last of her champagne and stood up. Madison and Alex both stood as well, hand in hand.

"I'll give you two a few minutes to talk," Jordan said. "Unfortunately, that's all you'll have time for."

When the door shut behind her, Alex's lips were on Madison's. Her body was ripe and willing to seize the bulge of his attention.

He cradled her cheeks, pulling away. "I hate it when this happens, but Jordan's right. I'm intentionally poking around in the dark, and who knows what nerve I've hit. The woman's not exactly my best friend. Well, not like she's yours."

Madison's eye roll earned her another kiss.

"But for the things I do know about the elusive Jordan Stone, she's rarely wrong. And somehow, in the most bizarre way possible, I think she cares about you." Moving an errant strand from Madison's face, he huffed. "You know the other thing Jordan's good at?"

On edge, Madison shot back her response. "Threesomes, apparently."

He laughed. "Timing. If she's saying this now, it's not too late to walk away. We could step back. We know Jack was a hero . . . maybe we don't have to know why. Not if it means putting you in harm's way. How about we pack up, go home, and plan the biggest wedding of the century?" With a tender peck, he added, "I'll do whatever you want."

Madison never tired of having Alex's arm around her. She leaned into him as they stepped outside the chateau to rejoin Jordan, drawing strength from his closeness. Her hives were building to an unrelenting itch, but she ignored it. And the passing wave of nerves and nausea settled quickly once she took a deep breath of fresh air.

"Well?" Jordan asked as she slid off the hood of her car. "Is Madison riding back to Paris with me or with you?"

Madison looked up at Alex, whose kiss descended on her in an instant, sweeping away all her panic and worry. At least, for the moment.

Pulling away, she faced Jordan. "I'm going with you."

Jordan's lips turned upward. "And I'm right again."

Stunned, Madison shot a suspicious look at Alex.

"I didn't bet against you, beautiful," he said.

God, those innocent eyes are convincing.

"No, I didn't bet Alex this time. Taking him for his goodies gets stale the second time around." Jordan grabbed a gift bag from inside the car. "Here. I made a bet with the universe. I like keeping score to see how well I know you."

Madison stuffed her hand through the layers of silver tissue, finding the gift bag held a box. Whipping it out, she glanced at it and quickly shoved it back beneath the wrappings. Heat rushed to her cheeks, causing Jordan's mild smile to grow to a grin of delight.

Alex made a grab for the bag. "Was that a—"

Madison fended off his playful attempts to snatch the goods as Jordan answered.

"A dual-headed, synchronized, G-spot and clit stimulator with thrusting power for her pleasure. Battery operated. Waterproof. Hypoallergenic. And a twelve-hour charge. I already tested it out."

Both Alex and Madison stopped in their tracks to absorb Jordan's last words.

"The battery charge. Not the toy," Jordan said, tsk-tsking. "Trust me, I need something a little more . . . imaginative. Now, we need to head back and Alex needs to go. But feel free to bust that baby out on our cruise back to the city, Madison." With a long wink at her, Jordan slid into the driver's seat.

Madison nestled into Alex's hold as he led her to the passenger door. Leaning in, she inhaled a whiff of the intoxicating scent of light cologne and heavenly man. Her failed attempt to hide the itch creeping up her arm was gently rubbed by his big hand.

"Hey," Alex said softly, "it's not too late to change your mind."

His wild embrace lifted her toes right off the ground into a warm, dizzying kiss. Every tightened muscle relaxed, and she melted into him. Slowly, he set her on her feet.

"Just like you can't fool me, I can't fool you." She held up her sleeve, giving some much-needed air to the small patch of hives. "If you and I left together now, we'd keep circling back to this mystery. Neither of us would be able to move on." After giving him a peck, she sighed. "It's now or never, and I vote for now."

His forehead pressed to hers. "Now, it is."

The passenger window whirred down, with Jordan loudly announcing, "Paco's getting impatient." She waved Madison's cell in the air, showing that several texts were awaiting her.

Alex's soft whisper caressed Madison's ear. "I love you. When you return to Paris, don't be surprised to see twice the guards. Have fun tonight."

With a final kiss, he let her in the car.

A second later, Jordan was tearing away down the countryside. Madison locked on Alex's handsome reflection until he vanished from view in the car's side mirror.

When an unexpected tear trailed down her cheek, Jordan's hand slipped into hers but swiftly retreated, leaving behind a black silk handkerchief. It was edged with the most unusual lace trim, elegant and distinctive. Madison used it to dab at her cheeks, staying quiet for most of the picturesque ride.

Studying the fabric and running her fingers over the lace and the single *J* monogram, Madison said, "This seems much too pretty for tears. Please tell me this didn't used to be your panties."

Jordan scoffed. "You think I bother with panties? It's like you don't know me at all."

I should have guessed. "Then let me get to know you better. Why did you do this?"

"Give you a vibrator? You're going to need something to keep you warm tonight. I'm pretty sure you won't let me take that role, though you and I both know that naughty little image must have crossed Alex's mind more than once."

Jordan's dark eyes stay fixed on the road ahead, though she reached out to trace a slow, seductive line up Madison's leg, stopping at her handkerchief. After retrieving the elegant black hankie, she withdrew her hand.

Entertained, Madison found herself warming up to Jordan's unique humor and perpetual flirtation. "I meant, why did you do all this? Me . . . and Alex? The palatial home of Alexandre Dumas?"

"I've got a better question." Jordan's smile grew. "Why did you come? The note was obviously from me. And even after our *touching* farewell the last time we met . . ."

Madison quashed a giggle, recalling Jordan slipping a business card into her bra on that occasion, and Jordan continued.

"You and I keep playing this sexy little game of cat and mouse. It must be love." She blew a sexy kiss at Madison.

The truth? No clue.

A hunch? Curiosity. Idiocy.

Take your pick.

Attempting to match Jordan's temptress vibe, Madison smiled back. "To see if you really know the color of my panties." *Actually true.*

"Pink," Jordan said, bored and not bothering with the pretense of a difficult deduction.

Shocked, Madison had no reply.

"I'm dropping you off a block from your hotel. Look." Jordan pointed to the familiar classic building ahead.

Taken aback at gently being dismissed, Madison exited the vehicle. Keeping the door open, she leaned in. "What was the second lesson? The one from Pearl Harbor?"

Jordan slipped Madison's phone into the gift bag, then dangled the bag on her finger, letting it swing hypnotically. "First things first. You asked why I did this." She extended her arm, letting Madison easily retrieve the vibrator-toting gift bag. "Let's call it a wedding gift."

Could Ms. Hell-in-High-Heels actually be bonding with me? Count me in.

"Then why not come to my party tonight?"

Jordan brushed the curve of her steering wheel, settling on gripping at ten and two. "Because crashing parties is more my style." She looked away, staring straight ahead. "And I have plans."

Eager to move on from the awkwardness of the sullen response, Madison repeated her other question. "And the second Pearl Harbor lesson?"

Back to her normal sultry self, Jordan let the answer roll from her crimson lips. "In a game of strategy, never underestimate the element of surprise."

With a lingering glance, Madison shut the door, dropping her shoulders as Jordan drove away.

CHAPTER 6

MADISON

Paris, France
The Peninsula Hotel

WITH A DEEP INHALE, Madison struggled to open her eyes the next morning. Exhausted, she blinked slowly at the ceiling, replaying in her mind the best bits and pieces of one hell of a bachelorette party.

Her memory wasn't fuzzy. She'd barely touched the copious amounts of champagne, cosmos, and inebriating shots pushed into her hands. Jordan's discussion had wreaked havoc on her appetite, turning her tummy into a roller-coaster ride of nerves and butterflies.

Her long yawn gave her a moment to flip through the more pleasant flash-backs of the night.

Madison's normally reserved clan of girlfriends held nothing back, corralling an entire stripper brigade to perform on her lap, and offered a thousand dollars to the hottest dancer. In half an hour, her diligent banana-hammock inspection made way for a winner. But it wasn't his banana standing out in her mind.

Hot and spicy, the winning dancer gave it his all. His unbelievable nice-and-naughty kiss brought the house down. Recalling the insatiable kiss, Madison smiled, but it stalled as a long beam of sunlight hit her eye. The sliver hitting her through the blackout curtains made her moan.

Grabbing her cell to check the time, she huffed as the face of the phone remained black. "Dammit."

"What?" her bedmate mumbled.

Startled but sedate, she looked over at the man resting peacefully buried under the covers. His black satin eye mask gave her a hot-pink wink.

Look at him. He must be exhausted after all that action.

Giggling at the unusually groggy Paco, she replied in a raspy voice. "Morning, sunshine. I forgot to plug in my cell. It's dead."

Effortlessly, moving only his arm, he swept his cell phone from the nightstand and handed it to her.

Madison stared at the black screen. Nothing. She pressed it back into his palm, then smoothed her hand over his. Tugging down the blanket, she kissed the cheek of the man who'd become a brother to her.

Well, except in those times like last night when he transformed into her hard-charging, party girl of a sister.

"Yours is dead too."

"Impossible," he muttered. "If both our phones are dead, we can't text our butler for coffee. And we *need* coffee."

A knock at the door broke through their bonding. Both grumbled at the thought of having to walk all the way across the suite to answer it.

"I *am* the bride-to-be," Madison said, using her best wheedling tone.

"And I'm recovering from celebrating the bride-to-be, downing so many cosmos, I stopped counting after six. Or seven. So we'll solve it the old-fashioned way. Rock-paper-scissors."

Amused, Madison agreed. "Deal."

Without moving from their spots, Madison watched as Paco held up his fist, waving it to the beat of, "One, two, three." With a V of his fingers, he hit her with scissors.

"You lose," she said, rolling over to smother a laugh, not bothering to let him know she hadn't played at all.

Heaving his body from the bed, Paco stood for a moment, jolted by the sound of another knock. Madison watched as he took out his irritation on the eye mask, fighting it free from his head and tossing it across the room.

She enjoyed the scene of an utterly polished man desperately keeping his balance as Paco made his way down the short length of hall, finally leaning against the door. He didn't open it.

Instead, he bent down to pick up a large envelope from the floor. "It's for you."

"Me? How would anyone know I'm in your suite?"

Madison sat up, plugging in her phone and waiting for it to charge. Paco shuffled back to her and tossed the envelope onto the down comforter. Without a word, he slid beneath the blankets, apparently going back to sleep.

Yawning, Madison opened the envelope and pulled out a few glossy photos. After a few blinks and rubbing her eyes, she decided to ignore her feelings. Calmly laying the photos on the bed, she grabbed the hotel phone.

"Yes, *bonjour*. Can I get some coffee and assorted breads?"

"And fruit," Paco murmured.

"And fruit," she repeated into the phone.

"And hair of the dog," he muttered.

Ignoring him, she thanked room service and hung up. To Paco, she said, "That's why we have a minibar." Sinking into the bed, she wiggled closer to him.

Frowning, he rolled over toward her. "What's wrong?"

She grabbed the photos and handed them to him, closing her eyes, unsure of what to think. When Paco looked at them and laughed, she sprang up.

"Really? You're laughing?"

"I am."

She snatched the image he was holding. "Alex, in the suit he was in yesterday, is standing in front of a naked woman in a hotel room. And . . ." Madison's voice took a pointed *aha* tone. "Here, he's removing his blazer. Getting more comfortable."

Paco laughed with obvious amusement. "You can't seriously think these photos are actually catching Alex in the act."

Frustrated, she muttered, "I don't." Throwing herself back on the pillows, she said, "But I can still hate it."

And hate it, she would. It was a setup, and not a photoshopped one. This was a real girl—with huge boobs—throwing herself at Alex. The young woman's body was perfectly posed for a handful of pics, possibly to be used in a scandalous exposé that could make headlines all over the world.

Silence stewed between them until Paco said, "Hand me your phone."

Irritated, she said, "It's charging."

He wrapped his arm around her, nudging her. "Come on. Mine's totally dead."

"Fine."

She did as he asked, dragging part of the ten-foot-cord with her phone as she handed it over. He opened it, having the privilege of unrestricted access to so much of Madison's life. Dialing Alex, Paco clicked on the speakerphone.

"Good morning, beautiful," Alex said, cheerful as ever.

"Good morning, handsome," Paco replied. "Madison just got her first taste of the game."

"Oh." Alex's good humor deflated. "What was it?"

"Guess," Madison said sharply as she piled pillows behind her back.

"Hmm . . ." Blowing out a long sigh, Alex said, "Images?"

She scowled, crossing her arms over her chest. "Yup."

"I'll bet they're still images, and not video. Of me. And the woman in my room last night."

"*Naked* woman," Madison said, gritting her teeth as she pointed out that teensy-tiny detail.

Frustrated, she teetered between two sides of anger. On one end of the cruel spectrum were these pictures and everything they represented. The man she loved and the life they cherished would forever be a target.

But how lightly he was taking it hit her harder. And pissed her off even more.

Here he was, Alex Drake, the global tycoon, who blew this off as not much more than the tail end of an unworthy business transaction. Apparently, years of being attacked had made him immune. She hated how he must have fought this alone for so long.

"Naked woman," he said lightly. "Her name is Shelly. Nice girl. You two would hit it off."

"Obviously. We have a lot in common." *Sometimes, I hate how much I love this man.*

A FaceTime request hit the screen. Paco held it up, giving Madison the option. She barely let the second string of chimes hit the air before clicking to accept.

Paco slipped out of the room, tripping over his own feet as he stumbled away toward the suite's living room. With an audible swear, he closed the bedroom door behind him.

Face-to-face with Alex's image, she clung to the traces of irritation that had swamped her a moment ago. *You might be unbelievably adorable with your warm eyes and that magnetic dimple, but I'm still peeved.*

"Madison, I'm sending you the video clip from the body cam Richard hid in my tie tack."

"You don't have to do that. I know nothing happened."

"No. You *think* nothing happened, because you love me and have faith in me. And your love and loyalty go without saying. But you have to see it. You need to know for a fact exactly why the photos look the way I can only imagine they do." He chuckled the last of his words out.

Calming down, she said, "Fine. Seeing is believing. Send me the clip. Can't wait." The ping of a text came from her phone, providing a link to a familiar secure DGI website. "Maybe I'll invite some of your top female fans and have a Facebook viewing party."

Normally, Madison would expect some witty retort and an extra dose of banter from Alex, but neither of them had the energy. Every mile of the dozen or so countries between them weighed on them.

"What can I do?" he asked softly, his sincerity ringing through.

In an instant, Alex had changed. In a steel-gray business suit that never failed to hold up appearances, he loosened his tie. The look in his eyes was unmistakable. He'd call everything off and sweep her away in an instant if he thought for a second she'd let him.

"Nothing." Madison's timid response was backed by a firm squint. "I've been typecast as the weakest link, and getting ominous envelopes with images of you in questionable activities is just par for the course." Forcing a grin, she said, "I'm fine. I'll just rent a post office box and let the floodgates open."

"Fine, huh?" He studied her, and she let him, giving him her best poker face yet.

I'm not fine. I miss you more than you can know. "Yes. Fine."

"Fine enough to watch the video?"

Her hesitation warmed to a full smile. "Yes. I promise. I'll watch your porno with nice-girl Shelly."

"I can't wait for your Rotten Tomatoes review." He took a moment before saying, "You know this is just the beginning. Is there any chance I can convince you to head home after Paris?"

Madison shook her head. "And miss all the action?" She raised the photos into view. Frustrated but giggling, she added, "Not a chance."

His gorgeous eyes hardened as he held her gaze.

Worry all you want. There's not a chance in hell you'll pull this off without me.

"I know what you're thinking." She teased him away from his concern, arching her body as she stretched and settled back into her pillow.

Instantly, the furrow in his brow relaxed. "And what's that, Ms. Taylor?"

"You're wondering how you can have your cake and eat it too. Send me home and still keep me happy."

Shedding his blazer, he corrected her. "That's not at all what I'm thinking." He slipped off his tie. "True, I want to keep you away from here because those photographs are just a warning shot. Someone wants us to stop digging up the past. But you know me, Madison. I won't shy away from a fight, and I wouldn't keep you from this one because it's more yours than mine. But," he tugged loose his collar button, "that's not what I was thinking."

The devilish turn of his lips set his tone to naughty. "What I was thinking is how I'd love to give you a few FaceTime step-by-step instructions on how I can have my cake and eat it too."

"Wait." Madison's breathless protest was weak at best. Licking her lips, she bit back an indulgent smile. "I'm in Paco's bed, and he's in the next room."

Alex lowered his voice to a sexy rumble. "Then lock the door. And keep your screams to a minimum."

God, I want this man.

Thrilled, she nodded. "Send Paco a DO NOT DISTURB text, and I'll lock the bedroom door in case he doesn't see it."

She rushed to the door, but before she could reach it, it opened after a quick knock. But it wasn't Paco.

"Mom!"

CHAPTER 7

MADISON

SHOCKED, Madison stared at the woman who'd just entered. In her modest travel clothes and casually curled shoulder-length hair, her mother filled the room with cheeriness.

Madison hugged Joy hard, seeing Paco standing back and apologetically pointing to the DO NOT DISTURB text as he mouthed, "*Sorry.*"

Aloud, he said, "I got word a gorgeous mother-of-the-bride was in the lobby looking for her daughter. I asked them to send her up here."

From the cell in Madison's hand, Alex's voice boomed. "Hi, Mrs. Taylor."

"Oh." Madison held the phone to her mother.

Joy grabbed it, waving a delightfully scolding finger at Alex via FaceTime. "Alex Drake, how many times do I have to remind you to call me Joy?"

"Just a few more times, and I'm sure I'll get it. You look wonderful. Had we known you were coming, we would have arranged your flight."

"Well, everyone kept sending me all the Facegram posts and Instabook shots from Madison's party. Even if I missed the festivities, I had to come. And I called and texted Madison, but she never answered."

Madison hid her smile at her mother's mishmash of social media platform names and gave her another hug. "Sorry, Mom. I wasn't checking my phone last night, and it was dead this morning. I still haven't checked it."

"No worries. I won't be in your way at all."

Too late. Her quiet shrug to Alex gave him all the excuse he needed.

"Madison, why not enjoy the day with your mom? The jet will be on standby and ready to go whenever you are, Joy. We'll make sure you're taken care of, and we'll make all the arrangements for your flight back home."

"Home?" Joy shoved her face closer to the cell screen, her protest firm. "I'm going with Madison to see you. In Shanghai."

"Singapore, Mom. And it's really a business trip."

"No problem. You all do business, and Zane and I will take in the sights."

His tone harsh, Paco said, "Zane?"

That hangover definitely made someone moody.

Madison kept her voice calm. "He's a family friend."

"And Jack's best friend at West Point. Ring bangers," Joy said.

A light laugh erupted at Madison's mother's mangling of "ring knockers," the slang term for graduates of a US military academy, but nobody corrected her.

"Look." Madison grabbed her room key from her purse and slipped it to her mom's free hand. "My room's just down the hall. Go on in and relax. Where's Zane?"

"He's arriving in Singapore tomorrow. He's stationed somewhere that way, and said he'd love to join us. He's a colonel now."

Whatever snide comment Paco was undoubtedly teeing up, Madison shot down with a glare. Her mother's voice beamed with pride. Like, that could have been Jack.

Maybe it could have been.

"Wow, that's terrific." Leading her mother out, Madison added, "I just need an hour or so, and I'll be right over."

"I'll take her," Paco said to Madison, then whispered, "Don't worry. I'll ungrump myself. You've got exactly one hour to . . . *get ready.*"

"That's all I need," she assured him in a voice low enough to keep from Joy's earshot. "I owe you."

"Use your new credit limit to grab me a pair of Louboutins, and we'll call it even."

"A four- or five-inch heel?" she teased.

With a distinctively adorable arch to his eyebrow, Paco glared. "Christian also makes men's shoes, but . . . whatever."

"Deal." Grateful, she kissed him on the cheek, nudging him and her mother with a gentle scoot out the door. Instantly, Madison flung the door wide, realizing she'd forgotten her virtual fiancé. Paco was standing there, holding up the still opened FaceTime call with Alex.

Even a world away, the gleam in her man's eyes was unmistakable, and deliciously sinister.

With an eager grin, Madison let out a breath. She snatched the phone appreciatively and shut the door. Delighted, she watched the man on the other end of the call peel the clothes from his chiseled physique. Magic Mike had nothing on Alex Drake under a time crunch.

"Why, Mr. Drake. Don't you look lickable. Should I get a Ziploc for my phone?"

"Do what you've got to do, beautiful, but you've got exactly sixty seconds to strip, hop in bed, and get on your hands and knees. Your shower will take fifteen minutes, then ten minutes for hair and makeup, since you'll pull all those luscious locks into a sexy ponytail that I can't wait to wrap around my fist. So I'd say I've got roughly thirty minutes to pleasure you multiple times, then give you a good three minutes to recover with a minute or two to spare." He displayed his wrist, anxiously tapping the face of his watch.

Without another word, Madison tossed off her clothes, assumed the position, and slipped her fingers in for a wet and wild race.

CHAPTER 8

ALEX

The Republic of Singapore
Changi Airport

EVEN IN THE dim light of late evening, Alex could make out every detail of his future wife as she stepped off the jet. Madison would be in his arms soon, but not immediately. This plan was moving into motion, and for the first time, he really hated it. Seeing her filled him with equal amounts of thrill and love . . . and fear.

As he'd instructed her, she'd pulled her tantalizing locks into a high ponytail. Her flowing skirt shimmied and danced suggestively around her thighs, as if the winds were commanded for his pleasure.

Patiently, he soaked in every movement before catching the passing sparkle of her engagement ring.

You're mine, Madison Taylor. All mine.

Singapore's sweltering heat and evening humidity hadn't been noticeable until then. His blood rushed with each glimpse of her thighs. But a second later, a rigid coolness overtook his needy cock. Tension traversed every muscle of his body, and his jaw clenched tight at the sight of her mother exiting the plane.

Pulling this off will be ten times harder with Joy here. Bothered, he tightened his crossed arms. *And Zane.*

Thankfully, Jess and Jaclyn had stayed in Paris, extending the girls' trip another day before heading home. Both workaholic women had no problem with ditching their men for a few days. But they weren't Madison, and this wasn't their fight.

With the woman of his dreams now before him, Alex pressed a chaste kiss to her cheek, then gave Joy a warm hug. Even though her presence made the situation more difficult, he was glad Madison had her mom nearby. And to Paco now joining them, he said nothing, not even bothering to shake his hand.

Alex was glad to have his own men in Singapore. These trusted agents within DGI performed an assortment of duties, from menial to lethal. Tonight, one of them played two roles: bodyguard and driver. At Alex's request, the lethal agent disguised as a chauffeur remained in the car, refraining from the normal duties of opening the doors. Unorthodox, but they needed to set the stage.

Instead, Alex held the car door open, encouraging Joy to enter the darkly tinted vehicle first. With the dark surroundings, it would be difficult for Joy to make out what was going down outside the car. If she did, they had a Plan B, but he hoped they wouldn't need it.

Once Joy entered the car, Madison smacked the large manila envelope hard against Alex's chest. He let the photos spill from her assault, scattering across the pavement.

Exaggerating his reaction, he dropped to one knee and painstakingly picked up one image after the other. Her legs still took his breath away as she stepped into the car, but he hid his admiration. Paco followed the ladies into the back. After returning all the photos to the envelope, Alex took his seat up front.

The ride was quiet, and he let out a sigh of relief when Joy nodded off quickly in the comfort of the luxury ride. Uneasy, he reached around to the back seat, deeply satisfied as Madison held his hand and squeezed. Her soft chuckle matched his as Paco wrapped their hands within both of his.

Though it had been tempting to rent a mansion in Singapore for privacy's sake during this trip, facing an audience head-on was the stronger tactic. When the world is watching, there's no better power play than to control the script.

In act one, Madison's natural reactions to a philandering Alex would disrupt their lives, putting them on public display for ridicule from the masses. They'd play it up. Let their opponent assume the upper hand.

And what the world didn't know about Paco far outweighed what it knew. He could play any role in this game, faking out any worthy adversary.

Likewise, what the world understood about Madison Taylor worked in their favor. She was young—nearly ten years Alex's junior. She was also gorgeous, naturally so, but she soared to stratospheric levels of sex appeal and attraction when she added even a light touch of makeup and the right outfit.

Short, flowy skirt . . . definitely the right outfit.

Madison's reputation for hard work and determination would be skewed under the scrutiny of the public spotlight, twisting her genuine ambition into nefarious social climbing. Which was exactly what Alex was hoping for to further his plan.

One gift-wrapped gold-digger angry at her fiancé, coming up. Now we've got a distraction.

~

At the Marina Bay Sands Hotel in the heart of Singapore, Alex and Madison took the presidential suite, ideally isolated from others. With Paco in the Merlion Suite, he was close enough without being on top of them.

Joy and Zane came with a whole new set of complications. Distancing them by a few floors would help shield them from the crossfire of potential messy events. Choreographing a semipublic breakup would take some maneuvering. Doable, but more difficult with Madison's mother and Zane nearby.

Joy's hotel butler met her at the front desk. After receiving hugs good-night from Madison and Alex, Joy was escorted by her butler to the elevator. With her out of the way, Alex readied himself for fireworks as a not-so-quiet Madison burst into character.

"Two days? I can't leave you alone for two days without you snatch-sniffing around."

On cue, Paco made a show of shoving them into the next available elevator. As the doors closed, his eyes narrowed on them. *"Snatch sniffing?"* he mouthed before the doors shut him out.

Facing Madison, Alex discreetly drew her attention to the camera behind him. She took it to heart, screaming, "God, you're an asshole!"

He covered his mouth, shielding a smile.

Between the heat of her words and the throbbing in his pants, the elevator was moving much too slow for his taste. "I swear. Those photos weren't real. I'm being set up."

"Sure you are," she spat out. "Because the master of conquests, Alex Drake, who's sampled more pies than Marie Callender, couldn't possibly settle for just one piece. What a joke."

"Me?" He towered over her, catching every rise and fall of her heaving chest. "What happened at your bachelorette party? You think I don't know about that kiss?"

Madison's lips pursed hard, holding back a laugh. Knowing, he pinned her down with the weight of his stare, leaning his arm against the wall. Her look softened to desire. With a gasp, her parted lips sucked in a breath. He couldn't take his eyes off her mouth.

Fuck. We're supposed to be fighting.

I can't think straight.

Where the hell is our floor?

The elevator opened.

At their room, Alex let her enter before him, then slammed the door for effect.

Shocked, she whirled around, laughing shyly as he slipped his arms around her waist, squeezing her against him. His firmness ached against her body as he descended on her hot, supple lips.

When he finally released Madison, she asked, "Is the show over?"

"Just the public one." Low, he said, "In here, we're alone."

CHAPTER 9

MADISON

MADISON ALWAYS LOST herself in his hungry stare. Alex Drake was more man than most women could handle. Unpredictable. Calculating. Dangerous. Two steps ahead of everyone else.

Sexy as hell. And all mine.

In his powerful hands, her body molded to his desire. He didn't rush her clothes off, instead seeming to enjoy brushing his fingers up under her skirt to caress the fullness of her ass.

The heat of his body seared through her, erasing every worry and doubt of the long day. She needed nothing but him.

Parting her lips, his tongue dove through with long licks and heavy breaths. Sliding his hand to her ponytail, he gave it a tug that woke a fire in her core.

"I need you, Madison," he murmured, his low growl vibrating across her neck.

Lightly, her fingers slipped from his torso to undo his pants. His heavy cock fell into her grasp. Lovingly, her gentle touch smoothed his stretched rod, cradling its weight. The bead of pre-cum at its tip begged for her mouth, and she licked her lips.

His hand cupped her jaw. "Just a taste. I need more than your mouth tonight."

With a sweeping kiss, he let her go. She dropped to her knees, eager to glide her tongue across his length and swirl it up to the tip. When he moaned, she swallowed him, taking him to the back of her throat.

Alex's dick was perfect, massive and stretched long, with the delicious taste that was his and his alone.

She sped up. Her greedy mouth sucked him harder, laving the firm muscle with her lips and tongue. Despite her deep, fevered bobbing, this man was holding back. He'd never give in like this after today. His way would be splitting her wide and riding her hard to kingdom come. *Pun intended.* But you can't blame a hungry girl for trying.

Moving her skirt out of the way, she tugged her panties down and dipped her fingers into her own wetness, satisfying her needs until he took his turn.

"Not for long, temptress," he said.

His low words were almost enough to push her over the edge. She slowed herself, timing the swirl around her clit with each progressive deep throat.

Unbinding her hair, he shook loose her wavy locks before sliding his necktie around her eyes. *God, that's hot.* His strong hands cradled her jaw as he pulled out. Light wafts of his cologne emanated from the tie, and her inhale was deep and noticeable.

"I need you out of these clothes." Sweeping her in his arms, he laid her gently across the bed, peeling the garments from her skin and caressing each area of newly revealed flesh.

His tongue licked down to her breast, causing her body to arch as her nipple ached for the heat of his mouth. After a hot, teasing breath, he took her in a long, languid suckle.

"I need you," she begged.

His lips trailed across her skin to her thighs. As his hands spread her legs wider, her body quaked. A whimper stuttered from her mouth.

Without warning, his tongue lashed at her swollen pussy, tearing her apart lick by lick, leaving nothing but the feeling of him. Bringing his tongue to a point, he entered her, fucking her sweetly until his licks moved to her clit. Two fingers now coaxed her climax. It was all she could do not to come on his hand.

"Please, Alex."

Slowly, he pulled away from her swollen folds, placing his shaft to her tender entrance. Drawing her hands above her head, he pinned them with the pressure of his grip.

There, he stopped.

"You called me an asshole." He scolded her with his deep voice.

Panting, she heaved out, "I'm sorry."

He pressed the rim of his crown just inside, then paused. "You've never said that before."

She needed him. *Now.* Aching but locked in position, her hips lifted into his.

Alex backed up just enough to withhold his penetration. The weight of his body pressed gently on her, keeping her still. His lips molded to her mouth, teasing, nipping, sucking.

And still, his cock didn't budge.

"No, Madison," he said, his voice dangerously low. "Not yet. You lied to me."

"What?"

"Don't deny it." His words whispered across her lips. "You're the only woman in the world to call me that and not mean it at all." His teeth tugged her ear. "Say it again."

Fevered, she asked, "Why?"

His words were on her neck. "Because I've never seen your pretty lips lie to me. And it's the hottest little white lie I've ever heard. Like the depths of our love is a secret." He kissed her hard, sucking her lower lip and breaking away to repeat his demand. "Say it."

She could feel him. The strong muscles of his thighs prying her legs wider. Ready to ram the whole of his shaft inside as soon as she gave in and uttered the tiny fib.

Ready, she held in a breath, licking her plump lower lip and letting the words he craved slip free. "You're an asshole."

Without mercy, Alex shoved himself deep into her, stretching her more than she could imagine. Days away from him had tightened her. After several thrusts, he slammed completely inside, forcing all of him deep within.

Again, he stopped.

"Please," she begged. "I need—"

His kiss covered her mouth. "I know what you need. But I can't reward a lie."

Her lips pouted hard, and he nibbled them to a smile. She gasped as his dick glided in and out, gently working her soaking core.

"Now tell me something true," he whispered.

Between desperate pants, she said, "I love you, Alex Drake."

His thrusts built, working the fullness of his cock against her trembling inner walls. Releasing her hands, he rubbed her clit with his thumb, building on his unrelenting thrusts.

Her legs captured him, and his moans were long and lasting.

Alex pumped harder. Faster.

In seconds, her screams shot across the room as wave upon wave of ecstasy crashed upon them both. He filled her with all he had, erupting several times before collapsing on her shivering body.

"You're the only woman I'll ever love."

Madison lay there, letting him slip the tie from her eyes. His soft kisses soothed her temples, making way to her ready lips.

"Our first public fight," she said with a sigh.

He rolled to his back, pulling her body to his chest. "Mm-hmm."

Holding her fingers to his lips, he brushed them softly between tender kisses.

Curious, she looked at him. "How did you know about the kiss?"

His chuckle was loud and sweet. "An anonymous informant told me."

Like an up-and-coming New York Times *reporter and my best friend.*

"Sheila?"

"You got it. Anonymous Sheila. The covert camerawoman at your bachelorette party."

"Can I see it?"

"Maybe. Have you watched my prime-time video yet?"

Embarrassed, Madison rolled her eyes. "Yes, and you're right. If I hadn't seen it with my own eyes, I'm not sure I would've believed it. Watching you remove your blazer to cover her naked body was . . ." At a loss for words, she finally said, "Chivalrous?"

He nodded at her quizzical confirmation of word selection.

"And I'm positive no one else will believe it either. Did you find out how she got in your room? Or who sent her?"

"Not from her, and I didn't want to press the issue. She wasn't an operative, just a pawn. But Richard worked his magic. We're ready. Anyone who enters our suite will now be caught by our own candid cameras."

Panicked and partially in disbelief, she shot him a glance. "Please tell me we didn't have an audience."

With a laugh, he said, "No. Our little porno goes to my personal cloud. No one has access but you, me, and Paco. He'll only look if he needs to. Or if the team sees that someone other than one of us has entered the suite. And we found the culprit who took those pictures. His hidden camera is now picking up the aquatic life of Marina Bay after a quick flush down the toilet."

Comforted, Madison lifted her smiling lips, which were instantly met by the smother of his hot kiss.

"Speaking of kisses . . ." He pulled up his phone, flipping to Sheila's text link. Sounding uneasy, he said, "Sheila called it 'the kiss of the century,' but said nothing else." Giving Madison a wary look, he asked, "You want to tell me what I'm about to see?"

"Nope." She giggled. "All I can say is it involves a hot, wet, steamy kiss with what I can only presume was the lead stripper of the evening."

Exaggerating his irritation, Alex tossed the phone aside, as if to give up before getting started.

Grinning, she put it back in this hand. "Oh no you don't. It's your turn. I saw photos of you peeling off your blazer in the company of a nude beauty. The least you can do is handle one little kiss."

Alex shook his head. "One little hot, wet, sexy kiss? Don't be so sure."

She held up the cell, giving him his own turn to click the video when he was ready. "And don't be discouraged because he walked away with a thousand-dollar grand prize for giving yours truly the best lap dance."

Blowing out a long huff, Alex hit PLAY.

She could tell it was nothing like he'd anticipated. Something about his expression seemed almost like he was sorry he'd missed it.

In the video, Madison had just finished receiving an anything-but-innocent lap dance from "Officer Nightstick." Promptly, he'd whisked her from the chair, forcing a wobbly Paco down in her place.

Speechless, Alex watched as one of his best friends got more hot-and-bothered attention than the bride-to-be. Paco seemed to be having the time of his life, a rarity for the man who'd slipped further and further into the monotony of adulting.

Before long, the enthusiastic dancer's performance was over, ending in a scorching kiss that lasted longer than the dance. The crowd quieted until the kiss ended, with a roar of cheers and applause as the hired talent bowed his way to a hasty escape.

With the video over, Madison smiled at Alex.

He smiled back, stunned as he set down the phone. "Is there any way in hell Paco isn't hot on this guy's trail?"

Cuddling closer, Madison answered. "Well, apparently he's a mystery man. Several dancers showed up—one more than was actually ordered. The agency that lined them up has no idea who the guy was. So, Paco's paranoia is in high swing, and he's even more determined to find the talented twerker. But he's got almost nothing to go on, with the man disguised and in dark sunglasses."

"Paco doesn't recognize him?" Alex's lips twitched. "Interesting."

Jumping up, Madison straddled him, provoking an excited grin from her crotch captive. "Oh my God. You know who it is."

"I absolutely do. Mark would too, if you showed him the footage."

Excited, she squealed. "And? Who is he?"

"Nope," Alex said. "I saw that kiss. Paco needs to figure this one out for himself."

"But you can tell me." Madison trailed seductive kisses down the muscles of Alex's torso, ready to persuade him with all kinds of adamant lip service.

Cradling her cheek, he drew her gaze. "You can't fool me, beautiful. Now I know what your lips look like when they lie." His eyes lit with a playful shine.

Tenderly nuzzling into his palm, she planted a sweet kiss to it.

"If you do manage to tear this secret from me, and you've got a *hard* tug-of-war ahead, you're sworn to secrecy. Agreed?"

Drawing out her response to emphasize her honesty, she said, "Agreed."

Confident, she went to work, extracting his deep, dark secret with her persistence.

CHAPTER 10

ALEX

ALEX WATCHED INTENTLY as Zane MacIntyre smothered Madison with an extra-long embrace in the center of the hotel lobby. It wasn't awkward. No, awkward was so two minutes ago. Madison tossed her hands wide with an *I give up* shrug followed by a giggle. Paco stepped forward to intervene, stopped by Alex's casual wave.

The similarities between Zane and Jack, Madison's brother, were striking. Almost uncanny.

Zane's piercing blue eyes shone bright against his light complexion and short, sandy-blond hair. He smiled easily from behind a rugged military demeanor, exuding a magnetic air of casual confidence.

Still, studying the man up close, Alex couldn't shake the feeling. *You're nothing like Jack.*

With an *mmm*, the man looked up at Alex, but didn't release his hug hostage. "Sorry, Al. I've gotta give my Frankie a super squeeze."

So now I'm Al? And he's calling Madison "Frankie"?

Grinning, Alex leaned in. "Well, I think you're neglecting another beautiful woman."

The second Zane unlocked his choke hold to switch over to Joy, Madison was back in Alex's arms. As she pressed her body against his, his lips met her ear.

Whispering, he asked, "You okay?"

Tightening her hug, Madison reassured him with a subtle nod. The crease in her brow didn't escape Alex's notice as he landed a kiss on her temple. The warmth of her growing smile was a relief.

Fuck what people think. I love this woman. And right at this moment, I'm showing her.

As Alex made a move for her lips, he was interrupted by a loud clap from Zane. Enthusiastically, the man rubbed his hands together. A second later, his hands were on Alex and Madison's shoulders.

Alex's glare was enough, clearly telegraphing, *You're lucky you mean anything to Madison.*

Zane dropped his hands and pocketed them. "So, what's the game plan today?"

Helpless, Alex shared a regretful look with Madison. "I have to work. But I can break away early. And Paco—"

"Paco needs to work too," Madison said quickly, interrupting. She ran a hand over Alex's chest, assuring him that her mind was set. If they were making progress today, Alex and Paco needed to divide and conquer.

At least you won't be alone, beautiful.

Smiling, Alex nodded back. "Paco and I will be working. Joy," Alex said to her with a grin, "I'm challenging you to shop till you drop and get this woman properly fed today."

Excited, Joy bounced in place with a light laugh, her thrilled squeal filling the lobby. "Exotic Asian food and shopping? Consider it done."

Pleased, he looked down at Madison, still nestled in his arms. "Your entourage is fluent in five or six languages each."

"Entourage?" Zane asked, making Alex smile.

"You heard right. We'll have two escorts and a driver to attend to any needs you all have. They'll give you privacy but be close enough. You know . . . in case anything comes up."

"That's not really necessary, is it?"

From behind, Zane laid his hands on Madison's shoulders, with an annoying and apparent massage before sticking his head next to hers.

Over her shoulder, he said playfully to Alex, "Come on, *Dad*. We just want to cut loose and relax." Jumping back, he added, "I'm fluent in French, Italian, and Chinese, and my karate chop's pretty killer."

Zane faked a Bruce Lee stance, then synchronized a few flexes of his biceps and pecs.

Madison jumped in. "Sorry, Zane. I'll feel better if they come with us. Besides, the more the merrier."

Alex couldn't help saying, "See, Zane? *Dad* doesn't make the rules." Looking at his bride-to-be, he found her pout begging for his attention.

Stealing the kiss he missed earlier, Alex held it for longer than he should have. But her fingers stroked his back. And her lips moved with his.

Alex hadn't lied. Where Madison was concerned, he never made the rules. He'd always be there for her, in any way she needed.

As her kiss lingered, his only thought was, *I'm not complaining.*

Tearing away, he settled for a last peck before releasing her, and looked around. "I guess they got tired of waiting."

Madison whipped her head around. "I can't believe they up and left because we smooched for an hour or two." Her giggle was infectious, and he laughed too as he glanced at the text on his phone.

"Paco says they're waiting in the car." Kissing her palm and smoothing it to his cheek, Alex gave her a stern warning. "Call me if you need anything at all. I'll be there at a moment's notice."

"Don't worry. I will."

Her final kiss was released with a sigh, and he held in her scent as she stepped out to the waiting pair of SUVs.

It was the one day Alex was grateful that Madison hadn't chosen to wear a skirt, opting instead for worn-in capris and a relaxed-fit T-shirt. The girl next door made casual look irresistible.

Perplexed, he watched as Madison leaned into speak confidentially to Paco. With a nod, Paco shut the door he'd been holding and led Madison to the traffic side of the car, ensuring she was safely in before heading back.

Even without hearing the conversation, they clearly both stayed in character. No hugs. No air kisses. Paco was just another employee. No discussions about their closeness. Not even a hint that they knew more than each other's names.

Once the vehicles were on their way, Alex waited as Paco returned inside. Undoubtedly, Alex's expression asked the question on his mind.

Paco didn't exactly have an answer. "I don't know for sure." Rubbing his chin, he said, "She said she wanted to sit on the other side, and I didn't ask any questions. And by the way, Joy says Zane's a colonel now."

Alex replied with an eye roll. "A ten-year colonel?" Paco didn't reply. He didn't have to. Their feelings were well understood and mutual.

Replaying the scene, Alex thought through the logistics. Joy was on the street side of the vehicle, and Zane was in the center seat. By Madison entering on the street side, everyone had to scoot over to give her room, moving Joy to the center and Zane to the curb side of the car.

"Hmm."

"My sentiments exactly. Maybe Zane's rubbing Madison the wrong way too." Both men smiled at the possibility.

Patting Paco's arm, Alex said, "By the way, that was *some* kiss the other night."

With a shake of his head and a mild blush, Paco sneered. "Fuck off." Straightening his suit, he stalked away.

Chuckling, Alex hurried to catch up. "Was it something I said?"

CHAPTER 11

MADISON

M adison sat in the car, letting her mom hold her hand. It had been four years since they'd seen each other, and talking always complicated things. When they did chat on the phone, they avoided topics that were deep. Or dark. And no mentions of Jack that would upset her. Madison never brought him up, keeping her conversations with her mom to topics like "How's the weather?" and "What are you reading?"

Joy didn't know much about Alex past the *billionaire* label, every mother's dream. Madison's dad vouching for him wasn't exactly necessary, and they all decided it was best not to bring up the remarkable connections . . . especially not—

Jack.

Looking at Zane, Madison found it hard not to think of Jack. They had the same height, the same build, though Zane had certainly enhanced his lean frame over the years.

Taking in how significantly bulked Zane was beneath his fitted navy-blue T-shirt, Madison wondered how Jack might have looked at this age. But Jack's eyes were so much deeper . . . softer and more sensitive. When it came to the guy anyone could talk to, Jack was that guy. Hands down.

But if Jack was everyone's confidant, Zane was the charmer. Even now, showering her mom with compliments and attention. It was great to see Joy smiling nonstop.

But calling me Frankie . . .

The nickname lingered in Madison's mind as she thought back to herself as the girl who couldn't get enough of being around her brother and his college roommate whenever they came home for holidays. Spring break. Could anyone fault a teenage girl for her first crush?

Everything was so right, and yet so strange at the same time. Her feelings were elusive, and something seemed off. Again, she fought to figure it out. *Frankie.*

Why had Zane come? It wasn't just that he hadn't called her Frankie in years. In fact, he hadn't called her at all—not even after Jack's funeral. It was understandable that he was closer to her parents, but just once it would've been nice to hear his voice for herself. To at least have him acknowledge her existence above a "give her my love."

Just like the hug. It was nice enough, but weird. Zane had never been overly affectionate. At least, not with her. In his defense, what guy in his twenties wanted to be stuck babysitting? But who knew what he'd been through over the years. People changed.

The old nervousness that used to cause Madison unrelenting hives was now stealing her appetite, resulting in a heavy dose of unintentional bridal fasting. Food had become decidedly unappetizing. But maybe some local bread would satiate this carboholic's needs. The upside of worrying was her waistline would be bridal-gown ready.

When the SUV ahead of them holding their security team signaled they were pulling over, theirs followed, securing two parking spaces that had been reserved for them. VIP was printed on the sign in English. Their bodyguard spoke a foreign language into his radio, then in English back to the trio.

"There are a lot of nice shops and restaurants here with beautiful views. Mr. Drake will take care of all your expenses."

Zane grinned. "I could use a Porsche."

"Ooh, me too," Joy said, joining in on the joke. "I bet I'll be a hell of a cougar with that."

Cringing, Madison covered her face. "Oh my God, Mom. I can see us double-dating now. Me and Alex, and you with someone younger than Zane."

Zane opened his door. Grabbing Joy's hand, he whisked her out, dragging her fanny along the leather seat. "Come on, cougar, let me show you the town. If I'm not too old for you."

Elated, Joy hopped out, giggling with delight.

Zane's single-finger summons coaxed Madison next. "You too, young lady."

Madison couldn't help but laugh, taking his hand and letting him skate her butt out too.

~

After a little food—very little for Madison—the trio was ready to hit the shops. Joy didn't exactly need an excuse to splurge with Alex's black card, grabbing one of everything before she headed into the dressing room.

With Joy busy trying on clothes, Zane turned to Madison. "Well, you're all grown up."

Shrugging, she said, "I guess it depends on your definition. Taller? A little. Adulting? Not by choice."

Zane looked around, glancing at the positions of the bodyguards. He lowered his voice. "Listen, Madison. I didn't want to mention this in front of Joy, but she called me. She's worried about you."

Puzzled, Madison asked, "She did?"

Well, that's a miracle. How Mom got his number is beyond me. I had to program my own number in her phone.

Zane nodded, laying his hand on her shoulder. "She's heard things about Alex and . . . look, there's no reason to rush into anything."

Patting Zane's hand, Madison forced a smile. "I'm not."

She *could* go into the details of everything they'd all been through—Alex and Paco, and even her dad. But looking into Zane's eyes, to her the difference was crystal clear. This wasn't her brother. Not even close. And something about the way Zane was rubbing her arm was sending her anxiety through the roof.

Shrugging him off, she moved across the store.

With a familiar arrogance that always rivaled his charm, Zane shook his head and laughed. "Seriously? You've known the guy for less than a year. His reputation alone should be a red flag."

"Which reputation?" she asked. "The one for building a multibillion-dollar global empire from scratch?"

Propping his hands on his hips, Zane snapped back, "No. For having more women on his staff than Mary Kay." Ignoring Madison's eye roll, he kept going. "Face it, Madison, he's a serial seducer."

Before she could object, Joy was front and center.

"What do you think?"

For a woman in her early fifties, Joy's dedication to yoga and running kept her in J-Lo condition. In a bright yellow bikini, sarong, and showing off the ample assets she'd passed on to Madison, Joy practically glowed in the revealing outfit.

His cheeks bright pink, Zane spun around. "Sorry, I've got to take a, uh, call." He raced out of the shop faster than a sneeze through a screen door.

Joy turned to her daughter. "Okay, Madison, it's up to you. Buy or don't buy?"

Definitely yes if it'll shut Zane up about Alex.

Staring down at her mother's feet, Madison said, "Outfit . . . two thumbs-up. But faded tennies from a decade ago means we're hitting the shoe store next. Hurry up and change, hot mama." Madison swatted her mother lightly on the rear as she headed back to the dressing room.

"*Psst.*"

Madison turned toward the sound.

Zane was back, peeking his head out from under a mannequin's arm. Wearing a pair of oversized dark glasses, he hissed, "Is the coast clear?"

Unable to stay irritated with him, Madison played along. Crossing her fisted hands over her chest in an *X*, she shot them down and wide, giving him the tactical signal for *safe—all clear.*

Standing taller, Zane slid the glasses to the top of his head. "Whew." His hand made a long wipe across his forehead. "I was worried she was eyeing me for a cougar call of duty."

"You sure she's not?"

Their polite smiles faded.

"Look, Mads, I'm sorry for what I said. No one wants you happy more than I do. I just feel obligated to look out for you. Make sure you're okay, and that you're safe." His hands rubbing up and down her arms seemed to be his way to reinforce his words.

Despite closing in on her for whatever he was about to do, she stopped him with a single word. "Mads."

Letting her go, he looked away, but she pressed for more.

"Yes, Mads. That's what you called me, what you've always called me since the first of a million times you teased me because I'd run off. You'd laugh, shouting—"

"Don't be mad, Mads." Zane ran his fingers through his hair, letting out a chuckle that sounded more nervous than anything.

A wisp of a memory clung to the nickname. She just couldn't hold it long enough to remember.

"But you're too grown up for a nickname like that," he said. "Too sophisticated. Too beautiful . . ."

Ignoring the compliment, Madison asked, "So, why did you call me Frankie this morning? You've never called me that. Usually, only my dad does." *And Jack.*

Zane shook his head as his eyes met hers. "I don't know. I guess I just wanted you to feel surrounded by people who care about you. People who know you. People who love you." His hand wrapped hers tightly. So tight, in fact, that despite being flustered, she had to pull back twice before escaping his grasp.

Nearly falling back into a carousel of shirts, she shook it off. "Mom has my credit card. I'll be waiting in the car."

Madison raced away, not bothering to look back.

CHAPTER 12

MADISON

FROWNING as she stared at their SUV at the curb, Madison decided the last thing she wanted was to be trapped in it if Zane chased her down.

"You all right, Ms. Taylor?" One of her very large bodyguards stepped over to her, still maintaining a professional distance.

"Yes, thank you. I just need a little . . ."

"Privacy?" He gave her a wide and genuine smile, a gentle giant transparent in wanting to help her.

Madison nodded, and her breathing eased at his quick understanding.

Taking her to the black vehicle parked in front of the one she'd arrived in, the bodyguard opened the back door. "This is our SUV."

He shot a glance to the driver. The car remained running, but the driver stepped outside, seeming to understand what was wanted.

"He's dying for a cigarette. I'll keep an eye on you. If anyone asks, you went to the bathroom and will be right back."

"You're a lifesaver. What's your name?"

"Jack."

Of course it is. "I love that name. Thank you, Jack."

Shutting her inside the luxury vehicle, he resumed his stance outside the store.

Quickly, Madison pulled out her phone. Feeling silly and juvenile, she just stared at it. As if by magic, a call rang and Paco's name flashed across the screen. Her smile was instantaneous.

"How did you know I needed you?

"Sibling psychic connection," he said, initiating a FaceTime connection.

Happily, she tapped the screen to accept. "Really?"

She'd only just seen Paco an hour ago, but he was a sight for sore eyes.

His eyebrow popped up. "No, *hermanita*. I'm good, but I'm not that good. Your bodyguard texted me. So, what's happening? I can be there in a hop and a skip. I don't even need the jump." Dropping his teasing tone, his handsome face grew stern. "What's going on?"

With a deep inhale, she shook her head. "I don't know." Meeting his concerned eyes, she said, "Really, I have no idea. I just feel . . . off. I'm worked up about what's going to happen. I can't eat. I'm run down because I can't sleep. Being with Alex last night was the first time I slept in a week. Well," a sly smile curled up, "I mean, *afterward*. If there's one thing that man is good at, it's working out my kinks."

Putting his free hand over his ear for a moment, Paco sang, "La-la-la, I'm not hearing anything about your kinks."

"Oh, whatever. I watched you lip-lock the dance-off king." She grinned as, for the first time ever, she witnessed Paco's natural bronze skin turn beet red.

"Whatever. It was just a kiss. He was fishing for an extra-large tip."

Naughty to the *n*th degree, Madison agreed. "Is that what he was fishing for? Your extra-large quote-unquote *tip*. Because I was watching, and I definitely did not see that."

Wide-eyed, Paco responded with utter shock. "Young lady, you need to behave. You're with your mother."

Grumbling, Madison tucked her hair behind her ear. "I know. And Zane." Shutting her eyes, she deflated.

"You sound upset. Did something happen?"

Her head shake was subtle. Her *no* came out almost questioning.

"Okay," Paco said with a long-suffering sigh, "can we bypass the long stretch of denial and skip to the part where you tell me what happened?"

Looking out the tinted window, Madison watched her mother and Zane leave the store and get in their SUV. This time, Zane got in first, obviously taking the center seat.

"I want to, but I can't. They're waiting for me, and I need to head over and play musical butts." When Paco glared at her on the screen, lifting a quizzical brow, she said, "Never mind. I'll explain later. Can I see you this evening?"

"Um . . . that might be difficult."

"If you tell me you've got a hot date with Magic Mike, you're forgiven."

"Well," Paco said, "one of us will be with a man with smooth moves, but it's not me."

Her eyes lit up, anticipating his next words.

"Alex has a surprise for you. But I'm not supposed to tell you, so you didn't hear it from me." Paco's large wink filled her with excitement. "So, hang in there. Or how about you ditch them, I'll ditch work, and we'll reconvene at the hotel spa."

"Tempting. But if Alex is about to make it all better, I can hold out a few more hours."

"Before you go . . ."

Paco's hesitation triggered more itching up her arm.

"You can't leave me hanging. Not today. Please, Paco, throw me a bone."

With a look of regret, he said, "Just watch out for Zane."

"Yeah, I'm trying. But how do you know about Zane? Or more importantly, *what* do you know about Zane?"

"Trust me when I say it's a long story. Or maybe not a long story, but not one for over the phone. We'll connect tomorrow. Unless you text me the bat signal . . . then I'll drop everything and be wherever you are. Pronto."

Sinking into Paco's words like a warm bath, she grinned. "You and Alex both. I love you. See you tomorrow."

"Love you too." Paco let her disconnect first, which she reluctantly did.

When she exited the car, Jack faced her, using the enormity of his body to block his hands, thumbing the question for *this door or that*. Thankful, she gestured toward her mother's side.

Nodding with understanding, he led her over.

CHAPTER 13

MADISON

BEAT FROM THE DAY, Madison couldn't abandon her companions soon enough. In the sanctity of the penthouse suite, she kicked off her shoes, exhausted from the strange cat-and-mouse games with Zane. *That man needs help.*

"Oh, Ms. Taylor . . ." The lull of a captivating low voice called out from the softly lit bedroom.

Madison perked up, all traces of fatigue vanishing at his suggestive tone. Following the glow, she found a barely clad Alex lighting candles near the bathtub.

Her gaze traced the lines of his body. She marveled at the dips and curves of the terrain of muscles. As he turned toward her, wearing only a towel tucked around his hips, the beauty of the scars across his chest reminded her of the man he was—the man she would marry. He was hers.

The soft curve of her mouth widened as she took in the nearly naked hunk. "If I'm getting a lap dance, I'll grab a chair."

Alex blew out the long stick of a match and set it down. "Haven't you had enough lap dances for one week, Ms. Taylor? Tonight, I'll start as your bath butler and end as your masseur. One bath and a full-body massage, coming right up."

Stepping aside, he pressed a button and the water in the tub vibrated, sending a swirl of bubbles to the surface. The air filled with the fragrances of lavender and mint. It was almost enough of a distraction that she didn't notice.

"Well, this isn't about to be a one-way street, Mr. Drake." Slipping into his arms, she welcomed a kiss before asking, "Should I get the bad news now, or later? And don't deny it. Your muscles are perfect, but they can't hide your tension."

Sighing, he dropped back his head in defeat. With a tight squeeze, he brought her closer. "We caught a break today. We're about to crack this mystery wide open. But . . ." The hope in his voice turned remorseful. "Those photos are hitting the papers tomorrow. Maybe tonight. Worldwide."

Undoubtedly, he saw her concern. Faking a brave face, Madison stroked his jaw, preferring to gaze at his mouth—too chicken to meet his eyes. "We'll get through this."

The bend of his finger pulled her chin up. The scrutiny of his glance was unavoidable. "Your poker face is so good, yet so atrocious. We could send out the video right away. Lessen the blow by being up front ourselves."

Silently, she let out a slow, frustrated huff. "No. This only works if we let them think we're hit. And it has to look real, like we're breaking up. So, no more lingering kisses in the lobby. No more googly eyes."

Joking, he said, "I make no promises on the googly eyes."

His kiss started soft, tenderly prying open her lips until his tongue invaded her fully. Deeper.

In a whisper, he reassured her. "Then tonight is our pre-emptive make-up session. And I'll assume I've got a lot to make up for."

With a heated sigh, Alex pressed his bulge against her. Her shirt couldn't come off fast enough.

The second her bra was gone, his lips warmed her nipple, teasing it with his tongue as he unfastened her pants and tugged them away. Her white panties he left on for the moment.

Skimming his fingers down her neck, he traced a long line past her breasts that ached for his touch. His lazy finger circled around her nipples, coaxing them into peaks.

"Alex." She moaned, her voice pleading as her hips pressed into his.

"*Shh.* I'm just beginning. We have all night."

Her head fell back as his finger continued down the length of her torso and the front of her core, lingering at her heat. Through the lace of her panties, he skated a light line of pressure up to her clit, then down again. Her wetness was evident. She didn't have to look to know his fingers were glistening.

"I want you," she said on a whimper.

"Yes, but tonight you're getting more than me."

Madison swallowed hard, her heart beating harder. *More than Alex?* He tightened a fist around the fabric between her legs and ripped it away. Her body jolted.

"You need this."

"Need what?" she said, panting, her words urgent. The fresh sting from the torn fabric assured that.

Scooping her up, he set her in the bathtub, then removed the towel from around his waist, dropping it to the tile floor. Her gaze dropped to his evident arousal, and his rod bobbed as if acknowledging her desire.

"Kneel down," he softly commanded, climbing in after her as he added, "And turn around."

With a dizzying tingle that affected every single cell in her body, she obeyed, facing the outside of the enormous tub.

His hand steadied her hip while the other pressed her back, urging her to lean forward. Her hands gripped the bathtub, and the vibration of the tub rumbled across her body clear to her pussy as two slow fingers slid inside her, then pulled out.

Above her loud gasp she heard him suck his fingers clean with a low, approving, "God, you're all I ever want." His grip on her side firmed as his heavy cock moved up and down her entrance. Then, without warning, he dove in to the hilt.

"Yes." Her hips bucked back, but now both of his massive hands were holding her still.

"Not too much," he teased, controlling his rhythmic thrusts, not giving her all of him again.

"More," she begged.

"I'm about to give you more." He pulled out, kissing her shoulders. The hot bubbling water was heaven around her body.

"Ahh," escaped from her throat.

Their bodies leaned forward together.

"Say when," he whispered.

"When? To wha—"

Just then, her body pivoted at exactly the perfect angle. A jet pounded water to her clit, resulting in a wild rush of sensations. She nearly collapsed under the power of the Jacuzzi.

Alex's strong arm wrapped around her, holding her up against it. "When?" he mumbled diabolically.

"W-wh—" Giving up, she let her stuttered word die away as her head fell back against his shoulder.

"If you want it stronger, we move forward. Softer? Move back."

Her nails dug into his arms. It was all she could do to keep him from shifting in the slightest.

His lips on her neck, he cupped her breast with a sharp pinch to her nipple, and her back arched. "Brace yourself . . . and don't come."

He threw her arms behind his neck, keeping her body stretched. The jet sent an erotic hum through her clit, lighting electric charges across her skin. Her core throbbed, clenching as the firm, hard head of his cock demanded entry. Her body rocked.

"Don't come," he warned again, low and demanding as he pressed his crown slightly inside her.

She shivered. "Please, Alex. I—"

"No. Not yet."

With another shove, the thickness of his dick filled her, stretching her wide as he carried its weight slowly in and out across her walls. His rhythm was unrelenting. Her hips moved, barely able to resist the explosive pleasure ahead.

Alex picked up the pace, thrusting as his fingers dipped down, spreading her lips wide to let the full force of the jet crash into her.

His command was low. "Now."

Her body complied in a wave of crashing explosions, one after another, shooting pins and needles from the top of her head to the tips of her toes. And still, Alex deepened his pounding, holding her trembling body as he pushed her to another rush of ecstasy.

"Again, Madison," he demanded, gruff and insistent. "I need you to come again."

Barely allowing her to catch her breath, he kept her body exposed to the pulsing stream of water. He was everywhere. Against her. Inside her.

Making her his.

His steady pace quickened, and again, his body nudged hers closer and closer to the pulse of the jet, inching her into a stronger sensation with every merciless thrust.

Madison's screams shot throughout the luxurious bathroom, echoing against the solid marble and glass of a room bathed in the glow of the city's sunset. A universe of stars filled her eyes, and every breath strained for the next.

His own climax surged, overtaking hers, taking her once again to another peak of pleasure so hard, she bucked back. In an instant, she was falling, one with him in every conceivable way.

They collapsed back into the swirl of lavender-scented waves and the endless luxury of massaging jets.

CHAPTER 14

MADISON

Waking up the next morning, Madison stretched, only to have the deep yawn forced out of her with a giggle. Arms of pure muscle scooped her backward into a spooned cuddle.

After a few tender kisses to her ear, Alex melted her with his deep, groggy whisper. "Morning, beautiful."

Snuggling against him and lacing her fingers through his, she sighed. "Morning."

"How about we face this day with a little breakfast?"

Hating the hell storm to come, she shook her head as she nestled closer, secure in his warm arms. His kiss on her neck brought a small smile from her lips.

"Not even a nibble?" he asked.

"Are we still talking about food?"

Pulling the blanket up a little higher, he reached beneath it to stroke her folds, already slick again. "Whatever will keep you here."

Alex climbed on top of her. The heat of his lips branded her skin with every touch, working steadily down. Her legs cradled him, relishing the weight of his body centered between her thighs.

With the worst timing ever, the chime of the doorbell rang softly. Both were determined to ignore it, until the pounding started.

"That's some insistent room service," he said, leaving a few extra kisses on the thigh he was moving away from.

"Maybe they heard this suite has a kick-ass tipper who gets hangry."

With much too short of a kiss, he said, "Don't move."

Her smile widened as he made the best of a robe two sizes too small. "Sure you don't want me to get it? They might misunderstand and think that's their tip." Her gaze suggestively lingered on his crotch.

When a new wave of pounding began, Alex rushed out of the room, calling back, "I've got this covered. And you're staying in bed as long as possible."

Resting her head back, Madison was ripped from any further relaxation by the ensuing commotion. Shouts rang through the penthouse, abruptly getting louder.

A second later, Joy burst into the bedroom, slamming the door on Alex.

"Mom! What are you doing?"

Joy paid no mind to her daughter's nakedness before grabbing her up into a suffocating embrace as she sobbed. "Madison, I know I haven't been there for you in the ways I should have, but I'm here for you now."

Madison caught her mother's hand clasping a crumpled newspaper. *Shit.* "Mom, it's . . ."

What do I say? There's no way I can tell her the truth. She'll have fifty questions that all lead to Jack. And then a hundred more questions will follow.

Even if I leave Jack out of it, if she knows Alex is being set up, her stubborn ass will be shouting his innocence from the rooftop, spilling our little secret for all to hear.

When Madison's silence took far too long, Joy handed her the newspaper. "He's a real piece of work, Madison. Who cares how much money he has?"

With a quick glance at the global business journal, Madison took in the headline that screamed:

Mega-Mogul Alex Drake's Marriage of Convenience

Wait. Convenience?

Madison scanned the article, flipping quickly to the center of the paper where it continued.

What the French toast?

There, in addition to the photos of Alex and nice-girl Shelly, was a spread of photos of Madison and Zane. The grab-and-hold in the store was caught by a paparazzo's camera. Zane's hands on her arms. Him holding her hand. In one shot, they looked unbelievably close, with her back to the camera and his head tilted just so.

Oh my God. It looked like a kiss.

A wave of heat rose past her neck, blazing across her cheeks. *Think fast, Madison.*

"Mom, can you hand me a robe? It's in the bathroom."

Nodding, her mother made her way to fetch it.

"You didn't see the photos, did you?" Madison called out.

"No." Joy's tone was apologetic. "I couldn't, but I can imagine what a snake like that man has done."

Crumpling the sheet of photos under the bed, Madison quickly refolded the paper. Joy returned and handed Madison a plush robe, which she promptly slipped on.

"Mom, I promise you, I . . ." She thought for a moment, choosing her words carefully. "I know everything there is to know about Alex. You have to trust me. I can take care of myself. And I need a really big favor from you."

"Anything, jellybean." Plopping herself on the bed next to Madison, Joy hugged her tightly again.

"I . . ." The consequences of her request could have a ripple effect for years. Maybe centuries. Feeling brave, Madison continued. "I need you to go home. You and Zane. Today."

And get out of the line of fire. If they know about Zane, they know about you.

Joy pulled away, hurt filling her glistening eyes. "You don't want me here?"

Squeezing her mom's hand affectionately, Madison met her gaze. "I know we haven't been close, and that's my fault too. I'm not pushing you away. It's just that Alex and I need to . . . work this out. Just us. Alone. Alex will have a jet ready to take you home this morning."

"I see." By her tone, her mother most certainly did not *see*.

But that didn't matter. Madison couldn't worry about Joy. Ironically, for the first time she understood how Alex and Paco felt—always wanting to keep her safe.

"I know you don't understand, but I have another favor. And this one's bigger. I need Dad to watch over you. He'll pick you up and take you somewhere for a while. To keep you away from . . . the paparazzi."

Joy frowned. "Madison, look, I'll leave if that's what you want. But your father and I haven't talked in years. I'm not going to hang out with Dan because you think I can't handle a few photographers."

Gently, Madison insisted in a way she hoped her mom would understand. "I need this. I've never asked you for anything, but I'm asking you for this. It's important. And Dad's changed. He's not the same as he was when we left. And I won't be able to eat or sleep unless I know you're protected. Dad's the only one I trust."

Sniffling, Joy asked, "What about Zane?"

Adamant, Madison made her position clear. "Zane's going too, but he's probably going back to his duty station. It has to be Dad. Besides, he's got a beautiful place in the city."

"In New York?"

Madison nodded. "It's a long story, but it's safe. No one will know where you are. No one will bother you. At least, not until things quiet down."

The questions clear from her mother's expression were getting to be too much. But a knowing glance exchanged between them. Some spark of understanding.

"There's something else, isn't there?" her mother asked. "And you can't tell me." Her tears shook loose again. "Just like your father, and just like Jack. You're in that world now too . . . aren't you?"

Madison fidgeted with the comforter, avoiding her mother's eyes.

Not waiting for an answer, Joy let out a slow breath. "I see. I know that look. No matter how many questions I ask or how much I press, you won't be able to answer me, so why bother?" Her despondent tone was heartbreaking.

Madison stood, ready to lead Joy out.

Taking her daughter in a rocking hug, Joy whispered, "Whatever you're into, you listen to me. I'm doing you a favor, so now you have to do me one, okay? Be careful. You'll always be my little girl. I can't lose you too."

Madison sniffed back the tears streaming down her cheeks. "Nobody's losing anyone. You've seen the guards. Alex won't let anything happen—to me or to you."

"Alex?" The knit in Joy's brow melted. "Maybe Zane should stay. He's got all kinds of fighting skills, and all those ribbons for shooting and weapons. He really wants to look after you."

"No." Madison responded a little too quickly, then dug deep for composure. "He's got his own life and doesn't need to get involved. He needs to go. You've got to convince him to leave."

Nodding, her mom stood. "I'll try. But the man has a mind of his own when it comes to you."

The strange statement needed clarifying.

"What do you mean? Is that why you called him?"

Their exchange of puzzled glances was interrupted by a knock.

Opening the door a crack, Madison breathed out a sigh, disappointment deflating her. In a three-piece suit that molded to his chiseled body like paint, Alex was obviously headed out.

"Did you wave a magic wand?' she asked him. "I thought all your suits were in here?"

"I didn't want to interrupt. And Paco always has a few suits for me on standby. He didn't mind me getting ready down there."

"You went to his room in *that* bathrobe?"

"Yup. Proud as a peacock." Alex lowered his voice. "Everything all right?"

Joy butted between the two, glaring and loud. "No. Everything is *not* all right."

With a poke of her elbow, Madison coaxed her mother to lower her tone to a half-pissed-off volume.

Curt, Joy said, "Madison's sending me home."

Madison fidgeted with the sash of her robe. "Mom needs to go back. Today, if that's all right."

Alex agreed, his relief almost palpable. "Of course. Whatever you need. The jet will be ready as soon as you are, Joy."

Without acknowledging him, she hugged Madison hard. Breezing past him, sniffling, she mumbled something under her breath.

As Joy neared the door, she spun. "And another thing, Alex Drake," she said as if they'd heard the first part of her murmuring loud and clear. "If anything happens to my daughter, I'll hold you personally responsible." Sobbing, she darted out of the suite, slamming the door behind her.

Shaking his head, Alex said quietly, "Well, that makes two of us."

Before Madison could apologize, his mouth was on hers. His tongue slipped through her lips, hasty in its sweeps to steal a moment just for them. His arms wrapped around her, and her plush robe couldn't stop his insistent cock from making its presence known.

He growled against her lips. "God, I love it when we're in a fight." When her hand slipped away, he asked, "Did we make up already?"

Dropping her forehead on his chest, she sighed. "We might be ramping up for another one. And not in a fun way. The newspaper—"

The playful glint in his eyes was unmistakable. "You mean our salacious marriage of convenience."

This man knows everything. "You don't seem concerned by the photos."

"Nah." He waved away her worry. "I already autographed a few on the way to Paco's room."

"But it looks like—"

"It looks like if Zane manhandled your wrist any tighter, you'd have to gnaw it off to get away from him. Do I need to have a talk with the overeager Mr. MacIntyre?"

Relieved, Madison shook her head and gave Alex a subtle smile. "I was worried what you might think."

"Hey." His comforting hands cradled her cheeks, and he met her gaze. "Don't think for a second I don't know the woman I'm with. And I do know you, Madison Taylor. Though . . ."

Unknotting her sash, he peeled open the robe, giving him the full-frontal view he'd always surrendered to. "I could always get to know you better." His kisses landed down her neck and chest, chasing away the dark worries weighing on her mind.

Slyly, she asked, "I thought you were heading out."

Losing his blazer and tossing away his tie, Alex gave her a diabolical smile. "I can't possibly leave now."

As he swept Madison off her feet, her half-naked body snuggled willingly in his arms.

"You saw that headline. And those incriminating photos." He kissed her growing smile, topping it off with the lightest nose-to-nose rub. "I feel a huge fight coming on."

CHAPTER 15

MADISON

Her desperate attempt to scurry away later that day had become an epic fail. Somehow, despite giving her bodyguards the slip, she couldn't lose this guy.

Wearing dark glasses and a ball cap, then ducking in and out of this shop and that, she'd unfortunately been discovered. And not by the growing swarm of paparazzi. Apparently, overzealous reporters eager for a big money shot had nothing on Zane.

He'd managed to keep pace, tracking her like a scientist triangulating her invisible sonar signal. And either she was going for a dip in the bay, or she was facing her obnoxiously loud stalker head-on.

Seriously, she had to do something, because the last thing she needed was him bellowing out her name in the middle of Singapore.

All he's missing is a loudspeaker and a Jumbotron saying "She's over here."

Tugging her ball cap lower to cover her face, Madison shushed him. "Didn't you say you were leaving?"

"A little white lie to keep your mom's FOMO under control."

With a conspicuous scan around the area, Madison took a breath. "Look, Zane, it's really not great if we're spotted together."

"But it's fine for you to be out here alone with photographers dying for a shot? What happened to your bodyguards? Leave it to Alex Drake—"

"Hey!" She crossed her arms over her chest. "Boundaries. You've got something to say, Zane, fine. Leave Alex out of the discussion."

"Fine by me." Zane's hands snapped to his hips.

With his heated glare bearing down on her from his six-foot-two stature, she staggered back a step.

Clearly, her reaction was noticed. The lines in Zane's brow smoothed, and the darkness of his eyes lightened, softening his words.

"Sorry, Mads." With a smirk, he added, "Maybe I should be the one with that nickname. Look, I . . . I haven't seen you in forever. And I never really connected with you. After Jack." He turned away, but she glimpsed the pain in his eyes.

Her hand brushed his arm. "It's all right. You were busy."

He shook his head slowly. "No, Madison. I kept busy, as busy as I could. To try to forget how lonely life was without Jack. And what could I say to you?" He blew out a long breath, his gaze unfocused in the direction of the bay. "Even across the globe, on his last mission, we kept in touch. Like brothers."

Clearing his throat, Zane stood taller as he faced her.

"Wherever he went, I kept an eye on him. Even when he went on his deployment, and his few weeks of leave to Italy. But I wasn't there for him, Mads." Zane grabbed her hand, smiling as he held it tight. "But I'll be here for you. No matter how much you try to lose me."

She couldn't help squeezing back. "Jack loved you, Zane. There was nothing you could have done."

"No? Then why do I feel so goddamnn guilty ten years later? And why do I feel the need to stick to you like a magnet?" He looked down at her hand in his. "See? I know any moment now, someone could snap a shot. Make your life hell. And I just . . . I can't let go."

"Well," she gave him a cocky smile, ready to rib him out of the deep discussion, "you're going to have to let go." Gently, she pulled her hand back. "Because that's my *wiping* hand."

Stepping back from her and throwing his hands in the air, Zack laughed. "Wow. That hand is definitely all yours."

His laugh died down quickly. "Listen, can we just spend a few hours together? I want to catch up, hear about absolutely everything we can cram in that time. When did you get your braces off? Who taught you how to drive, and how bad was it? Where was your first kiss? What made you move to New York?"

Barely holding back her grin, Madison agreed. "Okay, okay. But we can't stay out in the open."

Confident, he scouted the area and rubbed his chin. "Lucky for you, I know my way around Singapore. Come on. One of my favorite dives isn't too far from here. Singapore may be a pristine cosmopolitan city, but there are pockets of little China, little India, and lots of quaint spots where only locals go. Unless . . ."

"Unless what?" Curious, she dropped her guard.

"Unless you're no longer as adventurous with food like you once were, begging for anything except burgers and fries."

With a shy smile, Madison nodded. "Still a food adventurer but eating light."

If eye-rolling had sound, his was blaring. "Seriously? You can't tell me you're trying to squeeze into a wedding dress. You don't need to lose an ounce."

She shrugged. "Just not terribly hungry." *Covert activities do that to a girl.*

"Sounds like walking-down-the-aisle jitters. That's normal."

"As if you would know. Even George Clooney finally settled down."

Zane nodded, tapping his finger to the tip of her nose. "Only when he found the right girl."

CHAPTER 16

MADISON

M ADISON HAD her fill of a plain roti prata flatbread and some tea, but waved a polite pass to the oyster omelet and barbecue stingray.

"So, not as adventurous as you once were?" Zane took another bite of his fish, not minding the whole head attached or eye staring back at him.

The shake of her head was definite. "I am one hundred percent positive that at no point in time did I ever ask for such an . . . uh . . . exotic sampler. Nope, try as I might, I don't recall anything like this at Panda Express."

She checked her phone, discouraged at the lack of notifications. *Nothing from Alex*. Noting the time had flown, she said, "It's getting late."

Stuffing his face with anything left he could fit in his mouth, Zane gulped down the contents of his chipmunk cheeks with the last of his tea and winked. "Let's go."

As they headed out, Madison popped on her ball cap and sunglasses, and Zane did the same. The touch of sunlight captured a honey hue to his hair, and his smile sparkled. For a second, he was Jack.

And then the mirage vanished.

Hiding the tear that insisted on falling, she wiped her sleeve against her cheek. Blankly, she stared down the foreign street. "I have no idea how to get back."

"Well, the hotel is a hop, skip, and a jump down that way, but how about we take a slightly scenic route? There's fewer people or chances of someone recognizing you. And it lets me stretch out the last of our time together."

With a second disappointed glance at her cell, Madison nodded. "I'd like that."

And I could use the distraction. Where are you, Alex?

~

Taking in the city, Madison strolled slowly, noticing that wherever she stepped, Mr. Clean seemed to have just finished up. "I think this is the cleanest city I've ever seen. Like they polish the streets."

Zane nodded. "Not far from it. The leaders of Singapore are in a war against more than just dirt. On such a small island with a growing population, they needed a strategy to control trash and pests while keeping the health of their citizens optimal. They realized the root cause was the level of cleanliness, so they upped their game to what you see today. Whatever you do, don't chew gum. It's no joke. Fines. Jail time. It's what they do."

With an exaggerated gulp to swallow her imaginary gum, Madison nodded. "I'm good now. You sure know this country."

Arrogantly, he corrected her. "Sovereign island."

"Sovereign island," she repeated like a schoolgirl. "You must come to Singapore a lot. I didn't realize the Army had a presence here."

Zane shook his head. "There's a naval base."

When he didn't elaborate, she asked, "Did you switch teams?"

Indignant, he scoffed. "Not in this life." He caught her expression, answering her unsaid question with a grin. "You know me, Mads. My world is deep in the dark. If I tell you, I'd have to kill you. And you're far too beautiful for a quick kill."

His smile waned. "Seriously, though, there is something I need to talk with you about. But it can't be in public."

Considering it and checking her phone for what seemed like the hundredth time, Madison nodded. "We can meet at the penthouse. But we need to get there separately."

Zane agreed, leaning in and pointing down the street. "Head that way. As soon as the street opens, the hotel is on the left. I'll meet you at your room in twenty minutes. Give you plenty of time to use that wiping hand to do what it does best."

With an exchange of smiles and nods, they parted ways, and Madison headed back to the hotel.

CHAPTER 17

MADISON

The second Madison let Zane in her suite, his energy changed. The charmer she'd seen not half an hour ago turned grave. Solemn. Despite her offering him his choice of beverage, he waved her off.

Plenty of comfortable seats were scattered about the luxurious living area, but he remained standing. "Seriously, I'm worried about you."

Madison sat on the elegant sofa with ornately decorated silk cushions. Taking his lecture in stride, she calmly reassured him. "There's nothing to worry about."

"Yes, there is." Urgency pulling his brows to a tight knot, Zane muttered, "I know what you're trying to do. Jack's last assignment. You're digging around where you shouldn't be."

Although stunned, Madison put on her best confused face. "What?"

Playing her response off as surprised was weak, at best, but Madison gave it all she had. Pulling off a lie was one thing. Lying to Zane was another. He'd see right through it.

The guy had popped in and out of her life for years. Every holiday, Jack had Zane in tow. And spring and winter break, Zane was a second brother. *A really annoying, irritating-as-hell second brother who hogged all Jack's free time.* He even came down once on her mother's birthday. *No, twice.*

Half the time Madison spent with Zane, he'd ignored her. The other half, riling her up became his personal challenge. *That guy should thank his lucky stars for his good looks and Jack having his back to calm me down. Otherwise, my foot would have met his nuts on a regular basis.*

Madison had grown so much in ten years, but not at all when it came to Zane. She couldn't hide anything from him. When someone sees you at your teenage worst, is there any doubt they know you?

Maybe I can't lie. But I can act pissed off and irate. I didn't earn the nickname Mads for nothing. I doubt he'd even blink.

Switching gears, she huffed. "Zane, I—"

"Stop."

"I haven't said anything yet." She added a flail of her hands—an old habit from her early teens.

"And you're not going to. You're going to listen. I'm not an idiot, Madison, and I'm not your mom. There's no way I'm staying on the sidelines with my fingers crossed, hoping nothing happens to you. The sooner you deal with this, the better. I'm in this. I'll stay in the shadows if you want, but I'm not letting you take this on unless I've got your back."

Through with pacing, he lowered himself to the intricately carved wood coffee table in front of her. His hands wove together, wringing tightly. "So, either I'm leaving in the morning with you in tow, or I'm staying here."

Saying nothing, she blew out a long breath.

Zane studied her, rubbing his thumb against his chin. "Madison, this engagement to Alex Drake. Is it fake?"

"Fake?"

"Come on." The steep curve of condescension rose in Zane's tone. "The girl next door with a notorious womanizer? His claim to fame is having two different women a day for ten days straight."

"Really? Because as I've said, I believe his claim to fame is founding and running a multibillion-dollar global corporation."

And the rumor was fourteen days, but Alex only had sex with three of them. She thought hard. *Maybe four.*

Reengaging, she said, "It's not fake. It's—"

"Convenient?"

Unsure of a reasonably believable response, she shrugged.

"Because he's rich, right? And has some questionable connection to Jack."

She remained silent.

"You think I'm blind, Madison. You put on a good show, but the two of you fight like cats and dogs when you think no one's looking. And . . ." Zane paused, studying her as if to gauge the sturdiness of the speculative ice he walked across. "It's not exactly coincidence, is it? You—with the two of them. Like you'll do anything to cling to Jack. Even slip into Alex Drake's bed."

He knows about Alex and Paco . . . and Jack.

But Zane has a security clearance. And connections. He was Jack's roommate at West Point. And his BFF. Of course he looked into Jack's death.

A million thoughts crossed Madison's mind before Zane interrupted.

"If you're engaged, the only logical reason is Jack. Madison, I get it. Nobody wishes Jack were alive more than I do. So you're leveraging Alex's money and connections to investigate Jack's death, sniffing around dangerous areas you shouldn't be."

"If you know all that, it means you've been sniffing around it too."

Zane's nod was slow, his gaze fixed on the West Point class ring he twisted back and forth on his finger. "Why do you think I've stayed overseas so long? Not for my health. I hate the fucking humidity as much as I hate the desert. Years of nothing but a cold trail of dead ends." He pulled out his wallet, tugging out a keycard and handing it to her. "Until now. And I've got to trust someone. Madison, can I trust you?"

"Yes." She nodded definitively.

The keycard had a tiny gold Merlion on the bottom, just like the access card to their hotel room, and the one Alex brought to Chang. It was the whole reason they traveled to Singapore—to chase this elusive card and everything it had to do with Jack's death.

Perplexed, she brushed her thumb over the ridges of the raised emblem. "Your keycard?"

Zane hesitated. "Somehow, this is related to what happened to Jack." He leaned in. "This card can open any door with a keycard capability. Imagine it— universal access to anywhere you want to be. I could have walked right into your room. Or any room in the hotel."

"What?" She bolted to the door.

After exiting the suite, she tried the keycard. Nothing happened. Slower, she tried it again. The door clicked as it unlocked, and she walked in.

Zane stood across from her.

Her eyes widened. "An access key for . . . the world?"

"There's more. Not only will it open virtually any door, its use is untraceable. It doesn't leave a masked digital tag, where authorities can see when and who accessed an area. Not even an anonymous one. It leaves no footprint at all. You can slip in and out of anywhere completely undetected."

Unfettered access to anywhere imaginable. A game changer of epic proportions.

All she could say was, "Unbelievable."

"That card is everything. The most valuable thing I have, and the only tie I have to Jack."

With two steps, Zane closed the distance between them. She held the card out, returning it. Wrapping his warm hand around hers, he sealed the card in her grasp and rubbed gently.

"It's yours, Madison. A gesture of my faith in you, and proof that I trust you. Now I need you to trust me."

"Why wouldn't I trust you?"

Pocketing his hands, he stepped back. "Because I'm about to ask you for something, and the only way you'll do it is if you trust me. You wouldn't be here unless you had something. I need to know what it is."

Her poker face melted before his eyes.

"What do you have, Madison?"

Giving in to his demands, she shrugged. "Jack was holding something, but none of us know what it is." *Technically true.*

Zane grabbed her shoulders gently, his eyes boring into hers. "Do you have it?"

Without overthinking it, she said, "No." *Still true. It's back at DGI headquarters in New York.*

Lowering her to sit on the sofa, he joined her, not releasing his grip. "Promise me that if you get it, you'll hand it over and let me take it from there."

She gave him a stiff nod, but apparently, it wasn't good enough.

"Madison, promise me."

"Fine. I promise, Zane." *Easy enough. Not like I'm getting it anytime soon.*

Without another word, he gripped her harder. Before she could respond—or resist—he leaned forward and kissed her.

The shock sent her backward, but his lips stayed pressed to hers. More alarming than his forwardness was the slow streams of tears now sliding down her cheeks. The reaction was uncontrollable and so bizarre, that the subsequent wave of nausea following didn't seem nearly so out of place.

Everything about Zane's mouth on hers was wrong—in so many ways, and in no way at all. But it had to stop. For everything Madison was feeling, she might as well have been lip-locked with Jack.

And what about Alex? Was it the betrayal?

No. Getting forced into a kiss by someone other than the man she was madly in love with had become just another day in her on-again-off-again covert world.

Jordan had planted a big, fat, wet one on her that had gone on and on. And on. With a team of people watching, no less.

Including Alex.

Jordan used her, mostly for her own amusement, but it happened to be an incredibly pragmatic way to get them out of a bind. Jordan was Madison's first kiss with another woman, and as strange and uncomfortable—and even unnerving—as it was, it didn't move Madison to tears.

So, why am I crying?

Controlling her feelings was a lost cause. Figuring them out wasn't happening. But one thing was certain.

If his lips aren't off me in about ten seconds, the vomit is coming.

Ten.

Nine . . .

Zane's insistent kiss was quickly interrupted by the unexpected sound of a man clearing his throat from across the room.

Turning toward the door, Madison saw every tailored inch of him fuming from behind a raised brow. The sight of him filled her with relief.

"Paco."

He said nothing, turning his heated stare to Zane.

Zane's grip slipped away. Though he stood, his gaze stayed connected with hers. "We'll talk later, Madison." Without another word, he walked out.

Though Paco wasn't anywhere close to blocking the door, Zane's shoulder bumped squarely into him. Madison couldn't control the loudness of her gasp.

Shutting the door, Paco smirked. But when he returned his hard gaze to Madison, the semblance of an amused smile vanished.

CHAPTER 18

MADISON

MADISON'S EYES flew open wide. "Paco—"

His finger flew up, silencing her. His stride was slow and deliberate, and he finally stopped somewhere that seemed to make sense only to him. He pulled out a notepad, flipping it and scribbling on it quickly as he finally spoke.

"Look, you want to screw the nearest thing on two legs, be my guest. But if you embarrass Alex or DGI, you'll have me to deal with. And I'll be damned if we're losing hundreds of millions with a stock market plummet because the trailer whore on his arm can't keep her cunt shut."

Alarmed, Madison swallowed her discomfort, reading the note he held at his chest. The two words were in all caps and underlined.

PLAY ALONG

Play along? I'll do my best.

"Fuck off, Paco, and mind your own goddamnn business."

His smirk returned. Obviously pleased with her response, he resumed his scribbling at a feverish rate.

"You're not Mrs. Drake yet, sweetie. And if I've played the odds right, you never will be." Drawing out the last words, Paco flipped the notepad.

DON'T LOOK—CAMERA PLANTED BEHIND ME

Camera? Since when?

She needed answers.

"Oh, you don't think my marriage to Alex is happening. Why not, Paco?" She deliberately stretched out her next words. "Because of Zane?"

"There are so many reasons, Ms. Taylor. But yes, that son of a bitch just jumped to the top of my list."

Another flip of his pad, and Paco showed the note, his desperate gaze filled with pain.

ALEX MISSED TWO CHECK-INS

Two check-ins missed? If he's missed two, we're activating Delta.

Quickly, she recalled the short list she'd memorized.

Radio silence imperative.
Teams deployed.
Any member missing will be found at all costs.

She repeated the list in her mind, determined to convince herself.

Alex. Will. Be. Found.

At all costs.

Closing her eyes for a moment, she let out a silent frustrated sigh, finishing the list.

Madison to return home. Immediately.

She'd run through this list over and over for weeks, never imagining anything on it would materialize.

Staring at her ring, she fired back at Paco. "You know what, Mr. Robles? You do whatever it is you need to do. But I'm . . . I'm not going anywhere."

The veins in his temples throbbed unmistakably in response. His glare was daunting, but was met with her equally ferocious determination.

The GO HOME he adamantly tapped on his pad wasn't happening, and by his disgruntled huff, he wasn't exactly coming to terms with it.

"Look, Paco. You've obviously got fatter fish to fry than me, and I've got bigger battles than you. You're excused."

In a single swooping step, Paco stood before her and appeared to grab her jaw harshly. With her face twisted, playing it up for the hidden camera, she strained to see him. The gentle stroke of his thumb on her cheek nearly brought her to tears.

Paco's tone was low and menacing, the polar opposite of his tender, caring eyes. "Careful, Madison Taylor. You never know where a wrong step can land you. If I were you, I'd watch my back and be very, very careful."

With barely a nod, she smacked his hand away. "I could tell you the same thing. And to be clear, you and I aren't speaking again. Not without Alex between us."

"Don't worry." Paco let that hang for a second. "I'm going, but just one last thing." He hesitated, holding the pad tightly in his hand before slowly turning it toward her. "I might be out of sight, but I'll be watching."

The four words on the pad stole the air from her lungs.

ZANE WAS JACK'S FIRST

Her brother's first *what* was obvious. The rush of emotions hit Madison hard, but she'd have to deal with it later.

Paco needed to leave. *Now.* Alex was depending on him. On both of them.

Forcing herself to be strong, she rested the palm of her hand on Paco's heart, safely concealed from view. Her words were loud and booming for everyone's benefit, but only she and Paco understood the depth of the message.

Teary, she shouted, "Get the fuck out of here."

He whirled around and raced out the door.

The sudden swirl of fear and loneliness buckled Madison's knees. Her body crumpled back on the sofa, and her deep breaths were the only thing that stifled the sickening torment in the depths of her gut.

Repeating the small phrase over and over in her mind was all she could do.

Alex will be found at all costs.

CHAPTER 19

ALEX

SIDE BY SIDE, Alex and Jordan stood on a balcony overlooking the darkening city as it morphed into a galaxy of twinkling multicolored lights against the water.

Alex kept his cool, with a determined gaze forward to hide his speculating. An exchanged glance might expose his hand. Jordan also seemed just as content to lose her thoughts in the evening view, not letting any hint of emotion wrinkle her brow.

"It's like we're on a date," she said, sheer boredom leveling her words. Then a grin broke through. "Well, not like our first date."

A date he could never forget. She'd given him his name and made him the man he was today.

Is she trying to tell me something? Toying with people was part of Jordan's MO.

Maybe it was a clue, sure to help him if he could decode the cryptic message. Maybe, like so many believed, it was just another romp through her favorite playground—sadistic pleasure. Or perhaps it was something else entirely. The words were delivered without her normal armor of seductive banter, leaving the silence between them strange and sentimental.

Alex tempered his concern, controlling his tone. "What are we doing here, Jordan?"

Not really looking at her, he glanced from the corner of his eye at the armed guards who watched them. *His* armed bodyguards, who now had their weapons trained on him.

Their betrayal was anticipated, but the sight of his own men with rifles on him was still disconcerting.

Jack, the bodyguard, had a wife and three kids. An easy target. He could convincingly play the double agent, desperate enough to switch teams and vulnerable enough to be controlled. With the month of planning ahead of time, *check* and *check*.

The other guard, Nate, had a younger sister he was putting through New York University. Anyone with brains would know the swiftest path to an opponent was through their weakest link. A few photographs of a freshman walking to and from class, paired with a graphic and utterly disturbing threat, was all it would take to turn the man. Nate was also now part of the other side.

Each time Alex caught a glimpse of Jack or Nate, their bravery bolstered his confidence. Both had volunteered for this assignment—the pretense of working for the enemy while secretly watching Alex's back. And he didn't even have to ask.

Both went to Alex with an idea. Of course their plan worked . . . it was brilliant. Refusing their offer would do no good with these former operatives. They understood the risks. Jack's family was safely ensconced in a borough outside New York City, and Nate's sister was under 24/7 surveillance.

But there was a bigger cause at stake, a dual one—national security, and the ongoing work of DGI.

The men's bravery moved Alex beyond words. But for show, he pretended to be annoyed.

Answering his unasked question, Jordan flattened her lips, her tone dark. "You know how it is. Some things can't be avoided."

The Omega watch on her wrist reminded him of the time. The loose leash his captors had extended Alex gave him just enough freedom to stay on the balcony. He'd hung out there for most of the passing hours.

Without a doubt, his team would triangulate his position, with or without his cell. The hidden camera from Richard gave him that advantage, but its signal strength was very small.

Finding him would require sweeping the entire city in a slow, methodical grid of surveillance. Drones could cover a lot of ground. Even cars along the streets twenty floors below could help in the search. Being found would happen, but it would take time.

Staring forward, Alex drummed his fingers against the handrail in a practiced sequence. A quick tap followed by four finger drags. He repeated the sequence that translated to a single number—one. In a mixture of Morse Code and old 92 Code used to telegraph abbreviated phrases by railway personnel, the single digit translated to "wait a minute." But for his team, it simply meant "wait."

Wait. Stand down. Do not interfere.

Alex had to let them know he was unharmed, despite missing the check-ins. Rescuing him wasn't critical. His little movements ordered them back, insisting they do no more than stealth monitoring of his situation.

But when would they see it? Now?

Maybe not. At least, not for a while.

At some point, Richard and his high-tech reconnaissance team could pinpoint delayed satellite imaging once they isolated his position. If he wasn't in plain sight, they'd use this technique to gather the historic images, and his message would be received loud and clear.

He was unharmed, working, and needed more time. *To find out what the fuck all this is about.*

Jordan checked her cell, frowning with a quiet huff as she read a text. Pocketing the phone, she turned to face him. With renewed interest, he extended the courtesy, turning to fully face her. His adversary.

Maybe my friend.

Maybe . . .

The roll of that die was never predictable with Jordan. Her current mission would always be her number one priority . . . which was why she was so good at what she did, and so sought after.

Alex mused about the other more trivial factors that likely determined her allegiance. Money was a big factor, but would never be her only motivator. After all, she had a billionaire in her custody. If this were merely about cold, hard cash, the game would be over. Alex could pay whatever ransom was sought, quickly ending this kidnapping.

But there had to be other things persuading her interests. Power plays were undoubtedly up her alley. Trivial considerations like wardrobe and shoe selection had to be big influencers. And without a doubt, her level of horniness. In many ways, Jordan's motivations were much more raw and basic than those of other master manipulators. It was what made her so damn good.

As with so many times in their on-again-off-again acquaintanceship, Alex couldn't see past the persona Jordan pasted on. Out of respect, and because he was at gunpoint, he just stood there letting her look at him.

Her gaze washed over his body, contemplating something that, from her expression, couldn't possibly be sex. She scanned him, finally locking her dark eyes with his. Her lips pried from their pursed contemplation to speak.

"A three-piece suit. Smart choice. You'll be sleeping here tonight. I'd recommend staying in your suit, though I'm not sure how comfortably you'll sleep. I have no idea when you'll be moved, other than it will be in the next twenty-four hours."

Pushing gruff assurance past his lips, he said, "Don't worry about me. It's not my first overnighter in a suit."

"I figured as much." Starting at his shoulder, she smoothed her hand across his vest, moving in a slow serpentine path down to his torso. "Very smart choice."

Does she know? "Thanks for your endorsement."

"Don't mention it." She quickly lost interest in groping him and drifted away, waving indifferently. "Pick whatever room you like. The guards will rotate shifts watching you. And, of course, everyone and everything in here is monitored at all times." She blew out a tired breath. "I'll see you when I see you."

～

As the hours dragged by from evening to early morning, Alex lay awake. Preferring a ready stance of lying on top of the covers with his hands clasped neatly across his chest, he contemplated the ins and outs of the chess game to come.

No stranger to insomnia, he found comfort in not needing to doze off, though closing his eyes helped him think.

Eventually, his mind exhausted all the different if-then scenarios and came alive with another topic to ponder. *Madison.*

Their last moments together couldn't have been more perfect. *Will they be our last moments together?* He thought of her soft lips on his, her every move leading to her curves against his hands, her body beneath his.

Mental snapshots of the most beautiful woman he'd ever seen playfully bombarded him, one after the other. *I'll do anything for Madison. If it comes to it, I'll give my life.*

Blazing resilience fired back, and he quickly corrected himself.

With a knowing smirk, he breathed deeper. *That's not happening. Not today.* Stacking his hands behind his head, he settled into a cozy thought.

He didn't have the best team in the world covering his back. He had three. Three of the best damn elite teams ever assembled.

As quickly as he considered the magnitude of their capabilities, his complete faith in his team was vindicated. A small, almost indiscernible vibration emanated from his chest—a long pulse followed by four pops.

Breathing easier, he relaxed. The code back was exactly what he expected.

Six.

His team had his six. His back. And as soon as that reassurance sat warm in his mind, his thoughts veered back to Madison. In his estimation, Delta had been activated hours ago. Madison must be well on her way home.

Calculating the time and distance, he decided she would be safely back with her mom and dad in New York within a few short hours.

Thank God.

CHAPTER 20

MADISON

MADISON TURNED her wide-awake aggravation to the cell phone she'd kept clutched in her hand.

Two in the morning.

No matter how many times she looked, disappointment deflated her with each glance at her phone and no word from Alex. Her desperate mind zigzagged back and forth in a mental tug-of-war between Alex and Zane.

Zane was Jack's first.

The statement was declarative. Unyielding. A statement so bizarre, but held so much truth. It was, without a doubt, the memory she couldn't grab onto, like a cloud that floated into her thoughts, only to slip away when she reached for it.

For a fraction of a second, she could see Jack and Zane together. But just as quickly, the smoky vision would vanish.

Was it a thought she'd conjured up? Something to fill in the blank of all the years of not knowing her brother? Or could it actually be a memory? Her brother and his best friend, maybe embracing. Maybe more.

Deep down, Madison felt the tie to her nickname. *Mads.* Why didn't Zane want to use it right away? Did he realize it might trigger a memory? Her early teen years were a lifetime ago, but Zane's voice echoed through her memories. *"Don't be mad . . . Mads."*

What did she have to be mad about? *Puberty?* It had to be about Jack. Had she walked in on them? Would she have known what she was seeing? Confident there was something to her exhausted mental ramblings, she pulled on that thread.

If Zane was now making moves on her, maybe he wasn't gay or straight, but bi or fluid. *Anything's possible.*

Maybe this wasn't about her at all. He and Jack had been so close. Could he be trying to cling to Jack in such a strong way that Madison had become his only option? Had she become Jack's stand-in, forcing Zane to run straight to her?

With a tired smirk, she thought, *Straight to me. Funny.*

But that didn't explain why, on the one hand, Zane would plant a camera in her room, yet hand her a keycard worth more than the net value of Singapore itself.

Exhausted and confused, she kicked the covers and tossed herself to her side.

It's Zane. I've known him forever. Not since training wheels, but a training bra, for sure. And he and Jack . . . closer than—

Replaying her last thought, she quickly abandoned her trip down the yellow brick road of TMI. Jack and Zane. Together. At least it explained her reaction to his kiss.

Then she started thinking of kisses. From Alex.

Curling up in a ball on his side of the bed, Madison hugged his pillow tightly. She took in several deep whiffs of his lingering scent, letting herself fall into the quiet comfort of imagining Alex next to her.

CHAPTER 21

MADISON

BARELY SLEEPING AN HOUR, Madison held the pillow a moment longer before forcing herself out of bed. She made her way to the balcony in time to see the glimmer of early morning breaking far in the distance as the sun barely peeked over the horizon.

Going through the motions, she showered, dressed down in comfy travel-worthy jeans and sneakers, then packed. A crazy idea was taking shape, and she was going for it.

Looking around, she found her cell hidden in a crease of the fluffy down comforter. Once again, her stomach twisted with worry at the lack of a text or call from Alex. Shaking off her fears, she made a few imaginary swipes and clicks, then took the unopened cell to her ear, talking aloud.

"Paco? It's Madison. You win. I'm leaving Alex and going home. But I'm also taking back what belongs to me and my family. I know exactly where it is. Keep an eye on me all you want. You can't stop me."

That should do it.

Was Zane watching her? And why? She had to know. But that was only half the reason she stood in a hotel room, having an unusually loud conversation with herself.

She was taking a risk. A big one.

In order not to break the critical need for radio silence, she had to let someone know what she was doing. And Paco said he'd keep an eye on her. If she contacted him or anyone else on the team directly, there were too many ways to tap into their signal. Everyone's position could be discovered, and all their data compromised.

Direct contact was out. But maybe—just maybe—the team would somehow still have her back. *Fingers crossed.*

With all her belongings in tow in a rolling suitcase, her cell in her butt pocket, and the keycard Zane had given her safely in her bra, she headed out. Strangely, she didn't have to slip past any bodyguards. They were nowhere to be seen, undoubtedly asleep.

As she stepped out of the lobby, the early morning sunlight painted a golden hue across the grounds. At her request, the valet summoned a cab. Though there was a line of waiting city cabs, this one hadn't been in line.

A town car pulled up. The customary practice for VIP transit wasn't requested or expected, but a protest would have brought unnecessary attention to the complimentary service. The valet opened the door for Madison, letting her in the back seat before securing her luggage in the trunk.

A second later, the opposite door was opened. With a stack of bills in one hand and a disposable coffee cup in the other, Zane tipped the valet, speaking in a language unrecognizable to Madison, then slid in beside her.

Glaring at her, he spoke. "I told you, you're not doing this alone. And again, no bodyguards?" He blew out an exasperated breath, shaking his head. "So, where are *we* going?"

Once the immediate shock of his presence wore off, she calmly said, "The airport."

Zane nodded, again using that same foreign language with the driver, and the luxury vehicle rolled away.

The morning traffic bustled with a city waking up. Madison wasn't exactly a map wiz, easily getting lost in a circle. But the direction they were headed didn't go unnoticed. The luxury town car was speeding away in the opposite direction of the airport.

Choking back her panic, she studied Zane. And then his cup. Casually, she asked, "How did you know I was leaving?"

"You know me. Up before the sun. I already had a run and showered. Military men are always ready for the day. I was grabbing a coffee when I saw you leave and ran after you. Damn near missed you." His hand gripped her knee.

Forcing her gaze from the lid of his cup, she stammered out, "Lucky me."

She gave his hand a gentle squeeze, then pulled away. His gaze locked on hers, now studying her eyes.

Madison had seen this look a time or two. During a competitive family poker tournament, Zane had mystically read the cards she held. With a fixed stare back, she read him as easily. The opening of his pupils and darkening of his eyes meant he had her.

She couldn't hide these cards.

The squint of his eyes made way for a stiffer knit in his brow. In an instant, he seemed to realize it.

His mistake.

After glancing at the coffee cup in his hand, he shut his eyes a moment. Slowly, he turned his head to her, the heat of his knowing gaze burning through her thin facade.

The ready curse blew past his lips. "Fuck, Mads." Reluctantly releasing a deep laugh, he shook his head. "Goddamnnn. I never could slip anything past those big eyes of yours. You always see fucking everything, don't you?"

Madison tucked a strand of hair behind her ear as she swallowed her discomfort, clinging to her crumbling composure.

Staying silent, she watched as he held the cup to her face. She got a closer look at what she'd seen moments ago—the black plastic rim of the disposable coffee cup stamped with a dark red lipstick stain.

He shook the empty cup, crumpling it into a ball. Clearly, the cup's useful life had been exhausted.

Zane didn't bother backpedaling into another alibi. Having seen her imaginary phone conversation via the planted camera, he'd obviously grabbed the rushed prop in haste from somewhere along his path as he'd chased after her.

Holding her gaze, he held down the button to lower the window and toss the unnecessary cup away. The careless move earned him the wrath of their driver, who slowed the car and seemed to be pulling to a stop.

The shouting match between Zane and the irate chauffeur gave Madison a boost of bravery. As she reached for her door handle to escape, Zane yanked her arm. When she turned back to him, he pointed a gun at her.

Now worried not only for herself but the driver as well, she desperately looked to the rearview mirror.

The reflection of the driver's face told her nothing. His sunglasses hid the better part of his expression. But in the midst of him and Zane spitting heated foreign phrases at each other, he wiped the mirror—with a lace-trimmed black handkerchief monogrammed with the letter *J*.

Jordan.

The car stopped, and the driver exited to confront Zane, who was ready with his pistol. With the dark tint of the window, the driver wouldn't know Zane had a gun.

How can I warn him?

Zane's angry words kept her quiet. "Stay put."

Firming her resolve, she was ready to shout out a warning as soon as the door opened. But it was preempted.

As soon as Zane forced his gun through the opened door, the driver slammed the door hard on Zane's arm, trapping him for the moment. All she heard was the fervent scream from the driver. His voice was stern, unfamiliar, and distinctly Latin.

"Run, Madison. Now!"

Bolting from her seat, she sprang from the car as fast as she could, racing from what was becoming a louder scuffle between the two men.

Her ability as a half-decent runner filled her with uncertainty. She'd never outrun Zane in either speed or endurance. Still, she pushed on, rushing to a stairway on the far side of an overpass.

Taking the industrial stairs two at a time, she exited on what seemed to be an expansive pedestrian bridge, foot traffic surging endlessly in both directions.

A breath of relief filled her lungs as she found the population of runners, joggers, and walkers energetically engrossed in early morning activities. Scattered at various points along the huge concrete street were police officials. *Armed policemen.*

Looking back the way she came, Madison couldn't detect anyone chasing her. Zane could be right on her heels at any second, but accosting her on a pedestrian bridge crawling with cops was a bad move. She guessed a man like him didn't make many of those.

I've got to get out of here. But to where?

CHAPTER 22

MADISON

After a few miles of brisk walking, Madison could see her hotel. *What if Zane's waiting there for me?*

Playing it safe, she opted to back-door it to Paco's room. She touched her chest, ensuring the rigid plastic card remained safe below the light padding of her bra.

She didn't have her suitcase, but at least she still had that—a priceless universal key. Her salvation. Easy entry to Paco's suite—or anywhere in the hotel, she imagined. It was safer than her penthouse. At least she'd have an air-conditioned alternative where she could collect her thoughts rather than aimlessly wandering the streets of a foreign city.

The staff entrance was always left propped open, giving easy access to those needing a break or a smoke. It had become her secret passage. Energized, she picked up her pace.

The elevator required the swipe of a keycard, and as she hoped, the key worked. Normal keycards were programmed to allow access to specific floors, but she imagined a universal one would easily accommodate any floor. But no matter how many times she pressed the button to Paco's floor, it wouldn't light up.

Impatient and antsy, Madison swiped and re-swiped, trying the buttons for any floor, even her own penthouse floor. Surprising her, it lit. *Finally.*

Her comfort as the elevator ascended was met with equal amounts of confusion and fear. Again, she studied the key for a moment before the ding announced she had arrived at her floor.

With the doors opening, she didn't have time to second-guess her decision. Confident, she bolted off the elevator before she could stop herself.

"Hello, Madison."

CHAPTER 23

PACO

PACO HATED everything about the day, except for the stone walls now surrounding him. His love of secure facilities was vast. Something about being in the throes of restricted access thrilled him. Cutting-edge communications and limitless adventures always gave him a strange sense of home, belonging, and brotherhood. A fraternity for the clandestine and elite.

Sometimes it gave him the sense of being untouchable. Even invincible. But thoughts of Jack always dropped Paco's ass back to reality.

No one's invincible.

Paco could always hold it together with the best of them. Only a close few ever saw him sweat, and two of his closest friends were now missing.

Well, not really missing, but a far cry from being out of danger. Being one step ahead of an adversary was Paco's whole purpose in life, and his track record was flawless.

No one's getting the best of me. Never again.

But he'd been thrown one hell of a curveball. *Goddamnnmit. Why didn't Madison just go home? What the hell was she thinking?* After all his planning and prepping, hope could not be his strategy. But he couldn't be everywhere at once, could he?

He had a mission. Well, more than one with all the chaos. So, which mission was most important? There was *the* mission—to figure out what was so valuable it had warranted Jack Taylor's death, the whole reason they were in Singapore to begin with.

And then there was Operation Delta.

The code-red mission was called when Alex went missing, but everyone knew it was coming. Locating his best friend of ten years wasn't exactly a daunting task. To start with, he was Alex Drake, CEO of a multibillion-dollar corporation—one built by the sort of veterans who loved a piece of the action. The best of the best.

Then there was Paco's secret weapon, Richard. The world knew him as Davis R. Black, the CEO of Black Technologies. But to Alex and Paco, he was Richard—the kid with the coolest toys. Cutting-edge technology at its finest.

Richard's surveillance devices could take virtually any form, and included different capabilities that covered video, audio, and GPS tracking in air, sea, and on land. Finding Alex was hardly a challenge, it just took a little time.

Comforted, Paco reminded himself that Alex had his own search and rescue well under control. The ultimate control freak was orchestrating the search party from his own captivity. In true Alex form, he reined in his rescuers—insisting they lay low.

Had this been more of a garden-variety mission, Paco would have fucked with Alex just a little. Maybe sent him the code for "negative" or "gotta pee." But with Madison preoccupying Paco's mind, playtime was over. They hit Alex back with code number *six* almost immediately.

With that, Paco's mind could settle on the crisis of the moment. His impromptu third mission. The one nobody saw coming, and everyone should have seen without a doubt.

Madison. For all intents and purposes, his little sister.

Correction. His thick-headed, stubborn, insufferable, risk-taking little sister.

Paco had looked after her from afar for so long, doing it up close and in person was second nature. How, for the love of God, could he not see this coming?

He'd been working with the team on Alex's situation when Richard's camera caught everyone's attention. Madison's conversation with "Paco."

Watching the big-screen video, the eyes of every operative in the room turned to Paco . . . obviously not on the phone. Most secure facilities prohibited cell phones. But this one had enough cell-jamming protection, Paco could bring his in, but it would be useless. Wisely, and without violating strict radio silence, Madison communicated her message loud and clear.

Deploying a drone was instant, keeping watch over her was accomplished, but still didn't give the protection she needed.

Scratch that. *That I need for her.*

No dispute. Richard's toy was the epitome of high tech, but it wasn't exactly weaponized. His deal was reconnaissance. Surveillance. And on occasion, defense equipment. But bang-'em-up wasn't Richard's area of expertise. It was Paco's.

As they'd surveilled the town car, the incident at the bridge upset Paco more than he could reveal to the roomful of operatives. When the fight broke out between the driver and Zane, the team had to make a choice. Obviously, they were sticking with Madison. But once she'd returned to the hotel, finding her became a bigger challenge.

Without a doubt, she hadn't entered any of their rooms. But that was all they had to go on, and it didn't amount to shit.

"I need some air," Paco said to the team, and the men nodded silently, deeply engrossed with the emerging situation.

As Paco barged past the thick metal door, the wall of humidity and blinding midday sun stopped him. Within a few blinks, his eyes adjusted as the door shut behind him. Clear of the signal-blocking walls, his cell buzzed.

Urgently, he slipped the phone from his pocket, unsurprised that the caller displayed as UNKNOWN. Whether to take the call was a quick decision. *Answer.* Cloaked callers were just another day in the life. Paco had one too many anonymous moles and informants, but with any luck, this caller was Madison.

Never tipping his hand, he used his standard answer. "DGI."

"Mr. Robles. I don't have much time, so listen up." The gruff voice was spry, knowing . . . and familiar.

Leaning against the building, Paco held the phone closer. "The elusive Mr. Stone. Look, I'm dealing with something urgent at the moment—"

"It's a state we have in common," Stone said quickly, "and the clock is ticking, so I won't beat around the bush. I need your assistance, and I need it now."

Fishing his Ray-Bans from his top breast pocket, Paco slipped them on and looked around. "You've got three minutes."

"I'll take two. And I assure you, Mr. Robles, my emergency *is* your emergency." Stone's voice deepened, losing its cheer. "You and I have something in common. Jack Taylor. We both cared deeply for him, and the last thing either of us wants is for something to happen to his lovely little sister."

Paco didn't bother hiding his sneer. "A threat? It doesn't seem like your style."

"It's not," Stone said, his voice going from flat to compelling. "I could never harm Madison. After Jack's death, I swore I'd protect her. And as much as I'd like to think Jack's passing steered me to an unyielding intolerance for failure, I *am* about to fail. Unless you help me."

Stone let out a sigh. "This is as close to begging as I come, Mr. Robles. And I have to drop this call in about sixty seconds. Yes or no?"

Five seconds later, Paco said, "I'm in."

Instantly, a ping hit his phone. The text message contained a link that, when clicked, displayed a blinking dot on what looked like some sort of map app.

"Find the dancing dot?" he asked.

"Yes," Stone said, drawing out the *s* sound in some strange range between sleep and pain. "As fast as you can, Paco. Hurry."

The line disconnected.

Fuck.

Pressing his palm to the control panel next to the door he'd just left through, Paco waited the thirty seconds it took the sensor to register his pulse and body temperature as well as his palm print. That he was alive and relaxed were as important to the secure system as his identification.

The electronic protocols were satisfied. It unlocked.

Shouting, Paco addressed the team. "Keep me posted. I'll be back." He turned and left quickly, letting the door fall closed behind him as he headed to his vehicle.

CHAPTER 24

MADISON

As the elevator doors opened, Madison relaxed. Her initial startled gasp deflated to a slow exhale as she raced to the woman waiting outside the penthouse door.

"Jordan. God, I'm so relieved." With the keycard still clasped in her hands, Madison lifted it to the door.

Jordan stopped her. "I wouldn't, if I were you. We need to go."

With no option but to trust her best-frenemy-forever, Madison followed the woman who always rocked femme fatale to the *n*th degree. The light pitter-pats of Madison's sneakers on the emergency staircase seemed oddly louder than Jordan's five-inch heels, and she heaved heavy breaths to keep up.

"Jordan." Madison grew breathless, giving everything to push her feet faster. "Please tell me we're not running down fifty floors."

Jordan's voice was cool on what to her seemed a mild stroll. "Technically, it would be fifty-two floors. But no. Just two more floors. There's an emergency exit that I rigged not to latch. From there, we'll take a staff elevator to the basement, then outside to my car." Jordan looked back, the sparkle normally bright in her dark eyes seeming duller. "Now, tell me everything that's happened today."

With Jordan stopped and waiting for some form of acknowledgment, Madison nodded several times, saying only, "Of course."

As Jordan resumed leading her down a very premeditated trail until they were safely out of the building, Madison rushed through her account of every-thing that had happened. In a back alley, Jordan removed her leather jacket. She popped the trunk, dumping the sleek jacket in the black town car. It looked very much like the one Madison had been in that morning.

"Oh my God. Jordan, the driver! There was a man who saved me. We have to help him."

"What am I, Wonder Woman?" Jordan said dryly. "And just "a man"? Your eyewitness account needs some work."

"He had your handkerchief."

After a few blinks, Jordan gave Madison a blank stare. "It's the life we choose, Madison. We can't all have guardian angels. As you can see, there's only one of me to go around. And . . ."

Jordan lifted Madison's chin, undoubtedly to get a better look at the tears fighting their way free.

With a sigh, she continued. "You've once again managed to snare all my attention."

Horrified, Madison stepped back. Swallowing the bitter taste of acid rising in her throat, she shook her head. "Leave me. Go help him!"

Amused, Jordan challenged Madison with a smooth, seductive smile. "If only I took orders from you." Jordan eyed her jacket, apparently unhappy with laying it flat. She began a slow succession of folds, almost rolling it into a ball.

As aggressively as she dared, Madison grabbed her arm. "Hey. I'm not asking."

Jordan let out an amused huff but stayed focused, obsessively fixated on the jacket to get the folds just right.

Taking a step back and releasing her grip, Madison said softly, "I'm begging. Please."

Suddenly satisfied with the final succession of folds, Jordan sported a genuine smile of pride. "There. That's better."

Yeah. Looks great. You're a shoo-in for lead salesclerk at the Gap.

Stunned, Madison had to ask. "Did you hear me?"

As if suddenly aware of Madison's presence, Jordan turned to her.

"Hmm? Oh yes, I heard you. And I see you're not happy with my answer. Well, then . . . you'll be even less pleased with my actions." From the inside of her boot, Jordan withdrew a small-caliber handgun. Pointing it at Madison and waving it toward the trunk, she said, "Get in."

Not you too.

Resigned to the inevitable, Madison made a clumsy climb into the trunk, oddly prompting Jordan to lend her a hand. With every bit of mental sarcasm, all she could think was, *Thanks a lot.*

With the trunk closed and dark, save for small lights emanating from some strange source, Madison shifted around uneasily, the neat tucks of the leather jacket fitting nicely beneath her head, a makeshift pillow Jordan had to get just right.

Wow. The mind fucks keep coming.

Madison's alarm sent her heart rate high, quelled slightly by a cool wisp of a breeze. Following the soft stream with her fingers, she found a small hose where air-conditioning was being piped into the usually uninhabited space.

"Madison? Can you hear me?" Jordan's sultry voice came through crystal clear.

Must be some sort of jury-rigged speaker, like the A/C.

With a jerky brace against the walls, Madison held herself in place as the car began a bumpy start before smoothly rolling away.

As often was the case, Jordan didn't wait for Madison's reply before continuing. "Listen, normally when I'm moving a body in my trunk, I don't do detours. Then again, it's usually because they're dead, and if I don't move quickly, they'll start to smell. But don't worry. I'm taking extra-good care of you."

Grateful that the dark interior likely masked who knew what sort of stains, Madison couldn't help but take a few cautious sniffs. The freshness was unmistakable. *Brand-new car.*

Trapped and frustrated, she scowled. "Wackadoos always shower me with the wrong kind of attention."

"I heard that," Jordan said in a singsong voice. "Anyway, as I was saying, I need to make a short detour. When I stop, I'm sure no matter what I say, you're going to want to bang your fists, scream at the top of your lungs, and maybe even take out a brake light or two. Be my guest, if you don't mind getting killed as a result, because the very worst sort of people will notice you. Besides, you'll probably hurt those beautiful hands. I really prefer you preserve your strength. You're going to need it."

Right. Don't draw attention to myself because I might get killed by someone other than you.

"As usual," Jordan said, "you have no reason to trust me. But it's true. Scout's honor. I promise I won't keep you in there any longer than I have to. Oh, and there's a small bag along the floor toward the back seat."

Madison felt around, finding the Ziploc bag quickly.

"They're goldfish."

Squeamish, Madison withdrew her fingers. "Ew." *Why?*

"They're crackers." Jordan chuckled. "I heard they're your favorite. Worst-case scenario, perhaps they'll settle your little tum-tum. You know, in case you feel an upchuck coming on. This is a new car, after all."

Madison would love to throw Jordan's taunts in her face and puke on cue. But being trapped with the *eau du barf* stinking up the small space was the last thing she needed today.

In the dark and irritatingly comfortable trunk, Madison cursed herself with each nibble of the irresistibly tasty cheddar crackers.

Her idiocy suddenly dawned on her. *I have my cell.* Dragging it from her back pocket, she blinked, waiting for her eyes to adjust to the brightness.

Dammit. No signal.

Repocketing her phone, she froze, her anxiety ratcheting up as the car rolled to a stop. *What do I do? Everything Jordan told me not to do? Or remain quiet?*

Before she could settle the emotional tennis match bouncing inside her brain, she heard an unmistakable sound. *Gunfire.*

What if Jordan was shot? Who would know she was in this car? But if Jordan were shot, her assailant could be much, much worse.

Taking a deep breath, Madison decided to wait it out. At least for the moment.

CHAPTER 25

PACO

Ten minutes earlier

Following the blinking dot on Google Maps, Paco ended up in what seemed to be a private industrial center near the waterfront. The Straits of Johor gave him a sense of bearing, about thirty minutes due west from the heart of Singapore city.

After circling the perimeter a few times, he relaxed as confidence settled in. For the most part, the area seemed abandoned—well, except for that persistent flashing dot emanating from one of the buildings on the map on his cell.

He couldn't see another vehicle, but that didn't mean anything. Too many of the doors were warehouse size, where opening fully would allow an eighteen-wheeler through. Cars could be easily concealed.

Slipping his car between a mammoth dumpster and an outer wall of a building, Paco managed to keep his vehicle out of sight but still close enough for a quick getaway.

With a swipe of his finger, his cell screen was now missing the flashing dot. Realizing his cell lost its signal in the industrial lot, he flipped through his car's display. He pressed the Black Technologies logo, immediately launching the cell booster.

Back on his cell, the DGI master system was a click away. The encrypted database held insane amounts of detailed information, aggregating anything and everything. Today, he could isolate information about the building next to him. Thankfully, the detailed schematics were available, or at least the blueprints for how it had been constructed six years ago. And lucky for Paco, his flawless memory of images was sharp as ever.

The blinking dot could be on the first or second floor, but was definitely at the far end of the building. He'd have to make his way there. From the outside, the structure had enough windows to provide natural light to the interior, though the reflective tint assured him he wouldn't be able to see inside.

What fate awaited him?

A dozen armed men?

A decoy tracker attached to a note scribbled with "Fooled you!"?

Madison?

What or who the beacon had led him to, he hadn't a clue. And Stone clearly preferred to keep that little tidbit to himself.

Could Stone be getting him out of the way? Clearing a path to claim his own prize, leaving them high and dry? Or worse?

Oddly, Paco's gut told him *no*. The same gut that had told him beyond a shadow of a doubt a decade ago that Jack, and the rest of their team, were in imminent danger just minutes before that attack.

He blew a heavy breath from his lips. *Anything's possible.*

As he stepped away from his car, his apprehension pulled his gaze left, then right. Nothing. Except for the distant rumble of freeway traffic and a few bird tweets, the location appeared completely vacant and silent. No voices or footsteps. Taking a skeptical look back, he convinced himself his car was as concealed as it was getting.

Paco's pristine suit wasn't exactly tailored for prowling and skulking, but the stitching held a lot of advantages. If confronted by cops, both his ten-thousand-dollar attire and his command of Mandarin would give him the upper hand.

Then there was the custom vest. It matched the suit to perfection but was less of a fashion statement and more of a precaution. The skin layer of Kevlar could withstand a large-caliber handgun bullet—just another one of Richard's wonders.

And of course, the interior breast pockets held a handgun and extra clips, all without buckling the fabric from the weight. The look was seamless.

A smattering of standard doors gave him options, as several would lead to the area indicated by the blinking light on his phone. Fortunately, the most advantageous one seemed to take American Express.

One slide of his metal platinum card against the strike plate, and Paco was in. Before his eyes completely adjusted to the dimness, he detected sounds echoing through the halls. The commotion was coming from the back of the building, straight ahead.

Quietly but quickly, he moved down the length of the hall. The sounds were loud and clear because the door had been left ajar, without worry that anyone would hear the beating inside.

The loud smack of a backhanded fist broke through more than once before Paco could get a good look at the situation.

A man was seated with his back toward Paco. Handcuffs held his hands together behind him, which seemed to be all that was holding his slumped-over body to the chair.

Frustrated, Paco stayed put. *Who am I tracking?*

The man who'd unleashed the blows stayed in the shadows, just out of view. With a tired tone, he grumbled in French. *"Ne meurs pas encore. Je viens de commencer." Don't die on me yet. I'm just getting started.*

Paco instantly translated but recognized the man's French was far from fluent. Still, it made an impact.

As the attacker stepped into the natural light from a high window, Paco clenched his jaw. *What the fuck?*

Zane stood there, studying his own hand—seemingly unhappy to throw another bare-handed blow.

Paco had to stay back. Who was the man in the chair? Did Stone send Paco here for the captive, or for Zane? But none of it was about to matter.

When Zane pulled a small device from a duffel on the floor, Paco realized he'd just run out of options. The torture about to ensue from the fifteen-million-watt handheld stun gun forced him to draw his weapon.

That shit's not happening.

Using the door as a shield, he aimed the barrel of his gun at Zane's head and shouted, "Drop it, Zane."

"Robles." Zane lowered his hand but kept a tight grip on the weapon. "Hang on. You have no idea what's going on. Let me explain."

"Sure. Feel free to explain about some bullshit military mission . . . *after* you've dropped the weapon."

"This man is dangerous, Robles."

Sneering, Paco kept his aim steady on Zane's head. "Really? Your clear-and-present danger is the half-conscious guy handcuffed in the chair? Last warning. Put down the weapon."

"Whatever. Fine. But you're making a mistake."

As Zane squatted to lower himself to the floor, he made several overt movements to demonstrate he was putting the stun gun down. But Paco knew a thing or two about this situation.

For starters, no American military mission was sanctioned to torture people for the hell of it. Eastern Bloc and the Middle East? All day long. But the US at least made the pretense of using torture to satisfy the needs of national security. Nothing like that was going on here. And in some isolated warehouse in the middle of Singapore, this interrogation sure as hell wasn't military.

Second, Zane was a switch hitter—in more than one way. He was ambidextrous, completely adept at using both hands equally. While he tried distracting Paco's view by drawing attention to the stun gun wand in his right hand, it didn't go unnoticed that his left hand was reaching for his back—undoubtedly going for a handgun.

Paco was ready. He was also ready for the blinding light that hit him. This particular stun gun was also a flashlight, and he knew it well. The Bashlite not only could take down an animal or adversary, it was also equipped with 120 lumens, a quick-and-dirty disorienting tactic.

Fucking amateur.

Zane's bullet struck the door while Paco's bullet hit Zane somewhere high—perhaps his ear, judging by the way he cradled it as he ran off. The slam of a distant door followed by tire screeches meant Zane was peeling away.

The room was left dark and silent but for the labored breathing of the man slumped in the chair.

Cautiously, Paco headed toward him. Kneeling to get a better look at his face, he found the man's condition was shocking. His face was bruised and swollen, with ring cuts sliced across it. But more startling than any of that was the man himself.

It's him. Officer Nightstick. The dancer at Madison's bridal shower.

Paco racked his brain. There was something so unmistakably familiar about him, but for the man who never forgot a face, Paco couldn't place this guy. Well, other than from being lip-locked with him at the bachelorette party.

Struggling, the man took in a deep breath, then coughed again. Opening his eyes, he stared at Paco, not saying a word.

Softly, Paco asked for the man's name in what he assumed was his native French. *"Comment tu t'appelles?"*

"P." A second later, the man elaborated with a cough. "Pierre. My name is Pierre. But I go by *P*, and I speak English. *Y español." And Spanish.*

A small smile appeared with his last words. He seemed to be waiting for Paco to pick up whatever hint he'd just left.

Oblivious to whatever he was getting at, Paco returned the smile, more of a reassurance the man would be all right. "Can you sit up?"

Pierre nodded, forcing himself straighter in the chair.

Tending to the restraints, Paco had a few tricks up his sleeve for getting out of handcuffs but paused. On the man's wrist was a small tattoo. An ornate design that, when you looked closely enough, was two initials. *P* and *R*.

These were more than just initials. They were *Paco's* initials. Exactly the design of how he initialed everything under the sun, from invoices to approvals, to receiving packages . . . even to signing checks. He never used a signature. Just two little letters in an ornate circle.

More suspicious than before, he asked, "What's your whole name?"

The man's head fell back. "Pierre. Pierre Roca."

Clenching his jaw, Paco stood, drawing his gun and holding it to the man's temple. "Looks like I shot the wrong guy."

"It's my name. I swear."

Paco's disbelief couldn't be more transparent. "Pierre. French for *stone*. Roca. Spanish for *stone*. If your name's Pierre Roca, then I'm the queen of England."

The cold barrel of a gun pressed against the back of Paco's head, and the inescapable cock of the hammer froze him in place.

Her sultry voice toyed with him. "Nice to see you again, Your Majesty."

CHAPTER 26

PACO

IRRITATED, Paco huffed in defeat. Lifting his arms, he telegraphed his surrender to the woman holding his fate in her hands. "It's not a party without another Jordan Stone."

"No, it isn't." Jordan's assurance was strangely playful. "Now, Mr. Robles, hand me your gun." When he did, she said, "And I insist you do the honors."

What she wanted was obvious. The handcuffs undone.

"Those aren't my handcuffs, and I don't have the key."

Rolling her eyes, Jordan impatiently gestured with her gun. "I don't have time to argue about your hidden skills. You have something that will work like a key in a pinch. Use it."

Not bothering to protest, Paco took a knee and did as she'd requested. Pulling out something from his shirt cuff that looked more like a paperclip than a key, he worked. The locked metal released easily from *P*'s wrists.

"I'll take those." Not satisfied with just the cuffs, Jordan extended her hand lower, insisting on Paco's key as well.

Regretfully, he complied. They'd likely cuff him, but he had a few more tricks up his sleeve to get free. Now if they shot him, it was game over. *Probably.*

"Turn around," she said.

Of course they're not just going to shoot me in the back. Their kind loves staring their victim down.

A shot through the heart at point-blank range seemed totally their jam. It would be final. And how he'd do it.

If I have to.

With an indifferent pivot, Paco swung around. Hopeful, he held out his hands, ready for the cuffs. His shoulders sank as Jordan tucked the handcuffs he'd handed her into the back of her pants and slipped the key in her cleavage.

Fuck. I'm dead.

Instead, she retrieved his gun from her pocket and pressed it back in his hands. After uncocking the hammer, she tucked hers into her boot.

"I didn't have time to explain, and I needed you to free *P*, but I'm not killing you. Mostly because if I did, *P* would kill me."

The news took Paco by surprise, but questions were out.

She lightly stroked *P*'s head. *"¿Estás bien?"*

"Yes. Better than ever," *P* said, irate. "You shouldn't be here. Now what do we do?"

"Odysseus," she said, followed by a sigh and despondent look.

The stare they exchanged lasted only a moment, but its weight spoke volumes. Paco wasn't privy to the unspoken details, but some decision had been made.

P didn't seem pleased. "Then explain to Paco."

"You do it. I'm out of time," she said and turned for the door.

P stood. "Wait." Scooping her into a hard but brief hug, he smiled. "You're a real pain in the ass."

She gave him a smirk. "Only if you're very nice."

Finally, with a kiss on her cheek, he insistently whispered, "Go!"

Quickly, she left.

P turned to Paco. "You have a car, I assume."

Moving with a renewed energy, *P* rummaged through the abandoned duffel Zane had left behind. Grabbing a handgun, *P* released the clip, did a quick check to ensure it held plenty of ammunition, then returned the clip and slipped the handgun in his jacket pocket.

"Let's go. I'll explain on the way."

As Paco drove away, he ignored the incessant backseat driving of his passenger.

"You're going the wrong way."

Paco pressed on his predetermined course. "Yeah? Well, I'm about to drop your ass off at the nearest hospital if I get any more of your navigating. Now, in this order, you need to answer these questions. One, if you and Jordan both work for Mr. Stone, why am I coming to your rescue, and where the hell is he? Two, what's Odysseus, or most likely, Operation Odysseus? And three, who are you? And I don't want your fucking family history."

"Technically," *P* said, "that's four questions." Busy cleaning his face with a wet wipe from the glove compartment, *P* donned a charming smile with shining pearly whites.

Paco did a double-take. Rummaging through the corners of his mind, he flipped through memories like flash cards, determined to remember this man, and the fact that he couldn't was maddening. He knew him, yet he didn't.

P chuckled. "How about instead of torturing yourself, you let me answer the questions in the order that makes the most sense? Starting with who I am."

The proposition was too tempting. Paco hated giving up control, but he clearly didn't have it anyway. "Fine. Who are you?"

Grinning, *P* goaded him. "You really don't know?"

"Holy fuck, you're a masochist. You seriously want me to pick up where Zane left off?"

"God, you're gorgeous when you're mad."

What? Paco hid the heat rising up his neck and cheeks behind rage. "And you're deranged if you think I won't toss your ass from a moving vehicle. Last chance."

"Sorry." *P* nestled into his seat. "Life's short. I've never had a knack for filtering my thoughts. Occupational hazard. And I've wanted to meet you for a long time. Or re-meet you."

I knew it.

"So we have met." Paco shook his head slowly in frustration. "I remember every face I've ever seen, but I don't remember yours."

"Yes, you do. Your mind is battling to reconcile what you *know* with what you *see*. Come on. Trust your instincts. There are parts of me you remember, aren't there?" Like a professor leading a student, *P* continued. "Tell me. What's triggering your memory?"

Desperate to fill in this gaping hole in his mind, Paco took the bait. In a swift series of glances, he strayed from the task at hand, ignoring the question to lose himself in the man.

The mystery sitting next to him was attractive. Very attractive. With unfathomable strength, *P* had taken a beating that would break most men, comfortably springing back and ready for the next match.

Fuck, that's sexy.

"Fine." As if pondering something other than the biceps desperate to break free from *P*'s shirt, Paco muttered, "Something about your smile. It's weird."

P lit up with enthusiasm. "Ooh, give me weird, *guapo.*"

Ignoring the compliment of being called *handsome*, Paco focused. *You want weird. You've got it.* "There's something about the way your teeth . . . shine."

Unfazed, *P* licked his lips. "I like that my mouth has your attention. Go on."

Paco suppressed the unexpected throbbing in his pants and focused, desperate to make his vivid recollections sound as matter-of-fact as possible. "Your eyes. You were wearing reflective glasses as part of your costume at Madison's party, so I couldn't see them then. But now, there's something familiar about them. Like . . ." Unsure what to say, he hesitated.

"Don't hold back. Say it. What's flashing through that brilliant head of yours?"

Unbelievable.

Setting the ass-kissing aside, Paco held the thought. *P's eyes. His teeth.*

Then he blurted out whatever came to mind. "The sea. Salt air. Heat. Us— just like we are now. In a car. Home—"

Paco stopped at the last one, having another feeling. A strong one. He'd had it before, in the split-second instance of locking eyes while checking the bruises on this man's face, but he sure as hell wasn't bringing that up now.

Focusing on the road ahead, he considered the man sitting next to him. His height. His age. And again, those eyes. "You can't be . . ."

"Can't be who?" *P*'s knowing smile confirmed what Paco was coming to terms with.

Staring down the obvious, he finally released the name he'd held for so long. "You're Jordan Stone. *My* Jordan Stone, the one who recruited me. But . . ."

Nodding, *P* picked up where Paco trailed off. Enthusiastically, he said, "*Oui. C'est moi.*" *Yes, it's me.*

His ease in floating between French, English, and back to his native Spanish was alluring. Paco relished chasing his words. *How many languages is he fluent in? If he really let go, could I keep up? With his command of languages? Or him?*

Returning to the center of his puzzle, Paco still had questions. "But . . . you died. On a mission. At least, that was the last thing I could find out about you."

"I know. And I love that you were looking." Losing his carefree demeanor, *P* lowered his voice. "It needed to look like I was out of the picture. Let's just say that speaking my mind isn't my only occupational hazard, so I had to vanish. I needed a little work done to blend into the background."

"A *little?*"

P turned his face to the window, seeming engrossed with the passing scenery. "Does it bother you that I look . . . different?"

Paco's response was instant. "No. Even beaten to a bloody pulp, you're still a Latino Hemsworth, okay?" When *P*'s smile returned, Paco liked it. "Keep going."

"Fine." *P*'s ego seemed reinstated, letting him run through the pivotal points in their history. "You weren't just my recruit. You were someone I couldn't get out of my head."

Paco downplayed his surprise, pushing out a matter-of-fact response. "A crush."

"If only it were that simple. And it sure would've made Stone's life easier if that's all it were. After Jack's death, you laid down the law with the boys at the Pentagon. All those threats to expose operations. Take down the man. You were so adorable."

Paco blew out a long breath. One of his bravest plays had been relegated to a juvenile move. But thinking back, the truth of *P*'s words was apparent. *How did I walk away unscathed?*

"Are you saying you intervened?"

"A target was pasted on your back before you left the building. That's how the dominos fell. I couldn't let anything happen to you, so I backed you. Loudly. Threw out every threat I could. And Stone backed me. It was a hard line in the sand we could never undo, but it was worth it. Jack was enough of a loss. Either they left you alone, or it was war. Sometimes they left you alone. Sometimes it was fucking war. People got too used to my face, so I needed a change, to disappear for a while. In my line of work, there aren't a lot of options."

Distracted, *P* pulled down the visor, scrutinizing his reflection in the small mirror there to assess the damage from the beating he'd taken.

Still unclear, Paco asked, "So you had plastic surgery?" He quickly added, "No judgment. It looks fantastic."

With a sly grin, *P* said, "I'm glad you approve. And no, I didn't have plastic surgery. I had plastic *surgeries.* Perfection takes time. And my surgeon is going to kill me when he sees this. Until he swipes my credit card." With a flip, he replaced the visor.

"Hang on. If you and Stone are so tight, why did he call me? He didn't even tell me what I was walking into."

"He probably couldn't," *P* said flatly.

"Really? You were getting the shit beat out of you, and he couldn't do a damn thing?"

P's explanation was abrupt. "He called *you*."

After a minute of digesting the nonexplanation, Paco pressed for an answer. "What the hell was so important that he couldn't have your back?"

With a weighted breath, *P* answered. "Chemotherapy."

As they both sank into the heavy silence between them, Paco considered how quickly the tides could turn. What if it were Alex who had cancer? Or Dan?

Finally, in an odd and very natural way, Paco took *P*'s hand and squeezed. "I'm sorry."

Instantly, *P* wove his fingers through Paco's. "Thanks."

Not quite ready to let the feeling linger, Paco tried to withdraw his hand. But *P*'s determined, strong, and oddly tender grasp prevented it.

"Oh no you don't." *P* chuckled. "I've waited ten years to be this close to you. Listen, I've been through a lot today. I need the comfort of your amazing touch. If I can hold on for just a few more minutes, I'm sure I'll answer your questions much faster."

Paco feigned a huff, hearing the word *sucker* echo through his brain. He stifled any further response, holding back just how much he liked *P*'s thumb strokes against his knuckles. "Fine. Whatever. Next question. What's Odysseus?"

The gentle circles *P* made across the back of Paco's hand slowed. "Do you know what a Trojan horse is?"

Confident, Paco answered. He'd not only seen them in action, he'd effectuated a few over the years. "Sure. In cyberspace, it's a type of malware used to trick a user into executing a program. But the term stems from a historical reference. A giant fabricated horse was used as bait—a trophy—that was coveted by enemy forces. The Trojan horse allowed attackers to hide inside, wait for their opponent to bring it into their camp, and then attack them from within when they least suspected—while they slept."

"And the hero who lead the attack was Odysseus. Hence, the name."

Paco thought through the explanation. "You're implying that Jordan is Odysseus. But she wouldn't be able to infiltrate the enemy without a token of trust."

And then it hit him. *Son of a bitch.*

Paco slipped his hand from *P*'s hold, grasping his wrist and pressing his fingers against the beating of his pulse. "Does she have Madison?"

Before *P* could respond, Paco had his answer. The sudden spike in pulse rate told him as much.

"It's not what you think." *P*'s apologetic tone couldn't be less endearing.

In a surge of fury, Paco tossed *P*'s hand aside. "Then tell me what it fucking is. Now! Because killing you just came back on the table."

Retrieving his gun, Paco pressed it against *P*'s head. "Where's Madison?"

CHAPTER 27

MADISON

THE SLOWING of the car gave Madison a bit of hope. Not only that she'd soon be released from the trunk, but mostly because she had another pressing matter.

She didn't wait for her eyes to adjust. As soon as the trunk opened, she blurted, "I seriously have to pee."

"That's why we've stopped." Helping her out of the trunk, Jordan said, "Over there."

The building she pointed to could only be described as a stone outhouse in the middle of nowhere. Tall wild grasses led to a long cluster of trees far away. A jungle of some sort. The only view was across a body of water, on the other side of which was a distant land—probably Malaysia.

Shoving a handful of tissues in Madison's hand, Jordan pointed her chin toward the building. "You don't have a lot of time, and I doubt this place has toilet paper. As you've probably surmised, you can't escape. And I have a deadline."

"Deadline for—"

"For getting you to a rendezvous. And time's running out."

Beyond ready to burst, Madison hit the restroom. Grateful she indulged in yoga once or twice a week, she tackled the hole-in-the-ground toilet like a champ.

No dribbles down my leg. Didn't fall on my ass. Glass half-full.

Once again, she checked her cell. Nothing. The hope of any signal, even a weak one, remained a lost cause.

With no other exit, and a tiny window that maybe her head could fit through, her options were limited. She returned to Jordan, who spoke on her cell in a language Madison didn't recognize. With all the people speaking so many different languages, she was starting to feel like a child, not quite understanding what the grown-ups meant when they said things in code.

Seeing Madison, Jordan disconnected the call with a lavish wave of her hand toward the trunk.

With her lips pursed and shoulders slumped, Madison asked with a whine, "Can I just sit in the car?"

Jordan checked her watch, then slipped the oversized timepiece off her wrist. "As much as I love your company, I'm afraid not. But good news." From her pocket, she pulled out another Ziploc of goldfish crackers, giving them an enthusiastic shake before tossing them to the back of the trunk.

"And you might want to take a few sips of this before we get going." She handed Madison a small bottle of Perrier.

Suddenly feeling parched, Madison gulped down a few swallows before giving the bottle a stern glance.

With a roll of her eyes, Jordan responded to her obvious concern with an unimpressed glare. "If I'd slipped something in your drink, it would be too late anyway. The few gulps you just downed would be well into your system."

Still skeptical, Madison decided she was good.

Jordan asked, "Done?"

Weakly, Madison nodded.

Jordan's hand brushed Madison's as she took the Perrier away from her and enjoyed several long sips. With the bottle still half-full, she handed it back. "You sure?"

Now I feel stupid. Or maybe this is a Princess Bride trick, and she's built up a life-long tolerance to some bizarre poison. I am still thirsty.

With a shake of her head, Madison said, "I'm sure."

Resigned to her fate as Jordan's excess luggage, Madison climbed back into the trunk. Again, Jordan helped her in, easing her gently in place. The jacket pillow had been recently fluffed.

Nothing but the finest for this five-star kidnapping.

With a suggestive smile on her ruby-red lips, Jordan looked down. "Comfy?"

Beyond annoyed, Madison glared up at her. "Does it matter?"

Jordan's hand flew to her heart as if she were wounded by Madison's words. "Yes. It matters. It's important to me that when I put you in an uncomfortable situation, you're as comfortable as possible."

"Is that some sort of riddle?"

Without answering, Jordan took Madison's hand, wrapping a watch around her wrist and securing it. "You'll need that."

Madison glanced at it, noting it was the watch Alex had given Jordan in France. "Why—"

But her question was cut short. The trunk slammed shut, and she was back in the dark. Taking in a deep breath and huffing it out, she grabbed the crackers and munched in frustration as the car rumbled, then rolled off.

Soon afterward, the car stopped and the trunk lid popped up.

Daylight hit Madison's unadjusted eyes just as hard as before. After several blinks, she was again able to see. Jordan stood over her, offering a hand, but she wasn't alone.

As Madison bypassed Jordan's assistance and pulled herself from the trunk, she recognized some, but not all, of the armed men surrounding her. Half of them were Alex's guards—men she'd trusted until that very moment. Even Jack-the-bodyguard wore a badass expression, keeping his semiautomatic fixed on her as if he didn't know her.

Jordan slipped her jacket back on and lightly slammed the trunk. Madison turned to face a new noise. A helicopter was starting up less than twenty yards away. But this wasn't the executive-type luxury copter she'd become accustomed to.

With Alex Drake, they always traveled in style. Instead, before her was a foreboding monster of a helicopter.

Madison didn't know much about aircraft, but between living with her father and Jack as she grew up, she knew enough to recognize the weaponry strapped to the sides. Though the chopper looked recently painted, she could make out a word from under the black paint. In all caps along the side, the former owner's name was apparent.

Marines.

"Impressive, isn't it?" Jordan stared at the mammoth beast. "The Bell UH1Y, better known as the Venom, is one of the most lethal and tactical military utility helicopters around. Adaptive. Versatile. With unparalleled flexibility. A smoking sex machine that's perfect for a sunset ride over the water." With a grand wave to the chopper, Jordan smiled. "After you."

As soon as Madison climbed up through the large side door, her eyes locked on the handcuffed man sitting at the far back seat, and her breath stopped.

CHAPTER 28

MADISON

SHOCKED, Madison choked back the nerves constricting her throat. Seeing him across the helicopter bay after wondering and worrying was too much. Her knees threatened to buckle.

Alex.

"Have a seat." Jordan helped Madison to the simple metal bench nearest the open door.

It was the closest Madison had been to Alex in nearly two days, but he felt a world away.

Jordan took the seat next to her, donning a set of earphones with a mic. "Oh, pilot, how many are we waiting on?" Nodding at the response, she replied, *"I'll let you know when to take off."*

While they waited, Madison's eyes snagged Alex's finger signaling her. His small, slow strumming on his slacks was back and forth until it finished with a small dot. Then the rhythm started again. *Six.*

The code didn't make sense. *They have our backs? Or he has my back?* Whatever Alex was trying to say, it was clear he wanted her to stay calm. It was a great reminder.

Here's to hoping it will stick.

Looking around, she noticed the bay was still very much in a minimalist military configuration. Across from them, two armed guards sat—one with his eye on Madison, and the other watching Alex. She didn't recognize them.

After a few more minutes of waiting, a man hopped inside. Disturbed, Madison watched as Zane looked her up and down.

"Well, hello," he said, his words oozing with charm. He traced a finger down her nose, giving it a pop, just like when she was a kid.

She glanced at Alex, who gave her a subtle shake of his head.

Noticing their exchange, Zane smirked. "Oh, if Dad didn't wear the pants before, he sure as hell isn't wearing them today."

Zane cocked his head enough for her to get a good, long look. Horrified, Madison stared at the huge chunk missing from the lobe of his ear, and the trail of dried blood down his neck.

"I have a score to settle. It's with Robles, but I'll take it out on Dad. Which means I'll take it out on you." Handing an envelope to Jordan, he said, "You can go."

Crossing her arms over her chest, Jordan didn't bother reaching for it. "*That* wasn't our arrangement. I was given every assurance that my audition was for the man in charge. Not a plebe."

"You're speaking to him. I suggest you take it and go."

Giving him a skeptical look, she asked, "You're the Ghost Wolf?"

Zane nodded, narrowing his eyes. "And you should sound more awestruck than that. Careful, pretty lady. I might get offended."

Her chuckle was light. "I get it. MacIntyre. *Mac Tire*. Irish for wolf. Funny, you don't look Irish."

Glaring, he spat, "And you don't look like a fourteen-year-old whore rescued from a crack den in South America. What do you know? Looks can be deceiving."

Unfazed, Jordan relaxed her arms and eased back in her seat, unleashing her signature smile. When she spoke, her voice was sultry and compelling. "I'm a woman of action, and I only work with people who keep their word. You wanted me? You have me. I respect your work, but your techniques are too impulsive for my taste. You need to learn to savor the moment."

Snatching Madison's wrist, she checked the time, then threw Madison's arm back in her lap. "I suggest you get this show on the road," she said to Zane. "Our deal included a romantic sunset, and the sun's going down fast."

Zane's snarl melted, transforming to a smile. "Fine. But I'm not exactly a neat freak. Not all of us need the blood cleaned up."

"Well, I'm a fucking horrible maid, so it sounds like we can work together." Into the mic, Jordan said, "We're ready to go."

The lift of the helicopter swept Madison into a swirl of dizziness. She glanced at Alex, but he wasn't meeting her gaze. *Why won't he look at me?* Instead, his fervent eyes were fixed on Jordan. His silent stare seemed to summon her.

Standing, Jordan dropped the headset in Madison's lap. In her infamous sashay, she crossed over to Alex. Straddling his lap, she proceeded with a strange and what looked like an intimate conversation.

Madison couldn't begin to make out what they were saying with the roaring of the helicopter filling her ears. But her eyes popped open wide in absolute disbelief of what she was seeing.

What. The. Fuck?

Jordan wrapped her arms around Alex's neck and laid an impassioned kiss on him. Long and slow. Right on the smacker. Tongue and all. A lot of it. And to add insult to injury, he hardly seemed to mind.

Holy hell! He's actually kissing her back.

Concentrating, Madison listened harder as their kiss ended.

Alex's low voice came in clearly. "You don't have to do this."

But Jordan's response was muddled. All Madison could make out was Jordan saying, "I want to."

Imagining the worst, Madison froze as her anxiety hit an all-time high. *What if . . . Jordan's kissing Alex good-bye. Why isn't he doing anything? He's handcuffed, but is he drugged?* And the guards seemed to be enjoying the show, not bothering to watch Madison at all.

Despondent, she placed her hand over her heart . . . where it stayed. Then, in an odd motion of casually feeling herself up, she slid her fingers across the keycard's plastic edges.

The master key. It has to be worth something, doesn't it? Enough to trade for our lives?

Without another thought, she whipped out the keycard, wrapping her hand around it. Clinging to it for dear life, she wrapped her other hand around the seat harness, tethering herself as she neared the open bay door. Stretching her arm out over the vast ocean zipping past below, she held the piece of plastic into the wind.

"Hey," she shouted. "Unless you want this priceless all-access technology to be lost forever, I suggest you release Alex and turn this helicopter around right now."

CHAPTER 29

MADISON

Consciously, Madison tried to loosen her hold on the small card ever so slightly. In her tightened grip, the card's hard plastic edges cut painfully into her fingers.

Zane stepped toward her. "What are you going to do, Madison? Toss it, and you know you and Alex are dead. Well, Alex will be dead. Or better yet, how about we keep him alive . . . in a very drawn-out state of dying? That way, all he'll be able to do is watch every terrible thing I do to you."

When Zane stalked closer, Madison forced the breath from her lungs in a scream. "I mean it!"

Painting a look of fake fright across his face, he took another step.

Shit. What do I do now?

Jordan was now behind Zane. Just watching. Unlike Alex, who seemed preoccupied with his lap. Whatever was going to happen, it was all resting on her shoulders.

Zane took another step.

"I mean it, Zane!"

His stoic expression disappeared as he broke out into a full-blown laugh. "I can't keep a straight face. Seriously, go ahead. Drop it. What the fuck are you waiting for, Madison?"

Stunned, she said nothing.

Zane was now an arm's length from her, but didn't stay there. "Well? No? Just bullshit?"

Frozen, she didn't move, but the card cut even harder into her hand. A small line of blood dripped from her fist. An inch from flying out the bay, the only thing holding her in place was the harness binding her other hand. It strangled her grip, and she was losing feeling in her fingers.

"Let us go, Zane. And you can keep your precious card."

"Okay." He waved his hands in defeat, then added, "On second thought, how about I leave Alex alive and handcuffed while I take my time fucking you?" His hand shot out to grip her throat, and her tears fell instantly.

Pleading, she asked, "Why, Zane? Why are you doing this? You were part of our family. Jack's best friend. And your family has money."

His blue eyes lit up as his smile widened. "Jack," he said, sentimentally and exaggerated. "Don't you miss Jack? I did, when he left me to take some once-in-a-lifetime assignment. Jack never did anything for the money, and neither do I. It's about power, Madison. Real power. The power to reward your friends and demolish your enemies."

Scowling, Zane continued. "Jack could've taken me with him. They recruited three people—three! He thought he could ditch me and take the glory—war-hero shit—some holy grail of an assignment. Well, two can play at that game. And finding him on that mission wasn't exactly hard. That cocksucker told me everything, and I use that term literally." His eyes danced at the vile play on words.

"Jack wouldn't have told you where he was." Madison's protest was more than a feeble stall. She meant it. "Jack would never have endangered his mission by sharing classified information, even with you."

Zane smirked. "It's cute how you've really painted your brother as the great American hero. Well, rest easy, Mads. He didn't tell me where his mission was. He didn't have to. He was taking a quick break—they all were—to Italy. Him. Alex. Paco Robles. Not exactly hard to find. Or follow. All I needed to know was if and when he actually came into possession of the goods. And once I knew that, I had my own orders."

Madison trembled, but she had to know all of it. "What were your orders, Zane? And who gave them to you?"

"Let's just say whatever Jack had, it was really fucking valuable. I didn't need all the details. Piecing together what it meant was enough to have a few meaningful discussions with the right people. Some wanted what he had, but like you said, Jack was a vault. A few super-players were even content to make sure it never saw the light of day. I left the military and became a free agent for all the right sorts of people. The price was high, but the lifestyle was too good to be true. All I had to do was prove my allegiance."

Oh my God. Madison sank into the reality of what Zane had done to *prove his allegiance.* Her eyes welled with tears and she choked out a sob.

"How could you? You killed Jack, didn't you? You were a second son to Mom and Dad. And . . ." Madison looked at the keycard still clutched in her hand. Terrified, she looked back to Zane. "You killed Jack to destroy whatever he had. But the card—"

"You never could quite keep up with the big kids, could you, Mads? A master keycard? Really? Fuck, you're gullible. As gullible as the last . . . and the next. Like taking candy from a baby. You haven't been holding some magic, priceless treasure."

Grinning, he pointed to her hand, still desperately holding the plastic card. She looked at it, horrified at her own naivete.

"You're just like your brother. Can't see what's right in front of you." Zane's voice lowered as his lips curled into a smug smile. "All this time, you've been holding *Alex's* keycard. We took it from him as soon as we had him. I slipped it to you with a crazy story, and you bought it."

Zane scoffed. "Like I would trust you with my chewing gum, let alone some international treasure. And you did exactly what I thought you would. You tried the key on your own goddamnnn door. It was all the time I needed to slip a camera in your room, to know what you'd be up to. To see if Robles or anyone else would miss you if you vanished. The sad truth? Nope. No one would miss poor little Madison."

"If this isn't about a master key, then why kill Jack?"

Laughing, Zane shrugged. "Why not?"

Panic set in. He was psychotic. And there was no way he was letting her live.

"Besides, now I know you have one piece of the puzzle. The decoder. It's at Alex's penthouse, and with his wallet, I've got all his keycards. Full access. From the Google images, it looks like a nice spot in Manhattan. I can't wait to rummage through his stuff."

"But—"

Zane stopped her. "Oh, I know what you're thinking. I don't have both pieces. The decoder and what it decodes. Well, you want to guess where the other piece is? Drumroll . . ." His sound effects ended with a hateful stare at her. "They're with your mom."

No. "She doesn't have anything."

Leaning in, he snarled. "She's got Jack's dog tags. See, Jack had two things engraved in Italy. Something small, and his dog tags. You've got to ask yourself, why would anyone engrave their dog tags? Unless . . ."

Zane paused, letting her deductions catch up. "I thought your dad had them for a while, but nope. For all the stuff he did have, that was one thing he didn't have. Then, out of the blue, Joy mentioned Jack's dog tags. On Facebook. How she always slept with them under her pillow. Sweet, right?"

When Madison was about to speak, Zane shushed her with a finger to her lips. Then that finger wiped her tears.

"You can drop that card anytime, Mads."

The rush of dread paralyzed her.

Cornered, Madison had no choice but to let Zane move his hand around her neck. He didn't squeeze hard, but he did squeeze. She finally released the card to pull his strong hand from her throat. Struggling, she wrapped her other hand more tightly around the seat harness as he pushed her head out the door.

"That's it, Mads. You know the end is near. You're barely even fighting it. God, this is just too easy. Jack was always the better fighter. That's why I hit him from fifty yards away with an RPG. No chance he'd survive. Hey, things are looking up. In a few more minutes, you'll be seeing him again."

Madison's strength was no match for Zane's. He seemed to be getting off on prolonging the worst of it.

"Aren't you forgetting something?" Even with her voice loud to compensate for the rotor noises, Jordan's tone was coy and calculated.

CHAPTER 30

MADISON

MADISON WATCHED as Jordan slinked over and slid her hand on Zane's shoulder. "I believe we had a deal. I bring them in, and I claim the kill."

His hand squeezed harder on Madison's neck. She saw stars before he eased his grip.

"Fine." Zane pressed his mouth to Madison's, shoving his disgusting tongue deep inside as she fought for air.

She struggled, gagging from his assault, but ripping from his hold was impossible. He took his time, then licked the tears from her cheeks before setting her free.

Relaxing his glare, he finally huffed. "You're probably a piss-poor fuck anyway. Your kiss is a little too . . . timid. Jack got all the passion in the family. Definitely the better kisser." Turning, he addressed Jordan. "Sloppy seconds are all yours. But her parents are mine. On that one, I work alone."

Jordan nodded her agreement to his terms. Taking the headset but not putting it on, she gave an order. "Drop closer to the water. But for God's sake, don't try to fucking land on it. This isn't a Chinook." Tossing the headset back on the seat, she rolled her eyes and smiled. "Helicopter pilots—not exactly the sharpest tools in the shed."

Unwrapping the belt strangling Madison's hand, Jordan caressed her skin tenderly. "Better?"

Staring at the smiling face of an obvious lunatic, Madison gave her a weak nod.

"I love the way the last rays of sunlight are hitting your hair." Her thumb brushed Madison's trembling lips. "And don't listen to that asshole. You're the best kisser I've ever had." Jordan's lips pressed softly to Madison's.

Breaking down, Madison trembled, terrified at the unusually long and likely farewell kiss.

"Jordan, ple—"

"*Shh.* Don't say a word."

Releasing her hand, Jordan moved her fingers to the watch, pressing it until Madison felt something click.

"Wh—"

"I'll always remember you, Madison. Everything about you. The way you look against the sunset and the sea. The way you never lose faith that Alex Drake will come to your rescue. Even the childlike way you shied from my eyes at our last lunch, staring hopelessly at your glass of champagne . . . watching the fizzy little bubbles float to the surface. You'll always be that girl to me." She leaned to Madison's ear to whisper, "Follow the bubbles."

What?

Releasing Madison's hand, Jordan took a short step back. "This is good-bye, Madison Taylor."

In an instant, Jordan's open palm hit Madison's chest. The full-force shove tossed her out the bay door and into the vast and isolated stretch of sea below.

CHAPTER 31

ALEX

Twenty minutes earlier

ALEX HADN'T BEEN SITTING in the helicopter long, but long enough to know whatever was about to go down, it was important. The waiting. The guards. The superior military-grade helicopter armed enough to take out a village. He could feel it. This was it. He'd be meeting Jack's killer face-to-face.

But meeting the elusive Ghost Wolf wasn't enough. Alex needed to understand why Jack was killed. Get some insight into what happened. Risking his own life to do it wasn't just for Madison. Alex needed those answers too.

Studying Dumb and Dumber with their semiautomatics and protruding foreheads, Alex frowned, wishing at least one of his own inside guards were here. But a move like that would have been careless.

Whoever set this up was no idiot. Big reveals were final. You'd only use men you trusted, and you'd never trust someone you'd backed into a corner. If the roles were reversed, it was the play Alex would have made.

In the short walk from the car to the helicopter, he'd wrapped one cuffed hand over the other, repeating the message over and over. *One.*

Sure, it was risky. More reckless than he'd ever been. Although the humdrum couple of days he'd spent in captivity had atrophied his skills, today he was on high alert. *Ready for fucking anything.*

But if his team closed in too soon, he'd never know what all this had been about. And living without the truth had eaten at him, Paco, and Madison for far too long.

He was keeping the team away, but to what end? The helicopter was a bad sign. They were heading out over open water. Were they going to another country?

Alex clenched his jaw, worried about whether his team would be able to follow. *Drones only have so much range.*

A moment later, though, he realized that nothing had prepared him for what was to come. Seeing Madison walk into the bay, followed by Jordan, he froze and his plans disintegrated.

What. The. Fuck? Madison is supposed to be in New York. Under heavy guard.

It was too late. There was no way to signal his team.

Helplessly, he stared back at Madison's worried eyes. All he could do was reassure her and hope to hell they'd get out. Again, he laid out the signal. *Six.* He could see her confusion, but she needed to stay calm.

Who am I kidding? We're on a suicide mission. If we want any chance at all, we both need to stay calm.

After Zane entered and the helicopter took off, all Alex could do was hope to hell Jordan was on his side. But it was Jordan. Who could know for sure with her?

His intense staring caught her attention, and she prowled over, making herself comfortable in a straddle on his lap. To his ear, she said, "That's a magnetic stare you've got, Mr. Drake."

He didn't say a word, letting his clenched jaw and squint speak for him.

Jordan teased him. "Oh, come now, Alex. In so many ways, I made you. Gave you your name . . . and so much more. How about you show me a little appreciation?"

Her wide smile said everything he was hoping for. Relieved, he held back his grin. Held between her teeth was a universal handcuff key developed by his own engineers at DGI.

Welcoming her insistent lips, he let her slip the key through, but understood all too well the price of Jordan's favor. Her tongue fondled his mouth in marathon strides, in no hurry to end the staged seduction.

Somehow, her kiss turned tender, lingering a little too long. Intimately, he understood. And hated it with every fiber of his being.

Jordan's going to save us. By sacrificing herself.

Pleading, he gave her a hard but helpless gaze. "You don't have to do this."

Jordan's smile was warm. Her eyes glistened, but tears didn't fall. "You're sweet, Alex. You always have been. But you still don't know me at all, do you? I never do what I have to do, only what I want to do."

With a last kiss, she was off his lap, apparently deciding the conversation was over. Most likely because his fiery bride-to-be was now trying to take matters into her own hands.

Fuck. He needed out of these handcuffs.

Slowly and subtly, he pulled the key from his lips. Zane's horrifying confession focused him. He shot a glance at the guards, who were too preoccupied with Zane to notice him.

But he wasn't working fast enough, and Zane's hand was around Madison's neck. Alex's own big hands were doing him no favors. Working to remove the tight handcuffs with a tiny key proved harder with sweat dripping off his palms.

Dammit, I need another minute.

His gaze met Jordan's, and she stepped in. Again, the queen of distractions performed a show for everyone, giving him time to tear his hands free.

Slipping off his shoes was easily done without drawing attention. Losing them was important. Their weight in the water would work against him, dragging him down. But removing his blazer was crucial, and his short motions stretched out the normally quick task to an intolerable span of time.

A second after Madison was pushed from the aircraft, he bolted after her, shoving Jordan back as his desperate feet pushed hard off the bay floor. His jump had to be an Olympic qualifier—getting below Madison was critical.

The vest that Jordan so admired the night before was more than practical. Bulletproof was a great perk. But knowing he'd be on an island surrounded by water, he and Richard had considered the scenarios. Something floatable—even inflatable—might come in handy. Jordan's hand had probably lingered on him to feel the compressed life jacket within it.

Like all his inventions, the vest Richard had designed was pure genius. Its buoyancy was triggered by a sophisticated system that removed the oxygen from the water once it detected it was submerged. A slower process than the inflation of an airline vest, but it gave Alex the time he needed.

If only he could get deep enough before the vest would pull him to the surface. Hopefully, he'd be close enough to Madison to grab her before the vest would start lifting him up.

Alex hit the water feet-first as he'd been trained, holding a hand over his face.

With enough velocity from the jump and his own solid build, he sank quickly. Swimming frantically through the dark water, he could make out the light beaming from Madison's wrist. *The Omega watch.* She struggled to make it to the surface.

Helped by the vest, he propelled himself to Madison, grabbing her as they lifted all the way up, their heads breaching the rocking waves. Coughing up water, she clung to him.

"I've got you," he said, repeating it until her flailing arms and legs began to calm.

Alarmed by her shivers, he tightened his arms around her trembling body. Other than his own heat, there was nothing that would keep them warm, and the chopper was well off into the sunset. The nearest land was miles away.

"My cell." Her words were labored. "I-it's in m-my pocket. Maybe it's dry enough for a text."

Fishing the phone from her pocket, he kept the swearing to himself. *Dead.* Ready to swim for it, he fixed on the twinkling lights along the shore, but his ears trained on something. A noise.

A speedboat.

Shoving Madison's wrist into the air, he held it high, moving it back and forth to hopefully catch someone's eye. With any luck, the small light would be enough of a beacon to signal whomever was heading their way.

"Hear that?" Alex kept her hand high. "It's slowing. Hold on. They're almost here."

The speedboat killed its engines several yards off, tracing a spotlight back and forth across the waves.

"Over here," Alex shouted, now kicking his legs in long strides, taking him and Madison toward it.

A life preserver dropped nearby with a slack line to the boat. As soon as Alex grabbed it, he and Madison were towed in.

"Fuck, you have nine lives!" Standing on a small platform at the back of the boat, Paco held out his hands.

"Madison's freezing. She'll need help getting in."

P moved closer to assist Paco, and together they lifted her limp body effortlessly and wrapped her in a blanket.

Alex climbed in, happy to accept a big bro-hug from his best friend. "How did you find us?"

"The team had drones following each of you to the helicopter, but even with

Richard's range extenders, the drones couldn't keep up." Paco then looked at *P*, who pointed to Madison's watch.

"We zeroed in on the tracker I put on your watch. Someone activated it."

Grabbing Alex's arm, Madison whispered, "Jordan."

A second later, a boom rang out and a flash lit up the sky—an explosion at the far reaches of the sunset. The fate of the lone helicopter was cast.

Shrieking, Madison cried out, "Jordan!"

CHAPTER 32

MADISON

Manhattan, New York

IN THE TEN days since they'd returned home from Singapore, Madison was a zombie, going through the motions of keeping herself together. Each day was a torturous string of hours that slowly tore her apart.

Alex was right. Jordan had cared about her. Everything the woman did was choreographed to ultimately save Madison's life. And Alex's too.

The dive watch didn't just have the tracker . . . it also had a light. One so bright, even in the pitch-black water, Madison saw them—the bubbles. The insane reference that nudged her up to the surface.

"Follow the bubbles."

Jack had always had bizarre and fascinating stories to lull Madison to sleep. He'd spun bedtime stories from his mental Wikipedia of science and nature, not once giving in to the Brontë sisters' stories she always begged for. Too many of his tales were long forgotten, but one memory unlocked from the shock of the freezing water.

Deep, dark water is disorienting. People will swim in the wrong direction, desperate to get to the surface. Instead, they seal their fate, eventually drowning by diving deeper instead of heading up. But by the light of the watch, the bubbles were bright, leading her to air.

But so many things didn't make sense, and Madison couldn't reconcile them.

741

Why did Jordan keep her in a trunk? Bring her to the helicopter? To Zane? And why did she sacrifice herself?

It was senseless. There had to have been a better choice.

Perhaps there was. Perhaps there wasn't. And perhaps it didn't matter at all. Jordan made the ultimate sacrifice, and now she was gone.

Getting through her days was one thing, but Madison's nights were the worst. Alex just held her as she cried herself to sleep, no matter how many hours it took. Eventually, she'd doze off . . . only to wake from nightmares so unrelenting, the cycle would start all over again.

In that way, the tragedy was as much about Zane as it was about Jordan. Zane's face. His kiss. His charm. His threats. His hatred. Murdering her brother. Trying to kill Madison.

And for what? Which was more senseless—Jack's death, or Madison trying to find a shred of sense in the bizarre actions of a psychopath?

Each night, she worried about everything, even things as meaningless as waking Alex. Some nightmares just jolted her awake. For others, she'd be roused by her own screams.

But waking Alex? The man never slept. He took to working in their bedroom, ensuring he was always close when the dark dreams disturbed her.

The lack of sleep was making Madison sluggish. And depression was killing the diminished appetite she'd already been battling. But putting off her mom and dad any longer was impossible. They were coming to dinner that night, and they weren't taking no for an answer.

Dan had already been filled in on what happened in Singapore. But there was no reason for Joy to know anything else about Zane. Not hearing from him for long stretches was nothing new. Her heart needed a rest.

Out of the blue, Crystal, a freelance agent DGI used on their most sensitive operations, called to check on Madison.

Fine. You?

It was all Madison could do to carry on a normal conversation with the woman who'd become a friend.

With enough insistence, Crystal managed to coax Madison out of the penthouse for the first time since returning. Nothing big. A walk in the fresh air and some coffee.

Alex swore he hadn't said a word, but the coincidence was a little too remarkable. How could Madison say no?

"Crystal can be trusted. You can talk to her. About anything." She took his words of advice in stride.

Besides, the fresh air was appealing.

Madison's husband-to-be had to know she'd been holding back. Starting to clam up. The thought of burdening Alex and Paco with her pain broke her heart. She could tell them anything, but they had their own demons to battle.

It wasn't healthy to hold all her emotions inside, but clandestine shrinks weren't exactly something you googled. Crystal could be the next best thing if Madison gave her a chance.

The coffee shop Crystal had selected was well beyond walking distance, but Madison enjoyed the drive in her bright yellow Lamborghini. "The Big Banana" nickname was earned when Paco owned it. Somehow, the moniker didn't exactly roll off her tongue, but she loved the car, nonetheless.

Cracking her first smile in days, she shook her head. Under his custody, the nickname made sense. *I can only assume.*

As Madison parked on the lonely street, Crystal was waiting. For being in the city, the small stretch of road seemed strangely vacant. Isolated.

Less people-y. Thank God. I definitely need less people-y.

As soon as she stepped out, Crystal gave her a big hug, squeezing several tears out. "How are you holding up, kiddo?"

Shrugging, Madison stayed quiet.

With a kind smile, Crystal asked, "How about we take a stroll? There's a quiet park across the street, and a small coffee shop at the other end."

Barely nodding, Madison agreed.

During the walk, she shared more than she should have, but Alex assured her Crystal was a trusted agent. It was all Madison needed to let everything out. At the far end of the park, they each took a seat at the isolated coffee shop, enjoying the lush trees and singing birds at a quaint café table.

Tears streaming down her face, Madison took the tissues Crystal handed her. "It's over. Jordan's gone. But I can't let it go."

"Well, of course not."

Shaking her head, Madison objected. "It's like Jack all over again. I can feel it. Not understanding. Spinning my mind senseless with questions—too many questions. I've asked myself a million times—why? To everything. Her death. Why did she have to die? You know Jordan . . ." Solemnly, Madison corrected herself. "*Knew* Jordan. Why would she sacrifice herself like that? There had to be another way."

The waitress placed a cappuccino before Madison. The hints of green around the cup's rim intrigued her, along with a dusting of green powder on the leaf-shaped foam. But something was wrong.

"I'm sorry. I didn't order this."

The waitress said, "No? Well, you should have. It's a matcha cappuccino. Off menu. Frankly, you're a lot higher maintenance than people realize."

Madison froze. *I've snapped. Now I'm even hearing her, the ghost of Alex Drake's lover past. I'll just . . . act casual.*

Too afraid to look up, she preferred to keep her decline into madness to herself. That is, until a bag dropped on the table.

She looked down. The Ziploc was filled with tiny smiling goldfish.

Jumping up, Madison stood face-to-face with the waitress. The woman's normally ass-length jet-black hair was now stripped to platinum blond, softly layered just below her shoulders. But her lips spread wide in an unmistakable ruby-red grin.

"Still not eating?" Jordan asked.

Suffocating her in a tight hug, Madison touched and groped Jordan repeatedly. Sobbing, she asked, "You're alive? Real?"

"Real enough to start the clock if you keep feeling me up. Fair warning, I'm a cash-only girl."

Backing up, Madison looked her over again. "It's really you?"

"Of course it's me. Who else could pull off these heels?" She pointed a toe, showing off her latest six-inch find.

Madison firmed her grip, shaking Jordan lightly by the shoulders as if scolding a toddler. "You scared me. Don't do that again."

Obviously amused, Jordan grinned at Madison before glaring at Crystal. "At least someone missed me."

"Puh-lease." Crystal sighed. "You'd have to be gone a hell of a lot longer than that for me to miss you."

Shocked, Madison pouted at the insensitive comment.

Leaving a big kiss on Madison's cheek, Jordan rubbed her arm, then sat down. "Don't mind Crystal. She's just grumpy that I foiled her evil plan to kill me."

CHAPTER 33

MADISON

APPREHENSIVE, Madison couldn't take her eyes off Crystal . . . even as Jordan urged her to sit. "What's she talking about, Crystal? Did you have something to do with the helicopter crash?" When Crystal merely rolled her eyes, Madison raised her voice. "Answer me."

"*Shh-shh-shh.*" Jordan shushed her. "It's not her fault she's a lousy helicopter pilot. Not everyone can maneuver at night."

Pleased with her comment, Jordan smirked and opened the Ziploc of crackers. Before she could stop herself, Madison popped several in her mouth.

"Excuse me?" Offended, Crystal sneered. "*You* said you had it under control. *You* said you could take on two armed guards *and* Zane without my help. Because once again, *you* were full of shit. I had to rig the chopper, set the timer on the detonator, join in the hand-to-hand combat session so absolutely *everyone* was kung fu fighting, and get us out of there before the explosion."

Clearly bored, Jordan huffed. "I believe I said it's *not* your fault you're a lousy helicopter pilot. What more do you want from me?"

Confused, Madison watched the argument unleash. Watched their eyes. Their mannerisms. Their . . . *banter?*

Everything she thought she knew, she didn't. Nothing made sense, yet there it was . . . an unmistakable rivalry that could only mean one thing.

Wary of the two lethal women, she hesitantly asked, "Are you two . . . sisters?"

745

Jordan and Crystal looked at each other, both erupting into smiles and a knowing squint. Jordan fished a hundred-dollar bill from her cleavage and handed it to Crystal.

"Thank you," Crystal said. "I told you if we were together, she'd figure it out."

Still shocked over her own discovery, Madison repeated her words. "You are sisters? Really?"

"Twins," Crystal said.

"Obviously not identical," Jordan said, making a face at her sister. "I got all the looks."

"And I got all the brains," Crystal shot back.

Madison's head was already exploding by the bombardment of a wave of questions she was dying to ask. It made no sense, but then it made all the sense in the world.

Spirited. Competitive. Matched in fighting skills. Crystal was always one step ahead of Jordan—pushing all the right buttons at just the right times. And Alex had said Madison could trust Crystal.

"Am I the only one who didn't know?"

Squeezing Madison's hand, Jordan turned somber. "Nobody knows. Except Stone, *P*, Corey, and as of this morning, Alex. And it's important that nobody else knows. Ever. Our lives depend on it."

Shaking her head, Madison said, "Wait. Who's Corey?"

With a sly smile, Jordan threw out the answer. "Crystal's pet."

Crystal huffed. "We prefer the term *husband* in public. And let's not forget, he saved your ass."

"Just because I was with you." Expanding her explanation, Jordan turned to Madison. "He had a speedboat waiting for us."

Leaning in, Crystal added, "But Jordan's not exaggerating. We've come to each other's rescue more times than we can count."

"That's because some of us can't count very high." Jordan painted a look of innocence on her face, making Madison laugh.

"Fine. Let me rephrase. We've come to each other's rescue two hundred eighty-two times, and it's only because no one knows who we really are."

Keeping one hand on Madison, Jordan slid her other hand to Crystal. "No one understands the bond we share."

Madison tried pulling her own hand away, but Jordan held it tight, connecting them all.

"Why are you telling me this?"

Jordan raised an eyebrow. "Haven't you been paying attention? We didn't tell you. You figured it out, and I lost a hundred bucks."

Crystal answered more directly. "Madison, you're one of us. We're Finders. And sometimes we're Keepers. We're here to protect things and people. It's in our souls. And you now have both pieces of whatever Jack was protecting—"

"I'm not handing them over." Madison's words were hard and cutting. Heated, she pulled her hands to her lap.

Jordan continued. "We're not asking you to, because we know they're safe. And because the rule is whoever finds first—keeps. You are the Keeper for those items, to do with as you please. And we're here to have your back."

Madison considered their words, but she couldn't let go of the feeling the story was incomplete. "You kept me in a trunk and took me right to Zane. Why didn't you just tell me what was happening? Or at least let me sit in the car?"

Pursing her lips, Jordan explained. "I needed to keep you safe, and who knew for sure if I was being followed? I mean, other than with those asinine drones Black Technologies deployed. Seriously, I felt like I was being chased by fucking flying monkeys."

"They only follow witches," Crystal said, sneering.

"Just the West one. I'd pipe down if I were you. How about you keep busy watching for a falling house."

Madison refocused them. "That still doesn't explain why you didn't just tell me."

Jordan and Crystal looked at each other, and then at her, synchronized in saying, "Because you suck at lying."

Pouting, Madison accepted the truth. "Fine, I suck at lying. That sort of reinforces my point. Then why let me in on the fact that you're sisters? I'm freaked out about putting you two in danger. You're the amazing liars. You could have denied it and kept it to yourself. And for nearly two weeks now, we all thought Jordan was dead."

Frustrated, Madison ruthlessly grabbed several little goldfish, chomping them hard to ease her stress.

"That *was* the plan. Let everyone think I'm gone, then sail away into retirement. You seriously have no idea how hard it is being me. Everyone wants Jordan to fix their shit. Jordan, Jordan, Jordan . . . I can't get a moment's peace." The song in Jordan's voice landed flat. "But I now have new information, and it's going to keep me around for a very long time."

Sitting straighter, Madison frowned, ready for a serious conversation. "About Jack?"

"No. Not about Jack." Jordan plopped a gift bag in front of Madison.

Skeptical, she left it untouched. "Seriously, I'm grateful and all, but I really don't need another vibrator. Though, if it's any consolation, the last one was pure magic."

Madison reconsidered the gift bag.

"Wait. Are you saying it's about Alex? He has to leave again?" Shaking her head, she worried aloud. "I don't think I can be without him right now."

"No, it's not about Alex. Or Paco. Or your parents."

Crystal's words were reassuring, letting Madison breathe easier.

Uncharacteristically excited, Crystal nudged her. "It's about you. Open it."

Now curious, Madison peeked in. Whatever it was couldn't be seen through a monstrous wrapping of tissue. Pulling it out, she began unrolling the delicate, thin sheets of paper.

Jordan squeezed Madison's forearm before she could finish removing all of the tissue. Regret filled Jordan's eyes as she spoke. "I'm sorry I kept you in my trunk."

With a scolding tone, Crystal nudged her on. *"And?"*

Dropping her shoulders, Jordan continued. "And—" She sucked in a breath. "I'm sorry I brought you to Zane, made out with your fiancé, and threw you out of a helicopter into the freezing water. I would've come up with another plan if I'd known you were preggers."

Shocked, Madison sucked in a breath. *Pregnant? Me?*

Ripping the last shred of tissue paper from the box, she stared at the over-the-counter pregnancy test in her hands. Wide-eyed and her mouth agape, she shook her head in disbelief. "But I'm not—"

"You're usually Ms. Snacks-a-lot." Jordan's observation couldn't be denied. "Yet, you haven't been eating. Your hair is thicker, and you're glowing like the Eiffel Tower on New Year's Eve. And don't even get me started on your noticeably bigger and absolutely luscious boobs. I noticed them just as I tossed you out of the chopper, and I'm like, 'Fuck, I think I just threw a pregnant lady into the ocean.'"

Jordan's smile spread wide across her face. Crystal's was just as big.

A few happy tears trailed down Madison's cheeks as Crystal spoke.

"*This* is why we told you, Madison. Jordan and I thought about it—a lot—and we've made an important decision. Jordan is sticking around because we've decided to adopt you."

"The little sister we always wanted to torture." Jordan's grin switched to devious.

Crystal leaned in. "Not to torture . . . much. But to protect. You, and all the little Madisons and Alexes that come along."

"And maybe a little Jordan. I can teach her proper makeup techniques and mixed martial arts. Oh, and Farsi . . . and French!"

Loving how carried away Jordan was, Madison tossed a soggy grenade at her before popping the last of the crackers in her mouth. "Babysitting means you're changing diapers."

With a wave of her hand, Jordan dismissed the comment. "Crystal can change the diapers. I'll keep her fed. I'm sure she'll love these little cheddar crackers just as much as her mother."

Mother. The word lifted Madison to a stratospheric euphoria.

"I'm going to be a mother?" Giggling, she blurted out another revelation. "Oh my God. Alex Drake is going to be a father!"

They all laughed.

Jordan said, "Are you sure he's not already one?" She got a hard punch in the arm for that one from Crystal, which Madison thoroughly enjoyed. "*Ow.* Like you weren't thinking it too."

Perhaps in an effort to cover her guilt, Crystal recommended one hell of a distraction. "Madison. My penthouse—"

"*Our* penthouse," Jordan said, interrupting. "As if you could afford that lap of luxury on your own."

"Fine. *Our* penthouse is a block and a half away. How about we all pop over and have you pee on a stick. Just to make sure."

Jordan slid Madison's cappuccino closer. "But first you have to drink a few sips of this. Seriously, you're barely eating, and I slipped some protein powder in it. We've got to keep the baby and your boobs growing."

With a hint of a smile, Madison sipped, immediately swept away in the yummy goodness of her new favorite drink.

Crystal shook her head. "Damn, you're a mother hen."

Jordan proudly concurred. "I'm totally maternal. I'm making plans as we speak to retrofit my trunk with bumpers and a glow-in-the-dark mobile."

～

Madison kept a close eye on the timer as it counted down on her cell.

"Time's up, already." Jordan stopped her impatient pacing and took a few determined steps to the bathroom.

"Not yet," Madison said, playfully keeping Jordan away from sneaking a peek at the stick. "Thirty more seconds."

Crystal joined Madison, blocking the entrance to the bathroom. "And Madison gets to check first."

Jordan bowed up to her sister. "Brave words considering I have a gun."

Crystal crossed her arms over her chest. "Do *not* make me shove that pistol straight up your ass in front of the mother-to-be."

With the two femmes going toe-to-toe in a glare-off, Madison slipped into the bathroom. A few seconds later, she returned, bawling her eyes out and grinning from ear to ear. Her nod was all the invitation Jordan and Crystal needed to swoop her into a group hug.

"Oh my goodness." Madison's hold on the women tightened. "How am I going to tell Alex?"

Backing away, Jordan's sly smile was in full swing. "I think it's time for a bet. A hundred bucks on when Alex Drake will figure it out—all on his own."

Madison covered her naughty grin. Ecstatic, she said, "You're on!"

CHAPTER 34

MADISON

ENTERING THEIR PENTHOUSE, Madison stared, admiring it with fresh eyes. From the first time she'd stepped into the luxury suite, to her core, it had felt like home.

Now she could imagine her own baby taking his or her first tiny little wobbly steps along the rich wood floors. Wearing nothing but a diaper and a smile, their little one would weave around the comfortably elegant furniture, and even smudge some delightfully slobbery handprints on the infinity windows while curiously peering out at the breathtaking views of the Manhattan skyline.

Emotionally, she welled up and rubbed her tummy. The clanging of pots and pans in the kitchen tore her from her heartwarming reverie. Giddy, she strolled over to see Alex in the middle of making a ridiculously big feast.

"Hey, handsome," she said, thrilled at the sight of her man sinking deep into Betty Crocker mode.

Dropping everything he was doing, he took her into a huge hug, rocking her gently. Tenderly, he whispered, "You've been crying."

Looking into his worried eyes, she delicately cradled his jaw, relaxing his tension. "Yes, but I'm not sad anymore. I'm happy. Really, really happy."

Alex's brow smoothed, and his warm lips touched hers lightly. "I'm glad. And I'm guessing you, too, have received the privileged information."

She nodded, glee widening her smile.

Sweeping a few loose strands of hair behind her ear, he gazed at her tenderly. "Well, you'll be even happier tonight. I'm making all your favorites. Short ribs, mashed potatoes with roasted garlic, honey-glazed carrots, angel hair pasta with pesto, a strawberry-pecan-blue cheese mixed greens salad, and there's a surprise for dessert."

Grinning wide, Madison wondered if she'd just won the bet. "That's a lot of food for just us."

Cocking his head, Alex looked at her. "Well, I was hoping I could get your appetite up. And it's not just us."

The money's in the bank.

"Your parents are coming," he said. "Remember? And Paco, Jess, and Mark."

"Right. Of course." *I totally forgot.* "What time are they coming?"

"Seven."

"Seven," Madison repeated under her breath, checking the clock. *That's enough time.* "Is, um, anything cooking now?"

"Just the ribs. Low and slow heat. But I can whip you up something if you'd like some food."

"No. I'm not hungry for that." Eagerly, she moved her hands up the broadness of his shoulders and locked her hands around his neck. Her own low-and-slow heat sizzled in a kiss. After untying his apron, her busy hands made their way to his shirt.

His soft growl was on her lips as his arms pulled her tightly into him. "You *are* feeling better."

She nodded, unfastening his shirt one button at a time. His hands wrapped around hers, halting her renewed lust.

Frowning, he said, "We don't have to do this now. I know you love me. And I love you. But—"

Her fingers pressed gently to his lips. *Chivalry be damned.* "Hey. Just so we're clear, I'm heading to the bedroom, stripping off all my clothes, and indulging in about an hour of pure pleasure. I can either do it with you, or Maximus."

With a poorly hidden smile, Alex propped his hands on his hips. "And exactly who is Maximus?"

Beaming, she tugged another button free. "The toy Jordan gave me."

Without wasting another second, Alex whisked her into his arms and planted a soft kiss on her lips. "Maximus can wait. You're all mine, Madison Taylor."

"Yours to keep," she whispered, setting all her passion free in a lingering kiss.

In the bedroom, he sat her on the bed, but Madison immediately popped up on her knees. She had to catch a look at her boobs in the mirror across the room. Eager for a peek, she ditched her clothes in under a minute, leaving the great Alex Drake in the dust.

Her good long look resulted in a head nod, admiring Mother Nature's remarkable enhancement.

Jordan was right. My boobs are huge. Fascinated, she caressed them, wonderous in the weight cradled in her hands.

"God, you're beautiful," Alex said before suckling one with fervor.

A loud cry escaped Madison's lips before she could hold it back.

Wide-eyed and worried, he released her. "Are you all right?"

"Mm-hmm," she said, reassuring him. "Just a little . . . sensitive."

His lips curled up. "I'll be gentle."

Alex's hands softly caressed her breasts, lightly grazing her nipples. Laying her down, he again worked a soft circle of torture around her breasts with his lips, and his fingers glided down her center to enjoy her slick folds.

His lips. His touch. Every sensation crashed upon her in a symphony of lust and love for him. Her man was everything. Kind. Generous. Handsome. Daring.

And, God, his fingers . . .

Alex kept his pace, gradually pumping his fingers in and out. Slowing, he said, "Madison, are you . . ."

"Yes." She panted, grinding into his hand. Again, she huffed, "Yes!"

He knows I'm pregnant.

Working her faster, he asked, "Going to come?"

The words barely escaped his lips, and her screams filled the room in a colossal explosion. His momentum stalled as he let her float down.

Kissing her lips over and over, he gently withdrew his fingers. "I think that's a record, beautiful. I barely touched you."

With an innocent shrug, she bit her lower lip.

Glancing down her nude body, he marveled at her core. "And you're so wet."

Hungry, he dove down for a long, sensual lick from her core to her clit. Her sudden cry was more of a yelp, and again, he stopped. His concerned eyes met with Madison's pleading ones.

"Don't stop."

With a devilish grin, he raised a brow. "If you insist."

His tongue worked back and forth in intoxicating lines as she raked her nails across his shoulders. His groan vibrated against her, and he lapped at her until the tip of his tongue forced through her center.

Her climax ripped through every nerve ending in her body. He gripped her thighs hard, sending his tongue so deep, no amount of gasping could stop another wave from crashing hard. His lips drank her up, wave after wave, until there was nothing but the sweet ecstasy of his mouth.

Catching her breath, she sighed, "Oh my God."

"You're telling me. You're on fire." Alex scorched her skin, kiss by tantalizing kiss, making his way up her body until his lips were on her neck and his cock teased her entrance.

Desperate and needy, she clawed at his arms, wrapping both legs around him and pulling hard. But the solid muscles of his taut body held her off, keeping her at an unfair distance.

"Please, Alex. I need you."

"No," he said low, taking both her wrists and lifting them over her head. "I haven't touched you in weeks. I'm taking my time."

Gripping both her wrists in one hand, he used the other to caress a slow path across her breast, cupping it for a moment with the lightest kiss. It sent a shock wave through her, and she arched her back and wrapped her legs tighter around him. Controlled, he inched in.

Frantically, her body rocked, welcoming more of his dick as he stretched her wide. Working back and forth, he slowed, panting through his controlled breaths.

"God, Madison. You feel absolutely unreal. Like, I've never had you before. You're so . . ."

Gazing at her, his eyes sparkled brightly. Her hands slipped free from his grasp, cradling the hard lines of his jaw and pulling him to her mouth. The taste of her wetness was still fresh on his lips.

His thrusts dove deeper. Stronger. Pounding her into a surrender she never wanted to return from. His thumb glided around her clit, circling the sensitive nub relentlessly. Her hips shifted, and instinctively, he rolled to his back.

Delicately, his hands massaged her breasts as she rode his shaft to another peak of ecstasy.

"Yes, Madison."

His hips rushed to a rhythm that shoved every last inch of him deep into her. Gripping her thighs, he bucked to her magnetic moves. Her screams seemed to drown out everything but her own powerful climax.

Sinking back from the biggest orgasm yet, she wondered if she'd hogged all the glory. *Did Alex come?*

Relieved, she looked down on him. His eyes were sleepy, and his sexy half smile slight. Every part of his strong and magnificent body relaxed beneath her. Tenderly, her hands smoothed across the scarred muscles of his chest.

"I want to marry you, Alex Drake."

Shuddering his inhale, he beamed a wide grin at her. His fingers threaded through hers as he glanced at the ring sparkling from her finger.

Kissing her hand, he sighed. "Well, that's a relief."

"I mean . . . I don't want a big wedding, do you? Mom and Dad are in New York. Paco's here. All the people we love are here."

Alex's arms wrapped around her, pulling her body to his. Stroking her back and kissing her tenderly, he took a deep breath.

"Madison Taylor, you're my entire life. Tell me your wish and let me make it come true." With a sweet peck, he added, "It so happens that I know an ordained minister."

Despite the wave upon wave of climaxes she'd already experienced, her ecstasy was just beginning. Giggling and thoroughly delighted, she said, "And I know the perfect place."

CHAPTER 35

MADISON

AT SEVEN ON THE NOSE, Madison rushed to the elevator as it pinged, wanting to be the first to greet her parents as they arrived.

The sweet cinnamon scent of an apple pie warm from the oven came from the dish in Joy's hands. And it didn't escape Madison's watchful eyes that her father had a hold on his own hot dessert, his arm casually wrapping her mom's waist.

Grinning from ear to ear, Madison took the homemade pie, giving it a deep whiff and a loud *mmm*.

Joy grabbed Madison's elbow as she took in the penthouse, blowing out a long whistle of appreciation. "I've never seen an elevator go right into the apartment before. This place is swanky as hell."

Abruptly, Alex ended a call and headed over to greet them. His man hug with Dan was instant, but he kept a safe distance from Joy.

"It's all right. I know you didn't cheat on my daughter. And you probably ended up saving her life. How, I'll never know, if Dan and my jellybean have anything to do with it," Joy said as she yanked Alex into a tight hug.

"Well," Alex said humbly, "it was definitely a team effort. And she's saved my life in ways I can't even describe, so as far as I'm concerned, I'll be indebted forever." His comments earned him Madison's sweet smooch.

Giving her dad a subtle nod toward the kitchen, Madison carried the pie as Dan followed. Privacy was required for this conversation.

Strolling into the state-of-the-art kitchen, she couldn't take it anymore. "Well?" She let the word linger in the air like a song. Sliding the pie into the warmer, she perused the overflowing appetizers and charcuterie laid out across the marble island, finally settling on a small piece of smoked gouda that she popped into her mouth.

"Well what?" Dan patted her back, hiding the darkening pink of his face.

"Are you and Mom—"

Waving her off, Dan lowered his voice. "Hang on. We're just getting . . . reacquainted."

"Reacquainted, huh?" Madison enjoyed his embarrassment, but wondered aloud, "Reacquainted is good, isn't it?"

Dan smiled, nodding. "It's very good, but we've been apart a long time, and neither of us want you to get your hopes up. Joy's been through a lot. I wasn't the shoulder she could lean on before, but I want to be here for her now." Seeing Madison's teary grin, he continued. "Don't get carried away. One day at a time. Your mom and I have a lot of ground to cover. But I'll do whatever it takes to make it right."

After a light knock, Paco ducked his head in. "Am I interrupting?" The shake of her head was enough for Paco to push through the swinging kitchen door.

Patting Dan on the back, he quickly moved to Madison, tugging her into a brotherly embrace, then hitting her with the question creasing his usually wrinkle-free brow. "So, I hear I'm marrying you and Alex, which will be a first for me, what with the two of you being straight and all. And next weekend? What are you, pregnant?"

What are you, psychic?

Paco's chuckle immediately died when he took in her wide eyes. Checking the door to ensure no one else could hear, she shushed him.

"Frankie . . ." Dan's timid smile widened across his surprised face. "Are you?"

Slipping into her dad's arms, she nodded. "*Shhh.*" Her voice just above a whisper, she said, "Alex doesn't know. It's a surprise. But it's not why I wanted to marry him right away. After the last month . . ."

Paco grabbed her hand, giving her cheek a sweet kiss. "I get it. There's nothing like nearly losing your life to know what you want and going after it— full speed. But why the secrecy?"

Shrugging, she flashed him a devious grin. "There's sort of a bet." At Dan and Paco's eager expressions, she revealed the rest. "We're taking wagers on when Alex will figure it out."

Indignant, Paco crossed his arms. "Who exactly is *we*?"

With a gulp, she said, "It's a long story."

"I see." Paco's tone was daunting. A second later, he pulled out his wallet and fished out several hundreds from it.

Waving them before her thrilled face, he said, "How much? Dan and I are totally in. I'm guessing Mark and Jess will want in too."

~

Dinner was everything Madison could have hoped for. A tableful of family and friends, and the man of her dreams desperately trying to overfeed her.

And not because he had a clue about her baby-on-board status. It was just him. The guy who'd been caring for her long before the name Alex Drake ever entered her world. The man was built from so many broken and beautiful pieces, the result was an absolute masterpiece.

Alex slipped into the kitchen to get a surprise with Paco hot on his heels. Madison tried heeding her dad's words, keeping her hopes in check, but it was hard.

Her mom and dad were the happiest she'd seen in years. Hell, it had been years since she'd seen them together at all. And watching them now was like all the years of hurt between them had been wondrously erased.

Of course, life's not that simple. But with them hand in hand, Madison's hopes were sky high.

The unmistakable pop of a cork sounded, and Madison's heart skipped a beat when Alex and Paco entered with a tray of champagne flutes—all filled with their favorite Moët. Any concerns about drinking alcohol were instantly alleviated as Paco rushed her a flute ahead of Alex's exceptional service.

Pulling Paco down to whisper in his ear, she asked, "How'd you get the Sprite that color?"

"It's ginger ale," he said with a hurried kiss to her head.

With everyone holding their glasses ready for a toast, Alex spoke. "As you all know, Madison and I just returned from a journey that gave us a remarkable perspective on life. And as excited as I was when she agreed to marry me, I'm beyond ecstatic that she wants to do it sooner rather than later. So we've decided to get married . . . one week from today."

Their guests' roar of approval stopped as Alex clinked his glass with a fork. "But we've got everything nailed down except the location."

"I was thinking of a stunning little lakefront venue," Madison said. "Private, secluded . . . with just the people who mean the most to us."

Her hopeful expression didn't go unnoticed, and Jess ran up to her, squeezing her tightly.

"Of course! I can say definitively our home was made for beautiful weddings." Jess threw Mark an endearing look. "But we've got a ton of details to sort out, starting with the guest list . . . and your dress."

Welling up with emotion, Madison sniffled, glancing across the table at her mom. "I have a dress."

Before the words left Madison's lips, Joy's weeping turned to big-time sobbing. "Oh my goodness, of course you do. I'll have to rush home to get it."

Wrapping his arm around the mother of his daughter, Dan said, "I'll go with you." He finished the statement with a soft kiss to Joy's lips.

The onlookers were silent, letting the magical moment linger for as long as possible.

Finally, Paco lifted his glass. "To the happy couples."

Through everyone's clinking and congratulations, Madison couldn't take her eyes off Paco. Although the others might not notice, the sadness in his eyes was clear to her, despite his cheerful smile and jubilant words.

And on a wonderful day like today, that just wouldn't do.

CHAPTER 36

MADISON

"AND JUST WHERE do you think you're going?" Madison asked Paco as he prepared to go, the last guest to leave.

Mid-zip, he promptly stopped and took off his windbreaker, immediately returning it to the coat hook. "Absolutely nowhere."

With her arm linked in his, she sweetly coaxed him back toward his bedroom. "That's right, mister. You're staying here tonight. Alex is working late, and I need your company."

Grabbing her hand, Paco eagerly strolled back with her. "Then I'm staying put. You've got one hour to shower, hop in pajamas, fix the drinks, and meet me in my room."

"Done!"

Paco's bedroom in their penthouse had become his second home, complete with toothbrush and toiletries, a full wardrobe just in case, and a plush new bathrobe from an upscale spa. Madison found it amusing that he'd never go into much detail about his recent trip to the Four Seasons, Colorado.

Still, Paco traveled far less than Alex, who was out of town more often than even he cared for. During these girls-only pajama parties, Paco would grab two containers of Chinese noodles, though after the evening's banquet, the last thing on either of their minds was food.

Madison had become quite the bartender, keeping the Cointreau and

760

Luxardo cherries stocked for Paco's favorite cosmos. With the plop of a cherry in her own ginger ale, the drinks were done.

"A cosmo for me? You shouldn't have." Paying no attention to the pink drink in a martini glass, Alex took a sip of Madison's lowball. The exaggerated distaste making his eyes cross made her double over in laughter. "Bleh. Cherries in ginger ale? Your cocktail's missing something. Oh, I know. Booze."

"It's my new favorite drink." Her little white lie was true enough in the moment. Redirecting the conversation, she said, "Paco and I are having a girls' night since you have to work."

Taking her in his arms, Alex warmed her smile with a fiery kiss, releasing her only to ask, "I have to work?"

"Just long enough so I didn't lie to Paco." Innocently, she added, "I need to ask him about his love life."

"Oh." Alex let the word last until his lips were again pressing on hers. "Well, little matchmaker, I'd better get cracking on those reports."

But he didn't let her go. He seemed to be studying her.

"Is it possible you're getting more beautiful by the day?" Giving her an appreciative once-over, he asked, "Has something changed?"

Over-the-moon ecstatic, Madison could only nod.

Again, Alex looked her over, smiling curiously. "What?"

With a tender kiss, she whispered to his lips, "No hints." Grabbing the drinks, she headed back to Paco's room.

Alex frowned, asking, "Is it your hair?"

Delighted, she hollered back, "Nope."

In his room, Paco was happily sprawled on the bed, reading a novel. Snuggly warm in his own gray flannel pants, he'd donned a noticeably familiar purple Queen shirt.

"Funny," Madison said, "I have that same shirt."

"And now I have it. You know the rules. You let me rummage through your wardrobe every so often, and I do your toes." Snatching the case filled with the finest in Walgreen's mani-pedi goods, he showcased it, sweeping his hand across it lavishly. "And I always keep my promises."

Handing him his drink, she proposed a toast. "To family."

Tenderly, he repeated, "To family." Clinking his glass to hers, they each took a welcome sip, with simultaneous murmurs of appreciation. "Foot massage first?"

Squealing, she said, "Really?" Before he could answer, her butt was on the bed, feet front and center, ready for some pampering.

Paco pressed his thumbs into the balls of her feet, melting every sore muscle into submission.

"That's amazing," she said with a sigh. "You've never massaged my feet before."

"In my defense, you've never been pregnant before. Besides, I've got to spoil you while I can. Once Alex finds out, he'll hog pampering duty like nobody's business."

Her light laughter drifted away. "Speaking of romance . . ."

Paco's brows popped high. "Who was speaking of romance?"

"I was." After a cheesy grin and a moment of silence, she asked, "How's *P*?"

The carefree look on Paco's face dissolved into a sour expression completed with furled brows and puckered lips. "How should I know?"

Undeterred, Madison bit her lip, waiting for him to ease out his feelings.

Sneaking a peek at her eager eyes, he rolled his. "Pierre Roca's not who you think he is, Madison. He's impulsive, dangerous, reckless—"

"Easy. I need my feet to walk down the aisle," she said, begging for leniency as Paco's massaging hands turned aggressive. After a quick stop, he restarted, much more tenderly.

Apologetic, he asked, "Better?"

With a beaming grin, she nodded. "*P* is a lot of things, for sure. I'll give you he's impulsive and dangerous. Sounds sexy as hell and very much like someone I know. Happens to be devastatingly handsome, also like someone I know. Reckless? That's where we'll agree to disagree."

Fired up, Paco jumped off the bed, his wild hand gestures punctuating every word. "That asshole knew exactly what Jordan was planning."

"I seriously doubt that. *Nobody* knows exactly what Jordan's planning. Ever."

Pleading, Paco held Madison's hands, stroking her knuckles. "Madison, you were locked in a trunk, just outside the building I was in, less than thirty yards from me. We could've been working together. He nearly got you killed."

"That's unfair. Jordan nearly got me killed. And crazy as it sounds, it was because she was trying to help. She had me in the trunk for safekeeping."

Eyeing Madison's glass, he asked, "Are you sure you haven't been drinking?"

Thinking it over, she said, "That definitely sounded better in my head."

Giddy with laughter, she took another sip. "In her defense, Jordan actually made it as comfortable as possible."

Paco's unamused squint did the talking for him.

"It's true. And she only brought me to Zane when she was confident she could pull off a plan to save both me *and* Alex. Had she not helped, and *P* with her, the team might have been too late."

Paco gazed at his glass, finally taking a sip.

"Let me ask you something. You found *P* being viciously beaten by Zane . . . who was probably just about to kill him. Do you know why *P* was there?"

Paco's nonchalant shrug offered nothing.

"Because *he* actually saved me. Maybe you missed that on the drone footage, but *P* was the driver of that car. He's the one who took on Zane. He told me to run, basically taking my place as Zane's punching bag. And the only reason the two of you found us was because he put the tracker in the watch Jordan latched on my wrist."

Paco's thoughtful glance was encouraging.

"And one more thing. The reason Jordan even showed up at that building was because I begged her to help him, even though I had no idea how close they were. Paco . . ." Her voice choked up. "*P* wasn't expecting to be saved."

Paco's sip seemed to last a full minute as the gears in his head cranked away. With a final swallow, he shook his head. "It's just a bad idea, *hermanita*."

Madison loved how he adored her, but this *little sister* wasn't backing down. Defiantly, she shot out, "Why?"

"Maybe I don't find him attractive. Did you ever think of that?"

"Oh, the kiss viewed around the world says otherwise."

Fighting his smile, he offered a rebuttal. "Then maybe I'm not looking for a relationship."

"Now *that* definitely makes sense. I mean, you've had some of the nicest, most smoking-hot guys I've ever seen coming and going in and out of your life. And I've never seen any one guy twice. But just because you're not looking for a relationship doesn't mean you should turn away from one that's looking for you."

Deflating, Paco sat on the bed. His far-away stare inspired Madison to wrap her arms around him. When he finally spoke, his voice was soft with heartbreak. "You know why."

Squeezing him tightly, her voice was gentle, barely above a whisper, as if anything stronger would wound him. "I loved Jack too. We all did. But Jack would want you to be happy."

Teary, Paco turned away, but her palm on his cheek helped her reclaim his gaze.

"You—more than anyone—deserve to be happy. Besides, your initials are P and R. So are his. And you're from Puerto Rico. Tell me that's not one hell of a sign."

The realization hit Paco as hard as the booze. Bursting out with a laugh and a few big tears, he conceded. "There's no arguing with that logic, is there?"

Kissing his cheek, she said, "Not if you know what's good for you."

CHAPTER 37

MADISON

THE WEEK FLEW BY, and Madison couldn't fathom how the guest list had bloomed from ten to twenty of their closest friends into fifty. But apologizing to Jess repeatedly did no good. Jess and Mark were all in. It affirmed their motto . . . the more, the merrier.

"Jess, what did you mean when you said your home was made for weddings?"

Jess beamed. "Family weddings always happen here, starting with mine, funny enough."

Madison had to hear this. "Back before the mansion was here? You know, I don't even know how you and Mark met."

With a big hug, Jess headed out, saying, "Oh, it's a romantic, wondrous, dangerous story that's just what we need . . . for another day." Her eyes gleamed with mystery as she left to tend to the unending list of matron-of-honor duties.

From her seat with the glam squad, Madison could see out the picture window. The grand mansion nestled in an isolated area of the Adirondack mountains was picturesque, surrounded by sunshine and blue skies. Alex had his personal event planner take care of everything for the wedding, down to the last detail.

Rows of white chairs filled a small area in front of a custom arbor, over-flowing with white and blush roses and peonies, English ivy, and wisps of sheer fabric and satin. Against the crystalline lake and setting sun, no matter which way you looked, it was breathtaking.

As a glam team finalized her hair and makeup, all Madison could see was her gown. The simple elegance of the off-the-shoulder gown shimmered with the finest dots of stunning beads. It was an original design.

Madison first heard the story as a little girl, about how her mother and grandmother stayed up for three nights straight to finish stitching it by hand for Joy to wear in her wedding to Dan before his first deployment.

Welling up in happiness at the perfect, unaltered fit, she was given a playful scolding by Lisa, her makeup artist.

"I only have so much waterproof mascara. We need to make it last."

She nodded, denying the tears Lisa endlessly dabbed.

"Madison . . ."

The breathy adoration of her mother tore Madison from the spackle-and-paint session as Joy gave her the biggest hug.

"You're so beautiful. And you can't see the new stitches at all." Joy checked and rechecked the bodice, where she and Madison spent a little time last night sewing a small pocket on the inside.

"It's perfect," Madison said. "Did you bring it?"

Her something borrowed was one of Jack's dog tags, removed from its chain so she could keep it tucked in the pocket and close to her heart during the ceremony. Her mother had the other one, hanging from its chain and hidden beneath her dress.

Fussing with the gown, Joy approved. "And you've got my dress, so that's something old. What about something new?"

Madison flashed her engagement ring.

"Put that hand down. Are you trying to blind me?" Joy's laughter brought out Madison's. "How about something blue?"

Slipping a blue handkerchief from her bosom, Madison smiled as her pride bubbled over. It was her grandfather's, carried on his wedding day. Her father carried it at Jack's graduation from West Point, and at Madison's graduation from high school.

The steel-blue silk was plain and understated but would match an assortment of suit colors Alex gravitated toward. Her thumb lightly rubbed the delicate cross-stitch in one corner. On behalf of the Taylor men, Dan had agreed with the design she'd stitched along the border last night, not too floral or frilly. The three words read WORLD'S GREATEST DAD.

"I'm giving it to Alex tonight. I can't think of a better wedding gift for the man who has everything."

"But what about the bet?" Joy asked.

Astounded, Madison gaped at her. "And exactly how much are you in for?"

Indignant, Joy said, "I'm not. And what your father does with his money is his business." She winked.

"Well, I'm the only one who believes Alex will figure it out before the wedding night, but the countdown is killing me. If he doesn't figure it out, I might have to delay his gift. I think the latest guess is after we return from our honeymoon." Refolding it carefully, Madison slid the handkerchief back inside her bra. Once again, she checked her bodice, asking, "How do I look?"

Joy welled up. "You're getting married. And my baby is having a baby." As she blubbered, the makeup artist grabbed her with a "not you too" under her breath.

Watching her mom get primped and pampered lifted Madison even higher. It wasn't until her own wavy locks were set, and the veil positioned just right, that her reflection stole her gaze.

Hand over her heart, she whispered, "I'm getting married, Jack. And you'll be right here with me."

～

With the small orchestra in place and everyone seated, Madison saw Alex and her breath hitched. The gorgeous man at the end of a very long satin aisle was waiting for her.

The fabric path didn't hold much support against the grass beneath her feet, and her heels wobbled as she took a few hesitant steps. Grateful to be flanked by both her mother and father, she pulled their linked arms in a little tighter.

"Everything all right?" her dad asked.

Nodding with a smile, she said, "It's fine. A wobbly shoe brought me into Alex Drake's life. But I'm going to try not to full-out break the heel or fall on my butt this time."

At Dan's nod, the strings and harp began Pachelbel's Canon in D, and all the guests stood and turned toward her, smiling.

With her bouquet steadied, Madison took in an emotional breath. The fragrant roses sweetened her inhale, calming her unexpected butterflies. Her heart pounding out a steady, triumphant beat, she let her parents lead her to the man whose smile always set her at ease.

Something about seeing Alex in a traditional tuxedo was absolutely swoon-worthy. He'd always been a looker, but today he was the handsomest she'd ever seen him.

Well, except naked, of course. And that tie is definitely staying on tonight.

Surrounded by her bridesmaids and his groomsmen against the sparkling lake, Madison felt nothing could be more perfect. The approaching sunset cast the sky with rich hues of orange and gold against a bright blue backdrop.

Her beautiful brother Paco wore a tux very much like Alex's, but with an orchid gracing his lapel instead of a rose. It suited him perfectly as he officiated. His words were eloquent, but her attention just couldn't be held.

Alex lost the remarkable smile he'd worn just moments ago. The slightest furl crinkled his brow as he stared, then slowly dropped his gaze.

Uncertain, she mouthed, *"Are you okay?"*

But he wasn't.

Dropping his head into his palm, he said, "Stop."

CHAPTER 38

ALEX

FROZEN, Alex stood there, too stunned for words. He couldn't breathe or move. Paco's gaze bore into him, but he ignored it. He wanted a moment. *Needed* a moment.

The pounding in his ears was different, not the normal panic attack he had ways of working around. No, this was a whole new sensation, dropping him to a knee in front of an expectant crowd now gasping with surprise and concern.

Slowly, Madison lowered herself in front of him, tenderly caressing his cheek. Despite her worried gaze, all he could do was stare at her in disbelief. Nuzzling into her caress, he laid a tender kiss on her palm.

He spoke low, almost failing to form words. "Madison . . . I'm sorry . . . I just . . ."

Deep in his own thoughts, he hadn't noticed his own tear fall until her tender thumb was swiping it. *Could she be more beautiful?*

Unprepared, he took a few shallow breaths before stammering out, "Are . . . are you pregnant?"

Tears filled her eyes, and the crease in her brow smoothed. Her smile warmed his heart as she nodded.

Elated, Alex bolted up, lifting her high into a spin. He cut her delighted giggles short with his exuberant kiss, needing to feel the softness of her lips. He kissed her over and over as he returned her to her feet. Even with an exaggerated clearing of Paco's throat, this kiss wasn't over until he was damn good and ready.

Finally, Alex made an announcement to the crowd. "Sorry, everyone. We can proceed. I just had to stop for a moment when I realized I'm going to be a father."

Half their guests erupted in elated *aw's*, while the exclamations of the other half sounded deflated and disappointed.

Confused, Alex scanned the audience, noting several of them preoccupied with counting cash.

"Don't mind them." Madison gently stroked his jaw, grinning. "Our baby's college fund is in full swing."

Blubbering, Paco wiped his streaming tears as he handed Madison a wad of cash. She discreetly slipped it in Alex's pocket, and he seized another chance at a few more kisses.

After a needed breath, Alex rested his forehead to Madison's. "You ready to officially be mine, beautiful?"

"Yes," she whispered.

Alex rubbed his nose lightly against hers before he stood up straight. Once he nodded to Paco, his emotional officiant took the cue.

"I'm not sure where I left off, so let me begin again. Family and friends," Paco said, carrying his voice high across the canvas of smiling faces in the golden hues of sunset. "When I look at the two people before me, I see a man and a woman destined for each other. A small-town girl who unlocked the heart of a workaholic tycoon, and an unlikely hero who'd secretly cared for her long before they'd ever met. I've been humbled and honored to witness their love story. For ten years, I've watched each of you. From your struggles and hardship, your broken paths brought you together—finding love in the arms of each other, and keeping it forevermore. At this time, Dan and Joy will hand over the rings."

Dan held out the elegant band, teasing Alex with a quick withdraw as soon as his fingers reached for the ring. "You're not getting my daughter like that," he said, joking.

Catching on, Alex laid his hand on top for a shake—a military coin exchange. Instantly, Dan flipped their hands, landing the ring in Alex's palm.

Yanking him into a strong hug, Alex reassured him. "I'll take care of her."

Dan wrapped his arms tightly around Alex, choking up. "I know you will. And my little Frankie's the only girl in the world who can really take care of you, AJ. You've been family for a long time, and you've been through a lot. But I couldn't be prouder . . . because you might be making my daughter a Drake, but today you're one of us too. A Taylor. And my son."

Both men took another moment to connect, wiping their eyes and clearing their throats. With a pat to Alex's back, Dan smiled at the women, arm in arm and teary, who'd been watching them.

With everyone set, Alex took Madison's delicate hand, smiling at the stark contrast to her strength and courage. Sliding on the slight halo band next to her engagement ring, he said, "Madison, before you, I was empty—I existed in darkness and heartache, pain and regret. Now, every day is filled with happiness beyond what I could have ever imagined. Because of you, my life overflows with amazement and joy, endless adventures, and the deepest love. From this day forward, I vow to love and protect you. To comfort and cherish you. Today, in the presence of our family and friends, I make you my wife."

Kissing her lips might have been premature—again—but holding off another second was beyond his control. Her light sniffles caused him to wipe her tears before giving her his hand.

Slipping Alex's ring on his finger, Madison began. "Alex Drake, you swept me away with your protectiveness and caring, and took my breath away with your warmth. You captured my heart with every selfless act. You've stood beside me in ways no one else could. You're the man of my dreams, and from this day forward, I vow to love and protect you, to comfort and cherish you. Today, in the presence of our family and friends, and as Jack watches over us, I make you my husband."

Paco placed his hands on their clasped ones. "Looking at the love between Alex Drake, the man I'm proud to call my best friend, and Madison Taylor, my cherished *hermanita*, it is with the greatest privilege that I now pronounce you husband and wife. And *now*, Mr. Drake, you may kiss your bride."

The permission wasn't exactly necessary, but any excuse would do to take Madison in his arms again. As Alex's lips descended on hers, he forgot about anything and everything but the overwhelming love he had for her. The love of his life, and the woman carrying his child.

CHAPTER 39

MADISON

THE EVENING GLOWED with strings of tiny twinkling lights and a landscape dotted with candles. Although Richard and Jaclyn were inseparable, Madison handing over her bouquet to the beautiful bride-to-be somehow connected them even more. And they weren't alone. Jess and Mark. Her parents. It was like Cupid's cute little chubby butt was busy at work, shooting love arrows in every direction imaginable. The night was pure magic.

The dance floor was hopping with booty shakes and bare feet, and later, with softer, romantic ballads woven into the lineup. Paco twirled the bride in a well-rehearsed move.

As the music slowed, Stone cut in. "May I?" His distinctly weakened condition showed, but his bright eyes affirmed nothing was holding him back from the festivities.

Letting go of Madison, Paco extended his hand for a shake.

Instead, Stone placed a small box in his palm. "*P* asked me to deliver this to you."

Paco thanked him with a nod and gave them the dance space.

As Stone and Madison swayed slowly to the music, he said, "You make a beautiful bride, Mrs. Drake."

Mrs. Drake.

Madison's cheeks hurt from smiling so much that night, but his words pulled her exuberance wide across her face. "And I'm glad you were able to come. Jordan mentioned you were going to try."

Scoffing at her words, he said, "Trying is for weaklings. I simply do."

"Is that some lethal operative mantra?" she joked.

"No." After a second, he corrected her assumption. "Those, my dear, are the teachings of Yoda."

Laughing, she said, "Of course."

"You know, Madison, a very long time ago, I came across one of the most remarkable people I'd ever known. He was bright, loyal, a born leader, and someone who always sought the truth. At his heart, he was a Finder. And no matter what, he wanted my assurance that his family would always be safe."

Stone's kind words, obviously about Jack, endeared him to her.

"I'm part of a dying breed," Stone said, "and a good Finder is rare. In supremely uncharacteristic form, I'd like to make you a proposition."

Realizing he might or might not have spoken with Crystal and Jordan, Madison stayed quiet, intent on listening.

"You are in possession of both pieces of the puzzle, the decoder and the message. That puts you in a precarious position. You have power, but don't know to what extent. And you've become a target, but you'll never know exactly by whom."

"Mr. Stone, if you're trying to—"

"I'm not trying to do anything but perhaps give you a bit of mentoring. Jack's secret has stayed buried for ten years. It's your call whether you become a Keeper, or . . ." He stalled, mindfully checking the crowd around them.

"Or?"

His smile warmed. "Or continue your journey as a Finder. These aren't decisions we make. Life makes them for us."

Madison nodded with understanding.

"So," he said, "don't be surprised if *P* and Jordan are around. Crystal is, of course, a less visible part of the package. And every now and again, you and I may cross paths. We've all agreed. And frankly, our proximity might be enough to keep some factions away. No matter what you decide, you'll always need protection. Especially with a little one on the way."

Settling into his arms, she wrapped him in a tight hug. "Thank you."

Dropping a gentle kiss on her head, he said, "Like Jack, you'll forever be one of us."

"A Finder?" she asked.

"More than that," he said. "Family."

They continued their dance, but with a sudden shift of his weight, Madison could tell Stone needed to sit down. "Do you mind if I get off my feet?" These shoes are killing me."

He nodded his relief. She walked him to Jordan's table, where *P* also sat, with Crystal and Corey at a nearby table moved closer beside them.

Admiring Jordan's elegance, Madison couldn't believe how she managed to make a simple black pantsuit look remarkable. The elaborate diamond necklace she wore added a stunning touch. And her platinum-blond hair was now tinted a wavy honey-brown, styled to resemble a queen of the silver screen.

Trying to slip her a compliment, Madison said, "Jordan, you look absolutely—"

"Bored?"

Jordan's response earned her a cuddly hug from behind. Kissing her cheek, Madison could see the smile struggling for freedom.

Keeping her voice just above a whisper, Madison said, "You know what you need?"

"An enema," Crystal called out from the next table, gleeful in her mischief.

"A fifth of scotch?" Stone asked.

P raised a brow, smirking. "A three-way?"

"A date," Madison said matter-of-factly.

All of them stared at her in shock. And perhaps horror.

"Mind if we join you?"

On Alex's arm was a shapely blonde. Her simple strapless gown molded to her form in ways that suggested it had been sewn in place, but still laid across her body with an elegance that gave her a regal air. She waved a shy hello to everyone at the table.

Introducing her, Alex politely said, "Ladies and gentlemen, this is Charity."

Wide-eyed in her stunned trance, Jordan stood. Glancing between the two women, Alex tried but failed to hide his smile at the obvious electricity between them, and he returned to his bride.

Fascinated, Jordan asked, "How did Alex find you?"

Charity shrugged. "Alex knows everyone. How do you two know each other?"

Jordan's crimson lips smiled wide. "I'd love to show you sometime."

At the innuendo, Madison glanced away. But like everyone else at the table, she stayed glued to the conversation.

Charity dropped her gaze with a bashful admission. "Before we go too far, I need to tell you something. Charity's not my real name."

With a sweeping kiss that surprised the hell out of their rapt audience, Jordan whispered to Charity's lips, "Jordan's not mine. Is there anything here you need? Champagne? Cake?"

"Just you."

Without so much as a good-bye, the women left. Good thing, too, before they became the erotic floor show at Madison's wedding.

"It was nice seeing you again, Charity," Stone said. Looking at Alex, he added, "You're not the only one who 'knows everyone.'"

The air quotes from the elder Stone had everyone rolling with laughter. Alex's history with one too many a woman was legendary, but the hysterical comment nearly made ginger ale shoot out Madison's nose.

CHAPTER 40

PACO

Unable to move even a few steps without chatting with friends, Paco finally made his way to the bar. The fizzy tartness of his vodka tonic pushed an *ahh* from his lips as the small box Stone had handed him captured his attention.

Opening it, Paco found a ring. Fancy gothic letters spelling out West Point surrounded a small sparkling stone. He pulled the ring out, squinting enough to make out the name Jackson D. Taylor inscribed on the inside of the band.

How the hell did he get Jack's ring? Urgently, Paco scanned the room for *P*, who was clearly headed out, his coat on as he exited the foyer. As nonchalantly as possible, Paco darted after him in a subtle chase. But like old times, it took some doing to catch up with the man who could come and go with remarkable speed.

Rushing through the closing front door, Paco called out. "Going somewhere?"

P stopped but didn't turn around. "Home. I'm going to visit my mom before my next job." The torment in his tone drew Paco closer. "Did Stone—"

"Yes." Paco displayed the ring now gracing his right ring finger. "But why did you have it?"

P turned slowly. "I didn't. Stone did."

"A souvenir?"

P shook his head. "Motivation. Before Jack's last assignment, Stone told him how dangerous it was and gave him an opportunity to back out. I think the man was having second thoughts about sending his protégé into the wild.

Stone gets protective that way. Instead of skirting the assignment, Jack gave him the ring, with a confident 'I'll pick it up when I return.'" *P* took in a deep breath. "Whenever our investigating ran cold, Stone wore it, determined to do right by Jack."

"So, why not give it to Madison? Or Dan and Joy?"

"The rights of inheritance should first go to the spouse."

Paco frowned. "We weren't married."

"But that was Jack's intention."

Stepping even closer, Paco pocketed his hands. "Very few people know that, and I doubt any of them told you. How do you know?"

"I . . ." *P* paused a moment. "I did a lot of messed-up stuff when I was younger."

"Join the fucking club. Now I can guess the worst, or you can just tell me."

Frustrated, *P* let it all out. "Fine. Stone wouldn't tell me exactly where your assignment was. Obviously, he knew I liked you a little more than I should. Telling me *no* was his mistake. I built a small tracker, something quick and dirty that sent a signal once a day to preserve battery. I slipped it in your bag at Dulles. Back then, a Latin guy dressed as a baggage handler pretty much had free rein. I kept tabs on you in the Middle East, but I couldn't get too close there. Italy was another story. And . . ." He shrugged, pausing for air. Then with a huff, he admitted his wrongdoings. "Bugging your room wasn't exactly rocket science."

Despite Paco's wide-eyed shock, *P* didn't slow down.

"I just wanted an upper hand. Your assignment would be over soon. I'd planned to learn everything I could about you. What you liked. What you didn't like. What you wanted. Even, maybe, to know for sure if I could be the person to give you what you deserved. Like an idiot, I tried to start a relationship built on deception. Well, let's just say my punishment fit the crime."

"What do you mean?"

P's face crumpled. "I heard Jack's proposal. And enough of what went on afterward to know you'd accepted."

Suspicious, Paco glared, keeping his tone steady and even. Dark, but controlled. Accusation laced his words. "And what did you do?"

Snapping from the memory, *P* met his eyes, the blood draining from his face. "Nothing." Adamantly, he repeated, "Nothing. I swear on my mother's life. I left and went home. After the attack, Jordan found me and told me what happened. It was goddamnn Armageddon. Missions like ours never get compromised. It meant we were all compromised, and every one of our lives was at risk. The plan was for each of us to disappear."

Recalling their conversation from the car, Paco couldn't reconcile the disconnect. "But you didn't disappear. You said you backed me at the Pentagon."

P smirked, caught in the trap of his own recounting. "Predicting your moves was easy because you were my pet project. I'd studied you."

"Obsessively?" Paco's comment was only half teasing.

"I prefer the label 'thorough.' Anyway, trying to convince you would've been a waste of time. You weren't about to let this go. But you needed reinforcements, and without Jack or Alex, you were vulnerable."

"How did you know I wouldn't let this go?"

"Broken hearts tend to fight the hardest, and yours was shattered into a million pieces. So I grabbed two of the best reinforcements in the world. Stone would do anything for Jack. He was easy to convince. Jordan's allegiance was bought with a lot of begging, cash, and IOUs. We figured out your most likely courses of action, and I reactivated the tracker. Of course, you picked the worst possible scenario, hitting the Pentagon like an unarmed, pissed-off bunny stomping into a lion's den."

Really?

Apparently, Paco's thought pushed past his Botox, because *P* squelched an apologetic chuckle.

Repressing his own smirk, Paco nudged him for more. "I see. Saving my daring cotton tail became your new mission. If everything was so admirable and on the up-and-up, why not tell me what you did for Madison?"

P responded, his tortured gaze laying way to a heavy shrug. "Because it wouldn't matter. I knew Jordan's plan. And without a doubt, she had Madison. I could've told you and I didn't. I picked a side. And as much as I know you, Paco Robles, I know above all else that you need loyalty. Honesty. To know the people you love aren't being placed in harm's way for strategy's sake. I was none of those things to you, and I crossed an unforgivable line."

The hard truth left them both speechless. Paco watched him turn away, as if he could hide his sadness.

Checking his watch, *P* cleared his throat. "I need to go."

"Flight to catch?" Paco asked, disappointed with the sudden ending to the conversation.

P nodded. Without a look back, he walked away.

CHAPTER 41

PACO

PACO LET *P* take a few more steps before he called out, "Not even a good-bye kiss?"

Apparently, those five little words were enough to stop the man in his tracks. Paco's relief was swept away in an undertow of emotion as *P* rushed back, swift and strong, laying a deep, desperate kiss on Paco's unprepared lips.

He warmed up quickly, but as abruptly as the kiss started, it stopped.

P backed away, apparent uncertainty robbing his confidence. "You'll always wonder where my allegiance lies."

"No," Paco whispered, still catching his breath. "I won't. Jordan told me where you stand. She said if she killed me, you'd kill her. That seems to pretty much sum it up."

Their tease of a kiss rekindled, then frustratedly halted again. *For the love of God, now what?*

P's concern shot out in a breathy question. "Is this because of Madison?"

Smoothing a bold hand across the muscles of *P*'s chest, Paco kept his response casual. *Damn, he's built.* "Does it matter?"

Fervent in his gaze, *P* wasted less than a second thinking about it. "No, it doesn't matter. I'll kiss you . . . hold you . . . worship you. Do anything to be in your life. Give you anything I have and everything I am. But I need something too. I'll never keep anything from you again. And selfishly—unfairly—I need the same from you."

Meeting the seriousness of *P*'s desperate gaze, Paco blew out a breath. "Another fucking kiss and I'm getting ultimatums. Next, you'll be taking a knee."

Shaking his head, *P* stepped back, and Paco suddenly missed the glint that warmed his eyes just a moment ago.

Relaxing his faux irritation, Paco explained with an easygoing grin.

"Fine. The answer is yes, but not as payment for services. I've known people like you. Strategies bombard your overactive brain from early morning until late at night. You'd never go one-on-one with a dangerous adversary like Zane when he was armed. Which means . . ." Paco paused for effect. "You had a .45, right?"

A skeptical smile emerged as *P* nodded. "How did you know that?"

"I have my own love-hate relationship with them. They get the job done but tend to jam at the worst possible times, which you'd only know if you'd tried firing it."

P's grin stretched wider. "Over the shoulder, as concealed as I could. My eardrum might never recover, but I had no choice. I wasn't supposed to intervene. We didn't have enough information yet. He'd been clinging to Madison, so I kept close. But the situation was escalating fast. I knew enough about Zane MacIntyre to know, if he really was who we suspected, he could snap on Madison without much provocation. I'd seen the Ghost Wolf's handiwork before. The sick fuck loves torture and shops the images of his victims around to get work. So I took the shot." Dropping his head, *P* grumbled. "Nothing but an empty click. I hoped Madison saw my signal—that I was working with Jordan. Then I acted."

"So," Paco said, "you went toe-to-toe with Zane, even though you were matched in brute strength, and he was armed. In our business, that indicates only one thing. If your Hail Mary didn't work, you were ready to die for the cause. And for Madison. In my book, that makes you a good guy and a man of action."

Intentionally, Paco moved closer, feeling the heat of *P*'s body but resisting his lips. "Both are enough to pique my interest, even if it means you're batshit crazy and will fight a psychopath when your odds are piss-poor."

Staring at Paco's lips, *P* seemed equally determined to keep their mouths a tortured breath away. "It's probably a bad time to tell you I'm an adrenaline junkie."

Admiring the salt-and-pepper accents at his temples, Paco then stared into *P*'s magnetic dark eyes. *God, he's sexy.* "It's only fair you understand my reputation. I'm a notorious bachelor. I measure relationships in hours and days, not weeks. I bore easily and have grown accustomed to staying unattached."

P's eyes twinkled. "So, I'm the longest relationship you've had in a while?"

His hand slid around to the muscles of Paco's back, but hesitated in pulling him in. They both inhaled.

"Just so we're clear . . ." Paco licked his lips. The lingering taste of *P*'s kiss was delicious. Sexual tension like this made the man a smoking-hot unicorn.

Play it cool? Or like a player?

"The relationship clock hasn't started until I find every last tattoo on your body." Paco's devilish half smile shone proudly.

P's gaze washed over him before his mouth brushed against Paco's, teasing but just short of a kiss. "Does it count that I know where every one of yours are?"

Stunned, Paco had no comeback, giving *P* all the invitation he needed. The slow sizzle of his lips burned through Paco's last bit of resistance.

Paco kissed him back fervently, needing to know every dark corner of this man's mouth. Losing himself in the sweeping duel of their tongues, the thought of ever kissing another man suddenly became impossible.

A barrage of pops and small explosions slowly tore their kiss apart. Looking up, they found the night sky ablaze with sparkling fireworks.

With a shuddering breath, *P* exhaled. "Your kiss has me seeing stars."

Paco studied the scars *P* had sustained recently. His eyes welling with tears, he tightened his embrace. *I nearly lost him too.* "I think you need looking after. Maybe a little spoiling too. *If* you're good."

P's flirty words were at his ear. "Is it possible for a man to be good—all the time—yet never?"

With a chuckle, Paco surrendered to the light, irresistible kisses trailing down his neck. "Anything's possible. Remember how you asked what triggered my memories of you?"

Curious, *P* arched a brow and gave him a cautious nod.

"When I met you, all those years ago, I had the craziest feeling. And sitting next to you in the car, I sensed it again. It consumes me, even now."

Frowning his worry, *P* asked, "What is it?"

Tenderly, Paco said, "That you'd be good for me."

P's dark eyes warmed as his concerns seemed to melt away. "That, *mi amor,* is all I've ever wanted to be."

Their lips said everything without saying a word. Without a doubt, *P* was missing his flight.

CHAPTER 42

ALEX

"Madison?"

Unyielding energy pulsed through every tense nerve of Alex's body, but he tried calming down. Waiting was never his strong suit, and tonight—their wedding night—it was driving him out of his ever-loving mind.

Since he'd realized she was carrying his child, everything changed. She changed. But more than that, so did he.

From the moment he'd first laid eyes on her, Alex had needed Madison in his life. Not in a million years had he imagined how completely she'd become the center of his universe. Whenever they were apart, he ached with longing so intense, it was tangible. But tonight it was torture.

Was her delay premeditated, building the anticipation until he broke down the doors and took her in the middle of her closet? Was that a thing? A woman's fantasy? To have a man tear off her clothes in the middle of a massive walk-in closet filled to the rafters with couture clothing and high-end heels?

With his jaw clenched and his rod throbbing, Alex decided there was only one way to find out.

Shedding his boxers and stripped down to nothing but the bow tie her seductive eyes had insisted on, he stalked to the double doors. Before he grabbed the handles, the doors flew open.

Madison stepped to him, and Alex lost all thought.

Stunned, he took in the mesmerizing lines and voluptuous curves of her breathtaking body. Taking her hand, he kissed it, admiring the ring on her finger. The colossal diamond twinkled in the glow of a dozen candles, but the elegance of the thin band next to it caught his eye.

Under his breath, he marveled. "My wife."

Like a gift, he undid her cream silk robe, washing his gaze down her fitted lace bodice. The trace of a thong left just enough to his imagination, not that he needed it. Every inch of Madison had long ago been burned on his mind. And even with the subtle changes happening before his eyes, knowing her was his passion. He studied her, eager to keep up.

Alex's gaze followed her thigh-high stockings to her crystal-studded Louboutins. Smiling, he admired their height. *Six inches.*

No doubt Madison could rock a high heel, but she'd been suffering in one heel or another all day, and clearly these were completely for his benefit.

When she turned toward the bed, he said, "Stop where you are."

She paused, an uncertain giggle escaping her lips.

Lifting her off her feet and tucking her breathtaking body against his chest, he smiled. "Those heels are staying on, but your feet are done touching the floor tonight, Mrs. Drake."

His powerful arms laid her along the length of the bed before he delicately unlaced her bodice. His tender kisses discovered the new fullness of her breasts, careful to avoid her gorgeous pink nipples.

With a deep inhale, she arched her back. When he licked lightly across one nipple, she moaned. "Mmm . . ."

"Mmm, good?" he asked.

Her sweet smile encouraged him. "Mmm—very good."

Madison slid one knee over him and moved to climb on top, but the heat of her desperate kiss was more than his crumbling will could take.

"Oh no you don't." Alex glided his hand down her body to massage the inside of her thigh. "You're getting too hot to handle. I need to learn all the new ways to touch you."

Sliding the lacy fabric aside, his finger made a shallow dip into her center. Her hips bucked as he swiped her soaked folds, grazing her clit before sucking his finger clean.

"You're so much sweeter."

Teasing him, she shoved her thong down her thighs. Her own fingers slid across her ripe pussy, smearing her glistening wetness up and down. Spellbound, he let her needy hand play to her heart's content.

Before she came, she lifted her fingers to his lips. Sucking each finger into his mouth, he cleaned them of every last drop.

Low, he commanded, "More."

Alex's lips descended to hers, and his hand guided her movements, giving her a different rhythm for her growing pleasure.

"Yes," he whispered. "Like that."

He laid every kiss down Madison's body as tenderly as possible, tugging the lacy thong down the length of her legs. Her body broke out in a shiver.

"I'm close," she said, panting.

Harder than an obelisk, he gritted out, "Slower."

His hungry tongue dove inside her, and her eruption was instant. Her screams forced his lips to close in on her clit.

As her trembling legs straddled him, he moved a finger deep inside. Her fists tore at the sheets, and her heels dug into his back. Needing more, he pressed a second finger in. Her tightness was different, and rediscovering her body would become his new mission.

As Alex sucked her swollen peak hard, the hot walls of her pussy clenched down, pulsing his fingers to a stop. Her rapid-fire orgasm captivated him.

Her eager little body rebounded, with no intention of floating back down. Ready for another touch-and-go in paradise, Madison was already on her hands and knees.

Sweetly, she said, "I need you. Please."

Her begging was always his downfall. His best-laid plans were tossed to oblivion as the head of his cock touched her entrance. Before she could throw herself full force on him, he was ready.

Grabbing her hips, he laid a few kisses on her back. "Not so fast."

Alex kept his movement subtle, and her throat released a series of sweet, intoxicating moans. No matter how soft his touch, his featherlight fingers against her were sweeping her to the brink.

"Let's try something," he whispered, rolling her on her side and spooning against her back.

Madison whimpered, and he loved it.

"I need to know if anything is uncomfortable. Understand?" he asked, and she nodded.

Stretching her swollen walls wide, he shoved every inch of his length deep inside her at once. The urgency of his thrusts was fueled by each of her desperate screams.

Alex's body struggled, pulling away only to force his needs harder against her with each pass. Under his breath, he cursed the sweet agony as her body writhed for more of his thickness.

Her nails clawed across his thigh, and his momentary control was lost. Each thrust was a new rhythm brought on by the tender moans from her throat. Clasping his hand to the dew of her plump folds, his fingers rushed, sliding back and forth to match his strides.

"I—"

Her quivering lips and staggered breaths meant he was in for the euphoric race of his life.

"Yes!" He huffed out the word before crying out.

Alex rode the waves of their climax until his balls squeezed the last pulse from his cock. Completely spent, he breathed deeply. His pounding had been rough and hard, and maybe more than her sensitive body could handle.

Still struggling to catch his breath, he heaved through his words. "Madison, are you okay?"

Her response was quiet and stammering. "No . . . no, I'm not okay." After a few breaths, she smiled and continued. "It was heaven. I'm perfect."

Her giggles made him tighten his arms around her.

Laughing with relief, Alex kissed her shoulder. "You certainly are."

Gently, Madison glided her fingers through Alex's hair as he lay beside her. Through several rounds of sensual kisses, tender words, and losing themselves in each other's eyes, his hand hadn't moved from her belly.

"Are you ready for this?" she asked softly.

"Absolutely," he said with a chuckle. "Your man is about to go into full-fledged father mode. First thing tomorrow, I'm getting smarter on what to expect when we're expecting, and will get a construction crew out here to baby-proof the penthouse."

Madison wagged a finger at him. "You need to share the knowledge. Everything is a surprise. And apparently, there's an insane amount of medical appointments and blood work. No matter how shy I've been in the past, word on the street is that everyone and their mother will be looking under the hood."

With a cheesy grin, Alex asked, "Joy's looking under the hood? When did that become the word on the street?"

Madison threw her arm over her forehead. "I'm not sure when that headline broke, but just try and stop her. Oh, and whatever you do, do *not* google or YouTube anything without clearing it through me first. Especially crowning. You might never have sex with me again."

"What?" he asked, frowning with a curious furrow of his brows.

"Just trust me on this. Ten inches might have stock value in your universe, but it's got nothing on ten centimeters during childbirth."

Holding his hands so wide, his eyes rounded. Falling to his back, Alex raked his hand through his hair. "I take it back. I'm not ready for this." Looking back to her, he broke out in a big smile. "But I love an adventure."

The kiss he pressed to her lips was everything Alex was. Sweet and tender. Sensual and passionate. Complex in the extreme, but straightforward in his uncompromising love for her.

Each time her hands drifted across the scars on his chest, Madison loved him more. "I love you, Alex Drake."

Propping up on his elbow, he looked down at her, stroking her hair. "And I love you, Mrs. Drake. You're the love of my life."

Somehow, across a city of millions of people, their broken souls had found each other. Through the ashes of indescribable pain, their love bloomed. And in the midst of nearly losing their lives, a baby stole center stage as their most exciting adventure yet. Madison's happiness was unimaginable.

Forget the baby registry. All I need is love and support, lots of stories about Jack, date nights with the sexiest man alive, and a good night's sleep every once in a while.

Family is forever, love is eternal, and diapers don't change themselves.

Jess was right. The more, the merrier!

And Jess wasn't the only one who was right. Jordan, Crystal, and even Stone had nailed it.

Madison had the soul of a Finder, bringing together a collection of unique, talented people from all over the world. But more than that, her true north was as a Keeper, and all these amazing people were, beyond a shadow of a doubt, hers to keep. Forever a part of her life, and the ultimate guarantee that her child would be loved, adored, protected, and cherished.

This baby was everything—a new chapter in a life filled with over-the-moon happiness and undying love.

For everyone.

≈

Thank you for reading *Finders Keepers*! Alex and Madison have more adventures in store, and let's not forget Mark Donovan!

DEVIL'S CUT >> **https://www.lexxijames.com/devils-cut-amazon** - Book #5 in The Alex Drake Series

MARKED >> **https://www.lexxijames.com/marked-amazon** - Learn more about Mark Donovan and the love of his life, Jess Bishop.

≈

Subscribe to my newsletter to keep posted! Free hot romances & happily ever afters delivered to your inbox.

https://www.lexxijames.com/freebies

≈

If you loved The Ultimate Alex Drake Collection, check out Fallen: A Sinful Soldier Romance.

"Hot, combustible, sexy" ~Amazon Reviewer

For Jake Russo, abandoning the past became his only future. It should have been his burden alone. But he had one cross to bear. Watching over Kathryn Chase . . . in secret.
Her unangelic guardian paying back a debt.

www.lexxijames.com/booklink-fallen

"Laughter, love tears, suspense and danger" ~Goodreads Reviewer

~

How about something a little Ruthless?
Check out The Ruthless Billionaires Club.
www.lexxijames.com/ruthlessgames

"Tons of chemistry and passion ... Highly addictive" ~Goodreads Reviewer

ABOUT THE AUTHOR

Lexxi James is a USA Today bestselling author of romantic suspense. Her feats in multi-tasking include binge watching Netflix and sucking down a cappuccino in between feverish typing and loads of laundry.

She lives in Ohio with her amazing daughter and the man of her dreams. She loves to hear from readers!

www.LexxiJames.com

www.ingramcontent.com/pod-product-compliance
Lightning Source LLC
Chambersburg PA
CBHW070544310726
48982CB00010B/1471/J